The
*Travels of
Jaimie McPheeters*

The
Travels of
Jaimie McPheeters

ROBERT LEWIS TAYLOR

Introduction by John Jakes

MAIN STREET BOOKS
DOUBLEDAY
New York   London   Toronto   Sydney   Auckland

A Main Street Book
PUBLISHED BY DOUBLEDAY
a division of Bantam Doubleday Dell Publishing Group, Inc.
666 Fifth Avenue, New York, New York 10103

Main Street Books, Doubleday, and the portrayal of a building with a
tree are trademarks of Doubleday, a division of Bantam Doubleday Dell
Publishing Group, Inc.

First published by Doubleday & Company, Inc., in 1958.

Library of Congress Cataloging-in-Publication Data

Taylor, Robert Lewis.
    The travels of Jaimie McPheeters / Robert Lewis Taylor ;
introduction by John Jakes. — 1st ed.
        p.   cm.
    "Main Street books."
    Includes bibliographical references.
    I. Title.
PS3539.A9654T7   1993
813'.54—dc20   92-16490
                                                          CIP

ISBN 0-385-42222-9
LSI 001

INTRODUCTION

The Travels of Jaimie McPheeters is a work I rank right up there with *Lonesome Dove.* So did the Pulitzer juries, awarding the prize to each in its year of publication.

With that bit of background, I have a simple charge for you: Prepare yourself for a wonderful reading experience.

This is a novel that will entertain you royally. It will also—had I better whisper it?—teach you a lot about the mores, preoccupations, geography—and perils—of America at the time of the Gold Rush. The book is impeccably researched, but never pedantic. When you finish it, if you're curious to learn more about those who made the great overland trek to El Dorado, Robert Lewis Taylor thoughtfully provided a bibliography.

But *Jaimie McPheeters* is, first and last, a bang-up story, stirring and funny by turns. It's presented as a personal memoir; the reflections of a mature man recalling the supreme adventure of his life. This was a logical technique for Taylor to use, since Americans a hundred years ago loved to write accounts of personal experiences—an avocation which regrettably seems lost today.

Although based in part on the journal of a real gold-seeker, Taylor's novel reminds me in many ways of Dickens. The tale is long; packed with exciting incident; and built around a gallery of memorable characters, the most important being the wryly reflective Jaimie and his father, Dr. Sardius McPheeters (diplomate in Systemic Surgery, University of Edinburgh). Sardius is one of those complex, funny, touching figures who linger in the mind long after you close a book. He's a loving father but a poor provider; a man brought low by "gaming and tippling." He is the quintessential

American Argonaut, dreamily and desperately opting for a new start; the second chance. As Taylor puts it, Sardius is a believer in "the green pastures, the beacon on the hill." You'll long remember him, and his son, and others you'll meet on this journey from Louisville, Kentucky, to "General Delivery, Upper California."

Robert Lewis Taylor spent the early part of his writing career as a reporter for the St. Louis *Post-Dispatch*. Later he was a staff writer for *The New Yorker*. He authored three other novels, as well as highly successful biographies of Churchill, W. C. Fields, and Carrie Nation. He lives today in Connecticut. I think it's fair to say that *Jaimie* is his masterwork.

In 1963, the novel became the basis for a series of one-hour television dramas produced by MGM for the ABC network. Dan O'Herlihy was a superb Sardius, and his son was winningly played by Kurt Russell, then aged twelve. The venerable and dependable bible of show business, *Variety*, cited the boy actor as "a highly promising personality," but called the show a "doubtful" entry in the competitive arena of Sunday night broadcasting. This proved prophetic. The last episode aired in March 1964.

A life of only one season is not necessarily a reflection on the quality of the program, though. I remember watching it with our kids every week, and thinking it a pretty good show—though maybe I've always been a fan of film projects based on books. You can still catch episodes (in black and white) on cable.

Late in the morning, yesterday, I finished my rereading and closed the novel with a feeling of regret. I had left a long-ago world vividly realized by the author. I had parted from people for whom I'd developed a lot of affection and concern. I sat in the wind and sunshine, bundled under a Cunard robe in a chair on the upper deck of a famous liner making the Great Circle crossing, and I thought of journeys today. How little they require of us, beyond the money to pay for them. Unless there's a mishap, or you hate the sea, or blanch when there's nothing between you and the earth but 35,000 feet and the floor of a 747, contemporary journeys hardly call forth the best of a person's character.

In the world of Jaimie McPheeters and his father, however, there were not so many safety nets, backup systems, and traveler conveniences of the kind we take for granted. Indeed, even though there were plenty of guidebooks describing the route to California, many of them were spurious, written by men who'd never seen the trail. The way West was largely unmapped, hazardous, and often cruelly hostile. Going to California demanded a lot of heart; a lot of intestinal fortitude. It also called for more optimism—more sheer sentimental faith in a dream—than most of us can muster in this cynical world.

Taylor brilliantly captured the innocence and bravery of the people who chased the dream of California gold. You will love meeting them in this novel, and you will love traveling with them, and you will hate to see your journey end.

—*John Jakes*

Queen Elizabeth 2,
en route Southampton,
August 25, 1991

Chapter I

On the day when I first learned of my father's journey, I had come back with two companions from a satisfactory afternoon in the weeds near Kay's Bell Foundry, shooting a slingshot at the new bells, which were lying out in the yard and strung up on rafters. Struck with rocks, they made a beautiful sound, although it seemed to upset Mr. William Kay, the proprietor. His sign, "Maker of Church, Steamboat, Tavern and other Bells," hung over the doorway of his barnlike shop and had a row of little brass bells swinging beneath, squat and burnished, but these were hard to hit, and if you missed them, you were apt to hit one of the men working inside, and this was what seemed to upset Mr. William Kay most of all. So toward the end of the afternoon he pranced out with a double-barreled shotgun loaded with pepper and blistered Herbert Swann's seat as he zigzagged to safety through the high grass.

It was late—after suppertime—and I thought it wise to sneak up the kitchen stairs and avoid the genteel tongue-lashing and straightaway-to-bed that my mother favored for tardiness. But my baby sister Mary spied me from her pen in the back yard and set up a noisy clatter. Aunt Kitty, her darky nurse, was with her, scolding. In one leathery hand she held a leafy willow branch with which she was discouraging the early spring bugs. Bugs tormented her almost to distraction: gnats, deer flies, mosquitoes, midges, no-see-ems, things along that line.

This Aunt Kitty was so old she said she had come over from Africa, and she remembered how, as a girl in the slave ship, she had seen the urine run in green rivers over the between-decks planks where the rows of blacks were lashed to long poles. Once a week a man in a mask appeared with hand pump and hose and washed down the floor; otherwise there was no arrangement except two pails which were passed from one person to the next and were soon filled to overflowing.

My sister Mary wanted out of the pen, and Aunt Kitty wanted her in.

"I talking to old mister snake up in the bushes," she told her through the wire. "Snake say if you didn't hesh, he fixing to come down and bite. Said he wasn't aiming to bite me, say he going to bite you, though."

My sister made a squalling sound and shook the wire in her fists. She now had her eye on my billygoat, Sam, who was tethered to a tree near the woodshed.

Aunt Kitty put her face, all wrinkled like a monkey's, up close to the mesh and said, "Goat butt, baby go 'Yah-yah.'"

I asked, "Is Clara in the kitchen, Aunty?" Clara was the cook.

"Clara washed up and gone visiting to Miz Whitman's free Thelma."

"I was thinking I ought to have something to eat because I'm tired out from being late helping a sick man that got run over by a horse."

"People miss supper, they generly stays hongry till breakfast."

"Well," I said, turning away, "it's no more than I expected. That's what I get for trying to be upright and help other people. The more you do, the less other people care whether that person lives or dies."

As I walked through the twilight toward the kitchen, brooding on life's injustices, she called out, "Might be I put by a plate of chicken along with grits and cornbread and salat in the warming oven—for the cat."

Hurrying, I heard her jeweled African chuckle rise softly above Mary's pleas to the goat.

I got the food out of the oven and crept upstairs and ate it, sitting on the side of my bed. I enjoyed the cornbread and the grits and the chicken, both the wishbone and thigh, and wrapped up the salad greens in a paper and burned them in the fireplace. Then I lay down on the floor on my stomach and opened the register, which was merely an iron grating fitted into the wood to let the heated air up from below and was connected to nothing at all. Downstairs, in the family sitting room next to the parlor, my father and mother were having a discussion. I could see them, framed in the grating like birds in a pie, my mother sitting prim and stiff in her black taffeta dress with the white collar, and my father now standing over her, now pacing back and forth, with his string tie undone and his face shiny and earnest.

"I tell you, Melissa," he was saying, "this is the only way. I've gone into it painstakingly"—here my mother gave a little ladylike sniff of disbelief—"and I pledge you my solemn promise there's nothing more to it than picking up arrowheads out by the Indian Mounds—less, if it comes to that. After all, Indians were sprinkled around Louisville in limited numbers whereas nature in her blessed bounty has seen fit to strew gold over the Calif——"

"How does one convey oneself to these Elysian fields?" asked my mother in her dry, practical way.

"Why, that's the joyful part, that's the very thing I was hoping you'd ask," cried my father, his expression dissolving into a perfect sunburst of triumph. "This fellow Ware—Joseph E. Ware—has written it all down in a book—I've got it right here. Old Captain Billy Givens of the *City of Memphis* brought it down from St. Louis, where they printed them up, you know, and sold it to me at the most unbelievable bargain——"

"How much?"

"Believe me, Melissa, these books are going like wildfire in St. Louis. The people up there are fighting for them in the streets—I stole this one for twenty-five dollars, and only fifteen of it in cash at that: for the remainder, I lanced a carbuncle on his engineer's neck and gave them a partly used bottle of Blue Moss."

She sniffed again, unconvinced.

"Joseph E. Ware's *Immigrant Guide to California,*" he went on briskly. "It's all here—every blade of grass, every water hole from the borders of the Nebraskas to the Humboldt Sink and beyond. Or, if you prefer, there's the Santa Fe Trail, a southerly desert route said to be salubrious for those with nasal stoppages—covered in full in the book—or yet, if you've a freakish distaste for oxcarts and donkeys, there's the water passage via the Isthmus of Panama, a scenic holiday on such luxury vessels of the far Pacific as the *New Orleans* and the *California*.

"Now listen to this, on page 54—by George, this is a wonderful book; it ought to be required reading up at the University—'Upon your arrival at Chagres, take your baggage at once to the custom house, where you will experience but little delay. Then hurry out of the village, which is, ah, pestilential [no doubt a figure of speech]. Hire your canoe, which for expedition ought to be of small size. This is called a "piragua," is about 25 feet long, and navigated by a steersman and two rowers. The cost of boat-hire and men to Cruces ought not to exceed $12, unless, indeed, an increased traffic may have had the effect of raising the prices——'

"Fancy that, now," he said aside, shaking his head in wonder— "a mere twelve dollars for a canoe ride of fifty miles, and with your own rowers. This fellow Ware is an absolute trump."

"May I see the book?"

For a moment he looked undecided, then he handed it over, and if he'd had any suspicions that she was going to run it down, he was dead-right. Holding Ware's precious volume as if it had been plucked out of a garbage bin, she read a few passages aloud, but they were so tedious and uncomplimentary that nobody but a fool would have gone out of his yard, once he'd heard them. "It rains every day," she noted. Then she added that, " 'Bilious, remittent, and congestive fevers, in their most malignant forms, seem to hover over Chagres, ever ready to pounce on the stranger.' "

I don't mind acknowledging that when I opened the register, I was pretty excited, what with this prospect of gold-hunting, but my mother's remarks put a damper over everything, and made me wonder if my father wasn't possibly a little peculiar in the head. That was her style.

She was a good deal younger than him, beautiful, too—everyone in Louisville said so—but as far as I was concerned, he seemed like a child beside her, because of his bouncy spirits. Now that I think it over, he was one of the scatterbrainedest fellows that ever lived, and one of the nicest. He was a doctor, in very good standing, medically speaking, but he had a number of habits that appeared to give offense, though I failed to see that it was anybody's business but his own. For instance, whenever he got some money ahead, he usually went down to the shantyboats and had an enjoyable evening playing cards.

I've heard it said my father was a bang-up poker player. But there wasn't much chance of his winning, not with those cheats. Mostly, they were serious, hard-working professional men—thieves, forgers, cutthroats, small-time river pirates and a backslid preacher or two—as interesting-spoken a group as you would care to meet, but they could no more have gambled honest than they would have been comfortable in church.

Along with Herbert Swann, I'd climbed up many's the time and looked in the windows, which were punched out and had old raggedy pieces of burlap nailed over the holes. They'd be playing partners against my father, and such a lot of signs, winks, under-the-table kicks, bottom-deck dealing and aces flying out of sleeves you never saw anywhere. But if any hard-faced strangers were present, they would use the "sand tell," which was a deck marked with sandpaper so as to know the cards from their feel. And if by chance one of these out-of-towners got away with money, being a bigger cheat than what they were, it was considered an obligation to relieve him of it before he got five miles past the city limits. It was done out of civic pride; there wasn't any meanness in it.

My father beat them once in a while, through outrageous good luck, and then they were very polite and courteous, knowing perfectly well they'd get it back soon, with interest up to date. He recognized that they were cheating, of course, so he gouged them medically. For knife fights, blacked eyes and broken limbs, these shantyboaters, as civil as they might be in other ways, were in a class by themselves. And my father had all their custom. He was the only doctor they ever called. Mostly they'd send their cook, a big black man named Paddlefoot, up to the Marine Hospital with a note that gave the effect of having been labored over. One of these, rent down the middle, lies before me as I prepare this history. "Your esteemed old friend Jim Harbeson [it goes] has had the misfortune to lose the upper portion of his right ear through the medium of a bite at the hands of Ernie Caldwell, and would appreciate your professional opinion as to whether it can be sewed back or glued. He is bleeding freely but is not otherwise in distress since full of whiskey. Respectfully——" and signed by Ben Martin, the principal shantyboater of the district.

On these occasions, it was my father's way to turn over his appointments to an associate and rattle cheerfully down in his carriage, after which he treated the sufferer with great flourish, and charged triple his usual fee. What's more, he always collected it; then that night he came back and lost not only the fee but whatever other sum he had on him, along with his watch chain, or a ring, or a stickpin, or shirt, or some gewgaw of the sort. These articles he usually redeemed later. He got drunk, too, but not very often, and only because he didn't like being a doctor.

When my mother finished reading all the bad things she could find about Chagres, she laid Joseph Ware's book down with a contemptuous rustle of taffeta and observed that, "It certainly seems explicit."

"Oh, pshaw," replied my father. "I hadn't the least notion of going by that route anyhow, though it would scarcely discommode a man with a degree in Systemic Surgery from the University of Edinburgh to ward off a few mild vapors. These fellows get carried away, all writers do it. Let somebody sneeze and they try to turn the place into a pesthouse. I'd like to bet——"

Taking a grip on the register, I held my breath, for I knew what was coming.

"Yes, to be sure, *bet*," said my mother in the iciest kind of tone; then she went on to give out what betting and drinking, only she called it gaming and tippling, had done for our household, and if I had been my father, I would have gone down in the preserve cellar to live for a few days, I would have felt that low.

To upholster her argument, she left the room and came back with "the ledgers," a pair of big blue books she officiated over with as much pomp and mystery as if they had been the Bank of England. According to her figures, we owed money to nearly everybody in town, and it was all my father's fault. The minute she paid up in one place, she said, he skipped in and ran us into the hole somewhere else. And what was most bothersome was his new system, very sneaky, of picking up cash and putting it on charge accounts, all unbeknownst to her.

Watching him, I felt so sorry and sympathetic I would have run out and raised the money myself, if I'd known where to look, but I didn't own anything of value outside of my stuffed water moccasin, and the string of bear's claws I had bought off a Choctaw trader, and my deersfoot knife, unless you'd care to count Sam, but there weren't many people would have acquired him, he smelled so.

In one way, the whole situation seemed unfair. Here my mother laid out money by the cartload to the Presbyterian Church, with special donations to something called "Foreign Missions," which was in a yellow envelope—for the Chinamen, you know—and not one cent of it would do a particle of good to anybody we'd ever be apt to meet, and would likely work a lot of harm, getting the Chinamen stirred up and dissatisfied with their religion and not knowing which way to turn. And only last fall when I dropped in my nickel along with a message saying it was to help pay the transportation of a Chinese preacher over here, to even things up and give us a chance to compare notes, the Reverend Carmody brought it back to my mother and I got a licking, for something they represented to be "impertinence." But it was nothing more than ordinary common sense except they didn't have the good judgment to see it.

"Melissa," said my father when she was done, "it's even worse than you think. I can't to save me remember why, but I made a note of hand for five hundred dollars at old Parsons' bank, and now they want to call it in."

My mother sat in stunned silence.

"I was down at the Courthouse this morning," he went on, "and one of my connections there, a man very close to the County Clerk, if you know what I mean——"

"Mr. Axelrod, the County Clerk?" she asked in a low voice that sounded tired out and humiliated.

"I didn't say so. This connection of mine informed me that a number of creditors were banding together with the intention of obtaining an attachment. Now that illustrates what I have often said to you, Melissa, and, yes, I've tried to bring it home to Jaimie, too—that it pays for a man to keep up his friendships. If it hadn't been for this highly placed connection I mention, I'd never have known what those fellows were up to. As it is, I have consulted legal counsel, and if I should absent myself to go gold-seeking, there is nothing on this green earth they can—*what's that?*"

I'd heard it too—one or more men on horseback had reined up at our gate and were dismounting; I could hear the horses switching around in a half-circle the way they do after they've shucked off their load.

My mother got up and went to the window. "I imagine it's Mr. Parsons and a delegation of creditors. Very probably come to give you a last chance to straighten out your affairs. All the decent people in this city have tried time and again to help you turn over a new leaf. Reverend Carmody——"

"Never mind," cried my father, with a leap toward the kitchen. "If they have papers to serve, they'll find the bird flown. Tell them I'm upriver tending a woman that's down with chicken pox. Put them off for just twenty-four hours and they can address me care of General Delivery, Upper California."

I hung on long enough to see who it was, and sure enough it was old string-bean Parsons, looking uncommonly smug and self-satisfied, together with several others, all having as much fun as if they'd set a pack of hounds onto a cat. They didn't produce any papers, though; my father had been wrong about that. What they wanted was for my mother to place him in something called "moral chancery," which was to say, put him on probation like a mischievous child, with no drink, no cards, nothing but hard medical work and a schedule of paying off his debts.

Looked at squarely, this didn't appear too outrageous, particularly for a skinflint like Parsons, but their injured and gleeful way of telling it made me boil up with resentment for my father, who for kindness and understanding and real humanity was worth a hundred like them, with the Reverend Carmody thrown in for luck. I'd known him to labor all a hot summer day in a dirty run-down shack to ease things for some nice old darky woman who could as quickly have paid him as she could have been elected Governor.

Well, this Parsons mooned on, enjoying the sound of his complaints, and finally he worked himself up into such an aggrieved and sanctimonious state that he made the blunder of thinking my mother was on his side. "I know you won't take offense, ma'am," he said, "when I ask you to keep this conference private. My depositors would take it amiss to know that I had extended leniency to a man of Doctor McPheeters' kind."

When I saw her face, I didn't bother to wait for the answer. Mr. Parsons may have been, as people said, a good and crafty banker, but in the present instance he had sadly misjudged his audience. I heard afterward that my mother drew herself up to her full height, and she was by no manner of means short, and blistered this pious delegation with a defense of my father that more or less left them groggy, and ended up by suggesting that on any future visits they use the trade entrance instead of driving up to the gate. Mr. Parsons thereupon showed his true and natural colors by fishing out his papers, which had reposed all along in the pocket of his jacket, the miserable hypocrite, only he hadn't got anybody to serve them on, my father being absent, being, in fact, crouched just then in a thick patch of cockleburrs that lay behind the house.

I knew he was there, because I saw him when I went back to

collect up a hatful, thinking something ought to be done to make Mr. Parsons feel he wasn't neglected.

"Is that you, Jaimie?" he whispered.

"Yes, father."

"Have they left yet?"

"They're trying to."

"What's that you're doing, son?"

"Picking cockleburrs."

"Whatever for, my boy?"

"For Mr. Parsons and his friends."

There was a little silence; then I heard him begin to laugh. After a minute or so he took out a handkerchief and wiped his eyes. "Of course, of course," he said. "I'm proud of you, son. It's little attentions like these that make people remember you and want to come back. Always bear in mind that nothing's too good for a guest." Presently he began to laugh again, and he was still at it when I crawled out, loaded up with some of the nicest burrs in our patch.

When the party rode off, I was behind a tree, pretty much in the dark, though there was light enough to follow the action. Anyhow, what I couldn't see I could hear well enough. It often works out that way, I've noticed: when one set of senses lies down on the job, another reports in and takes over.

By a lucky chance, Mr. Parsons' stallion seemed to be the one most briskly affected. After backing up several feet, it paused to scrape his right leg against a shaggy-bark hickory, which is the very worst kind of tree for that sort of accident, then it ran fifteen or twenty yards down the side of the road and stopped with its forelegs spraddled out, shooting Mr. Parsons over its head into a gully of moss. Up till then, I had no idea he could be so chatty, and to tell you the truth his remarks gave me a fresh outlook on bankers, and made me appreciate them more than before. Even so, his statements were pale and sickly compared with those of Mr. Whitmore, who was mounted on a roan mare, because he and this mare separated almost immediately, in such a way that Mr. Whitmore was left in an awkward position upside down on our gate. Of the entire delegation, the only one that showed any skill as a rider was Mr. Crawshaw, on a big gelded buckskin, and to his credit he stuck on for several miles down the river road, or as far as the farmhouse of a family named Thornton, which picked him out of a ditch, but when he got home, around dawn, they said his clothes and hair were so caked over with mud and brambles his wife had to use a trowel before she could make a positive identification.

Horses will nearly always behave like that if you place burrs under the saddle. There's no use trying to reason with them; it's a prejudice that likely goes back a long way, and could be explained if anybody had the time to sit down and puzzle it out. As for me, I felt that I had helped out all I could for the moment, so I climbed on up the back stairs and went to bed.

Chapter II

Early the next morning my father and mother were at it hammer and tongs, trying to work out what to do. It was my mother's claim, not complimentary, that he was too addleheaded to look after himself on any kind of journey longer than ten or fifteen miles. "Jaimie would have a better chance of getting to the gold fields than you," she observed.

"Then let me take him," cried my father, darting to a curtained east window of the house and peering out with great caution. On the theory that Parsons would probably try to wriggle through the shrubbery, perhaps carrying his papers in his teeth, he had all the shades drawn upstairs and down. Except for the kitchen, where Clara and Aunt Kitty were stationed, for intruders, with an encouragement to use skillets if necessary, the place was as dark as a tomb.

"Why not?" he demanded, having satisfied himself that the azaleas along that side were free of enemy activity. "One year, two with bad luck, and we will return to this astonished city, laden with the treasures of Golconda, respected, envied by all, denied credit by none, including Goldswaithe the tailor—confound his parsimonious hide—he refuses to release my trousers, with or without the new patch—and, in a word, solvent forever."

Not wishing to overhear what was none of my business, because there are few things lower down than an eavesdropper, I had stretched out on the floor behind the sofa with a book, only a few minutes before. I was reading in it here and there so as to shut out the sound of the voices, but it was an uphill job being a sort of championship long-winded poem by a man named Milton, though if any of the lines ended in rhymes I failed to locate them, about a group of angels that talked all the time and couldn't make up their minds whether to settle down in heaven or in the other place.

Try as I might, I couldn't quite drown out the conversation, so when I realized what my father was saying I sprang up in a hurry and told my mother I had to go.

"You've got to let me," I cried. "You've said yourself my eyes are as snoopy as a hawk's at seeing what I shouldn't, and if it came to finding gold——"

"Jaimie is enrolled for next autumn at the Male High School," she said crisply, directing her statement at my father.

Well, there you were. I was already educated to the point of absurdity, but no, she had to have more. Here we saw the perfect example in my father, who had been hauled up as a boy in Scotland and put to doctoring over the plainest kind of objections—he had run off twice and burned down part of a schoolhouse another time —and he'd been miserable ever since, because he wanted to be a smuggler, you understand, like everybody else along that coast, and engage in a respectable trade that brought in a steady living. He used to swear, and I believe it, that if a person had normal curiosity all they needed to teach him was how to read and make change. As he said, though, he didn't much mind knowing Latin and Greek, because he often got tired of cursing out medicine in English.

My mother spoke up to announce that she had talked every- thing over with Professor Yandell, a know-it-all up at the University who had all the ladies blathering over him at teas. "Jaimie's studies will include Rhetoric, Belles Lettres, the Classics, and Modern Lan- guages," she said. "We can decide on the University course later."

Now I knew I had to go. Not only the Male High School, but another round on top of that. There wasn't any sense in it. By the time I got out, I'd be too old to do anything except retire, and you didn't need an education for that.

"Jaimie's not the type," said my father. "Maybe you've forgotten the unholy ruckus he had with Mental Arithmetic at the Secondary School. You're trying to turn him into a milksop—you'll break his spirit."

Tossing her head with a considerable show of firmness, my mother replied that, if she could help it, I would be fitted to take my place in "the cultural life of Louisville, and share in the city's advancement." Well, I thought, if you ask me, they've gone too far with this Louisville already. It was overdeveloped and blown up with commerce and business so you could hardly get across the streets any more without being run down by teamsters. Why, they had eight brickyards in Louisville in 1849—I saw it in a bragging pamphlet that was got up by some merchant or other that seemed to have a good deal of time on his hands. There were three pianoforte manufactures, too, and three breweries, two tallow-rendering houses, an ivory-black maker—for use in refining sugar, you know—eight soap and candle factories; three shipyards; two glue factories; and four pork houses that slaughtered upwards of seventy thousand hogs a year.

And if you were looking for steam machinery, they had twelve foundries that made the best on the river, or so the pamphlet claimed. There were rope factories, flouring mills, oilcloth factories, three potteries; six tobacco stemmeries, a paper mill, and a new gas works that lit 461 street lamps over sixteen miles of main. Not only that, it had a gas holder measuring sixty feet in diameter and twenty-two feet high. People used to ride out Sundays to look at it, but the superintendent said it was a nuisance because he couldn't keep the children off. In the end, they were obliged to hire a watchman, but he was bullyragged so steady that he sort of went out of his head, so to speak, and they had to place him in a hospital that made a specialty of such cases.

Another thing they had, not mentioned in the pamphlet, was an epidemic of cholera, and it was this that finally convinced my mother and sent me on the journey to California. My father brought it up toward noon; he had just remembered it. It was lucky for us he did, because two cousins of my mother's New Orleans plantation clan had died of cholera when she was small, and you only had to mention that disease for her to get the nervous jumps.

"Two more deaths reported yesterday," he went on cheerfully, "and not down on the river this time but right smack in the middle of the Fourth Ward, not a stone's throw from this house."

She was shaken, and he recognized the signs, for he observed that, "Hannah's well out of it—we'll have to write her to stay on in Cincinnati for a few weeks."

Hannah was my sister. She was off visiting, as she most always was.

My mother went over to a window and stood looking out awhile, holding the drawn curtain a little way back. "All right," she said at last. "Jaimie can go, but only until the plague [she never could mention cholera by name] has run its course. Let it be understood that he will return next autumn in time to begin at the Male High School."

I remember those words very well. She didn't know any more what she was asking than my father did, and that was about as little as possible. A good many classes have assembled and graduated since that morning, and they did it all without me. Neither can I say I'm sorry; we learned some things you couldn't find out at the Male High School if you were to go there for two hundred years, which I estimated was about the time it would take me to finish up, if I buckled down and worked at it.

First off, my father dashed upstairs and came back with some little shiny books he'd gathered up on the sly and said they must be his "Journals." I have them here now—they are of duodecimo size, as they call it, in brown hand-sewn leather, and filled with a lacy kind of handwriting, very tiny, that often traverses a page in two directions, the one set of slants on top of the other at right angles, so as to save space. This crisscrossing of lines was popular with the period, but such pages are vexatious to read, and require the use of a glass.

No matter how much trouble, these Journals are interesting, and filled with excitement. Practically any place you read, something good is about to happen tomorrow. The same is true of his letters, only more so. Nobody ever lived that could touch my father for producing perky and misleading letters, and he himself acknowledged, one day when we were nooning at the foot of Independence Rock, that their tone was somewhat "crouse an' canty," which he said was the phrase of a Scottish poet named Burns, who had written a good deal of material about small animals. Here at the foot of one letter—to my sister Hannah—is a grainy smear of gold dust affixed to the page with mucilage. All is now black with age and weather; at only a spot or two do pinprick glints of yellow shine through to bolster up his tale. But I was there, and I chance to recall that this particular dust was washed by an Ohio man, and came to us in exchange for a pair of surgical shears, with which he intended to set up as barber at a Feather River camp. In those weeks, you could have thrashed out our clothes with a flail and not found a grain of dust, for my father had taken to "crevicing," a system he'd picked up from a friendly oracle with the Wolverines. The rotary motion of pan-washing made his head swim, he said. This crevicing was just the thing: you walked up a dry creek bed with a knife and a spoon and dug nuggets out of gold pockets in the shelves. "It's as simple as opening a bank," he went on. "Any fool can do it."

Well, if this was true, we'd soon be rich, I figured, because no ordinary fool could have got us out there in the first place. But to give my father his due, specially since everybody was always running him down, he was as methodical as clockwork once it was decided we were going. You never saw such a bustle; the whole house was turned upside down. He made a little speech, full of pomp and reassurance, telling my mother how comfortable and well off she would be, and said, "Now you have the income from the old gentleman's estate—God rest his peculiar New Orleans soul; he let a fortune slip through his fingers when he declined to finance my Convalescent Home for Drunkards—and this house with inclusory chattels will be intact during the period of my separation. To sum up, you and the family are secure."

Then he sent her on a trip downtown, with his "holograph

power of attorney," which was a piece of note paper with his name signed to it in a looping flourish, with a number of curlicues, to "liquidate" his account at the other bank, only when she got there, there wasn't anything in the till except an overdraft of eighteen dollars, so she drew out her own money and cashed in two bonds they had put by together, which he had overlooked somehow, and altogether raised nearly four hundred dollars. When she got back, she handed it over with the same kind of look I once saw on the faces of some relatives at a funeral, just before they screwed down the coffin: mournful but resigned to the loss.

The next thing was to "fit out the expedition," as he called it, because he said we would leave early the following morning, before the usual rising hour of process servers. So he hauled out some lists which he had mostly made up from Ware's book, and appointed Willie the yard boy to do his buying, with the precaution not to get any two articles from the same store. "We must avoid indications of an evasion," he said. All afternoon, Willie tramped back and forth, piling up stores in the woodshed, and before he was done, he had bought two soft gum rubber ponchos, a waterproof can of matches, an India rubber spread for putting on the ground under blankets, two knapsacks, some lye soap and candles, a skinning knife, two pistols with ammunition, some outdoor cooking utensils, a belt ax, a sewing kit, and a number of other things, some of which we couldn't have used in a million years.

By this time, my father was hopping around as full of directions and information as if he had been prospecting for years. He had begun to use the word "we" to mean the old-timers around the California gold fields, including himself.

"What's the skinning knife for—Indians?" asked my mother, whose tongue had been getting a little more sarcastic as my father swelled with importance.

"Game. We often find that fresh meat puts new heart in the emigrants, especially if provisions are running low."

"Who's to shoot it?"

"I'm reckoned a fair shot with both rifle and pistol," he said a trifle huffily.

He had an old Hawken rifle a trapper had turned over instead of paying for an operation on his groin, which had been caught in a trap while sleeping, and he said we would take this along, but I didn't much care for the idea when I found out I'd have to carry it. Herbert Swann and I had sneaked this rifle out in the woods one day and shot it off. It was so long we had to rest it in the crotch of a sapling, and it weighed about a ton and a half, give or take a couple of pounds. When we pulled the trigger, it kicked us both back into a slough, and the ball zipped through some sycamore leaves and out into a little clearing we had failed to notice and knocked two slats out of a tobacco shed that was several hundred yards away and should have been out of range, but wasn't.

My father couldn't carry the rifle because he had his hands full. Besides his knapsack, which was stuffed to the top with Willie's things and some articles from the house, like blankets, clean linen, razor, and such, he was taking his surgical bag.

This appeared to put my mother out more than anything up to date.

"Whatever for?" she said. "You can practice medicine right here in Louisville."

"I'm a doctor," he replied with dignity. "I owe it to the Oath of Hippocrates to be prepared for any emergency."

The way it turned out, he was right, as he often was at the most unlikely times. Toward dusk our gear was assembled, and with the fading of the warm spring sun the spirits in our household sank a notch, too. I went out in the back yard to say goodbye to Sam, because they were going to take him to a farmer to keep, as soon as we were safely gone. It was cooler this evening, and Aunt Kitty had brought Mary in from the pen the minute the sunshine left. So I untied Sam and put him in the pen instead, and gave him two lumps of sugar, along with a chew of tobacco, which he enjoyed as much as some people do, though he was obliged to swallow the juice, being without any means to spit. I had tried to teach him many's the time, but somehow he never got the hang of it, and my father remarked that I might as well throw it up as a bad job, because a goat's instincts, together with his machinery, were all for moving edibles in exactly the opposite direction.

Going back to the house, I heard Aunt Kitty call, "You, boy," and I stopped to see what she wanted, under the big crooked oak where I had my treehouse.

"You fixin to go journeying, ain't that so?"

I replied that we were off to California to seek gold but that she mustn't say so to anybody before we had left, not even to Man, who was her son that my mother had freed and worked across town in a foundry.

"I talkin' to *you*, you hear me?"

"Yes, ma'am. I hear you."

"I gazed in the boiling pot—see some real bad things."

She had this black iron pot, with bleached catfish and chicken bones in the bottom, and she could tell the future from the way the bones jumped around and arranged themselves.

"We'll get rich in California," I said. "I'll buy you a nice present to bring back."

In the corners of her wrinkled-up eyes two large tears formed and rolled down slowly, then dried up for want of support.

"You lookin' at Aunt Kitty for the very last time on this yearth."

If I had felt unsettled before, I was miserable now, and I swallowed hard to keep from crying and throwing my arms around her skinny waist, as I had done dozens of times in crises.

"Day you study to come back, I be in the ground, long gone to my good home."

I snuffled, half angrily, and said it wasn't so, and then she held out her hand with something shiny in the palm. It was a buckeye, polished like old mahogany, with several marks burned in blackly by a poker or other iron tool. In the top there was fastened an eyelet and screw, and through this, for wearing round the neck, passed a fine-mesh chain.

"Conjure man give me this charm, say you to keep it close by, and shine it to your cheek if need be."

I knew what a buckeye was, of course, but I didn't realize they were useful for charms. Aunt Kitty had cures for nearly anything you could name, and when I was bad cut by a sickle, she stopped the bleeding with cobwebs and soot. When my father came home, he said it would have stopped anyhow, but I reckoned that was just professional jealousy.

"It's pretty," I said. "What's it do, Aunty?"

"Time to find out when sperets come."

"But how do I know they're coming? *When* do they come?"

"Sperets work they mischief in the dreadful night."

"Well," I said, "I'm usually asleep in the night. I don't hardly wake up at all in the nighttime."

"Conjure man say this charm good for bears and such; you rub it, come a bear—hear?"

"All right, Aunty, and if it doesn't take hold, I'll just go ahead and use the rifle."

"I'll use a broom on *you*, give me any more sass."

She was the thinnest-skinned darky there ever was about charms; you couldn't say boo about one of her remedies, even, but I happened to know they didn't always work; the strength went out of them now and then. Only the year before, the conjure man had brought in the Jackson County madstone, from way over in Illinois, for a white peddler that had been dog-bit, and the man went ahead and died just the same, howling and snapping at water, with the stone strapped directly over the bite, exactly as prescribed.

When I got back to the house, everything was ready except that my father was trying to jam two big medical volumes—Andrew Fyfe's *Anatomy* and Lizars' *Surgery*—into his knapsack, with my mother standing alongside, wearing an expression of scorn.

"It's the silliest thing I ever heard of—walking all the way to California carrying two heavy books."

"You never can tell, Melissa," he said, using his knees with great vigor. "Some poor sufferer of the not too distant future, prostrate

28

on the alkali plains, may owe his deliverance to these very selfsame volumes."

"The more I think it over," she went on, "the more I'm convinced that I've agreed to a fool's errand. I have a feeling I'll live to regret this night."

There was such an earnest ring to her voice that I sent a curious glance her way, and I'm glad I did. She fitted into the room, you might say; the one seemed to go with the other, they were that upright and graceful. Maybe because of this last look, I find the room easy to remember: the black iron fireplace with its fancy marble mantel, the faded Persian rug—a family heirloom from New Orleans—the horsehair sofa and chairs, each with its starchy-white antimacassar, which last were supposed to keep off the Macassar oil that people had taken to putting on their hair, and the cheerful old wallpaper of steamboat and cotton-bale design.

Just when I was getting into a nice sentimentally frame of mind, almost wishing we weren't leaving, she said, "Sardius, before you go to bed, Jaimie is to have the caning he was promised yesterday morning, before all this came up. He was smoking catalpa beans again, out by the woodhouse."

Wouldn't that show you? Her husband and son were preparing to enter the wilderness, probably to be devoured by wolves or red Indians, and she must insist on the regular rules of the house. Well, in itself the caning amounted to very little, as usual. My father viewed the smoking of catalpa beans as both harmless and dull. I had dried out a considerable parcel from last summer and stored them in a handy place in the cellar, comfortably removed from the rats, which seemed to favor them. According to custom, we climbed the stairs in silence, to all appearances mournful and low, and I went on into my room. From beneath a mattress in his, my father extracted his latest copy of *The Turf Register*, then brought it in, tightly rolled, and fetched the bed several noisy whacks, whilst I voiced a few piteous howls, meanwhile proceeding with the removal of my clothes.

The sheets were cold, the wind howled round the eaves. I went to sleep and dreamed a mixed-up sort of dream about bears and buckeyes, and cockleburrs and Mr. Parsons, and at one point, far out on the prairie, my father had Fyfe's *Anatomy* open beside a sick Indian that was stretched on the ground, looking indignant, and he was saying, "There's no need to argue—you'll have to give up catalpa beans." I tossed and turned, sleeping very shallow and restless, and it seemed like no time at all before my father was coming down the hallway with a lantern and shaking me by the shoulder. It wasn't just a dream, then. Dawn was an hour away, of a clear, cool, sweet-smelling morning, and we were off to California.

Chapter III

Dear Melissa:

I take up my pen for this first letter home with a very heavy heart. The temptation is strong to consider the events in chronology, but the suspense of waiting for bad news would be too cruel. I must face up like a man, though a foolish and misdirected one, it appears, and tell you that Jaimie is gone, presumably lost off the boat and drowned during the night before we arrived at this sleepy little river-bottom town.

No amount of upbraiding and reproach, of reminding me how right you were (and always have been) can make me feel worse than I feel. For the rest of my life I must bear the stigma of knowing that I have, in effect, caused the death of our boy. Had I listened to you, and borne my responsibilities, this terrible thing would never have happened. I beg you to tell Hannah as gently as possible, and be no more bitter than you must. At this moment, all I can think of to say to you is that I'm sorry, sorry, sorry.

Now, your first shock over, I shall try to describe what happened in such detail as will make it all clear. As you know, Willie delivered us in the rig to Portland; dawn was breaking as we arrived. The boat I'd booked stateroom passage on, the *Courier*—a packet for St. Louis—was lying in the canal, though far from ready to go, despite the advertised sailing time of 8 A.M. It was nearer 11 when our cargo was aboard and the plank taken in. You may imagine what a fever of anxiety I generated during this delay; we alternated between disposing our luggage in the astonishingly small cabin assigned us (a mere closet, with wooden bunks one above the other, next to the ladies' quarters in the stern) and pacing the upper deck, myself watching the communicating roads, as the morning wore on.

When at last the whistle blew and the huge stern wheel began to turn (disconcertingly near us), we thrashed out into the broad Ohio, greatly swollen by the Spring rains, to the shrill squealing of pigs, the alarmed lowing of cattle, and not a few drunken hurrahs, these varied articulations rising from the lower deck, where not only the poorer passengers but an assortment of livestock were quartered.

Under the circumstances in which I write, I realize your impatient lack of interest in the trip, as such, so I hasten to the unhappy time which has saddened and impoverished us both. But first I must relate an incident that may or may not have affected Jaimie to some reckless adventure in the night, some ill-advised nocturnal ramble to soothe his mind, for he witnessed a sight frightful to the most seasoned adult and doubly so to a lad barely in his teens.

The entertainments of this vessel fell into two divisions, separated by the daylight hours and those of darkness. In the first instance, time was passed by the upper-deck gentry in firing off pistols at objects afloat in the river, with wagers of prodigious size riding upon each round. At night, poker games even more ferocious commanded their attention. Faithful to my new vows, I abstained from both pleasures. Amongst this convivial group was a Mr. Streeter, portly, ruddy-faced, amiable, grievously fond of spirits. The fact is, I might say without doing him injustice, that this worthy quite evidently began his refreshment immediately upon arising, for he appeared at breakfast in the most exuberant humor, and with his face bearing the warm glow of a particularly fiery sunset. He had, we were soon informed, by none other than himself (for he was a powerful talker), sold a substantial business in the textile line, in Pittsburgh, consequent upon the death of his wife, and was now en route (as we were) to the frontier, there to find opportunities for prospecting.

Pitiful to relate, this unfortunate was not destined to go very far. On the evening of the third night, he was attracted to the boisterous merriment of the saloon, and was there cursed by as whimsical a fall of cards as it has ever been my lot to see, and I believe I might (ahem!) pose as an experienced observer. Well, with each worsening of his luck, he absented himself for a hand or two, in order to consult John Barleycorn, thus, I assume, deadening his pain. Upon coming back, he would produce a leathern pouch of capacious size, from which dribbled a steady stream of gold coins onto the green baize and into the willing hands of his co-travelers. At length, after a monstrous failure, at a point when the table held no less than a thousand dollars, our Mr. Streeter, now far gone in drink, muttered thickly and excused himself, as it developed, for the very last time.

It may have been ten minutes later that we heard a terrible cry, a shriek from the innermost recesses of Hell, it seemed, and felt a soft, padded thumping that appeared, suddenly, to stop all way on the boat. There followed a rushing of humanity, crewmen and passengers, and then the chilling shout, "He's tumbled into the blades!" Poor, wretched man! In his dulled and heedless state, he had made his way toward his cabin and stumbled over the taffrail and into the churning wheel. With the engines cut and the *Courier* sliding down in ghostly silence, broadside to the stream, two roustabouts ran out onto the fanways and removed Streeter's broken body from the dripping paddles. You would scarcely believe it, but he was yet alive, his legs in multiple fractures, the skin and hair removed from one side of his head, an elbow protrudingly nakedly, and his insides in Heaven knows what condition of rupture.

For all this, I had some slight notion he could be revived. Perhaps the protective effects of the spirits lengthened his life. You may imagine that I was promptly impressed into service. Indeed, the Captain—Captain Macready by name, a sturdy Scot himself, with friends in common with my cousins near Linlithgow—entreated me so piteously to succor the victim that I saw tears glisten in his eyes.

We contrived a makeshift hospital in the wheelhouse, for reasons that you shall see. In my mind, the immediate necessity, aside from staunching the appalling flow of blood from his head, was to set the elbow and legs before the sedative benumbment of whiskey and shock wore off. We were twenty-two men passengers, apart from the crew, and strong, yet we could devise no effective means of pulling out those legs in such a way as to persuade the bones back into alignment. Accordingly, working as fast as possible, I rigged cables to the wheel, in a similiar fashion to the ancient instrument of torture, and, with members of our company holding the victim firmly by the shoulders, extended the right leg to something like an advantageous position; alas, midway through this operation our patient awoke with a bloodcurdling scream, struggled himself momentarily to a sitting position, then fell back—stone-dead.

Captain Macready had him taken ashore at Cairo, a collection of drab dwellings at the confluence of the Ohio and the Father of Waters, with provisions for the remains to be shipped back to Pittsburgh on the next boat out. He was packed in sawdust in an icehouse there, and this was all that mortal man could do in his behalf. Miserable creature, how much better if he had stayed to perpetuate that thriving business of which he boasted so proudly!

This, Melissa, brings me to the time of our personal sorrow, the disappearance of Jaimie, and it is a sore trial for my hand to form the words. The hour was nearly midnight when Streeter went to his reward in the wheelhouse of the *Courier*, with Jaimie among the horrified onlookers peering through the glass. The accident had occurred at nine, as he and I were preparing to leave for bed. When finally we got into our bunks, we were, I am sure, distressed and wakeful. I fell into a sleep disturbed by visions of that grotesque shape in the paddle wheel (some of Streeter's clothes were even torn from his body, such was the violence of the blades) and I awoke early, at the first streaks of sunrise. I sensed rather than noticed that Jaimie was not in his bunk. Springing down, I verified that this was the case, and with agitated heart, flung on some clothes and searched the deck, thinking to surprise him in an early morning stroll. He was nowhere to be seen. Frantically, now, I rushed through the ship—into the saloon, the engine room—room by courtesy only; it was all but exposed to the elements—through the lower deck, and at last to the Captain's cabin. We combed the ship; he was gone.

By now, what with one shocking mishap piled upon another, Captain Macready was in a condition bordering on collapse. His eyes were bilious and his face the color of paste. Disregarding his schedule, already badly upset, he turned about and we searched both the Illinois and the Missouri banks, as well as several channels formed by islands, for a distance of twenty miles back. It was absolutely hopeless, as all hands knew; and I shall ever honor Macready and tender increasing homage to the country that gave him birth, for the costly pretense he made for my feelings. Even at the best, a thirteen-year-old plunged without warning into that icy sea of mud (it runs at the rate of six miles an hour) would have little hope of survival at this early season of the year. And with the Mississippi now at flood—miles wide in most places—his chance of making shore would be impossibly reduced.

However, the Captain put in at two landings—one consisting of three ramshackle two-storeys and going by the preposterous name of Thebes, and another called Grand Tower, from a huge projection of rock that rises in mid-river, where we left word (and I money) against the chance of the boy's being heard from. And then, Melissa, in my resolve to leave no stone unturned, I debarked at this hamlet of Cape Girardeau. For six days I have ranged both riverbanks by horseback. I have ferried back and forth four times. I believe I can say with veracity that no resident within some hundreds of yards of this ugly brown torrent has gone without notice of my quest. If Jaimie is alive, he will be found; that is my solemn promise. But it would be selfish and unfeeling to arouse false hopes. The boy is dead, and I alone am guilty. Conscience-torn, reduced by fatigue, I yet see nothing to be gained by turning back from my journey. And so, my dear wife, having made this calamitous start, I now resume my way toward California, with a grieving heart, and with the hope that, in God, you will find some means of forgiving,

> Your devoted husband,
> SARDIUS McPHEETERS (M.D.)

Reading that letter over, now at this later date, I feel a lump come to my throat. It isn't a bad thing to be wanted, and I only wish I could have showed up for the funeral services that my mother held afterward. The Reverend Carmody, they say, was at his very oily best, and he went praising and glorifying along perfectly straight-faced and sincere, as if I'd located the Holy Grail. Judging from the remarks he'd made about Herbert Swann and me in Sunday school, which were mostly on the opposite tack, the funeral must have placed him under a pretty brisk strain.

Another possibility was that he got me mixed up with somebody else. There were two church funerals that week, one for me, who was absent, and another where they had a resident corpse, with all the trimmings, a new boy in town that had a good record and was what they called a Model of Deportment, but he was knocked down by a beer wagon while he was holding an umbrella for two old ladies crossing the street, so he wasn't much better off than if he'd been the town nuisance, as far as I can see.

Aside from that, the sermon for me was purely wind wasted. At the moment when Carmody was mooing about Jehovah's Blessed Cherubs and Infants Now at Peace, I was thrashing through the Missouri backwoods as loaded up with troubles as old Job, the sheep farmer they kept picking on in the Bible, which was one of his favorite characters. The way I fell off that boat was this: I was lying there in the bunk, downcast and moody, and philosophizing over Mr. Streeter's bad fortune, and wondering what had become of his gold. Nobody had mentioned it at the rescue, and I happened to remember that he had that bag on him when he left. So I said to myself, there's the remainders of a couple of garments stuck in the back corners of those fanways—I saw them when they took him out—and what if the gold's in *them*? Furthermore, in the morning they'll notice those clothes, so why wouldn't it be a good idea to haul them out now and save everybody the trouble? In addition to which, if the money *is* there, somebody will only collar it. Or when they settle the estate the lawyers will gobble it up, because many's the time I've heard my father say that a lawyer is nothing but a burglar with a license to steal.

Right away, it made me feel good to know that I might prevent a burglary, so I slid down quietly from the bunk, and pulled on my shirt and mohair trousers, because it was cool out there now, and tiptoed around to the stern. The moon was up, and the boat was full of sharp shadows that made me jump, they favored humans so. In the soft light, the river looked big and still and silvery, not muddy and dipping with high-water whirlpools, the way it was in the daytime. Off on the Missouri side I could see a smudge of bluff bank, but on the Illinois side, where there was nothing but low bottom land, all under water, I couldn't make anything out at all.

Hanging on carefully, but excited too, I slipped back along the narrow board runway beside the big wheel and felt down in the corner. Sure enough, soggy and torn, a piece of Mr. Streeter's jacket was wedged there. I pulled it out an inch at a time, to keep it from falling in the river. It was the left-hand half, as you'd face him, and had two pockets, one outside and one in, and in this inside pocket I found his leather pouch. After the poker games, it didn't feel so very heavy, but it gave a nice jingle when I shook it, so I stuffed it into my shirt and turned to go.

And right there is where I had my bad luck. The river was on such a rampage, and had torn so many things loose along its banks, that trees and logs and boxes and barrels and dead pigs and even houses were spinning downstream almost anywhere you looked. One night the captain had tied up to a cottonwood at the foot of a bar; other times in the dark he stayed out of the channel, seeking the cleaner water, removed from the trash line.

But now there was a grinding bump and shudder, while I had both hands loose stowing the gold, and I toppled off that runway like a tenpin. I lit on my back, outboard of the wheel, thanks to goodness, but popped back up in its wake, too choked up with muddy water to make a sound. The river was deathly cold and looked as black as night; even so, I saw a darker shape, and it was this same tree that had caused all the trouble, riding low in the water, with leafy branches sticking up, only now it was about to do me a service. For I couldn't have swum fifty yards in that ice water without support. Already my feet and legs were numb clear through, and my clothes weighed me down like sand.

The spot where I fell in was just north of Tower Rock, I've found out since. This was the worst place on the river between St. Louis and Memphis, a big upthrust block of stone dividing the river, surrounded everywhere by whirlpools that sloped down as much as six feet, big enough to upset a skiff, and a current almost like rapids in a hilly stream.

Well, the first thing I knew, the tree I was hugging—I was too weak to haul myself up—bobbed and ducked, twirling half around, then scraped its way over some rock and we were ashore, so to speak. Panting and shivering, I crawled past a pebbly shelf and into some prickly grass. It was bitter-cold; I've never felt such a cold, before or after, even in the western mountains.

Said I to myself, I'll freeze to death if something isn't done, so I got up and began stamping and squeezing out the water and hallooing for help, not knowing it was an island. But it was; I made sure of that soon after, stumbling my way up a little path to the top, where some scraggly pines grew, from where I could look all around, seeing nothing but water in the moonlight. Some clouds sifted in front of the moon, now, the way they usually mass up before dawn in that valley, and I wasn't any longer sure which was the Illinois shore and which the Missouri.

But I went down the path again, because I knew what I had to do; no matter how painful. I'd freeze, or starve, or both, if I stayed on the rock; neither was there much chance of boatmen snooping around before the river dropped—it was too roiled up—so I had to get off while I could.

My tree was still there, held against the rock by the current, and I pulled it up a little farther. Then I hunted around and pretty soon found a piece of drift for a paddle. Wading the tree down one side in the shallows, I jumped up on the trunk near a low branch, and perched myself astride, all but my feet high and dry. It was a tolerable craft, somewhat inclined to wallow and roll, particularly when the bottom branches scraped, which they did before we floated clear, but it was the only boat in sight, for all that.

Very cautiously, I dipped my paddle now and then, waiting for the rolls to level off, and eased us ever so gently toward Missouri, which was the nearest bank, being to the right. We were booming

downstream in black, empty space, with never a light showing anywhere, nor a sound to break the stillness. It was awesome, and grand,
too, but somehow I didn't care for it as a vacation. Working my
paddle, nearly shaking my bones loose, I thought of my warm bed
in Louisville.

Chapter IV

Presently the sky clouded up and I couldn't see any farther than I could spit, but before long I heard a twittering of birds off to the right, so I reckoned that daylight was coming. I was close in to shore; still, no matter how I paddled, I couldn't seem to land.

I thought, the river bends here and the channel sets in toward the bank, but there's a strip of backwater eddy, and I can't push the tree out of the current, not without a sweep. So I knew I'd have to swim for it. I waited till the blackness was graying a little and I could see the trees going by like scenery in a play; then I splashed off my perch, still holding the board, and struck out kicking. It couldn't have been more than a minute or two, though it felt like an hour, before I was out of the channel and into the easy water, and after that I made good time for the bank, which was bushy and steep along here.

Drifting down, I caught a root, pulled it out with a spray of dirt in my face, grabbed another that was grown all over with thorns, and finally nailed a willow that held fast, with me on it, too played out to move. I lay there getting my strength back, blue to the chin with cold. Then I dragged myself up the bank through gravelly mud and brambles, and you may believe that my clothes were a sorry sight when I finished.

Nothing on top but dense woods and rocks, no road, or even a footpath anywhere. The only thing for it, I judged, was to strike out inland; there was bound to be a farmer somewhere, if I had to walk to Timbuctoo. But I was so stiff with cold and exhaustion I fell down every few feet, and the last time I didn't count on getting back up. When things can't go much worse, they generally take a turn for the better, and now I had a windfall of good luck for a change.

Up forward in the woods, still dark in here and dripping with damp, I caught sight of a glow, a flickering of reddish light, very near to the ground. If this was what I thought, I could praise the saints and take a new lease on life. True enough, lightning had knocked over a dead sycamore, and the trunk underneath, eaten out in a charred hollow, was still smoldering, as it probably had been for days. I was down on my knees in a second, feeding it whatever dry leaves and sticks I could find. In no time at all, I had a blaze going that would have warmed up a mummy, and with my clothes, what rags were left, spread out on the tree to dry.

Well, this was all right. I turned around slowly, naked as a jaybird, roasting one side after another, letting the heat sink clear into my bones. When you come right down to it, there's nothing like a fire for putting the spunk back into a body. Looked at in some ways, my situation didn't exactly call for a celebration—I was standing pelt-bare in a strange woods out in the middle of nowhere—but I felt fine and ready to push right ahead.

When the clothes were dried stiff, I put them on—though they were powerful scratchy and raw—and kept going inland, watching the trees for moss, trying to head due west. Maybe an hour had gone by—I was getting hungry, and a little cold again—when I waded out of a backwater slough, climbed a high ridge thick with walnuts and oaks, and came down into a clearing. In the center, on a grassy knoll by a stream, was a miserable-looking farmhouse: warped gray clapboards, both doorsteps gone—burned for firewood, likely—roof very patchy and rough, with the shingles all curled up, no more foundation than rocks piled up under each corner, pigpen close enough so that everybody could enjoy the smell, and a chicken house just behind that, with a saggy lean-to adjoining. No paint on anything, nor decorated up any, rusty old kettles and tools lying out in the yard, a well with a wheel up above, some faded garments

—denim jeans, a pettiskirt or two, an old yellow sunbonnet—blowing on a line, a double rank of firewood spread over with scraps of dirty canvas, and early morning smoke winding out of a hewnstone chimney, the lonesomest sight of all, somehow.

A woman of about forty with gray streaks in her black hair was bending over the well, working the wheel, which needed oiling and gave off a dismal shrieking that set a person's teeth on edge. Off in the woods somewhere, I could hear an ax ring, a regular chunking, with now and then rests in between. It must have been seven o'clock; the sun had just blinked out above the tree line, looking as though it had maybe arisen too early, and didn't feel quite up to scratch.

"How do, ma'am," I said, stepping down. She stiffened up straight, like she'd seen the chief of the Cherokee nations, and stood studying me over, head to foot. By and by she said:

"Where in all git out did *you* come from?"

I opened my mouth to make up some kind of lie, but nothing came handy, so before I knew it I had told her the truth, with a little embroidery work dropped in here and there, to keep from getting rusty.

"A St. Louis packet, hey? And gold there, you say. I hadn't heard of it."

I said the gold was in California. "Out by the Pacific Sea."

"That'd be a tolerable stretch, I expect."

"Close on to two thousand miles."

"Hush up," she said with a crooked smile, not believing it for a second. In a little while she said I could come in, her man would be along directly; they were about to have breakfast, only she said they were fixing to vittle. They had been here in Missouri less than two years. She told me her husband was "Ioway-born," and I never let on I didn't know what that meant, but I guessed he was sick.

"He's up in the woods cutting sprouts for a fence," she said, leading me into the house, which was chinked-up logs inside the clapboards—a big room that looked like the remainders of a cyclone, and a loft up above that leaked straw. "The rabbits are so pesky they've et everything except the rocks. Between they and the crows, I don't know whether to puke or go blind."

At this uncommon sort of complaint, I stammered out a few words that I hoped were sympathetic, meaning I hoped she'd think it over and decide to do neither one, and said I imagined it was a pretty hard area for farming, not knowing in the least what I was talking about but just aiming to hit on something agreeable.

She almost bit my head off. "Hard! You'd say so if you could see. The land ain't fit to clear. I'm from across the river south of Grand Tar, and my family can grow a stand of corn, pick it, shuck it, store it in a silo and raise a litter of pigs while my husband's getting his plough in the ground. No, if you want Missouri, take it and welcome."

She was about the fullest of grievances of any woman I ever met, and to hear her tell it, it was all her husband's fault. He didn't like the Illinois bottom because he claimed the river swoll up every second year and washed the topsoil away. But I got the notion pretty soon that he moved across because he couldn't stand her relatives' jawing, and if they were as gabby and positive as the representative he married, he would have done better to settle in Peru.

"You can say what you like, he's got his pints, but Ferd ain't sociable," she told me, and then she grabbed my arm and hissed, "Be quiet now—here he comes."

All this time, I had to wrestle myself to keep from snatching and eating a string of onions that were hanging beside the fireplace, my stomach was so hollow after the walking and swimming. Even so, I was warmed up again and feeling better.

The man came in, stomping his feet, and glanced at the woman —who was throwing some knives and forks on a split-pine table— and then at me, pulling up short. He looked sour, and had a scowl on his face, which was deep-lined and pock-marked from the small-pox. "Who in thunder's that?" he said finally, in what I supposed was the hospitable style of the neighborhood. She told him my story, getting it middling-right, although she said I was from Cincinnati, and when she finished he showed it had affected him by remarking, "Humph." It must have cost considerable effort, but he motioned me toward the breakfast table, and we had a loaf of salt-rising bread and something she called side-meat, but you couldn't fool me on things like that—I had done too much trapping —and I spotted it for woodchuck.

After breakfast he said he reckoned I wouldn't mind earning my keep, so he handed me a snaggley-toothed saw and took me up into the woods. There was a pile of about forty saplings lying there, the lower ends sharpened, and he said I must saw some more the same size and he would trim them up with the ax.

While I worked, he chewed tobacco and eyed me carefully, as if he had something on his mind. Presently he commenced to ask foolish little questions, like:

"Yore paw got any size to him?"

I answered that my father was a large man, husky and able, and with a temper to frighten a bobcat, because if this fellow was planning any deviltry, I wanted him to feel he might expect trouble later.

"You look stout enough," he observed after a while. I nodded and kept on sawing, wondering what was next. It had turned into a kind of game, and went along like this:

"Often sickly?"

Then, after my no, a few chunks of the ax, a pause or two to spit, and:

"Weight how much, did you say?"

I told him, and in a minute he inquired, with a sharp look: "Much of an eater?"

"One of the poorest eaters in Ohio—they used to complain about it at home, and give me tonics to fat up."

Chunk, chunk, pause, spit, chunk.

"Don't favor meat, I suppose?"

I said I never cared for it, hardly ever touched it, only a piece now and then to thicken my blood, but I'd take a piece to oblige him, if he preferred it, and many thanks for the offer.

44

"Tain't no offer," he said, and then he asked:

"Did much ploughing with a mule?"

I was enjoying myself now, being convinced that he was an outright lunatic, though harmless, and I rattled on, as overblown as a rooster.

"Very little," I said. "Back home in Cincinnati my father was the county sheriff, and I mostly helped out with the hangings and such."

He chunked away for several minutes, stopping to spit at a beetle, which got out of there in a hurry, and asked:

"Say he reckons you drowneded?"

I was sure of it, I said, but it didn't matter because I intended to push right on to St. Louis and find him. In a way, I was telling the truth, because I knew my father had a letter of introduction to a friend of my mother's family, a Pierre Chouteau, who was one of the biggest traders in St. Louis, or so they said.

"Maw expect you back soon?"

"Not so you could notice it—we were counting on two years at least."

He seemed satisfied with these answers, and we worked until noon, when we went back to the house and had some more sidemeat, this time with compone and collards. In the afternoon we carried down the saplings, and he loaded me up till my knees buckled, after which he kept asking me boneheaded things like: "Tired?" "Wears you out, does it?" and "Appear to be much of a heft?"

I *was* tired by now, and it was in my mind to damn him and his saplings to perdition, but something about him, a shadow of meanness in his dark, broody face, made me think this mightn't work out very well. The more I mulled him over, the better convinced I was that he had something up his sleeve, so after supper, as soon as they mentioned how late it was, I volunteered to get a fresh bucket of water. Once outside, I streaked to the well and raised two or three wails from the wheel, then tiptoed back and peered in the window, listening hard. They had their heads together, as thick as three in a bed.

"I can easy get him bound out, Agather," he was saying. "The judge'll take my word against his'n, and besides that, he's counting on my vote. We need somebody on the place, and this boy's stout—I put him to the test. He ain't real bright between the ears, but if it's hauling you want, why teach a jackass to sing? He'll do, or I'm mistook—it's the chance of a lifetime."

So that was it! Here I'd been playing him for a dunce, and he'd been using me for bait, all the time. He was going to apprentice me, and bind me out to him for maybe seven years, the way they did, and I'd have to like it or lump it.

As soon as I could, I said I was ready for bed—they had given me a blanket and told me to sleep in the loft on the straw—but the woman picked up the bucket and says, "I thought you went out for water."

Confound the luck, in my anxiousness to overhear them, I'd forgotten to fill it. The man flashed me a suspicious look, and they exchanged a glance that gave me goose-pimples, but I spoke up and said, "I stumped my toe coming in, and the water splashed out, but I thought there was enough left to drink. Here, I'll get some more."

"Leave it lay," he said; then he added irritably, "Git on along up —there's work to be done tomorrow."

I didn't need to be told twice. I skinned up the ladder and made a show of slapping down the straw and scrunching up a bed. Then I heard one of them blow out the lamp, and I waited for them to begin breathing heavy, so sleepy I was near about dead. But they were restless. Twice I could hear them talking, and once I heard the man get up and drink out of the bucket.

Suddenly I snapped awake—the moon was up; I had dozed off for no telling how long. I was in a sweat for fear I was too late; that I would be an indentured servant and punished by law if ever I broke away. I crept to the trap door—all dark below—and started down the ladder, skipping the fourth rung from the top, which was loose and creaked—I'd counted on the way up—and padded silently across the room. If Ferd had had trouble getting to sleep before, he was making up for lost time now. His mouth was wide open and he was dredging up noises that sounded like a pig stuck in a rail fence.

The woman, a shapeless lump beside him, was having a dream, something about how hard the ploughing was, for I heard her threaten to take a spade to Gomer, which was the name of their mule.

Out in the smokehouse, I borrowed some matches and a piece of sowbelly, and with my blanket over my shoulder and some shoes on at last—a pair of buckskin moccasins that didn't seem to be working but were too big and needed rags stuffed in them for comfort—I lit up the hill and on into the woods. I wanted to take his shotgun, but I didn't think it would be polite, and if there was one thing my mother was a stickler on, it was to be courteous and mind your manners while you were in somebody's house visiting.

So I took his hatchet instead, which was stuck upright in a stump. While we were sawing, the day before, I'd pumped him about the way to get to St. Louis, and he took me back a piece and pointed out a wagon trail to St. Genevieve, which he said was about halfway, "give or take a hundred miles," but I imagined this was a joke. The trail was grown up with tree shoots, and the ruts filled in with weeds, but he said it was traveled a-right smart in the summers. It would have been used more, he said, except that when they busted up the river pirates around Cave-in-Rock and Natchez, some of them drifted up here and were always accommodating and would cut your throat without charge.

This was travel news on about the same level as Ware's *Guide*, but I hadn't any choice, so I struck out, wishing I knew what time it was. Unless I misjudged my late host, he would rip around in the morning, and cuss, and of course blame everything on his wife, and maybe give her a couple of licks; then he would follow up the St. Genevieve trail for about five miles, mostly to avoid working. After that he would lose interest. So if I could do ten miles before dawn, I was safe. Or anyway, that's what I figured.

The trail was in the deep woods mainly, and sometimes hard to see, but once in a while it came out into a mossy glade of scrub evergreen, and then it was bright and pretty in the moonlight. Even in the big woods the paleness sifted down, because not all the trees had leafed out yet, and the ground was speckled with light. Very little sound except an occasional hoot owl, and the rustle of small animals—night-prowling possums and coons, along with foxes hunting them and a soft wind that swayed the trees and breathed through the high-up larch boughs, lonely and sad, like spirits flying by.

I made good time, and wasn't scared, only at bushes crackling too near at hand. I thought I must have walked for two hours, and was so sleepy I'd begun to stumble. It was cold, too. This wouldn't do, so I knew I'd got to take a nap. At the next open place, I went off a hundred yards or so, keeping the moonlit clearing in view, then made a small fire in the shelter of an oak, well out of sight. Rolled up tight in the blanket, I lay down and melted into the leaves.

Chapter V

"Turn him over! Shake him up!"

"It's only a boy."

"Never mind that—prod him out of there."

I sat up, then sprang to my feet, stupid with sleep, but with an icy grabbing of my heart, too.

They were an old man, hatless, with tumbled gray hair, two younger ones—a tall, sallow fellow dressed in gambler's black, neat even here in the woods, and a beefy, yellow-haired brute with as ugly a face as you'd be apt to meet ouside a jail—with a pale, black-haired girl of eighteen or nineteen. They were mounted on poor-looking horses, the girl riding double behind the beefy man.

"Well, you had to investigate, now you know the long and short of it," said this last. "Put a ball in him and let's be along, else he'll describe us for sure."

"Hold your tongue," replied the old man in what I thought was a very careless tone, considering the difference in their ages and size. "If I was you, Shep, I wouldn't try to think. You haven't had the experience."

The old gentleman got down—he was taller than I thought, and straight as a slat. He said, "Now let's have a chat, sonny. What are we doing out here in the woods, eh? Don't be afeard. Speak right out."

My teeth were chattering at the talk of shooting me, but I had begun to take heart a little, and felt brasher.

"I'm mighty glad you found me, sir. I was lost—I got separated from my Uncle Jessie and the others. They were on their way to

Memphis to see Uncle Jessie's stepbrother, Merle, that runs the brewery."

"Hold on, hold on—you're running away with yourself. Who's this Uncle Jessie? Why ain't you home with your maw and paw?"

"I'm a poor foundling boy," I said, using a word from out of an English book they handed us at the Secondary School, a very good story that I'd read through four or five times. "He isn't my blood uncle—they left me on his doorstep, in a basket, one night when it was snowing and sleeting. I was near about froze when they found me, him and my Aunt Harriet, his second wife; the first was shot while poaching hares."

This didn't seem to fit the occasion, but I was stuck with it, so I let it go, and anyway it was in the book.

The old man looked up at his companions and said, "Durn me, if this boy ain't the champeen long-distance talker of Missouri, and they was *all* born with a flappy jaw hereabouts, if I'm any judge." Turning back to me, he says, "Son, your tongue waggles like a billygoat with the St. Vitus."

I didn't relish the compliment, specially when the beefy man spoke up to suggest that, "Let's cut it out and improve his looks." Behind him on the horse, I could see the black-haired girl stiffen up and look frightened and miserable.

It took me only about five minutes to make up my mind that these were common highwaymen, dangerous, too, and that I'd better watch my step, and not get frisky. Even so, I was beginning to fix a sort of plan in my mind.

The three of them had drawn off for a consultation; now the old man came back. Just as I thought, he'd been working on my story, and didn't altogether care for it.

"You say you was separated from your Uncle Jessie? Now how in the name of common sense can anybody with the brains of a muskrat get lost on a wagon trail? And why didn't they send back to search?" He put his face down—I hadn't noticed before what a wild glitter his eyes had—and said in a tone that made me gulp,

"Son, if you want to live long and die hearty, you'd better spit out the truth and spit it out quick."

Before I could answer, he said, "Now ain't the facts that you're an apprentice and have run off to shirk toil? Ain't that so? Talk up, or by Jupiter, I'll——"

Seizing my jacket, he gave me a yank that put a crick in my neck, and I began to blubber.

"I couldn't stood it any longer. I was black and blue the whole first year. He beat me up regular, whether I deserved it or not, and didn't give me anything to eat except cold leavings from the second table."

"That's all well and good; the point is, what's to be done *now*?"

I tried to look pitiful, but he went on:

"My partner here, Mr. Baggott, who's known for his merciful ways and love of children, favors putting a bullet in you, so you won't have to suffer any more. What do you think of that?"

I commenced to sniffle again, and said I hoped they would spare me—I couldn't do them any harm, but only wanted to escape in peace, so that nobody would take me back for the reward.

The old man's ears pricked right up.

"What reward? See here, who was you bound out to, anyway? And whereabouts?"

"Mr. Chouteau, sir," I said, wiping my eyes on my sleeve. "Up in St. Louis. He's the wealthiest merchant in those parts, and the meanest. He placed a reward of two hundred dollars on me out of spite and revenge, because he couldn't have wanted me back, seeing how he treated me."

"How'd *you* know about this reward?" he inquired suspiciously, putting his face down again.

"I hid out for two days under some pilings by the river, foot of Market Street. I saw the notice on a handbill when I was out nights rummaging through garbage cans."

It sounded good, dropping in Market Street like that, as if I'd been around there for years, but I remembered it from hearing my father ask my mother how to get to Mr. Chouteau's establishment.

They had drawn off for another pow-wow now, and when they came back they said I must go along with them toward St. Genevieve "for protection," else I might meet up with some "hard cases" and get hurt.

"But I'm traveling in the other direction, sir!" I cried in alarm. I told them I was aiming to go south as far as New Orleans, and find honest work there, with maybe a chance to go to school on the side, which was all I'd ever wanted since I was old enough to know what I was doing. These last words got sort of stuck in my throat, but I finally coughed them out after a little difficulty.

"You'll do what you're told," said the old man, and Mr. Baggott, possibly out of his love for children, unslung the rifle he had tied to his saddle, humming a little tune.

As he did so, the girl behind him suddenly spoke up for the first time. "Don't you touch him!" she cried in a low, fierce voice. "The child's had enough trouble. Leave him go on his way."

All right, I said to myself, you're not here because you like it. You need help, and I'll try to see that you get it.

Baggott's reply to her outburst was to turn half around, rising in his stirrups, and in a quick, sure motion strike her across the mouth with the back of his hand. In the woods stillness, the smack rang out like a report.

She gasped a shocked, "Oh!" and put her palms to her cheeks, but said nothing more.

Paying no attention, the old man vaulted back on his horse, surprisingly nimble and springy. Jerking its head around—it had been droopily trying to find grass—he said, "Get up behind Slater," which I judged was the one in black, and when I had done so, he called out, "Come along," and we started along the trail.

For about an hour we rode toward St. Genevieve, with the sun coming up over the pines to our right, and everything sparkling and dewy and fresh in the morning sunlight. Once in a while we came up onto a high baldy knob where we could see the river, broad and silently moving, and across the way parts of the Illinois shore, like drowneded islands now in the big floodwaters. I was glad I didn't live there. You could smell the river—that cold, muddy-bottom smell, mixed up with dead fish and swamp rot and tree stumps. But it was mighty pretty just the same, and made you want to get out on it in a skiff or a raft and slide down, stretched out in the sun and watching the spring-rise sights. I had done it on the Ohio many's the time, sneaking away on the sly. You could make a tolerable raft, to hold three or four boys, from out of two big logs and a few drift planks, unless they had got water-soaked and sumpy.

Presently we called a halt so the girl could go over in the woods, and as she did so Mr. Baggott got off a few coarse jokes, calling after her a time or two, to inquire if she needed help, and advising her to watch out for snakes. The old gentleman said nothing, merely sitting without stirring, darkly thoughtful, but Mr. Slater muttered under his breath. He and I had exchanged no words of any kind. Riding along, I'd been stiff and uncomfortable, not finding anything to hang onto except his waist, which I didn't like to bother for fear of making him mad and being shot. So I held onto his coattails, in case there should be an emergency of the horse shying or like that.

Getting on toward noon, we stopped to eat, and I learned some more about the party. About the first thing that turned up was that the old gentleman, who went by the name of John, claimed to be John Murrel, the pirate and outlaw. I was acquainted with this Murrel, or leastways with the real article. He had been written up in a paper-backed book I'd got off a shantyboater for two stringy rabbits from my traps. According to the reports, he had ended up by going around trying to coax all the slaves to rise up against their masters and kill them with axes and hoes, upon which he would run a "southern empire," with whiskey and women for all. It might have worked, too, but one of his partners named Steward told on him, and the people around Natchez charged forward and placed Murrel in jail, where they hoped he would be less of a nuisance. After that they had a kind of picnic, going overboard on the other side, as reformers generally do, and hung all his friends, and some of his acquaintances, and several strangers, including a number who were just passing through, and wound up by flogging everybody else in sight. Then they called it a good day and said they wished they had a conspiracy to put down more often.

Anyway, Murrel sat in prison for ten years, if you cared to believe the book, and when he got out he was real woozy in the head. He stated that he would be a preacher from now on, which was about all he was fit for, I reckon. In the ten years, he had loaded up on scriptures until he had some kind of verse to cover everything, and the last they saw of him as he staggered off into the woods, heading north, he was shouting and singing and waving his arms, calling on the Lord to tidy up this or that situation, dropping in quotations as he did so, and a few of the citizens around Natchez felt down-right sorry to see him so reduced, for he had been a dignified and upright figure when he was a pirate.

From that time—four or five years back—he had disappeared completely out of view, but now here he was again, up in Missouri, or allowed to be, though I didn't much believe it. Neither did Mr. Baggott and Mr. Slater, I judged, because they always spoke to him very mocky and overcourteous, as if they were addressing a poor, addled humbug who was out of his mind and should be humored. But they were afraid of him, too. His eyes were so crazy and flashing that a person realized there wasn't any more bluff to him than there is to a spider.

We let the horses forage, and sat down on a couple of fallen trees. The girl, who they called Jennie, was so pale I thought she was sick. It was too bad, because she had a sweet face, with black hair and curling lashes and very white, even teeth, and a gentle, interesting expression, as if she had known better people once. She lay back against a limb and closed her eyes, refusing to eat, and Mr. Slater put a coat over her, saying, "The lass is beat out. We ought to hole up somewhere and rest."

"Don't mind her," said Shep. "She's likely got something in the oven. They mostly do after they get to be ten or eleven."

"You have a rough tongue, my friend," Mr. Slater told him, and the old man suddenly threw back his head and cried, " 'Oh, thou oppressed virgin, daughter of Zirdon: arise, pass over to Chittim; there also shalt thou have no rest.' "

"Mighty pretty," said Shep. "I imagine you learned it when you was thieving and murdering down along the Trace. Or was that from one of the Sunday schools they had in the Pinch Gut?"

His mouth was so sneering, and his tone so raspy, that I made sure the old man would pull out a revolver and kill him, but he appeared not to hear. Instead, he consulted a very dented silver watch with a stained face, and said, "How far do you make it to St. Genevieve?"

"In the neighborhood of two mile, so we better look peart," replied Shep. "People will be driving hogs in to market."

"I don't know when I've encountered such a run of threadbare luck," the old man went on. "In the book of Daniel it is set forth that the Lord will provide, but I'm blessed if He ain't been snoozing on the job. Them last two bunches couldn't a raised enough cash for a basket of turnips. All we got was the pleasure of knocking them on the head and this girl here, and that only because of Joe's fastidity notions."

I had been eating on a piece of pork which they took from a saddle bag, saying nothing about the sowbelly I had in my pocket, or the gold, either, you can bet—just listening and wondering what they aimed to do next.

Slater's name was Hard-Luck Joe Slater—I found that out when Shep took to ragging him about gambling. Slater would have liked to have been an honest gambler, but he never could catch any cards, so they said. If he came up with an eight-high flush, somebody else snatched the pot with a nine-high flush. It had gone on so long it turned him sour. It was disgusting to him, and broke his spirit. He began to cheat, but he didn't have any luck at that either, because they always nabbed him and gave him a knuckling.

He and Shep, who was a mule skinner by profession but graduated to be a mule thief, which was quicker, had joined up with the old man in Memphis, in the Gut, or Pinch Gut, and had been working the Missouri side of the river as far north as St. Louis. I wasn't clear about the manner of work they did, but I had the idea that Reverend Murrel had backslid since they let him out of jail. Or maybe he hadn't located a pulpit yet and was filling in the time.

Back on the trail, we rode for about an hour and arrived at a fork where several roads came in, with St. Genevieve not far off. "This'll do," said the old man. "We'll lay up in that clump of alders, and the first one makes a noise'll have me to deal with."

I began to get scared, not knowing what was going to happen, but if somebody had told me, I wouldn't have believed it.

Pretty soon a farmer and his wife hove into view driving a broken-down wagon with one tire iron flapping loose. It was Saturday; they were going in to trade. The wagon was filled with produce and sausage bags, but looked ornery and poverty-struck. In our sheltered place in the bushes, the old man raised his hand and whispered, "Leave them pass. What we're after's a party going t'other way."

Jennie, I noticed, had her eyes closed and her lips were moving as if she might be saying a prayer. Shep looked impatient, and Mr. Slater, as usual, sat his horse like a man without a purpose. The sun was high, and the bugs were out; I was itching to get at a couple on the back of my neck, but I didn't dare. It was a handsome day, one of those clear, breezy spring mornings when the sky is a blue well, without a bottom, with now and then puff-ball clouds floating in it like blossoms off a snowball bush. If you stared up at it, it somehow made you thirsty. Altogether, the scenery was too cheerful for trouble, so I guessed they were fixing to buy provisions.

"All right," the old man said quickly, bringing my mind back to earth, "here they are. Shep and I'll ride out first."

Around the bend, out of the woods, came a very clean and bright-appearing young man with his wife, one of those red-cheeked, plump girls that can work a man down any day in the week. They were riding horses, and behind them followed a wagon hitched to two mules and driven by a youngster of eleven or twelve. Two other children were in the wagon, both little girls; they could have been twins.

"Howdy, folks," cried John, and up he rode, digging his heels into his mare with little nervous nibbles. Shep was right beside him, having put Jennie down to the ground, and we followed along after.

"Good morning, neighbor," answered the young man, very friendly and open. "Heading for St. Genevieve?"

"Not till you tell us how you fared. We require to fodder up, but we was aiming to make the best bargain we could."

"We carted in a passel of beaver pelts," said the young man, "and they commanded a tolerable price—better than what I figured on. If you've got skins to trade, Ross Sylvester's your man. He's honest, and he pays cash."

I didn't think Shep would be able to keep his jaw buttoned up very long, so now he said, "There's a fancy side-saddle for you," and rode toward the wife to examine it. His manner was bold and yet cringy and polite, too—nothing a person could complain about, but not comfortable, either. He prodded his mare on up till its flanks rubbed against her stirrups, and laid his hand on the saddle horn, which was silver-studded, like the rest of the leather.

The young man's face kept its friendly look, and his slouch was still easy and loose, but his eyes changed ever so slightly, becoming —I don't know how you'd say it—*tight*-looking.

"Yes," he said, "her uncle that was in the Texas troubles brought it back from Mexico. We've been offered a heap for it, but she won't sell."

"Well, now I don't blame the little lady, indeed I don't," said Shep, grinning at her and touching the brim of his hat. "It's just a perfect fit—very snug and firm. I don't know when I've seen a better-filled saddle."

She stared directly at him, cool and contemptuous, and showed without saying a word that she no more cared what he thought than she would a pig in a pigsty. She had pluck, and no mistake.

But he couldn't leave it alone. He had hit on a line of palaver that suited him, and he meant to squeeze it dry. He said:

"Why, the two was made for each other; there ain't a wrinkle anywhere." Then, turning to the husband, he said, "How old was this uncle? If you ask me, that saddle was cut to measure, and it wasn't done in only one fitting, neither."

"Come on, Joyce," said the young man shortly. "Stir up the team, Todd, we'll be getting along."

"Hey, now!" cried Shep in offended alarm. "That ain't what I call neighborly. You're a-going to hurt this old fellow's feelings"—gesturing toward John. "He's touchy, he is—there ain't hardly any telling what he's apt to do next."

" 'God shall likewise destroy thee for ever, He shall take thee away, and pluck thee out of thy dwelling place, and root thee out of the land of the living,' " said John, and pulling out a pistol from under his coat, he shot the young man in the middle of the forehead, the bullet making a small, neat, blue hole. I remember thinking how queer it looked without any blood whatever. Then I saw Mr. Slater's coat coming up toward me; the tops of the trees spun around in a whirling circle, faster and faster, and everything slipped away into blackness.

Chapter VI

When I came to, that monster was bending over the dead man, on the ground, going through his pockets. Shep had the woman by both wrists, but he was making poor shift of it, for his left cheek had four bloody scratches from eye to chin, his jacket sleeve was half torn off, and he was being kicked about the shin and knee. At the sound of the shot, the team had reared, and the boy, standing up and sawing at the reins, was trying to calm them.

"Go, Todd!" the woman cried. "Lash the mules—streak for home and fetch your Uncle Ned!"

I don't know when I ever saw a cooler performer than that boy, even among the shantyboaters, who were a rough lot and didn't care a fig for human life, theirs or anybody else's. He cracked a blacksnake whip down on the team, shouted "Gee—on!" and fell backward over the wagon seat, so abruptly did the mules leap forward and yank him out of there. The twins, in the back, were screaming, but the boy, steady and white-faced, was as businesslike as if he tackled this kind of thing every day.

"After him, Shep!" the old man cried. "There's nothing here—they've got their plunder in the wagon."

With a curse, Shep dropped the woman's arm and spurred his horse in the direction of the runaway, but he hadn't got more than fifty yards before a shot rang out and his hat flew off like something jerked on a string. He hauled up, almost pulling the mare back on top of him, which would have been a very good thing, in my judgment.

The boy had dropped his reins and let the mules head for home on their own. Then, lying on his stomach, he had snatched up a rifle and taken a pot shot as deliberate as a professional hunter's, and if it hadn't been for a bump in the road he would have bagged game, though nothing you'd care to eat or even have stuffed and hang over the fireplace. The last I saw him, disappearing into the woods, he was ramming home a charge for another try.

Shep gave out that he'd had enough. He shouted back, "Catch him yourself—I ain't hankering to have my skull ventilated by no shirttail boy."

It was nearly over now, but not quite. Finding herself freed, the young wife, still without tears, grabbed an ax that was slung in a pack on her husband's horse—he'd likely been riding ahead, cutting shoots off the trail—and wheeling around sent it spinning at the old man's head. Murrel or not, he took a lot of killing. Quick as a youngster, he rolled over and over on the ground, like a snake that's been hit a lick with a stick, and when he came up he emptied his other pistol into the woman's left breast. Before she slumped off her horse, I watched the red stain widen out like spring water bubbling up.

If I live to be a hundred, I'll never forget that day, either the killings or what came after. When Shep got back, he and the old man checked up and found that the total haul was eight dollars silver, a couple of trumpery rings from off the woman's fingers, and a good hunting-case watch that the young man was wearing on a braided rawhide thong.

"There was more cash than this—bound to be if they traded goods," said John. "I'd like to get my hooks on that cotton-haired whelp."

Shep took the boots off the dead man and said they fitted him like a glove. He tossed his, which were scuffed up and full of holes, and had a piece of bark in one for a patch, into the bushes and walked around as blown up as a peacock. You would have thought he'd been elected to Congress, he was so pleased.

John took the eight dollars, and Slater got the watch. They opened it up and it struck the hour—two cheerful little dings as saucy as a grandfather clock—and on the inside were two pictures, one of the man and his wife at their wedding, looking happy but warm, and another of the children. The twins were mere babies, but the boy Todd had the same sober, grown-up look as when he had whipped up the mules, half an hour before.

I wondered where he was, and if he reached home. Evidently Shep had the same idea, because he said, "We'd better hump ourselves—that boy'll be back soon, and he'll bring help." It was curious, but the miserable bully had got the fear of God put in him by that close ball, and now, as I write, I think he must have had a foresight that he and the boy would meet up again sometime.

But now they must dispose of the bodies—"to destroy the evidence"—for John said he had studied law in jail, along with the religion that had been his salvation and made him see how wicked he was in the old days, plotting uprisings and drinking, and he said they had to have a corpus delecty before there was any crime.

"If they find a corpus delecty in this case, they'll have to dive for it," he stated. "For anybody of the true girt, there was only one answer, and that's the way we'll do it."

So they took a sheath knife and ripped both bodies clear down the stomachs and pulled out all the intestines, and then they filled the spaces back up with rocks and sand and dumped those two poor unhuman shells into a slough that had steep, muddy banks.

Both Shep and John were red to the elbows before they were done, but they washed up as offhand as a pair of coal miners. It was sickening, and horrible, but I'd seen so much that day, I was kind of numb, you might say.

After a while, we headed on up the trail, with no sound but the irregular clopping of the horses, and now and then Jennie crying a little. Right then, I made up my mind to get even for that boy Todd if it was the last thing I did. Still, you understand, my own case was nothing to brag about, not yet. But I was alive, and madder than a hornet, which I've noticed can serve as well as courage in a pinch. I had my hatchet that I'd lifted from the farmer stuck in my belt, and I figured that when we stopped to sleep, I'd get up in the middle of the night and bash in their heads. I was just sore enough to do it. But the more I thought it over, the better it seemed to wait and work my original plan.

When we pulled up to camp, the old man said he called it about seven miles to St. Louis and that we'd ride in early in the morning to collect the reward. I wailed and took on and begged him not to do it, but he quoted four or five verses from the Bible, mostly having to do with a man named Joab, who had a fight in a tree, and told me to shut my trap.

That night, sitting around the fire, drinking "coffee" made from evans'-root, he fell to talking about the old days, and he said: "No boy ever had the advantages of upbringing that I did, and I thank God for it. A blessed mother is heaven's earthly reward, and mine was a jewel. She was the wife of a boneheaded innkeeper, and she taught me to steal before I was ten. It was her guidance that made me rise up to success. She had the flair for hospitality, and when she tucked in a guest, she generally bottom-warmed his bed, to be sure he'd sleep, and then I would prize my way in and empty his pockets. She gave me my start, you might say.

"At the height of my nigger-stealing I was that genteel you wouldn't have recognized me. I bought my boots and hats in Philadelphia and had my clothes tailored in New Orleans, meanwhile laying over at Mother Surgick's to frolic with the girls. My pantaloons were strapped on, top and bottom, and my shirt was fastened with ribbons and buttons of gold. I had a silk hat with a rim three quarters of an inch wide and boots of pure calf on my feet. And if it ain't too much for your stomick, have a look at me now."

Leaning forward, he seized a brand and stirred up the fire, and in the upward shower of sparks he looked as pious as old Moses himself, with his white hair flying and his eyes crazy and hot. I could see Shep glance at Slater, who was gazing broodily at the embers, and then at the girl, who sat as white and still as death. "Yes, sir," said John, "I was a roarer, born and bred, and I flung money both to the right and to the left—I was famous for it. There wasn't hardly a law I didn't break, from murder to treason, and do you know what first laid me low?"

He began to rip and rave and foam and grit his teeth and haul at his hair till I thought he'd tumble over into the fire.

"—why, they took me up for horse-stealing, like a common beggarman in the street, me that was plotting to rule an empire. They sentenced me to twelve months in jail, gave me thirty lashes on my bare back at a public whipping post, made me sit two hours in the pillory three days running, and at the end of the third day brought me into court and branded my left thumb with the letters 'H.T.' for Horse Thief."

Leaping to his feet, he flourished the thumb with a shriek that made the woods ring. Both Shep and Slater jumped back out of the way, and the girl woke up with a whimper.

So it was true, then. The mark, now fine white lines, showed up clear against the dark grime and broken nail of his thumb, and I fancied I could see dried crusts of blood from his work earlier in the day. He *was* Murrel, just as he'd said all along, and here I was stuck with him. Shep and Slater must have had something like the same idea, for they stood back staring, as sober as gallows birds facing the noose.

"All right, John, all right," said Shep nervously. "That's over and done, so why don't you turn in and get some sleep? Another screech like that and you'll have half of St. Louis on our necks."

"They strapped my hand to the railing at the judge's bench, and brought in a tinner's stove and set it beside the sheriff. Then he took up the red-hot branding iron and placed it against my thumb. Some people in the back of the room—they came and thanked me later for the entertainment—said they could hear the sizzle of meat frying and see the smoke plumes three or four feet in the air. And I never twitched a muscle. Men came up and shook my hand afterwards; they said it was the finest display of gall they'd seen in the history of Nashville court punishment."

"Sure, John, sure, John," said Shep, who was getting back some

63

of his impudence. "There never was anybody like you for a thumb roasting—we all know that."

The old man didn't heed him but kept on with an account of how that was nothing, that two of his confederates who were nabbed later, at the time of his long prison term for conspiracy, were stripped, lashed all over with nettles, tied face up naked in a skiff and set adrift for the flies to finish the job. Speaking for myself, I'd heard enough, so I crept back out of sight and pulled my blanket up over my ears. But I wasn't easy in my mind. Through the covering I could hear the droning of the madman's voice, and occasionally the fire popping, and once, after I'd been asleep, I reckon, I sat up sharp with my heart in my mouth. But it was only a hoot owl or a bear—it's curious how much alike they can sound, it takes a real old woods rat to tell them apart—and I lay back down, very quiet. John still sat by the fire, bending over and moaning with his head between his knees, and the others were sleeping nearby. I could have split his skull easy with the hatchet, but no, I thought I'd wait for the morning. They'd earned that reward in St. Louis, and I wanted to be there when they got it.

Chapter VII

We were up before dawn, mostly because it was too cold to sleep. The fire had gone out, and the horses were stamping around, noisy and restless. There *had* been a bear in the woods during the night, and nothing else I know of will give a horse the jimjams quite as fast. Bears will attack a horse, if they're feeling ornery enough. Years afterward, I met a man who'd been all around, in India and Africa and run-down places like that, and he'd had a lot to do with lions and tigers, but he said he'd rather tackle them any day than run foul of a bear in a grouchy humor, which is their natural outlook.

Anyhow, the horses were ready to shove. You can't fool them about things like that. If you think so, try and get one to step out on a rotten bridge. You could settle down on the bank and raise a family before he'd budge, they've got that much sense about danger.

Slater's horse, which might have brought seventy-five cents for glue, now had a lame front leg, along with mange, colic, coughing fits, heaves, saddle sores, fistula, and a sway-back, so we had to go slow. Shep grumbled and took on, and John snapped at him once or twice. I was thinking we'd better get to St. Louis soon, else there'd be an explosion. Tempers were worn thin, and probably it was from their jackass notions of eating. They didn't have anything but the piece of salt pork, and it had turned right green around the edges. If a body was really pining for a case of the bloody flux, I can't think of any better way to get it than load up on pork, especially after it has passed its prime, and I've heard my father say the same.

Off and on, I went over in the woods and nibbled on my sowbelly till it was gone, so I made out all right.

"We'll spruce up in St. Louis, once we get the reward," said John when we stopped to clear the trail. "I don't mind acknowledging that I've contracted a case of the gripes. It's odd, too, for that pork's as tasty as any I've come across lately."

"Yes, it's delicious," said Shep. "It tastes like a piece of boiled pickaninny, and not necessarily the best cut, neither. As commissary of the expedition, you make about the poorest out of anybody I ever met. More than that——"

He was meaning to blather on, not being able to stop once he'd struck something agreeable, but the old man suddenly straightened up in the saddle, with a wicked glitter in his eye.

Slater said soothingly, "I suggest we save our strength for the ride in. Things'll look better in St. Louis."

Shep gave a short, harsh laugh, that sounded as if he was about as amused as if somebody had sawed off his leg, and shouted, "Listen to Hard-Luck Joe the missionary. Why, he's getting to be a regular psalm singer, and I shouldn't wonder if it wasn't the influence of this little lady here." He turned and gave Jennie a playful nudge in the bosom. "Ain't that so?" he asked her. "Ain't it true you've been casting calf's eyes at our old friend Joe?"

Hanging onto the coattails, I could see Slater's back stiffen up, and I was amazed, and a little scared, when he said in a low tone, "Take your filthy hands off that girl."

"Well, now," said Shep, riding his horse up to glare down at us out of his little mean yellow eyes, "was you looking for a test of strength with me? Was that it, Joe?"

Slater sat steadily for a few seconds, then dropped his gaze. "I'm no fighter," he said at last. "Have it your own way."

"That's enough," said John. "Break it off and let's be moving. Time to cat-fuss when we've collected the reward. Slaughter each other and welcome—I'd admire to hold your coats."

Getting on toward noon we came to a sizable stream that ran into the Mississippi, which I heard them call the Maremack, or sounds to that effect, and it had a rude log bridge over a narrow part, with a toll gate. An angular man wearing a straw hat and a pair of corduroy jeans with one gallus busted got up off a bench, a foot or so at a time, and said, "Howdy." His face was neither friendly nor unfriendly; he just waited. Leaning against his bench was a rickety old squirrel gun.

"Your bridge?" asked John.

"I wouldn't hardly say that," said the man, "but it's on my deeded land, I sawed the lumber, whittled the pegs, put it up, could take it down if so minded, but hope to hold it till the rightful owner proves his claim."

"What's the toll?"

"Regular charge is fifteen cents a head, children and horses free, but I'll admit the entire group for half a dollar, and nobody stung either way. Or I'll take produce if you've got it."

"Seems high," said John. " 'The rivers, yea, the seas and the fishes thereof, are possessions unto God the most high.' "

"I'd be the last to deny it," said the man, "and it may be you can get Him to put you across in a boat. Otherwise, you'll have to swim for it, which ain't unenjoyable, if you've got the time. Best place is down about a quarter of a mile, clear of my land."

At this offhand and disregardful address, I expected to see John rise up in his sanctimony and let loose some thunders, but he said, "Can you make change?"

Not answering, the man jingled some coins in his pocket, after which John drew out a long, baggy leather pouch and removed a folded-up bill. What he'd done with the eight silver dollars I had no idea. The gatekeeper eyed the bit of paper with great interest; then he picked up a loose-leafed book from under his bench and sat down to study. "I reckon you won't mind," he said in a minute, "if I just thumb through Bicknell's *Bank Note Detector*. You couldn't hardly imagine a handier little pamphlet, and put out every week for only two dollars a year. It's only because I know you're honest that I want to help you, and"—running his finger down a list—"why, yes, sir, bless my soul, here's the number right here—now what do you think of that? Counterfeit! Not worth the paper it's printed on. If it hadn't been for you and I checking this out, I'd been left sucking hind tit; wouldn't you say so?"

"Open the gate," said John in an easy voice.

Shifting the gun very leisurely up over his knees, the man said, "I'm near about wore out, getting up and down. Why don't you open it yourself?"

It was as good as a play. For the first time since I'd struck these scoundrels, I could sit back without caring what happened. As much as I hoped John and Shep might come to grief, the gatekeeper's smart-alecky manner was almost as raspy. Maybe I'd seen too much blood lately; whatever it was, I didn't altogether mind how it came out.

"Are you refusing to open the gate?" asked John, still very quiet, like some old prophet about to deliver a judgment, as I'd seen them do on some pictures we had at home. The man was chewing on a cud of tobacco, and now he leaned over and spat, then wiped his chin deliberately with the back of his hand.

"I could see you were smart when you first rid up."

John sat like a statue, I held my breath. After what seemed a long time, he thrust his hand into his pocket, the gatekeeper swung the rifle up sharply, and John threw down one of the silver dollars. It lit on its edge and rolled up against the man's foot. He leaned over, picked it up, and bit it.

"Hand up the bank note," said John. "I'll want to turn it in to the authorities."

"No hard feelings," said the gatekeeper when he slouched over with the troublesome bill and fifty cents change. But John made a signal to Shep and us, and we wheeled our horses around. Before we stepped on the bridge, he said to the man, "You should go far—you've got chance on your side. You want to tell your children and grandchildren about the lucky day you had in the spring of '49."

For my part, I doubted if that gatekeeper would go much farther than he'd gone, his tongue was too loose. But I'll say this for him—he had grit. After we'd clattered over his poor excuse of a bridge, he called out, perfectly cocksure, "Keep an eye peeled for a shifty-looking party of queersmen. The constables have been searching hereabouts, and would favor your help."

Now that the danger was past, Shep yanked his horse's head angrily and said, "Let's shut that clodhopper's mouth. I've heard about all I can stand. We can pull up around the next bend and I'll sneak back through the woods and draw a bead on him from the rear."

Which was, I expect, just about his notion of a fair fight. John merely clucked at his horse, and we jogged on.

We rode into St. Louis in the middle of the afternoon. Now that a showdown was near, I commenced to get nervous. What with the douse in the river, no sleep and skimpy food, not to mention murder and kidnapping, I wasn't in what you would call hearty condition. I felt sickly, and was sweating. I was so low down and poorly I might even have swallowed one of Aunt Kitty's conjure draughts, which were aimed for just this kind of thing, or so she claimed. But I had tried one on Sam, after he'd eaten an umbrella handle, and he only rolled over on his back with his feet stuck up in the air, not much better, and maybe a little worse, than before he was treated.

When a few scattered log huts hove into view, with warehouses and docks strung far out up the river beyond, John stopped and gave us a lecture. "Leave me do all the talking," he said, aiming his remarks mostly at Shep, who, with his horse, was looking impatient. "There won't be any trouble—nobody knows us around here. Only don't say anything you don't have to. Least said, soonest mended has always been my motto throughout my career, and barring ten or fifteen years in jail, I wouldn't change a particle of it."

Then he rode up to me and said, "You let on there's anything amiss—just one peep—and I'll turn you inside out and start you off afresh. And stop the snuffling; we're doing you a favor if you only knew it. You can skip out again once we're clear of the town, and maybe this time steal a horse and ride off in style. You'd better hang up for twenty-four hours, though, else it wouldn't be ethical to collect the reward, and I want everything aboveboard. I may set up for merchant later on in this town; I like the looks of it."

From where I sat behind Slater, I couldn't see anything to rave about. After the outlying log huts, with enough pigs to populate the universe, we passed through what I've since heard was the old French quarter, being a very cramped up section of narrow, crooked streets, or lanes, and queer, high-balconied houses with ladders reaching up from the ground to the top rooms, and everything tilted at crazy angles, as if the dirt underneath had settled here and there, leaving the buildings now leaning backwards, more often forward, with their heads together, like old ladies gossiping.

Clattering into St. Louis through these dizzy passages, like the crooked man walking his crooked mile in the rhyme, we attracted little enough notice for all our rough appearance. Suddenly it came to me that, if my story held water, I ought to know the location of Chouteau's trading post. I had a panicky flutter, guessing somehow that the same thought was puzzling John at that instant, and sure enough, here he came reining up and riding back.

"Joe, go on ahead with Runaway"—he'd been calling me Runaway all day now, getting worked up for the collection—"he'll point us in, and without any monkey business, neither, if he wants to have breakfast tomorrow."

But I was a second and half ahead of him. "I'd sure enough like to," I said, "because I know which side my bread's buttered on now, but I'm mixed up and addled coming in from this direction. Going out, I stowed away on the carriage ferry and went down on the Illinois side through the American Bottoms."

My face wasn't more than a foot from that murdering old lunatic's, and I could see in his smoky black eyes that he only half believed me.

"Then what were you doing on the Missouri side below St. Genevieve?"

"A farmer running trot lines put me over in a skiff for rowing and baiting hooks all morning."

70

"Sounds likely."

I felt good again. I was so free I almost spoke up and dared him to make something out of it, for we were right smack in front of a noisy bar where the street was full of traders and rivermen and a handful of Indians. I had only to set up a cry for these blood-thirsty hellions of ours to be in a peck of trouble. But I knew what I had to do, so I kept mum.

Presently John made a sign to stop, and he got down to have a confab with an aproned man with a very reddish-purple face in front of a barbershop. I saw this fellow gesturing and explaining away as excited and impatient and angry-looking as the Frenchmen in Louisville always were. Then John got back on his horse and we pushed on out of the French quarter and into a section, going up-hill from the river, of new board houses and warehouses, all raw and ugly in the afternoon sun, and such a lot of hammering and banging going on, and dogs barking, and dirty-faced children yell-ing, that you'd have thought it might raise the dead, only they wouldn't have stayed up long, not after they'd had a look around.

The barber's directions must have been sound, because we made a few turns, and at the end of a long street arrived at a very broad store building with two galleries and warehouses to either side and behind, the whole advertised by a split-log sign that had a white-birch rim all around, saying, "Pierre Chouteau, Jr., Fur Trading and General Merchandise." An air of bustle and energy lay over this place, with clerks pushing through the doors carrying armfuls of supplies, others running from warehouse to warehouse, wagons loading at side doors, and a dozen or so horses tied to hitching posts out front. A darky boy of about my age, dressed in an out-landish costume of black silk hat and scarlet jacket, was serving as hostler, watering the horses from a wooden trough, then tying them up, and from the number of coins I saw spun his way, along with gibes and a playful cuff or two, I judged he must have been making as much money as old Chouteau himself, and was likely a partner in the business.

When we dismounted, I found that my legs were trembling. I

made as if to run, but John caught me with a low hiss, "No, you don't, you tricky scamp. Get on in there and be quick about it!" I hung back, whimpering, then let him shove and yank me along, with the others—Shep, Slater and Jennie—coming up behind.

A good many men, bearded and tobacco-chewing, were ganged around in the big room downstairs, jawing and spitting on the floor, and hitting one another on the back, and I saw piles of skins, shiny and blue and brown, tied up carelessly with string, lying on both counters and floor. It was the big season, with the winter's trapping over, and bottles were going it here and there in celebration.

John caught a clerk by the sleeve and asked where we could find Pierre Chouteau, but got only a hurried pointing of a pencil up at a little office balcony in the rear. So we made our way on through the crowd and climbed a low set of stairs, and there was our man, talking to an ugly old trader wearing a patchy coonskin cap with one ear flap hanging down, as brisk and courteous and full of manners as an ambassador at court.

"I'm an old scut and as crooked as the devil's claw," the trader was saying, as if this was something anybody might be proud of. "If they think they can glom onto what's taken me ten years to thieve from the Indians, outright and open, then I'm a suck-egg mule, and you can tell them I said so."

"Indeed I will, I understand perfectly, Mr. MacFarlane," replied Chouteau with a polite shake of his head. "You've been most wrongly used."

"A suck-egg mule—in them selfsame words; they ain't spoken lightly."

"I'm sure they aren't, Mr. MacFarlane. Good day to you, sir."

He was taller than most Frenchmen, slender, with dark, flashing eyes, very carefully dressed, and with an easy manner, as if he had long ago decided not to be bothered by trifles, which I have noticed is the way with most people of importance. When Mr. MacFarlane had backed off, still protesting his desire, under certain conditions, to be a suck-egg mule, whatever that unfortunate animal might be,

Mr. Chouteau turned toward John and said, "Did you gentlemen wish to see me?"

"When you learn our errand, I think you'll say so," said John, and I couldn't help comparing his rude speech and appearance with the graceful style of the proprietor.

"In that case, perhaps you'd better state your business."

I had been partly hidden behind John and Shep, but now John reached back and jerked me forward, saying as he did so, "Here he is, the ungrateful imp. We collared him below St. Genevieve, and if I was you, I'd count up to see what's missing."

Chouteau gave me a calm, unhurried scrutiny, then looked back, perfectly unruffled, at John. I could have spoken up if I'd wanted to, but I was enjoying myself too much, and preferred to drag out the moment.

"Do I understand that I should recognize this boy?"

John's face fell as if he'd been kicked.

"What's that? Who are you, anyhow—where's Pierre Chouteau?"

"I believe I am the only Chouteau, certainly the only Pierre Chouteau, on the premises."

"Ain't this the runaway apprentice you advertised for?"

"To the best of my knowledge," said Chouteau, "I have never seen this boy before in my life. Neither am I aware of having advertised for a runaway anything—boy, horse or dog."

I almost laughed out loud, it was such a pleasurable occasion after the days of bullying and violence from those monsters.

"What is this?" screamed John. "What's going on here?" Then, when a glimmer of the truth worked its way through his rage, he lunged forward and seized my throat, crying, "By God, I'll wring your neck like a chicken's——"

My eyes had begun to pop out and everything was swimming when I noticed a peculiar thing happen to his hands. Across the backs, just under my nose, there suddenly appeared a thin, gaping, wet-pink crevice which filled with blood that welled up and spread out all over, even running down his wrists. Unseen by me, whilst I was fighting for my breath, Jennie had snatched a paper knife from Chouteau's desk and given him a slice that probably went a long way toward evening up old scores.

He let go all holds in an instant, and I got back my vocal cords at last. But the only word I could think of was "Murderer!" so I shrieked it out with all the force I could muster, and when John, with Shep right behind him, sprang down the stairs, I yelled out to Mr. Chouteau that I was Jaimie McPheeters, that had fallen off the boat, and that these frauds were nothing but thieves and killers.

"*Stop those men!*" he cried. and I added my bit with another "*Murderers!*", which I seemed to have got stuck on. Then I looked back and saw that Jennie was sitting down in a chair, weeping, and that Slater had never moved so much as a finger to escape. He just stood there, gazing somberly around, as much as to say that no matter what lay ahead, he had gone as far as he intended to go with scum of that kind.

The scene below was rackety and scrambled up. Most of the fur traders were very comfortably refreshed, with whiskey, and welcomed a diversion, in particular an entertainment as lively as this. Two men unloading skins made a dive for John, who dodged, and they caught Shep's arm instead, but he brought up a knee hard and slipped out. Then they darted first this way and that, running back and forth in little spurts, like some people I'd once seen dancing at the opera house in Louisville, not quite real, and finally, leaping up on a table, they went through a window, sash and all, with that maniac Murrel leading the way.

"A hundred dollars if they're taken alive!" cried Chouteau, and the traders poured out the door in pursuit. But they were seconds too late. Grabbing the two likeliest horses at the hitching post, the murderers sprang into the saddles, as the darky boy tried to hold them back, and ran him down in a wild thunder of hooves and mud. When we burst outside, he was lying very still, almost white-looking, in a rut, the gorgeous silk hat smashed to tatters, and the scarlet coat very muddied and torn.

Chapter VIII

Independence, Missouri
June 10, 1849

My dearest Melissa:

I have arrived here at the last outpost of civilization. This is the jumping-off point; beyond lies the wilderness—the prairie, the alkali plains, the desert, the great Rocky Mountains, and Elysium! (or California). All is going forward at a tremendous pace. My hopes have never been higher, and were it not for the heart-felt absence of Jaimie, my spirits would be hard to contain.

As it is, I have made progress in several directions. Let me assure you it is no easy matter to accustom oneself to the raw exuberance and whimsical *humors* of the frontiersmen with which this town is jammed. The seams of Independence are bursting with the most varied and boisterous humanity it has ever been my lot to encounter. I think it is the total lack of restraint that sets the trailsmen apart from their fellows, and I append an anecdote in illustration. We are blessed, or cursed, here with two butchers, both of them thieves, though one, a certain Mr. Schmidt, surpasses in dishonest ingenuity his competitor, Mr. Burke, who is merely a run-of-the-mill rogue and not destined, I fear, to rise very far above petit larceny. (For clearness, I interpolate that the general fleecing and gouging of these poor, credulous emigrants is a public scandal and should be acted upon by the authorities, as I have stated emphatically upon several occasions.) To resume, our precious Schmidt made the tactical mistake of selling to an encampment of drovers, at an outrageous fee, a gigantic cut of horse under the representation of its being beefsteak.

Vengeance was not long forthcoming, and I marvel yet at the

diabolic wit of the man who wreaked it. The head drover, a huge bearded fellow with mischievous, deep-set eyes, waited until the mid-morning hour, when Schmidt's emporium was filled with housewives; then in he burst with a dead cat, which he banged down upon the counter. "That makes nineteen," he said. "Since you're busy, we'll settle up another time." And he thereupon ran out of the shop.

You ask, how did I make my way to this riotous sink of predatory butchers, prank-loving plainsmen, lamblike emigrants and other oddities of humankind (including Indians), many of whom would have remained in Louisville only long enough for the constabulary to usher them out? In the interval since my last dispatch, my eyes have been opened to a new manner of life, rude and bustling, but one which will advance the torch of progress to the outermost limits of our nation. After combing both banks of the Mississippi on my futile quest, I took a packet from Cape Girardeau to St. Louis, where I called upon your family's friends, the Chouteaus, and was received with every courtesy. Indeed, Pierre Chouteau, Jr. (his father or grandfather founded the family's fortunes, I believe), insisted that my belongings be removed from the Planter's Hotel, a sprawling edifice with wings and dreary hallways not unlike our own Marine Hospital (though, thank God, with greatly improved fodder) and installed in the principal Chouteau residence, a stone mansion set in spacious grounds and supported by numerous outbuildings—negro shanties, warehouses, and the like.

You, who have looked askance at my venture, will be pleased to know that Pierre Chouteau himself is interested (by indirection) in the rush for gold in California. Moreover, he displayed for me a letter from the much-sung scout and now storekeeper far out on the overland route, Jim Bridger, the legend of whose exploits has reached Louisville long before now. I asked and received permission to copy out the document, with the notion that I should profit by a knowledge of, and visit to, that wily frontiersman later on in my journey. Thus I quote from it in part:

"I have established a small fort [writes Bridger], with a blacksmith shop and a supply of iron in the road of the emigrants which promises fairly. In coming out here they are generally well supplied with money, but by the time they get here they are in need of all kinds of supplies, horses, provisions, smithwork, etc. They bring ready cash from the States, and should I receive the goods ordered, will have considerable business in that way with them, and establish trade with the Indians in the neighborhood, who have a good number of beaver with them. The fort is a beautiful location on Black's Fork of Green River, receiving fine, fresh water from the snow on the Uintah Range. The streams are alive with mountain trout. It passes the fort in several channels, each lined with trees, kept alive by the moisture of the soil."

Upon my taking leave of Chouteau (and he with all his connections send you their best "souvenirs") I sensed that he would have liked nothing better than to buy a share of my expedition. He made no outright mention of it, canny merchant that he is, but I have a very good instinct in these things. Though grateful for his interest (still implied) I kept silent, not being willing, even for a friend and benefactor, to convey a valuable property for a song. *For I will without doubt establish a handsome estate in the California gold fields!* Nothing can stop me now, and I only wish I could imbue you as well with my excitement for the adventure.

Chouteau saw me to the boat, as I took deck passage (in my new caution for economy) at four dollars for the 450-mile journey up the Missouri of three days and a half. And this good man has volunteered to press further inquiries along both banks of the Mississippi to Cairo, out of concern for our beloved Jaimie. At my offer of money for this work, he declined stoutly, not wishing, I feel sure, to jeopardize my chance of success by even a small depletion of my store. He *knows*, does Chouteau, that my acquisition of wealth in fabulous quantity is only a question of weeks; indeed, I am surprised that he could restrain himself from speaking out for a partnership. But the French of his class have ever had a delicacy in matters financial, in happy contrast to the boorish greed of their menials, who would cheerfully poison you over an inadequate tip.

I shall not vex you with details of my ride up the Missouri. Suffice it to say that I was in a fever of anxiety to arrive at Independence and strike onward into the wilderness. The days dragged slowly, and the sight of that silent, mud-swollen stream proved at length a lively irritation. No words of mine can depict the scenic primeval grandeur, the monotony of the rivershed, the ugly, sluggish movement of this cold, vast coil of mud writhing its way toward the sea.

To my surprise, we were disembarked at a port six miles from Independence, having tacitly been led to believe that our passage would deposit us on the edge of the town. In company with others, I made haste to protest, but our Captain, a man of demeanor so languid that he seemed in a permanent doze, even at the wheel, had the impertinence to suggest that if we wished to carry the boat overland, he would set us down in the public square, "since there ain't any water to float it on betwixt here and there, leastways none that I've seed." The atrocities of grammar together with the offhand incivilities of these Westerners can be immensely trying. They appear impervious to the usages of cultured society. When we informed the Captain that, on our return trip, we would forsake his boat and proceed by horse, he shrugged his shoulders and replied, within earshot of several ladies, "It's yore —— [a portion of anatomy usually designated medically as the *postus fundamentum*]; flog it all you please."

We were able to stow our gear (I was, and still am, traveling with both Jaimie's and my kits) in the wagons of some freighters, then we treated ourselves to a trudge over ruts and stones of six miles! Before it was over, I was gladdened for the experience, for it was the beginning of my conditioning for the long, long trek that lies ahead. It did not put me out of countenance when I stumbled and went head first off a log spanning a stream, and I was exhilarated when a wagon wheel passed over my instep, inflicting nothing more serious than a painful sprain, with no fractured bones that I could discover. These happy portents, I feel, are an augury of what is to come. Having used up my capacity for adverse luck, I am doubtless due for a long season of good fortune, and the foregoing will serve as examples.

Independence, when we arrived here, in excellent spirits, having recovered fully from the little peeves attendant upon wet clothes and bruises (I was lucky enough to fashion a capital crutch from a kind of yew that grows in abundance hereabouts), proved to be an unsightly, temporary sort of place, composed mainly of frame houses and buildings, with now and then one of brick rising amongst its fellows like a poppy in a bank of weeds.

All about us the country, fertile and picturesque, undulates like a broad sea-swell, its various timbers—oak, maple, cottonwood, elm and sycamore—forming darker oases in the polychrome carpet of prairie wild flowers. For that rolling immensity, the Prairie, begins here. I rode out with acquaintances to its veritable edge—ahead lay the lonely, treeless reaches of blossom and grass, waving, wind-rippled, a few silent birds circling overhead, a botanic desert solemnly brooding. The grasses are not yet high, nor the flowers blooming in their later wild profusion; black patches showed through the green and yellow, adding to the impression, at this season, of bleakness surpassing the British moors.

The town itself numbers a thousand souls, in a permanent way, but swelling this population are the swarming hundreds of movables: the traders, trappers, drovers, mule skinners, emigrants and adventurers. Not only is Independence the point of embarkation for the California-Oregon Trail but it also provides the last stop for those taking the southerly Santa Fe route, so that large numbers of Mexicans and half-breed Indians are seen daily lounging over the town. These latter have dusky complexions, are dressed in filthy costumes, and are mounted on raddled mules and horses, presenting altogether as shabby an air as can be imagined. They will beg or steal, being equally insensitive to blows and curses. One Indian, a fine, straight young fellow, several cuts above the others, approached me two days ago, holding out a paper envelope. Suspecting the usual trickery, I made haste to detour around him, but he spoke up in very passable English. "Me Sioux name Che-Tom-W-Ku-Te-A-Ma-Ni, the Hawk that Hunts Walking," was the crux of his address. I stopped, curious about his next overture, but with a firm clutch on my purse, you may be sure.

"White doctor go with wagons—make trails into California?" I replied that this was indeed the case. "Mr. Reese [he is our local minister] put writing for Hawk to father,—Doctor carry?" For a minute I was nonplussed; then I divined that he was petitioning me to act as mailman. But what a hit-or-miss arrangement!

"Where do I find him? What is his country?" I asked, and he pointed toward the west, with all the accurate fervor of the government mail system; then he said, "Many suns," opening and closing his fingers several times. Now an Indian's "sun," for measurement,

I have learned, is approximately fifty miles, or what the average of them travels in a day, to that I was able to put his "Sioux father" somewhere in the region of South Pass, or far, far out on my journey. And when I asked for his father's name, in the interest of making delivery, what finally emerged in English, after the usual crackle of Indian syllables, was "Black Poddee."

To sum up, I tucked the curious dispatch in my coat and promised to hand it over to Mr. Poddee just as soon as I ran across him, and so we parted, the Hawk and I, with much arm-waving of mutual esteem.

I have found cheap lodging at the home of a storekeeper, Mr. Wilson, who with his partner, Clarke, is the principal outfitter here. True to my new vows of temperance and abstention, I am commonly off the streets by sundown, not unhappily so, since they are filled with rowdies, oxen, mules and a general congestion of such clamor that to make one's way is scarcely feasible. The migrant element among us abides largely in tents, without plumbing, and a lively stench flavors our prairie air which would otherwise be sweet with the scent of larkspur, wild pink, verbena, indigo and lupin. So carefully have I trod in the paths of righteousness that I attended, yesterday, a basket social prepared by the "lady Masons," and Sunday I was at the forefront for the services of the Reverend Mr. Reese. I must confess that I deemed his sermon badly overstrained in pathos; at its end he consigned us all either to the grave or to perpetual exile, a summary dismissal that I felt to be in bad taste, since many of his listeners were soon to depart under conditions that would make either alternative a strong possibility. To clear our nostrils, we sang some verses to the tune of "Old Rosin the Bow," and left, having abandoned all hope of salvation.

In my next epistle, I shall relate to you, and to my dear Hannah, the details of my setting out. I must join a "company," either as member or passenger, in the first case to own a share of the chattels—wagons, oxen (or mules), tools, arms and provisions—and in the second merely to join one group of families, called a "mess," for an agreed-upon sum of money. In seeking to make these arrangements I have had the most incredible windfall of fortune. And it must be confessed that I owe it all to the benign influence of religion.

On Sunday, following the melancholy accusations of Rev. Reese, I so far broke my rule as to look in on one of the gilded Palaces of Chance, filled with commiseration for the poor misguided creatures there in thrall, and hoping to aid them in some small way. The prevalent game was something called "Sledge," an importation from the prospecting camps further west, and surely enough, one pale young man, with a look of terrible depression, was losing what I imagined to be his priceless all, a grubstake probably got together by doting family and friends.

Watching this pitiful spectacle, I became aware that the Rev. Reese, together with his Superior, would have wished me to guide this lost sheep out of the field of wolves and into safe pasture. So I took a hand, much against my present instincts, and began to support him in bucking the combination playing against him, for it grieves me to tell you that, as in Louisville, there are those unscrupulous enough to snare any innocent who comes their way. In all, it cost me upwards of forty dollars before I had succeeded in indicating to my pallid friend the true nature of things, upon which he quit abruptly, with, I trust, enough left of his store to reorganize and continue as planned. As for myself, I considered it money spent in the service of the Lord, via Rev. Reese, and I'm sure that you would have been proud, Melissa, to see me thus forcing myself to an enterprise which I now condemn as heartily as yourself.

Moreover, had it not been for a calamitous fall of cards, I stood to make a potful, again in the name of Providence, for I am certain that the Heavenly wisdom would have applauded any clipping of these wolves. But as the book tells us, He moves in strange ways His wonders to perform, and in brief, He saw fit, at a moment of climax, to slip me the jack of spades when any small heart would have provided His humble servant with upwards of three hundred dollars.

So much for that. I feel cleansed and purified at having made this worthy sacrifice for a weak brother-in-need.

And now the stroke of fortune: Before I left, I permitted myself to be stood a very small, or medicinal, draft, or glass, of spirits, following the inviolable custom of the house in providing a "nightcap" to clients whose contributions to the entertainment have not been niggardly. Ranged alongside me at the counter, or bar, were a rough-hewn pair with hearts of gold, the prototypes of fighting men who have made our great nation what it is. One, a cadaverous, white-maned, rather elderly fellow with piercing black eyes and an inborn sense of piety, informed me that they were raising a company to be called "the Merinos," and that they would welcome me either as member or passenger. His companion, a bluff, meaty giant with some recently healed scars on his cheek, clapped me resoundingly on the back and cried out that with my capital and their brains we'd "get our share of loot and more." At first glance, this seemed hardly complimentary, but I later realized that what he meant by "brains" was experience. These honest bravos have the look of competence; they will meet any emergency, I am sure of it. And, Melissa, your sympathy would go out to the patriarch, for as we left, with plans to meet in two days, he sped me on my way with a ringing passage from the Bible—"Unto every one that hath shall be given, and he shall have abundance; but from him that hath not shall be taken away even that which he hath."

Can you imagine better luck than to have fallen in with such selfless benefactors? Wish me Godspeed—things move forward with almost unsettling celerity. But more of that anon; for now I close, to hie myself to the post office in quest of a stamp "for 300 miles or beyond"—price ten cents! Thus the penalty for wayfaring. Bless you all, and be sure to remember in your prayers,

Your devoted husband,
SARDIUS McPHEETERS, M.D.
(in Systemic Surg.)

Chapter IX

I think they might have spared Slater if it hadn't been for the killing of that hostler. The boy was popular; he cheered folks up and made them laugh, and tempers were pretty high when he got ridden down. Especially when Jennie and I told our stories. We didn't lay any blame on Joe, but I've noticed that lawyers have a sort of wormy way of getting things out of you before you know it. We had to admit, then, that Slater was in with John and Shep, and was along during the murders.

So they threw him into a low, square, red brick building, which was the county jail, and said they would try him the next day and hang him the day after that. "I'm aiming to give him fair play," stated the sheriff, a man with a belly so fat he probably hadn't seen his feet in years, as we stood in his office with Mr. Chouteau and some others. "There's been a lot of loose talk about old Judge Lynch around here, but no man, and I repeat, no man, be he white, black, green or striped, is going to be hung in this county without a trial beforehand." Then he said they had to hold the trial tomorrow because the circuit judge would be in town that day, but had to make an election speech in St. Charles the day after.

Except for Mr. Chouteau, who I noticed was looking on with a kind of distaste, everybody said this was as fair as anyone could wish, and they said they knew Slater would feel better at the hanging to have had a trial first, with a regular judge, and so on. Then they organized what they called a "posse comitatus" and went tearing all over town, and out in the outlying districts, looking for John and Shep, and they didn't leave a stone unturned in their efforts to locate them, but hauled in a number of suspects that were about as likely a bunch of candidates as a party of Eskimos, including a harmless pair of traveling evangelists, several men drunk in a saloon, and a darky that had been sitting on the riverbank fishing. They shot a man in the leg, too, and he wasn't doing anything more serious than riding along on a white horse without any hat on, which they said tallied with the description and he shouldn't have answered up so brisk when they told him to dismount and undress.

Mr. Chouteau took us out to his house, which was a stone mansion grander than anything I ever saw in Louisville, and on the way told us about my father's visit and how they had gone to all that trouble to find me. I felt bad that I'd caused my father the grief, because he had enough worries without adding me to the list, but I was glad they missed me, too. So I explained some about my adventures, but I didn't exactly put it all in, especially about the gold, for I've observed that the less jawing a person does about his money, the longer he's apt to hang onto it. Which was the perfect opposite of my father. If he found a million dollars' worth of diamonds, he'd collar the first ten people he saw on the street and tell them all about it, and maybe give them each a handful to make them believe it. But that's the way he was—he wanted everybody around him to be in on whatever he did.

Mr. Chouteau introduced us to his family, a middling-large group with several children, and he told the ladies, who were very nice and kind, with shiny black hair in coils, and the laciest kind of clothes, what a hard ordeal Jennie had been through. So they put her to bed, with servants, as gentle and considerate as if she'd been a duchess, and waited on her, and gave her broth to drink, and I noticed when they took me up to see her the color had come back in her cheeks; she looked pretty.

I felt a little stiff, not knowing what to say as I stood beside the big high bed, canopied over with ruffles and silk, there being two of the Chouteau women in the room, watching, but by and by she smiled and put out her hand and took mine. "You're a good,

84

brave boy, Jaimie," she said, being probably a little out of her head. "I'll look after you till you find your pa."

We talked awhile, then, and agreed that I should visit Slater in jail, to see if we could make things easier for him. "He was an honest man once," she said. "I'm sure of it." Before I went out of the room, they got up a letter to my mother, telling how I'd been found, but leaving out the awful parts, and I added a paragraph saying I was homesick but not suffering, to make them feel good, and wound up by hoping that the children in school were learning as much as I was, but doubted it. I was itching to inquire if Professor Yandell had any courses about how to swim out of the Mississippi River in May and, maybe by use of Mental Arithmetic, make his way to St. Louis with a group of murderers, but I fought it down. I had yet to see anybody gain anything by being smart-alecky with my mother; somehow it didn't pay.

The cooks in the kitchen fixed a box of fried chicken and deviled eggs and cake and things like that, and Mr. Chouteau slipped in two bottles of wine. Then in the evening I was taken to the jail and they let me in Joe's cell. He was sitting on a bench playing solitaire, and seemed in neither lower nor higher spirits than usual, but that's the way he was—his face hadn't any more expression than a ham.

"Well, boy," he said when he saw me. "You've hauled us all down, but if it hadn't been you I expect it would have been something else. The odds were against us."

"I've brought you a box of food and wine."

"It might surprise you, but the prospect of being hanged has taken my appetite. Still, I'm obliged to you—have an egg?"

I gulped and said no, I'd already eaten my supper.

"*Warden!*" he cried, and slapped on the wall. Presently a shiftless-looking fellow wearing very dirty clothes slouched up to the bars and said, "Here, here, what's all the racket?"

"A piece of fried chicken for a cigar—fair exchange."

"Don't try any of your murdering tricks with me," said the

turnkey, but I noticed that he looked hungrily at the chicken, all the same.

"Oh, come along, don't be shy," said Slater. "Say two pieces, with an egg thrown in."

The man disappeared and came back in a minute with three long, black, sort of twisted-up cigars that were thinner than any I'd seen, and he said, "Put the food through the bars first." Eyeing the other two, Slater offered to play cards for them, against the rest of the lunch, and after some haggling he dealt out two hands of showdown poker, one on the inside of the cell and the other through the bars on a hat. But not with his own cards; the turnkey got a deck from the sheriff's office. I'd never known Slater to be so happy and outgoing. He acted more like a man about to have a monument unveiled to him, and I had to shake myself to remember that all the merriment was because he was in danger of being hung.

Sure enough, he won the cigars, after dealing the cards out twice, with a lot of flourishes and gestures that were meant to look professional, I guess. When the turnkey had left, feeling pretty sour, he said, "Now what do you think of that? I cheated him both times and got away with it. He didn't notice a thing. It's the perfect note to end up on."

He lit a cigar and said he would tell me his life story, and he said, "I was born in the meanest brothel in New Orleans, and my mother hated me from the minute I arrived. Now you may ask yourself, how can this fool enjoy himself so much when he's in such bad trouble, and I'll tell you. This is the most notice that ever was taken of me in my whole life. There aren't many would admit that sort of thing, but I'm so near finished it doesn't make any difference. As a boy, I grew up loitering around low dives and running the omeriest kind of errands, and most of the things I did wouldn't be fit for a decent boy's ears. Over all, I had less than a year of schooling, in a convent, but when my blessed mother got her own place she took me out and put me to work as can-rusher and linen boy.

"I learned my educated speech from the high-born people that came there. We had the very best custom, even the Mayor, and professors from out of colleges. And all the reformers that now and then started clean-up drives would always come back once they'd made their first visit. I'll say this for my mother; she ran a fair house and never tried to hurry a customer, or encourage the girls to wink him in.

"A gambler taught me to deal cards, and I broke away when I was fourteen to go on my own. I think I can rightly say that the first thing I ever did to be proud of was stand still when those two swine ran out. It must have been my father's blood, it couldn't have been my mother's. Who do you suppose he was? I often wonder. He'll stir in his sleep tomorrow night, for his wandering boy's about to mount the scaffold."

"You didn't do murder," I broke in, somehow affected and mixed up by all this poor, silly speech. "They'll find you not guilty, they're bound to."

He held out the hunting-case watch that was taken off the farmer they killed below St. Genevieve. "A gambler has instincts," he said. "Someday you'll be going along and you'll say to yourself, that fellow looks familiar, and it'll be the towheaded brat of those people we slaughtered for a few baubles down the road. Give him back his watch."

I was angry at myself, for I was about to cry, though knowing he wasn't worth it, so I seized the watch sullenly and got up to leave.

"One more thing," he said. "The girl Jennie. Shep killed her folks, all of them, in a shanty in Illinois. He propped logs against the doors and burned it after he'd caught her down at the spring. John was planning to put her in a crib in Memphis. You look after her—take her to your paw and see she's well treated."

When I left, he had opened a bottle of wine and lit another of his cigars. He seemed perfectly content, so I figured that he realized they couldn't convict him on evidence as flimsy as what they had.

But at the trial next day they didn't waste much time, but got right down to brass tacks. It was in a dingy brick building with a courtroom of ugly benches and a raised platform at one end where they had a pine desk, very high and important, for the judge. He was late getting in, and seemed in a poison bad humor, and kept looking at his watch, as if it was our fault. He had on a checkered waistcoat and a pair of steel glasses and he kept drinking water one glass after another till I began to wonder if he hadn't eaten something that didn't agree with him the night before.

Jennie and I were witnesses, so we told our stories, but neither of us laid anything real bad against Slater. They didn't have a jury, but said it would be better not to, in a case of this severity. Besides, they agreed it would take too long to raise one, with the judge leaving tomorrow and all. A prosecutor, who they said was employed by the county, out of taxes, got up and made a long speech, and in the middle he crooked a finger at a colored boy in the rear who had a big armful of books, with paper markers sticking out of them, and when he brought them up, the prosecutor read out a lot of tiresome long references that he said were "precedents."

They mostly showed that when a man shoved in with a group and that group did something contrary to law, he was just as guilty as they were. "This defendant is an accessory not only before the fact but after the fact," said the prosecutor, and the judge said, "It will be so taken into account in the summing up."

At the beginning of the trial, they had asked Slater if he was represented by Counsel, and he got up and stated that he couldn't afford it, he only had a few small coins and the clothes he was wearing, unless they would care to make him a price on a deck of marked cards he had, along with a pair of no-seven dice. Both the judge and the prosecutor had a look at them, but they said there wasn't any sense making an offer, they were so clumsy a child could spot them, and so they told Slater he was just out of luck, he'd have to defend himself. Then the judge added that it was generally the custom for the Court to appoint a counsel in cases of this kind but there was only one lawyer qualified in the area and he was over in Illinois having some land surveyed.

While all this went on, I noticed Mr. Chouteau, sitting next to me, stirring around angrily from time to time, and now he muttered that this was "a damnable farce" and that the people ought to stop it. Later on he told me that the administration that was in then was corrupt and run-down, and that it would likely be voted out at the next election.

Anyhow, they heard all the witnesses, which were Jennie and me, along with the people that were in Mr. Chouteau's store, and then the judge asked Slater if he was ready to present the defense. Slater got up, looking interested and relieved that they'd noticed him, and said that the defense was built around the fact that he hadn't killed anybody. Then he sat down, and the judge thanked him, as he said, "for making such a clear and well-organized defense, without taking up the Court's time a-wandering off on side issues." When he came out with this piece of poppycock, Mr. Chouteau stirred around so I thought he was going to get up and leave, but somebody reminded him he was a witness, so he sat back down again.

Afterwards, the judge banged his gavel and spent ten minutes "summing up for the jury." He explained first that although there wasn't any jury in this case, he would prefer to sum up just the same, because it was the only part of the trial he enjoyed, and besides, he had got kind of used to it. So he told the jury to be sure and avoid prejudice one way or the other, and not let Slater's ratty appearance tell against him, but only consider the evidence, and that in the sight of God, Slater and a man like Pierre Chouteau were equal, and when they were born you couldn't tell one from the other. Then he went ahead and fixed the time of the hanging at eleven o'clock the next morning.

I'm not going to dwell on that day, for it wasn't something you'd care to remember, in spite of the fact that nearly everything they did was mostly comical, if you consider it apart from the final misery for Joe. First off, the sheriff, who'd received a lot of criticism lately for hanging people in a bored and listless way, announced he was "going to do a job on Joe Slater that will make St. Louis go down in history." Boiling it down, then, they turned it into a regular celebration, with a procession and hawkers selling candy and pamphlets about famous murders of the past, and somebody dug up the old book about Murrel, which they said told how Slater got his start, only his name wasn't mentioned in it anywhere—I remember well enough from reading it. A kind and thoughtful delegation came down to the jail early, bringing some elegant new clothes, including a stovepipe hat and a frock coat, for as one of them said, "It would be a crying shame for a man to be the poorest dressed figure at his own hanging." The hat had black crepe paper wrapped around it nearly to the top, which was fashionable just then, but everybody said it would be especially appropriate in the present instance.

But the most ridiculous thing was when they asked Joe if he had any last wishes, and he said yes, he'd admire to take a steamboat ride. So they dressed him up and went parading down Market Street, with Joe and the sheriff in front, all blown up with importance, and they got the ferryboat out and a whole passel of them rode across to Illinois and up and down both banks, with the sheriff and others pointing out landmarks and telling him their plans for this and that piece of real estate, just as if Slater would be on hand to see it.

The sightseeing tour took so long, and ate up so much of the morning, that everybody agreed it would be better to have lunch before going ahead. So they went to the Planter's House and had a whopper of a banquet, also out of taxes, and Slater tanked up on punch so that his legs were kind of rubber, you might say, and that's the way he went to the gallows, which was a very good thing, in my opinion.

Mr. Chouteau said that, all in all, it was the most disgusting exhibition that administration had put on yet, but the sheriff stated that he'd taken a canvass and hadn't found anybody with a complaint worth mentioning, excepting possibly the corpse. "I hope it will end all this talk of skimping," he said. "From now on maybe they'll realize that when we hang a man in St. Louis, we aim to hang him in style."

That night at the Chouteaus' it was decided that Jennie and I should take the boat for Independence, where the wagon trains formed. "If you find your father gone," said Mr. Chouteau, as generous and considerate as always, "you come back and we'll see you home to Louisville. Your trip got off to a stormy beginning, but perhaps that means smooth sailing from now on."

I hoped so, but I really didn't believe it for a minute. I was too used to trouble, and as it turned out I was right.

Chapter X

It was very early in the morning when we said goodbye to the Chouteaus, with the ladies sniffling and taking on in their fussy, kindhearted way. They had got the cooks to put up a basket lunch that would have fed a family of ten back and forth to Russia, I reckon, and it weighed so much we had to carry it together. This was lucky, for the cooking on that boat had gone to rot and ruin, mainly because the regular cook, which was a darky, had had a misunderstanding with a lady acquaintance in town, and her arguments had been set out in the form of five or six punctures with an awl. So that, making a joke, they said his goose would be cooked for quite a spell.

Consequently the captain had a substitute take over at the last minute, who was a man regularly employed in swabbing down the engines with a bundle of waste, which had got to be such a habit that when he changed jobs he just put it on platters and poured gravy over it and served it to the customers, or anyhow that's what people said.

The Chouteaus also gave both Jennie and me some new clothes, but I didn't care for mine. They were a pair of blue pants that buckled below the knees and a jacket with a belt and a cap with a button on top, which Jennie said was a very modish outfit and I ought to be proud. But I wasn't very long in figuring that over in Illinois, where she came from, the styles might be fifteen or twenty years behind, so I cut off the buckles, to let the pants hang down, and lost the belt off the jacket overboard, and got rid of the button, so that pretty soon I was comfortable again, and didn't stand out from the herd.

The trip was interesting but dull, if you know what I mean. That is, it was interesting to look at all that muddy water and those cottonwood bottoms for about ten minutes, but dull if you kept it up much longer. Right off, I found out that the girl Jennie was very well named; I knew now how they worked it out. When it came to balkiness of disposition, there wasn't scarcely anything to choose from between her and a mule. Not that she wasn't sweet; I think probably her sweetest expressions were when she was having her bullheadedest notions. Here I'd been living free and easy for a while, without my mother or Aunt Kitty bossing, and now I had to do things to suit this Jennie. In books I've read, I notice that they do a lot of talking about so-and-so's "character," making the point that hardly anybody's what they seem but that everybody's pretty deep and shifty. I can well believe it.

To look at that Jennie, you would think an angel had come down to help brighten things up, and put us in a happier frame of mind, but let me tell you what she did. The first morning we went in to breakfast, being a wide assortment of food with a crust like a stove lid—fried ham, fried bacon, fried cornbread, fried mush, and such like—she thumbs'd down when one of the passengers, very accommodating and polite, offered me a cigar. I told her I'd been smoking catalpa beans since the diaper stage, almost, but she only gave me that sweet smile and stated that cigars were for grown men, and anyway ought to be smoked out in the middle of a field, so that as few as possible would get suffocated.

Before we left the Chouteaus, there was talk about getting us different cabins, but Jennie said it was a waste of money; we could make out with upper and lower bunks easily enough. Besides, as it turned out, the boat was crowded. I didn't entirely understand all the ruckus, but they said it had something to do with "delicacy." Then they said it was all right because of the great difference in our ages—she would be like a mother to me. When we got ready for bed the first night, it began to seep in what they were talking about. They were afraid she would pester me to death, and she almost did. To start off, it was, "Have you been to the bathroom, Jaimie?" then, "Did you wash your feet, Jaimie?" and "Have you brushed your teeth yet?" I told her I'd been cleaning my teeth, when they needed it, with a willow twig, which is what Indians and such use in the woods, but she had a new pig-bristle brush, along with some salt, so I had to troop back and do it all over.

Not only that, but she made me put on a nightgown to sleep in, as free as if she owned me. Furthermore, I didn't care to have her loitering around when I got ready for bed. But she said she'd been raised in a one-room cabin with five brothers, and not to be silly. Even so, there are some things a body wants to do in private, and undressing is one of them. She herself was as open as a statue in the park, and likely imagined that she looked handsome in her pelt, only she didn't—she was soft and round where she should have had muscles, and I'd bet she couldn't have sprung a rabbit trap if her life depended on it. When I was tucked in below, and she had snuggled down above, she asked me to say my prayers, but I told her I didn't know any, so she said one for us both, blessing everybody she could think of, including a number of persons that were strangers to me, and ended up by hoping Slater would find a comfortable berth in heaven. I felt a little better, then, knowing she was off on the wrong foot, and so went to sleep.

Now I want to tell you how we found my father. At the end of the boat trip, we got a ride with a family by the name of Matt Kissel, who was a man about three pounds heavier than an ox, standing six feet and a half high, with mild, clear-blue eyes like a baby's and a half-smile on his face. He and his wife, a little woman that they would have to peg down in a strong wind, were traveling to California to be farmers, along with their four children, which they said were named after books of the Bible, being Deuteronomy, Leviticus, Lamentations and Micah. But when I looked in a Bible lying in the captain's saloon, I judged that they'd picked the worst stumpers in the list, so I asked Mrs. Kissel about it, saying what pretty names the boys had; and she said her aged mother had done it "to foment character." She said her mother's idea was that if the children could swallow those names, and learn to live with them, they could overcome anything, and probably turn out to be President.

Anyhow, the Kissels had a team of six oxen and a wagon on the boat, together with tools and seed, and they said they weren't interested in gold, but hoped to find a fertile valley in the new land, since their own place back in Indiana had washed down a river—house, sod and good will. They were a nice family, and Jennie said the same. We crowded into the wagon, me on the seat beside Mr. Kissel and Jennie in the back with his wife, helping to attend the collection from the Old Testament.

This Kissel was about the scarcest talker I ever met; I couldn't get him to fasten three words onto another. He seemed to live way down inside himself, perfectly sunny and serene, and hadn't any need to jaw it all over like most people, who spend half of their time explaining what they do, to make themselves feel good. I liked him. You couldn't imagine anything that might make him mad. He was too big to be bothered by humans, even if he didn't like them, and whatever circumstances he was in suited him just fine.

At one point on the rutty mud road to Independence, the oxen, who were frisky and hard to manage from being cooped up, shied at a thrown-away tin and the right front wheel sunk up to the bed in gumbo; we were stuck. Now a thing like that would have prodded a perfect gusher of speech out of my father. He would have confounded this and damned that, and quoted some poetry to cover the case, and philosophized, and then, before he ran down, likely philosophized somebody into taking care of it for him.

Kissel got rid of his smile, I'll say that for him—he broke into an outright grin. Then he summed up the predicament by remarking, "Sticky," and very patiently took two planks out of the wagon, with Deuteronomy, Leviticus, Lamentations and Micah tuning up in the back. Springing down, nimble as a cat, he kind of laid them across the firm and also the soft ground, put a foot on each plank, and before I knew it, bent underneath and lifted up the whole front end, bogged-down wheel and all. Then he edged us over into the tracks again. I guess what struck me as wonderful, and I think about it still today—I mentioned it to him only last month—was that he didn't even ask me to hop off and lighten. He disliked to inconvenience me, you see.

On the edge of the town, being mainly tents and rickety shacks, we stopped a man carrying a jug and I mentioned my father's name, but didn't get any satisfactory reply. What he said was, "Go ahead in if you've a mind to—I'd sooner live in hell with my back broke." I puzzled it over quite a while, hoping to get a connection, but finally decided to try somebody else. We went on, being often blocked by other wagons, and horsemen, and people in the streets, and lumber carried this way and that, and got down toward the thickest part of the town. I didn't care for the looks of it, it was so raw and noisy and mixed up, but there was excitement to it, and it somehow made me anxious to get along on our trip. All that liveliness was catching. The Kissels were looking for a site to place their wagon, but they wanted us to find my father, too. Anybody else would have let us shift for ourselves, now, but Mr. Kissel, in an uncommonly long speech, stated that, "She'll stay put for a while," meaning that California would wait and there wasn't any hurry.

I hoped my father hadn't gone yet, but I needn't have worried. We rounded a corner, in a nice section, and there he was, right in the middle of an argument you could have heard out on the salt flats. A knot of grave-looking men and a woman or two with shawls over their shoulders stood on the steps and porch of this brick house, with a confab going on. Swallowing hard, I took Mr. Kissel's arm and pointed. My father was talking, as he generally was, and we could hear without having to strain. He was spruced up very neat, had his surgical bag in one hand, had one of those heart-testing cones around his neck, and was wearing what my mother called his "consultation manner." That is, he was full of concern and importance, and to look at him, you'd never guess he was probably itching to get out and consult a deck of cards. But right now he was really worked up, for we heard him say:

"I've made my diagnosis, and you hear my advice—go in, operate. Don't waste another minute."

A nice but vacant-appearing old fellow alongside him on the porch, also in neat black clothes, shook his head with great vigor and said:

"It is entirely without medical precedent. On top of that, the weight of local opinion is against you. Both Doctors Shipway and Munson concur with me one hundred per cent—the patient has a septic pregnancy. My suggestion is to place a sharpened ax under her bed; it may ward off hemorrhage."

"Pregnant! Why, there isn't a single indication, aside from the swelling. That poor woman is no more pregnant than I am."

"Until I've had a chance to examine you, preferably in my office," said the old fellow, "I wouldn't care to make the comparison," which they all agreed was a sound good hit, and caused a lot of chuckling and back-slapping among the rougher-dressed men in the yard.

"Listen to me a moment," said my father, his face shining with seriousness, "I saw this sort of case over and over as a medical student in Scotland. Same history, same symptoms. In their ignorance, they called it pregnancy, too, and they lost every last patient, the blithering fools."

"To my knowledge, the abdomen has never been opened by the best metropolitan surgeons, either in this country or in Europe," said another of the doctors.

"Then let's break new ground here in Independence. That unfortunate young housewife will be dead before morning."

Still another man on the porch, who I took to be a preacher, because he had a funny, rolled-up black hat on and was holding a Bible in one hand, now spoke up to say, "The official position of the Church is negative. The Lord has no wish for his unordained servants to defile the sacred caverns of birth."

At this, there was an angry muttering aimed at my father, and some threats of violence if he insisted on going ahead on his own. I saw one man, with hair that grew down in front like a chipmunk, loosen a pistol in a holster and grin at his neighbor.

"All right," said my father. "I wash my hands of the case, but hear my prediction: The woman has a cystic growth which is surgically removable, with no more risk than she's taking right now. This operation will be performed within your lifetime, and I hope your consciences are sorely smitten." Then he walked to the door and shook hands with a haggard, grieving young fellow that was likely the husband. "I'm sorry, I did my best," he said, and strode down through the crowd. He'd gone twenty or thirty yards up the street before I found my voice.

"Father," I called out. "I'm up here—on Mr. Kissel's wagon."

I saw his back stiffen up; then, with a little shake of his head, as if his ears were playing him tricks, he went on without turning around.

"It's me—Jaimie," I screamed, leaping to the ground. Then he was down on his knees with the tears running down his face, and clasping me in a hug that cracked my bones almost.

My father was a great man in his way, and I told that about the operation mainly to show how easily he could get on the bad side of people over things he was right about all the time. Where I live now, writing our story, I don't much keep up with events, but I'd like to bet that that same operation *was* done not long afterwards, just as he promised.

"Providence has answered my prayers, boy," he said, wiping his eyes. "I'd never given up hope, not for a minute, but I'll have to own up that you've taken the wind out of me. I think I'd better sit down."

So I led him back to the Kissels and introduced him to everybody, and we had a general cry together, with a good deal of nose blowing, particularly by Jennie and Mrs. Kissel, and then my father got up on the seat beside us and was soon his old self again. In fact, he remembered pretty quick how outraged he was about the cyst, and went to the length of explaining it all to Mr. Kissel, using the most technical terms, just as if Mr. Kissel knew the difference between a shinbone and a corpuscle, breaking off now and then to say, "You understand me?" or "You follow that, do you not?" And each time Mr. Kissel smiled in his slow, quiet way, which had the effect of encouraging my father to push right ahead with more.

That night, sitting around the campfire where the Kissels placed their wagon on the edge of a grassy field, I told him about our adventures. And when I got through, Jennie told some of hers, but you could see she wasn't very eager, so nobody pressed her. We had a meal of three chickens cooked on a spit over the fire, with Mr. Kissel doing the work, and my father telling him how, and everybody agreed that they were about the tastiest chickens we'd ever run across. My father said it certainly beat the food he'd been eating at his boardinghouse, which had consisted for the past two days of boiled pieces off an old saddle Mr. Wilson had taken in on a trade. But I judged that this was one of his exaggerations.

He'd got Jennie a cubbyhole room at the Wilsons', and toward ten o'clock, happy and worn out, we said good night to the Kissels, excepting for the Old Testament group, which was mainly asleep, with some yowling now and then to keep their hands in, and went on home. But before we did, we made an agreement to all travel together to California in the same company, because Mrs. Kissel said they'd admire to have Jennie along, just like one of the family. I haven't the least doubt they'd have taken in five more without a word of objection, for that's the way they were. There wasn't anything small or selfish about them any more than there is about an elephant.

And I was relieved later to hear my father declare in the strongest terms that this family of Kissels deserved the best, and that he intended to throw a considerable amount of gold their way the minute he staked out his claims.

Chapter XI

Right after breakfast the next morning we picked up Mr. Kissel, leaving Jennie at the wagon to help out, and went off to meet my father's new friends that he said were so gracious toward him in the bar. But first, full of style and flourish, he had to drop into the office of the Independence *Expositor*, where he introduced us to Mr. Webb, the editor, and to a Mr. Curry, who had been one of the editors of the St. Louis *Reveille*. "Mr. Matthew Kissel," my father said, with a kingly sweep of his hand, "a leading agriculturist of Indiana."

I never saw anybody who could have so good a time with such thin material. Now his outward excuse for going into that office was to "insert an advertisement for the recovery of a mislaid watch fob," but his real reason was simply that he felt high-spirited and wanted to bring together some people he liked.

Anyhow, he inserted the notice, after first putting on his spectacles and surveying the table of rates, making an expert show of deciding on the proper space and type, and he wrote it out himself, longhand: "Lost, probably in Church or in the Last Chance Saloon and Entertainment Estab., 14 Kt. gold watch medallion, struck off by Lazarus of Louisville [this last was pure humbug—Mr. Lazarus ran a brokerage shop back home and sold whatever people brought in to pawn], carrying profilian bust of the late G. Washington, Pres., U.S.A. Substantial reward for return of this cherished family heirloom. Dr. Sardius McPheeters, M.D. (in Syst. Surg.), Box 137, this newspaper."

Then he asked Mr. Webb if Box 137 was spoken for, and Mr.

Webb said no, that they didn't have any Box 137, or even Box 1, or 2, but he would make a note of it, and it would be all right. Then we all shook hands around and left, after Mr. Curry had attempted a polite inquiry of Mr. Kissel on the subject of erosion. It went along very much like a dentist trying to pry out a wisdom tooth that had got wrapped around the jawbone. Something like this:

"Excellent soil back your way, I understand, Mr. Kissel?"

(Smile and a slow nod from the latter.)

"Adequate rainfall?"

"More at some seasons."

"But not too much, I hope."

"Mortal damp."

"A plenteous rainfall can be a downright curse in regions near our larger streams. You are probably fortunate to be situated high and dry."

"It washes."

"But not to the point of actual damage, I have no doubt."

"Some."

"By erosion?"

"Washed it all down the river."

"Pardon?"

"The whole farm. Also the house. Along with barn, silo, wood-rack and pigsty."

It was about in here somewhere that Mr. Curry concluded to let go his holds on erosion and change the subject, and I didn't much blame him, for it was pretty clear that he'd got off on the wrong track. So we passed some notes on the local weather, which was good at the moment, but worse at other times, they said. After getting that settled, we made our way on down the street.

My father's two friends were living in a tent in what was beyond doubt the meanest part of town, being peopled by as handsome a set of cutthroats as you could meet short of the Louisville shanty-boats, but my father said it was because they were so rugged and outdoorsy they felt cramped in anything civilized. So we made our way through a litter of lean-tos, tents, wigwams, and worse, and there, tending a blackened coffeepot hanging over a fire on a forked green twig, were John and Shep. They looked even uglier than usual, if possible.

"Gentlemen," said my father grandly, stepping up, "I want you to meet——" and right there I gave out with my best lung blast and yelled, "*It's the murderers!*"

Well, it was a lively scene. Those villains straightened up pretty quick, and Shep made a motion to go for his gun, but John stopped him, and after an effort to get hold of himself, said:

"The boy's mind's affected—it's a case of mistaken identity."

I don't think I ever saw my father look so unhappy. "Surely there's a misunderstanding here——" he began, but I didn't aim to let anything interfere with putting those fellows where they belonged.

"I tell you, these are the men that kidnapped me and killed the farmer and his wife!"

"It's his word against ourn," said Shep, "and even if it wasn't, there ain't no St. Louis sheriff that's got jurisdiction out here."

"Hold your tongue!" said John; he said to us, "I've never been one to ruffle up at the babble of infants, but I draw the line at criminal slander."

My father spread his hands in a soothing way and said in a low tone, for a curious crowd was beginning to gather, "I'm sure this can all be straightened out—the lad's been ill; he's not responsible——"

I was in such a fit at not being believed, even by my own father, that I was stamping my feet the way they say people do in books, but then I thought of something. It was all as clear as daylight, and I don't know why it hadn't occurred before.

"Wait a minute! We'll go get Jennie—Jennie can tell you, if you don't believe me."

"Now you just do that, son," said John in an easy voice, looking as though he pitied me in my sickness and distress. "That's exactly what I'd do—I'd go get Jennie, if there *is* a Jennie. And if there isn't, why you come on back. There'll be no hard feelings—we don't hold grudges against children out of their heads."

"This is all very embarrassing," said my father, mopping his face with a handkerchief, "and I want you to know I'm grateful for your attitude——"

"Don't think about it, humor the boy, doctor; go right along and fetch his Jennie. We're entirely at your disposal."

But I was dragging my father off by his coattails, and urging him to hurry, so we left, and in all that time I don't believe Mr. Kissel had changed expression by the flicking of an eyelash; he just waited. And somehow, thinking it over as we half ran back to the wagon, I was mightily relieved he'd been along.

Jennie turned pale when she heard the news, but the way she snapped on her bonnet seemed to me a very bad sign for those scoundrels. I was in a sweat to get back, but sure enough, following her mule's custom, she insisted we get the law officer to take along, and by the time we located him, playing faro in a saloon, we'd wasted upwards of an hour.

I didn't need to be told—they were gone, bag and baggage, when we got back at last to their tent. The deputy—he was a deputy something-or-other—took out a notebook and asked a lot of ignorant questions of the people nearby, but he did manage to establish, by accident, mostly, that John and Shep had scooped up their traps, packed their mules, and skedaddled.

The deputy closed his book with a wise look and said, "There was a mule company going out at noon—they've likely joined it."

"Well, stop them! Get after them!" cried my father, who had finally worked himself around to believe that he'd thought they were the murderers all along.

"We haven't got the facilities," said the deputy. "Moreover, they've omitted to lay themselves open to charges, as far as I know. And I ain't the one to deliver them to St. Louis—are you?"

So we trooped on back to the wagon and talked it over. "What's to be done?" asked my father, glancing around at us all, as helpless as a baby in this crisis. Then Mr. Kissel spoke up to make his first voluntary statement of the morning. "Leave them be," he said, "and have some cold chicken."

It seemed like a very good idea; besides, it was time now to get ourselves organized on to California. That afternoon we made a tour of the companies forming, and next day we signed on, as passengers, with a group called "the Beaver Company." But I'll let my father's letter of June 20 take it up from there.

Encamped on the Little Vermilion Creek
June 20, 1849

My dearest Melissa:

We are stopped to rest, on a Sunday, beside this beauteous stream that races clear and limpid over a red sandstone bottom. All is proceeding with delightful ease, save for those few inevitable hitches that plague the most seasoned expeditions. You will recall that in my missive of Tuesday last, I expounded on our Heaven-sent fortune in recovering our boy, and laid forth in detail the events preceding the flight of his tormentors. As to those last, they have shown a clean pair of heels. May they be swallowed up by an inhospitable desert: *Fiat justitia ruat caelum* [Let justice be done though the Heavens fall].

To acquaint you with our actions of the interim, I shall resume my chronicle from that point. In concert with the Kissel family of which I spoke, not neglecting the girl Jennie, who escorted our Jaimie to Independence, we have joined the Beaver Company, comprising thirty-three "messes," or family groups, each in its own ox-drawn wagon, and are actually on the overland trail to California. Gold in abundance awaits at the end of this simple journey; and be not misled—it is there for all to dig. We have that intelligence from the remnants of a mule company, four in sum, who crossed us in return only yesterday. They had got as far as Bridger's Fort, where some are recuperating, a few settling permanently, and these four, as stated, going back, but all with wondrous secondhand tales from California. I hasten to add that their failures have no bearing on the certain success of our mission. A number of troubles, easily avoided, beset them, namely that they started before the grass was properly up, their pack mules had a tendency to run off and unload independently of human aid, they lacked a knowledgeable leader, and they were too easily affrighted by thieving Shawnees and Pottawattomies.

We of the Beaver Company are blessed with a paragon of trail lore, bearing the name of Buck Coulter, who was hired in the dual roles of hunter and trail "boss." I find him a tolerable companion though gruff and unsuggestible, even something of a tyrant in his way. There can be no question that he fancies his knowledge of pioneering to exceed that of the Almighty himself, and he has laid down petty rules and duties without recourse to sager counsel. Be that as it may; we shall see.

Our means of locomotion is walking, Kissel's and mine and Jaimie's, with the women, and the children—a melodious quartet rather heavily freighted with Biblical labels—inside for the most part. Mrs. Kissel is one of those stringy, tireless, uncomplaining samaritans, thoughtless of self and devoted to the whole of humanity. Her husband, a giant for strength and size, exerts less conversational strain, as we plod along, than any other man of my recollection. A superficial person might consider him a fool, but there is much more in his pithy comments, such as "Pretty," "Careful!" and "Pass the bacon," than meets the eye. As to the last member of our little group, it is hard to know what to say. This girl Jennie is as fresh and sparkling as a rosebud, now that her spirit is mended, but I must add in fairness that the lovely petals are protected by a thorn. Masked over by an innocent smile, she has a caprice of steel. It is painful to recount that only last night, before supper, she announced that she felt it time to wash both Jaimie's and my underwear; moreover, she stood flintly by until we had gone in and handed them out. Woe betide the young man upon whom her managerial glances light, and already she has widened her sphere of influence to include the melancholy Brice—Adam Brice, whose wife, the sufferer from the cyst, died exactly as I predicted. In his despair, he sold his home and business, a sizable icehouse, and has elected to make a new beginning apart from the scene of his loss. His wagon traveling in tandem behind us, our women, the all-embracing Mrs. Kissel and the immovable Jennie, help attend his wants; indeed, we mess together.

In making our decision to go, we were compelled to choose between mules and oxen. The two animals, having a strong mutual aversion, are seldom mixed for purposes of expedition. The mule was never born that could resist the chance to kick an ox, especially if tied, and oxen take keen pleasure in crowding mules out of any available grass. Our choice was easily arrived at for the reason that the Kissels already had oxen, though they would cheerfully have relinquished them for the general weal and, I have no doubt, switched to reindeer or kangaroos with no serious loss of composure.

The selection of oxen is a fortunate one, I feel. The more I see of mules (and I shall explain in a moment why my vision is thus enriched daily), the more taken I am with the lowly, toiling, virtually tireless ox. Light oxen under six years of age are the ideal beast of burden— I hear this everywhere and have it, in particular, from no less an oracle than Buck Coulter himself, whose marvelously short, graphic expletives dealing with mules shall not be set down here.

We Beavers are presently joined for a few days by a mule company, called the Hornets, organized by Colonel Ralston, an outfitter in Independence and comprising forty-eight mules (six for each team) and a bell-mare, which latter is supposed to keep the former from straying, but I regret to say that a whole congress of mares ding-donging day and night could scarcely keep these pestiferous beasts on the straight and narrow. And indeed they have slowed us perceptibly.

As to our health—it is excellent. In buying our provender we were warned to allow for an appetite on the road of almost twice that at home, and such has proved the case. The sight of our Jaimie in the early morning, at "catch-up" time, would warm your heart. His attempts to eat all the bacon in Kissel's wagon have been remarked as courageous beyond the call of duty. In this connection (of food) I should add a note on Jennie, who has appointed herself the implacable custodian of us all, if the truth were stated bluntly. On the third morning out, she announced that the frontier's morning fare of fried bacon, coarse-flour biscuits and, occasion-

106

ally, beans, should be enlarged to "a rounded diet," and she began, surprising us all, to forage on her own.

It appears that back in Illinois, where she came from, poor waif, her father and brothers were ardent hunters of small game, and in consequence she is a shooter on a level with Boone and Crockett. So she said, and you may imagine our hearty but good-natured laugh at the concept of this slender blossom stalking like Diana through the forests. But her reply was only a slight tightening of the lips—a mannerism I have come to identify with the donkey's bray—and she took down Kissel's double shotgun, which is suspended from a sling in his wagon, and walked out into the prairie, alone, despite earnest advices from several men on the danger of becoming lost in this silent, billowy vastness. Upon her return, some two hours later, she had eight brace of prairie plover (an excellent roast bird, tender as quail) and an apronful of eggs. Perhaps the great stickler in this incident was the fact that she had only fired seven times. And at Kissel's well-phrased inquiry of "Oh?" she said carelessly, "Five doubles and two triples."

Enjoying this repast that evening, and foregoing the usual dinner of "salt junk," or pork, we looked at her with something akin to tenderness. And I must say that in Brice's glance, as he filled his mouth with breast and dripping drumstick, was a glint of speculation. Since that happy beginning, our starchy Nimrod has produced in addition, duck (when once we camped beside a broad flash of water), prairie snipe, and hare; and from a stream whose name escapes me she drew an abundance of large catfish. Each evening, now (since we must contrive to camp near water) she and Jaimie set out "night lines," so that often for breakfast we have an abundance of these last finny viands. Only once have we boggled at her supplemental fare. When, yesterday, having skirted the train at a distance of three or four hundred yards for an hour, she marched in with three prime rattlesnakes, we declined to make ourselves available. "It cooks up as good as eel," she said with the old steely look, but I rejoice to tell you that we only stared back, unmoved. So that in the end she was obliged to cast the horrid creatures into the weeds, and I honestly feel that she was relieved to do so, for a good many of her actions spring simply from a stubborn notion of being in the right. Rattlesnakes may in fact provide a delicacy for the gourmet's table, but for my part, I'd as soon eat a platter of bats.

Now I wish to add a paragraph on our expenditures and general finances, then close, with a parting observation about one of our number who I think is likely to cause us concern, a young swashbuckler fancying himself a great rough, who rides out looking for Indians while wearing two huge revolvers strapped to his waist.

In Independence, before our start, we conferred with the best men of our company, also with the talkative Coulter, and agreed that Ware's *Guide* must be passably accurate about the necessaries for the trail. Accordingly I made arrangements for storing in Kissel's and Brice's wagons, paying them for the privilege (over their lively protests) the following articles: One Additional Rifle—$20; One Pair Pistols—$15; Five Barrels Flour, 1080 pounds—$20; Bacon, 600 pounds—$30; Coffee, 100 pounds—$8; Tea, 5 pounds—$2.75; Sugar, 150 pounds—$7; Rice, 75 pounds—$3.75; Fruit, dried, 50 pounds—$3; Salt, Pepper, etc., 50 pounds—$3; Saleratus, 10 pounds—$1; Lead, 30 pounds—$1.20; Powder, 25 pounds—$5.50; Tools, etc., 25 pounds—$7.50; Mining Tools, 36 pounds—$12; Tent, 30 pounds—$5; Additional Bedding, 45 pounds—$12.50; Cooking Utensils, 30 pounds—$4; Lard, 50 pounds—$2.50; Matches—$1.00; Candles and Soap, 50 pounds—$5.30.

These are supplies for one year for three persons and come to a total of $170.00, so you may see I am now traveling very light with regard to coin of the realm. Out of common charity, Kissel and Brice and I concluded to divide the cost of Jennie's travel amongst us, making the above calculations subject to a considerable rebate. Also, in her tearful gratitude, the girl herself has sworn vows of recompense, and if I am any judge of character, she will indeed return these loans if it is her last act upon earth. And so we set out, a sturdy band of hopefuls, undaunted by the prospect of difficulties and trials. The way thus far is not hard to scout—the wagon ruts of other emigrants before us lie plain in the mud and weeds.

We are now eight days on our journey and have covered nearly 120 miles. Within a hundred miles from Independence we were "blooded," as they say hereabouts, by having to cross the Kansas, or "Ca" (Indian) River. All went smoothly, thanks in the main to a ferry operated by two businesslike Shawnees: Fare—one dollar per wagon; the horses and loose stock we swam across, losing only a pony of no great value. In the main, the members of our company are honest, stable, God-fearing men—only one of us, the youth I referred to, provides real anxiety. But he is a protégé of Coulter's, yet in his teens, a swaggering, sneering bully, already well muscled and tried, and given to strutting around ever with a chip on his shoulder, hoping to provoke a row in which he might employ the use of his guns, at which he is said to be precociously adept. Appeals to Coulter have produced only coarse laughter and the propitiatory remark, "He's full of beans and his tail's high." Which, when you come to think of it, solves little or nothing. This odious, pimpled, troublemaker is called Dick McBride, and I fear that before he is done he will have disrupted a poised expedition.

But everything will come right, and Providence will work His miracles to the greater glory of all, and certainly beyond doubt for the enrichment of the undersigned, whose golden re-entry of Louisville (no longer by stealth) will be hailed, I predict, as of historic import comparable to Caesar's return from Carthage. And by the way, it has been in my mind to donate, as a gesture of good will, a new wing to the Marine Hospital, a ward to which the poor and needy may apply without cost for therapeutics. Unless you feel it bold, I suggest that "the McPheeters-California Public Clinic" might be a fitting honorific. Concurring, would you, my dear Melissa, make representations to Mr. Birdwell, the architect? It would be a refreshment to have the plans waiting and ready upon my arrival (spare no expense). And so, with this joyous consummation in view, I lay down my pen for the nonce, having to go join some of my fellows in the rescue of a wagon that has skidded down an incline and fractured a singletree. With the most devoted salutations to you, my faithful wife, and to my darlings, Hannah and Mary, from,

Your adventurous husband and father,

SARDIUS McPHEETERS (in transit)

Chapter XII

There was a meeting at Coulter's wagon that night to hash out the argument about stopping to rest on Sunday. It was Coulter's notion, and I submit that all his statements were put forward in an iron-jawed style which riled others besides my father, that lying over on Sunday, resting the oxen, would save us days in the long haul.

But there was a good deal of grumbling. The people at this stage of the trip were anxious to get on and begin taking out the gold. Except for the Kissels, nearly every group had some pet scheme to use the money on, and some others had debts to pay, like my father. He, by the way, now had his head full of the McPheeters-California Public Clinic, the idea having popped up by accident, and he was filling notebooks full of the most elaborate plans, including rooms for "Hot-Water Therapy," "Isolation," "Homeopathy," and I don't know what all, and I expect there wasn't enough gold in the universe to take care of it, but he charged right ahead as if he already had the money in his pocket.

And he consulted Kissel, too, in the idiotically sober respectful way he always did, and if the answers he got back were just as woolly-headed as usual, he paid no heed.

"How do you feel about having female nurses in attendance during operations on the male genitalia?"

Kissel thought it over, knocked out his pipe, and replied, "I wouldn't let it bother me."

"You're quite right!" my father cried, smacking one knee. "Once again, you've gone right to the heart of the thing. I'd been worried about it before, but I see it now. Go right ahead, and not be concerned. Many thanks."

Well, when they'd straightened out that knotty question, we got up and headed for Coulter's meeting. But we went early, to have a look at the Englishmen with the mule train. The stories about them drifted in every day, and I'll own up that they deserved it all. The main one's name was Coe, but it was considerably more complicated than that, being, as they said, "the Honorable Henry T. Coe," but what the Honorable was for, I hadn't any idea, unless it was because he didn't cheat anybody when he bought the mules. The fact was, everybody said, Colonel Ralston had gouged his eyes out, near about, and everything else this Coe did turned out just as hilarious, though sour financially, so I guess that was it.

Anyway, we got up to his camp and sure enough he was sitting there in an overstuffed rocker, wearing white kid gloves, just like they said.

"Doctor Sardius McPheeters, your servant, sir," said my father in his grandest style, walking forward to introduce himself, with his hand stretched out.

"A pleasure," said Coe, without rising, and taking the hand as a king might accept a gift from some cannibals out of his provinces. That is, he grasped it limply, put it aside, and reached for a silken kerchief, as if to brush off any contamination. Besides the gloves, he was wearing a pair of gray striped trousers and a black coat.

My father coughed, being taken down a little, and introduced Kissel, Brice and me; then he went on to state that he'd taken his medical degree at the University of Edinburgh, so that he thought he should pay a visit of "British solidarity."

At this, Coe thawed slightly and even called to a negro youth, who went by the name of Othello, and said to fetch some ginger beer.

So it was true, then. They'd told it all around that this Coe was traveling to California with twenty-six cases of ginger beer, and he had it here stashed away in his wagon—I sidled over and peeped under the canvas. It tasted good, too; he wasn't due to get much farther with it, but I'm jumping too far ahead.

Sitting down, they had a talk about the exaggerated hardships of traveling to California, and this Coe said he was keeping a journal and meant to write a book, to be called, *An Amble over the Rockies and a Stroll through the Diggings*. When Brice remarked that the title might prove to be a little breezy, considering other accounts of the ride yet before us, Coe waved with disdain and said:

"Oh, these fellows told me I was a bit of an ass to wear kid gloves and carry ginger beer, but it's necessary to keep up appearances. I make no doubt they'll have the desired effect upon the natives."

It seemed to me he was the greatest fool I'd ever met, and I go to this trouble to show him because we saw a good deal of him later. He had his mule skinner, Othello, standing at an iron pot cooking what he called a "leveret," which was nothing more than a young jackass rabbit, and the Honorable Coe called him over to demonstrate him.

"Othello, how do we discipline a balky mule?"

He was a solid, shiny fellow with a head like a bullet, and he said, "Sah?"

"How do you gentle a mule?"

"I take and butts 'em, sah."

"Show these gentlemen. Pick out the worst one, say Gnasher. Pretend to pack-saddle Gnasher."

The negro took up one of the heavy wooden packs and approached the mule, which switched around suddenly and lashed out with both heels. But the boy was an artist for nimbleness. While we sucked in our breath, he backed off a few feet to charge in like a shot out of a cannon. What kept his neck from breaking, I have no idea, but his head hit the mule's side with a thud like a bass drum. The animal just stood there and quivered. It wasn't happy at all. And it didn't make a move a moment afterward when Othello threw the saddle over its back.

"That'll do," said the Honorable Coe. "See to the leveret. You know," he went on, "that noisy villain, Coulter, gave me a foolish method of subduing these beasts, and I rather think he did it on purpose. He told me to throw Cayenne pepper in their eyes and push them into the river."

"Did you try it?" asked my father.

"Tried it on Parliament—that's the slow one."

"With good results, I trust?"

"The bounder bit a hole through the third finger of my right hand."

Everybody sympathized with him and said how ornery a mule could be, no matter how well you treated him, and then we went on over to Coulter's, because it was time for the meeting to start. The Honorable Coe tagged along, after telling Othello to look in once in a while on Vilmer, which was his valet, he said, but had taken down sick owing to the wretchedness of the food.

"I'll be happy to attend him, as a courtesy," said my father, brightening up at the prospect of occupying the limelight for a while.

"Why, that's good of you," said Coe, "but a Doctor Merton had a look at him only this morning. He reported that all hepatic action had ceased and gave him some morphine and senna leaves. He said if he didn't rally in a couple of days, not to count too much on having a valet for the trip."

"Singular diagnosis," muttered my father, and we made our way through the oval of wagons. Coulter and most of the men were grouped around his campfire, with Coulter standing up and his side-kick, McBride, not far away. Coulter was a big fellow, about the size of Shep but not red-faced that way. He was dark tan and black-haired and always looked blue around the chin, as though he needed a shave, though mostly he didn't—he shaved every day. He had on a buckskin shirt with a fringe, and a pair of coarse linsey-woolsey pants that narrowed down into boots, and a very beat-up hat with a broad brim and a thong underneath, so as to keep the sarcastic look on his face from being blocked off, I reckon.

"To get things started," he said, looking around, amused, "I understand there's been some beefing about my orders to hole up Sundays."

A nice-looking elderly man in very decent clothing, a Mr. Kennedy, with a party from Missouri, spoke up to say in a polite tone, "Not beefing, Mr. Coulter. More properly, you might say a difference of opinion."

"What's yourn based on?" inquired Coulter. "You made the trip often?"

Kennedy reddened up and stammered something about common sense and ordinary judgment, but Coulter paid him no attention. "When I signed on as nursemaid to this bunch of milksops, I did it with the understanding that I was to be boss. But if you insist on committing suicide, you're entirely free to do so. However, I ain't planning to be in on it. I resign, and you can keep my salary—a hundred dollars and found. Dick and I'll be riding back in the morning. You're on your own."

I noticed the Honorable Coe sort of looking down his nose, as if somebody had hauled some garbage into camp; now he said, "Your judgment may be sound, but your manners could stand improvement, Coulter. In England, impertinence like yours would be answered with a day or two in stocks."

There was a general gasp of shock, and some tittering from one or two men in the rear, hidden in the shadows. I couldn't believe my ears—here was this Honorable Coe, dressed up like a dandy, with a sprig of artemisia in his buttonhole and usually giving out the sissiest kind of speech—and he spoke up to this roughneck as if he was dressing down a groom.

But the biggest effect it had was on McBride, who wheeled around, white-faced, and demanded in a gritty kind of tone, "*What did you say?*"

"You can call off your whippersnapper, too, Coulter," said Coe, taking no notice. "I don't recall ever seeing an upstart so badly in need of a birching."

Stripping off one of his gloves, which he wore like a gunfighter,

McBride moved forward two quick paces and slapped at Coe's face, but my father stepped between them and took the blow on his shoulder.

"*Go on! Draw!*" McBride half screamed, adding a few choice curses. "I'm going to make you sorry you opened your dirty mouth."

My father and one or two other gentlemen said some soothing things, and held him off, for he would have shot Coe sure, and then Coulter came over and jerked the boy away, saying, "Get in your tent."

With a good deal of boldness, I thought, Kennedy spoke up to complain. "In addition to the Sunday delay, Mr. Coulter, not a few of us are sick and tired of being bulldozed by that bad-tempered young ruffian. We refuse to put up with it much longer."

Coulter amazed us all by breaking into a grin and saying, "To tell you the truth, I'm a little sick of him myself. Now I propose that we keep our heads and talk this out. My reasons for the Sunday rest are perfectly simple. I've never been over this route, as I acknowledged candid and frank when I hired out, but I've done trail riding in other directions, including the Santa Fe, and I've yet to see a wagon train that didn't profit by a day-a-week layover. The oxen are refreshed, the equipment can be patched up, and folks just seem to get back their strength generally. Several of you set such a store by Ware and his guidebook, I'm surprised you haven't taken his word. He says, and I think I remember it right, 'Never travel on the Sabbath; we will guarantee that if you lay by on the Sabbath, and rest yourselves and teams, that you will get to California 20 days sooner than those who travel seven days a week.' "

Well, this seemed to impress most of them; they shook their heads and said maybe they'd been a little hasty, that they must have read Ware's comment but had likely forgot it.

"That's all fine and good," said one man, "but what about this squirt, McBride? He's pining to gun somebody. We're about wore out on it; speaking for myself, I've got saddle sores."

"I'll make you a promise. If he hasn't changed his tune in a week, I'll ship him out. He's the son of an old friend, and I vowed to take care of him."

"That sounds fair enough," said my father, and a few joined in to agree, but I noticed that some still looked unconvinced. They looked worse when Coulter said, in his old raspy voice, "If you've had your say, I suggest you drift back to camp. The dew's coming up and you may catch a cold."

He was hard to figure out. Sometimes he seemed sensible and almost human; other times he was as irritating as sand in your porridge. Neither did it make him more popular, as we left, when he took a swig from a bottle he carried on his hip and cried out, like a mother putting some half-witted children to bed, "Good night, sleep tight, don't let the bedbugs bite." We heard his hoarse laugh back in the darkness as we made our way to the wagons.

Chapter XIII

We rolled out of bed at 3 A.M., caught up the oxen, hitched, and had breakfast, squatting around the fire, still in the deep dark. We always had firewood laid out from the night before, and the women made breakfast in silence, feeling a little poorly and not quite up to snuff, the way women do in the mornings. It was best to leave them alone. Jennie was apt to snap your head off, and even Mrs. Kissel took on a kind of mournful note, which was aimed at the general misery of being a woman, I judged, and not centered on any one person like her husband. So the smartest thing was to let them pitch in and work; it's my observation that nothing's as handy for taking the kinks out of a woman as work.

Shivering a little, for these early mornings on the prairie were cold even in June, we had bacon, left-over biscuits, and several cups of black coffee, and I noticed that Brice, the pale, thin-haired young widower, still wasn't eating much. But Jennie would fill his plate and shove it in his hand whether he wanted it or not. There's no telling what might have happened otherwise, because Brice couldn't seem to bounce back from the loss of his wife. Mostly he said little, answered questions pleasantly, and always was willing to help, but it was as if he didn't have any push of his own. That is, he would half kill himself if somebody told him what to do, but he couldn't *start* anything. I believe he would have sat over a dead campfire till the buzzards got him. I'd heard him in the night, too, whimpering—dreaming, or lying awake thinking of home.

It was a fresh, clear morning with the stars out in smears and clusters. Off in the distance you could hear animals barking, coyotes or wolves, and the oxen stamped around, lowing, ready to move. It felt good to be a boy and off adventuring. I remember eating an uncommon lot that morning, and I'm glad I did, for it turned out to be an unusual day, and required strength. As my father finished his one-man conversation—he was always bubbling over at 3 A.M., in the gabbiest of spirits, but since nobody else cared to talk, he just rattled on alone—Coulter rode by on his Indian pony to see that we squashed our fire. "Get it out—every last ember," he called from the saddle. "Rain's been scarce and you've never lived till you've seen a prairie fire on the roar."

"Confound that detestable bore," my father fumed when he was gone. "I don't know how much longer I can swallow those pompous advices."

I think Coulter, to my father, represented all the spoil-sports in the world rolled into one. At exactly the wrong times he kept sounding warning notes that pricked my father's happiest dreams. For instance, on the second day out, we bought a white horse from the mule party that was dropping back, and paid only a few dollars for it. He was so blown up with pride at turning a bargain that he talked it all over camp, referring to the animal, for some reason, as "horseflesh," a professional word he'd got out of the *Turf Register*, I judged. And then Coulter exploded this bubble, too. As they passed, Coulter riding his mean-looking pinto and my father, as he said, "superbly mounted" on "Cream," which was the name this white horse went by, Coulter held up a hand to stop him and remarked:

"You'll probably have to shoot that horse when it gets a little hotter."

It wouldn't take much imagination to see the look on my father's face. "Things must be well in hand if you can take time from your duties to play the clown," he said.

"No joke. White horses aren't worth a dried lizard skin on the plains. They attract bugs. Bugs will pester him out of his wits."

"In that case," said my father, so angry he was ready to swap insults like a child, "Cream and your mongrel can start off even."

"Color aside, Indian ponies are the only ones can stand the strain."

"I'm obliged for your counsel," my father said stiffly, and rode off.

Well, when we got scraped up after breakfast, with both wagons ready to move, he said I could ride Cream for a while, and we waited for "Gee-whoa-haw!" It came at last, and the wagon at that end wheeled out of formation and took the trail, behind Coulter, and, after him, McBride, who rode a range stud about as savage and low-down as the owner.

The wagons at night were driven into an oval, like this:

It made a good barricade against Indians, Coulter said, and could be defended against a large force. The cooking was done outside the enclosure, and the cattle turned out to graze until dark, then brought back inside. Later on, in the bad Indian country, the cattle had to be staked to feed outside, but we weren't there yet. So far, all we'd seen were Shawnees and Pottawattomies, with a few Otoes and Kaws, a poverty-struck bunch that wanted to come up and beg, but Coulter wouldn't let them. "Never let an Indian in camp," he said. "Never under any conditions." Even at that, he was easier about them than his "protégé," who was itching to kill a few and notch up his guns.

"A man orta put the smelly devils in their place, once he gets the chance," McBride told us.

Twice Coulter had to haul him off when he tried to ride down little traveling groups within a few yards of us. Coulter also made a speech in which he cautioned about straying off from camp. He told Jennie she was playing "ring-toss" with her life by going out to hunt. "Indians along here are mainly harmless but they'll swallow up a straggler and leave nothing but his bones. And in your case," he went on, looking her impudently in the eye, "they'll breed you to half of the tribe. If that's what you're after, go ahead."

She shook her head in disgust, but I noticed she stayed within shouting distance of the train for several days.

While my father walked along beside Kissel, I rode Cream on up ahead, past the train, almost to Coulter, who had taken what he called the "point," a word he'd got in Texas—say two hundred yards in front. McBride was nowhere to be seen. It was about four-thirty now, and a few pale streaks, the false dawn, showed in the East where the real dawn was about to break. Looking back, I could see one or two wagons with lanterns out, where people were sick, maybe; but mostly it was dark.

We'd left the Vermilion (our crossing had been made Saturday afternoon) and were headed for the Big Blue, a jump of twenty-four miles without water or wood. To save Cream, I slid off and walked for half an hour or so, until it really began to get dawn. Suddenly, out of the mist up ahead, far beyond Coulter, a number of shots rang out, noisy and jarring in all that silence. Two nearly together and then, a moment later, a third.

"Whoa-haw!" Coulter yelled back, waving. "Hold up the train!"

I leaped up on Cream, not wanting to miss anything, and streaked forward at a gallop, and behind me I could hear others coming a-horseback. Through the mist that hung in the hollows over the prairie I saw Coulter fanning his horse with his heels, his body not rising an inch from the saddle; he could ride and no mistake.

We whipped over a rise, down an incline, and out onto a barish spot, where I could see something on the ground. Coulter was off and running before his horse stopped. Then I saw the trouble; it was McBride, standing with a revolver in each hand, and before him, on the patchy grass, a terrible sight. An Indian woman sprawled there, both hands clutching her breast, which was rising and falling in gasps, and worse, at her feet lay a little boy of about seven, black-haired and handsome, holding a toy deer made out of deerskin—shot dead through the neck—and a girl one or two years younger with her head blown apart so bad I couldn't to say honestly look at it.

As we stood there a second, maybe too stunned to move, the woman arched up with her back, quivered a little at the top, and sank slowly down; she had died. Then I heard rather than saw Coulter's heavy fist meet McBride's face with a thwack, and his cry of, "You crazy damned murdering fool!"

Not much damaged, McBride scuttled around on the ground like a crawfish, to a crouching position, and made a motion to draw one of his guns.

"Go ahead," said Coulter. "Pull it out. Get it two inches out of the holster and you'll eat it, bullets and all."

"You're not my father," the boy screamed. "What business you got telling me what to do?"

Coulter reached down with both hands on McBride's coat and jerked him up so far he had to let him back down to stand. "You loud-mouthed tinhorn, are you trying to get this train masacreed?"

"Nobody hits me and gets away with it."

Sick as I was, I enjoyed seeing Coulter yank away his guns, then kick him about ten feet in the direction of his horse, saying, "Ride back to the wagon—get inside and stay there." Picking up his hat, which had fallen off, he added, "Move off that wagon seat, I'll stake you out and rawhide you in front of the whole camp."

By this time, more of the men had got up, including Mr. Kennedy and some others I knew, and they dismounted, looking grave.

"This is a fine business, Mr. Coulter."

Coulter was down on his knees beside the woman and made no direct answer. "Traveling Pawnees," he said finally, "and pretty far south." He stood up. "What's done's done, but we may see trouble before we're through. Pawnees aren't Pottawattomies or Shawnees. They've been chewed up some by the Sioux to the north and the Comanches south, but they can still raise a fight. They ain't apt to swallow this lightly."

"What do you recommend?" asked Mr. Kennedy.

"Get a burial detail started and keep the train moving. Maybe we won't be blamed, but I've got an idee we're under watch right this minute."

They dug one long grave and laid out that poor woman and the young ones in blankets, side by side, and left the toy deer in the boy's hand. Then Coulter made them smooth over the grass with leaves and twigs, as if nothing had happened, and carry the extra dirt off and throw it away. Some of the men protested, saying it was downright un-Christian to give them unmarked graves, but Coulter shut them up sharp.

When the train caught up, I got off Cream and told my father and the others what happened, and Mrs. Kissel and Jennie snuffled a little; they said what a pity, and how they'd like to get their hands on McBride.

Well, not long after that, somebody noticed he was missing. Coulter searched in his wagon and had others look around, too, but the boy wasn't to be found. His horse was gone, also, but his hat was still inside the wagon. There was nothing to be done except go on, so we plodded ahead slowly, over the faint ruts visible through the weeds. The sun sailed up high—it was hot today —and making it worse we spent an hour climbing one of those swells, like young mountains almost. From the summit was spread out a sight I'm not ever apt to forget. Indians were massed across a valley as far as the eye could see, waiting. They were mostly braves, but I could spot women and children, too. Coulter waved down the train, and we stopped.

Our menfolk made their way forward to get instructions. "I don't think it's an attack," said Coulter, standing by his pony, watching.

As he got the words out, there came a scream from the other hill that brought goose-pimples out on my arms. It was followed by one after another, rising and falling. Then I saw that the

Indians in front had washed away, sort of, to show what went on in the center. To a long pole stuck in the ground, McBride, stark-naked, stood trussed by thongs that passed under his chin then around his wrists and ankles. We could just make it out from that distance. But he wasn't quite all there. Two braves with knives that flashed sun glints were busy beside him, and I could see large raw patches that were red where he should have been white.

"They're skinning him alive," said Coulter.

I stopped my ears to shut out the screams; I couldn't stand any more. Two or three men in our group uncovered their heads, and I could see one's lips moving. Another went back to make the women stay in the wagons. And after that, we just waited, standing in the sun, with the prairie and its flowers all around, beautiful and wild, and no movement anywhere except the work going forward across the hill. They said McBride's screaming died down to crying and begging before they finished, and for a while almost to nothing—long silences and between them short cries that rose up into wails and sent the birds flying.

When it was over, and the Pawnees had retreated from the dripping body that was still alive on the stake, Coulter and a few of our group with strong stomachs, including my father, who hadn't one, followed up the hill as the tribe vanished into the waving grass.

It seemed impossible, but McBride recognized Coulter out of what face he had left and began crying, "Kill me, kill me!"

"Anything to be done, doc?" asked Coulter.

"Not a thing," said my father. "Thirty or forty minutes at the most."

Coulter unholstered his long-barreled .45 and shot McBride through the head with no more expression than if he'd been finishing off a deer. Except to say, "We'll double the herd guard every night till we're over the Platte," he never mentioned this Indian meeting again. But I judged he felt sore and miserable for falling down so bad on his old friend's child. Even so, it was concern wasted, as I saw it. Nobody short of a saint could have reformed that snarling pest, and I heard several of the men say the same. He was born for trouble, as a good many are. If we could only see it in advance, the kindest thing would be to kill them in the cradle.

Chapter XIV

After this, all members of the company stuck close to camp. Nobody "straggled," as Coulter called it. He said again there wasn't any real danger of an attack along here but the skulkers would murder anybody lagging behind. He also counseled us to keep an eye peeled for Indians trying to sneak their way in at night. "They ain't so much aiming to kill, but they'll come thieving," he said. "And they're powerful slick at inching along unseen—more like a snake than a man."

Jennie quit shooting way out from the train; what's more, she never went alone. Sometimes she took me, me toting two of my father's pistols—that is, if Brice was busy with other duties. It was plain to see she had set her cap for that poor fellow; he hadn't any more chance than a rabbit surrounded by snares. But the funny thing was, he didn't seem to take notice of her at all, except to be polite, and grateful, and to thank her when she rammed a piece of pork down his throat when he was daydreaming instead of eating. Things like that.

Hunting, she and I would ride to the front, doubled up on Cream, not far from Coulter, so as to get a chance at game before the train stirred it. But it really didn't make much difference. The birds, plover and such, were so thick you could have brought home a mess with a butterfly net.

Seeing us, as he walked his pinto ahead, Coulter was always entertained, and generally called over three or four sarcasticy things like, "Watch out you don't flush a bobcat now," or, "I'll bet the bears are skedaddling out of here," or maybe a kind of half compliment: "If I had those pretty black locks, I'd figure to hang onto them."

Jennie couldn't stand him. She said he made her sick, and she tossed her head whenever he tried to be sporty. Thinking it over, I figured he was too outright a man for her; what she wanted was a puny thing she could nurse, and Coulter was about as likely a candidate as a buffalo. And what her peeve was centered on, maybe the most noticeable mark of his roughness, was his hairy chest. "Why doesn't that fractious critter button his shirt?" she would say. "It's indecent."

There wasn't any problem of that kind with Brice. He hadn't any more hair on his chest than a catfish and his head would be in the same boat, give a couple of years. No, if you were speaking of hair, Brice was as decent as they come, though for my part I didn't think he looked any better than Coulter, and he probably wasn't anywhere near as warm in the winter.

We went up hunting, Jennie and I, and I trailed along behind, with Coulter over fifty yards or so breaking trail and watching us out of the tail of his eye. It was pleasant. A breeze was in our faces, so we couldn't hear any sound of wagons, and nothing else disturbed the scene. Now and then a grasshopper got up and went winding on a few feet, the way they do, and faint bird cries, complaining about us being there, came down from where they soared high overhead. Plovers in clouds kept getting up, and Jennie peppered away, swinging the double gun from side to side smartly, like a man, and she never got any single birds, either—she was a crack shot.

But today she wanted to pry about Brice, so I had an enjoyable time, getting even for her bossiness.

Says she: "Your father's mentioned his wife, I reckon?"

"Some."

"I understand she was a skinny little thing, peaked and drawn out."

"Not the way I heard it."

She looked back at me, sort of mean, and said, "What did *you* hear?"

"She had red hair and was plump and handsome. There wasn't anything skinny about Mrs. Brice, rest her soul."

"They say she had a mournful disposition and fretted him like all get out."

"On the contrary, she was as gay as a cricket. She was about the sweetest thing in skirts. Everybody says so. Always obliging, never arguing. You couldn't got her to bawl out a man to save her."

"Still and all, I've heard it told, she wasn't much of a hand to work."

"Work! She wore her fingers down to the joints, almost. Scrubbing, polishing, picking up. And when that was done, she'd go down and pitch in at the sawmill. As far as work goes, you've seized on a champion in Mrs. Brice. She didn't hardly do anything else."

"You act like you knew her. You didn't know her a whit better'n me, and I didn't know her at all."

"I *feel* I'd known her," I replied. "She was that kind. Some people just naturally are so good and loving and unheadstrong that their memory goes right on. I don't imagine anything could take its place, ever."

She was so mad she blasted away at a bunch of birds and missed both barrels, clean. I knew better than to say a word, then, for the back of her neck was as red as a turkey's and to tell the truth, I'd said too much already. But she *was* the bossiest human I'd ever seen, and my father indicated the same, but following his style in such matters, he couldn't say so direct but referred her case to a play by a man named Shakespeare, saying she needed taming. And then he dwelt for a while on the wife of a man called Socrates, who he didn't bother to place, though I judged he had something to do with the mule train, as there was a fair number of foreigners amongst them.

Anyhow, I was sorry I'd put her out so, because I liked her, down underneath, and she truly was handsome, with her shiny black hair, her rose-petal mouth and her face with its high color. So I made up a lie and said, "Jennie, Mr. Brice was asking how old you were the other day. He seemed mighty interested."

"Oh, hush up," she said, so I figured she saw right through me. She was pretty smart, for a girl.

But I didn't worry long. Knowing Jennie, I was certain she'd get him, if he didn't choose to cut and run, and take a chance on living with the Indians instead. But if I'd looked ahead and seen the truth, I probably wouldn't have believed it.

You might say that the trouble with McBride turned the corner of our luck. Up to then, everything had been smooth, except for miscalculations that weren't anybody's fault in particular. Since the very first day, near about, we'd found that things didn't altogether jibe with Ware's book. Where he said was grass there often wasn't grass at all, and in a lesser way the same was true of water. The blame wasn't really his, but the men cussed and took on and said what they'd do to Ware if they ever caught him out in the gold fields.

My father had been one of the loudest in his praise of the *Guide:* now he joined the rest and worked out a gaudy piece of sarcasm, telling it all around that the book was fiction. "One of the greatest fiction writers of our generation," he said. "The man's deep, so deep the publishers swallowed it hook, line and sinker, and put the *Guide* out as fact. No, the one I'm sorry for is Ware himself. He's produced a little masterwork, which would have taken its place beside *Robinson Crusoe* and *Tom Jones*, if understood, and he's being abused for writing an erroneous book of fact."

Well, as often in my father's case, he carried this idea so far that people more or less lost the meaning of it, but he had a good time anyway. He finally had it that Ware was a New Yorker and had never been farther west than New Jersey, so he pretended to be more interested in the book than ever, and would read a passage like, "It has been the practice of most immigrants to drive cows along with them for their milk," and would exclaim admiringly, "Capital! First-rate! What an imagination!"

In case I forget it later (for a person's apt to leave out of a book important bits that he meant to work in toward the end), I might say that Ware met up with a sorry fate. In a way, he was killed by his *Guide*. On the trail with a company (I disremember going which direction) he fell sick near Fort Laramie and was abandoned by his friends. They left him to lie for two days by the roadside without water, provisions, covering, or medicine, as a payment for not being accurate in his book. That is, they didn't feel at all grateful for the hundred good things he told them, but punished him for the hundred and first. He crawled on his hands and knees two miles to a pond and was found by another company, burned black by the sun, but he died before they could help him. A young man not yet past his thirties.

It's likely our group would have served him the same, because they didn't fancy his statements at all. But what really happened was this: Grass *had* been there when Ware wrote his book, but trains coming afterward had destroyed it, and various water holes he told about had dried up or been polluted. I remember on our first day, after a long dry pull, we reached one of Ware's landmarks and people jumped out of their wagons to run ahead, with the oxen and mules taking on, too, and when we got to the pond, we threw ourselves down to see a dead ox in the middle, blown up with gas to twice his size, and the flies and the vultures just having a picnic.

From that first day, too, we found nearly all the wagons to be overloaded. In deep mud the oxen pulled till their cords stood out, causing no more than a gucking noise of the wheels. So the families began throwing away things they could spare—bedsteads, springs, heavy kettles, and so on. And we saw right off that others had made the same mistakes. Within five miles of Independence we commenced to run across a regular warehouse of furnishings, and I suppose that's what attracted the Indians. I noticed extra wheel tires, axletrees, wagon irons, a sheet-iron stove, two ploughs, and, for some reason, a coat and pair of gray broadcloth pants.

We passed our first grave three days out—a pile of stones from a dried-up creek bed, a rough wooden cross, and a board saying, "Master Richard Wiggins, Lebanon, Ky. Died May 7, 1849." Around it were scattered a lot of baby clothes, so we judged the party was already concerned about getting rid of the excess, for I imagine that mother would have hung onto those things forever, if she could.

Well, we'd been seeing this condition all along, but now it was getting worse. In swampy places our wheels bogged down deeper and deeper from the loads, as the oxen got tireder, and finally we stopped for a confab. Within the last hour, we'd passed three more graves, including one that said, "Ben Robbins, a Colored Man," and the trail was strewn over with coffeepots, ironware, candlesticks, a perfectly good Collins ax, buckets, and, at last, food. There were piles of beans, a side or two of bacon, one or two sacks of flour, and such like, and you take it all in all, it scared our womenfolk. To make it worse, Brice was ailing. My father tested his temperature, looked at his tongue, and asked him some questions, then made him ride on the wagon seat beside Mrs. Kissel, because he said he was suffering from a suspended action of the liver and if he didn't watch out he would have a case of dry shucking.

We pulled up for council, and after the men had coopered a wagon tongue that had split going uphill, Coulter said, "We've got to lighten, else we're going to bog down on this prairie and stay, and there ain't enough gold here to stick in your eye."

He was back in his old sneery ways again, and he said, "I happen to know one wagon is almost full up with bricks. Now it would ease me to learn what they're for—do we eat them or use them to play beanbag with?"

This Mr. Kennedy, who was a slender, gentle-looking soul to be sure, but would have spoken up, I think, with spunk enough to spite the devil, said, "The bricks are mine, Mr. Coulter, I thank you for your interest. When my wife joins me later, she'd like a fireplace of good Missouri clay."

"That's very sentimental of her, I'm sure, but your wagon's the first down every day—we've been delayed all I've a mind to."

Mr. Kennedy swallowed bravely and said, "I'll make whatever adjustments are necessary for the general weal, of course."

"Then dump them out—there might be a Pawnee family hereabouts that would favor a chimneystack on their wickiup. And that brings me to this frippery Englishman, the dude in the undertaker's gloves. Is he here—Moe, or Crake, or whatever it is?"

The mule train that was supposed to catch us, so Coe and his group could hook on and leave, had never showed up, so we'd more or less adopted Coe as our own. He was tolerably digestible, though odd.

"If you were addressing me, my man," he said, stepping forward, "have the goodness to use the prefix, 'Mister.' "

"That ginger beer," said Coulter, not much taken down. "Pour it out. Your wagon is one of the worst offenders. Buying mules was boneheaded enough, but the belly-wash is a step too far."

"Coulter," said Coe, smoothing his gloves, "there's an axiom that conferring petty authority on an ignoramus will turn him into a swine. Your case is illustrative."

"Pour out the pop-skull," said Coulter.

"You may be damned, sir. I'll do nothing of the kind. If my luxuries must go, they will go in style. The ginger beer will be served at an open house, or wagon, this evening before dinner. With the single exception of our friend here, you are all invited."

That night the people gathered at Coe's wagon, very shy and tongue-tied, most of them, and Othello, the colored mule-butter, passed around the beverage. Coe had dressed him up in a sort of uniform, being a pair of dove-colored trousers, which looked uncommon odd against his bare feet, and a brown coat that I later heard was the valet's, who was still sickly and unable to stand.

Coe himself sat in his rocker and lorded it with even worse pomp than my father's, and that was bad enough. My father seemed to have got it fixed in his head that *he* had arranged it, and he brought people up to be introduced, got little conversations going, and went around inquiring, "Have you tasted it?" "Do you care for it?" and "Take another—there's plenty."

The object was, as they said, to get rid of all twenty-six cases. So there was enough to go around and to spare. The fact was, the emigrants tackled it in such hungry and starved-out good humor, after nothing but black coffee and water, that they kind of over-did it. I believe the first ones to vomit were two children who crawled over into the weeds and had a very sour time for a while, or until they were asked to shove aside and make room for some wagon drivers that had swallowed several bottles in a row. My father was then called to peer down one woman that had neglected to say she had kidney trouble and was on a diet, and one boy about nine got a cork stuck in his throat, which called for a plumbing treatment to unstop him. It made you proud to see how they waded into this excess-baggage problem, and it was certain to me they would do very well in the gold fields; they had good stuff in them, even before they drank the beer. A considerable number went right on swilling out of pure politeness, long after their thirst had been knocked out for a week or more, and altogether they disposed of twenty-two cases, four bottles. After that, they ran up the flag, and as they sipped along at the end, wobbly but game, Coe began pouring out the rest, after he had offered a panful to two mules and an ox, which declined.

Coulter came over at one point and looked on from a distance, but he went away again shaking his head as if he'd been watching a pack of lunatics. And I can't much say I blame him. It was about the ridiculousest sight ever seen on that prairie, and probably stands up so to this day.

As hilarious evenings often do, this one had to end up in trouble. During the drinking, the people had thrown off their worries, except for what was going on in their stomachs, and had forgot the hardships and miseries that were mounting up on the trail, when someone called out, "Look at those fool dogs skylark!" Everybody turned around, and it *was* peculiar. Two or three families—an Irishman and a couple of others from, I believe, Illinois—had brought dogs along. They called them wagon-dogs, because the owners had formerly been cart drivers, you see, and the dogs were trained to trot along underneath, and not stray. Anyhow, Coulter had made a few grouchy remarks, but the dogs hadn't caused anybody any fuss.

But now, two of them seemed to be chasing the third, and they were bending down and humping themselves, too. I never saw dogs so wrapped up in their work.

"Hold on!" cried one of the men. "That's no dog—it's a wolf!"

It was heading right for us, and a minute later, with the women shrieking and the men scrambling up from the ground, it burst right into the circle, and we could see, with a kind of horror, that its jaws were slobbered all over with foam.

"*Get back! It's mad!*" my father yelled, and such a turmoil of boxes turning over, screams, and kids yowling, with the dogs trying to close in, you never heard. But that Mr. Kennedy, who *was* the grittiest man I ever met, and the mildest-looking, seized Coe's stick and walked right up, lashing as hard as he could. The animal —it was lean and gray and had poor, scraggly fur—took half a dozen blows on the head and then jumped up and bit Mr. Kennedy several times, with quick, nervous snaps, on both arms. He fell back, the dogs held off for a second, and there was a report like a thunderclap.

"It's better off dead," said Mr. Kissel, blowing the smoke out of Coe's shotgun that he had taken down from its sling near the wagon seat. In his hulking but limber and easy way, he had sent both barrels clean through the wolf's chest, and it lay breathing its last on the ground.

While the owners held back the dogs, everybody came back up again, and examined it, and said what a close call it was. Then they congratulated Mr. Kissel, who only smiled his slow, peaceful smile and said yes, it seemed the thing to do.

But we were bounced back to earth by Coulter's familiar raspiness.

"Well, doctor, and what's to be done with our precious Mr. Kennedy?"

In the hurly-burly, people had forgotten the bites he took. He was sitting back weakly in Coe's chair; Coe and Othello were cutting away his sleeves, and Mr. Kennedy himself had about the awfulest look in his eyes I ever saw.

"Tell me the truth, doctor. What are the chances?"

My father bent over him and looked very closely at his bites, but the way he did it, in spite of his best effort to be offhand, was answer enough for anybody—the damage was done.

"I won't deceive you, Mr. Kennedy. But you needn't be too downcast, either. You've been bitten by a rabid wolf. You stand a chance, perhaps only a slight chance, of contracting hydrophobia. Not everyone's who's bitten gets the disease—not by a long sight. Compose your mind; we'll do everything possible."

Then he and the Dr. Merton that Coe had mentioned about his valet drew aside for a consultation, after which they asked the women and children to leave, and they cauterized the wounds, using a white-hot poker stuck in a campfire. Mr Kennedy was given a tin cup full of rum before they started, and they laid him unconscious in his wagon after it was over.

That night, my father and Dr. Merton had a long talk in the latter's tent, over a lantern, and I pinched back my blanket to look when he came in to bed. He didn't seem happy.

Chapter XV

We'd been on the trail eighteen days and had left behind us the Sweetwater Creek, a large gully with wooded banks, full of stones "that have a green slime moss on them which is eternally floating with the current." This last part is from my father's diary; he had been keeping it with a kind of doggedness that wasn't usually noticeable with him except in the business of playing poker.

Other people have since read these Journals and called them works of importance, and one man wrote that, "McPheeters quite obviously realized that what he was doing had literary and historic value." Whether that's true or not, I know he says things in his diaries a lot better than I say them in this book, but I've got a running start now and can't back out.

For instance, he throws in little bits that make you picture the country, and as I read back, I see that I haven't really described it at all, but have maybe got too wrapped up in ourselves. In his entry of June 21, he speaks of finding "a cockleshell in the limestone," and the next day he walked aside to pick "foxglove bells of lilac color, also a round ball of the cactus tribe." And again, "some fine bloody bells three feet high." For a physician, he had an uncommon interest in nature, and his booklets are filled with the carefulest sort of attention to plants: "There are some beautiful lilac-colored leaf daisies with orange-colored hearts. There is also a small pod with two or three seeds just the size of clover seed; its leaves are trefoil, each about an inch long and hardly a quarter inch broad, lanciform, just as I remember the leaf of a sensitive plant."

Sometimes, taking his writing materials, he would stride up ahead, past Coulter, who he didn't bother to nod to any longer, and seating himself on a hummock, study the train as it wound its slow way forward, the men cracking whips and crying, "Gee-haw!", children romping along throwing stones, the women stiff on the seats in their sunbonnets, scared but determined.

In dry areas, we raised rolling billows of dust, and for these reasons, and others, the oxen bellowed hoarsely. My father writes, "Gravel and sand began to mix with the slate stone [in the streams]. It must be like sharp grindstone to the cattle's feet. None of our cattle or mules has ever been shod."

Mr. Kennedy lay sore in his mess's wagon, after the unhappy attack of the evening. Some of the people said he seemed low in mind, and thoughtful, but they had to hold him from getting up to help with the chores. I don't know what it was, maybe all the things like Mr. Kennedy, McBride, the dismal trouble with the wagons, and Brice laid up, but suddenly I was taken by a yearning to get out in the prairie alone. I wanted to shake off the miseries for a while. The day was fine; only a few puff-ball clouds broke the solid blue, the weather was soft and warm, and the bees were just going it in the blossoms. The more I thought it over, the more I couldn't wait to get off by myself.

Coulter had showed us a map, part of a Mormon Way-Bill that they sold to emigrants, and for the rest of the day we'd be going in a wide curve to the left, fetching up, as they hoped, at the Kanza Creek. Says I, I'll just slide out and take a short cut, and see what's in that prairie, away from the trail. With a little luck, it wouldn't even be noticed—I often took some food in my jacket and spent the day visiting up and down the train. So this time I collared a few slam-johns and some bacon, took one of the pistols with several loads, took my hatchet that I'd borrowed from the people in Missouri, and was ready to explore.

My sack of gold was in one of those pouches the emigrants sewed all over the roofs of their wagons. Inside, you could usually see upwards of a dozen of these patch pockets, for storage, you know, and Mrs. Kissel had made me one of my own. So I'd stuffed cotton in the bag, to keep the coins from jingling, and sewed it up there, saving it for I don't know what. Two or three times I'd been on the point of telling my father, but somehow I couldn't get it out. It's a funny thing—I don't know any better lip-buttoner than what gold is; it will dry up a man that's ordinarily as gabby as a magpie, and I was to see it often like this later.

I looked all around. Jennie was bossing Mrs. Kissel, Brice dozed in the sun on his wagon seat, and my father was up ahead gathering prairie peas that the women made pickles of, to ward off scurvy. All was clear. Now at eight o'clock the train already was moving in the slow bend that Coulter said would continue all day, so at the first dry creek bed, I slipped off, looking, I hoped, like I was searching for a handy place to go to the outhouse.

Leaving the creek after two or three hundred yards, I found walking easy through the grasses and flowers. It was exciting. All around me the green swells rose and dipped as far as the eye could see. From my father I was learning the plants, and I could pick out verbena, spiderwort, wormwood, and larkspur, and along with them the currants here grew thicker than dewdrops.

I watched the sun, to keep my directions, and had a good time. Some said that ravening animals, wolves and such, trotted free in these grasses, so I watched out sharp, but I saw nothing more wicked than prairie dogs, and nobody bothered about them. Still and all, I found this heaving prairie, this greenhouse carpet of a world, so bright and many-colored, and sleepily harmless in appearance and in sound, in reality a wild thing, a kind of pretty spider's web where a good many dangers lay unseen.

Crossing a creek bed, skipping stones in the puddles, I passed between some boulders and fell backward at the dry whirring we'd all been told to expect—the rattle, like peas shaken in a gourd, of the rattlesnake. It had been coiled and asleep on a rock baked hot by the sun, and had followed its frightened nature by striking.

The fangs sliced clear through the heel of my boot. But when it drew back its head to try again, I scrambled up and left. I could have killed it with a stick, but I decided not to waste the time. And I soon learned to watch out for grease spots on flat rocks, for it was here that these snakes had lately been coiled, sunning.

Some prairie hens went skittering along; we'd been warned not to chase them. They played a teasing game with the emigrants, it was said, and led them into the prairie to be lost. But a wild turkey shot out in front of me, and I went after it pell-mell with my hatchet. It was funny. He would get up with a noisy flapping, but he couldn't fly only a few yards, and down he'd come again, with me right behind. More than that, being uncommonly fat, he couldn't seem to make more than one good rise, but his shanks were very lengthy, and I was soon piped out. It was too bad; I'd counted on taking back a catch for the roasting pan, because a good many people like these turkeys, although I heard one man say that, "The tarnation critter would soak more butter in basting than it was worth."

It was just after I chased the turkey that I noticed the sky had clouded up; I couldn't any longer see the sun, though I knew where it was from some copper-colored streaks. Well, this wasn't any worry —I knew my directions all right, but it would have been nice to see a few trees, as landmarks, and to climb for a look around. For the first time I had a naggy feeling of how big this prairie was, and how empty of friends. You could have walked to China, almost, and nothing might hinder you, but it wouldn't help you, either.

The weather had begun to act downright odd. The sky wasn't dark—it was patchy, with copper slants through clouds that were boiling-black in the middle and blue or silver on the edges. And a stiffish breeze had started to blow. I said to myself, confound the luck, I didn't bring my poncho, so I'll likely take a drenching. So I walked up a creek bed, hoping to stumble on something clever, and sure enough, here was a bend where flash floods had washed out a great slash of bank, and a grass-tufted rim hung over.

It was a kind of gravelly cave, and suited me fine, with enough shelter for three my size.

Well, the rain wasn't long in coming, and how it zipped down! Everything happened fast on this prairie. One minute all was sunny and mild, and in the next the clouds were ripping and raging and tearing everything apart. I didn't feel quite so fond of it as formerly. Crouching down in my cave, I watched the sky over the lip of the opposite bank, waiting for things to quieten. The rain stopped for a minute, like turning off a faucet, and the wind picked up to a screech, coming in swoops and gusts. It made a strange sight on the prairie—the grasses first tossing and waving, then flattening out like a wagon bed. There would come a broad ripple uphill and down, as if a giant roller had passed over, invisible to the human eye. It was awesome.

Presently the sky lightened up and I felt so cocksure, being dry, that I skipped out for a look around the horizon. Then I noticed a very peculiar thing; I hope I never see another. Far over to the left, some of the black clouds had rolled up into a kind of funnel, with the spout hanging down, and it came lazing its way over the fields, pretty as a picture. You felt comical to see it dance and jump, now touching the prairie, now lifting a little, but making fair time, too, in my general direction. For a few seconds I didn't connect up the roaring I heard with the funnel, but all of a sudden this wind spout curled down and touched a high clump of bushes, maybe two hundred yards off, and where they had been before they weren't any more.

I'd turned to jump back under the bank when the air became filled with such a hullabaloo of noise, rocks flying, twigs and leaves and sand sweeping past, and general bedlam breaking loose, that I couldn't really think at all. Neither could I breathe—there wasn't any air in the middle of that column. I heard some thuds like cannon fire and saw several creek-bed boulders weighing about half a ton slam into the bank, but they hadn't hit me, thanks to goodness. The next thing I remember was the grassy bank above tearing loose with a sound like cloth ripping, and then I didn't remember anything at all. The last thing in my mind was a flutter of panic that I was about to be buried alive. Then everything went black.

I haven't any way to tell when I opened my eyes again. It must have been hours. The sun was shining, the birds were twittering, and that bright, two-faced prairie looked as innocent as angels painted on a church pane. I started to move my arms but couldn't. I was buried to my chin in rocks and earth, and my head felt like stevedores had been drumming on it with a maul. It was easy to wiggle free, though, and I crawled out to take inventory. All intact, except for a lump on my head the size of a walnut, and the hair around it sticky with blood.

But now I had a new problem. The sun was so low, and things were so shuffled around, both inside my head and out, that I'd lost my bearings. I brushed myself off, ate two slam-johns, threw them back up right away, and struck out over the prairie, hoping to hit the trail somewhere, in front of the train or behind; it didn't much matter which. My head ached, and I stopped pretty often to bathe it in cold water.

It's hard to tell the feeling of being lost in an unfriendly place like a prairie. The first thing you want to do is run real fast and catch up; then you have the suspicion you may be running in the wrong direction, so you quit. Once I came across a bare patch where filth showed that Indians had been camping there, and not long since, judging by the flies.

Well, I wasn't anxious for a ruckus with Indians, so I took a little more care, climbing a hillock and looking all around before I ventured out into a high openness. It was baffling. Often I'd say to myself, now I've seen this before, but I'd find another place that looked just the same, so I knew I was wrong. I commenced to get mad at my bad luck, and kicked a number of rocks and shrubs, but there wasn't much profit in it, because my feet were sore enough already. About this time I had the notion I was being followed, so I disappeared behind some bushes, stooped down and waited.

In a minute or two, a gray shape, and then another, flitted cross-ways over a hill I'd just left. Wolves. Now I *was* scared, and knew I'd better find that train soon else I'd put in a lively night. There still wasn't any tree to climb, either. An hour or so passed, the sun sank, and I was about ready to lie down and call everything quits. I was all tired out and knotted up inside, which took the form of cussing myself for being such a jackass as to leave the train in the first place. Here I am, I said, causing everybody concern, not only one time but twice in a row, and laying myself out as dinner for some prairie wolves in the bargain. It was just what I deserved. But I hoped I gave them indigestion, all the same. I fired the pistol back once, daring them to come on, but there wasn't anything in sight, so I only wasted the powder and ball, in addition to which I imagine they had a very good laugh.

Dark came down like a curtain, and now I *was* stuck. Still, I could see a little by the early stars, so I plodded on, singing and talking to discourage the wolves. It must have been nearly midnight—I was getting giddy with tiredness—when I saw a glow of campfires up ahead. I gave a shout, remembered to say my prayers of thankfulness, and broke into a run, my knees buckling at every piece of uneven ground.

Then I had a thought—all these people were probably frazzled out from searching beside the trail, and were likely down in the mouth. They'd dropped off to sleep with their worry gone for a while, and it wouldn't do them any good to be wakened. I made up my mind to find my father's tent and creep in without a sound. Then, in the morning, we'd have a reunion, with a hearty breakfast, and I wasn't so apt to get a going over, either. But it was hard to sort things out in the dark. Our tent had one pole that was crooked and longer than the others, so I studied them all against the slightly less dark of the sky; it must have been upwards of half an hour before I found it. I crawled in through the flap, my head reeling, and curled up on a piece of buffalo robe. Somehow, in the fog of my played-out wits I remember thinking how powerful the tent was now, and concluded to suggest that we give it an airing. A tent *can* get pretty brisk on the trail, and a buffalo robe isn't exactly perfumery to start off with. Then sleep closed in, and I didn't any longer care.

Chapter XVI

Dear Melissa:

Again I have the painful task of reporting to you that a slight accident has befallen our Jaimie. Do not be too disturbed. He has not this time been swallowed up by Father Mississippi, nor seized by outlaw ruffians—he has simply disappeared into the prairie.

I must acknowledge that my concern is tempered with irritation. All is now clear; you were right from the start, as indeed you have usually been in the case of our children. *I did not do my duty by that boy!* On occasions when you directed me, in the commanding style that I regrettably connected with your late father (whose lack of foresight in declining to finance my Convalescent Haven for Drunkards unquestionably hastened his death) to whale him for what seemed to me trivial indiscretions—smoking catalpa beans, burning down the woodshed, dosing Professor Burr's cushion with oil of mustard, selling church hymnals to a peddler—I made only a hollow pretense. Confession, they say, is good for the soul, and I must admit to you, now, that after we performed the funeral march up the stairs, I only whacked his bed with a rolled copy of ~~The Turf Register~~ The Compleat Supplicant. A few licks judiciously place might have spared us all, and him, these present unhappy experiences. *Tempora mutantur, nos et mutamur in illis* (The times are changed, and we are changed with them).

Lest you think me unfeeling or harsh, it seems evident that our boy's *sortie* into the brush was made voluntarily, as a lark, and was not the result of kidnapping, as in the case of young McBride, which outcome I described to you (with some elisions) last week.

His hatchet is missing, likewise one of my pistols, with several rounds of shot, together with a plug of Kissel's tobacco, and other articles that can only point to a selfish, whimsical frolic among the scented rushes. I hold this to be a plain dereliction of duty, and for once, as much as it plagued me, I was forced to agree with the odious Coulter, who said (and I beg you to indulge his untutored frontier idiom), "That sprig ought to have his ass-bone [sic] kicked up between his shoulder blades."

Coulter's ire was provoked by my insistence on stopping the train for a search. For upwards of two hours we lay idle while the men deployed in the verdure. Increasing Coulter's pique was the fact that no less than three of our number, in so doing, themselves became lost, and it was only through the happy circumstance of one woman's having a conch shell, native to (I believe) the Caribbeans and employed by the natives there as a tocsin, or horn, that we could summon them back into the fold. Gunshots had only snarled matters, since everyone was firing both inside the prairie and out.

But no Jaimie. He is off on a willful excursion, and we must pray for his safe return. Should that transpire, and Coulter in spite of himself assures us that it will, I have luckily secured a ladle, wrought in iron, that will be every whit as effective as any rolled-up edition (including the Christmas number) of ~~The Turf Register~~ The Compleat Supplicant.

If he does *not* turn up—but I refuse to consider that proposition at all. Indians are unpopulous in this region; and such as frequent here are often of mild and amiable temper. Wild beasts of the prairie are dangerous only in packs, or when goaded to rashness by famine. All will eventuate with success; do not doubt it for a second.

So, having disposed of the worst, I can deal lightly with the bad. During our wait and search, there occurred, adding nothing to Coulter's pleasure, a storm of such unbridled fury that we were like to be wiped out *in toto*. It was Coulter's surly contention, based on zero, that had we been two hours "forwarder," the tempest would have missed us altogether. My rejoinder was (and rather well taken, I thought) that had our position been indeed advanced, we might have taken the full brunt of the winds, and so perished.

I topped this assertion with a ringing gibe from Horace, in the native Latin, of which he knows nothing, unless he has familiarized himself with the E Pluribus Unum on coins, and he left in disorderly retreat.

As to the storm, it has shaken the nerves of even the sturdiest. There are those (not including the undersigned) who now feel that this arduous and terrible ride is not worth the dubious rewards at the end. For myself, I cling steadfastly to the knowledge that, in California, nearly all is gold that glitters, and I wish you to proceed with the McPheeters Public Clinic, although perhaps the actual business of ground-breaking should be deferred against my return, to be held with suitable ceremony—the golden spike (railroads), ribbon-slicing (statues), speech by the Mayor (unpreventable) and the like.

On the morning of the storm the wind blew high, though it was nothing more in effect than a hot blast of temperature. About one o'clock, however, strange meteoric appearances began to present themselves to the north (the opposite point to that from which the wind blew), gradually becoming more widespread and livid; when suddenly a small black speck emerged from the horizon, and, with the quickness of thought, the wind ran round to that quarter, increasing to a perfect hurricane, scattering hats, laundry, and clothing, and detaching the odometer which trails from the wagon of a Mr. Meeker, to check our daily mileage. Several of the wagon covers were rent to shreds, one vehicle was turned clear over, and the unhitched stock, being badly scattered, went galloping about, snorting and puffing, and keeping us busily engaged for some while to look after them. The din and confusion, the mingled screams of the ladies, and the terrified cries from the cattle—were past describing. To add to our dismay, a kettle of coals in the overturned wagon ignited the underwood, and a lake of flame spread out, threatening to engulf one and all in its depths. By good fortune, the rain, which came in erratic torrents, soon extinguished this, and we managed to pick ourselves up and regroup.

Only God knows where our Jaimie was crouched during this ordeal by nature. I have a strong fancy it skirted him entirely, for it took place some hours after our discovery of his absence, and he may have been far into the prairie. Upon his return, as stated, I hope to apply the ladle to the improvement of his education; he wants it sorely.

This morning I stripped myself of my flannel *for a very good reason* and put on a clean shirt. I have always been careful, but some of the company have sat on my buffalo robe. Thus far the women of our wagons—Jennie, Mrs. Kissel—have beaten out our washables in first one stream and then another; indeed, this "soap and knuckles" system of laundering is the standard for the train, but I should tell you that some of the wayfaring dandies among us, not excepting Coulter, have been guilty of the plagiary (if I can call it so), of mangling after the manner in which the Bedouin Arab cooks his steak—by placing it between his posterior and the saddle and setting his horse to full speed.

Now I must finish by relating an anecdote concerning the above-mentioned leader of our train, whose meteoric changes of mood, and, yes, surprising depths, will never cease to amaze me. We have held a meeting in which it was stated by several worried members that the diet of all could be greatly improved by the accession of fresh meat. And it was here, at this point, that our Mr. Kennedy, whom you will remember because of the wolf bites, spoke up firmly, as is his wont, to say, "Under the articles, Mr. Coulter, you were to provide game for the train, as one of your collateral duties."

At the sound of his words, others gave vent to their feelings, bitterly denouncing him for what was generally considered his defection.

"The articles called for game to be hustled by me *and* McBride," said Coulter, sitting quietly, the familiar sneer on his roughened countenance, atop an upturned barrel.

"Surely you don't hold *us* responsible for the boy's death!" cried Kennedy.

"Leading the children out of Egypt's a full-time job. Who's to look after your didies while I'm off stalking?"

You may well believe, dear wife, that this swarthy fellow often seems one of the greatest charlatans alive, besides being uniquely offensive. The thought struck us at the same moment—Coulter was no more hunter than the callowest child among us, but had deceived us when hiring out as guide. This intelligence, while a shock, rendered us bold.

146

"I don't believe he *can* hunt," said one of the younger men, a farmer as grand in stature as Coulter himself.

You have probably noticed that the instant a formidable person, like a leader of an animal pack, shows weakness, the cry goes out for the kill. So it was now. Heretofore, Mr. Coulter had been approached with diffidence, even with fear, but now, as he made no reply to his accusers, the epithets flew fast and thick.

And here was an odd thing. Perhaps the only person who did not leap into the fracas was Coe, the mincing Britisher who had ragged him so recklessly before. Instead, I saw Coe regarding Coulter with a suggestion of a smile, and it came over me that this latter had no *need* to defend himself. He was as comfortable as if he were receiving the plaudits of the multitude. The English can be an exasperating race, but they have (and have always had) a sharp awareness of courage. I must tell you, Melissa, that I feel indebted to Coe, because my translation of his look saved me a fair amount of money.

"I can't hunt—is that the general verdict?"

"You're a fraud and a cheat," said the young farmer hotly, "and for two pins——"

"You've got it all decided, don't want to change your minds?"

"A change of leadership would be more to our liking."

"Well, I'll tell you what I'll do," said Coulter in his annoying way. "I'll take on a few bets I can be back here before sundown with fresh venison, as bad a hunter as I am, and if none of you big talkers can't put up, I suggest you shut up."

This was on a Sunday, and several hours of daylight were left. Even so, most of the men laughed aloud and pressed forward with sums from their meagre treasure. The lanky farmer laid down eight dollars; Mr. Kennedy stepped into the casino with five. The sole member who declined to make a risk was Coe, who continued to survey Coulter with amusement tempered by regard. For once in my life, I let discretion take the reins, and I, too, kept a firm hand on my purse.

Well, when all the wagers were down, Coulter got up leisurely, still wearing his derisive smile, as if he had dismissed a class of idiot children, and walked over to his wagon. I could not help but admire his tread; physically he is unusually graceful for a man of his height and breadth of shoulder. He steps along as silent and wary as any Indian, but to offset what might appear to be a compliment, I'll add that he has a disposition to match that of the surliest Indian alive.

So we followed along at some distance, curious about his preparations. What was our surprise when he emerged from his wagon carrying his rifle, an ax, and a large piece of bright red flannel. He proceeded to cut a sharpened sapling six feet high; then, with a sardonic wave, he pushed forward up the trail.

It was two days before we learned all the details of this abominable rogue's "hunt." For the outrageous truth is that Coulter came back at dusk dragging two sizable buck on a pair of poles interlaced with thongs—what the Indians of some parts call a "travois." Yes, he had slain the animals and won upwards of a hundred dollars. And at collection time he declined to say how the job was done. But inevitably with a man of that stamp, he had to confide it afterward, amid triumphant guffaws, to one of the men, a drover with a pronounced "gallows complexion."

Employing an old plains trick, our rascally Coulter merely set up shop on a likely knoll two miles distant, thrust his sapling into the ground with the flannel tied to the free end, concealed himself in the bush, and awaited developments. They were not long forthcoming. Several deer that were attracted by the waving rags crept forward timorously to explore, and two of their number were dispatched for their pains.

What on earth can you do with a fellow of that moral stature? Quite clearly he stooped to a low form of subterfuge, and you might have thought the least he could do would be to refuse the money won. But no, not Mr. Coulter. He pocketed every last farthing, and with the pithy observation that, "Lessons ain't learned easy on the trail," followed by the equally noxious statement, "Thrift is a virtuous quality, you gentlemen ought to cultivate it," he retired to his meal and couch. There, in microcosm, you have the species of leader to whom our fortunes are committed.

Notwithstanding, all is potentially well. These trivial distractions will soon be resolved; of that I am certain.

Your devoted (if peripatetic) husband,
SARDIUS McPHEETERS (M.D., Univ. Edinburgh)

Chapter XVII

I lay with my eyes half open, staring at the top of the tent where the sky showed through in the smoky gray of first dawn. It was puzzling; I couldn't figure it out. Then I thought, this isn't Sunday—why aren't we up and moving? It was still dark inside and I had an itch to spread the good news about how lucky everybody was to get me back. But that hole worried me; I didn't know why. It was along about here that I became aware of a real lively stink, like a barn where a skunk had taken up residence and later moved by general request. It was fragrant but unsudden.

I raised up, and the minute I did, a flap was thrown back and an Indian woman, not young, and not pretty, either—she looked like a dried persimmon—stuck her head in. Beyond her I could see other women getting a fire going. When she spied me she dropped the flap quick and grunted, and as soon as she did, I out with my knife and jumped across in the dark and ripped a four-foot slit down the tent wall. But it was no use. I felt hands like iron on my ankles; I was caught.

They dragged me out in the open and looked me over. And at the same time, scared as I was, I had a look at them. Since that morning, I've read a lot of books about the noble red man, how keen his eye is in the woods, how silent he slinks along, how brave in the face of danger. Well, the specimens I had here looked mighty run-down and seedy. If there was anything noble about them, I didn't notice it. Most of the men, when they crawled out, scratching, draped over with store blankets against the bitter cold, were potbellied—from not getting any exercise, I reckon; the women did all the work. What's more, their presence was so powerful, from rubbing rancid fat on to stave off the bugs, that a person had to stay upwind if he wanted to be comfortable.

The women weren't much better. When the fellow that had grabbed me hauled me out, the women all rushed up and commenced to spit on me. To relieve the monotony, a few hit me with sticks, but they were kindling twigs for the fire and didn't hurt. I disliked being spit on, though—the practice hadn't been common in Louisville—and I spit back at one old squaw that had several teeth missing. It turned out to be the wrong thing to do. She dipped a calabash gourd into a kettle of boiling water and threw it on my leg. If I hadn't been wearing a pair of stout denim trousers, I'd have been laid up with bad scalds.

The next thing those spiteful old witches did was take off my clothes, which they passed around, grunting and cackling. This left me as naked as a jay, and I wasn't at all easy. There were several girls of about my own age or a little older there, and they seemed to titter more than when I was covered. I was cold, too. The men had crow-black hair parted evenly in the center, with braids hanging down on either side and a gaudy single feather stuck up from the crown of a few. Red and blue grease paint badly smeared showed on a couple of faces, and some had strings of beads or other decorations. One, that seemed to be a chief, had a silver medallion of President Jefferson, maybe presented to his grandfather or somebody, and another wore a necklace of bear's teeth and claws. I didn't see any more animal decorations, though, and if you came right down to it, I imagine there were more bears walking around the woods wearing strings of Pawnee teeth than the other way around. These fellows *might* have been great hunters; if so, they disguised it by their looks.

By and by they quit tormenting me, and everybody sat down around kettles to have breakfast. There must have been two hundred members to the tribe altogether. It was interesting to watch them. The way they worked it, each one had a knife and they dived in and speared a hunk of meat; then, holding it between their teeth, they sawed it off at the lips. It was a wonder they didn't get cut.

Sitting there, I got so hungry I couldn't stand it, so I grabbed the elbow of the man that had nabbed me and made motions toward the kettle. At first I thought he was going to haul out his tomahawk—he didn't change expression any more than a halloween mask—but suddenly he dipped into the pot and hauled out a leg bone. What it was a leg off of I have no idea. Nor do I have to this day; some kind of grouse, or hen, likely. He gave me a rickety knife with the handle knocked off one side, and I fell to work.

Well, the pot didn't *look* inviting, being all a-bubble with various pieces of meat—wildfowl, venison, woodchuck, dog, and the like—but I took a bite hoping I wouldn't throw up. To my surprise it was as flavorsome a dish as ever I ate back home, and our old Clara was the best cook anywhere around. It was sweet meat, so tender it was falling off, and the soup was rich and full of strength.

I finished the leg, then figured I would forage on my own; the meat had been tasty but scant. I stuck my knife in to fish for the thigh, but this time the crazy old fool cracked me over the head with the handle of a dog whip. My ears rang like church bells; for a second my vision was crossed like a cockeyed person's. There wasn't any figuring these Indians out. One minute they invited you to dine, and the next they hit you on the head for enjoying yourself. The blow kind of took the edge off my appetite. I started to get up, but they pushed me back down again.

When breakfast was over, they gave me a pair of worn-out buckskin pants and made me help the women clean up, along with some other children. They were taking down wigwams and packing, ready to move, and I had a chance to study them, now that the sun was up and warming my bones. These people were dressed mainly in hides—deer hides, buffalo robes worn as capes, and such—but there was a good deal of store cloth, too: calico, cotton and denim. I wasn't long finding out where this came from. Neither the men nor the women wore any of the headdresses that always appeared on Indian pictures back in Louisville. Mostly the squaws had a kind of buckskin bodice, not very tight, and attached to this was a skirt of the same material that hung to the knees. Some of the younger women were pretty, and wore leathern hose embroidered on the side with beads. These were laced to moccasins made out of the tougher parts of the skins. A few girls had on eardrops, and others wore rings stacked up in piles on their fingers. Before sunrise, both the men and the women had been wrapped around with snow-white blankets of wool.

Even if I'd wanted to, I couldn't help much with camp-breaking. Right after breakfast, the old man tied rawhide thongs between my ankles that gave me walking room but would have been as much help running as carrying a cannonball in your hip pocket. They cut in, too. I never saw such an unsociable fellow. Although I'd got over my fright a little—I was pretty sure they planned to burn me when the women started cooking—I still wasn't entirely peaceful in my mind. Nobody seemed friendly, not even the children. There had been a couple of dozen campfires for the two hundred people, and back almost out of each firelight was a circle of skulking, patchy-furred dogs. And if somebody sawing off meat ran into a piece of bone, or a saddle horn or a belt buckle or something, and then threw it over their shoulder, didn't those dogs pounce on it in a fury! But nobody paid them any attention.

In an hour we were ready to travel. I wondered if they intended to leave me behind, but no, they brought over a foolish-looking man of about forty with a slack jaw and a nose that was mashed kind of flat and twisted to one side, like a rudder.

"Anglish," they said, and pointed to him with pride. He grinned and said, "Am spoke Anglish once prisoner for catch stealing. Many beatings." Then he introduced himself by name, which was a number of sounds, very bothersome, that ended with oo-sah. He said the English of this was Afraid of His Horse, which appeared to me to give him a poor sort of reputation, but I didn't say so.

"What name to she?" he said, and after a second I figured he meant me.

"Jaimie."

He made a ripping noise, together with some coughs and gurgles, and I learned afterwards it was his way of laughing.

"If you don't like it, you know what you can do," I said, being fairly sure he couldn't understand, whereupon he became fierce and pulled out a tomahawk which he laid against the middle of my forehead, the blade pressing into the skin.

"How much peoples in wigwams with wheels?"

It was plain enough he meant the wagon train, so I said, "Ten thousand," hoping to discourage them.

He struck me such a blow with the flat side of the tomahawk that I fell to the ground, stunned. When I got up he'd worked out figures in the dust that were amazingly close to our number. I made up my mind that a joky and carefree manner with these monsters was about the silliest thing a person could do. And I got a further idea of how free they were of ordinary feelings a few minutes later when we started to go.

A wrinkled old woman commenced to howl and strike herself on the head and breast when the tribe took up a single-file away from camp, so I pumped Afraid of His Horse about her trouble. After some fits and starts, he got across the statement that she was "too much older," and was being left behind. Later on, I found that nearly all these Indian tribes—Sioux, Crow, Bannock and Cheyenne included—disposed of their old folks when they got to be eighty. The unloading was done in various ways, none of them appetizing. The usual Pawnee system was to take the old person and set her, or him, in the center of a circle, and, covering her over with blankets, shoot arrows into her from all around the ring. After this the body was burned and the ashes strewn in the wind, which they called giving their soul back to the Great Spirit. But this particular bunch of loafers, being short of arrows, were too lazy to shoot them up on tomfoolery. I inquired why they couldn't pull the arrows back out again, but they said this might be offensive to the spirits.

So they bound her feet and hands and left her behind. "Much wolves get fat," said Afraid, grinning, as if he'd like to view the festivities. I swore to myself I'd serve him the same if I ever got a chance; anyhow, the poor old lady could have done worse. Some of the tribes, bored for lack of amusement, dug holes for the elderly people and buried them alive, making jokes and having a good time as the dirt was thrown in.

When we first took up the trail, I had hopes of hooking a knife and cutting my foot bonds, but they knocked this out in a hurry. These Indians had gone to seed, all right, but they were tricky, too, possibly because of early training. Right off, when we started, they cut a limb three feet long and placed it across my shoulders; then they tied my hands. Afterwards they unloosed my foot straps. That is, I was free to come and go as I pleased, but I didn't feel encouraged to strike out across the prairie trussed up like a goose on a spit.

I shuffled along, first with one group and another, looking them over for further reference. A man they said was a chief, though I couldn't pronounce his name, neither did it seem to have any English equal, walked in front carrying a bundle of what I took to be sticks with wampum wrapped around. This was his sacred bundle of chieftainship, which made him the keeper of the people, as I understood it. After him came the "braves," so to speak, and then the squaws driving horses pulling travois, some with papooses on their backs; then the children romping along. At the tail end were the dogs and the other livestock. A few braves were mounted, but most made their way on foot. All in all, it was about as ratty a procession as you'd see in a lifetime.

Well, it wasn't long before I figured out where they were heading. These people made their living by scavenging in the wake of wagon trains, picking up things thrown away. Taken all around, it was a low kind of calling, but it was rewarding, too. As my father stated in a letter, the emigrants all started off with more than they could haul, and the process of shucking down to weight commenced a short way out of Independence.

We crawled along, an Indian village on the move, chief in front and everybody hopping from side to side seizing on valuables. It was pathetic but catching. I don't know why, but found things are better than articles you acquire by honest effort; they're more prized. If my hands hadn't been laced up high, I could have collected enough to open a store. It wouldn't have had any customers, though; there was enough on the ground for all.

The farther we got, the slower we went, because of the load these vultures took on. And right here I want to say a word for that chief. I've written a lot about how reduced the Pawnees were, but I'd make a poor book if I didn't give credit where it was due. This chief wasn't any chief by accident. He was the sharpest-eyed fellow in the tribe; some said he was the fastest runner, too. And his age, as nearly as I got it, was fifty-seven. One reason I mention this is because he was the first man there to pounce on something of real value. We hadn't filed out on the trail two minutes before he darted to one side and came up with the remainders of a very nice striped silk umbrella, with only a few rents of any size and a couple or three spokes sticking out. Moreover, he knew exactly what to do with it. The day had turned cloudy cool, but he got the umbrella up, after sticking himself in the eye with a spoke, and sailed up the road as pleased as a girl with her first party gown. Still and all, conditions weren't perfect. The main trouble was, he had his chief's bundle under one arm, and the umbrella kept folding up and hitting him over the head, so he stumbled and fell in the bushes now and then, since he was more or less proceeding blind, but he stuck to it like a man, weaving back and forth, flapping like a bird, and having a very painful time altogether. Everybody admired him, he had got so involved.

Dead cattle were strewn along here thick enough to walk on like steppingstones. And we came to mounds of thrown-out beans and bacon and flour, and every utensil you could name, including pots and pans and a ten-gallon water cask. I wondered how much had come from our train, up there ahead, and how much from others. The first pile of bacon we came on, these potbellied Indians hove to and organized a feast. It wasn't more than ten o'clock in the morning, but they dug in as if they hadn't eaten for a week. The bacon was spoiled to the point where it was kind of slippery, and the stench would have frightened a polecat, but that made no difference to these fellows. They grabbed up pieces—soapy lumps, rather—and stuffed them in, and a good many ate the beans, entirely raw. I've seen some vomity sights among Indians since, particularly with the Utes, which live on a caterpillar mash, and the Diggers, which will eat anything as long as it's filthy, but these Pawnees fighting the flies for that bacon topped everything.

Once they were filled, they lolled awhile in the shade; then we went on again, picking up as before. The women were anxious to find cloth, and the men did a fair amount of arguing over harness. But they all decorated themselves in some way. I saw one woman wriggle into a copper band off a keg, to make a nice belt, though it seemed to pinch her and made her bulge out above and below, and the tallest brave of the bunch made a tolerably good pendant out of a teething ring. They were the simple-mindedest fools I ever met, and I swore I'd be rid of them soon. But it wasn't so easy. Without seeming to, they watched me. By and by, this Afraid of His Horse, who I got chummy with when he wasn't cuffing me, let out that they hoped to trade me for horses.

"Don't count on it," I said, exasperated almost to death by the bugs that lit in places where I couldn't get them with my hands tied. Nearly everybody else, except some of the nicer-looking women, had that rancid fat rubbed on, but I'd rather had the bugs any day.

"Wagons people pay."

"I doubt it. They're overstocked on boys, and horses are pretty scarce. You're barking up the wrong tree."

"Four horses, possible with five."

"Not one red cent. If I know my father, he isn't the kind to throw away money on a boy when he can buy a horse."

"Then maybe burned at stakes."

I changed my tune when he said this, but I was so cocksure, I thought he was bluffing. Later on I knew better. I never got used to the contrary ways of these Indians; their thinking was just the opposite of ours.

For instance, when I had to go to the outhouse, they sent a young girl along as a sentinel. They said she was some kind of chief's daughter, but that's what Indians always say. Anyhow, this girl was called Pretty Walker, about two years younger than me, not ratty-looking like the others. I complained so much about being trussed up, they finally removed the harness and fixed my feet again. And this time I could take steps about a foot and a half long. I don't know which was worse—having my hands up all day or crow-hopping along like a quail protecting its eggs. But as I said, this girl Pretty Walker left the trail with me when I had to go out, and we didn't make it at all.

I told her to stay behind a tree.

She shook her head and pointed to my feet.

"I couldn't undo these thongs in a month of Sundays," I told her.

But it wasn't any use; she couldn't understand a word. No matter how clear I pronounced things, nor how loud I hollered, she never caught on. She was more than ordinarily thickheaded even for a Pawnee. What's more, she had the audacity to throw some of that Indian talk, which sounded like cocking a rifle, at me. She was pretty brash; I'd like to have seen her taken down a peg.

"You'll have to shove along a way, otherwise we're stuck," I said, but she only smiled and said approximately, "Moo-wah-rick-tok-goo-sah," which I took to mean, in a general sense, no.

Finally, after a good deal of palavering, I got her to stand behind a tree, and then things went better. Afterwards, I found out that Indians nearly all set a pretty young girl to watch a prisoner like that, the idea being that the braves are too dignified and the squaws are too busy doing the braves' work. Also, a young girl is supposed to kind of lure a prisoner from *trying* to escape, but I didn't understand this part.

Certainly it didn't work with me. The minute I was behind *my* tree, I tackled those rawhide straps as fast as I could. It was no good. The skunks had tied them and wet them, so that they'd drawn up like fiddle strings.

When I got back out, she smiled again—she had very nice white even teeth, so I imagined she was as much of a bore with the willow twig as Jenny was with the brush—and said on the order of "Na-noh-kik-tik-seh-goony-la." Then I realized she was suggesting I'd tried to escape, after more or less giving my word. I turned red and got angry. It was exactly the style of these Indians; they wouldn't trust their own mothers. It's the way they're taught; they haven't got the morals of a coyote.

That evening when we made camp, I struck up an acquaintance with a boy of my own age named, as they said, Shorter than the Crane. He was playing with a brown-and-white-spotted puppy and didn't mind when I stopped to pet it. I had just finished hunting firewood with the women. Shorter seemed fond of the dog, and affectionate toward him, and I began to think a little better of the tribe, or at least the young ones. This pup was frisky and cute; he made me homesick for Sam. We threw some sticks, which he failed to bring back, and told him to sit up, which missed connections, and nudged him to shake hands, which he ignored, and then we tried to balance a piece of meat on his nose, but he ate it. He was a real nice pup, and could likely have been trained, if anybody had had thirty or forty years to lay aside for the job. Shorter had patience with his stupidness; he took him in his arms and cuddled him, and was as crazy about him as any boy with a dog.

Then an old squaw who had got a fire going grunted something, and the boy stood up and took the pup and hung it over the flames, holding it by the tail. The puppy twisted and cried out, very shrill and piercing, while the boy and the squaw carried on a conversation. Then, when it was dead and all the hair burned off, they gutted it and put it in the pot with the other things for supper. Feeling uneasy in my stomach, I went over in the weeds for a while.

It was all I needed. I made up my mind to get away that night if I had to murder everybody in the tribe, including Pretty Walker. These weren't humans, they were monsters. When it came time to eat, I poked in the kettle, then fished out a bird—a quail or a partridge—and when nobody was watching, put it on a stick and roasted away the stew smell. I could have gone without eating if I'd wanted to, but I was hungry.

Before the sun fell below the prairie horizon, both women and boys set fish traps—woven baskets—and night lines for catfish in a stream nearby. I went down and watched them, hoping somebody would lose his footing and start to drown, so I could throw them a rock. But I hadn't any luck; they were as nimble-footed as a goat. They placed these woven baskets in little places below falls and the like, where leaping trout would fall back, as they do. Some of the boys fished with fiber lines and hooks of thorn or wishbone, using worms or bits of rag for bait. Under other conditions, I might have joined in, but I couldn't see any fun to these people now. So after a while I went to bed, in the same wigwam with the old fellow that had caught me. I couldn't exactly make out how I stood. I believed, now, that Afraid of His Horse was telling the truth about trading me for horses, but there was a question about who owned me, whether the first man or the tribe. Generally speaking, things like food and necessaries were shared, but they had private property, too. So I figured he might get his pick of the horses.

The only thing you could recommend about this collection of camp-following hyenas was their tents, or wigwams. They were nearly eighteen feet high, shaped like a cone, twelve feet across at the bottom, and held upright by straight poles called lodge poles, which were drawn together at the top, leaving a hole for smoke to get through. Over the lodge poles they had tanned buffalo robes stitched together to form one big airtight skin. A fire was made on some raised ground in the center, and what smoke couldn't get out swirled around and made things tough for the mosquitoes. It also made things tough for the sleepers, because if it was a windy day when the draft didn't work, they lay on their robes and spent their time sneezing and coughing. What between the bugs singing in a rage for blood and the people suffocating, it made a very melodious night. Still and all, these wigwams were workable dwellings, roomy and rainproof, and if it wasn't for the odorous nature of the residents, a person could live inside in comfort. They were pretty on the outside, too, some of them. A number of Indians that seemed to have more energy than the others had decorated the hides with paintings, very spidery and graceful, of hunting scenes—mounted braves shooting arrows into buffalo, deer running, and things like that. They were handsome, and would have made a nice decoration on the wall of a library or study back in Louisville.

Going to bed, I noticed two more buffalo robes inside, and wondered who the new sleepers were. This old rascal who'd grabbed me, named Sick from Blackberries, had a wife once, according to what Afraid of His Horse told me, but she cavorted with somebody else when Sick was off hunting, so they gave her a perfectly straightforward trial, but she was guilty, right enough, and had a papoose to prove it, so they cut off her nose. Since then, she and Sick had been pouting at each other, Sick because he had another mouth to feed that he hadn't sent for, and she because she missed her nose, which seemed natural. Just the same, she was required by law to fix his meals, and did, though he had a stomach-ache most of the time, so everybody figured she was poisoning him.

Anyhow, I turned in, ready to put my escape plan into action. My feet still were tied with drawn-up thongs, and Sick had fastened them to a lodge pole, but I figured I'd pretend sleep and steal his knife sometime in the night. After that, I could cut loose, slit the tent again and hike out of there. I'd get back on the trail, which was only a few hundred yards away, and follow forward until I hit the right camp this time. It was a good program.

But I had a pesky hard time to keep from going to sleep. Outside I could hear the summer night sounds, cicadas, locusts, crickets and such, and the stream made a soft rustling that lulled you so you could hardly hold your eyes open. Way off somewhere I heard a hoot owl going, then a wind came up and made a kind of song in the grasses. Tired like that, it was more than I could stand.

Next thing I knew I heard voices and two more Indians were in the wigwam. Sick with Blackberries was sitting up talking with them. They were young, lean fellows, and it was easy to see they'd had some kind of adventure. They were stark-naked except for a knife string and flap, and they'd thrown a couple of wolfskins to one side. I didn't understand at all, particularly since one of the men had a red, bleeding furrow alongside of his head and the other had hurt his ankle. They'd been up to something. And all of a sudden they took it out on me. Saying a word I'd come to recognize as "white" or "paleface," they began to kick and beat me. I covered my head with my arms, but they yanked them away and slapped me hard several times. Then they kicked me in the ribs and stomach until I got dizzy and wasn't wholly conscious for a few minutes.

When I got back my senses, they had finished tending their injuries and were on their way to bed. I lay as far removed as I could, in a kind of corner, sore and miserable and homesick. I wanted my mother to tell these mean dogs where to head in—she could have done it better than anybody—and I wondered if Sam was happy at the farmer's. I cried a little. Then, after a while, I went to sleep and dreamed it had all been a dream—we were home peaceful and safe, my father was off for the Marine Hospital, my mother was in the back yard chiding Aunt Kitty, Sam was eating a pair of linen drawers off the line, and I was up in the cool summer morning, barefoot in the dust, headed for Herbert Swann's.

Chapter XVIII

Several days ran by, with me watching for a chance to get away. But these Pawnees were crafty about some things. So far, they'd made no motions to trade me, and I was beginning to wonder what was up. At night, I had to sleep with the old man and the two marauders; in the daytime I worked alongside the women, with Pretty Walker close at hand.

You couldn't say we were friends, but we had an understanding. As long as I didn't make any move to escape, we jollied together and tried to talk with the Indian words I was learning. Once in a while we played games with the others, but my heart wasn't really in it. After the business of the puppy, I wouldn't have trusted this bunch as far as you could throw a buffalo. Sometimes in the afternoons, after a morning scavenging the trail, the women would sew garments and the men smoked something called "Kinek-Kinek," out of red stone pipes. For a short space, or until the effect wore off and they returned to their natural state, it seemed to make them less ornery, and not quite so cautious. I kept my eyes peeled and sure enough, on the seventh or eighth day, I got what I was looking for—a knife, and a beauty, too. It was a silver-mounted bowie, in a case, lying beside the trail. When I spied it shining in the bushes, I was walking near Afraid of His Horse and in front of the girl, with my feet tied to a line. I didn't waste a second but pretended to stumble on a rock and fell headlong, covering it with my body. And when I got up, grumbling and brushing myself off, I had it safely inside my waist. Now all I had to do was get away from the band, cut loose, and shinny up the trail toward the train. It was rumbling along somewhere ahead, no telling how far.

But I didn't get a chance all that day, and not that night, either. One bad move in the tent with those devils and I'd never get another whack at it; I knew that well enough. So I had to bite down on my anxiousness and wait, but I do believe that's the worst amusement on earth, if you've got something to do at the end. I once read in a schoolbook how some people in India manage to put in time resting in a kind of trance, brain perfectly empty, nothing stirring at all, but by and by the article let out that they were standing on their heads. I lost interest; it seemed extreme, somehow. Besides, it wouldn't have won favor in the important places like railroad depots, so what practical use was it?

The first thing you knew, the tribe ate so many beans and other scooped-up truck they had to knock off a day to recover. A lot of these western tribes had stationary summer lodges as well as winter lodges, but this gang mostly just marched along, breaking camp when an area got thinned down on things to steal or beg, so kept moving nearly all the time. But today we loafed around, the women catching up on chores, the men either asleep or crawling off for a quiet vomit—because the beans and bacon had been so wormy even the birds passed them up—and the children playing the usual games, which were an imitation of adult meanness of some kind: clubbing dogs, shooting toy bows or spears, using ropes, and the like. By and large, they were an unusually woodenheaded collection, and had names to match. The biggest boy in our bunch of about six was called, "Luh-sah-cov-re-culla-ha," meaning "Particular as to the Time of Day," but the name was such a stumper, I didn't call him very often.

The children looked on me as a novelty, a kind of slave-prisoner, and had fun snarling up my feet with a shove and making me fall. Other times, they let me join in, mainly to laugh at my clumsy arrow-shooting and such. Well, I didn't mind being the tribe jackass as long as I had hopes of advancement.

We played in a rocky stream bed with steep mudbanks on the

sides, and I edged farther and farther away from camp. Shooting the arrows, throwing the spears, me hopping along like a mother bird leading intruders away from chicks, we went around a bend and out of earshot, I judged, of the main tribe of braves and squaws.

About the only one that didn't take joy in tormenting me was Pretty Walker, so I'd begun to have an idea she might let me escape after all. She wasn't any bad-looking girl, for an Indian. She kept her black hair coiled in two long pigtails, and her skin was smooth, not dark and pitted the way some were. In addition to that, she was clean; she kept so by bathing. I knew it for a fact because she once slipped out of her hide blouse and skirt and splashed in the river right before me. Stripped down that way, she didn't look as young as I thought, but rounder, like Jennie, and it was disgusting to see anybody so proud of growing up like that, ahead of other children. She didn't have any more modesty than my goat Sam.

The girl's most noticeable trait was the way she looked at you. People generally are shy or scared of each other, I've observed; and no matter how friendly they seem, their eyes always change a little if you peer at them close, then pull down some shutters in back. This is maybe because everybody wants to show themselves in a particular kind of way, the person they'd like to be, and whatever they say is put forward carefully to make up the picture. But not this Pretty Walker. She looked clear into you and saw everything you felt, so you could loosen up and be comfortable. She said my name in two parts, "Jay-mee" and I could have been sore about it, but wasn't. Just the same, she was an enemy, appointed by the tribe, and I knew where she stood. Most always. At other times, her hazel-colored eyes, deep as a well with no bottom, seemed waiting for a signal.

We played tie-'em-up, with Particular as to the Time of Day taking the lead. He was the noisiest Indian I ever met, then or later, bossy and cruel and loud. He tied everybody up, and I could have got loose but didn't try hard on purpose. It was my game; I had suggested it, and the idea was to keep him happy with it for a while. We took turns, and sure enough, blown up with brag as he was, I got mine. I tied the four boys, working just as fast as I could, smiling and talking all the time, and when I came to Pretty Walker she shook her head, no.

"Get loose," I said to Particular, and gave him a push backwards. There wasn't a one of them that could have fought free in less than an hour; I'd have bet any money on it.

Pretty Walker stood looking on, with a puzzled frown. Grinning, now, I flashed out the bowie and cut the thongs between my feet.

It isn't easy for an Indian to turn pale, but she did, after which she ripped back her bodice with both hands and closed her eyes— showing me where to plunge the knife.

"Hurry up," I said, and seized her by the arm.

For about two minutes, she fought like a wildcat, until I got her down on the ground and held her, but I had the feeling she was doing her duty, and not really meaning it.

"Come on, you fool," I said, and pulled her up roughly. This time she was ready to go, and we crept and ran as silent as we could up the creek and out of sight. The last thing I heard was Particular howling like a coyote for his father, but his father was two miles off and upwind at that. So I just let him howl; it sounded kind of meloderous.

I estimated we'd have an hour's start, but I hadn't counted on the weather. We hadn't been going ten minutes before it began to pour rain. It was warm—I didn't mind it—but it came down so thick you couldn't tell where you were going. This was about the worst luck I'd had since I left home, and nearly all my luck had been sour, or so I felt right now. As soon as the creek bank shallowed, I got us out of these rocks and turned in the direction the trail ought to be. We picked a path in the grasses and pushed, and how it did rain and lightning and thunder! But it was good for one thing —in this sop we wouldn't leave any more track than a snake, nor be easier to find. After a mile or so, when it hadn't slackened any, I figured we could find shelter without running much risk. One thing, we didn't want to overshoot the trail in the downpour, and besides, we were beat out. In a little hollow I found scrub pine growing and cut branches with my knife to make a lean-to. It was perfectly snug when we crawled in; I'd laid the branches over each other in such a way that the water poured off, exactly as we used to do on the riverbank back home. We were nice and dry, except on the ground.

It was interesting to be there with this girl who wouldn't have been considered bad-looking back home, if she was white. But as far as conversation went, she was a total loss; she was worse than Afraid of His Horse. She hadn't learned only a few words and they didn't seem to fit in somehow.

"Are you sorry you came?" I said.

"Jay-mee."

"We ought to catch the wagon train tomorrow, if we have any luck."

"More whiskey."

I figured this was something she'd heard the men say, and paid no attention. It was hard to puzzle out how much she knew. I wanted to give her the benefit of the doubt, so I decided to go on a way, no matter how ridiculous it sounded. There was a chance she might get the hang of it.

"My father will take you in and adopt you, if you behave your-self."

"Indians stink."

I couldn't think up a good argument, although she herself didn't have any bug fat on; I'd noticed that from the start. The trouble was that, so far, she was only repeating odd words they'd picked up from white men, and a low grade of white man at that. But she was enjoying it—I could tell from the way her eyes and teeth gleamed in the cloudy dark.

"We'll find the trail and camp just off it tonight, then go up fast tomorrow."

"Dirty horse thieves."

"You won't have to work so hard among white people."

"How about it?"

"We'll find gold in California, and all be rich."

"Come on, honey."

I could see she was running out of words, so I thought I'd take one more whack at it and give up for the day. It would be foolish to tire her out; she might get discouraged. Neither had she done too bad on the first attempt—she was coming along fine.

"It's eased off," I said, sticking my head out. "We'd better make up some time."

"Go to bed plenty cloth and beads."

It couldn't have been more than noon, so I knew she was overstrained, and no wonder, on her very first lesson.

"Come along." I took her by the hand.

"Jay-mee dirty horse thieves more whiskey."

We went out in the drizzle and headed for the trail. Considering her foundation, I was very well satisfied with her progress. There were half a dozen girls in Louisville to my knowledge that couldn't have done anywhere near so well. She wasn't any slouch, for an Indian.

We angled toward the trail, or where I thought it was, and sure enough, we struck it after two hours of beating bushes that reached clear to our necks at times. I didn't care for them; it was too easy to step on a snake. It rained off and on, too, coming down in sheets after a lull that made you think it was over. The water hit you so hard it seemed to come right on through the skin. I don't recollect when I was ever so wet before, even in swimming.

When we got to the trail, I was careful not to strike right up. If I knew that tribe, they'd fan out and cover every bet, and the trail back to the train was the best of all. So we went along, parallel, about a hundred yards off, creeping very cautious and quiet. It was lucky we did, for in a while we heard voices and dogs barking, and there they came, about twenty of them, tracking in the wagon ruts, sicking the dogs and looking in a poison bad humor, what with the rain and the inconvenience. I recognized Sick from Blackberries, and Afraid of His Horse, as well as several others; they were that close.

We crouched behind a bush and watched, trying to keep from

breathing. For a minute I was all a-tremble for fear the dogs might spot us, but it was too wet. Besides, I doubt if they could smell much outside their own precinct; whatever was around, unless it was something as hearty as a skunk, would be drowned out by the bug fat and by the braves' natural stink, which laid over everything in range, and had a kind of paralyzing effect on the nose. So they passed on, grunting, motioning, making little darting runs from side to side of the trail, bending over low. Now and then they fetched the dogs a kick, and it seemed to put them in cheerier spirits.

"They're going on by," I said, holding the girl's shoulder to keep her from getting up too fast. One of those buzzards *might* just look back and ruin everything.

Except to whisper "More whiskey," which didn't seem to cover the case, she didn't say anything, but I could tell she was having fun seeing the tribe outwitted. I hate to say so, but if this Pretty Walker had been a boy, and, of course, white, she would have been downright companionable. There was something enjoyable about her, of a sort I'd never noticed in Herbert Swann. She made you feel *warm*, somehow.

It was along toward four-thirty now, and getting dark, what with the rain and the clouded-over sky, so we had to hole up. It was colder, too. I hoped to go to bed early and be up around midnight, to get a good jump while the tribe still slept. In spite of some night marauding they do—horse-stealing, camp-raiding and such—an Indian isn't any account before dawn, on account of the spirits. When the dark closes down, and the spirits begin to whisk around, he prefers to crawl in his wigwam till things blow over. Dawn is his great time; that's when he attacks, and I wanted to be home long before then.

For another hour we followed beside the trail, then I said, "We've got to fix up a shelter—sleep," and did "sleep" in the sign language that all the tribes understand—hands folded alongside, the head tilted over. I figured I was in for a number of references to whiskey with a few sidelights on horse thieves, but she caught on right away.

168

What's more, she grabbed my arm and pointed with great excitement in a direction just right of the trail ahead.

She began to pull me along, and, after a bit I gave in, she seemed so positive she was right. In about twenty minutes we came onto a beautiful fast-running stream, green and with smooth white stones in the middle, and beyond it was a clearing of pasture grass and upwards of fifteen wigwams. I dropped like a shot and pulled her down with me. But she kept jabbering and pointing and insisting, the way women do, so I rose up again to have another look. Well, I thought, maybe she's right—nobody appears to be around.

Nothing troublesome in sight, no children playing near the stream, nobody fishing, no women working, no smoke coming from the tepees. This was one of those villages that Indians left to go hunting, then.

"They come back?" I said, not really expecting an answer.

"No, no, no, no." She took a stick and made some marks in the mud so that I could get the idea. First she made a straight line: ▬▬▬▬▬ that I finally saw was the horizon, then a round globe: ⚛ that was the sun; and then she made thirty marks in a row and pointed several times at the sun.

They wouldn't be back for a month. Or so I understood it. Now we were away and free, I felt uneasy about crawling back in a wigwam, but the girl looked so shaky and cold and almost pretty, if white, with the rain running down her forehead and dripping off her nose, that I took a deep breath and said, "Very well—go ahead."

She took my hand and led me forward, past some old campfires, past a cut-off sapling with a bundle of jerky meat in the crotch, past a broken turkey-wing fan on the ground, toward what I guess she thought was the best wigwam in sight, scribbled all over with paintings, some of them uncommonly raw according to my way of thinking. It was cozy inside; you couldn't deny it. To make it more so, the rain still dribbled down, and darkness was coming on now. These tepees are roomy—they're as wide as a small cabin, and when they've laid buffalo robes on the ground, and cut a trench around outside for drainage, you're as comfortable as you are in any parlor. This one seemed to have lost its smell, too.

Right off, the girl found a bow with a stick-drill and a box of dry tinder and got a fire going on the raised earthen mound in the center. We fed it kindling from a pile in the corner, then she went out to cut jerky for supper. She made a broth of herbs that she took from a pouch in her bosom. We had a good meal.

But I wasn't *entirely* at ease sitting here in the firelight. It was different than being with a boy; I didn't have the same feeling about it, for some reason. Still, I didn't make any objections when she fixed our sleeping robes near each other; it wouldn't have been polite. She seemed so helpless, being away from home, and even, in a way, captured, that I put my arm out of my robe and held her hand. It seemed to me the least I could do. And when she wriggled across and went to sleep with her black hair on my shoulder, I was proud of myself because I didn't throw her off. A little service like this—being kind to your inferior instead of taking advantage— was what gave a person character; I'd heard my father say so on many an occasion.

I snapped awake; it was clear daylight. Through the smoke hole I saw the sky, deep blue, and outside I heard the birds twittering, happy the storm was over. I turned in a hurry to sit up, but my hands were tied. And so were my feet. The same kind of rawhide thongs as before, dipped in water, too.

I called out the girl's name several times. I yelled, "Pretty Walker —come and cut me loose!" but I didn't get any answer. There wasn't a thing but the birds stopping their noise for a second, the stream splashing over the stones, and a scratching of the flap strings loose in the wind.

I should have known, I suppose, but I had a big lump in my chest, as if something good had gone, now in my fourteenth year, that might not come back again ever.

Chapter XIX

From the McPheeters Journals

July 12, 1849

This day encamped beside the Platte, near Grand Island in the Nebraskas, where the soda encrustations begin. To bridge a gap of days, occasioned by other duties and by the absence of Jaimie, our route has been up the Little Blue, which runs in a southeast direction. The channel has been no more than ten yards wide, but its periodic overflow deposits sand and detritus of such thickness that the grass does not penetrate through it.

For this period our luck has held good; we begin to smell California and hearken to its beckoning promise. The trail has been firm and easy, diverging at length from the Little Blue to ascend high bluffs overlooking the Platte. No trouble, but Indian signs plentiful: cottonwoods to either side have been stripped of their bark—indication of Indian ponies feeding there, as is their wont. No flowers here; numbers of antelope and curlew.

Wood for our campfire came tonight from the island half across the river. Though broad (and sluggish), the Platte is deceptive about depth. In no place did it ascend higher than our chests as we waded. For purposes of navigation the Platte is a nullity.

Mr. Kennedy's bites, at first healing with great vigor, now show inflammatory symptoms, with tingling and itching. These are uncharted regions. Not subscribing to quackery concerning "madstones," or other witchcraft, I am powerless. As with the secret spark of life itself, there is a point at which science leaves off and Providence assumes the burden. We must commend Kennedy's plight to His almighty wisdom.

July 13

This day had an encounter that saddened us, and disturbed our womenfolk. During the morning we were hailed by a detachment of six soldiers, under a Captain Duncan, all in civilian clothing. They were riding trail in search of four U. S. Dragoon deserters from Fort Laramie. These latter villians had committed a depredation which aroused all the decent people of the Fort. Heading east and skirting an emigrant train bound for Oregon (consisting of sixty-six wagons) they came upon a lone woman washing clothes at a stream. The deserters forced her to give up her possessions— some pieces of trumpery jewels and a hand trunk—and ravished her, one after the other. The poor creature's husband was only a few hundred yards distant, tending his cattle, but upon her first attempt at an outcry, they stuffed her mouth with a stocking then tied another round her head. Her husband finding her in a condition of swoon, raised the alarm, and the emigrant leaders called at the Fort in protest. At this writing, there is some doubt whether she will return to full rationality.

July 14

No signs of our son. I reproach myself for not staying behind in search. But where? The prairie is a vast sea in which a single being can be swallowed up without rippling its gay and deceitful surface. But I cling to the notion of his having fallen in with roving Indians, the noble red men, who will restore him to us soon. And after that— the ladle! Coulter seems positively glad of our distress, and makes coarse remarks about "smart-aleck quality" endangering the safety of the train. I verily believe he would turn his back if the boy were spied grappling with wolves within view of the camp itself. He is a *hard* and *unfeeling* man, hounded by personal devils. Probably he is disturbed for some reason, even dating as far back to his youth. But we shall see. The fire has fallen to a bed of faintly glowing coals. I can write no more. Tomorrow we pass Fort Kearney. To Morpheus!

July 15

This day traveled up the Platte bottoms, frequently near its bank. The bed remains expansive, with numerous green islets, while on the opposite side the plain appears to be sand. All presents a barren aspect, largely lacking in grass. Behind us, offering no inducement to tarry, lies Fort Kearney, a string of log huts inhabited by a scattering of unshaven, unshorn soldiers whose uniforms are crazily patched. Their lounging gait foretells a soul weariness of this station in the wilderness. Some few of the worse element among us sold them whiskey at a dollar for the half pint.

The sun blazes fiercely; the water in our canteens is at blood heat. For coolness, we are obliged to sew them up with flannel.

Have today seen our first buffaloes—a black smear, moving slowly, some miles distant. Bleached bones of buffalo are now apparent on the trail; indeed, the white skulls of those great beasts are of a form of post office, whereon the emigrants inscribe messages, one train to the other. A second courier is the cleft stick, in whose crotch advices about Indians, water, grasses, and like may be found. Thus does man's inherent neighborliness manifest itself in this desolation. In addition to its use for meat, the buffalo is valuable as the staple for fire fuel in these parts. "Buffalo chips"—dried manure—burn like tinder, making a further quest for wood unneedful.

July 16

I am worried about Mr. Kennedy. As little as I know (nay, as any of us know) this dread disease, his condition appears alarming. Besides the inflammation around several of the bites, with tingling and itching, the areas now are afflicted with intermittent numbness.

A patient's report to his physician is privileged; Mr. Kennedy has been to me in confidence, filled with apprehension. While I can confide this to no person, I feel justified in committing it to a Journal meant, in my lifetime, for no other eyes than my own. Who knows—these jottings, upon the possible maturity of rabies, may play a small part in the understanding of cases yet to come.

Seated on robes by our campfire (the others having retired) Kennedy discussed his emotions, an astounding revelation. He senses a powerful evil a-stir within him, a swelling of the most malignant and deadly forces. Poking thoughtfully with a stick at the embers, he said, "I have been a soft-spoken and deliberate man," and all of us who know him as an emigrant will endorse that sentiment gladly.

And yet, this gentle, courageous fellow now is swept with wild gusts of alternate elation and despair, and is racked with intense sexual excitement. You may imagine that these phrases did not come easily to one of his sensitive disposition. In fact, I cannot conceive that the words "sexual" and "quickly aroused" have passed his lips since his boyhood, even in the intimate embrace of his wife. He scarcely knows himself. He has never been unstable, but now he is subject to mental depressions, restlessness and fears. These are joined to periods of full quietude, such as the one in which he related to me his story.

However, I took uneasy note that, as we ended our discussion, his talk was unnaturally rapid and verbose. The words tumbled out one after another, the articulation was abrupt and jerky. He seemed in a state of barely suppressed tension, and upon wringing my hand to leave, his eyes glowed in the dark like an animal's.

Poor, unhappy man! I fear the worst. Tomorrow I shall confer with the others. Something must be done. But what? Only a miracle can now save him.

July 17, 1849

Dear Melissa:

It grieves me to write you a melancholy letter when my others have been, I believe, uniformly cheerful and bright. First I must say that Jaimie has not yet put in an appearance. I am still positive that he will turn up soon. But now I have the sad duty of chronicling the tragic events in the case of Mr. Kennedy, who was bitten by the rabid wolf. In my Journals I recorded the gradual deterioration of his physical and mental health in the last few days, the inflammation of the affected areas, their tingling, itching, irritation and numbness; his emotional instability, his deep depression—and the day before yesterday all this came to a climax.

We had stopped to noon on a bank of the Platte near the head of Grand Island, and were resting in the shade, the day being excessively warm. Suddenly there came a dreadful shout—it was a man of our company, a taciturn and bearded drover, who, in the act of leading his horse to the stream, had come upon a very shocking scene. Unable to proceed, he froze in his spot, then voiced the shout previously mentioned. We—Kissel, and some others and I, including Coe, who is now a friend—rushed to his side and stared in the direction he was pointing. Below, on all fours in the mud, snapping, uttering sounds of a sighing or sobbing character, enough like the baying of a dog to make the hairs rise on one's neck— was our Mr. Kennedy. He was in the throes of virulent rabies, or hydrophobia, the dread disease in full career. It was a sight to sicken strong men; and several of our group were thus affected.

For once, Coulter proved a help rather than an irritation. Causing the women and children to be sent away from the scene, he raised a tent, and thither did he and Kissel and Coe and I convey the raging victim. At this time, Kennedy did not appear to know us. Neither did he make any attempt to bite us, as I had understood might occur at certain stages of the madness.

But if Kennedy was oblivious of us, I for my part scarcely recognized him. His countenance was contorted with an anxiety so terrible it twisted his features grotesquely. His brow was feverish, his mouth oozed saliva at either end. His eyes were wild and staring, and he continued to respirate with sobbing and sighing. It was almost too much for my nerves, and I have been the (reluctant) witness to a vast catalogue of human ills and disasters.

Placing the unfortunate on a cot, Kissel remained unperturbed, save for an unaccustomed tightness of his lips, Coe was ashen, and Coulter, much as I hesitate to say so, was his usual catlike self.

"The show's all yourn," he said to me in his delicate frontier idiom, and I fancied, at least, that there was a contented look of malice in his face.

"He is beyond the physician's help," I replied, and I'm afraid I said it a little stiffly, considering that another's troubles and not petty feuds were the critical business at hand.

Within half an hour of the first violent seizure, Kennedy had emerged from his rigor and was speaking quite rationally. He was cognizant of his plight, and described, at my apologetic request, his symptoms immediately preceding. His appetite had departed entirely, along with his gift of sleep. He had severe recurring headaches and extreme, compulsive, ungovernable nervousness. Telling us this, he begged for a tablet and pen, saying he was desirous of inscribing a last message to his wife. That he could think of others at a time like this! I believe him to be, to have been, the very best man of our train.

My dear wife, it would have wrung your heart to attend that gallant and frightful effort. We propped him up, Coulter with a hand behind his back, and he undertook the incredible labor of saying goodbye to a wife and two children to whom he was apparently devoted. Such phrases as "we shall be rejoined in a realm where even the streets are paved with gold," "assure the boys that my death was an easy one," and "find a good and kindly man to take my place in your heart" had the tears running down our cheeks, and I verily believe that Coulter himself was moved, for I heard him snort angrily a time or two, and make a motion as if brushing away a fly.

The paroxysms now became more frequent, and the writing was suspended until each passed. In all likelihood, I shall never be present at another such exhibition of courage. The sufferer's agitation quickened greatly toward evening: anything could send him into fits of writhing and crying—sudden movement, strong light, even a breath of cool air. He would be seized with convulsions, then make a plea for water, only to meet the offer of a drink with the most maniacal revulsion. Indeed, the mere mention of water occasionally brought on a fresh paroxysm, during which we held his arms and feet to keep him from doing himself an injury. Between fits, he struggled to a sitting position on the edge of the cot, then doggedly continued his missive to that wife whom he will not see again.

In the twilight, I stepped out for air, to witness the emigrants standing in little groups, with that air of hushed and reverent yet interested expectancy that one usually notes in the closing chapter of a life. I have watched crowds on the banks of drownings, at scenes of horrible injury, at explosions of human violence that left an inert shape on the floor; it is hard to define what is writ in the faces of the spectators—pity, surely, and yet a morbid curiosity about the hypnotic secret of death, and, I believe, embarrassment. It repels and attracts us alike. Our menfolk were silent; the women in their sunbonnets whispered together, the children romped heedless and undisturbed. To be sure, one thrust his head under the tent once and inquired of Coulter—"What's the matter, mister, is he mad? Will he bite you?"

Kennedy's breathing became increasingly difficult in the late evening. This together with insane excitement while threshing in our grip—screaming, spitting and, finally, snapping, giving forth dog-like howls that chilled the blood—marked the last hours of the victim. When he showed signs of tetanic spasm, as well as the emission of a visceral secretion that he seemed to dread swallowing, I became prepared for the end. There is no way to describe the awfulness of his suffering. Coulter at length sprang up from the cot, as shaken as I have seen him, and with a savage oath drew his revolver.

"Give him something to knock him out or by God I'll end his troubles with a bullet in the head."

I had previously tried a sedation of morphine, which had failed utterly in its purpose; now prepared a second and more substantial dose. It was all in vain. With a howling scream that must have startled the wildlife miles away in the bush, Kennedy sat bolt upright, breaking the hold of Coe and Matt Kissel, and expired in a foaming paroxysm. It might be said that he choked to death on his own spittle.

When he fell back, we noted with a thrill of horror that his wide-opened eyes stared with a look of animal frenzy—his face held more a wolf's aspect than a man's.

It was some time before any one of us four could regain composure. I think that Coulter, in his crude way, summed up the general feeling when he said, turning aside abruptly, "The meanest skunk alive don't deserve to die that bad."

So, Melissa, I have been obliged to recount a tragedy of the trail, the terrible reward of one hopeful who will never see any gold fields but those he mentioned in his letter. His memorial lies before me as I write. It was broken off in the middle of a sentence: "I meet the end that God has ordained for me cheerfully and willingly, knowing that there is a divine pattern that shapes our ends; I cannot tell you, dearest wife——"

What he could not tell, we shall only be able to surmise. But I have a fancy that she knows. The rest of us now must push forward and be of stout heart. And, indeed, so must you, my faithful consort. All will eventuate for the best (as stated earlier).

Your harried but sanguine husband,
SARDIUS McPHEETERS (M.D.)

Chapter XX

The Indian girl was with them when they came to take me back. It was all I could do to look at her, but she didn't seem put out at all. She said my name the same way, and then smiled, so innocent and happy I almost forgave her. Then I thought, maybe she did it because I was maybe going away off and wouldn't see her any more. That must be it. Right away, I felt better, and even gave her a sort of grin when she looked up, starry-eyed as a baby.

The men threatened me with tomahawks and made a number of references to burning, that I had come to recognize in Pawnee, but otherwise did me no mischief. I judged they had been given orders about the horse trading, and had decided not to damage a valuable piece of merchandise, which would be the same as damaging the horses themselves.

Back at camp, it was easy to see some kind of preparations were afoot. They were getting ready for a feast. The braves had put on new paint, and some of the women were spruced up, even having washed their hands and feet in the stream. Scarcely anybody paid me any attention. I didn't see Afraid of His Horse anywhere, and Sick from Blackberries, when I walked up to our lodge, only grunted and looked the other direction. That didn't bother me any; I didn't like him, either.

All over camp there was the kind of holiday air you get at a church social, where everybody brings a basket full of good things to eat and they set up long tables end to end on the lawn in the summer and the congregation goes at it together, diving into each other's contributions—fried chicken and devil's food cake and potato salad and watermelon and lemonade in an open-end keg with smooth cakes of ice, maybe twenty-five or fifty pounds, floating inside, and the women making compliments about each other's cooking, but running down their own, you know, while you can hardly stand up for the children whooping across the lawn and crawling under tables. It made me sick to think about.

Well, these Indians were getting ready for a basket dinner, too, but it wasn't the same kind. Toward noon there was a hullabaloo of people running and pointing, and sure enough, over the hill here came another such bunch as I was with, and in the front right behind the chief were two white men, and they were John and Shep.

I almost sank through the ground. It was all up with me now, because if the Indians didn't tomahawk me, Shep would be certain to shoot me, to settle old scores. But they rode on into camp, and when they saw me, Shep sang out:

"Well, as I live and breathe! If it ain't our old friend that we owe so much."

"You've come to a pretty pass, boy," said John, looking down from his horse, thoughtful and grave, and to prove it he added a scriptural verse that was aimed to cover the case: " 'How sharper than a serpent's tooth is an ungrateful child.' "

"How do you do, you're keeping well, I hope," I said, as fresh as I was able, what with my heart going the way it was. To tell you the truth, I was so tired of trouble and downcast from Pretty Walker's treachery, I'd as soon they got it over; I was that reduced.

"We'll tend to your case later," said Shep.

They turned away with some of the leading men, and it was then I saw the reason for all this hilarity. On the end of some ropes, behind horses, they had three other captives, all Indians, and they were scalped. The raw, red, dripping tops of their heads was more than a body could stomach, but I couldn't keep my eyes off them, somehow. These men were Crows, I found out later, the worst enemies the Pawnees had, and the fiercest fighters of any western tribe. How these mangy dogs of mine managed to capture them I don't know—took them asleep while apart from the tribe, I reckoned. Anyhow, all three were conscious and seemed perfectly resigned to what was going to happen.

The capture was such a big event to the Pawnees that two or three branches of the thieving tribe had gathered to make merry. They had an entertainment arranged in two parts, but I didn't find out the second part till evening.

I should say that I was now shackled hand and foot and couldn't have run off if they'd pointed out the direction and given me a going-away present. As soon as I was safely trussed up, Particular as to the Time of Day and the ones I had fooled came up and spent a while slapping me and pushing me over. Then they turned to the principal show, which was being arranged by the men.

First off, three stakes were set up in the center of our clearing, and dry brush, but not very much, was placed around each. Then the prisoners were gagged and bound and withes fastened around their waists and under their arms. In that way, they were tied to the stakes.

When everything was ready, the squaws rushed up with torches of dug-up fat wood and lit the twigs. I wondered why there was such a scarce amount of brush, but they had a good and typical reason. These poor devils weren't going to be killed right out but would be roasted to death slowly, so as to cook the flesh for eating and save the muscles for bows.

I can see that scene now, when the troubles of our journey are behind us. The captives weren't able to scream because of the gags, but low moans could be heard, piteous and eerie, and they strained against the withes until their veins stood out like cords. It was heart-rending, but I still couldn't seem to look away. I put a cloth to my nose, but it didn't work; that stink of burning flesh was everywhere—I smelled it later that night on my clothes when I went to bed, cooked into the cloth, like something oily and rotten.

How could anybody that called himself a human watch a scene like that with enjoyment? But as the smoke rose up, and the moans and threshing around increased, the braves undertook a jerky dance, with war whoops and brandishing of weapons, and there began such a general uproar that it echoed over the prairie like the Judgment Day. I never heard anything like it for pure outright lunacy. And the children joined in, too. It was one of the happiest games they'd ever played; they laughed and shouted every time a particularly pitiful moan stood out above the others.

I thought to myself, I'll bet that girl draws the line at this kind of thing. Even if she turned me in, she was good fun when we ran away, and her smiling in the rain was something I liked to think about. I looked all around, then saw her sitting cross-legged on the ground not far from the stakes, leaning forward, with her mouth slightly ajar. When my eye caught her, she wetted her lips with her tongue, and her eyes got a little glaze to them, very strange. She seemed in a trance, almost; with her arms hugged close around her breast and the upper part of her swaying back and forth like a snake that's raised its head to watch something in the bush.

I closed my eyes, sick all over again. When I opened them up Shep had slouched away from the circle of dancers, bending low to kneel down beside her. He whispered something in her ear. She came out of her trance with a shake and grabbed his arm suddenly, as if she had seen him before and was glad to find him there. He whispered something, and they got up together, then walked very quickly to her wigwam and disappeared through the flap.

I thought about snatching a brand from the fire, then running over and flinging it inside, but the dance stopped and everybody rushed forward to the stakes—the poor wretches twisting in the bonds had finally died.

I didn't join in the feast that followed. Unnoticed, I crept into Sick's wigwam and after a long time fell into a shallow doze. But the shrieks, and the stamping, and the cries of the happy children outside kept sifting through; I didn't sleep much, but woke up, wet all over with sweat, three or four times.

That night they had the main entertainment, and they made me come out to watch. The festivities got started sometime before dark and lasted two or three hours. There had been a strong tribe of Indians called the Mandans ten or fifteen years before, as I learned a long time afterward, but they'd been weakened and nearly wiped out in fights with the Crows, Cheyenne, Sioux and Blackfeet. Along the way, though, they had developed some very fine customs, everybody said so, even their enemies, and these Pawnees had picked up a few. What we had now was one of the meanest, the "ordeal of manhood," as they said, known as O-Kee-Wah.

The tribe took seats on the ground before a long, stout log they had slung across two crotched upright poles about eight feet high. Shep and John were there, on either side of the chiefs, and the doctors, or medicine men, were dressed up with wolf heads and jewels and feathers and things to rattle in their hands, and seemed prosperous, as if they'd established a very good practice, with customers that paid up on schedule. They were fussing around, making signs in the air, hissing, and going through a lot of ridiculous contortions, and pretty soon the braves led out two boys of our tribe, fourteen or so years old. I knew one of them well enough—his name was Buffalo Horn. Along with some others, he had offered me a drink at a water hole once but it turned out to be alkali and near about burned my mouth out. The second one I'd seen around but didn't know well, thanks to goodness.

Right now these fellows didn't seem so brash; it appeared to me they weren't looking forward to O-Kee-Wah of the Mandans. Well, once the boys reached the center, the braves took up a kind of chant, while the medicine men hopped around and yowled with about the poorest bedside manner ever developed, then, when the noise died down, the chiefs got immediately to business. They stripped those poor youngsters clear naked and laid them on the ground, after which the medicine men knelt down with sharp knives and cut long deep incisions in the upper chest muscles on the right side, down far enough to expose the tendons.

Nothing was done to kill the pain or make it easier—no whiskey, no powders, nothing. One of the boys started to whimper but there was such a grumble from several braves that he stopped. They both looked like death all the same. Their bodies turned rigid, their eyes rolled up, and their fingers clenched the grass.

Bad as this was, it was only the beginning. You might have thought they had showed manhood enough for a few years, but the real test hadn't come yet. In a few minutes, after recovering a little, they were given something to drink out of a gourd and then propped upright, bleeding like pigs, and supported by braves on either side.

When the next part came, I closed my eyes tight and tried to remember something pleasant to blot it out. Mumbling, making signs in the air, and twisting around, the medicine men came forward and, holding some thongs, probed deep down inside the wounds, pulled up a big tendon on each, and tied them to thongs. A noisy shout went up as the boys were hauled up and suspended from the log, dangling, you see, from their own chest muscles. Both were still conscious but they appeared to be dying; their tongues, black and swoll-up, stuck out to the side like somebody that's been hung. But the medicine men daubed powder from a long-handled brush on the wounds, and where blood was gushing a minute before, everything now dried up and stopped. It was uncanny.

Those boys weren't out of the woods yet, though. One of them cried out, then bit it off quick at the chorus of growls. The other, Buffalo Horn, fainted in a minute or so, his nose began to bleed, and they cut him down. His partner hung on a few moments longer; he was the winner, then. Both had showed manhood, the braves said, but Buffalo Horn, fainting first, hadn't shown quite as much as the other fellow.

By the way the medicine men pranced around, as the boys lay unconscious, I judged the demonstration had been a success. Anyway, the tribe was so set up and warmed by this butchery that they were kind of taken out of themselves. I won't tell *all* that happened during this nonsense, but it wasn't nice to see; it even lacked considerable of being decent. Shep and John had got out some whiskey, which frisked things up more, and while Shep was putting in most of his time with the girls, John sat silent and glum in the edge of the firelight, lost in broody thought, just as before. Well, he *had* come down a peg since the days when he was Murrel, the pirate, and wore fine clothes. As far as I was concerned, these animals were the lowest note in the scale. If you wanted to make a joke about anything so ornery, you might say they had finished last in the human race. I never saw any others like them, before or since, for outright calculated cruelty.

Well, things were so noisy and rambunctious that everybody got thirsty for *more* amusement—half killing the boys hadn't been enough—so a couple of drunken braves spied me trying to crawl aside and dragged me forward to run between two lines. This was one of their favorite ordeals; Indians are always cooking up a bone-crusher of a test for somebody else.

They formed two rows, including the squaws and children, and after taking off my foot bonds made me ape it through them, one end to the other. While I did so, they hit me over the head and shoulders with whips and sticks. It was painful; I was all over bruises. This might have gone on till they killed me—they were that fired up—but a lucky accident ended it: a visiting chief, that they called Standing Bear, was goggle-eyed-drunk by now and was doing a kind of solo dance off to one side, twirling his rifle to show what a dangerous fellow he was when aroused, and sure enough he proved it by gyrating so fast and dangerous he whacked his gun against his knee and it went off and shot him through the side, the bullet making a clean hole front and rear.

This broke up the party. When the Indians saw they might get shot themselves, they more or less lost interest. There was a big racket made about the punctured chief, too. You might have thought he was the King of England the way they took on. Squaws enjoy wailing anyhow; they've got so many stored-up grievances they go all to pieces when something official happens; it's like an overloaded dam giving way.

They carried this Standing Bear, who wasn't any longer able to stand, onto a blanket by the fire and the medicine men got ready to save him. If their prancing and face-twisting had seemed odd before, they let go with everything now, on this emergency case. One threw some root dust into the air and yelled "Goo-Wah!";

then he bent over and looked at the wound, but it must have been the wrong diagnosis, because the blood kept right on seeping out the back. Another took two gourds with dried peas inside and shook them, very hard, in the injured man's face, but all he got was a pretty brisk cussing, because this chief was a tough old nut and had troubles enough without any folderol of that sort.

I stuck around, curious. I was relieved to be shut of the gauntlet, and hoped it wouldn't start up again. In a couple of hours all the bleeding had stopped, and the chief looked sweaty and feverish. I knew these signs from having been around my father on cases. And by midnight it was perfectly plain that the old scoundrel was dying. He was breathing very hard, with wheezing noises, and seemed puffed up. I knew what had to be done—I'd sat in once at the shantyboats when my father treated just such an accident.

It went against my grain to do a service for these monsters but I didn't think it could hurt any to help a chief. So I hunted up Afraid of His Horse, who was trying to wheedle a drink from a visitor, and told him I had strong medicine to draw devils out of Standing Bear's wound. Being drunk, I thought for a minute he had decided to hit me, just for practice. When it finally soaked through what I said, he left and told what braves were sober enough to listen, and they called me over.

We talked through Afraid, first the leaders, with the doctors, asking questions and then me answering. I said my father had been the biggest medicine man in Louisville, and had cured up much worse cases than this, and had once fixed a man that had been shot through the stomach with a cannon ball. This was a lie, of course, but I couldn't see anything wrong with stretching things, and anyhow it was a pretty good lie, and cheered me up. So they held a meeting with Afraid, who turned to me and said:

"Medicine men ask what father wear on head?"

This Afraid of His Horse was such a confirmed jackass that I couldn't be serious with him very long, even when I knew he was apt to whack me. So I said, "For house calls he wears a derby made of rooster feathers but for the Marine Hospital he favors an opera hat with a goat's head on top."

They went into this, not understanding, praise the saints, and then Afraid turned back.

"Medicine men no believe—say how father fix coughing broth?"

"It's a professional secret—I can't let it out, but I'll say this—it's got something to do with tree frogs."

Another confab, and back again.

"Medicine men say any spiders mixed in?"

"Not any more—they've gone out in Louisville. It's against the law to use medical spiders in Kentucky now."

Then I sort of overdid things, because I had got too cocky, being as I was having so much fun, and said, looking stern, "If you want to know something, those quacks of yours couldn't pass the examinations in Louisville. They'd be arrested for practicing medicine without a license. Why——"

I knew it. You could fool Afraid part of the time but you couldn't do it forever. He fetched me a clout that sent me sprawling.

Well, the leaders of the tribes put their heads together for a few minutes, then they beckoned me over, and didn't those medicine men look sour! But your general run of Indians, though stupid, comes a long shot from having complete faith in humbugs of that kind; they recognize a lot of it for just what it is—low-down trickery and superstition. Anyhow, the average medicine man, or shaman, isn't anything more than a general practitioner, of no account in specialized cases, and everybody in the tribe knows it. Still and all, these medicine men aren't always wrong. For instance, a few hours later I checked up on the incisions they made in those boys and you could scarcely see them. Some of the Indian medicines were sound; there wasn't the least doubt about that.

I asked for a thin willow twig two feet long; then I borrowed an India silk handkerchief from a girl I'd seen wearing one, and boiled some water. It took a few minutes to strip the bark off the willow, leaving the yellow wood slippery and bare, and after this I pared down the joints. For a minute, I thought the chief had died, for he gave several astonishing gasps that raised his chest up and down, and when I bent over to look he seemed purplish in the face. I was scared, because if this old polecat skipped out before I began work, they would blame me sure. So I hurried up and wrapped the India kerchief around the wand and dipped it in boiling water, waving it around to cool off a little, then worked the willow in and down, having to force it because the hole had closed back and clotted the blood. As far gone as he was, the old man felt that plunge, for he raised his shoulders clean off the ground and gave out a howl to rouse his ancestors. I never heard such a shriek. And only a few hours before, he had been one of the mainstays against letting those boys make any sound at all.

Afraid of His Horse, with some others, were bending over nearby and I motioned them to help me roll him on his side. For once, they seemed to catch on, and when we got the holes exposed, both entrance and exit, I went right ahead and rammed the rod through. When its end, soaked in red, appeared in the rear, I grabbed it and pulled, missing fire twice because it was so slippery. But it came, and made a little sucking sound when the end popped out.

There was a loud "Ah-h-h!" as a perfect gusher of clogged-up blood that I'd heard my father call "coagulated" came pouring out on the ground. I let it flow, then got two squaws to make hot packs and put them against the holes. We carried him into his tent, where he lay for better or worse.

I felt a little weak, so I said I was going to bed, not even bothering to ask. Nobody tried to stop me.

Next day I was up bright and early, and scooted over to the old man's to see how he was getting along. Inside his wigwam were several women, and what do you know? He was propped up smiling and taking full notice. Lucky for me, the treatment had worked; he was much easier. But when I wanted to inspect the holes he wasn't any friendlier than ever. What's more, before long he called in the medicine men again. They got down on their hands and knees to sniff, then shook their heads as if they'd known it all the time. And for all the credit they gave me, I might have ranked down amongst the nurses and bedpan squad. So be it. I was still alive, and that was what interested me most.

Well, the next day after this, I had the suspicion that something concerning me was up. I kept seeing John and Shep conferring with the chiefs, talking through Afraid of His Horse, and pretty often they stared in my direction and shook their heads. Along toward evening, John and Shep came over, Shep looking satisfied and happy, as if one of his neighbors had contracted the leprosy, and sat down where I was tied.

"We've got your hash all settled, you sawed-off piss-ant," he began, but John interrupted. "Clamp hold of your tongue—leave me talk."

Shep pulled some tobacco out of his shirt pocket. John went on: "You probably ort to know that your train ain't to say on fire to regain you. They're sick of you—that was proved last night."

"What do *you* know about it?"

Shep raised one of his wagon-tongue arms and said, "Lean back a piece so I can box one of his ear flaps loose. I never had any use for this squealing whelp since we first rooted him up in the woods."

"—leastways they so informed one of our Pawnee brothers [they were brothers now, were they?] when he entered your camp under a flag of truce."

"Last night?" I cried. "What are you talking about?"

"Their object was to collect three or four horses, but your Mr. Coulter laughed in his face. I doubt if you'd bring a pound and a half of dried beans on the open market."

"I don't believe you—what else did they say?"

"Some of the others stated they'd like to see you stood up within sight before further palaver."

"They'll pay," I said, relieved that the first part was mainly a lie.

"The Indians smell treachery, and they're right. I've failed to note anybody on that train," said John with his old pious look, "that I'd trust with a pair of wore-out suspenders. They're a bad lot, born bad, raised bad, lacking the true religion, and the whole stamped plain on their mugs. It makes me ashamed to be white."

"What else?"

"In a word," said Shep, "since our friend can't seem to get at the point for clacking like a magpie, we've bought you outright—two dollars silver, a quart and a little over of whiskey, and half a dozen plugs of niggerhead. If you ask me, we've been took."

" 'The Silver is mine, and the Gold is mine, saith the Lord of Hosts,' " cried John; then he added what seemed to prove just the opposite: "I'm calculating to get a thousand dollars for you, cash. I figure it'd be worth that to your paw for the privilege of tanning your hide."

"He hasn't got only about three hundred dollars left," I blurted out.

"I'm obliged for the information," said John drily; and I could have bit my tongue off.

They had bought me, all right, and were fixing to take me away the next morning, early. Only it wasn't apt to be pleasant. Shep filled in the rest: "We'll contract to turn you over if they meet our offer, but there won't be nothing in the articles to say we deliver the goods *intact*. Speaking for myself, I've got a grudge to settle. Maybe we'll take an arm off at the shoulder; better yet, we'll put an eye out. You and Mr. Chouteau try and work yourselves out of *this* fix, hey?"

They'd do it, too. I looked at John, hoping he might say no, but his face was as set as a rock. Bloodletting and violence meant no more to him than eating and drinking. He didn't relish it, especially, but he didn't mind it, either.

That night I went to bed feeling the lowest I'd felt on the trip. I couldn't see any way out. Now that I wasn't their property any more, Sick from Blackberries courteously held back from kicking me when he came in, but somehow I wasn't consoled. I wanted both of my eyes; I would need them when we started to look for gold. But that time, talked about so often, seemed more and more remote. It was like the mirage they have on these plains—as you go on reaching out, it fades farther and farther back in the distance. And then one morning it isn't there at all.

I must have drifted off to sleep; when I woke up, smelling something wrong, bright starlight winked down through the smokehole. Outside, the camp was deathly still; then I heard a horse whinny. For some reason, my heart began to thump and I made to sit up. But a rough hand fastened over my mouth.

"Quiet, quiet." It wasn't any more than a hiss.

I knew the voice, but I couldn't find him in the dark. Then he shifted into the starlight, soft as a snake, and it was Coulter, right enough. Even here I could see the old sardonic look on his face. No matter what he did, he seemed to despise you for doing it.

"What——?" I started, but he clapped his hand on my mouth again. He didn't do it easy, either; the palm hit me like a slat.

"Raise up slow and careful—don't bump anything."

Then I thought, by George we're not alone in here, and at that second I saw Sick from Blackberries sitting up and watching us from across the tent. I could make out his eyes shining, a kind of smile on his face.

I gasped, pointing, "Look *out!*"

Coulter's voice had its usual sting. "He won't mind—there ain't any way for him to move his head without it falling off."

I could see now—the throat laid open more than halfway around, from one ear to the other. It looked sickly; mean as he was, I couldn't help feeling a little twinge of misery.

Coulter whispered, "Come on," and parted the slit he had made in the tent. Within a few minutes, treading tiptoe, dodging the campfires out to the bushy fringe, we were back on the trail and running toward Coulter's horse.

I was free.

Chapter XXI

Everybody was glad to see me next morning when we caught up to leave, although there was grumbling by neighbors that I had caused trouble. My father burst into tears all over again and said it was his fault because he hadn't been both father and mother to me, but things now would be different. He had a rusty old iron ladle he'd got as a present for me, as he said, and stated that it would be useful in digging sand on the riverbanks. It seemed like an odd sort of gift, but I took it anyhow, and said it was just what I needed.

Then he walked forward, after the train began rolling and the light came, to thank Coulter, because last night Coulter had eased me into our tent, very quiet, and told me if I woke anybody up, he'd take me back to the Pawnees. He was such an unpredictable coot he might have done it, too.

Well, I followed after my father, meaning to say something on my own, and presently we saw Coulter stalking along, treading soft and graceful, leading his horse in order to save it, two hundred yards ahead of the first wagon. Suddenly it came to me that, no matter how he galled people, he was a very lonely man.

"Mr. Coulter," my father called, coming up behind, "could I have a word?"

"Well, if it isn't the doctor," said Coulter, looking amused as always. "Making your rounds, doc?"

"Mr. Coulter, I wish you to know that, despite past differences, which I deplore, I am grateful to you for restoring our boy. We are deeply in your debt, sir." He had taken off his hat, and his face shone with earnestness.

"They tell me the dude Englishman's valley handed in his dinner pail."

I guess this Coulter was probably the perversest tomcat ever manufactured, and the least gracious. I hadn't heard about Vilmer, though; it was news to me about him dying, though he had been sick since they joined. But it was true; he'd died during the night and they planned to bury him while nooning.

"Your indifference to human emotions is a pose, Mr. Coulter. You're a good man; I know it."

"What with him and Kennedy," replied Coulter, "you ain't running a very high assay, doc. You'd better change your medicine. If I get a sore toe, I'll make my will for sure."

"With complete disregard of your own safety," my father continued, as determined as ever I saw him, "you went into that Indian village and performed a miracle of skill and courage. However little you may value what I'm saying, and whatever happens in the future, I shall honor your name."

Looking up, I was thunderstruck to notice that Coulter was sweating. Little drops of moisture stood out over his forehead and upper lip. For some reason, he wasn't comfortable. He was like a backward child that is being teased; as big and rough as he was, he seemed embarrassed; he wanted us to leave. We had got off the subject of business and touched him in a personal place. And somehow I had the feeling that it wasn't any small thing; I couldn't understand it at all.

"We'll go back, Mr. Coulter," said my father with great good cheer, "but we hope you will join our mess for dinner this evening."

"Yes, of course. I don't generally come without a printed invitation, but this time I'll let it go. Would a swallow-tail coat be satisfactory?"

"Our women are fine cooks."

"I'll make out on sowbelly and beans. I've got a train to run."

"Perhaps you may change your mind. Drop in at any time, tonight or later. You'll always be welcome."

I was proud of him. People in Louisville were always talking him down for one excuse or another, because he wouldn't fit into the mold, you see, but he was the kindliest person on earth. It was funny; he was firm in some ways—he was going to like Coulter now if it killed him—and weak in others. But mainly he just wouldn't face things. Once, after a big row, I asked him why he drank, and he said, "I have an abnormal fear of being snake-bit, and try to keep prepared"—passing it off as a joke.

Well, he *hadn't* been drinking, or gambling either, as far as I knew. Troubles or no troubles, we were moving toward the gold fields, so my mother must have been wrong. Things weren't simple, though. I didn't know it then, but my Indian adventures would bother my dreams and wake me up screaming for months to come. The sight of those roasting Crows, and the boys strung up by their tendons, will likely disturb my sleep as long as I live. Many nights I woke up, covered with sweat, to see my father sitting beside me, tired as he was, speaking in a low, soothing voice and bathing my face with a rag soaked in water.

But now we were rolling through new country, our problems eased for a time. It was fun.

I sat beside Mrs. Kissel, who was curious about the Indians and said, "I hear tell the women are untidy around the house. What's more, one of the neighbors forward—her husband's him that wears the gray beaver and has bleeding piles—said she heard the girls go about uncovered above the waist. She got it from a Mrs. Dawson, who had a cousin that went west and married a half-breed Shoeshine."

"I believe it's Shoshone," I said. "The women I saw seldom ever wash their bodies, and the only shift they make in the wigwam is to pull a person out when he's died. The stench gets so fierce it commonly tans the hide walls."

"You don't say. And with food to match, I reckon."

I was sore at those Pawnees, so I laid it on a little, telling her about the boiling pots and the odds and ends inside. "You can imagine how a stranger feels fishing around in the soup and coming up with a foot or a pair of ears."

"It's scandalous, them not washing and all. I suppose they do have divine service. Indians or not, they're the Lord's sheep, same as us, and entitled to His guidance. What denomination are they, mostly?"

This Mrs. Kissel was so goodhearted she would give you the frock off her back, barring modesty, but up to now she hadn't been ten miles away from their farm; she told me so. Her husband had started as a hired hand of her father's, and lived right across the river. She got attracted to him because he wasn't loose-tongued, and didn't interrupt while she talked. She appreciated it because she generally talked all the time, and before Kissel there wasn't anybody to speak of would listen. Neither had she read any books except the Bible, and it had kind of warped her viewpoint. That is, she knew exactly how old Jehosophat was when he took office, which was thirty-five, and most of the material connected with Uriah the Hittite, but she wasn't up on any news much later than that. It placed a strain on the conversation. There were times when, much as I disliked stretching the truth, I had to invent along to keep things moving. But we had got on the subject of religion now, so I had to be careful.

"Pawnees?" I said. "They aren't *any* denomination. They're got their own, and it's about the crudest worship you ever struck. You probably wouldn't believe it."

"Well, if they're worse than the Campbellites, I'd like to know. Do they immerse or sprinkle?"

"Neither. When a child joins up, and not all of them by any manner of means *do* join up, they generally notch his ears."

"Goodness gracious me! I take back what I said about the Campbellites. What about prayers? Do they favor an open meeting or lone efforts while on their knees in a closet? *Deuteronomy!* You leave go of Micah's hair or I'll call your paw!"

I glanced back at the quartet, which was swatting each other with everything except the water barrel, and said, "As far as prayers go, they don't bother at all unless they're in some kind of a jam, such as a rain drought, when they customarily burn a dog."

"Burn a d——! Well, I never as long as I lived. Those poor creeturs need help, and the next time we camp within hollering distance, I'm going to visit among them and read Scripture."

She meant it, too. She was just that unselfish. But I told her the Pawnees would welcome her into camp, hold a short prayer meeting, and unhook her scalp.

"They're past saving," I said. "There wouldn't be any use to bother. You don't know those skunks like I do. I've been there; I've *seen* them."

"Why, they wouldn't harm a messenger from the Almighty! Surely when they saw I was toting a Bible——"

"Bible! They'd use it to start fires with. Why, they were having a kind of revival while I was there, and some visiting preachers came in, and they ate them. Didn't give them any show at all."

"*Ate* them! They were likely starved, the poor wretches. I'll take a side of bacon along, and some beans. It's pitiful to think of a people so racked by hunger they'd eat a preacher. It's almost sacrilegious."

I got down off the wagon to walk awhile. Why argue? She was so good she couldn't see bad in anybody. If we ever *did* run across an Indian camp, she'd take her Bible and go charging right in. There wasn't any doubt about it. I made a note to tell her husband and a couple of others, if it became necessary, and they'd likely get a rope and hog-tie her. It was the only way.

Walking forward to catch my father, who was talking to Kissel and Brice, I had a chance to smell the country, which was interesting along here, though not so green and growy. It was different. The prairies lay mostly behind us—we were pushing into the alkali plains, the soda wells, and salt flats. We'd heard about them, nothing cheerful.

On my right the Platte rippled along in the sun, with little islands full of trees sticking up here and there. It was an odd river—one night it rose seventeen inches. The trail lay on a grassy bluff, but close to the left the grass thinned out and became poorly. We began to see the prickly plants they called cactus; an emigrant's wife, a Mrs. Goodings, had sat on one a day or so before, somebody said, and some women had to take her behind a bush and put her in working order. At the time of the accident, her husband surveyed her and stated he wasn't up to the job; he said she resembled a kind of "double-barreled pincushion"; those are the very words he used.

In a while we should reach the junction of the north and south forks of the Platte, where there's a well of pure spring water, icy-cold. A notice of it was stuck in one of those post-office buffalo skulls. Everybody looked forward to this well. On the trail you drink whatever's handy, but you don't get used to it. People take good water for granted until they haven't got it any more.

Well, my father, when I caught up, had Ware's *Guide* out and was going at it strong. Now that the grassless patches were over for a while, and Ware had hit a right thing or two, he was back on him as admiring and complimentary as if he was quoting from the Old Testament.

" 'To the head of the island, twenty miles, the road is good,' " he read, showing the book to both Kissel and Brice, as if they wouldn't believe him for some reason. "That's been borne out, I think you'll agree; he's a hundred per cent accurate so far, and here's what's coming: 'From the "head" to the forks of the Platte, ninety miles, the emigrant can supply himself with fuel from the island, or with buffalo chips. Buffalo are sometimes plenty here.'

"Exactly what yesterday's note said. The day I purchased this book was my lucky day," said my father. "It's an aggravation to me to think how little faith some people have. Not two weeks past, half the men in this wagon train were damning and blasting the *Guide* as if it were the devil's handbook. Yes, and Coul——"

He'd almost forgot his new vow and jumped on Coulter again, which was as natural as eating to him, but he caught himself just in time.

196

"Yes, we three and Coulter—that was the hard nucleus of the steadfast group. I admire him for it; he's nobody's fool, is Mr. Coulter."

Brice had been stumbling along in a reverie, but it soaked in now what they were talking about, so he spoke up. "That was a humorous turn of yours about the novel, doctor. I remember it well."

A thing like this didn't faze my father. He cleared his throat and said, "I repeat, and I'll repeat it again and again. A novel constructed from the material in Ware's book could be a unique contribution to the world's store of great literature. Think of it—the classic ingredients of the work—the new country, hardships, the rough characters, the little humorous incidents along the trail, the inevitable call of romance among the youngsters, the suspense before finding gold, the disappointments, and, at last, the great discoveries, riches, and the full life to follow."

He whisked out a note pad and jotted down a memorandum. "By George, I've got to remind myself to block out such a book while we're still on the trail. I'll complete it in the first free time after our strike. 'Do—novel—based—on—Ware's—book—and—journals—of—self,'" he wrote, reading the words aloud. Then he snapped the notebook shut, looking entirely satisfied, as if he'd already finished the novel and it was on its way to the printer's. That was his style; he had more fun talking about it than other people did writing it. And before long he wouldn't know whether he had written it or not. To hear him tell it, the McPheeters-California Public Clinic was finished and doing a booming business among the hard-up and downtrodden.

After these weeks on the road, Brice seemed perkier, though not certain where he was, and Kissel looked as quietly contented as ever. His ox's strength was admired all up and down the line, and was put often to use. He was employed as a kind of human hoist. Whenever a wheel got off or a wagon sank in the mud, he was generally called upon to demonstrate. It was something of a game; they made bets on how long it would take him. But try as they

197

might, they couldn't get him to make a lift for purely sport. It had to be needful; otherwise he would only smile in his slow way and swing on back, maybe whistling a little tune. As somebody remarked, Kissel was about the only member of the train that Coulter respected enough to address without sarcasm. It wasn't because he was afraid of him, either; he just respected him. Kissel was a kind of private man; it made him different. Usually, people can forgive a person anything except a desire for privacy. But Kissel still lived his sunny, private life; he would have had privacy in the middle of a riot.

They made interesting companions for my father, Kissel and Brice, because what he wanted was an audience, and a good deal of the time there wasn't any way to tell whether these two were listening or not. It aggravated him sometimes. Brice, now he was picking up, had a habit of going off into recollections about Independence, and he said, interrupting some remarks of my father's on the Mormons, "Yes, sir, it was a nice little business, only it was really two businesses—ice at one season and the sawmill in the other."

"Dogmatically," stated my father, as we began a long bend in the river, "the Mormons divide the religious world into two sections, themselves on the one hand and Gentiles on the other."

"—as a usual thing, we started cutting in late December, when there was four or more inches of ice on the low ponds, where it's colder. Drive down to the edge in wagons and saw all day, then load up and back to the warehouse. It makes a pretty sound, cutting ice—clean, regular and gritty. We always had plenty of sawdust to pack in, of course, because of the mill. That was my wife's father's idea; he had more ideas than a dog has fleas, except he never put any into execution himself. He took to bed in his middle forties, and never got up. He ran out of motion—that was his word. He said it drew all his strength to remain upright. But he wasn't the complaining kind; he just laid there, eating, reading books, jawing with whoever came in to visit, many of them frolicky young girls of the neighborhood—because he was friendly and helpful and would listen to anybody's troubles—and never took on at all. He finally died of pneumonia. The doctor said he'd been laying down so long his lungs filled up and forgot to empty. He——"

"Mormons," continued my father, "have suffered perhaps the most grievous persecutions yet known on this continent, and for a young country we have produced some notable samples. In Missouri and Illinois a number of Saints were whipped so severely that their bowels had to be swathed up to prevent their falling out. In addition to that——"

"Yes," said Brice, again, remembering things better now, "it was a nice little business. We would pack the cakes deep in the sawdust, and through the hottest summer there wasn't enough shrinkage to notice. It was fun getting it out, too. You'd take a long iron goad with a hook on the end and push a cake down a little railway to the platform outside. Once moving, you could trot a two-hundred-pounder along like coasting. But you had to watch out, because if the goad slipped and stuck in a tie, with the butt braced against your stomach, you'd go out like a light. It's happened to me more than once. I figure that next year we'll work up a better system—maybe fix a hook and chain for pulling. That ought to serve very well. What do you think, Kissel?"

Matt had been walking along, staring at the river, half hearing both palavers, but he turned politely and said, "Yes, I believe you're right—winter's the best time for sawing up Mormons."

I looked at him curiously, but if there was humor, it was unintentional. He was lost, a long way off, probably thinking about the green pastures in Oregon or California.

My father now got me aside to inquire if I didn't think Brice's condition was a little worse, because he talked so, and said, "It isn't natural, it has a compulsive quality that I, as his physician, find alarming. On top of that, nobody else can get a word in edgewise. I may have to prescribe something for it."

He had struck a good vein here, and would likely have gone ahead to mine it out, but a rider came galloping back to report that some cattle were scouring again. My father immediately put on his bedside manner, which was a kind of low, concerned humming, agreeable to him, being the only part of medicine he enjoyed, including the collection of bills. It was automatic, and as quick to arrive for a cow as for a human.

When he left, I went back to Brice's wagon, which Jennie was driving, and climbed up on the seat beside her. She had her hair tied up with a red ribbon, saucy and trim, and wasn't the same girl who'd been on the river trail with John and Shep. She'd come to life, and it might even be claimed that she had overdone it, because she got bossier and more muley-headed around every turn of the road. Right now she took it mighty amiss that I had gone off with the Indians. You would have thought I did it to spite her. She was so forward I couldn't help ragging a little.

"Some people I could spit on think they're pretty smart, strolling off and fretting everybody like that."

"Pa said you missed me. He told me you sat in the wagon crying every night."

"I said good riddance to bad rubbish, if you want to know."

"It wasn't my idea—I did it as a favor to a mutual acquaintance of us both."

She sniffed. "Lay it on somebody else. The fox is the finder, the stink lies behind her."

"What's that mean, Jennie?"

"I don't know. My mother used to say it, and that's enough for *you*."

"It was Brice," I said. "He came to me private and asked if I could find him an Indian wife, cheap. He wants to get married and naturally can't find any candidates around here. He said he was prepared to go as high as three dollars for anybody that didn't look like a false face."

She boxed my ears sort of playfully, but it stung all the same.

"I've had enough of your sass about Brice, the poor addled man. You ought to feel sorry instead of going around making fun."

"I *am* sorry for him," I said, "and I did my level best, but there were only three single girls in the tribe, and one of them had two children and the others wouldn't get married for less than four dollars. And it had to be cash *before* the ceremony, too."

Instead of being sore, she only looked thoughtful. Then she turned her head toward me, her face shining with some kind of idea that had come to her. When she wasn't nagging you to clean your teeth or change your drawers, she could be handsomer than anybody.

"Jaimie, you remember how I looked after you on the boat from St. Louis?"

Wondering what she was up to, I nodded cautiously.

"We're friends?"

It was pretty clear now she was aiming to give me another bath, so I started to scramble down, but she caught my wrist.

"Friends ought to have secrets. I want you to do something, and not tell a living breathing soul, cross your heart and hope to die, but who I say. Promise?"

"It's useless," I said. "I stood out in a pouring rain for two days. There isn't any more dirt on me than there is on a duck. I can't *take* any more water; my skin won't stand it."

"Nobody wants to give you a bath, numbskull. You do what I ask, hear?"

It was hard to decide. So I said, "I don't know—I'm pretty busy just now."

"I want you to tell Mr. Brice to meet me *outside* the wagon circle, on our side, but not near the Kissels' wagon, at nine tonight. After dinner, before everybody turns in. You want to help him, don't you?"

"Help him what?"

"Have a good life again, spite of his wife's dying and all."

"He seems in very good shape to me," I said, more or less thinking out loud. "No women pestering him, free to get as filthy as he likes, excused from eating greenery. I don't believe I could figure out any way to improve on Brice's condition, so if you'll just ex——"

She spun me around, and I felt a little guilty to see she had tears in her eyes.

"You stop your mischief. This is important. There isn't any time I can talk to him, no time at all. In the day he's with the men, and at night I can't go in his tent. I want you to *do* this."

"All right, Jennie. I'll tell him."

She threw her arms around my neck and kissed me. I did get down, then, in a hurry. She'd gone too far. I said I'd do her a favor, but it was typical of her to take advantage of it.

I got my chance just before supper, when Brice was helping stake out the oxen. But it wasn't easy. He was in one of his fuzzy moods, and didn't seem to catch on at all.

"Mr. Brice," I said, "I know somebody that wants to talk to you real bad, right after we eat."

"That's nice of you, son, but I'm not very hungry."

What could you do with a fellow as mixed up as that? Practically nothing he said was sensible. It sounded all right at first, but a piece was usually missing.

"She informed me to notify you particular. It's important. She's got some things on her chest to get off."

"My wife and I haven't been dining out of late. She's expecting another baby, you know."

Suddenly, without even thinking, I took the bull by the horns; it was time somebody did.

"Mr. Brice, your wife's dead. She died back in Independence and you came with us, to go to California. Remember? This person that wants to talk to you is somebody else."

He straightened up and shot me a look. Somehow he seemed a lot older than when we started.

"I remember. I was reminiscing for a minute. That can be a bad habit. Who is this person?"

"Jennie. She'll be outside the wagon circle at nine, but she doesn't want anybody else to know."

"I remember Jennie. She's going to California with us."

"Nine o'clock," I said, and left, hoping he'd turn up but not counting on it. He'd arrive someplace, I supposed, but it would take a bloodhound to tell where. No matter how much they pretended, this fellow had lost his handhold on the situation. For the first time, I wondered if, after all, he wouldn't be better off with Jennie. It was a terrible thing to wish on anybody, but this was an exceptional case.

First, though, a queer thing happened that night at supper. We were sitting around the fire—it was getting deep dusk, being now in the middle of the summer—when a figure strode up out of the shadows, and it was Coulter. After his sneery talk, he was about the last person I expected to see, and I think he was surprised at himself, because he gave a short laugh and said, "I was going by." My father sprang up, filled with pomp, and cried, "Sit down, Mr. Coulter—you honor our humble board." The others, except Jennie, all gave him a friendly greeting, but Jennie kept her nose in the air and didn't say a word. It would have been reasonable for him to sit next her, where there was space, but she shifted over, so he sat on the other side of the fire. When Mrs. Kissel fixed him a plate of biscuits and beans and side-meat, he said, "I've et," after which he went right ahead and sailed into it like a man starved, not looking up once.

Oddly enough, he cast a little uneasiness over us all; we talked too much and too fast, to cover up the silence. He was shy. It didn't seem possible, but he felt uncomfortable with everybody being so nice to him. My father explained it later in a medium-brief lecture of several thousand words, on the order of a medical report. He had the notion that what troubled people in grown-up life could be told by things that happened when they were young, and he said, "Coulter's disposition and attitudes are a challenge—I hope to probe them as time goes on."

But right now, Mrs. Kissel asked how Coulter had "persuaded" the Indian in the wigwam to loose me, saying, "I hope you appealed to his Christian charity, Mr. Coulter."

"Well, not exactly, ma'am," he replied at last, his mouth full of beans. "I slit his gullet."

Mrs. Kissel drew in her breath with a little yip, and Jennie looked so mad I thought she'd like to slap him.

It was dark now, and Coulter had finished his meal, so he laid down his pan, then fumbled in his buckskin shirt to draw out a plug of coal-black tobacco. It looked vicious. "Chaw, ma'am?" he said to Mrs. Kissel politely, and held out the plug. I'd never known him to be so courteous before; it was a side of his nature that was new to me. Most men would have gone ahead and bit off their own chew first, but Coulter, to give him credit, thought of the women first.

"Thank you kindly, I don't think I will," she said, and Jennie, when her turn came, only said, "Humph!" The men nodded no and pulled out pipes, all except my father, who unloaded his usual number of windy remarks, this time about Havana cigars. He said he wished he had one, which was a lie, because he never smoked anything at all, and after this, when the plug was offered to me, I reached for it and Jennie slapped my hand. By the firelight I could see Coulter's strong teeth flash a grin against the background of his dark, swarthy face.

But he didn't say a word from that moment on; he just sat, perfectly rigid, staring across the fire in the general direction of Jennie. My father filled up the gaps. During the last days, as we'd headed toward Great Salt Lake, he had got wound up on Mormons, so he continued for about half an hour, telling about their habits and beliefs, most of it made up, I reckon, and the rest borrowed out of a book somewhere. But if you hadn't known better, you might have thought he had organized the sect and was the owner and general manager.

Right in the middle of a sentence, Coulter got up, said "Thankee," and disappeared into the darkness. It was my bedtime, but I had something to do, so I crawled through the entrance of our tent, wriggled out under the opposite side, and ankled off up the train in a hurry. Most everybody had gone to bed by now; the fires were burned low. No sound but the insects wailing about summer and a hoof-stamp now and then, where a horse or an ox was restless after the long hard pull of the day. I stepped over a wagon tongue to get outside, then crouched down behind a bush, waiting for Jennie.

Chapter XXII

In a way, I felt responsible for Brice; besides, I disliked seeing him bullied. If things got to the point where he needed help, I planned to stroll up as if I was taking a breather and say good evening. That might show this bossy creature I was on watch, and maybe even up for gouging me out of a chew.

But I wouldn't have believed she had so much cunning if she'd explained it to me beforehand. She was so sly I felt kind of paralyzed, there in the bushes, and couldn't open my mouth before it was too late.

In a few minutes, along she tripped, as fresh as a daisy. The moon wasn't up, but it was a light night, if you know what I mean. Stars were out in smears, and everything looked pale rather than black. The wagon tops reared up like sailboats and even the grass seemed a lighter green than it was.

She stopped, glancing all around, and sure enough, here came that woolly-headed Brice, hatless, sleeves rolled up, hands in pockets, muttering to himself. I figured he was probably sawing ice and that unless stopped he would keep on walking until he fell in the river.

"Thank you for coming, Mr. Brice," said Jennie, stepping forward. Her voice was soft and she had put on a frock that my mother would have called scandalous because it drooped so low in front. She was practically bulging out of it, up there, and for a slim girl, there was a disgusting amount of her to bulge, in that particular way. But if she was hoping to lure Brice, she'd made a mistake because he paid no more attention to her than he would a Jersey cow, though there was a pretty strong resemblance if you cared to look them over, which I didn't.

"Miss Jennie?" he whispered, peering around in his idiotic way.

She wiggled up closer, bulging even worse. "I wanted to talk to you—about your wagon."

"I haven't had a chance to say thanks. What you've done, looking after things, has been a real godsend, now my wife's gone."

"Mr. Brice, I'm just as interested in your home as if it was my very own."

"You'll have your own one day soon, Miss Jennie."

"Oh, no—not unless someday, years and years from now, I got married. It wouldn't be respectable for a single girl to keep house. People might think she was—fast."

Right here was when I should have stepped out and spoken my piece. This Brice was already in over his head, and it was my duty to toss him a rope. But I was struck dumb to see just how low-down she could work it.

"I meant marriage, of course, Miss Jennie. Any man would be lucky to win you."

"Mr. Brice, you make me giddy. I don't know as I truly understand you."

"What I meant," said Brice, trying to collect his poor wits, "was that you *ought* to be married, of course, before you, before——"

"Do you really feel that way? Are you *sure?*"

"I've never been surer of anything. Why, marriage is a sacred institution——"

"Mr. Brice," said Jennie, stepping up so close he could look right down on her, "you've set my heart hammering. You're so impulsive it—it scares me."

"I certainly don't mean to scare you," he said, putting his hands on her shoulders, but still trying to avoid the bulge. "Why, you're shaking!"

I'd like to bet she's laughing herself sick, I said, but to save my life, I couldn't seem to budge. I never before realized just how stealthy that girl could be. I almost admired her, she was so treacherous.

"Mr. Brice—Adam—what can a girl do but say yes? You've swept me right off my feet. And all the time, I thought you were dodging me. You strong, silent men are *deep*."

"Why, Miss Jennie," said Brice, trying feebly to unhook himself a little, because she had grappled him around the waist, being helpless and scared, you know, "I hadn't thought, that is, up until now it hadn't occurred——"

"Don't say another word"—and she made a teasing motion of putting her hand over his mouth. "You aren't going to talk me into any more foolishness tonight. My knees are so weak I want to go lie right down, but I'd better do it in *my* tent." She gave a saucy little laugh.

From where I crouched, Brice looked warm and stupid in that bear hug. It was odd he didn't fight his way out. Being considerably taller, he could have got a headhold on her and wrestled free, easy. On the other hand, he could have kneed her in the crotch. Or if nothing else worked, he could have tripped her over backwards and run for it. Then, by appealing to Coulter and the others, he might have got a guard put on his tent and been tolerably safe for a while. But he just stood there; and he'd even come to look as if she wasn't unenjoyable, bulges and all. It was nauseating. I made up my mind to wash my hands of him.

The way it turned out, I broke things up, but not the way I planned; besides, it had gone too far for human aid. She was mashing herself up against him so shameless that I got embarrassed and looked away, toward the wilderness. And there, plain to see, framed against the sky, were two wolves creeping up on us, not thirty yards away. They had a funny gait, though, more jerky than is common among animals. I opened my mouth and yelled as loud as I could: "Injuns!" and the camp, silent before, turned into a perfect cyclone of noise and confusion.

It couldn't have been over a minute before Coulter came riding down, but by then three or four men had run out with lanterns.

"Over there! Two men in wolf skins; they've cut for the river."

The figures had stood up in a flash, cast off the skins, and gone knifing through the bush toward the Platte, which showed broad and pale below. Jerking out a gun, Coulter put the spurs to his horse and plunged in after them, but the growth was so dense he jumped down and clawed ahead on foot. Several others were right behind, and I was close on their heels. It wasn't good judgment to get very far toward the front, because lead was zinging around everywhere, now: two or three hotheads blazing away at nothing, as a few always do. A person could have got shot easy, if he'd wanted to.

Just then the prowlers broke out into the open and across the muddy flats for the water. We all saw them at once; you never heard such a barrage. One fell to his knees but kept crawling, the other dived into the water and disappeared.

I got there behind two men with lanterns. This buck had been reamed through the back with a buffalo gun; the bullet had angled up to come out near his collarbone in front. He was done for. Still and all, he pulled out a knife and slashed feebly when the first of the men arrived. Lying on his side in the mud, in the yellow circle of light, he looked familiar. With one foot, roughly, Coulter rolled him over; it was one of the young men in Sick from Blackberries' wigwam. He'd been very uppity once, kicking and slapping me around, but he didn't cut much of a figure now. A buffalo gun is .50 calibre and makes a nice hole. You could have poured sand through this fellow as easy as you could through a funnel.

Coulter got down to inspect him, and said, "Just to settle an argument—have a look at that. Now who was it claimed I didn't scratch pay dirt?"

So this was where they'd been the night they came into the wigwam notched up. Clutching a braid of hair, Coulter lifted the head to show a half-healed wound, a furrow still red and bare.

Seeing this, several of the men spoke up to say they had been hasty, and a big farmer offered him a plug, remarking, "When I opined that you couldn't hit a cow in the ass with a handful of salt, I may have stretched it some. I'll eat them words."

It was a handsome apology, nobody could have asked for better, and Coulter looked satisfied. He said, "We'll leave the thieving skunk propped up on the trail. Maybe it'll serve to show we mean business."

They cut a pole and went back a ways, removed from the wagons, and nailed the corpse to it, upright. Coulter himself did most of the work. Some of the religious men complained a little, saying it was heathenish, and as bad as the Indians themselves, but Coulter jawed them down. There wasn't anything shy about him while he was busy on a job. Before we turned in, he rode by Jennie and Brice, still standing side by side, and reined up a second. I wondered how much he'd seen.

"It's a crying pity when Indians sneak around breaking up lovers' meetings. I may have to speak to the chief."

"It surely is crowded here tonight," Jennie said to Brice.

I went over in the bushes and found the wolf skins. It was my intention to keep them for souvenirs, or maybe to sleep on, but my father heaved them out on the end of a stick.

"I can't recall when I've encountered anything so rancid in the course of my medical career," he said. "They're probably infested with vermin, too. What with the denizens that normally take shelter on a wolf, plus those indigenous to the Indian, along with the hybrid produced by intermarriage, you can imagine the conditions that exist. I doubt if there's a disease on the face of the globe that isn't carried by one of them. The fact is——"

He would have gone ahead till he'd worn it out, but I said good night. I was sort of sore. I didn't believe there were any bugs on those skins, and what smell was there seemed soothing, and removed your mind from other troubles. Unless I'd been living with the Indians too long, that is. I could easily have taken one of those skins back for my mother to put in her bedroom, because she generally kept the windows open all the time anyway, and besides, Sam was tethered right below, so that the aromas would intermingle, and nullify each other out. In addition, I'd aimed to give the other to Daisy Coontz, which was a girl in my room at school who could chin herself five times. It would have made her a nice bonnet or muff, and there wasn't any chance her parents would object, because she was always running off and hiding, and this way they could locate her in the dark.

We spent the next day approaching the fork of the Platte, and at suppertime Jennie announced her betrothment, as I believe they said, to Brice. He appeared pleased, but he had the good sense to turn red when everybody crowded around with congratulations. I stated how much I admired him for talking her into it, knowing what a job it must have been, and Jennie gave me a wicked look.

"I've been meaning to have a word with you all day, you bothersome scamp," she said, but I ducked out. I couldn't think of any handy reason why I was nearby when I yelled at the Indians.

From the McPheeters Journals:

July 26, 1849

The wedding pair have set the locale for the festivities as Chimney Rock, a grotesque configuration of limestone that rears its head several hundred feet a fortnight ahead on the trail. Camped this day at junction of north and south forks of the Platte. All members partook copiously of the fresh, icy waters of the well here. It might be said that they partook recklessly, for the result has been an epidemic of violent retching and diarrhea. Together with Doctor Merton, I administered restoratives to slow the traffic into the brush, which has been congested, even giving rise to disputes over priority of position.

Buffalo within view in great abundance, some straying nearly close enough to mingle with our loose cattle. Though familiar with the chips, or *bois de vache*, we have had our first encounter with the meat, which in reference to the fat young heifer seems superior to the finest beef. A Mr. Bedloe, retired with a competence from the undertaking trade, this morning shot a young straggler that was dismembered by the versatile Coulter, in the presence of the company. In the end, only the men were permitted to remain; the business of removing the hide and intestines proved so onerous that Coulter's speech became laced with expletives of a unique piquancy. A number of husbands were observed herding their mates, at a rapid clip, to some sanctuary beyond earshot.

Coulter at length severed the choice cuts, which included a strip of flesh along each side of the spine, from shoulders to rump, the tenderloin, the liver, heart, tongue, hump ribs, and an intestinal vessel commonly called by hunters the "marrow-gut." Speaking anatomically, this is the chylo-poetic duct; it contains an unctuous matter resembling marrow and is unquestionably the greatest delicacy I ever tasted. Also, their genitals here on the frontier are put to excellent use. Everything, both choice and ordinary cuts, apportioned out fairly.

And what a sight that night over the campfires! Fresh meat; it quickens the spirits of all. We feasted like aldermen. We will take the trail tomorrow, along the south fork of the Platte, with revived courage.

July 27:

Buffalo everywhere, as far as the eye can see. The herds number in the tens of thousands. These shaggy creatures, so awkward and lumbering, will provision and clothe America in perpetuity; there is no doubt of it. The most confirmed pessimist could not envision a lessening of these endless black smears from horizon to horizon. The buffalo will be part of our West to the end of its destiny.

Again have been required to treat cattle. The alkali scours them sorely, as the Mormons going before us found. They (the cattle, not the Mormons) should be salted often, and if sickness develops, treated with thin slices of fat bacon dipped in salt and thrust down their throats. The dose: one pound of fat bacon per animal. Should this fail to work, add brandy and black pepper.

Traveled along south fork of the Platte, hoping to ford tomorrow. In the main, the trail has kept to the river, which narrows here. Nooning, Kissel and I found the powder kegs to be shrinking from dryness, and leaking powder. An ingestion of the spilled contents by the Kissel children, Deuteronomy, Micah, Leviticus and Lamentations, appears to have had no ill effect; on the contrary, they are filled with crackling good spirits being somewhat more vocal than formerly. Nevertheless, I have agreed to watch them for several days, and have cautioned the Kissels to prevent their approaching any open flame. While their stomachs may be conditioned to black powder, for reasons not now understood by medical science, mechanically there may be danger of a backfire. In any case, *no one should attempt to carry powder in kegs along this route!* It should be transported in strong, tight tin cans or canisters.

Besides the disturbing number of dead cattle and oxen along the route, we now pass live animals which have been left behind, too crippled or exhausted to proceed. Poor dumb beasts; they have nothing to look forward to save poisoning in the alkali ponds or slaughter by the Indians.

Distance made this day, as recorded by the odometer: seventeen miles.

July 30:
We have forded the Platte, with no more than trivial mishap. This ford was at what they call the California Crossing, a wide traverse of the bottom in normally shallow waters. As luck would have it, the river was on the rise, making the many areas of quicksand difficult to find. Before sallying forth with the wagons, a number of men themselves waded over, seeking the best route. One horse mired down to its head in the sands, but was speedily extricated with ropes.

The actual width of the river is half a mile, while its depth seldom exceeds four feet. As a precaution, which occasioned grumbling, Coulter ordered a double team—as many as eighteen yoke—hitched to each wagon. The tedious business of hitching and unhitching has made the operation spread over a day and a half. In my opinion, he was proved right. We suffered many incidents, no serious losses.

Before the undertaking, we camped near the remnants (and filth) of numerous other encampments. The scattered heaps of cast-aside articles gave it the appearance of a Rag Fair. The point of it all is that this quicksand, which lies everywhere in greater or lesser degree, will suck down, and swallow, a wagon if it pauses for as long as a second. *Once started, it must keep moving!* In consequence, the loads of all trains preceding have been lightened before entering the river. In a stroll about the camp, I noticed a jackscrew, boots and shoes, a tar kit, a shirt with a fine pleated bosom, a bolster filled with feathers, a broken crystal glass, a Britannia teapot squashed as flat as a scone, nineteen sides of bacon with beans in huge piles, chains, bolts and harness—enough loose iron to set up a blacksmith for life. There was a fine camp kettle, a deer-skin trunk, barrels, boxes, mounds of salt, a large crucible, and strangest of all, a split-bottom rocking chair sitting by the roadside. I had to shake off the feeling that it was occupied by a wayfarer somehow invisible, and might shortly begin rocking.

The business of lightening gave rise to a dispute that was settled by general vote. A sawmill owned jointly by several families presented such a problem that it was abandoned for the common good. Regrettably, there was born bitter ill feeling that has not yet passed away.

The crossing was begun at first dawn. The second wagon set in motion overturned to send its contents hopping down the steep. These were regathered laboriously, Coulter encouraging the process with refreshing examples of his peculiar idiom. As to our wagons, they completed the trip with smoothness, though in the struggle for footing the oxen were pushed to their last extremity, their sides sobbing with distress. We had taken the precaution to caulk both beds with calico strips and lampwick, but the water bubbled on in. By good fortune it was warm, not at all displeasing to the touch. Toward noon a hullabaloo was raised when someone pointed downstream to a sand bar where lay the body of a middle-aged man. After a head count, we agreed that he was none of our group. But only a few minutes later we observed Jaimie swimming stoutly toward the bar; hallooing brought no response. He was seen to clamber out, kneel, then make his way to the far shore. He returned with a purse carrying the identification of one Edwin Lorch, of Prairie du Rocher, Illinois, and said that the clothing was heavily freighted with sand, so that the victim must have stepped in a sink hole, only to be spewed back later.

I was strongly tempted to borrow back the ladle I presented the boy and administer a drubbing, but upon mature thought this appeared to be unethical. I may do it tomorrow. His activities throughout the day left much to be desired. Coulter at one point rode up to inquire if I would "have the goodness to make that pestiferous muskrat leave go of the oxen." It seemed he had been riding back and forth by means of clinging to the oxen's tails. When I reproached him, he said it acted as a kind of rudder, and kept them on a straight course. I fear that the child has not enough to keep him occupied; *I am resolved to begin giving him daily lessons in Latin.*

While completing the crossing the second day, our wagons helter-skelter on both banks and over the river, we saw a band of fifty Sioux appear to cross simultaneously. Though scattered, we were galvanized to defense, but their attitude was pacific, even aloof. These were fine-looking Indians, a vast difference existing between them and the others we have seen to date on the route. The braves were large and well formed; incongruously, they were mounted on very small horses. The squaws led pack ponies with both dogs and papooses perched on top, and other children, clad only in nature's raiment, toddled along beside.

Except for one deputation, stately and gelid, these Sioux never by so much as a flickering glance took note of our presence. When once they had crossed the stream, the chief and two others came forward to dicker about guns. They were not begging. All Indians, it seems, prefer the flintlock to the percussion rifle. Flint is readily available, while they have often great difficulty to secure caps. The result is that they try constantly to trade. After facing their horses toward us, the chief, with what I took to be a fleeting smile (for their reputation as fighters is fierce) made the sign for "Sioux"—the edge of his hand across the throat. Contemptuously undismayed, our Mr. Coulter replied by walking his horse back and forth at right angles to the trail—the plains sign for "come to me." Then, when they arrived, he informed them in brisk terms that we did no business with Indians, adding with unnecessary rudeness, "Vamoose."

It was, in its way, an unsavory encounter, but the fault could not be laid to our visitors. Mr. Coulter is a uniquely able man, but his own mother could scarcely deny that he has all the genteel polish of a cougar. And his detestation of Indians verges on the maniacal. He is a diverting study.

A brief medical note: Assembled, ready to move, on the opposite bank, we found many of our people ill. The influence of the alkali has affected us all. As senior physician present, I gave a lecture on health, advising a low diet and cooling aperients, stating in addition that I had decided against bleeding, and suggesting that those ill suck linen rags soaked in vinegar. Green goggles were found for a few suffering from opthalmic irritation of dust and sun, and cambric mouth veils were provided for those with coughs. I concluded with advices on bathing: Cleanliness and frequent baths, I said, are your best preventives of sickness, but I cautioned against bathing if fatigued and recommended as the best hour for this exercise around nine or ten in the morning; one is stronger then than at other times of day. My further directions were, heed not the coldness of the water if it is soft; and after leaving the water, begin an active rubbing with a coarse towel, until a reaction takes place in the skin; dress rapidly, drink a long draught of pure water, and commence a smart walk until perspiration ensues; then cool gradually and fix the mind on subjects of pleasant good cheer.

Hearing these remarks, the sufferers appeared to brighten. But I am disturbed about our prospects for harmony. The train seems in danger of being rent by factionalism. The group which abandoned the sawmill, headed by Matlock, the big farmer, clings stolidly to itself. And overshadowing all, the sandy road grows rougher, the oxen more exhausted, the loads harder to move, our supplies much depleted through lightening, and the grass worn and scant. What shall we do if our food gives out?

Traveling to California is a heavy, laborious business!

Chapter XXIII

Approaching Chimney Rock
In Transit to California:
August 12, 1849

My dearest Melissa:
      This is penned as the writer sits on a rocky eminence some distance up the trail ahead of the train. The day is sunny and bright, and the atmosphere clear and springlike, enabling the viewer to observe that lofty phenomenon of nature some forty miles distant called "Chimney Rock." We are to have a wedding there.

I write from an exuberance of spirits, occasioned by the fact of everything proceeding so splendidly. The trail, while not actually improving, and even deteriorating in some trifling respects (the wheels now sinking into the sand to a distance of ten inches), still is passable. The oxen, though not refreshed to the point of rambunctiousness (some numbers of them dropping by the wayside from time to time), continue to pull the wagons with commendable zeal, considering the absence of both grass and good water. Our supplies, which seem capable of holding out for many days yet, offer a healthful, athletic diet which yet permits none of that over-nutrition, with its consequent obesity, heart strain and overburdened kidneys, that proves so disturbing to the practicing physician. *I am happy to tell you that there is not a single case of gout in camp!*

As to the grass, you will rejoice with me when I say that, for all practical purposes, there is none. Indians in large numbers will never frequent this area, because of its arid desolation. So that, on one of our most important scores, we are almost entirely free of anxiety. The finding of water has turned into a species of romp, in which both children and adults participate. From every viewpoint, including the therapeutic, it is well to have a diversion among people so closely bound together, and the seeking of aqueous potation, in this soda-encrusted stretch between the north and south branches of the Platte, serves admirably. Example: while passing, yesterday, through an area of unbelievable sterility, with high winds whipping the sands and soda dust like furiously driven snow, someone spied to our left a stream of fresh-running water. You may imagine with what whoops of delight all members ran to throw themselves full-length beside this limpid fountain. Alas, one mouthful was sufficient to produce nausea. So the game must continue. I am thinking of offering a prize to the first who makes a successful discovery. The waters of the Platte itself are drinkable in an emergency, but they exude an unpleasant, foetid odor, highly offensive, as does the atmosphere hereabouts. This has been uniformly viewed by the train as a healthy symptom, for it has spurred the enthusiasm of all to proceed as rapidly as possible to California, or to any place except here.

In the broader sense (as stated) we are thriving bountifully. After crossing the south fork, we descended into the valley of the north fork through a pass known as Ash Hollow, being a dry ravine with a few stunted ash trees, the entrance signalized by a log cabin of historic import. Erected by trappers caught here by winter snows, it has been converted into a general post office, and its walls inside and out are covered over with manuscript, advertisements for lost cattle, directions and suggestions, messages for oncoming trains, and a variety of advices. Inside, we found a rich cache of letters, with pleas to parties traveling in both directions to assist in conveying them to the nearest Government post office.

We had here an altercation which only highlighted our underlying harmony. The train paused for some time at the cabin, to profit from the pointers and, needless to say, to reject out of hand the several recommendations that we retreat before we perish. Mr. Coulter (who will be associated in your mind with my unshakable admiration from the start) was hailed while reading a bill near the front door, by our bellicose Illinois farmer, Ed Matlock. It was the contention of the latter, a very large and lank man, with a bony face rather longer than life-size, unkempt yellow hair, and small, gimlet eyes, that we should hold a meeting to consider the notion of "packing." That is, abandoning the heavy wagons and loading our supplies on the backs of either oxen or, if possible, mules, for which we should trade at the first opportunity (such advices were plentiful at the "post office").

I should say that Matlock has harbored a grudge since the Platte crossing, when Coulter insisted that he and his cousins, a numerous and shaggy lot, no credit to the general appearance of the train, leave behind a sawmill that others agreed was too cumbersome to transport across the river without risk to human life, oxen and wagons.

"We're still rolling," said Coulter, without taking his eyes from the bill. "Motion rejected."

A good many of our people—myself, Brice, Jenny, Coe and others —were nearby when this occurred, and we gave a gasp of dismay when Matlock seized Coulter roughly by the shoulder and spun him half around.

"Look here, I'm sick of your bulldozing," cried the farmer. "Me and my cousins'll do what we durn well please."

"Speaking for the train as a whole," said Coulter pleasantly, "we'll continue for a while with the wagons."

Knowing Coulter, we thought this a moderate and unobjectionable reply, but the farmer, quite apparently smoldering with resentment (partly dating from that painful day when Coulter conducted his notorious "deer hunt") now chose to become personal.

"How come you know so much?" he cried, walking forward till his sun-blistered nose was thrust almost into Coulter's face. "I'll own up we joined the train late, so I didn't git to make inquiries. If I had, we'd a joined another. Where'd you spring from, Big Mouth?"

"I was hired by popular vote."

During this uncomfortable discourse, Coulter simply stood easy and relaxed in his loose slouch, wearing a half-smile. But his face went white as chalk at the farmer's next remark.

"I've heard a few stories—we haven't got no hankering to trail after a man that's murdered his own kin."

Coulter looked as if he'd been struck. He stepped back a pace, then, the words hardly audible, said, "All right, you've chose yourself a fight."

At this, a number of the cooler heads intervened, but Coulter threw them off. "Not this time," he said, peeling out of his buckskin shirt. "Doctor, I'll thank you and Kissel to go forward and make the arrangements. That rise up yonder'll be handy ground enough."

You may imagine that I tried to dissuade him, but he was as firm as flint. Matlock having appointed two of his cousins—rough, bearded men nearly as big as he—to act as seconds, we conferred briefly. I must confess that the formalities of such a rough-and-tumble were entirely foreign to me, but Kissel, to my amazement, stepped out of taciturnity and said, "Heel and toe, no gouging, no butting, stand up fair till one hollers enough."

The larger of the cousins, as uncouth a man as ever I've seen in my life, with bacon grease spattered down the front of his filthy denim shirt, spat tobacco juice contemptuously and said, "You prefer the body planted here or pinted home in a box?"

Kissel regarded him with his baby-blue eyes, then uttered the first unfriendly statement I'd ever heard pass his lips. For some reason I can't explain, this burly cousin had offended his dignified concept of farming as an occupation.

He said, "Mister, you talk a good fight."

"How tall be you, Fatty?"

"Six feet six, give or take."

"I didn't know they piled dung that high," said the cousin, and I leaped in between as fast as I could move. For a moment, I thought we had a *second* battle on our hands.

Matlock stripped, and we led the way up the knoll, the children running behind, screaming, "Fight! Fight!" dogs barking, the women taking a stand at a distance where they could not be accused of unseemly curiosity, but able to see a little, too, and over all that air of serious, hurried portentousness that such physical encounters always breed. It's infectious; it stirs up the blood; one finds oneself on the point of bristling out of sympathy, and even looking around for somebody giving offense.

When the two faced off, bare to the waist, there was apparent a certain disparity in bulk. Matlock is a huge man, of a fish-belly whiteness of skin, with the corded, sinewy muscles common to one who has done hard labor, with lifting; and Coulter, swarthy, deeply tanned, though as sleek as a panther looked helplessly slight by contrast.

"Pining to back out, Big Mouth?"

"I'd rather make it free," said Coulter.

"Free it stands."

The farmer's answer was offhand enough, but his expression showed a momentary unease. You could scarcely blame him. Coulter's face, in anger, is one of the least reassuring sights on earth. There was no bluster, no contortion of features, no tension, no nervousness; his eyes had the flat glitter of a rattlesnake's, his nose was splayed out in dilation, and his mouth a line incised in granite. To put it mildly, he looked extremely dangerous, and I believe that Matlock, for the first time, suspected that he may have been hasty. Nevertheless, at Kissel's cry of "Fight!" he came out, weaving back and forth, his hands working in the air, not unlike a swimmer's pawing through water, and suddenly aimed a heavy, unsporting kick at the vulnerable area of Coulter's crotch. Had it landed, it might well have crippled him for life.

What happened next remains blurred in my mind. Coulter's actions were performed with such rapidity that they confused us all. I was strongly reminded of the classic notion of a wolf striking at the throat of the slow-moving moose. In conversations that evening, nobody remembered precisely the sequence of events, but all agreed that the meeting could not properly be described as a fight. It was murder and sudden death, or would have been had there not been general intervention.

Slipping aside, Coulter—I believe—caught Matlock's foot and gave it a sharp, quick hoist that flipped him up off the ground then dropped him down with a jarring thwack on his back. Our farmer looked shaken, but he had little time to recover, for Coulter lit on him like a hawk swooping on a peewit. There was a silent flurry of thrashing arms and legs, and we heard a crack like that of a dry stick breaking. Matlock screamed, scrambled out of the melee, and rose swaying to his feet, his left arm hanging limply at his side. But Coulter, too, had sprung up and now he dropped his left shoulder and swung a short blow with his right fist—the hand moving only a few inches—that caught Matlock flush in the face. We saw with horror that his nose was mashed almost perfectly flat; only the nostril apertures, streaming blood, remained to make it recognizable as a nose. Needless to say, he went down, slack in every joint, a dull, glazed look in his eyes. But before he hit the ground, Coulter was on his back with what I believe is called a scissors hold of the legs around his middle, the fingers of his right hand dug firmly in Matlock's eyes. In a "free" fight on these plains, the conqueror has a moral right to blind the vanquished if he chooses.

However, there came an interruption in the form of the Matlock cousins. Others also were about to protest. But the larger of the cousins suddenly whipped out a knife, swung it up in a high arc, and had started it down toward Coulter's back when Matt Kissel seized his wrist and twisted the blade free.

"You want something, too, Fatty?" cried the cousin, and aimed a blow at Kissel's head. I have the impression it landed, but it appeared to make no difference. This quiet, oxlike man clenched his fist in the cousin's stomach, gathering together the tight belt and loose flesh, and picked him up bodily. He held him thus, several feet in the air, with one hand.

"You're all het up," said Matt. "Get un-het."

"No hard feelings," gasped the cousin, and our fight was over. It had been of unique violence while it lasted, and I have no doubt it will become a plains legend. Of special curiosity to me was its aftermath. Coulter, brushing himself off and all but returned to normal, though still breathing hard, said, "Just for the record, I wasn't aiming to douse his sight."

Regarding him stolidly, Kissel replied, "I'm glad to hear it."

Then Coulter made his remark that brought a general laugh: "Mr. Kissel, I hope we never have to tangle; I couldn't figure out a worse afternoon's work."

"No occasion," said Matt.

We walked on down the hill. The Matlocks took charge of their injured warrior; his nose and the splintered bone in his arm would have to be set. It seemed to me that all things considered, he had got off very lucky. The thought was faintly disturbing.

But as I said, Melissa, this trivial dispute, in clearing the air, simply emphasized the essential solidarity of the train. It is true that, next day, the Matlock faction and a few others of like disposition split off from the parent group, determined to go it alone. But for the rest, our resolve continued unabated. Ahead lies gold, gold to wallow in, to fling out of the carriage as one proceeds (with credit restored) over the streets of Louisville. By Fort Laramie, only a comparatively brief distance up the trail, we shall have gone halfway! After that it is only a pleasant stroll across a few deserts, some salt flats, and then the Rocky Mountains. Could any prospect be more enticing?

With loving greetings to you
and my darlings, and in the
very best of spirits, I remain,
SARDIUS McPHEETERS (M.D., etc.)

Chapter XXIV

People kept talking about the fight and before long they threw the blame on Coulter. All except our bunch. Nobody came right out and accused him of anything, or made trouble, but when somebody said the Matlocks had been valuable additions to the train, that was all they needed. Before the ruckus, there wasn't hardly a soul could stand those clodhoppers, or their womenfolks either, but now you would have thought they were a collection of missionaries. It was disgusting.

My father said it wasn't worth worrying about; it was just part of the general cussedness of humans. He said they'd go baaa-ing off in another direction as soon as something occurred to them.

"I've seen this sort of perverseness in elections. A man will be in office, doing fine, honest, upright, hard-working, even noble, as far as you can find that quality in a politician, and the opposition will put up a known scoundrel that hasn't a thing to recommend him except noise. But if he brays long enough and loud enough he'll bray himself right in. People are prepared to believe anything about a person as long as it's bad."

Even Jennie acted sulky and said that Eloise Matlock had been going to be one of the bridesmaids at her wedding, but now she'd be a bridesmaid shy. I figured that, at the outside, she'd spoken to this Eloise two or three times, so mostly she made it up to spite Coulter.

What actually galled the train was the country we were crossing, but it seemed handier to take it out on the leader. Here between the two rivers the soil was so sandy and dry the air was full of flying particles nearly all the time. It was enough to suffocate you. The wind was high, too. People wore kerchiefs wrapped around their nose so they could breathe without drowning in the dust. This went on for two days and then we had a rain that freshened things up some. The wind dropped, and it was lovely. There was even a faintly green, grassy look roundabout, and directly ahead was this Chimney Rock, standing straight up like some old temple. Everybody was so grateful for the change that several men came out flat-footed and promised to stop abusing Coulter for a while.

We'd be at the rock in plenty of time for a Sunday wedding. This appeared to cheer everybody up. Weddings do that, I've noticed. The ones already married are happy to see somebody else hooked, and the bachelors are naturally relieved that it isn't them.

What with one thing and another, I felt good. Jennie had said she would appoint me a "flower boy," because there were only three girls of the right age in the whole train, and although there wasn't anything growing around here except milkweed and cactus, I hoped to have some fun, and maybe throw a monkey wrench in the machinery somewhere along the line. This smart-alecky female had it coming.

But that night when we camped, my father brought out a nasty-looking little green book he'd borrowed off a man whose wife had been a schoolteacher but reformed, and said he was going to teach me Latin.

"Now, my boy," he said, getting me off to one side and putting on his spectacles, "you've been idle long enough. We have a duty to your mother, and we'll start discharging it right here."

"Yes, sir," I answered, feeling about as low as I'd felt since the day they sprung Mental Arithmetic on me at the Secondary School.

"You're familiar with the general meaning of Latin, its basic definition and purpose, that is?"

"I've heard it mentioned," I said, "but not very favorably. Nobody's said anything good about it in *my* presence."

"If you persist in being facetious," said my father, looking over his spectacles, "I'll be obliged to give you a birching."

"I'm only telling you what I heard."

"Very well, then. Now, first of all, what exactly *is* Latin, in your mind, as we sit chatting?"

"I may be a mile off, but I think it has something to do with the Greeks."

"You're off, all right, but not too far off at that. This is a very good start. It was the Romans. I'm proud of you, son. Taking another step, I assume you realize that Latin is a dead language?"

"Why, no," I said, being considerably set back. "I hadn't heard that. How did it happen to die?"

"We're getting a little off the track. Latin, the classic tongue of the early Romans, is now a dead language. We can begin with that premise, and go right on from there."

"I certainly don't want to cause trouble," I said, "but I'd feel a good deal more comfortable to know why it died. Who killed it?"

"Nobody killed it. Several races intermingled along about that time, and the language simply got swallowed up. That's all."

"You mean the Romans quit speaking entirely?"

"The Romans, as such, were no longer Romans, and so used the tongues of the people with whom they intermingled. See here, my boy, do you want to get on with this or don't you?"

"Well, I guess I don't," I said, brushing myself off and starting up. "I'm sorry the way it turned out, but I hadn't any idea Latin was dead. Maybe we can do something else later on."

"I'll tell you what we *will* do," said my father warmly. "Unless you've got back down here in about three seconds and tackled this thing in good spirit, you won't be sitting down for a week."

"That's all right," I said. "I didn't understand. I thought you were giving me a choice. I'm perfectly willing to push ahead with this Latin, dead or alive, but I can't see what use it is."

My father shook his head. "Of what use is *Latin?* Is that what you mean?"

"I'm not apt to be transacting any business with dead Romans, so why bother?"

"Latin," said my father slowly, "is the basis for our own richly eloquent language of English. Many, many words have been carried forward in almost their exact, identical form. To a dedicated student of philology, the two are almost interchangeable."

"Oh, well, then, in that case, hand me the book. I hadn't realized we might switch back. I see what you mean. I'd be in a pretty pickle if everybody shifted to Latin and left me stumbling around with English. I couldn't understand a word."

I made a motion toward the book, but he held it back. "My boy, I'm going to give you one more warning and then I'll have to cut a sapling. Any further attempts at levity will erupt with very serious results."

"I'm sorry to be so ignorant," I said. "You go right on with the lesson."

"That's better. Now, Jaimie, my lad, the first thing we should realize, before proceeding to grammar, is that a knowledge of Latin opens up for us a wealth of grand and lofty literature. Does the name Caesar convey anything to you?"

"There, at least, I'm on solid ground," I said with pleasure. "As it happens, I know him well. He's the old darky helper that sweeps out at Briscoe's Feed Store. He sharpened a pocketknife for me only about a week before we left. He must be near onto a hundred and fifty years old; I'm not surprised all his friends are dead."

My father took off his spectacles and wiped them. "I don't know," he said at last. "Maybe the simplest thing would be just to move on to grammar." He opened the book and pressed down the fold so he could read. "Here we are, son. From here on we won't have any trouble."

"I'm anxious to get it now that I understand what it's about."

"Of course you are. Now the first thing to consider is the order in sentences: subjects, objects, verbs and the like. You follow me, do you not?"

"I can understand it's important to keep order in a sentence, just as anywheres else."

"That was a joke, wasn't it, son?"

"I guess so, father."

"You weren't planning to make any more jokes, were you, Jaimie?"

"No, sir."

"Well, then. In Latin we find that the verb comes last. If they should say, 'The Indian fired the rifle,' how, in your view, would they say it, with reference to order?"

"Simple enough," I replied, feeling a little easier. "That's one of those trick questions. We had them in school. They wouldn't say it at all, you see. There weren't any rifles around then, and the Indians hadn't been discovered yet."

He took off his hat and swabbed out the band. This was curious, because the sun had practically gone down and it wasn't hot any more, leastways not hot enough to sweat. Then he said an interesting thing, but it didn't seem to have anything to do with Latin.

"I don't believe I've ever before had a due and meet appreciation of the late Job."

But in a second he went on briskly. "What they'd say would be, 'The Indian the rifle *fired*.' You may take my word for that; I'll get affidavits if necessary. Now let us consider a sentence in the actual language, in Latin itself. Listen carefully. *Agricola in horto est*. What do you think of that?"

"It's very nice," I said. "I like it. I'm surprised they let it die out."

"*Agricola* means farmer, *horto* means garden, and *est* means is. Now put them all together and what do we have? In other words, son, translate the sentence."

"The garden is in the farmer."

He didn't appear to care for the way it was going, because this time he snatched off his hat and threw it on the ground. "Confound it, boy, there must be *something* you can learn. I never saw such a student. An outsider would get the notion you were a complete jackass. Why do you say the *garden* was in the *farmer*? Perhaps you'd care to explain it."

"I figured it was toward the end of the season and he'd eaten the garden up. It seems perfectly sensible. After going to all the trouble of planting it, he'd be a fool to let it sit there and rot."

I could see we had about finished the lesson, because he got up, a little carefully, as if he was in some pain, and rubbed the back of his neck, working his head all around. "I think that ought to wind it up for today, son. I've marked out a section here, having to do with the verb 'to love'—'amare'—no, you needn't make any comment on it; I'd rather you didn't. Over the next few days, take a shot at learning the conjugation: 'Amo, amas, amat,' etc. Frankly, I don't think it will pan out. What we may have to do is get another book and start back a little farther, in English: 'A' is for Archer, 'B' is for boy, and so on. It's been a very instructive experience. The only thing about it that bothers me is why I ever paid school taxes in Louisville. It's a perfect example of municipal larceny. You can come along to supper—S-U-P-P-E-R, to eat, or dine, whenever you've washed up."

I watched him go. Somehow, he seemed to walk a little *older* than usual. But I felt relieved all the same. It had been a very close call. And in case you might have the notion that I wasn't being helpful, I'll say now, again, what I've believed all along: There isn't a particle of use in making all that fuss over a language as dead as Latin. If you ask me, I'd saved us *both* some trouble.

When we arrived at Chimney Rock, everybody let down a little. It wasn't very remarkable when you thought it over. These people had been under a severe strain for weeks. What with Indians, sickness, boggy roads, and the loss of their supplies, which they saved and scrimped and bargained for, and beneath it all an anxiety about the strange new land ahead, they were ground down pretty fine.

About ten miles before reaching the rock, we came across another odd formation, being what they called "the Courthouse," because of its resemblance to the Capitol at Washington, so they said. If you squinted up your eyes, you could imagine a main building with wings on either side and a big dome on top. It gave you a funny feeling. Particularly so when my father said that all these formations—the high bluffs on the riverbanks, the Courthouse, and Chimney Rock itself—were all of a soft stone that would crumble away in years to come, and not be there any more. You could believe my father on things like that; when he was sticking to scientific facts, without any need to embroider, he showed an amazing knowledge; I've heard several very smart people say the same.

Seeing the Courthouse, I had an urge to explore it, so I went ahead of the train and climbed up part of the outside. It was ghostly: dead chalky white, with places as smooth and finished as the finest building, but other parts ruined and moldering, like some old lost city. I couldn't stand it very long; every little pinnacle or wall I climbed, I expected somebody to jump out on the other side. Things were too quiet. I thought I heard a clock ticking way down deep, too, and Aunt Kitty once said it was a sign somebody was about to die. I was beginning to get a case of the nervous jimjams, so I turned to scramble out of there in a hurry. But as I half slipped around one of those white-dusty corners, I almost swallowed my heart; I must have come within an inch of fainting. A very old, wrinkled Indian man was standing on a flat place, erect as a tree, arms folded, face entirely stiff, waiting, and at his feet sat a young girl not more than eleven or twelve, eyes cast down in a sort of sadness.

Well, I'd seen enough Indians; I knew what they were like, so I looked around for the others. But these appeared to be alone.

"How, cola!" said the old man in a voice that almost croaked, as though he hadn't used it lately. He held up one arm.

I trotted out what I remembered of Pawnee, to ask what he wanted, hoping it was peaceable. Then, with a rapid-fire flourish of signs, and a lot of words I mostly didn't know, he managed to indicate that the girl was for sale. He wanted to barter her off, cheap, but I couldn't get the details or even figure out the price.

As best as I could, I said we weren't in the market for any marked-down Indians, male or female, and I'd thank him to stand aside and let me pass on back to the train. But he had the persistence of a dog that's too hungry to be driven off, and followed right along, towing the girl on the end of a line. It was ridiculous: I'd go a few feet, stop, look back, and shout at him to leave; then take up the march, half climbing and slipping, and do it all over when we came onto more level ground. There wasn't any way to shake him; I never ran across such an old donkey.

So the best thing was to continue on down toward the train, which was winding up the plain almost even with us. It looked bedraggled, I noticed, not so white and smart as when we left. In a minute, I made up my mind not to palaver any further with the old man—it wasn't dignified—but would join up and leave him slide. But my father and Buck Coulter were walking ahead a ways, having a talk, and they were set back when they saw me.

"My boy, you've got company," said my father.

As might be expected, Coulter's two cents' worth wasn't quite so genteel.

"Arapahoe," he said, with a sniff; then, raising his voice, "Skee-daddle."

The old man came right on, then pitched into the same tirade he'd given me, pointing at the girl, who stood aside, waiting, as if she'd done it often before. Altogether, I guess, he unloaded about ten thousand words. But first he took out of his shirt a short flag-staff and unfurled a flag with an eagle and "E Pluribus Unum" on it. And after this he handed over a letter written by a French fur trader, vouching for his friendliness.

Coulter's comment on the last was, "Very pretty, I'm sure. Maybe I'd better take and hit him over the head with a pistol butt."

"I hope not, Mr. Coulter. It doesn't seem courteous, somehow. What exactly is he after?"

"He wants to get rid of the girl." Coulter asked a question, seeming at home in the language, and when the answer came, said, "She's a Sac and Fox, from up towards Wisconsin."

After another exchange, he said, "She was taken by Sioux when a baby and since then been with Cheyennes and Arapahoes."

A third passage, and, "His family's wiped out, says he can't afford to keep her any longer. He wants to trade her for a red blanket."

"What an extraordinary wish," said my father.

"Most of it's lies, I reckon, but the last part's true. These skunks will do anything for a red blanket. They'll rent you their daughter, then stand by and watch. It amounts to a disease."

My father asked her name; I thought it an odd question. And when Coulter turned toward the old man, he said, "No, ask the child herself."

She raised her head to look Coulter steadily in the eye—there wasn't anything hang-dog about her—and spoke in a very low voice.

"Po-Povi—Water Flower," Coulter translated. "She says the Cheyennes gave it to her."

"Poor, miserable, neglected child," said my father. "What will become of her, if he hasn't any luck with us?"

Coulter grinned. "A bunch of bucks—Sioux, or Crows, or Shoshones—will chip in and keep her for sport. Till she wears out. Then they'll pass her along to the Diggers and the Utes."

My father straightened up with an air of decision. "Then that settles it. Mr. Coulter, I've decided to buy the child. Up to now, Jaimie and I have depended on the bounty of Jennie and the self-sacrificing Mrs. Kissel. This child can help with the chores from now on; she looks strong and competent."

"And when the job's done, and we've lit in California—what then?"

"If she's the good, decent girl she appears, I'll see she has the best upbringing possible."

I almost exploded. This was the most idiotic notion my father ever struck, and he was kind of genius for foolishness. Here I'd told him all, or nearly all, about the trickery of that Pawnee girl they called Pretty Walker, and now he was trying to take on another exactly the same: both were young and pretty, both had been captured, and, as likely as not, both had a disposition as black as the ace of spades. It was more than I could stand, and I told him so.

"Son," he said, putting an arm over my shoulder, "I don't often go contrary to your wishes, now, do I?"

After a moment, I said, "No, I guess not."

"You will doubtless recall the spankings I adminstered with *The Turf Register?*"

I nodded, feeling sheepish, because he *was* as good a father as you could have, and the most fun, too, if you came right down to it.

"Jennie's getting married tomorrow. And Mrs. Kissel doesn't look well, according to my doctor's view. And in the further cause of common humanity, let's give this unhappy waif a home and the attention of some goodhearted people. Now what do you say?"

I couldn't do any more than nod again.

"You may be making a mistake, doctor," said Coulter. "An Indian's ways ain't necessarily your ways. Even a kid this age."

"I'll take the chance," said my father stoutly.

Coulter turned to the old man and asked one more question. "Well, that much is all right. She hasn't been used yet. The old villain says she's still a maid, and he'll up-end her and prove it if necessary. If you ask me, I'd let him do it. You can't be too sure."

I wasn't entirely clear what he meant, but my father turned a bright red; then he stammered, "Surely, Mr. Coulter, you aren't suggesting that I, that this child——"

"Doctor," said Coulter, "I've lived rough and I think rough. I don't know what limits a gentleman like yourself might set on a purchase of this kind. It's up to you"—he grinned again—"and time."

"Absolutely outrageous!" my father burst out, fuming, and we went down the train to get the old Indian his red blanket.

Chapter XXV

Sunday we had the wedding, and it turned out fine, but not quite the way Jennie planned it. Still, it was a very pretty wedding—everybody thought so—and if the bridegroom didn't exactly know what was going on, that could be laid to medical reasons and wasn't any reflection on the bride.

As I said in the last chapter, people let down a little when we got to Chimney Rock, but my father, for the first time since we left home, let down so far they couldn't get him back up. It was an embarrassment; he felt very bad about it, as I'll tell in a minute. But first I want to put down, from his Journals, what he wrote about this Chimney Rock, because it shows that weak or not now and then, he was strong on a whopping variety of subjects. Maybe that's what made him so unsure. It takes a very smart man to realize how many things there are he will never know.

He wrote that "this circumambient rock has long since largely melted away, the argillaceous part to fill in the river, the sandy part to add to the plains," and spoke of a "serrated wall of freestone." And then he said that there are "four high elevations of architectural configuration, one of which could represent a distant view of the Athenian Acropolis; another the crumbling remains of an Egyptian temple; a third, a Mexican pyramid; the fourth, the mausoleum of one of the Titans." And he wound up by setting down that "the illusion is so perfect the viewer can imagine himself encamped amongst the ruins of some vast city erected by a race of giants, contemporaries of the Megatherii and the Ichthyosaurii."

I don't mind taking pride in those words. Some of them couldn't

233

be pronounced by the smartest professor, and as for spelling them, I doubt if you could have got it done in one college out of five. Any man with that much reading behind him deserves to drink pretty well what he pleases.

But I'd better keep moving, and not maunder, because a neighbor with a very good education, and a piece of sheepskin scribbled over with Latin to prove it, was reading these pages the other day, and said I wasted too much time on "irrelevancies" and should "get right on with the action."

So we set up camp in the shadow of Chimney Rock, toward the middle of Saturday afternoon, and the people knocked off to visit. The Honorable Coe came down to our wagons and sat around, talking to my father about Britain, and they agreed that the weather at that moment, which was misty, would be called a "dawkie" on the Scottish coast. This curious fellow had become friendly with us, in his thawing-icicle way. As well as he could, he was trying to work himself out of the clammy, strangulated, nose-tilted outlook of Englishmen and be one of the group. They're a funny race; I've heard my father admit it. He said when you first meet them, they draw off as though you're trying to borrow money from them, but when you get better acquainted, they generally borrow money from you. Anyhow, Coe sat down on an upturned keg, and he had a bottle of sherry he said he'd "been saving for a propitious moment." But could he open it himself? Oh, no. That might be letting the bars down, you see. Othello, the bullet-headed darky, came along, dressed in the idiotic costume of the late Vilmer, and drew the cork with as much flourish as if we'd been at Buckington Palace.

Coe had put on his elegant white gloves, but they didn't have a formal appearance any more. Two of his fingers were sticking out of the ends, there was a long tear on one back, and the other was stained with axle grease. He waved them around with the same style, though, and that was what mattered.

I could see my father eyeing that bottle, and wondered what would happen. Maybe it's crazy, but I felt sorry for him. It's entirely possible I've pictured him wrong in some ways. A stranger might have dismissed him as nothing but a lovable humbug, but there was more to him than that. I realize, now, after it's all over, that he was crushed down by responsibility for going on this trip, and especially for taking me along. He *had* got us into it, what with the slipshod dodging of his problems back home, and now, you understand, he wasn't quite so sure he'd be able to get us out.

So he eyed Coe's sherry, and pretty soon he gave a long sigh. Finally he said, "Sir, I'm a teetotaler, born and bred. If there's one thing I can't abide the sight of, it's rum. I know you won't hold it against me when I tell you I consider it the devil's partner. But neither can I stand a blue-nose—I know because I'm regarded as one myself, back in Louisville—so I'll join you, delighted to, in a beaker of light wine."

Then he added a couple of sentences, being unable to resist throwing in a quotation or so, out of the Bible, from a man called Paul something-or-other—I didn't catch his last name. It had to do with drinking wine to keep your stomach from getting out of whack. "So you see, scriptural authority exists," my father added, and grabbed the little crystal tumbler that Coe held out. Matt Kissel was there, and Brice, too, whittling vacantly on a stick, and they both took a glass, Brice looking up eagerly and Kissel, after a start of hesitation. In a few minutes, he poured it out behind him; I saw him do it, but nobody else did. He *was* a teetotaler, but he wouldn't have hurt anybody's feelings for a wagonload of gold.

During my father's absurd discourse on his soberness, I saw Coe regarding him with puzzlement. Coe was a sissy-looking man, by frontier standards, but by now people knew he wasn't a sissy inside. What's more, he was nobody's fool. His troubles rested mostly on keeping up the appearances, and mules.

Once my father collared the glass, he held it carelessly aside, to prove he didn't need it. You would have thought he might accidentally tip the liquid out, he was so disregardful. But when, in response to Coe's toast to the bride and groom, he lifted his glass up, he took a bite out of that sherry that left nothing but a brown bubble in the bottom.

"Splendid. Really splendid. An elderly sack from, I assume, the region of Jerez de la Frontera. I had an uncle who wintered there."

"You surprise me, doctor," said Coe. "The Spanish climate can be beastly."

"He didn't go for the climate," replied my father, warmed up a little and returned to his natural self. "He went down for the sherry." Set up by this nonsense, he said, "Following his middle thirties, I doubt if he was ever aware of any change in the seasons."

"It's a way of life," said Coe drily. I could see that, having made up his mind to something, he intended to nurse that bottle slowly, but he might as well have hauled it out in a wigwam full of Apaches. I once heard a man say my father could be the most engaging companion and conversationalist on earth when he tried, and now he would have charmed a bird off a limb. He spoke (I believe) on something called Bizzanteen architecture (with reference to Chimney Rock); Aztec fertility symbols, which it wouldn't serve any good purpose to repeat here; the emigration of some Israelites out of Egypt, led by an early trail scout and lawyer named Mose, who I judged was a pretty tough old bird, not unlike Coulter; and then he gave out notes on a couple of sick poets name Sheets and Kelly; established links between man's historical development and the grape; and wound up, as usual in this period, on the Mormons. By this time, all the wine was gone, and Coe was probably wondering what hit him.

But that wasn't all the activity of that night for my father. After Coe graciously refused an offer of dinner, saying that Othello had a stewpot boiling and would be put out by his absence, my father took up his medical bag and said he was going off to attend a man suffering from frostbite. This seemed uncommon odd, in the middle of summer, so when Kissel looked up in his mild way, he changed it, with some hemming and hawing, to "frogbite."

"Yes," he said, gathering confidence, and likely convincing himself, seeing the state he was in, "I grieve to tell you that one of our number, a Mr. Belkins—small man with a gray goatee and a limp— has had a very serious encounter with a frog."

"*Bitten*—by a *frog?*" inquired Brice, looking even fuzzier than usual.

"Did I say bitten? I don't recall it."

"Maybe he was kicked," I suggested.

"Listen, my boy," said my father sternly. "The cheapest kind of wit in the world is that enjoyed at other people's expense. No doubt it seems ludicrous to you, hale and young and ready for your supper, but I can assure you it's no joke for that unhappy sufferer, Mr. Beldings——"

"Belden."

"—for Mr. Belden, lying up there perhaps at death's door. No, this is no ordinary case——" and then a solution occurred to him, for he said, "The fact is, it was a *horned* frog, one of the most dangerous predators of the West. *That poor fellow has been gored!*"

He left, and I sat shaking my head. I wasn't only embarrassed, I was annoyed. But I saw that both Mr. Brice and Mr. Kissel were smiling; they liked him, and enjoyed his foolishness, and that made it better, somehow.

After I'd misfired on the Latin, my father gave me a long talking-to about helping out with chores, so I went over to where Jennie and Mrs. Kissel and that Indian girl, Po-Povi, were cooking, and they said they needed fresh firewood. Jennie sent the girl along with me. Now there wasn't the least doubt in my mind that this Po-Povi—Water Flower, if you cared to believe her translation, which I didn't—was just as wicked as Pretty Walker, but I couldn't to save my life hate her. She was too sad.

My father was right about one thing, though. She was a worker; she didn't have to be told twice, she pitched in and put things to order. Mrs. Kissel said she had "more elbow grease" than five white people, and she mothered and fussed over her so gentle and kind you'd have thought she was her own blood kin. But what you wouldn't expect was that Jennie was crazy about her, too. When I got to figuring this out, I decided it was partly aimed at Coulter and me, because we were always running down Indians. Her liking of Po-Povi, you see, was a reproach to us.

We walked off toward the river, but firewood was scarce in this bare, alkali, wind-swept land. The girl had put an apron on, and when I asked her why, she said it was for "*bois de vache.*" As my father stated in his Journals, that's what the French fur traders called buffalo chips, and I wondered how much she had seen in the course of being dragged from one tribe to another. She could speak tolerably good English—quite a few words, though sometimes twisted—but to tell the truth she didn't speak at all unless necessary. She would bring us harm later—I felt sure about that—but she'd been given bad treatment, all right, and she wasn't much more than a child.

I studied her on the quiet: she was perfectly straight and had a nice line to her back; and while she carried her head high, her eyes seemed always to be cast down. Her hair was done up in the usual two pigtails on either side, and her lashes were long and silky. Her skin wasn't red, as people claimed about Indians, but was about the same shade as Coulter's, though smoother. She had on the same buckskin blouse and skirt and leggings, but without pretty bead-work, and she hadn't a single ornament whatever: no bracelets, no rings, no fancy belt, no velvet headband, no feathers, no copper wire, none of the things that make life rich to an Indian woman. She didn't need them. Her handsome carriage would have stood out, no matter what she wore. For a second, seeing the resemblance, I had a stab of pain about the Pawnee girl. We could have been friends.

But now I was itching to know what this Po-Povi thought of her new situation.

"Where did you live?" I asked her.

She looked over her shoulder and said, "Back, beyond."

"Behind the Chimney Rock?"

"Sometimes in a far country."

"How many suns?"

"Farther than the eagle flies without rest."

Afterward, I found out that her talk, when she made any, often was put in pictures that involved nature's things like eagles, clouds, sunsets and such like, and in other terms that came from Indian myths and legends, what my father called "the aboriginal fables of origin," going back to their great god, Glooscap.

I'd thought that sort of stuff was mostly in books people wrote about Indians, to make it sound like poetry.

For all she was aware of me, we might have lived a thousand years apart.

Along the riverbank was a scraggly line of drift, and I gathered an armful of sticks that didn't seem waterlogged; the girl found an apronful of buffalo chips. What buffalo were doing in this wasteland I didn't know, but later I learned that they crossed and recrossed the Platte forks going from place to place. The herds were smeared over the plains in such numbers that they spilled out everywhere.

Dark was closing down before we got back. Everybody was having supper late, because I suppose it was the first time they had felt like taking a breather. Up and down the line we could see fires glowing, and I heard a snatch of song. A wedding was tomorrow, we had come a long way toward California, things were peaceful for the moment, and spirits were generally high.

Since the first buffalo killed by Mr. Bledsoe, Coulter had organized a system of hunting one down nearly every other day. Mostly he did it himself, with help from the drovers. It wasn't pretty, but it was exciting: they'd ride into the fringe of a herd, bending low on the necks of their ponies, and fire buffalo guns almost against the animals' sides. Often you could see a blue ring of powder burn on the hide.

So we had buffalo meat all the time, now, and tonight we tackled it with a kind of holiday appetite. Even Brice was hungry, because he probably remembered it was customary to eat a hearty meal before they sprung the trap. I knew where my father was, well enough; he was up at the drovers' wagon, with Coulter and the rest of that rough crew. For the purpose of mischief, it was as close as he could come to shantyboating, and as a matter of fact, it was a little too close for comfort.

239

This Indian girl started to gnaw in the usual cannibally way of her bunch, but Mrs. Kissel set her right.

"Now, child, you don't want to take the chunk and worry it like a sawyer—put it on your plate, so, and cut it with a knife and fork. That's better. You'll get onto white ways soon, and you'll thank the blessed Lord for it."

I could see the girl's dark, clear eyes shine in the firelight, and for just an instant—a flicker and then gone—I thought she looked like smiling.

When supper was over I made up my mind to go forward after my father, but gave it up. I doubted if it would do any good. So I helped Po-Povi fix up a tent he had got her from a man that picked it out of cast-off rubbage, and saw that she was set. She'd slept with Jennie before, but now Jennie was getting married. I couldn't see that this made any difference, and said so, said: "Your tent's big enough for all three of you, and more. You and Brice could simply shove over, and there'd be room enough for four or five adults and a family of buffaloes. It's pure selfishness."

"You poor ninny," said Jenny, blushing, "don't you know *any-thing*?"

As usual, she'd dodged the issue. That was one of the main troubles with this schemer; she never could stick to the point.

When we got the tent fixed, I said, "Good night," and the girl said something in a language I didn't understand, so I concluded she was crazy. All Indians were crazy, more or less. But in a minute she stuck her head out of the flap and said, very low, "Doctor have trouble?"

"He's had it before. It comes on him regular."

"Po-Povi wait to make medicine."

"You'd better go to bed. He's a doctor, and if he can't cure himself he'd better hand in his bag."

"Indian medicines good for strong water."

I remembered the stuff they rubbed on those Pawnee boys, how it healed the slices in their chests, and wondered if we couldn't have some fun and maybe do good at the same time.

"I'll help you," I said. "I once worked with a very reputable Pawnee witch doctor, who stood practically at the head of his profession, and my father's taught me a lot, too. Where do we go?"

She took me by the hand, and on the way out, I snagged a lantern. After checking on Brice and the Kissels, to be sure they were bedded down, I let her lead me back toward the river. Inside my waist, I'd stuck one of my father's pistols, in case she was planning any monkey business. I didn't mean to be caught napping twice. But her aims were entirely medical.

On an ordinary night, we'd have as many as four sentinels out, but in this place, without any bad Indians around, and with festivities on hand, nobody saw the lantern at all. We were free to roam as we pleased.

She kept her nose practically to the ground, like a beagle, and I moseyed along beside, carrying the lantern. To tell the truth, I felt kindly toward her for taking such an interest. It wasn't *her* stomach that was involved, and if it had been me, I'd let it slide: the sicker he got, the more good it would do him. But she gathered little leaves here, and a berry or two there, and dug some roots at the water's edge, and peeled bark off of what looked like a willow shoot. To help out, I turned over some things I found, but she rejected them all. It made me sort of sore. One of them was poison sumac, she stated, and the other was something called "loco weed," that they try to keep from giving horses.

Well, it was pretty dark, even by the lantern, so I might have been wrong, but she could have been wrong just as easy. So every now and then, on the sly, I gathered up whatever she missed, for if I'd learned anything from those Pawnees, it was that nature is the best healer. You can't go wrong if you stick to the natural growths. They're laid right out for you, free of charge. All you have to do is pick them up.

When we arrived at one of those soda ponds, being a little backwash slough with a white deposit over the top, I collected a pocketful of dust that goes by the western name of "saleratus," which is practically the identical same thing as baking soda, and really first-rate for undigestion.

In about an hour, she had enough to suit her, and said we could make a very tolerable brew that would likely ease him when he came home. I had enough, too—my pockets were near about filled —so we went on back.

By now I was wrapped up in the work, and felt happy for my father. He was in luck; not many people backsliding like that have an unselfish bunch out moving heaven and earth to help him. I stirred up the fire and put on a kettle and she spent a long time mixing and testing. And when she turned around to throw out a beetle that had got in by mistake, and regretted it, by the look of him, I added *my* stuff. So we really had an uncommonly powerful remedy going; I was proud of it. It was maybe the first one like it ever brewed. And if you can judge anything by the smell, there was enough strength in that pot to clear up an epidemic of the bubonic plague. I never smelled anything like it, before or since.

"We've done a good job," I said when we finished. "I think that ought to hold him. I'm well satisfied with it. I doubt if he ever drinks anything again, even water."

The girl said the odor wasn't exactly what she had in mind—it seemed heartier than most medicines she'd fixed—but I didn't bother to mention my additions. There wasn't any reason for it. It would only produce argument, and if there's one thing I can't stand, it's wrangling with females. Even my father had lately commented on the uppity ways of women, after Jennie made some kind of statement about "equality." He said in a few years about the only field closed off to women would be fatherhood, and he imagined they'd find a way to get around that, too, before they were done. Jennie only said, "Stuff!" and "Vulgar," but I figured he was probably right: you couldn't fool him on scientific things.

We waited up another hour or more and then went to bed—it was beginning to look like a tiresome long haul. But it didn't seem I was asleep over a minute before I heard somebody singing, "Angus McGregor, Helpless in the Heather," which struck me as a very good choice, and then I heard a heavy sound like a thud, and then a moan, and a man's voice in a tent saying, "What in the name of Jupiter's going on out there?" So I got Po-Povi, who was already awake and dressed, and we ran over and picked him up. He had tripped on a guy rope, you understand, and taken a header into one of those slit trenches they dig to keep the water out.

He seemed to be enjoying himself, though when we got him on his feet, saying, "Shhh!" so as not to wake everybody, he appeared to drag his left leg, and said it was paralyzed. But in a minute he forgot about that and asked where's his hat, somebody had stole his hat. "There's nothing lower on earth than a hat thief," he said, then he started to sing about Angus McGregor again, so we hustled him right along to the tent. But he was sick before we got him laid down, and we had to wheel him outside and empty him. When we got back I said, "Conditions are perfect for the medicine. It's a good thing you thought of it; I want you to know I appreciate it."

She didn't waste time on polite gabble but helped me get to work. We had him down on his buffalo robe, partly moaning and partly trying to sing the second verse of the song, which wasn't really fit for a young girl's ears, so whenever it began to come out, I sort of stopped him up for a second with a sock, taking care to let him breathe on schedule. But now we had the problem of trying to get the medicine down, and it was a puzzler. Whenever the girl tried to pour in some out of a cup, he thrashed around and spilled it. We were about strapped for a way out, when I said, "There's only one solution—we'll have to use the coal-oil funnel. It's just the ticket." She looked doubtful, but there wasn't time to complain. I got the funnel and shook it out carefully, because of course we didn't want coal oil in the remedy, and put the end in his mouth, and after that we waltzed along. He spit the first dose straight up in the air, like a geyser, but after that it appeared to go much easier. There wasn't any doubts about it; that medicine took the fight out of him in a hurry.

I don't much like to tell the next part, but I've got to own up and face it. Along toward 3 A.M., with me asleep on my robe and Po-

Povi gone to her tent, my father began to make some very peculiar noises, like a volcano that's about to give notice. Then he raised up and said he was dying. He looked so white and sober I believed it, too. So I got the girl and we talked it over pretty fast. She knelt over him, and looked confused. "Don't worry," I said. "It isn't your fault. The medicine's taken him wrong—it does that sometimes. I'd better go for Doctor Merton." I was back in ten minutes, but I must say that this Dr. Merton appeared to be in a poor humor, and said he hoped it wasn't any kind of joke; he'd be obliged "to make representations in the proper quarter."

But it wasn't. He took one look at my father, counted his pulse, tested his temperature, listened to his heart with a heart cone, and told me to rouse Mr. Kissel at once. We sat outside the tent, Po-Povi and I, and waited. I'll have to admit I was a little worried. It's entirely possible that nobody but a doctor should make medicine; I realize that now. But to give her credit, I believe the Indian girl was on the right track. Somewhere along the line, I'd thrown the remedy out of balance. I don't know where I went off but I guess I learned a lesson.

It was nearly dawn when Dr. Merton came out, rolling down his sleeves. "It's all right," he said. "He'll live. But I don't mind telling you it was a very narrow squeak. You woke me just in time; another half hour and it might have been a different story."

He said my father appeared to have swallowed a very powerful alkali, "on the order of lime or lye," and that there was evidence of further poisons that he hadn't come in contact with during his professional career. "Altogether," he said, "it's been a very singular case, though there are aspects of it I hope to illuminate more fully later on."

I didn't hope so. I said my father had drunk some whiskey up at the drovers', and had likely got hold of a piece of tainted meat. "Mr. Coe also gave him some sherry," I said, "and it looked old to me. All the printing had faded off the label. I'll make any bet that bottle had gone bad."

"Interesting explanation," said Dr. Merton, and left. I didn't say anything else; I wasn't feeling very brash.

Well, they had the wedding at noon, and I took good care not to get out of line. They had three little flower girls, and me, but I said I wouldn't put on a dress to see the Queen of England get married to King Solomon, so they let me wash up and join in anyhow. A man whose name I've forgotten with a wooden leg played the fiddle, and played it very well, too, and some of the women had baked a real winner of a cake, with what they called "matrimonial devices" on top. They handed it around; each person got a piece, even the children.

Some way or other, this wedding had a different effect on me than what I'd imagined. It was pretty. Jennie looked as handsome and blushing and smiling as a bud that's just opened up, and softer, you would say, than usual. They had wax candles, just like a regular wedding, back home, and with that awesome high Chimney Rock in the background, it was kind of solemn. The officiating was done by a Reverend Mr. Campbell, a tall, baldish man with hair in his ears and a voice on the order of a soothery foghorn, mellow and churchy, and an interesting way of coming out strong on the last letter of a word, making it more important, such as "folks-ah," whilst rocking up on his toes at the same time, and he read a beautiful service. Weddings *can* get at you; there's no doubt about it. I hate to say so, but for removing all the frivolity out of a person, they've got it over funerals.

The only things that went wrong, from Jennie's side, were that my father, who meant to give the bride away, was flat on his back in bed, and that Mr. Kissel, the best man, was also laid up, with a severe cold and fever of over a hundred. It was rotten bad luck, but my father called her in and said he'd fixed everything so nobody would suffer; the festivities wouldn't be hampered any. He said he'd appointed Mr. Coulter to act in his place and that Mr. Coe would be best man. "The two most distinguished personages of the train. And God bless you, child. I'll be thinking of you as I lie here in my pain."

Well, *wasn't* she mad? For a man as intellectural about some things, my father could be an awful fool when he tried. If he'd gone to work and picked Benedict Arnold to give the bride away he couldn't have made a worse choice than Coulter. Her eyes just blazed, and her color was so high I thought she'd explode. But it was too late to do anything now—there weren't only a few hours left— so she flounced out and went about trying on the elegant dress Mrs. Kissel had made with her own hands, the good, kind soul, with all the other things she had to do, too.

When the Honorable Coe heard about his last-minute substitution, he was as pleased as punch. He was a very fine-mannered man; everybody said so. And from that point forward, he practically took over the wedding. He declared that everything must be in order according to the rules. He had a book on ettiket, as they said, and he brushed up on his duties as best man; he told them he'd done it twice before but had become rusty. Digging into it deeper, he saw there were some problems to get over, if you went by the book. For example, he was supposed to either get the railroad tickets for the groom or hire a carriage for him if they stayed in town. It was awkward. There weren't any railroads around for miles, and the only carriages in sight were these big old lumbering wagons, and they were full of things like pots and pans and rocking chairs and children and garden scythes and such like. So he had to give that part of it up. Then he read, aloud, that the main duties of a best man were to be " 'valet, expressman, and companion-in-ordinary,' " but since Brice wasn't going anywhere to speak of, there wasn't any packing to do, so Coe just concentrated on being a valet.

And he did a bang-up job of it. I saw so many people congratulating him after the ceremony you'd have thought it was him that got married instead of Brice. He had on striped pants and a frock coat and a flowing pearl-gray tie, and he dressed Brice up just as gaudy, out of his own wardrobe.

I don't want to make Coe sound silly, because he worked like a dog at this wedding. His heart was in it; he gave it class. Jennie told me the other day—I mean a long time after this—that what Mr.

Coe did in his officious, pompousy way provided her with something nice to have always about this wedding.

Those words make me realize what I should have known years before, that Jennie really cared for that poor, bewildered Brice. She looked upon him as something that needed mothering, and cherishing, and if she mistook it for love, a lot of others have done the same thing, just as my father said. They *both* needed somebody, so it was all right.

At the last minute, she decided to have a maid of honor and she dressed little Po-Povi up in a real linen dress that set off her dusky skin and made her nearly as respectable as a white person. She was proud-looking; her eyes practically sparkled for a change, and instead of being somber, her mouth was curved in a half-smile.

When the wooden-legged man, who I think they called him Jim Hardesty—he'd once had an argument with a buzz saw, and lost—struck up the wedding march, everybody got downright teary. I could feel the goose-pimples coming out on my arms. Coe, with his long blond mane and moustaches carefully brushed, and Brice at his side, marched up the little aisle they formed, stately and grand, and then Jennie came forward, with her hand resting very lightly on Coulter's arm. For once, there wasn't any frippery about this roughneck. He didn't only seem deadly serious, he looked almost angry, and his face had turned a funny kind of pale under his tan. I couldn't understand it. But Jennie *was* beautiful—only a fool could deny it—and I had some guilty thoughts about the ways I'd plagued her. All at once it came to me that she meant as well as could be expected. She was bossy and peckish, but she'd gone through a lot of troubles, and lost her entire family. Looking at her shining, strong-featured face, and thinking what a good shotgun shot she was, I almost loved her.

The Reverend Mr. Campbell read the service and pronounced them man and wife. Coulter started to turn away, but after Brice had kissed the bride, he took Jennie by the shoulders roughly and gave her a kiss that made everybody gasp. It really shook her. And when he let loose, she slapped his face. In a second, everybody had passed it off as a joke, and Coulter disappeared. Then they tackled a fine wedding luncheon, or as good as you can manage with the sort of fodder we had, and Jim Hardesty fiddled for dancing all afternoon long. It was the pleasantest time these people had seen in weeks. Nobody got drunk, if you except my father's indisposition in the tent; nobody got in a fight; nothing broke down anywhere. It was as peaceful a wedding as the frontier had ever seen; I heard one of the drovers say so, but he didn't sound happy about it.

That night, all worn out, I crawled into our tent, and lay there, suffering a little but not knowing why. I felt blue, now that it was over.

"Is that you, son?"

I said, "Yes, father."

"Wedding went off like clockwork, didn't it?"

"Yes."

"Bride got a lot of fine presents?"

"Yes, father."

He himself had given them a handsome silver carving set he'd picked up somewhere along the trail and carefully saved away for just such an occasion.

"You still there, son?" It was such a stupid question that it sort of broke the camel's back, so to speak. I began to whimper; I couldn't help it.

"You come over here," he said, and I did so, and hung on. Maybe you think it's sissified, but all of a sudden I missed my mother.

"Now, Jaimie, boy, I know you're ashamed of me, and I don't blame you, but I want you to believe it won't happen again. You'll be grown soon—you're shooting up fast—and you'll understand that adults, in their way, are fuller of flaws than children. We'll make this trip, and we *will* get the gold, and we'll go back to Louisville in a hurry. You'd like to see your mother, wouldn't you?"

I said yes, rubbing at my eyes with my sleeve. "You'll see her, my boy, and you'll see her soon. Now before we go to sleep, let's dream for a minute about the good fun that lies ahead. When you make your strike, you know, you build an oblong, sloping, 12-foot trough that they call a 'Long Tom'—for the water that does the washing—and at the bottom of it you have a piece of flat, perforated sheet-iron, resting directly over what's known as a 'riffle box.' "

He went on, painting the pretty pictures, cheery and optimistic, just as always, and inside I think he was dying. We seldom know anybody until it's too late.

Chapter XXVI

During the next few days we encountered any number of people turning back, for one reason and another. It was discouraging, because we began to have troubles, too. We were now in the Western Nebraskas, moving up the north fork of the Platte toward Fort Laramie and the junction of the Laramie River. We had mostly passed the plains, and were in a kind of foothilly, boulder-strewn land that lay before the mountains. There was grass, but it was cropped down and eaten away because they said a caravan of Mormons was up ahead, and they wouldn't only consume the blades but generally took the roots along with them, and felt sorrowful if they had to leave the soil.

Anyhow, the grass that was left was full of stickers and burrs, and crawling all over with crickets so fat they made good targets for a slingshot. I had a very good time all one morning, counting up as many as twenty-five solid hits, until a small granite pebble, no bigger than your thumb, and certainly nothing to make a fuss about, glanced off a rock and hit a Mr. Millsap behind the left ear. After they got him back on his feet, he spoke up pretty brisk, being probably in a bad humor about something, and my father made me put the slingshot in the wagon.

The area all about was so rocky and coarse, and graveled everybody so much, that Coulter told us to put on heavy boots if we had them. So my father traded for a pair of cowhide boots with a party returning to Ohio, but he said they were too stiff and rubbed his right ankle above the "malleolus internus."

The road had become littered with dead oxen. The more that

died, the harder the wagons were to pull, because now we were going uphill considerable, too. One of Mr. Kissel's animals dropped dead in its traces and another lost its cud. But when we stopped to noon, near a very mired-up quaggy place, they gave it a piece of fat bacon dipped in salt, and it was soon chewing again. But nobody looked very glad, neither in our own group or up and down the train.

The third night out from Chimney Rock, camped on a plain beyond a place they called Scott's Bluffs, where we could see the peaks of the Rocky Mountains in the distance, we had an electric storm that scared everybody half to death but hardly did any damage at all. The left rear wheel of one wagon was smoked up where a bolt hit a bush nearby; that was all. But that lightning squirted around as if the whole sky was on fire. Nobody in the train had ever seen anything like it. For about an hour it was as pale as day and the air just quivered; the lightning was going all the time, never any let up. There was such a crackling and hissing of current that it crawled along the wagon tops in a blue-white liquid, and rolled and dripped off nearly everything in sight. It's a wonder we weren't all killed.

Lying flat on our robes but with the tent flap open so we could see, my father made some remarks about a man named Ben Franklin, who had gone out in such a storm to fly a kite, he didn't say why. Drunk, likely. I didn't pursue it. My father had some most amazingly ignorant patients, and there weren't half of them ever paid up from one year to the next. But I remembered now there was a family of Franklins, poor white trash, filthy and uneducated, used to sell catfish out of a peddler's cart in Louisville, and one of them was said to be a half-wit. That was it, then; that must be this same Ben. Why, a child would know better than to take a kite out under conditions like these.

From here on toward Laramie, things got worse; even Coulter seemed downhearted. The wife of one man, a Mrs. Gurney, died of galloping pneumonia, and a number of other people were sick in their wagons. It kept my father and Dr. Merton on the jump all the time, and many a time way off in the night, I'd awaken, struggling up not quite to being conscious, the way you do, and hear somebody whispering in his ear that a person needed tending. He looked worried, and he was so peaked and drawn I wondered if he wasn't apt to get sick himself. But he kept encouraging people, and telling them how close we were to California—though we hadn't got halfway yet—and finally, in a burst of confidence he wrote my mother a letter that for plain, downright humbug surpassed anything he'd come up with yet. I know because he read it to me and asked me if I thought it "misrepresentational." I was tempted to tell him it was nothing but a pack of lies, but I didn't have the heart. In the business of writing one of those letters, he always worked things around to believe it himself, partly, so was in a better frame of mind.

It was an interesting letter, though, and laid stress on everybody's "exceptionally robust" health, their bouncing good spirits, and their all-around satisfaction that they'd decided to come. He gave it to three men from Oregon who were heading back to Missouri and raise a flock of sheep to drive out. They said they'd post it, the first chance they got, and in return my father tested one of them that he said was anemic and advised him to take a long sea voyage and rest up. The honest truth is that, along in here, he was so ground down and overworked he was sort of addled.

Even so, he hardly let a day go by without writing an addition to his Journals, and in these he was as honest as anybody could get. I believe, today, that down underneath he felt he could excuse everything—debts, drinking, skylarking off for gold, all the doubts that plagued and chafed him—if he would leave behind a good, true, faithful document of pioneering that people might read later and profit from. As he saw it, this was his contribution now, far more than doctoring, and he put into it every ounce of uprightness that formed the core of his disposition.

On the twentieth of August he wrote that, "The road is getting heavy with sand; it's a dead, heavy pull, and we are compelled to rest the oxen often. As a person walks, his foot slips back one or two inches. We have passed Horse Creek, over a sandy, barren country. Now must use sagebrush for fuel, as the buffalo are, for the moment at least, behind us. We are finding the carrot seed troublesome. It sticks to both blankets and clothes . . ."

And a few days later, after riding Cream up a slope a mile or so ahead, he sat down on a rock and wrote: "Because of the saline incrustations, I have noticed little ulcers in many of the horses' noses. At first, I was fearful that these might develop into full-fledged cases of glanders, but all of them responded well enough to a treatment by washing in a weak solution of alum.

"The sand in places has been very loose, and often blazing-hot. The wheels now are apt to sink in as far as eighteen inches, making such a dire pull for the poor, exhausted, uncomplaining oxen that we are, again, discussing the common alternative of 'packing', that is, shifting our cargoes as well as feasible to the backs of mules and continuing our journey on foot. Coulter himself mentioned this only yesterday, and I foresee that a crisis in our resolution may develop at Fort Laramie, a more or less civilized outpost some miles distant on the trail. The wagon wheels, being constantly immersed in hot sand, are taking punishment of the most damaging kind. The felloes and naves shrink, the tyres loosen, and the spokes rattle like a bag of bones. For a while we were able to cure this by wedging and submerging them in water, but they are now far advanced on the road to disintegration."

We reached Fort Laramie several days after this last entry, and found some excitement. Camped on the plain all around were upwards of three thousand Sioux, their horses staked out grazing, and about six hundred lodges sticking up like a harvest of tied-together corn shocks. It was a sight to behold. But before we got to them, we went by Fort Bernard, which wasn't any more than a lopsided building made out of crude logs with holes punched in them to shoot through. Nearby, as Coulter rode up, followed by the first wagons of the train, stood a drove of mules tended by some Mexican Indians that kept saluting us by flashing the sun off a broken piece of looking glass. It was annoying; I could see Coulter trying to hang on to his temper. For once, he did it tolerably well.

We stopped there only a few minutes, while some of the men talked about mules to a Mr. Richard, who was the principal of the post, as they called it. He was a big, red-faced man with white hair, not overly clean, not what you'd call sober, either, although the sun was perfectly high overhead. He invited us all to stay the night, meaning to sleep in our tents as usual, I judged. You couldn't have herded all those people into the Fort without a very rackety jamboree, and one of the men of the train, a crude fool that cracked the rawest sort of jokes whenever anybody got near enough to listen, which was seldom, said, "I wouldn't care to take the chancet. My ol' woman ain't no rose, but she's all I've got, and if we was to bundle in that cubbyhole she might scoot into the wrong bag by mistake. Could be I'd wake up brother-in-law to a Navahoo."

This was certainly a poor joke, and three or four people told him so, said it was "indelicate," but it didn't faze him any. He bit off a chew of tobacco and had a very good time laughing; then he left, saying he was going back to tell his old woman, because he knew she'd enjoy it, too.

We moved on to Laramie, where the members of the train wanted to lay in supplies, those that could afford them, and make plans about what to do from here. A celebration was concluding when we pulled up; the Sioux had been doing a war dance inside. Somebody said the big encampment was because these Indians were planning to attack the Snakes and Crows, who were their natural enemies. They spilled out of the adobe gate in whooping bunches, shaking tomahawks and having a merry old time, and it wasn't long before we saw they were mainly drunk. The women, too. These women were throwing themselves around in any old way, shaking their hips, and making gestures at our men in what several people said were "disgusting," and "indecent" attitudes.

They weren't any bad-looking women, either. A light copper color, some rouged on their cheeks, and dressed very rich, many of them, with buckskin worked up somehow so as to make it a creamy white, wonderfully soft, and with shirt, pantaloons and moccasins decorated all around with porcelain beads of many colors. How these last shone and sparkled. Jennie said they were brazen hussies, and Po-Povi, walking beside me, seemed nervous at so many of her kind; she wouldn't look at them at all.

Well, one of these women—not more than a girl—came up suddenly and flung her arms around Brice, who couldn't have been more surprised if she'd peeled off her clothes, and Jennie cracked her smartly over the head with a skin reticule full of knickknacks. It was a beautiful lick. That girl's eyes actually crossed—she was right in front of me and I saw them—and her legs wobbled her all around in a circle. I noticed Coulter move his right hand easily toward his revolver, but nothing came of it. The braves thought it was a prime good joke; they almost died laughing, the way a drunk's apt to. Several of them walked forward, in mock interest and sympathy, to feel of the girl's bump, but once they'd touched it, they collapsed with hilarity. This was just the kind of fun they liked. If the girl's neck had been busted, they would have declared a national holiday and feasted for a week.

Still and all, these braves made a fine appearance: big men, fierce and proud. Later on, somebody in the Fort said there were eight to ten thousand Sioux altogether, of all nations. They claimed lands that extended over hundreds of thousands of square miles, but a lot of others claimed them, too, so there was always fighting. But the Sioux generally got the best of it, except when they found themselves odds-even against the Crows. The Crows were the toughest fighters anywhere, and the cruelest, if you want to except the Blackfeet, who were born with the outlook of a mountain lion and got steadily worse as they grew older. Among other things the Sioux claimed was this Fort Laramie, so the white men that ran it, called the American Fur Company, let them go right ahead. It didn't bother anybody to be claimed; it didn't cost anything; and it made the Sioux look better to other tribes. The only objections the Indians ever had around the Fort were to the crops that people occasionally set out. For some reason, these Sioux were powerful down on farming. They were buffalo hunters and didn't cotton to agriculture. So once in a while, to keep their hand in, and make their claim more valid, a bunch rode down and scattered the crops. In that way, they could maintain friendly relations and not have to massacre anybody; they'd showed who was boss. What's more, they kept a handy place to buy whiskey, this way, and sometimes muskets and rifles. But only a few braves that I saw had guns; most were armed with knives and tomahawks, bows and arrows, and such.

The Fort itself was made out of the meanest kind of adobe, or sun-dried brick, undecorated, formed in what they call a military quadrangle, the walls having watch towers on the corners, and the gate protected by two brass swivel cannons. Along one side of the court, built into the walls, were offices and storerooms and mechanical shops, like a smithy, and against the opposite wall was the main building. The whole enclosure took up about three quarters of an acre. A few raggedy soldiers lounged here and there, with more Mexicans and Indians, a handful of traders, and trappers, the remnants of wagon trains that hadn't made it, and altogether the scene wasn't by any means one to perk up your spirits.

Well, while my father and some others went over to pay their respects to a Captain Cooper, and to the head of the Fur Company, a man named Monseer Burdeau, we loafed around and took in the sights. A few of our people bought things, but it wasn't easy because the prices were so high. Coffee, sugar and tobacco were a dollar a pound, flour was fifty cents a pint, and they claimed whiskey was a dollar a pint, but I didn't price it. Coulter rode his horse in to get the forward off-hoof shod, and did considerable grumbling at the blacksmith, which seemed like a poor idea because this fellow was about as broad as Mr. Kissel, though shorter, and had arms like young oak trees. He was wearing a pair of hide pants, a jersey, and a leather apron all marked up with burns, from flying sparks. His naked arms and shoulders were covered with red fur as thick as an ape's, but he hadn't a hair on his head. Perfectly bald and shiny, not even a fringe around the edge. It often works that way, I've noticed. Remove the clothes off an entirely bald man and you'll find that, in the line of growing hair, his strength was laid out elsewhere. On the other hand, I never saw a bald Indian or one with any hair to speak of except on his head; they've struck a nice balance that way, and seem advanced over the whites.

We had come abreast the little shop, noisy and jammed, where they sold whiskey, when out rolled two or three Indians and a couple of white men, and I opened my mouth, because they were John and Shep, but Shep stepped up to Coulter, as brash as you please, and sung out, very sneery:

"Well, if ain't my old friend and neighbor, Buck Coulter!"

I'd never seen Coulter look so. He looked sick. But he stood his ground, though not with any feist in him, while Jennie and Po-Povi and I and some others sort of washed back to give them room. All right, Mr. Baggott, I thought, this is where you get what's coming. There won't be enough left to shovel up and carry outside for the coyotes.

"Now what might you be doing out here?" said Baggott. "Come to try your hand with a bow and arrer?" This seemed to strike him as funny, for he gave a rude laugh before going on. "What's the dodge, Buck?"

"No dodge," replied Coulter very low, glancing around uneasily, as if he'd prefer to conduct this conversation in private.

None of us could believe it.

"Speak up, Buck. You don't act very friendly to your old boyhood chum. It ain't genteel. Cat got your tongue?"

Coulter took off his hat and wiped his forehead with his sleeve. "Let's get a drink."

"I don't like to drink when I've got to face a party all the time. It's galling to the nerves."

Coulter started to turn away, but Shep called out, "Don't tell me you've got yourself a train, Buck. Have you writ home lately? Maybe you ought to tell these people about your brother. Where you going, Buck? Why, I've never seed you so jumpy."

He bellowed out his laugh as Coulter lurched past us and, shouldering aside some Indians, through the gate. I felt so low I could have crawled off and cried. I noticed that those of our men who were nearby looked grim and shook their heads. I reckon we'd come to think of Coulter as a kind of hero, no matter how raspy he was, and now he'd turned tail before a drunken bully like the meanest sneak and coward.

I could see tears in Jennie's eyes; then Shep saw her, too. He took in the rest of us for the first time. A little of his bluster faded off—you couldn't deny that, but he cried, "Well, what are *you* aiming to do? You won't find any law out here."

Jennie blazed right out: "Wait and see, you bloodthirsty beast. We'll have you tarred and feathered and ridden out of this Fort. *Doctor! Doctor!*" and taking Po-Povi's hand, she started running toward the offices across the court.

"Come on, you noisy blabbermouth," said John, speaking up at last. He took Shep by the arm and dragged him aside, but before they left he wheeled back to me.

"Look here, boy, I wouldn't advise you to make trouble, you hear? It might be onhealthy."

I'd be a liar if I said they didn't scare me; I'd seen them do murder, and a poor, young wife and her husband laid out on the ground with their guts out; but I had my slingshot with me, and lots of people were about. What's more, I hated those monsters more than I ever hated anybody before. I almost got insane with it when I saw them, and didn't altogether make sense.

"Shut up," I yelled. "I'll do what I please, you dirty scum. My father and Buck Coulter'll see you hung before we leave here." And then I did something I'd never seen anybody do, except the Pawnees. It just seemed to come natural. I stepped forward and spit in John's face. It refreshed me a good deal.

"Why, you damned imp——" he broke out, reaching toward his belt, but I jumped back and yanked out my slingshot and fitted a smooth round rock to it that I'd been saving in my pocket, and hit him, thud, directly over the right eye. The rock hung there a second, then dropped. He fell forward on his face in the dust like an old tobacco shed crashing down.

I didn't wait around any longer, then. I took to my heels as fast as I could go, and a minute later found where my father and the others were. I was shaking all over and had flecks of saliva, dry and cottony, in the corners of my mouth. It was the first time in my life I'd ever tried to kill somebody, and I didn't feel so good.

Two or three of our men that were right behind me started telling about it, and between them and me, and Jennie raising the roof, there was a rumpus in that office, you bet. Everybody was shouting at once, and crying, some of the women, and asking questions, but above it all that Captain Cooper, a tall, thin, gray-eyed man with a very sallow face—no red in it anywhere—raised his voice, perfectly steady and firm, and folks calmed down a little. Some people can do that as natural as breathing; you can't learn it; it's born in them. A nearsighted idiot could have spotted this Captain Cooper for a leader a mile off. His manner wasn't stern, but you wouldn't have taken any more liberties with him than you would with a loaded rifle.

"It's a ticklish situation," he said, after my father had snatched down a musket from a rack and shoved it over to Kissel. "There isn't any civil law here, neither is the Fort to say under outright military rule. What's more, we're surrounded by thousands of Sioux warriors that let renegade carrion, like Baggott and Murrel, live among them peaceably—in effect under their protection. I assure you of my sincere desire to help, but we must proceed with extreme caution."

My father wrote down in his Journals what Captain Cooper said, which was that "the Rocky Mountains have their white as well as their copper-colored population. I would estimate the former as from five hundred to a thousand, scattered among the Indians, and inhabiting, temporarily, the various trading posts of the fur companies. Adventure, romance, avarice, misanthropy, and sometimes social outlawry play their part in enticing or driving these persons into this savage wilderness. After taking up their abode here, they rarely return to civilized life for long. They usually contract ties with the Indians that are sufficiently strong to induce their return, if

259

they occasionally visit the settlements. Many have Indian wives and large families. Polygamy is not uncommon. They conform to savage customs, and on account of their superior intelligence have much influence over the Indians, frequently directing their movements and policy in peace and war."

"Captain," cried my father when he'd finished, "something's got to be done! We can't let those scoundrels get off scot-free. Why, they barricaded up the entire family of this child here"—he laid his hand on Jennie's shoulder—"and burned them alive in a cabin."

"Sir, we'll do our best. If we can persuade them from the hands of the Sioux without a commotion, I'll return them to St. Louis under guard, no matter what the legality of it. That much I promise. Mr. Chouteau's reputation is well known out here, and his correspondent, Bridger, is a personal friend of mine."

Well, we all agreed that this was as handsome as anyone could wish, so we trailed back to our wagons, with some of us, including my father and the Kissels and Coe and the Brices, accepting an invitation to dinner that evening in the Fort. On the way, we talked about Coulter's odd actions, but nobody could think of anything handy to say. It cast a damper over us all.

When we reached the train, people were standing around in little knots and clusters, and sure enough, they were discussing the trouble, too. Coulter was nowhere to be seen. The general opinion, as people got the whole story, was that he had neglected to do his duty in protecting the train. I heard some angry mutters about throwing him out, and there were others that wanted to haul him before a "summary court."

My father and Mr. Coe soothed them down for now, but there was a lot of determination to bring matters to a head. I can tell you truly, I wasn't much looking forward to tomorrow.

Toward twilight, the Kissels bundled the children in their wagon and made arrangements with neighbors to check them once in a while. Then we went to the Fort and had dinner. Mr. Cooper was there, and Monseer Burdeau, and other gentlemen of the American Fur Company. It was mannery and elegant, with wine that had been carted clear across the plains. I'd a had a glass except that Jennie reached over and took it away. It wasn't her wine, it wasn't her dinner, it was none of her business in any way, but she had to shove her nose in just the same. Marriage didn't seem to have straightened her out.

"Your boy, ma'am?" inquired one of the guests, a man wearing a frilly white shirt with sideburns, and Jennie answered back, very tart, "No, I didn't have any babies when I was seven, thank you for asking."

The food was an improvement over what we'd been eating, but it was cooked pretty careless, not like Mrs. Kissel's, which had *flavor*. No matter what she cooked, it had flavor. She could have made a stew out of cactus and rocks, and nobody would have had any grounds for complaint. Still, she never seemed satisfied; nothing turned out right, according to her. The bread generally had a "sad streak," things fell that were supposed to rise; if she reached for the salt, it turned out to be sugar; and she never really got a good "do" on anything, to hear her tell it.

My father stated that this was the usual dissatisfaction of the artist. "It takes two men to paint a picture," he said. "One to do the job, and another to stop him when it's finished. My advice to you is, if Mrs. Kissel gives evidence of satisfaction, sprint, don't walk, for the stomach pills."

Anyhow, here tonight we had boiled corned beef, cold biscuits, fresh buffalo meat, venison, salt beef, and milk. It was a regular feast, because they'd got in some flour, after being without it for upwards of six weeks.

"We eat what we can get," said Captain Cooper. "After a while it doesn't seem to make much diff—— What's that?"

All of us heard it—a whoop from outside somewhere, more of a scream than a shout. The men scrambled up, some taking the pains to excuse themselves, and we ran out. The night was coal-black, but in the direction of our wagons the sky was aglow with red. It was scary-looking; fire always is. It's a sight I'll never get used to. It knots up your stomach.

When we reached the gate, we could see greasy yellow smoke boiling against the red, and outside, we heard a babble of people yelling and running, wagons being moved, horses rearing and neighing, and men bawling directions.

By the time we got there it was over. Nothing remained of Kissel's wagon but a skeleton, where the iron parts held it together. The furnishings and household truck were no more than pieces of char, black and ruined.

Then we heard Mrs. Kissel cry, "My babies! my babies!" and I almost sunk through the ground. All four of those children were in that wagon while we had dinner, with only the neighbor to check.

She tried to charge into the middle of the smoke, but her husband grabbed her and held her, lifting her up, kicking, and turning her away from the ruins. It was enough to make you sick.

Then I heard a man cry, "Doctor, over here, doctor!" and I scrambled my way through some people to where they had something laid out on the ground. It was a welcome sight, I can tell you. Propped up in a row, making a noise which came pretty close to drowning everything else out, were Deuteronomy, Leviticus, Micah and Lamentations, and sitting beside them on the grass, his head almost between his legs, as two women and a man tore away burning pieces of cloth, was Coulter.

"He did it all himself," one of the women called up to Mrs. Kissel. "He went after them, two at a time, and brought them out, and now look at him."

Coulter was a sight. Nearly all of his black hair had burned off, his forehead was cracked and purple, he hadn't any more eyelashes than a snake, what little clothing was left still smoked, and his hands were dripping blood. I probably shouldn't mention it, but his pants were so far gone that he was completely exposed, you might say. And with a man the size of Coulter, he was more exposed than most. But nobody appeared to mind or take any notice. Then a soldier from the Fort covered his lower half with a blanket.

Mrs. Kissel knelt down amongst her brood and swept them all together at once, and Mr. Kissel leaned over beside Coulter.

"Can you hear me, Coulter?"

Coulter raised his head a little, trying to look up.

"Is that you, Kissel?"

Everything was quiet; the people wanted to hear what was said, but some of the women were taking on a little, and two or three men, including my father, blew their noses.

"You'd better call the roll," Coulter told him. "I think I counted four altogether."

"Coulter," said Matt, "you're more of a man than any ten in this train. The next one raises his voice or hand against you"— he turned and looked around slowly—"is going to have me to whip."

Coulter gave a dry kind of chuckle that ended in a cough; then he said, "I wouldn't envy him, I sure wouldn't."

My father and Dr. Merton walked forward now and took over. They, and others, picked Coulter up and made to carry him to the Brices' wagon, but Captain Cooper stepped up and said, "I'd be pleased if you'd take him to my apartment."

I saw Jennie's pale face watching as they carried him away. I figured maybe she thought she was even at last for all the rowing they had done; she always seemed to hate him so.

When they were gone, we got the story. That neighbor woman, Mrs. Hughes, had looked into the wagon the second time when, on the way back to her own, she noticed two men, one old and lank and gray-haired, the other an oversized, red-faced hulk, picking their way up the train, inspecting the wagons as they went. She saw them particular, for they appeared shifty and spoke in low whispers.

Ten minutes later, she heard a cry of "Fire! fire!" but when she and her husband and others went running, the Kissels' wagon was already roaring.

Coulter, horseback, arrived a few seconds later. He took the news on the run, then spun himself off the saddle and right through the burning canvas.

Everybody stood talking, and one of the men who was so outspoken against him before, said, "It was the bravest act I ever witnessed. Speaking for myself, I'm mortal ashamed I backbit him to begin with. A man ort to withhold judgment till he's sure."

That seemed to be the sentiment all around. There wasn't any harm in these people; they were only average. Most of their bad thoughts came out of fear, and to tell the truth, that's what causes most of the troubles in the world.

It didn't take long to figure that John and Shep had fired the wagon out of spite, because Captain Cooper had sent notice among the Indians that he wished to see them. Whether they knew about the children, nobody could say, but for my part, I imagined they had.

But there was something else on my mind, and I had to work fast. My bag of gold coins, that I'd got when the man fell in the paddle wheel, several centuries ago, was in that wreckage, and I wanted it. In addition, we'd be needing it, now. Little bits of wood were still burning as I began sifting through them with a rake. One or two people asked what I was doing, so I said Mrs. Kissel had lost an old family heirloom, a cameo brooch, and wanted me to find it. When they offered to help, I said Mrs. Kissel had given me fifty cents for the job, so I'd better do it myself if it took all night. It almost did, too. The coins had turned black, but they weren't melted; they were all in a little pile, under some barrel hoops. I fished them out, juggling them back and forth, because they were warm, and stuck them in my pocket. And when I stepped out, I saw that almost nobody had gone to bed. They were still standing around talking, women talking to women, and men to men, now and then breaking off to threaten various children that kept popping out of bed.

The feeling ran pretty high. The same men that had been so hard against Coulter before were now itching to go after the new villains. They sent a deputation to Captain Cooper and demanded that he dispatch troops on a search. But Cooper said it would be unwise, because the Indians might boil up all around us. "Let things quieten down a little," he said. "Then we'll try to sneak them out on the sly."

The deputation came back, and everybody grumbled, and said it was a case of typical Army procrastination. Then one man said he'd be durned if he knew what he paid taxes for. "Here we set this Army up, living off the fat of the land, fresh meat every few days, flour once a month, and wine for company—all out of my pocket—and when an emergency arises, where are they? Nowhere. And what will they do? Nothing. For two cents I'd move to Mexico."

My father said it would be quite a loss, but he imagined the country could rise above it. Then he told me, "I'll bet that fellow's never paid a dime's worth of taxes in his life. Whenever you hear somebody making any noise about his 'rights,' you can be sure he's got a very thin claim on them. Moreover, if the Army called for volunteers in a crisis, our belligerent friend would vanish in a cloud of dust."

My father stayed with Coulter all the next day, and also treated the children, who had burns that weren't very serious. Coulter was a different proposition. "He'll be scarred," my father said. "Eventually, it may clear up, but I'm afraid he's bound to be marked, both face and hands."

Comparatively, this wasn't bad news. For a while, there were doubts whether he'd live. He was burned bad. But they covered him over, head to foot, with an oily salve, and gave him morphine for the pain, which they said would come in about twenty-four hours.

Po-Povi gathered some bark and soaked it in scalding water, and when my father and Dr. Merton started to throw it out, Coulter came to and objected. "It works, it works," he said. "I've seen it myself." Then he and the girl exchanged a few Indian sentences, and she took a rag and bathed him all over with the bark water. Anybody else might have been embarrassed, but she paid no more heed to his nakedness than if he'd been a horse. Before she was finished, Mrs. Kissel came in to help, sitting beside his bed all one night, but they wouldn't admit Jennie because they said he was in a state of "intermittent excitation" and it wasn't good for a girl of her years and position.

"Tommyrot," she snapped. "What do you think I married, a mummy?"

But she didn't get her way this time—Captain Cooper saw to that, and I couldn't have been more pleased.

She said, "Men are numbskulls—they're nothing but children, full of vanity and self-worship. If they only knew how women laugh at them."

"Why don't you get some of the stuff and go home and rub it on Mr. Brice," I said.

She boxed my jaws again; confound the girl, I couldn't seem to learn how to duck on schedule. But I left her as mad as a wasp, and that was worth something.

The second morning after the burning, I was in the courtyard of the Fort, and a splendid big Indian came stalking along, followed by a train of girls and other braves. He was so outstanding, I asked who he was.

"Black Poddee," a loafer told me. "One of the big chiefs around this area—rich as Croesus."

The name rang a bell. It was unusual for an Indian, because they mainly depend for their names on some kind of description, like the activities of animals. Many Indian names are so forthright they never get into books. On the other hand, they don't have any curse words; there isn't anything in the Indians' language like the profanity in ours. It's a defect, and has slowed them up in dealing with the higher civilizations.

But I remembered now. My father had told me about the young brave, back in Independence, who'd come up and given him a letter to deliver—pointing in a general direction toward the West. We had forgotten about it long since. But I knew where it was;

it was in my father's knapsack. The Kissels had lost their main plunder in the fire, but we'd all taken a few necessaries out of the wagon for camping, and my father and I'd put most of our truck in our tent.

So I went back, curious, and fetched the letter for this chief, who was in the smithy buying iron for arrowheads. Metal was better than flint, which would break if it struck a rock, but iron could be used over and over.

I stood in the doorway while a young Indian palavered with the blacksmith. This Black Poddee didn't seem to speak English at all, or maybe he wouldn't. Some were like that; they figured it was below their dignity.

"Two robes," said the blacksmith, seizing a maul and whacking a wagon tire that lay on the coals. When the sparks flew up in a shower, everybody jumped except the chief. "Two robes, take it or leave it," continued the smith. "Take it for a bargain. Iron ain't easy come by—it don't grow on bushes."

This was a lie, of course. You could go out on the California-Oregon Trail and pick up enough iron in a day to shoe all the horses in Nebraska. But that hairy baboon of a blacksmith had a whole box of end bits he'd cut to the right size, and here was where the trouble lay. Indians didn't have tools for cutting and sharpening.

"Two robes. You want it? Tell you the candid truth," said the blacksmith, "that box is spoke for. If I was to sell it, I'd be going back on my word. A very good Snake friend of mine——"

The chief raised his hand in a gesture so grand and princely we could see he was tired of haggling. He made a sign to the young brave, who said, "Two robes." They picked up the box, and I waited till the party was outside.

"Mr. Black Poddee?" I said, with a kind of quaver in my voice. I was scared of this fellow. His face hadn't any more give than one of the rock bluffs along the Platte.

They stopped, and he turned slowly around to look me over. Then I hauled out the letter and addressed the interpreter.

"Tell chief I have a letter. It was handed my father and me in Missouri." I waved toward the east. "Many suns across the big river. Letter is for Black Poddee."

For a second the chief's eyes blazed—I wondered if I'd made him angry—then he answered me himself.

"Who has given letter?"

"An Indian young man"—I made the sign of hand across the throat—"of the Sioux people."

When he reached out, I placed the letter in his palm. He opened it and read it through, without needing help. Then he smelled the paper, crinkled it to get the feel, and looked through it at the sun. After this curious business, he read it again. I watched him carefully; his face changed; it didn't seem so rigid any longer. Finally he folded the letter and placed it in his shirt.

I hoped he was pleased, but he had finished talking to me. Instead, he spoke to the interpreter, who turned and said:

"You bring news of Black Poddee's son, who is thought dead while the moving birds fly three times."

"I'm glad he's alive," I said. I couldn't seem to think of anything smarter.

The chief again spoke to the young man.

"Black Poddee asks name of boy with yellow hair who has carried letter to Sioux lands."

"Jaimie."

"Black Poddee wish Jay-mee come to Sioux camp tonight when sun go behind mountains. He will send guide to wagon train."

I was embarrassed. I didn't hanker to visit another Indian camp under any conditions. But I was afraid of hurting the chief's feelings, so I gulped and said, "Yes, sir. I'll be glad to—I mean I'll ask my father."

This Black Poddee stared at me hard for a second, then they wheeled and walked off in their soft, graceful way toward the gate. Confound the luck, I thought, I've done it again. Everything I touch turns out to be trouble for the train.

When I looked up my father, he was so busy with Coulter he didn't rightly hear me.

"Yes, yes, go ahead," he said. "Do what you think best. Now run along and don't bother me."

That was exactly what I wanted to hear. I'd cleared things, so nobody could say I'd gone without asking. Neither did anyone know I was going. It worked out fine. Honesty *is* the best policy; I've always found it so, but a person often forgets until it's too late.

Toward sundown, I began to get fidgety, wondering what I was in for. I recalled a mention of my yellow hair, and figured that these Sioux aimed to add it to their collection. Even so, I was stuck, as I already said. It was too late now. I'd given my word, so I just waited.

About six, Mrs. Kissel and Jennie started the fire, and all our gang except my father, who was at Captain Cooper's, were on hand to help. This included the children. Before, they'd been fed early and put to bed by dark; now there was only the one wagon left, and things weren't quite as smooth. But nobody complained. When Mrs. Kissel said, "If you think it over, it wasn't nothing but furniture," her husband added, in a rare burst of speech, "If a man's got an ax, he's got furniture." Then he added, as an after-thought, "And I've got an ax." He was right about that. An ax in Mr. Kissel's hands was like a thing alive. He handled it the way another man might handle a pocketknife.

I sat in front of the fire, watching Po-Povi, who was handing things to Mrs. Kissel. Then, after a while, I looked over Mr. Kissel's head, and a copper-colored fellow, naked to the waist, hair beautifully groomed and oiled, wearing a beaded headband that gave off glints in the firelight, was standing there with his arms folded, waiting.

"Excuse me, I've got some business to transact," I said, and got up to follow after the Indian. I saw Mr. Brice's mouth drop open, and heard Mrs. Kissel's "Land sakes alive!", then we were swallowed up in the duskiness.

This fellow was hard to follow. He blended in with the shadows.

Besides, I'd been staring at the fire, so the dark looked blacker than it really was for a while.

I yelled, "Hold up, will you?" a couple of times, and he waited, perfectly good-natured. After what seemed like forty-five minutes or so—we must have covered nearly two miles—we got to the Sioux village, which was spread out over several acres. Campfires were going every place I looked.

The chief's lodge was on a rise, with the others in a circle around it. In front, several burning flares were stuck in the ground, so that things were almost as bright as day. This wigwam of his, the biggest of the lot, had a high flag sticking up in the center, with bright colors and things drawn on it.

Looking around, I saw that the whole tribe was out, dressed up, as handsome a bunch of people as you might see in any city back East. It looked like a celebration, and I didn't feel comfortable; I'd seen how these things went in the Pawnee village. But I had very little time to worry, because my guide stopped before the gaudiest lodge and, pointing, said, "Black Poddee."

I stooped down and crawled in, and there sat this old chief, dressed up with a lot of feathers, with a pot on the fire, three wives behind him, and four dignitaries on either side. They were smoking a pipe, and when I was seated, they passed it along to me. I took a couple of puffs and would have been perfectly happy to puff on, but they took it away and handed it to the next man. Then they offered me some hunks of meat from the pot, on a sliver of bark, and I wolfed them down fast, being hungry after an exciting day. It tasted like jerked beef, tender and good. I made up my mind that the whole style of Sioux was different from the Pawnees; these people were clean, they smelled clean, and their lodges were tidy. What's more, they appeared friendly and courteous. Just the same, I'd heard how bloodthirsty the Sioux were, and I wondered if they were fattening me up before the feast started.

After we ate, Black Poddee got up and led us outside, where we sat down in a row. Then some of the prettiest girls I ever saw came forward and did a dance, but it wasn't anything special. They just padded around in a circle, chanting, with their hands clasped. And after this, some children set up targets and showed how they could shoot bows and arrows. They did it very well, getting eight or nine hits out of ten. Suddenly, they whisked the targets out of sight, everybody sat down, and things got deathly still. I said to myself, the main part of the show is about to commence, just like the Pawnees, and sure enough, Black Poddee rose up, pulled out a knife, and pointed it up at the heavens, while everybody gave a big shout.

I was so scared I couldn't get my legs in working order. I wanted to run but couldn't. You could have heard my teeth chattering fifty feet away. The chief now reached down and drew me up to my feet. Very slowly, he raised his knife again, then he cut a slice across his own wrist. Before I knew it, he'd cut one across mine, too. For some reason, it didn't hurt. Placing his cut wrist against mine, he said in a loud voice:

"Now Yellow Hair is blood son of Black Poddee."

This was a very pleasant surprise. They weren't going to kill me at all; he'd made me an honorary member of his family, entirely legal, with blood, and that wasn't the end. When they'd put salve made of bark and buffalo marrow on my cut, he led out the handsomest spotted pony you ever saw, and handed me the reins, which were worked out of braided buckskin.

"For me? You mean mine?" I said, being practically addled with good fortune.

"Yellow Hair bring son to Black Poddee," he said. I shook his hand, shook hands all around, then wrote out on a paper, as he asked me, a statement that the chief and his tribe were good, friendly Indians.

The moon was up, so I could see to go back. And didn't I go back in style! I jumped on the pony, which was frisky and switched in a circle, but I hauled in to show who was boss, then called out thanks. At this, Black Poddee came up and shook hands all over again.

"Black Poddee lodge, Yellow Hair home."

Looking them over, I felt just a little choked up. People *can* be nice to each other when they choose. They don't do it often enough. Here these Sioux had gone to work in an hour's time and wiped out my bad memories of the Pawnees. It goes to show that maybe you shouldn't generalize, as they say, but should judge people on their own merits.

Then Black Poddee slapped the pony sharply on the rump, and I was off home, swelled up with pride, as happy as I ever remember being in my life.

Chapter XXVII

Next morning everybody was bowled over at my story, but they hadn't much time to discuss it, because at a pow-wow last night, it was settled that my father and the Kissels should get mules. We'd have to "pack," as they called it. Jennie and Mrs. Kissel and the quartet would ride in Brice's wagon. It was the only way.

But as they talked—my father, chiefly—I noticed Mr. Kissel looking embarrassed, and contributing even less than usual. Then he said, "You folks had better go on. Mother and I'll prefer to turn back."

"You *what?*" cried my father. "Now see here, Kissel, this was your expedition in the first place—the rest of us just tagged along. You *can't* turn back!"

Kissel was perspiring, but he stuck to his guns. "Mother and I've talked it over; we'll turn back."

I had a thought, then, and spoke up, though my father had sworn me not to interrupt grownups during a conference.

"I may get a licking for talking," I said, "but it might be the Kissels haven't any more money."

My father's face looked like a balloon that's been punctured. "Oh, I see."

Before he went on, Mr. Coe, who was sitting by, but not taking part, got up and took off his hat. He looked fussed, as my mother used to say.

"Possibly it's poor taste to mention it," he said, "but the fact is, dash it all, it's ridiculous to put so many strictures of form on the subject of money. What I'm trying to say, so very badly, is that

I'm rather rich, in a moderate sort of way. Always have been. Vulgar, but there it is. Fellow left it me in a will—total stranger. Some sort of uncle, I believe they said. So, if you don't mind——"

Mr. Kissel said, "You're a good and generous man, but we can't take a loan that mightn't be repaid. It wouldn't be fit."

Clearing his throat, my father now got off some of his usual rubbish. "If it comes to that, and not to detract from the typical gesture of our esteemed friend, Henry Coe, I myself——"

I interrupted; I couldn't help it. I knew exactly how much money was left; and realized that because of Mr. Coe he was planning to bull right ahead and suggest that, he was rich, too, which could do nobody on earth any good, and might bring harm to several.

So I dug into my pocket and dribbled those pretty gold pieces out on the ground. I'd shined them up; how they twinkled in the sun.

"Son," said my father, turning white, "step over to one side. We'd better have a chat."

"It's all right; they're mine." I told them about finding the injured man's jacket, and how I'd stowed the coins in the wagon pouch that Mrs. Kissel made me.

"If the Kissels won't take it outright," I said, "I'd like to call it buying a share in their venture. Digging gold *or* farming!"

Mr. Kissel gazed around in his slow way. Then he shook hands and said, "Lad, you've got a partner." And after that, he said, "Thankee, all. You're real friends."

This was as long a speech as he commonly made. Mrs. Kissel told me so afterward; she said in some ways it beat his proposal of marriage, which was so brief she almost missed it.

Coulter would be ready to travel in two days, riding in a wagon for a week, so we went back to Fort Bernard and bargained for three mules, with pack saddles, some large canteens, coffee, beans, bacon, tools and other gear. It took all one morning. These Mexican Indians were sharp, and a Yankee working with them, a Mr. New, was worse, because he never disagreed but had a way, mild and accommodating, of saying, "Why, yes, it'll bear pondering," as if he'd let us know in a week or two, while he understood perfectly well we were in a raging hurry.

My gold came to four hundred and forty dollars, more than we needed, and Mr. Kissel said we'd plough the rest into seed, come California. This didn't exactly suit me; I'd planned to buy a sluice box and get rich washing gold, but I didn't complain; he was too happy.

We pulled out on a Friday, a nice, cloudy day, cool for traveling. The rest of the Kissels' oxen were hitched to the Brice wagon, which had also lost one, and we had our new mules going. Everybody's supplies were built up, and their spirits seemed revived by the layover. Coulter was riding in a wagon belonging to the drovers, one they'd figured on selling in California. They do that—haul things out, sell, and come back light. And make a very nice profit, if the trip goes well, and they're still alive.

For some days we went along, quiet and peaceful, except for packing and unpacking the mules. No matter how we arranged them, in an hour these packs would slip around to swing under the mules' bellies. It was a botheration, but it must have been worse for the mules, because on about the third day, they appeared to get sick of it; they began to act up. First thing you know, they'd run down and stand in a stream, or jump up and down stiff-legged, till the packs fell off altogether. One kicked a man they called Muttonhead Braden near a clump of greasewood. My father had to tend him; he was colored up like a rainbow.

The road kept moving up, still in sandy soil, still within view of the Platte, too, but getting closer to the summit of the Rocky Mountains, now. We passed the Black Hills, and camped one night on Beaver Creek, where there was good grass, with lots of trees—cottonwood, willows and such—and signs of antelope and deer. That evening, the women gathered wild green peas, and we felt charged up after eating fresh vegetables for a change. My father was in his glory, picking various new plants to show around, often using their Latin names, as if the English wouldn't serve, and among others, he collected sunflowers, wild daisies, and "wild heliotrope," but he got in an argument with Dr. Merton over this last one.

I forgot to say he'd swapped Cream in on the mules, at Fort Bernard, because the white horse attracted flies and other bugs, exactly as Coulter stated. The poor creature was all over welts. Bugs didn't bother my spotted pony, which I'd named Spot, after discarding several names that didn't suit him. Spot struck just the right note, somehow, though my father inquired if I didn't think it was too subtle, which I figured was some kind of joke.

Anyhow, this Spot and I hit it off fine. Coulter called me to his wagon and said, "You may not know it, but you've got a real horse there. You can't wear an Indian pony out, ride him all day." I was glad to hear it, and asked him how he felt. He didn't look so good, all bundled up in oily bandages, with his black hair gone. I was sorry for him, all right, but I couldn't get out of my mind about him backing off from Shep.

But I heard more about that soon. Some bad things lay just around the next turn of the trail. We didn't know it, but we had nearly finished one long leg of our journey. Our lives were going to be changed, but I'd better let my father tell what happened.

Beyond Independence Rock
En route to California
Sept. 25, 1849.

Dear Melissa:

There may be a hiatus in my correspondence, owing to new plans which we, our particular group, have decided upon. Alterations have taken place. The Lord in His wisdom has seen fit to point us in a different direction, and in the nick of time, too. It bears out what I have tried to emphasize to you and the children: trust in Providence; in the long run, He'll see you through. I recall numerous examples. With apologies, there was one occasion on a shantyboat, in my unreformed period, during the course of a contest at cards. I had need—it bordered on a religious yearning—for a jack of spades, to complete what is known (professionally speaking) as "an inside straight," and I shut my eyes in brief prayer, calling the Supreme Dealer's attention to the fact that, minus the jack, my family were in for something of a shock, financially speaking.

Did I get it? Did that jack drop like a gentle rain from Heaven? It did not. In actual fact I drew the deuce of clubs, which was of no use whatever, and seldom is to anybody (unless you're playing with "wild" cards, of course, and then you must remember to hang onto it, as being valuable). The point is, had I drawn that jack, gambling might have gripped my soul like a vise, causing me to end up a ne'er-do-well in the backwashes of Louisville, instead of in my present fortunate condition.

First of all, to clear up our mystery about Coulter. Nine or ten days out from Laramie, traversing rough country near the Independence Rock, a gigantic elevation surrounded by soda ponds, I walked forward to see Coulter, who is up and about, regaining his hair, his scars healing, and in general convalescent. Finding him driving a wagon, his strength far from fully returned, I climbed to the seat and made conversation on general subjects for a while. Then, seizing the bull by the horns (the metaphor is apt in this case), I said:

"Friend Coulter, at the risk of provoking your ire, I'd like to ask a question. I have a theory and wish to test it out."

"The air's free over the desert," he said. "I haven't heard of any ordinances corking up speech."

"My theory is," I went on, despite this odd rejoinder, "that you weren't physically afraid of that ruffian Baggott, not this much"— and I snapped my fingers—"but were cowed by something possibly quite trivial out of your past. I speak medically, as your personal physician, in the hope of finding a solution."

Astonishingly enough, he turned quite pale. Then he wet his lips with his tongue and said, "Some things are better left as they be."

"I disagree. Seen clearly, out in the light, they often appear foolish, and without the significance that has built up over the years."

"Not in this case."

"There's no way to tell till it's tried. You've never told us where you came from, Coulter. Where were you born?"

After a long pause, he said, "Western Kentucky."

"Your father, what'd he do there?"

"I never saw him. He was drowned, duck-hunting, when I was in the crib. He waded out into the river after a bird and stepped in a hole, wearing boots."

"What was your mother like?"

"She had a hard row. She did a man's work to keep us fed and growing."

"Us?"

He snapped the reins at the oxen, and said, "Camp time, soon. Time I was back in the saddle."

"How many in the family, Coulter?"

For a minute, I thought he would refuse to answer; then he said, "I had a twin. His name was Phillip. People called him Sandy. He was fair, where I'm dark."

"What did Baggott mean when he said, 'Why don't you tell them what happened to your brother?' "

"Twins aren't always like. He was bigger than me, smarter, as good-looking as they come. My mother favored him; she couldn't help it, and you don't have to believe it, but I didn't blame her. He was the leader of the boys around there, and the funny thing was, he didn't try to be; he just was."

"What happened?"

I don't think he heard me. After being pent up so long, the words were tumbling out.

"—and if there was a game, with choosing up, he was chose first, always, every time. There wasn't anything he couldn't do better than anybody his age, or even older. Neither could you flinch him, no matter what. One time there was a sycamore slanted out over the water's edge, and we climbed up and looked down—this was in the summer barefoot time—and nobody would jump. Then Sandy went off that limb like a frog. I'll bet it was seventy feet high. After that, of course, I *had* to do it, but my head hit a piece of drift, and it knocked me cold. I came to on the riverbank; Sandy had pulled me out."

"I see," I said. "But it was natural to resent him. Nearly anybody would in the circumstances."

"Resent him? I liked him better than anybody I ever knew, or am apt to know again."

"Then I really don't understand, Coulter."

"Not long after our twelfth birthday, my mother gave me a hiding for something Sandy had done—he didn't know about it—and that afternoon we played Injuns in the willows down by the river. We were both tricked out like savages, with sticks and such in our caps, to blend in with the bushes, and had bows and arrows we'd made. The bows weren't bad for kids—they had a nice spring. For arrows, we'd smooth down a piece of ash and tip them with odd-shaped pieces of tin we'd find lying around at the tinsmith's—ends they'd cut off, you know.

"Playing along the bottoms, we flushed up a deer, a very good head, and watched him jump in the water and head downstream, swimming high, head and shoulders out, the way they do.

"Sandy said, 'He'll climb out below. Run down and head him off, and I'll trail along and meet you.'

"Making a big circle, I waded over a stretch of backwater, and in a minute, sure enough, I heard the deer stomping through sand. I didn't move, but I remember thinking, I'll snag this fellow and Sandy will be proud. He was always bragging about things I did, whenever I did something.

"But there wasn't time for woolgathering, for the leaves gave a rustle, his antlers poked into view and I let drive——"

He stopped.

"Go ahead, Coulter. Get the whole thing off your chest."

"I shot him directly through the left eye socket—the arrow sank nearly up to the feathers in his skull. He was dying when I ran up, but when I leaned down, he said, 'Tell Ma it was an accident—tell her I said so.' A few seconds after that, he was gone.

"I held him in my arms till I was sure, then I ran into the river and tried to drown myself. But it isn't easy, not for a boy that age. You keep coming up, and whether you want to or not, you swim. And after a while, you get sick."

"Coulter——"

"I'm not quite done. My mother never spoke a word directly to me from that day forward. I lived at home three more years, and she never addressed a sentence to me in all that time. If something needed doing, she'd say like, 'I hope extra firewood will be chopped for the wash while I'm gone.'

"She believed I did it a-purpose, out of jealousy, and nearly everybody else did, too. I was the target for every child in town. They'd yell 'Cain slew Abel! Cain slew Abel!'—having likely heard it from their parents.

"In the long run, I took to fighting back, and naturally that showed they were right. I had a vicious streak; it was a throwback in the blood. That's what they said. So when I was fifteen, I left for good. My mother'd got married again, to a man that knocked me around, her, too, and I ran away one night after they'd gone to bed. I never went back. Some years later, I heard she'd died of consumption. On her deathbed, one of the women bathing her face asked if they ought to try and reach me. 'I only had the one son,' she said. 'I had one boy, Phillip, that was murdered.'"

I'm ashamed to admit it, Melissa, but I couldn't think of anything to say for quite a little while. Finally I said, "Coulter, that's a terrible story, terrible. But——"

"Maybe you'd care to step down now, doctor. I haven't any doubts you'd dislike riding with a murderer. Everybody else has, whenever they heard."

"Coulter, if I may be so bold with a man who could whip me with one hand, you're something of an ass. The incident you describe was an accident, just as your brother said. By the way, what a wonderful boy he must have been. These things happen every day, something like them, somewhere on earth. In your case, you let it grow, and fester, and take possession of you, with some cause to be sure. But tell me something—isn't this the first time you ever went over the story to an outsider?"

"I've never laid tongue to it since the day I told my mother and she beat me unconscious with a poker."

"How do you feel—at the moment, I mean?"

He gave a long sigh. "Doctor, I can't say why, I'm not smart enough and haven't the education, but it seems like somebody's just rolled a mountain off my chest."

"I'm delighted," I said, getting down. "Now listen to me. I'm going to repeat your account, word for word, to our people. Then I want you to come have supper with us at seven."

For a second, he looked uneasy again. "Maybe tomorrow—I've got to catch up on——"

"*Tonight*," I said firmly. "You're within sight of getting out of the woods. But you've got two or three more steps to take. Flinch now and you're finished."

Turning to leave, I added, "Coulter, do what you think Sandy might have done."

He looked angry, then relaxed.

"I may be dropping in," I heard him call as I walked back down the train.

Now I'd better move on in a hurry. Sad events should never be dwelt on. We tarried two hours at Independence Rock, "the registry of the desert," so called because of the names, initials, dates and origins scratched on it by parties coming before us. Climbing up as far as they could, Jaimie and Po-Povi chiseled a memento there— two names, a boy's and an Indian girl's—for the generations to come to marvel at. Do you suppose that inscription will be legible a hundred years from today, when the warm shroud of earth is pulled long since over us all? Will some gay band of picnickers, come out from the cities that have risen here, puzzle over those words: JAIMIE McP. and PO-POVI? What were they like, the two who left those clumsy letters? Where were they going? And what became of them after they left?

This is foolish speculation. Beneath the blasts of desert wind, the spire itself may crumble within a few decades. This is harsh and pitiless country.

Five days out from the Rock, beyond the Devil's Gate, a thirty-foot fissure in a mountain wall, and approaching a granite canyon, Coulter came riding back with every look of concern. He offered no salutation, which was unusual, but spurred his horse rapidly to the rear. Then he galloped up the other side, shading his eyes to peer first at one frowning wall, then at the opposite.

Plainly he had no fancy for what he saw, for he set about closing up spaces between wagons, in tones by no means gentle.

Jaimie, on his spotted pony, rode up and said, "Coulter smells Indians—he doesn't like the canyon."

This was hard to believe, for Indians along the way had generally been peaceful, barring our boy's mishap and the infrequent raids by night.

Watching anxiously, we saw a faint puff of smoke behind the canyon wall, off to our right. It was followed by two others in quick succession, then nothing at all—empty sky where a second before something had been burning.

Events now came rapidly. Pointing to a high rock, Jaimie shouted and we saw silhouetted against the blue expanse a motionless figure, then two shots rang out from somewhere in the train ahead, and Coulter came galloping back, very fast, sitting his horse twisted to one side in the saddle, the better to address us: "Circle! Circle wagons—this is an attack!" Above the confusion, we could hear him repeating it all down the line—"This is an attack, this is an attack."

One's first reaction to the words is a chilly gripping of the bowels. It is difficult to grasp that in a few moments you may be shot at, and perhaps wounded or killed. Fortunately there was little time for reflection. The dust rose in clouds around us as thirty-odd heavy "prairie schooners" wheeled into the defensive ellipse, horses and oxen rearing and complaining, men cursing and sawing at the reins, a tempest of frightened movement in an otherwise silent desert. Coulter skidded up to leap off and begin inspecting guns, and then he placed women behind wheels and boxes and covered children over with planks and tarpaulins. His manner was neither impolite nor gentle, and only a fool would have argued; he meant business.

Up ahead, nothing yet in sight. Then Coulter said, "We've got a visitor."

Down the canyon passage an Indian came riding, alone, on a fine-looking horse. He was coming along fast, but a hundred yards or so before reaching us, he swerved his horse suddenly, nearly falling, to plant a garlanded spear in the sand. Then he galloped back and disappeared around the bend.

No sooner had he disappeared than several dozen others, the advance guard, the head men, trotted out from the bend ahead to survey us impassively. Our Mr. Coulter now walked forward boldly, with his customary look of contempt when dealing with Indians, leaned over and picked up a handful of dust. He held it high, for all of them to see, then threw it down.

Then he returned, not running, but he didn't tarry, either.

"That's it," he said. "They gave us a challenge, and I took it up. Get yourselves ready; they won't be over a minute or two."

And only a few seconds later, "Here they come."

Two files, straddling us, swept past close against the canyon walls, difficult to see, because the sun was directly overhead and both sides were shadowed. Several arrows fell inside our enclosure, but none caused damage.

"Don't fire," Coulter sang out. "Not on this pass. Hold up; it makes them nervous." He ran, bending low, from one group to another, and his serene indifference to this crisis, and our enemies, began to rub off on us a little.

At the far end, they collected, whooping, and gathered for another run.

"Crows, with Snakes amongst them, black as niggers," muttered Coulter.

Not having attracted our fire, they spread out from the walls this time, and we looked them over. Some were large and well made, others appeared poor and bedraggled. Many were entirely naked, while the bodies of a few were covered with the skins of hares sewn together. In general, their hair was long, they had aquiline features, and the average height, I should say, was five feet six or seven inches. And Coulter was right about one thing—a sprinkling —Snakes, or Shoshones—were as dark as our Louisville negro.

I seized up an arrow that struck the sand not far from my feet, without force, having been fired high into the air. It was crudely wrought, poorer in quality than those of the Sioux we had seen, but it was strongly tipped with iron, procured at some trading post, no doubt.

"Now, lads," said Coulter. "They'll be careless this run. Pick a man well out in the sunlight, and if you ain't a dead aim, *hit his horse!*"

One of our number cried, "I draw the line on that, it ain't humane. I'll shoot for the man."

"You do that, Wilson," said Coulter, "and that yellow-haired tyke of yours'll have herself a honeymoon with twenty-five bucks."

The man stepped back angrily, but I noticed that when the lines came down, screaming with such frightful effect as to have paralyzed a less hardy group, he took cool aim and dropped a pinto mare head over heels on its rider. My physician's eye could spot the signs of a broken neck—the tilted head, the threshing of the lower limbs, the whole body flopping like a chicken before he died.

One notes these small pictures against the larger screen of battle.

I was loading and firing the Hawken rifle, a cumbersome weapon which rested between the spokes of a wheel. These Indians were shooting guns as well as arrows; I saw a man hit, though not badly, across our enclosure.

"How many altogether?" I asked Coulter during one of his low-crouching sorties.

"They've got us about six to one. And they've picked a nice day for it." He looked ruefully up at the sky.

The heat in our canyon was growing unbearable. A sun that seemed ten times life-size blazed down without pity, and not a breath of air stirred.

We had four casualties on the next two passes, none fatal; a youth hit by a ball in the shoulder, two men wounded at almost identical spots in the groin, and a scalp injury, unserious but bloody.

Over the uproar, I could hear Coulter bawling for the dozenth time, "Pick a horse, pick a horse—forget the man."

By now I was no longer firing, but had quit by request to tend wounded. Jaimie, lying beneath the Brices' wagon, was shooting a borrowed revolver, and Jennie was working careful, methodical havoc with one of Kissel's rifles. Mrs. Kissel loaded for us all. Our situation was quite plainly desperate. In a battle of attrition, into which this was degenerating, we were hopelessly outclassed. Our number would be so reduced that we could expect a direct charge long before sundown; I heard Coulter say so, in a tone not meant to be generally audible, to one of the drovers.

Still they came on, in endless supply. On the next pass, several bucks formed a cluster, reining up, and giving a bloodcurdling huzza, headed straight at us. All of our men on that side rose instantly to their feet to draw careful bead, but a stark-naked Indian, accoutered only in head feathers and paint, still got inside our circle, leaping his horse over barrels and boxes between the wagons. Yelling bloody murder, he began thrusting left and right with a lance, but his moment of glory was short-lived.

Kissel rose towering before him, there was a flash of steel against the sun, and we heard that curious ripping sound that one makes when a watermelon is split with a knife. With his ax, Kissel parted the Indian's skull from crown to chin; it was cleft as a pine faggot is divided for the fire. It was a sight, I assure you, that I shall carry to my grave.

With complete lack of emotion, as if it were a farming chore he had to do, Kissel then seized the brave by the waist and hurled his remains outside our fort. His shattered skull was a trifle too much for civilized stomachs.

Coulter came over, brushing the sweat out of his eyes with his sleeve; an occupational hazard with this kind of fighting. He'd been everywhere, plugging up holes, speaking both comfort and direction, and occasionally reproach, looking after the women, rearranging barricades, gentling stock—I saw him draw two arrows from the backs of oxen, hit by those high, looping shots that were meant to distress mainly by annoyance—and keeping our spirits alive by a perfectly callous disregard of danger to himself.

Now in the lull he stopped beside us for a second. "God damn these Crows," he said, adding a few details which I'll refrain from setting down verbatim. "We've dropped a bunch, but they won't haul off. Any other tribe, they'd pull up for a while, collect the dead, maybe wait till tomorrow. That's what the Snakes'd do, left to themselves."

I asked how long he thought we had.

"Three more passes and they'll try to ride in. They're calling, doctor; who's that hit? Damn the luck, it's that swamp rat Billings, from Georgia. He and his wife are the best shots we've got."

In the next few minutes, I tried counting the Indians fallen. Twenty-six horses were down, on both sides, some still kicking and many crying horribly. Around these, sprawled in every attitude of death, were forty-odd braves; the number being difficult to figure, because not a few were all but invisible beneath mounts. Other horses, riderless, had taken to flight. And a fair proportion of the men down were moving, trying to rise, clutching an injured part, crawling in one direction or another. One fellow, wounded in the eyes, fascinated us all by coming slowly, on hands and knees, directly toward us, his sense of orientation gone.

I heard a pistol crack from beneath our wagon, and peering downward, saw Jaimie's eyes a-gleam with excitement. And the next instant he had drawn a knife and started forward. I grabbed his collar and shouted, "What is this? What are you trying to do?"

"I thought I'd take his hair," was the incredible reply.

I drew back to cuff him, but I was too late. The faithful Jennie had already performed that service with neat, graceful competence.

Twenty minutes later, Coulter scrambled rapidly around the enclosure, passing out hand weapons of every variety—axes, knives, his own tomahawk—gained God knows where—mallets, hammers, clubs, anything to repel the concerted rush we all now expected. Raising his voice, he cried, "They're coming in, men. We'll stand them off—we can do it. If we don't, save a ball for the women and children. I'm proud of you—you've done your duty like men—everybody here. Now let's give them hell!"

A little cheer went up for Coulter, and he looked sheepish.

Then we tensed, waiting, and I'll confess that my bowels were constricted in knots. The Indians were massed together, forsaking their lines, working themselves up for the signal, with whoops, yells, screams, and a rattling of weapons. Over everything rose an odd, high whine, eerie and unsettling. "Pay no mind, boys," cried Coulter. "They've got some eagle-bone whistles, aimed to scare us out of putting up a fight. Get set, hold your fire, and wait for their signal."

I rejoice to tell you, Melissa, that it never was given. Behind us, emerging like a mirage, a cloud of horsemen as impossible to count as leaves on a tree, approached in such numbers as to choke the canyon from wall to wall. There were hundreds—we could hear the rolling thunder of their hoofbeats before even the Crows spotted them.

"Now *wait* a minute," said Coulter, shading his eyes.

Coming on, they seemed familiar, though they were Indians beyond a doubt.

Under the wagon, Jaimie cried out, "I know him! It's Black Poddee, that gave me the horse."

I should guess that fifteen hundred or more Sioux comprised the charge that swept over the luckless remaining Crows, driving them past us, with a great deal of slaughter, on up into the canyon and out of our lives.

An hour passed, and we assembled before our wagons. With massive dignity, Jaimie's friend rode slowly toward us holding out his arm.

"Yellow Hair that carries letter," he said in English.

"I'm here, all right," spoke up Jaimie, looking self-conscious as the center of so much attention. He walked forward and the Indians in the front rank dismounted. The chief shook hands in the white man's fashion, then this fierce and amusing old fellow drew out the paper Jaimie had signed, attesting his friendliness. At that moment, I believe, everyone in the train would have been happy to swear in court that Black Poddee was the greatest man in America.

In half an hour they were gone, to join other Sioux in the holy crusade against the Snakes and Crows, and we filed wearily back to the wagons, elated but depressed, too, in the awful emptiness that follows a battle, the anti-climax to perhaps the sharpest of all human experiences.

"That's like Brice," remarked Coe, who had stood unruffled beside us, exchanging shot for shot, as debonair throughout as a man grouse-hunting at an English country estate. "He's taking a quiet nap against the wheel as if he fought Indians every day of his life."

And then Jennie's, "Oh, my God!"

An arrow pinned him to the hub, passing through his neck from back to front, severing the carotid artery, and, I think, snapping the bone itself. We drew it out later—a vicious thing, with a long, smooth stem, a bright turkey feather, and a heavy iron tip.

He was quite dead; I doubt if there had been an instant's pain.

We disengaged Jennie, who had clasped him around the back, weeping like a tired child, and lifted her into the wagon. Our casualties had been heavy—ten killed and eighteen badly wounded, plus many animals dead or waiting to be finished.

Who had gained from this senseless encounter? Coulter says that many Crow squaws tonight will gash their breasts and amputate their fingers in mourning. We have met, injured each other horribly, and drawn off, both sides poorer forever for a witless act of violence in the sun.

And now, Melissa, we have been compelled to make a decision. The train—its remnants, that is—will proceed together to Fort Bridger, there to split up. The Kissels, Jennie, Coe (the good man has put aside his personal interests in our behalf), Po-Povi and ourselves will go to the Great Salt Lake, Citadel of the Mormons, and spend the winter recouping. Mrs. Kissel is ailing. While she doesn't complain, she quite obviously lacks strength to continue this cruel trek to California. She would be in her grave before snow fell.

So—we will rest over the winter among the followers of Brigham Young. And with the first buds of Spring, the first flight of birds toward the north, our group, rested and refreshed, shall be off once more, headed for those beckoning fields of gold to which we have addressed our energies and our resolution. My spirits have never been higher; and your son is the picture of radiant health. I remain, strengthened by adversity, on the brink of colossal fortune, your devoted swain,

SARDIUS McPHEETERS
(*in slightly decelerated transit*)

Chapter XXVIII

From what I'd heard of these Mormons, I didn't care too much about them. Besides, we were supposed to be off adventuring after gold and not holed up with a bunch of mule-headed religious nuts. My father always claimed that people who took on about being pious would bear watching. "I wouldn't trust one for a second," he said. Back home, he was barely civil to the Reverend Carmody, and when we left church each Sunday, he'd take his watch and slip it into his trousers pocket before shaking hands on the way out. He was only having fun, but my mother said it was irreverent and pointed up his deficiencies before God. But the preacher they'd had before Carmody sat up praying with the wealthiest old man in the parish when he was down sick of malnutrition, being something of a miser, and finally prayed so hard that when the man died, they came to find out he'd changed his will. And right after the burial, the preacher collected his inheritance, turned in his stole, and moved to Philadelphia. He'd been popular around Louisville, but nobody heard from him again until two years later, when he got into the news from being shot. So I don't intend to dwell on that winter with the Mormons, but will just hit the high spots—there *were* a few—then get right on to California.

After the fight with the Crows, we reorganized and moved on fast to Fort Bridger. Within a few days, we'd left the Platte forever. Nobody was sorry. It seemed we had been within view of this sluggish nuisance for as long as we could remember.

We followed the Sweetwater, within sight of the Wind River Mountains, over a country a-swarm with mosquitoes, and finally began the long rocky climb toward the snow ridge that "divides the Continent." That is, the rivers change directions here; the ones on the East flow toward the Eastern sea, and those on the West empty into the Pacific.

For several days in a row, there was little grass, but the ground was carpeted over with thistles, on which the oxen and mules fed, though without much appetite. Food for the immigrants was scarcer. Mostly people still were refreshed from Laramie, but Coulter kept trying to bag game, which could often be seen on these rocks up above. Twice he shot antelope, but the wolves moved in and devoured them before we could get there.

Several women came down with fever, so my father and Dr. Merton were hopping again. The upward pull was affecting both people and beasts. Part of it, my father said, was anxiety, fear of the summit we were approaching, which they called South Pass. But when we arrived, it was no worse than the road before, and was nineteen miles wide. We hardly knew we'd got to the top, but if you ran or moved fast, you knew it well enough, for they said the altitude here was over seven thousand feet high.

From the top we went along a level road two or three miles, then started a gentle descent to a gushing fountain known as Pacific Spring, very cold and good, being the last water for a long time. And after this we passed over a dry brown plain with what they called buttes—reddish-brown knobs of sandy rock—standing straight up like mushrooms. My father said they were once islands in a great inland sea, but he got into an argument with two other men about it, and was kept busy all afternoon.

Camped beside the Big Sandy, and started on a stretch of twenty miles without water or grass. Everybody was in a grouchy humor when we reached the Green River, which was nearly three hundred feet wide, and the fording was done to considerably more cussing than had formerly been noted on the train. People were so tired out I almost felt glad that our bunch was calling it off for a while.

On October twelfth we rode into sight of Fort Bridger, where we were to part, and of course there was some sniffling and carrying on. People went around shaking hands, and wishing good luck, and I honestly think we nearly backed out. But Mrs. Kissel now had to spend part of the day lying down, and my father, to do him credit, was bound and determined to get her back to health.

Coulter was going on with the train. "I hired out to deliver it to California, and that's where I'll deliver it," he told us. He waited a bit after we'd said everything, then followed Jennie to the tail of Brice's wagon. Having a little free time on my hands, I crawled underneath to rest up.

It was funny; Coulter had quit being so sarcastic with us, but he still spoke to Jennie with a kind of joky ragging.

"I'll be back, once I've got the sheep in the corral," he said.

"Indeed: you don't mean it. And leave all that gold behind?"

"I'm not much of a hand to go scratching in the ground like a squirrel."

Jennie gave a sniff. Now she was beginning to recover a little, she was handsome and lively. And since she'd been married, she was different, somehow. She had lost her sharp look and was softer and rounder. But there wasn't much improvement in her manner toward Coulter. He got her back up, no mistake, but I thought she liked him, too. It was a different kind of liking than what she'd had for Brice. I heard one of the men say she hadn't any more use for Coulter than a Jenny had for a Jack, but I didn't know what he meant.

"I hear gold-mining's hard, back-weary work," she said. "I don't doubt you'd shy off. Gallivanting's more your style."

"If a man's without ties, he might as well roam. A man, that is, not a doddering mooncalf——"

"You say anything against Brice and I'll slap your Indian's face."

"I wasn't talking about Brice, so maybe I'll give you a real excuse." He grabbed her shoulders and kissed her hard, pushing her up against the tail gate so that she went limp, leaning over backwards, with her legs apart.

When he let go, she caught her breath and hissed, "You vulgar roughneck. You ought to be ashamed. Leave me be." But when he turned half around, she said, "Where are you going?"

"California—remember?"

Jennie began to cry, she was so mad, and said, "Go ahead. And don't come back, hear?"

"You want me to kiss you goodbye again, just for luck?"

"No, I don't! You catch me letting you. Not ever! Just once, then—not that way—all ri——"

Then she broke loose, hanging on a second, and gasped, "You'll have to stop. Damn you—I'd like to kill you!"

"I'll be in Salt Lake City by Christmas."

"I won't be there."

"You'd better."

"I'll marry a Mormon."

"I'll make you a widow."

When he left, she put her head down against the board, breathing sort of hard, but she took it up again in a minute and kicked the wheel. She was an interesting case. Still, I couldn't make out what was bothering her, and anyhow I was rested up, so I left.

Before the train rolled on for California, Coulter took the men of our group to meet Jim Bridger, who he said was an old friend. If my father was right, Coulter'd only had a handful of friends since his childhood, and these were such hardened old geezers they wouldn't care whether he murdered his brother or not. Being friends, they'd simply have figured he had a good reason.

One was this Bridger, and another was a scout named Carson that Coulter said was somewhere on the Oregon Trail this year. He hoped to see him soon.

Coulter told us that Bridger's Fort, where the Mormon route to Salt Lake splits off from the California-Oregon Trail, was on Black's Fork of the Green River, where it took the fresh waters from the Uintah Mountains. He said Bridger himself was one of the toughest birds alive. "In 1834, he came out of a fight with the Blackfeet at Powder River with two iron arrowheads in his shoulder," Coulter said, "and a Doctor Whitman removed them while Bridger sat on the grass, smoking a cob pipe and playing mumbledy-peg with a soldier. Injuns carried the story all over the West. In appearance he's as mild as soup, but don't be surprised at his stretchers. He ain't any bad hand at storytelling; fact is, he's famous for it."

The train had camped on one of the three river forks surrounding the Fort, and we walked on in, Coulter and my father leading the way, Kissel and Coe behind them, me bringing up the rear. The first thing you noticed was how foxy Bridger had been in his location. The Fort was plopped down on an island in the middle branch of that stream, and we had to get to it by flat-bottomed boat, though we could have waded, they said. When we reached the island, the Fort wasn't any beauty, but it seemed solid for defense, being encircled all around with a strong stockade that had a heavy gate in the middle. The construction was picket, with the lodging apartments and offices opening into a hollow square, like Laramie. On the north side a corral was full of animals—mules, horses, oxen, ponies, and the like—and Bridger's house stood in a southern corner—a long cabin of very ordinary appearance for a man so well known, calling himself a military Major to boot.

We observed that the proprietor of this seedy dwelling was now within view on his doorstep, and I'll copy down what my father said in the Journals: "A man of middle stature, lean, very leathery of countenance, wearing a fringed buckskin shirt in indifferent repair, also a low black hat, and on his face a look both of deeply ingrained mischief and studied innocence; small eyes, close together but incredibly sharp and black, nose beaky, neck wattled, mouth set as if determined to avoid laughing at some epic jest."

At the time of our arrival, he was lugging a big brass spyglass, which we understood later was with him most always. He knew everything going on in that area, and the Indians never understood how he managed.

His meeting with Coulter was somewhat out of the common, as such formalities went. It departed from custom.

As he stood there, in an easy slouch, holding his telescope, we could see two fat Indian women in the doorway behind, and at their feet a number of copper-colored brats.

Bridger lifted his glass, though we were now only twenty or thirty yards away, and fixed it rather rudely on Coulter's face. Then he gave every appearance of alarm, as if the Fort was under attack. It set my father and the others back a notch, especially Coe, who had a pretty stiff notion of manners, even after all these weeks on the trail.

"Get the children back!" cried the proprietor to the Indian women. "Shut and bolt the doors—bury the silver." He stepped spryly aside and whisked the telescope out of sight behind the door, coming up with a very long rifle instead. His attitude was concerned, if not downright menacing.

Coulter, for his part, fell into this nonsense as if he'd done it before, and called, "I wonder if you could direct us to the person in charge of the Fort. We understood old Bridger was killed by a couple of Arapahoe children."

"Keep back," said Bridger to the women, who had yet to move a muscle in obedience to his commands. "Don't show yourselves. It looks like Coulter."

"Put down that rifle."

"Come up, Coulter, but come slow, and don't move your hands."

Coulter now grinned and said, "By God, if you aren't the worst-looking sight I ever run across. Have they quit sewing buttons on shirts?"

"What's happened to your hair?" asked Bridger.

"It got singed."

"You haven't a particle of business outside the Fort without a guide. I've told you before, only you won't listen."

"These are friends," said Coulter, introducing us. "They want to make serious talk, so cut out the piffle."

At this odd point in their reunion, they shook hands, but each did it as though the other was an object of miserableness almost past belief.

"I didn't figure on seeing you again," said Bridger, "wandering around unattended."

Inspecting him with an air of pity, Coulter said, "I'd almost forgot what an ugly old squirrel you are. It's always a shock. Why in hades don't you shave? It might help some."

"Come in, gentlemen," said Bridger, "make yourselves to home. I'm starting a new house next month, of imported Vermont marble, but the workmen aren't quite ready to go."

I found out later this was a lie; in fact, the proprietor of Fort Bridger practically never told the entire truth, if there was an opportunity to make up a better story. Coulter said that was the way he got his amusement, and my father added later that what he was, at heart, was "a first-rate working humorist, a rose wasting his fragrance on the desert air."

When we went inside, Kissel stooped over to avoid striking his head and Bridger introduced two Indian women as his wives, saying their names were "Durn Your Eyes" and "Drat Your Hide." None of our group had the impoliteness to inquire if he was joking, but these were the authentic names, according to Coulter, thought up by their husband several years before. The women were proud of them.

We got down to business and explained that we wanted to go to Salt Lake City for the winter. Then my father suggested that we would never make it without a guide. "He'll do it," said Coulter, addressing us, although Bridger was sitting at his elbow. "Once in a while there's work to be done around here, so he gets away and hides whenever he can."

"I'm not in good with Brigham Young right now," said Bridger, in a serious vein. "He says I've been selling firearms to the Utes; what's more, he'd admire to annex my Fort. It so happens I was meaning to go over and have a talk with him; you can ride along and welcome."

This was wonderful news. He would be leaving the day after tomorrow, when his partner, Vasquez, returned from a trading trip. Meanwhile he said we might enjoy seeing the local sights. Then he promised to take us, women and all, to a stream up in the mountains that he said had the fastest current in America, but he cautioned us beforehand not to stick our foot or hand in, so that we wouldn't be scalded. "Water running that fast works up a power of friction against the bottom and sides," he said, eyeing us with a kind of squint. "During the spring thaw, the temperature's close to biling."

Walking us down to the ferry, he rode over with us. A number of Indians were camped on the far bank, as well as the remnants of another train—three wagons altogether. "They're stopping here," Bridger said. "They like the country and mean to settle. They're a mighty smart bunch—got everything they need right in their own crowd, butcher, baker, blacksmith, cobbler, and all like that. They didn't pick a single man unless they needed him for a purpose."

Sitting beside the nearest wagon, sunning himself on a stool, was a gray-bearded old man so ancient and rickety you'd have thought he might fall apart any minute. I could see my father trying to fight down the question.

"What'd they bring the old fellow for?"

"To start their graveyard with."

On the way back to camp, Coe said, "Did you hear what he said about that stream? I don't believe it for a minute; it doesn't stand to reason."

"That man Bridger," replied my father, about to burst, "is the most preposterous humbug and liar I've met in the course of a lifetime devoted to the study of such creatures. I don't believe anything about him. I don't even think he's an Indian fighter."

"Well," observed Coulter, "you can't say I didn't warn you. But you corner him, and I wouldn't be surprised if he'd fight."

All of us except Jennie stood beside the train as it pulled out, waving handkerchiefs and calling our last goodbyes. We had exchanged names and addresses, the way people do, and made vows of keeping in touch later on in the gold fields, knowing in our hearts that we weren't apt to meet again, ever. The passing of time eases the best intentions; it's sad but true.

Coulter would return to Salt Lake City. When he said so, I believed him. But not Jennie. "That's the last we'll see of that critter," she said, angrily fighting back the tears. "He's purely worthless." Standing apart, she turned around when he grinned and waved, riding by. "You performed me a service," he had said to my father. "I'll be along back to see you through to California."

Then he offered one last piece of advice. "A word about Bridger, now. Never mind his yarn-spinning. Trust him as you'd trust your mother. You wouldn't know it, but he's guiding you because I asked him. So keep this in mind; never forget it. Trust him absolutely. There's just about nothing he can't do. And now—goodbye, all."

My father spoke up with real affection. "Coulter, we regard you as a member of the family. It'll be a happy day when we see you back." Kissel crushed some of his bones with a handshake, and Mrs. Kissel broke down and sniffled; even Coe looked distressed to see him go.

So we split up. It was a mournful pass to come to. I found myself holding Po-Povi's hand, with a good-sized lump in my throat. It was like watching all our hopes and plans go fading off in the distance. Would we really get to California? I didn't much think so any longer.

Chapter XXIX

Led by its owner, we pulled out of Fort Bridger before dawn on the day promised, prepared for a hard passage to the Great Salt Lake, much of it over scorched desert and soda flats.

Major Bridger was in a cheerful humor, but he cautioned us that the country was humming with Indians and that we must keep a sharp lookout.

He placed Coe's wagon, still mule-drawn, in the front, the Brice wagon with children and Mrs. Kissel next in line, and our new pack mules, Kissel's and my father's, in the rear. The men were supposed to go on a kind of sentinel duty, roaming the flanks and dropping behind but never getting out of eyeshot. I trotted on Spot up forward near our guide, who rode an Indian pony as raggedy and careless as himself.

By dawn we were well beyond sight of the Fort, keeping to the eastern fringe of the mountains. This route, a short cut by the Great Salt Lake, was coming into use by the bolder of the California immigrants, but the majority still clung to the old trail that continued to Fort Hall and the Humboldt River.

It was October, now, but it was a blistering-hot day. Before us stretched an empty waste as forlorn as the eve of creation—no trees, no water, no grass, no growth except artemisia, or sagebrush, and I didn't care if I never saw that wiry shrub again.

When it was full light, and the sun broiling down from about fifty yards high, we began to see the same old thrown-away furniture and wreckage. And before the day was out, dead oxen again, along with graves: "E. Pritchard, Died July 28, 1849." My father picked up a novel called *The Forger*, by a man named G.P.R. James, and read it walking along, occasionally laughing at something funny, but when Bridger pointed in his dry, squinted-up way at a file of Indians that had taken up the march beside us, scavenging, he put it hurriedly away.

The Indians were Utes, all but naked, so ratty and poor they made the Pawnees seem elegant by comparison. In the afternoon, at a time when the trail lay close to the hills, we passed a village of Diggers—outcast Utes—a breed so low they acted more animal than human. Bridger stopped to show a few dwellings; they were nothing but holes in the ground, a fox's den, with a crude lean-to over the weather side. My father made a hasty sketch of one; I have it now: a shallow pit in which a stark-naked woman crouches, eyes wide and frightened; beside her a bowl of roasting crickets; and hung against a pole, in a skin pouch laced to a board, a papoose wrinkled and shrunken. One of the scavengers now came up with hand thrust out, saying, "Chreesmas gif, Chreesmas gif," but Bridger shooed him away.

"They beg in Brigham Young's city," he said. "They ain't dangerous unless they got an advantage, and then they'll kill you with pleasure."

The scout had been businesslike and silent, considering his reputation for talking, and I think my father was relieved. Bridger placed a strain on him. He never knew how to act when the tall tales began. Only twice during the day did our guide pull any nonsense, and as Mr. Coe said, these two made up for everything. Once, rolling along a perfectly straight, well-marked trail, in what seemed like the middle of the desert, Bridger stopped and glanced to the right and left, as if checking his bearings. Then he uncorked his spyglass and had a careful look around. After this, he wheeled his horse off the trail and began a wide, bothersome detour, finally ending up back on the road.

"I durn near made that same mistake again," he said with a chuckle. "I've bashed up me and my horse twicet already."

"What is it? Why'd we leave the trail?" demanded my father, as the others rode up, sweating in the sun.

Bridger pointed back. "It's that pesky road-block—a mountain of pure glass. You can't see it unless you get right on top, almost."

"Where?" cried my father. "Surely you can't be serious. I can't see a thing."

The trouble with this fellow was, his departures from normal were so crazy and unexpected he caught everybody flat-footed. That's what made my father so mad.

"First time I encountered it, I fired at an antelope and didn't ruffle a hair. I laid down a regular bombardment until I found out what was the matter. He was standing on the other side."

"A mountain of transparent glass," said my father, with heavy scorn.

"You'd better have a last look. You don't see them often. There ain't more than a handful in the entire West."

"No, I expect not," said my father, about to blow up again. "How do you like it, Coe? Pretty, don't you think?"

Falling in with the humor, Coe shook his head. "You couldn't convince me it's glass. If I know anything about gems that mountain's solid blue-white diamond."

"You don't say," said Bridger, studying Coe with new interest. "Well, now, you may be right. Next trip out, I'll bring a jeweler with an eyeglass and have him look her over. Be worth a fortune, if it wasn't flawed."

"Get up," cried my father, swatting one of the mules. "We've got a journey to finish." But in an hour, he'd forgotten the mountain and made the mistake of asking Bridger what he knew about California.

"I've got a fair knowledge of it," said Bridger. "I've been out three times, and enjoyed it, but wouldn't care to live there."

"Why not?" demanded my father, bridling slightly.

"Well, sir, I'd in nowise relish the longevity. No, when my three-score and ten's up, as they say in the Book, I'll be ready to call her off."

"What do you mean? What the deuce has longevity got to do with it? California's just like every place else."

"Not exactly. There's a difference in that respect," said Bridger. "A few die on schedule, give or take a couple of decades, but the majority'll go right on without a hitch. You never know they've aged. It's the climate. Take the case of a man I know out there, name of Psalter, living north of Sacramento. If I remember right, he'll be two hundred and fifty-five in November. He's a tragic example, but there don't seem to be any help for it. When he got to be two hundred, he was plumb wore out, wanted to die and get some rest. But he couldn't make it, no matter what. He went to the priests and begged permission to commit suicide, but they thumbsed down on it—said there wasn't any scriptural precedent.

"Then his youngest sister—she couldn't have been over a hundred and fifty and hadn't been paid any attention to before, being the baby—came up with a fine idea. 'Why don't you move away, get out of the state, maybe that'll work?' she said. Well, sir, he was tickled pink. He arranged all his affairs and journeyed over into Nevada, and sure enough, he died, within a month. But he'd left in his will he wanted to be buried in California, so they plopped him down, after a beautiful service, in the Sacramento graveyard, with a marble slab to seal the bargain: 'Horace E. Psalter. 1594–1794. Rest in Peace.'

"However——" Bridger paused and squinted sideways at my father.

"Yes, of course. I quite understand," said my father in disgust, as if he was talking to an idiot.

"Yes, sir," said Bridger. "The climate was too much for him. He wouldn't stay dead. He came back to life, and being a husky sort of fellow, he busted the box and pushed right out. He was perfectly resigned, last time I saw him. Says he don't aim to make any more tries—he'll stay on and die in California if it takes till Doomsday."

My father looked at him steadily for about a minute. "I want to thank you for the anecdote, Major Bridger," he said at last.

"You've cleared up a good deal of confusion in my mind about California."

"Any information I've got about it, you're more than welcome. Situated where I am on the trail, I'm apt to hear more than most. I'll try to think up some other points by and by."

"Pray don't bother," said my father stiffly. "There couldn't possibly be anything else of importance."

The third day out from the Fort, we crossed the Wasatch Mountains and then came within view of Salt Lake, an eighty-mile sea with a number of very high islands thrusting up from its calm, silent waters. Thousands of waterfowl—geese, ducks, gulls and bigger birds on the surface, but they made little or no noise. Along with the fact that not a solitary tree, not so much as a two-foot bush, rose from the land nearby, it gave the region a feeling of being more dead than alive.

Before supper, Po-Povi and I walked to the shore and tasted the water, which was brackish and bitter, puckering up your mouth, but in appearance it was as clear as a spring. You could see the bottom sloping down a long way out.

Before we left camp, Major Bridger stated that a person couldn't drown in this lake, unless they fell in upside down, but he said it used to be a lot saltier, and more buoyant. Then he began a story about trying to drive a stake in it with a maul, back in '32, but my father interrupted. I don't think he could of stood any more, not right now.

Later this fall, a group of Army engineers, sent from Washington to survey the Mormon territory, boiled down five gallons of water from Salt Lake and made what they called an "analysis." My father copied it out in his Journals: "Out of the 5 gallons were recovered 14 pints of salt; the exact composition as follows:

chloride of sodium	97.80%
chloride of calcium	0.61
chloride of magnesium	0.24

sulphate of soda	0.23
sulphate of lime	1.12

100.00"

We rode into the Mormon capital the next morning, but I'll let my father's letter, written some days afterward, tell the story:

Plodding toward the amazingly treeless citadel, we beheld a party of men at the outskirts, dressed in buckskin or homespun, with black hats and chin whiskers, in an obvious attitude of toll collection, blocking the trail. This being an unheralded development, I queried Bridger, who said, "They've likely thought up a new dodge for raising revenue."

"Hold, brother," said the foremost of these, stepping into the road. "Be ye Saints or Gentiles? Are ye from one of the other settlements?"

"These good people ain't Mormons," said Bridger, "but they favor the Mormon ways and hope to pass the winter in Deseret, to recruit their strength."

"Oh, ho," said the leader, taking a closer look. "It's Bridger. The Prophet [meaning Brigham Young] preached a fire-and-brimstone sermon against you only this week."

"I'm mortal sorry to hear it," said Bridger. "It's a waste of his talents. The devil gone on vacation hereabouts?"

"Blaspheme not," one of the others spoke up sourly; then they came to the point and demanded a tax of one per cent on all the goods we were bringing into the city, barring spiritous liquors, which were taxable at half their sales price.

This was a bitter blow, but there seemed no other way except to pay it, which we did, spending an hour haggling over the settlement.

Bridger was the last through, and he caused offense by shaking out on a paper a pile of brown shreds, measuring it with great solemnity, adding a few particles, taking some away, and generally showing concern over the amount.

"What is this rigmarole?" asked one of the collectors impatiently.

"Baccy," said Bridger. "It's all the goods I've brought, and I think you'll find that pile right dead on one per cent, though I'll weigh it if required."

The leader swept it onto the ground. "Pass on, ye godless, unserious man." Then he added, raising his voice as we filed past, "Let me give you a word of advice. You won't find any house to live in. What with Saints coming in from the European Stakes and the ones in the Sandwich Isles, plus all the gold immigrants wishing to rest, Zion's crammed to the curbs. You'll be obliged to sleep in your wagons."

Undisturbed, Bridger called back, "I expect Brigham Young'll make a particular effort for such an old friend."

What a sight as we entered! The city is designed on a magnificent scale, being four miles in length and three in width, with very broad streets at right angles, each over a hundred and thirty feet wide, bordered by sidewalks of twenty feet. The blocks are forty rods square and are divided into eight lots each containing an acre and a quarter of ground.

By ordinance, the houses must be back twenty feet from the street and the interval planted in suitable shrubs and trees. Alas, to date no trees have grown, and this lack presents a most depressing scene, which is relieved by the canals that run along most of the streets, somewhat in the spirit of Venice. These irrigations have been led in from the River Jordan, which runs to the northwest and creates great fertility on that level plain beyond the city.

Mountains ascend in terraces on the north and east, and from their base a warm spring is conducted by pipes to a large community bath, a structure that has been said, (quite wrongly, I find) to embrace conduct of the most orgiastic kind. A surly itinerant (a disappointed gold-seeker) assured me "on my oath" that the elders there commonly bathe and fondle young girls of the congregation twice or thrice weekly, to prepare them for "plural marriage," but this account I now know to be apocryphal in many details. Indeed these religious fanatics (for such it must be admitted they are) have been shamefully abused throughout their comparatively brief existence.

As you may know, the sect was organized by one Joseph Smith, of Vermont, by profession a house painter and glazier, who had the good fortune to be visited by an angel, who informed him that, should he care to travel to a hill near Palmyra, New York, he would find buried the prophetic records of a tribe of Jews who had immigrated to America in the time of Zedekiah, circa 600 B.C. (This latter movement would appear to be something of a miracle in itself, since history has no record of these wandering gentry that I am able to discover.)

In any event, Smith made all haste to Palmyra and located a square stone box, as he reported, but upon attempting to break into it, he was felled by an invisible blow whose origin was celestial. The trouble was simple: he was not yet ready for so portentous a revelation. Indeed, it was not until after four years of penitence that Smith was permitted access to the box, which proved to contain not only certain holy weapons but a number of golden plates, united by rings and scribbled over with writing. These Smith declared should be the Book of Mormon, the foundation of his new creed.

Apparently, Smith was a restless fellow, uniquely jumpy in the development of his religion, so that we next find him in a wood in Pennsylvania, baptizing, (and being baptized by) a convert named Cowdery, in the Susquehanna River. Also present, as witnesses, we are told, were a number of spirits who had made their mark some years before in the mortal phase, including Moses and Elias. The scene now shifts to Fayette, New York, for no reason that I can discover, where the first real organization was made, in 1830. And then, when the student has perhaps become geographically adjusted, we find a monster temple in construction at Kirtland, Ohio.

Here, we should observe that the Latter-Day Saints, for such they called themselves, were not overly popular with the neighboring commonalty, or non-Saints. They were unwinning. And while I believe the Mormons to have been treated shabbily often, there exist arguments on the other side. Without doubt, they have been in their travels as inflexible, bigoted, and mulish as most religious fanatics, and made no attempt to adjust to any host community where they settled.

At any rate, Ohio proved *not* to be the promised land, so, leaving the monster temple incompleted (as was the Tower of Babel, earlier), they shifted to Missouri, a place revealed to Smith in a vision as being "the new Jerusalem . . . the spot where the Garden of Eden bloomed, and Adam was formed." Grievous to relate, the lay residents there cared practically nothing for the vision, and doubts were even expressed that the area, a horticultural blank, was the original Garden of Eden. Persecutions followed; many Mormon leaders were imprisoned for "treason," which was, of course, absurd, and in one jail a number of confined Saints were served, as food, roasted flesh of their colleagues. (The cruelty that "civilized" people can practice upon each other often passes belief.)

So, at length, Smith led his flock out of angry and small-minded Missouri to the town of Nauvoo, in Illinois, where for a space prosperity smiled. Their community grew to a populace of twenty thousand souls, all with a corner on salvation, you may be sure, and a more industrious group probably never lived. But even here they aroused resentment by their flinty notions of dogma, their unbending superiority, and their practice of "plural," or "spiritual," marriage, which I shall develop at a later date. At every turn of the road, these hardy folk met bad luck besides making many bone-headed blunders on their own. Nauvoo, for reasons I do not properly understand, became a center of horse thieves and counterfeiters, along with the godly pursuits, and what was the inevitable result? Why, everybody threw the blame on the Mormons. It was as natural as breathing, though maybe there were cases of justification, too. Upshot was that Joseph Smith and his brother Hyrum (with the subsidiary rank of Patriarch) were murdered, shot down, while trying to leap from the window of a jail in nearby Carthage, in 1844.

Brigham Young, as the Lord's Prophet and Seer, with the official title of First President, took over the reins, no enviable job for anybody with normal instincts for self-protection. And shortly afterward the Saints had what must be remarked as perhaps their first wholly workable notion: they would remove to the Western wilderness, far from the haunts of men, and pursue their theological star in whatever manner they thought fit. In brief, they foresaw that they could live in tolerance, peace and good-neighborliness as long as they didn't have any neighbors. Accordingly they began a laborious march from Illinois and Missouri, with the heartiest assistance of most residents along the route—this latter frequently taking the form of rocks, broken bottles, dead cats and scattered gunfire—and made a temporary, if unwelcome, stop at Montrose, Iowa, where they were received with every discourtesy. But they wrought improvements in organization, then, acquiring wagons and livestock, pressed forward toward the setting sun, finally arriving on the far bank of the Missouri River, beyond the limits of state jurisdiction. But their troubles were by no means over. Beyond reach of the States, they ran afoul of the Federals, in the form of an undoubtedly biased requisition from the U. S. Army of five hundred Mormons "for military service against the Mexicans." Still, the Mormons were not actually conscripted; we must give the Government that much, at least. They were "ordered to volunteer." Be it said to their credit that these tough-fibred men, who had as much interest in the Mexicans as they did in the inhabitants of Central Borneo (and most assuredly were not mad at them) patriotically took leave of their families, under conditions of extreme privation, and did their military stint with distinction. The women, children and old persons, meanwhile, sustained life by dining off berries and roots and living in sod huts or caves. As might be expected, a good many sickened and died; their cattle, too, starved or were stolen by Indians.

Elsewhere it has been noted that faith conquers all, and in 1847, with the men returned, we find the Mormons again on the road for the West. An advance guard reached Salt Lake on the twenty-first of July. From this point their prodigious outlays of energy made progress a certainty, although there was a period in that winter, before crops were grown, when they ate the hide roofs of the dwellings they had erected. The main body of the sect arrived the following Spring, and the city was begun in earnest. Crops were sown, grist and sawmills erected, elaborate irrigation carried out, construction of homes and common buildings commenced on a large scale, and a "provisional State Government" devised, with a petition forwarded to Washington asking full recognition for the new "State of Deseret," the mystic word taken, in some fashion, from their Book of Mormon, and signifying, with ear-catching lilt, "Land of the Honey-Bee."

So much for history. (As I read over the foregoing, I see that I have fallen into a vein verging on the flippant. This does not imply disrespect for the Mormons. It is simply that I have suffered, through my lifetime, from an inability to view with seriousness any extreme form of organized religion. It is something beyond my comprehension as a reasoning man. But I hope to keep an open mind as our adventures progress in this God-fearing land of the Mormons.)

Altogether, the population of Salt Lake City now numbers eight thousand, being disposed in neat, clean houses of adobe, or sun-dried brick, which makes a warm shelter in winter and a remarkably cool retreat in summer, a season that can turn most intemperate in this valley.

A huge square has been appropriated for public buildings, and a shed upon poles erected to accommodate upward of three thousand persons. This is known as "the Bowery," being intended to serve until they have completed a Great Temple, an edifice that I am informed will be the largest house of worship on earth.

These dedicated if stern and curious people remain infused with bustle and drive. Already they operate a mint that issues gold coins of the Federal denominations, stamped, without assay, out of dust brought in from California. Whether this is legal, I cannot say, nor do they seem to care. Apprehension regarding the opinion of others is not one of the Mormon weaknesses.

When once we entered the city, Bridger took us to the Bowery in search of Brigham Young, who at length sent word that he was, at that moment, "unavailable for palaver with the Gentile, Major Bridger."

In lieu of this exalted personage, we gained the ear of an elder, one Ezra T. Benson, a dry, practical-looking man with sandy hair, wearing steel spectacles, who at first said there was no rental space to be had in any dwelling. Then he advised us to return later, as he was occupied in forming a committee, together with the Prophet, to carry out certain town road projects. Though not personable in the English social, or charm, sense, Benson appeared unhostile and even helpful within his limits. He is an earnest, able man, and his descendants, Mormon or "Gentile," will make their mark in the America of the future. Before we left, he informed us that a large room in the southeast corner of the State House has been converted to an eating establishment for the accommodation of emigrants and laborers on the public works, to be called the Deseret Boarding House, where one may obtain a meal of milk, bread, butter, radishes, onions, and slaw for a few pennies. Thither we repaired for a noon repast of welcome fresh vegetables and dairy products, items we have missed very sorely these past four months.

Later— We are in luck. Having wandered separately over the city for hours, we returned to the Bowery and found that Coe, in the interim, had obtained a large "double" house—such structures are common in the practice of plural marriage—from a Welsh family that will go to the gold fields for the winter. That is, if my suspicions are correct, the family is now *able* to go, with the sum that Coe has advanced for their dwelling. I queried him about this outlay, but with his usual close-mouthed attitude toward money, he simply murmured that it was "modest" and that he "actually" disliked taking advantage of the Welshman, a silent, gloomy fellow named Llewellyn. We are told that Brigham Young is incensed over the family's decision, feeling that the California gold fields are the source of much evil, and that he has extracted a promise from Llewellyn to return next June, win or lose, upon pain of excommunication. Young's hatred of the loose morals prevailing in California borders on mania. In a recent sermon, we are informed, he rallied the women of Salt Lake about Paris fashions, and I quote verbatim, as follows (with apologies): "Just because all the whores in San Francisco wear funny hats is no reason why we must wear them. If they wore piss-pots on their heads, no doubt you women would feel obliged to follow suit."

(I shall say a word shortly about the shocking freedom of profanity which these Mormons enjoy, presumably by official sanction, since their leaders are among the very worst offenders.)

Young in the pulpit, by the way, never omits a chance to play down the Californian allure and often reads unfavorable items seized upon in newspapers from the region. In Sunday's address, it is said, he read that, "There are too many people here, and they are still coming—ten by water to one by land. The lucky man who strikes a good lead, and can keep it a secret, will get rich, while there are twenty barely making expenses."

After which, he read additional notices to the effect that, "A Yale college graduate is waiter at one of the principal hotels, and a Philadelphia reporter has turned scavenger at San Francisco."

I of course discount much of this as being Mormon bias.

For now, to sum up, we are established with every comfort. Coe and his negro servant, with Jaimie and myself, inhabit one half of our low, solid dwelling that is flanked on one side by a canal and on the other by the broad street. We have a commodious bedroom, Coe has another, and the darky sleeps on a mattress of shucking in a storeroom opening off the kitchen. On the other side, with no communicating door, are the Kissels, in a bedroom, and Jennie and Po-Povi in the second. Our evening meal we take together. Breakfasts shall be done separately, and our lunch must be eaten, at least by Kissel and me, of sandwiches while on the job. Yes, I have a promise of work, as clerk in the General Merchandise Emporium of Elijah Thomas. We are in a thriving way of business and have just nailed up a bulletin, at the Bowery, describing a recent arrival of goods: "Prints, Mull Muslin, Variety of Shawls, Painted Lawns, Ladies Hose, White and Colored Stockings, Linseys, Ginghams, Cotton and Silk Cravats, Silk Tussie, Gents Comforts, Kid Gloves Cold, Side Combs, Tuck Combs, Merinos, Me De Lains, Coat and Vest Buttons, Jackonetts, Redding Combs, Broad Cloths, Cassamiers, 'Redy Made' Clothing, and Tea."

We expect a sizable run on these in the pre-Christmas trade.

Kissel seeks work either on a private farm or on the "public works." (Without here exploring fully the Saints' system of tithing, I will say for now that each man must deliver up, in addition to a tenth of his income, a like percentage of his working time to labor in the common fields.)

Coe will devote the winter to his projected book, *An Amble over the Rockies and a Stroll through the Diggings.* Jaimie's fortunes of the period are not yet decided.

310

So, my dear wife, we are well arranged, as the French have it. Of all the possible methods of getting to the gold fields, this is unquestionably the best. I only wish I had thought of it in the beginning.

Your undaunted (and many-faceted) spouse,
SARDIUS MCPHEETERS;
(Ass't to E. Thomas, Gen. Mdse., S.L.C.)

Chapter XXX

Three days after my father wrote that letter he got into a fuss with Brigham Young. They took a dislike to each other right away; they didn't waste any time on it.

The way it happened was this: across the street lived a family that had an unusual situation. The case was one in a million. Brigham Young himself said he doubted if there'd be another such mix-up in the Mormon settlements for the next hundred years.

A woman by the name of Rachel Diddler lost her husband, Merle, and in a few months she married another, a much younger man. In fact, he was so noticeably younger that she was called "giddy" from the pulpit, by one of the elders. But that didn't bother her; she went ahead and married him as soon as they got permission from the Quorum of Seventies.

Well, her daughter, a plump and pretty but shy girl of fifteen, was living with them, perfectly grown-up and ready, as they said, and under the system of plural marriage it seemed natural that the stepfather should add her to his collection, as a second wife. Across the street they put up this double house, exactly like ours, and had everything working fine, though a little out of the ordinary. The mother and daughter were now sisters, in a way, and on equal terms, but the mother wasn't a small person and didn't mind at all; she quit giving the girl orders, because you don't boss your married sister, of course, and everybody was happy.

Then they ran into bad luck. The young man—he wasn't more than twenty—went out with a party to punish some Utes and got killed, shot through the stomach with a flintlock. Well, *his* father, who was thirty-eight, had been living with them, being a widower, and had taken a shine to the daughter because she was serious and ungiddy, like him, and wasn't always trying to go to parties, the way her mother and his son used to.

So, after a decent interval, of about three weeks, *they* got married, and this changed things a little. The girl was now her mother's mother, and when she had a baby, a boy, which they named John, he was her mother's brother. It was confusing; everybody said so. And they all felt sorry for the mother, and hoped she'd eventually settle down so that the father, who was both her son-in-law and father-in-law, might marry her, too, and get things more or less back to normal. And even if he didn't, she had the right to "claim him" by the Mormon laws, and *demand* that he marry her, on the ground of "the privileges of salvation." If he refused, he had to show "just cause and impediment" why it shouldn't be done, or else by considered "contumacious and in danger of the Council." But meantime they were all getting along very well, though it was another demotion for the mother, who, as stated, was dropped back from sister to daughter this time, when she had started out as mother, right on top of the heap, in the first place.

Anyway, late one night the baby had a fit and turned blue, and the daughter came running over after my father, who'd done some talking about being a physician, with a degree from the University of Edinburgh. It was only a case of simple spasm, he said, and he placed the child in a tub of cold water, which brought it around in a hurry.

Well, Brigham Young heard about it and blew sky-high. He called at our house the following evening, which was a lowering of him in his position of Prophet and First President, and would never have happened if it hadn't been an emergency involving a Gentile.

We were in the middle of supper when we heard a rat-a-tat on the door, and when Po-Povi opened it, it was Brigham Young himself. But we didn't know this at first. He was medium tall and firmly built, and had the air of a man used to being obeyed. His hair was light-sandy, with eyes to match, and his expression, though stern right now, might have been pleasant and mannerly on other occasions, I thought. After his blast about fashions, I was surprised to see he had on a very bright flowered waistcoat, and other garments just as stylish.

My father sprang up, dropping his napkin, and cried, "Come in, sir. Come in. You're the roofer, I imagine. Llewellyn said you'd be around. If you'll just step this way, I'll show you the trouble. I hope you brought your own ladder."

"I—am—Brigham—Young," said our caller in a tone like the low notes of a pipe organ, spacing his words out slow.

"Brig—— Well, now, I call this courtly. We *are* honored, sir. Draw up a chair, take a bite with us. I want you to know," said my father, adding a little more pomp as he heard himself orate, "that we are highly appreciative of our chance to visit your splendid city. We've been extended every courtesy, notwithstanding our divergence of faith. This is Mr. Kissel, of the Baptist persuasion, the Honorable Henry T. Coe, representing the Church of England, Mrs. T. Adam Brice, Methodist, Miss Po-Povi, a worshiper of the non-denominational Manitou, and self and son, Neo-Presbyterian, or free-thinkers. An open mi——"

"My visit concerns itself with the heresy committed in the name of healing last evening across the street," said Young. "Perhaps you'd care to explain it."

"To be sure," said my father. "Gladly, though it's hardly worth explaining. If Your Excellency is interested in medicine, I can call to mind any number of cases far more compelling. For instance, I remember a very obese darky woman in Louisville, a 'Mrs. Washington,' legal husband unlikely, who had what appeared to be a carbuncle on her——"

"Hold!" cried Young, raising one arm. "Enough. Since you're a Gentile, newly arrived, we'll assume for once that you are ignorant of the Word. In the territory of Deseret, all real followers of the True Faith are healed by God. Let that be understood now and forever."

I could see my father getting his back up, and Major Bridger had cautioned us in particular not to take issue with the churchmen. He'd made a real point of saying so, with his eye on my father when he said it.

"There was no question of a *fee*, you understand," said my father, a little huffily. "Mrs. Diddler's daughter, Mrs. Cravat, came running to ask assistance, and I gave it gladly. I would respond so always; it's part of my Hippocratic oath."

"Gentile McPheeters," said Young, "I've counseled with the High Priests about this party. We have made exceptions enough already, mainly because you appear to be people of substance who will probably join us eventually. But hear the Word now. Only Elders of the Church of the Latter-Day Saints are empowered, through God, to heal the sick, halt and sore. There is no practice of medicine here except the Divine laying on of hands. Another example of this quackery will cause your removal, with companions, from Deseret. The Prophet has spoken."

My father's face was red as a beet, but he made a stiff bow, then stood aside to let Young pass out the door, which he did with no further word, not even the usual goodbye.

"The intolerable boor!" cried my father when the door slammed. "Prophet! Seer! High Priests, and laying on of hands! I hope he breaks a leg and calls me to set it. I'll tell him to get a couple of boneheaded elders. He'll change his tune when something happens to *him*. His kind always does."

Sure enough, we found that some Mormons *did* use doctors, who'd been in practice before joining the Church, but these back-sliders were said by the priests to be "lacking yet in a full measure of the faith." The Prophet kept pounding at everybody's duty to "ask for the Elders' hands," all right, but my father's tantrum contained a kind of prophecy of his own about Brigham Young, as I shall tell later.

"It's their land," said Kissel unexpectedly. "And their faith."

"Kissel's right, doctor," agreed Coe good-humoredly. "While here, let us observe and annotate. We have a priceless opportunity to document this curious movement for the world."

"By George, you've hit it," cried my father, sitting down and looking more satisfied. "The only way to stop that charlatan is to get the word, the real word, to Congress. I'll write an exposé of this mumbo-jumbo that will scorch that imitation Moses right out of business."

"That wasn't precisely what I had in mind," said Coe drily.

In the next few days we got settled in and began our work. Mr. Kissel didn't get his farm job at the start but signed for a week of labor at the new college, the University of Deseret, which was being laid out on the lower terraces of the mountains north of the capital, a place known as "the temple city." They had a big stream running through the center, called City Creek, and this was being conducted here and there in the college grounds, for irrigation, to beautify the campus with all manner of decoration: "water jets," botanical gardens, groves of unusual trees, even bath and swimming houses.

They meant to make this University the finest anywhere, and the handsomest. Kissel pitched in first at a big square given over for an athletic field and equestrian ring. I went out with him the first day, and it was jolly to see how he relished getting back in harness. The sun rose up, so he stripped off his shirt, and how his shoulder and arm muscles rippled and jumped! Removing some pesky root, he'd flash his ax high, which made him look exactly like some old wrestler in one of those Roman or Greek pictures. A number of Mormon men stopped to admire him, and then a couple of women, bringing lunches, but these were hustled right along. Another emigrant working there, a red-bearded Irishman whose family lived in a wagon on the outskirts of town, said he reckoned these were members of a sizable harem, but were likely far down on "the servicing list," but I didn't know what he meant. Anyway he was a rough, rude fellow, always spitting, and worse; and once, he relieved himself directly before everybody, not bothering to turn his back. There was grumbling about it, because the women were still there, and pretty curious too.

Oddly, the boss on this job was a Gentile, who had been hired to

316

come out by Mormon recruiters. They did that right along—rounded up artisans and other skilled men with the promise of high salaries and cheap land to buy—"for two or three shillings an acre." The boss liked Kissel and told him he could work on the astronomy observatory when they finished the athletic field, if he wanted to. They were erecting an engineering building and a big agricultural department and a school that would teach "the living, spoken languages of all people throughout the earth."

As I said, this was going to be a show place, and no mistake. They even had plans for a "Parents School," for the heads of families, and Brigham Young himself had announced he would enroll as an ordinary scholar, which people said showed his true size, because there wasn't any record in another religion of a Prophet going back to school like a boy in knee-pants. One or two said you'd have waited till Doomsday before Mohammed or Buddha or one of those fellows could have buckled down so. This Parents School struck me as a very good idea. It was what had been needed all along, the one big missing link in the Louisville education, for instance. If parents were obliged to turn up, and sit sweating through all those classes, watching the clock, listening to a group of pea-brained bores dribble on about William the Conqueror, hounded and harried by truant officers if they knocked off to go fishing, they'd likely get their skin full of it quick and tone down the whole system.

The trouble with parents is, their memories get rusty. And as soon as they forget, they change. The truth is that parents are nothing but children gone sour. This school was well advised, because it might yank them back over the years and make them see things clearly again, as children do unless overeducated.

As far as my parent was concerned, the one working at Thomas' Emporium, he was having a picnic of a time. He was happier than he'd ever been doctoring, because now the responsibility belonged to somebody else. Moreover, he enjoyed meeting the people. He had spruced up his clothes, bought a marked-down vest from the proprietor with a hole in it, laying the cost against his salary, and placed a very splayed-out blue flower in his buttonhole. He was a sight. And when somebody requested a yard of muslin or half a pound of tea, how he spread himself. No stranger could have told him from the owner. Thomas sort of took a back seat, being entirely willing to do so because my father was a born salesman. He really made things move. He'd peter out on it presently, as I knew from past experience, but right now it looked as though he might empty the shelves by New Year's. Before a week was out, he was on speaking terms with practically everyone in the city, Saints *and* Gentiles.

But he simply couldn't resist pulling old Thomas' leg about religion. During a lull one morning when I dropped in, he said:

"Brother Thomas," (all the Mormons called people brethren and sisteren, even outsiders) "I've been deep in study on theology, but I'm having trouble with your definition of Gentile. Perhaps you could enlighten me."

This Thomas was a skinny old buzzard with a turkey-gobbler neck that slid up and down when he talked, which wasn't often, unless it involved cash.

"In what way, Brother McPheeters? I'm not a priest nor an elder; I'm only a humble Saint."

"The stickler in my mind is this: what, exactly, *is* a Gentile?"

"Why that's clear enough, unless I'm mistaken. Anybody who is not a Saint."

"Does that include Jews? In other words, where do Palestinian Jews fit into the picture?"

Brother Thomas replied with some heat. "Jews, as they call themselves, are not actually Jews. They're mixed up on that. The Latter-Day Saints of the Church of Jesus Christ are the only true descendants of the Tribe of Israel."

"You mean to say, then, that Jews are, in fact, Gentiles?"

Thomas was getting a little rattled, but he said, "You've oversimplified things, but I do know this—*all others besides Saints are Gentiles*, so stated in the Book of Mormon."

"The Saints, then, are the only authentic Jews, is that correct?"

"I've never heard it stated in just that way. I don't believe you

318

have it right. I don't think the priests would put it as you have put it. I do know this: there was a trader through here, a very likable and honest man, named Solomon Isaacs, but he got into a dispute with one of our people, not overly popular, who called him a 'dirty Gentile.' Isaacs was boiling-mad and took it to the Council on the ground of slander. He said if it was necessary to be cussed, he had a right to be called a 'dirty Jew,' according to the traditional view of his race, which he had got used to, whereas the other jangled his nerves. I disremember how it turned out."

My father leaned over the counter, like a lawyer in court, and said, "Do you, Brother Thomas, consider yourself a Jew?"

"Why, of course not," he answered indignantly. "There isn't a drop of Jewish blood on either side of the family. We're Scotch-Irish, and English, right on back."

"Then you're a Gentile?"

"Naturally. Confound it, do I *look* Jewish?"

"So—you're a what, did you say?"

"Gen— *Saint*," cried Thomas, turning pale. "See here, Brother McPheeters, I don't know the purpose of this, but it isn't healthy talk. Just you get back to work—there's a customer, so drop the nonsense and get busy."

"Good morning, madam, good morning," cried my father, sweeping forward in his most flourishy manner. "What can we do for you? We're running a special on Gents' Hose and Gaiters. We're pushing them, three sets for the quarter. On a somewhat different level, we've got a secondhand piano knocked down very reasonable. Two No. 3 steel buttons? Certainly, Sister. That will be three cents. And we thank you. It's warm for this time of year." He bowed her out, and I left. I'd heard all I cared to for one day.

Two nights later we went to Service at the Bowery. Emigrants were permitted to attend, but not to take part. It was interesting, though fuzzy in spots. I never saw anything quite like it in the religious line. One of the main Mormon notions was that people should approach worship in a cheerful and happy spirit, so as to let the good thoughts in, and they often told how Joseph Smith, in

Missouri, would greet a pious, long-faced convert by offering to wrestle him in the middle of a public street. In that way he eased the tension and made way for the good fun to follow.

To me, this bunch seemed contradictory. They preached sport and jollity, holding dances, parties, hayrides and all, but for those who broke the rules there was an underlying threat of punishment that was downright scary. They *were* scary, these Mormon leaders: there wasn't any bluff to them. Several times that winter they sent out posses to overhaul and return, from hundreds of miles off, backsliders who had crossed them in some way, even women.

Anyhow, before this service at the Bowery, they had the Nauvoo Brass Band out, and it played anthems, marches, and waltzes, preparing the minds for the sermon to follow.

When everybody was assembled, the bishops and the elders filed in, and things opened up with a Mormon hymn: my father copied it down:

> *Thrones shall totter, Babel fall,*
> *Satan reign no more at all;*
> *Saints shall gain the victory,*
> *Truth prevail over land and sea.*
> *Gentile tyrants sink to Hell,*
> *Now is the day of Israel.*

There were other verses just as ornery, and the people joined in and made the windows rattle. I looked at my father, who had a hymn book open and was braying like a jackass, though why he should have been so eager to jump on the Gentiles, I don't know. It was unsettling; you could hear him above all the rest. He always sang so back in Louisville, too, in a kind of falsey-strained voice that was supposed to sound pious, I reckon, but he didn't have the religion of a polecat, as everybody knew.

After the hymn, the people sat down with the rustly stirring they always make at an intermission in church, joggling the books in the slots, fixing their skirts, rearranging their feet, clearing their throats, and so on. Then Elder Ezra T. Benson gave a report on his committee's road-work, saying how they'd drawn on the Treasury for the money appropriated, and after that an elder got up and made a long-winded string of announcements, some of them downright curious. He led off by saying that the California Lion had recently been seen, and even killed, in this Valley, according to reports, but he got a general laugh by remarking, "It's only a rumor; I haven't saw one myself. I'd be obliged if somebody would show me a stuffed skin." Some of the Mormons around us—men scrubbed up with their neck skin red and cracked from working in the sun, women in bonnets, twisting and turning to see what their neighbors had on, same as congregations everywhere—laughed so loud they almost busted their sides. They enjoyed a good joke as much as anyone.

The announcements droned on. On Tuesday, two gardens had been damaged by emigrants' cattle, which cost the owners seventy-four dollars in fines. Would the emigrants kindly camp a little further from the city, "thereby saving their money and leaving the vegetables to grow? Thank you." An Elder Bullock had married a young couple named Throgmorton during the week, and afterward supped on green peas. The Council of Health would meet Wednesdays hereafter, and give advice gratis, from 3 to 4 P.M. The Utes were getting uppity again and had attacked a Snake village nearby, burning six lodges. It looked as if they might have to be punished some more. The Stake of Zion in the Sandwich Islands was prospering, according to the latest report of Apostle Parley B. Pratt there, and soon would be sending Hawaiian converts to Salt Lake City. As to the Stakes in Europe, converts were piled up in those countries—specially England and Wales—by the hundreds of thousands, waiting to come to America. Thirty-five thousand were said to be collected at Liverpool alone. The slave trade on the African coast was very brisk just now, the average price of souls on the current market being thirty-two dollars. Thursday evening a concert would be held at the Tithing and Post Office, "when we shall endeavor to introduce a variety of sentimental and comic pieces which will be new to the people of Deseret generally, together with some original pieces. Those who love music will have the privilege of enjoying it for a few hours, at a small cost."

And so on.

While all the talk went on, a Welsh interpreter, a squatty little man with a bald head and black-rimmed eyes, from maybe not yet getting all the coal dust out, stood in the left-hand aisle and interpreted. There were several hundred Welsh Mormons in Salt Lake, and more in other settlements of America, not yet arrived out here, and most of these couldn't speak English, made noises that sounded like somebody plucking the strings of a bass violin, with a lot of "*lud wud duds,*" and such like. So they had this Welsh interpreter in church.

After the announcements, they said we were in for a treat, in addition to the regular sermon that evening, which was by an Elder Griggs. Brigham Young himself was going to say a few words. This was always enjoyable, because he *was* a good speaker—exciting, and what Coe described as "occasionally eloquent," and because of his superior profanity. All of these Mormons used words that other people would consider scandalous, but Brigham Young had the widest vocabulary. He could make the best swearers among them sound dull. People envied him, but they weren't jealous. A thing like that is a gift, and, to give them credit, these Mormons were open-minded enough to recognize it.

This evening the Prophet's remarks were about "the new fornication pants," which buttoned up the front. A lot of us didn't entirely get his drift, though I saw some women turn red, but his way of stating it was enjoyed by all. "The Church is against these pants," he said, but I won't tell everything he said. "They're an invention of the devil. They make things too easy; it's a temptation, and takes your mind off your work. I heard of a case in San Francisco where a man's hardly had his buttoned up since he got them. If I can help it, the Latter-Day Saints of the Church of Jesus Christ will wear pants that open on the sides; they're plenty good enough, and speedy enough, for us in Salt Lake City. And I hope the women don't encourage things to the contrary."

It's hard to get the religious flavor of his address into a book meant for family use, but he *was*, as stated, an uncommonly interesting speaker. My father put some exact phrases into his Journals, but he marked that section "Private and Personal," and later we met a Lieutenant Gunnison, of the Army Engineers, who planned to write a complete, honest book on the Mormons, but he said he would only "mention the profanity in salvo, and not do any sharp-shooting." Still and all, he *did* put in some pretty raw stuff about Joseph Smith, on a take-it-or-leave-it basis, but I'll tell all that in good time.

Elder Griggs now arose and bored everybody half-witted with a windy discourse on "doctrine." I don't think a soul understood it, least of all Griggs. It was about the so-called Melchizedek priesthood, and somebody named Michael, who had hair made out of wool, which sounds likely, and the Noachian deluge, in the days of Peleg, and a place called Beulah Land, which I searched for in a geography book, but couldn't find anything closer than Bolivia, so I reckon that's what he meant. Altogether, it was as sapping an ordeal as I could remember. Neither was I able to get in position to snooze; the seats were too hard.

After this, they came to the best part of the service. These Mormons believed that when the spirit moved a person, they were apt to burst out in an "unknown tongue." So a period was set aside toward the end when one after another could get up and make whatever noises came natural. Sometimes it was perfectly straight-away, in English, and concerned with misdoing or temptation or sin. But often all hell broke loose, so to speak. This evening a young farmer sprang to his feet, was recognized by the chair as Hiram Snow, and told (did it very well, too) how he had been on a hay-ride and the younger sister of a friend of his wife's had persisted in tickling his nose with a straw, lying there against him in the hay, and as they rode along, he had a very strong notion to slip his hand inside her shift. But did he do it? "I did not," he said. "Only once, and not very far. At the eleventh hour, the dear blessed Jesus whispered in my ear— 'Leave that virgin be. She can get you into a peck of trouble.' "

It was noticeable from the people nodding their heads that they approved of his upright behavior under stress, and he sat down looking self-satisfied and noble. This airing of people's secrets may have been healthy; you could just feel the room crackle with excitement. Then a stout woman in an outlandish feathered bonnet jumped up, lay back her head like a chicken's and began to holler, "Whoodledee whoodledee whoodledee geezledee geezledee gum." It was outlandish. It gave me the goose-pimples. I commenced to look around for the exit, because it seemed like a pretty good chance they'd wind things up in a general free-for-all. But presently she tuckered out, and with a dying cackle or two, which sounded like "Goozoo, goozoo," she flopped down, and her neighbors began to fan her, very anxious and kind.

Right here we found that any other member of the congregation, hearing this kind of uproar, was legally entitled to get up and claim that God had made him that person's "interpreter," and sure enough, a fellow did just so. "Sister Crenshaw was trying to convey that the dear Lord visited her in a dream last night and told her to forgive Sister Whitesides for calling her a big-mouthed frump," he said. "Praise be for the glorious revelation." Everybody baaed "A-men!" then another woman rose up, weaving from side to side, and said exactly as follows—both Lieutenant Gunnison and my father wrote it down:

"Melai, meli, melo, melooey."

But as soon as she fell back, a very waggish-looking young man that I'd noticed before, because of his mischievous eyes, got up straightaway to cry:

"Dear me, dear me. I don't interpret it fully, but Sister Burkhardt has just said, 'My leg, my knee, my thigh, my——' "

There was a shocked gasp from the audience, not at the word itself, because anybody was apt to say that around here, but because her mind was straying in such coarse regions whilst in church.

The general feeling was that this young fellow had made up his translation in the interest of sport. And afterward we heard he was hauled up before the Council to be punished. But he stuck to his story, insisting that his interpretation was "in the spirit," and they let him off with a rebuke.

No matter how you viewed it, this was a bang-up meeting, full of surprises. I don't recall when I ever enjoyed church quite so much. If you buckled down on this Mormonism, it seemed like a very good thing. If it didn't do anything else, it kept people from getting overly bored.

Chapter XXXI

It was now so late in the year that Mr. Kissel decided to let the farm job go. He continued working at the University while my father helped Brother Thomas tend store and Mr. Coe got a good jump on his book. Late one night, when I was supposed to be asleep, I heard them talking about sending me to school, and my heart skipped three or four beats.

"It isn't as though the boy were usefully engaged," said my father. "He and the Indian girl go fishing, and he helps Othello with chores, but the bald truth is that he hasn't nearly enough to keep him busy."

I didn't waste a minute next day, but went down and got a job on Brigham Young's pet project, his silkworm nursery, where they'd had a sign out: "Boy Wanted." This scheme didn't figure to break my back, either. It was nothing but a big room that had a lot of wire cages with imported silkworms in them, chewing away on mulberry leaves. It wasn't fit work for a man, so they'd decided to hire a boy instead. All I had to do was feed the leaves to the worms. In other words, keep a sharp eye out, so that when a bunch gnawed its way clear—throw in some more leaves.

Eventually this way they were supposed to come up with silk. But somehow they never did. The Prophet dropped in now and then to check—it was his favorite place, almost. He'd look at me pretty sour, as though I'd misfired on the silk. It was annoysome. I didn't have anything to do with it; I couldn't *make* them give silk, and I told him so, said, "You can drive a horse to water, sir, but you can't make him drink."

"Very apt," he remarked, not amused.

I said, "I'll tell you what I suggest, if you don't mind—I suggest prayer. If one or two of the leading elders got down on their knees and worked with these chaps, same as with a convert, it might get them over the hump."

"Confine your attentions to the leaves," he said, and left.

Even with this job, which took six hours a day, I failed to get off scot-free on the schooling. Mr. Coe volunteered to my father that he'd tutor Po-Povi and me awhile each evening before supper "in English literature and the classics."

"That's handsome of you, Coe," said my father. "It's like you. But I'd better warn you what you're up against. The boy's basically fine, plenty of common sense, good bone structure, but he hasn't an ounce of learning capacity. Head's solid concrete, more like a gorilla than a human."

"Oh, come, doctor. He seems perfectly intelligent to me. The fact is," said Coe, his eyes twinkling, "I've noticed that there are times when he appears to outwit us all."

"After an hour's Latin he had the impression that Julius Caesar was a handy man in a Louisville feed store. To give you a rough idea."

"Let's try him, if it suits you, and the Indian child, too. It would give me pleasure."

I was so blue, I'd have jumped in Salt Lake—if there'd been any chance to sink. I talked it over with Po-Povi, and right there I found what she was really like. I'd had the feeling all along there was something treacherous about this Indian; now I knew it.

"Yes," she said. "I wish to. I speak in the white man's tongue as a bird flies with a broken wing."

"You *want* to go to school? On *purpose?* If I had time," I said, "I'd tell you what they tried to do to me back in Louisville."

But it didn't do any good. We had the first lesson that afternoon, and I hate to admit it, but it was fun. This Coe was a born teacher. With him, it wasn't a duty; he enjoyed what he was telling. He read about a man named Robinson Crusoe, who got lodged on a ripping good island, then spent all his time trying to get off, like a lunatic, and then he told us about the green English countryside, and a big house named Blandford Hall, and finally he read us a poem called *St. Agnes Eve*. It was beautiful. I never realized about that sort of thing before. In Louisville they missed the whole point of these poems. They picked them to pieces. Count the similes, rake out the metaphors, how many feet in a line? It hadn't anything to do with literature; it was more like carving up a pig.

"That's all for today, Jaimie, my lad. You got on splendidly."

I felt embarrassed; I didn't know what to say. Finally I blurted out, "It wasn't as bad as I thought—nowhere near."

"Same time tomorrow. Cheerio for now."

He kept Po-Povi after school, so to speak, because he said he would teach her to read. Her face was shining when I closed the door. I'd never seen her so happy. A man old enough to be her father.

A month or so ran by. Winter came early to the valley of the Great Salt Lake that year. In November we had our first snowfall, a dry, white powdery dust driven by a chill north wind. Our adobe house was warm and snug, we were saving up our money; the mules and Spot had been hired out to a farmer; and the wagons stashed in a safe place. Our impatience to wait for spring was almost forgotten. In fact, we would have been content except for Mrs. Kissel. She couldn't seem to get her strength back. But it was practically by force that my father managed to keep her in bed.

On November fifteenth we had a short note from Bridger, delivered by an Indian boy who stole a silver candlestick before he left: "Hoping this finds your party well and harmonious with the Saints. You will never meet an abler or friendlier people, but they're notiony. *It would not do to cross them.* I am making a winter trip to Salt Lake City, exact time undecided. Trading here good, especially in gray wolf pelts. I have twenty-five hanging outside the house. It may be you heard about our cloudburst of October. No serious damage, but the island washed thirty yards down the river. Both wives seasick during the trip."

Then this curious addition: "By now, you may be visited for proselyting purposes. Be firm but courteous. If possible, strike an attitude of permanent indecision. If things develop that you need advice, send word by Brother Hugh Marlowe. *Brother Hugh Marlowe. Don't fail to do it fast.* When read, destroy this note."

And a final P.S.: "Messenger bringing this is a brother of my younger wife. He has established some local reputation as a pickpocket and sneak. Generally thought to have a bright future. He should go far, unless plugged. Undersigned will replace what he steals. Kindly prepare inventory. J.B."

True to the prediction, we had two visitors one evening soon—a Brother Muller, a heavy, pimpled, loutish fellow with stained and jagged teeth set in a wet, half-opened mouth, and Elder Beasely, a church leader. They dropped in, took chairs stiffly, holding their black hats in their laps, and talked in an aimless, dull way about crops, building, and Indian troubles for half an hour. We knew about this Beasely, who was dark and smug-looking, though dour, as if he had a stomach-ache, but nothing about Muller. Beasely was the one who'd tried to destroy the Utes' food supply during the middle of summer. In the driest season, the Utes commonly burn off the untilled fields of the Valley, along with the mountain slopes that have cover, to roast the millions of crickets there. These they gather up, then mix them into a thick, gummy, purplish paste, and eat it all winter. For a delicacy, Major Bridger said, this paste had it over the yellow-juicy grubs that the Worm Eater Indians favor. Beasely's idea was to punish the few hostiles by burning off the fields and starving the whole tribe to death. But Brigham Young called the plan "inhumane, indoctrinaire, and generally unworthy." Beasely was the leader of a very nasty faction among these Mormons, which recommended harshness, and even violence, whenever possible. He was also thought by some to be the leader of a secret and terrible society of Mormons that was organized in Missouri, called the Big Fan. The object of this bloodthirsty bunch, which had recognition signs and private words, called Key Words, was to hunt down and murder all backsliders: converts who got sick of Mormonism and left the Church. The boy that told me this said if I ever peached on him, he'd likely be killed. He said the society was now known as the Danites and that the persons they did away with, including some Gentiles, too, for one reason or another, were said to have "slipped their breath." This boy's mother and father were against such goings-on, but they never said so outside the house.

Twice, to our knowledge, Beasely had insisted on the full church punishment, decapitation, for plural-marriage brides who had been caught misbehaving. But he didn't win out on this, either. Nobody was decapitated during our stay, though a few women were stripped entirely nude and lashed with a cat-of-nine-tails, by their husbands, in view of Beasely's committee. Somebody said he seemed to relish it, being uncommonly religious even for a Mormon, and would grow flushed and sweaty, while shouting prayer aloud in a kind of frenzy as the naked women twisted and screamed. But when it was over, he was limp and loose, as if he had really driven the devil out. Most everybody was afraid of him, he was so religious.

Anyway, here he sat and butter wouldn't melt in his mouth. It took him a tiresome while to get to the point, but Brother Muller, who was a German-Swiss, said little or nothing at all. Except for John and Shep, I don't know when I ever took a heartier dislike to anybody.

"Brother McPheeters, Brother Coe, Brother Kissel," said Beasely, "we have welcomed you all, we have opened our gates and our hearts. You have asked for work, and the Prophet has given you work. Won't you, now, open your hearts to us? You say you seek gold—where is a richer lode than the strength in these sweet, well-watered fields? Acres and acres—a valley of five hundred miles—and ready for tillage, practically without cost, for any and all converts to the true faith."

Brother Muller leaned over and tugged at Beasely's coat. "Say it about the girl."

330

"After the baptismal immersion, Brother Muller has expressed his willingness to have the widow"—he waved toward Jennie, whose eyes began snapping with anger—"sealed to him in wedlock." In view of the difference in their condition—Brother Muller part owner of a thriving brewery on the one hand, and on the other a husbandless pauper—his gesture is generous; it's more than that—it's Saintly. It is typical of Brother Muller."

"I like ones with something to get a-hold of," said Brother Muller, showing us his bad teeth. He didn't address anything directly to Jennie, but that was in line with the Mormons' feeling about women. Women were considered inferior by the Church. If there was only one seat available, nobody would dream of giving it to a woman. She must get up and turn it over to a man. And she must never try to go through a door ahead of a man, otherwise the last part of her through was apt to get a whack. Women were only "child-tenders," and should not be made the objects of "Gentile gallantry and fashion."

I could see Jennie starting to get up and explode, but my father made a soothing gesture, and said, "We are honored, greatly honored, Elder Beasely, by your invitation to join the Church. But I feel that you, one of the intellectual heralds of your faith, will appreciate that this step should not be taken lightly. You would never respect us if we changed our devotion as casually as we change our garments. We view Salt Lake City with admiration, but we need time for study. To be converted to a new faith is to be reborn; some of us have not, ah, shed the old skin."

Well, that was a pretty good speech; we agreed on this later, particularly Mr. Coe, who said, "It was an effort worthy of a Burke. It embraced all and promised nothing," but it didn't seem to solve anything for Elder Beasely.

Getting up, he said sourly, "The Council will be disappointed. May I submit hope that you will reach a decision soon?"

My father and Mr. Kissel stood up, too; though Coe remained languidly seated.

"Please tell them we shall re-examine the worship we have lived with all these years," said my father, coming pretty close, too close, to getting off a piece of sarcasm. "You see, it may take a little time. We always thought we were happy with the old forms."

Elder Beasely looked at him sharply. Finally he said, with just the gentlest hint of a threat, "The Council is satisfied you will make the wise choice. In fact, we'll pray for it. Salt Lake City is undergirt with prayer."

Before they left, Brother Muller announced to nobody in particular, "I don't like to be put off, once I'm ready to wed. I'm itching for it. Some like them tender and raw, but there ain't nothing like a fresh-broke-in widder, with handholds, for cutting up didoes on a wedding night."

I knew the signs; my father was precisely at the end of his tether, but he stepped in front of Jennie, to keep her quiet, and said, a little more loudly, "It's a pleasure to meet such a high-minded connoisseur of romance as Brother Muller. Old-world courtesy is always refreshing, especially so in the wilderness. I'll wager Mrs. Brice will be hard to contain over the next few weeks."

Elder Beasely turned a dark, muddy red. "Thank you, sir. I shall report your remarks, verbatim, to the Council."

My father bowed them out, with, "Pray do so. Good night—gentlemen."

Coe burst into laughter, but Jennie hit the door with one of her shoes. On solemn reflection, though, the men felt uneasy. When Mr. Kissel said, "We'd best repair our fences; these people are dead-serious," he summed up the general sentiment.

Salt Lake City
Dec. 21, 1849

My Dear Melissa:

As suggested in my last message, we are finding it increasingly hard to maintain good relations with the Saints. These people can be irksome. Four times in the last weeks, we have been visited by a ruffianly oaf, heavy, sensual and coarse, named Muller, whose amorous propensities have been aroused by the sight of our Jennie.

He sits, making comments that are perilously close to vile, while eyeing her with thinly concealed lust. This makes for a delicate situation, since Muller has some influence and is exerting great pressure to accomplish his unworthy end. This he can do only if she abandons her present religion and adopts the Mormon faith.

Needless to say, there would be no question of her doing so by volition, so the aim of Muller, and friends, is to persuade, or subtly threaten, us *all* into conversion. To be perfectly candid, though our fever about gold remains high, we are feeling the strain. Were it not that the mountain passes are piled high with snow, and if Mrs. Kissel were well, we should be tempted to decamp.

In my capacity as associate merchandiser (I'm confident there's a vice-presidency for me there if I choose to remain) I meet everyone, give or take, and I've become acquainted with a Lieutenant Gunnison and a Captain Stansbury, both cultured gentlemen of quality, who are sent here on a governmental mission, surveying the Salt Lake Valley and generally exploring the region. Captain Stansbury, of course, will prepare for Congress, and the Army, a full report in book form of his findings. Lieutenant Gunnison, a man of strangely philosophical leanings for a career officer, is even now engaged in writing a *History of the Mormons,* with particular emphasis on their theology, practices and present social condition.

Invited to the billet of these gentlemen, I held a long discussion of our problem. Both are fair-minded and see merit in the Mormons' basic character and aims. But both acknowledge a certain grim inflexibility in the cult, though they feel that time will soften both the outlook in general and the inexorable punishments which the Saints now mete out for transgressors.

Lieutenant Gunnison has kindly permitted me to copy a few paragraphs of notes that bear on these traits, and he says, at one point:

"Of the parties organized in the States to cross the plains, there was hardly one that did not break into several fragments, and the division of property caused a great deal of difficulty. Many of these litigants applied to the courts of Deseret for redress of grievances, and there was every appearance of impartiality and strict justice done to all parties. Of course, there would be dissatisfaction when the right was declared to belong to one side alone; and the losers circulated letters, far and near, of the oppression of the Mormons. These would sometimes rebel against the equity decisions, and then they were made to feel the full majesty of the civil power. For contempt of court they were most severely fined, and in the end found it a losing game to indulge in vituperation of the court, or make remarks derogatory to the high functionaries.

"Again, the fields in the valley are imperfectly fenced, and the emigrants' cattle often trespassed upon the crops. For this, a good remuneration was demanded, and the value being so enormously greater than in the States, it looked to the stranger as an imposition and unjustice to ask so large a price. A protest would usually be made, the case taken before the bishop, and the costs be added to the original demand. Such as these, were the instances of terrible oppression that have been industriously circulated as unjust acts of *heartless Mormons*, upon the gold emigration.

"But provisions were sold at very reasonable prices, and their many deeds of charity to the sick and broken-down gold-seekers all speak loudly in their favor, and must eventually redound to their praise. Such kindness, and apparently brotherly good-will among themselves, had its effect in converting more than one to their faith, and the proselytes deserted the search for golden ore, supposing they found here pearls of greater price."

This, you will agree, sounds fine, but Gunnison observes later on:

"Thus they allow that mistakes have been made by some individuals in carrying out their doctrines; for instance, many have supposed that the time was come when they should take possession of the property of the Gentiles, and that it would be no theft to secure cattle and grain from neighboring pastures and fields, thus, despoiling the Egyptians, and we are told by themselves that such conduct had to be forbidden from the public desk. This instance of wrong application of the dogma that they are 'the stewards of the Lord, and the inheritance of the earth belongs to the Saints,' shows that some foundation exists for the charges against them, on the score of insecurity of property, in Illinois and Missouri—and that abuses can easily arise from their principles, when residing near people of other religious views."

Both Gunnison and Stansbury recommend, for us, a policy of diplomatic stalling until Spring, when, after the thaw, we can remove in peace. For my part, I am not convinced that this will succeed. A Mormon spurned is a Saint blasphemed, and trouble is almost sure to follow.

Frankly, Melissa, I feel very strongly that their system of plural, or "spiritual" marriage has bred unconscious contempt for the whole institution. If Muller wants Jennie badly, he should have her—that, in essence, is the official attitude. That she might evince preferences in the matter is of little concern. This polygamous structure is furtive and dangerous *as practiced*. I say this in spite of a doctor's suspicion that it could be of immense therapeutic value in reducing, or even banishing, boredom and monotony in marriage, a condition that certainly produces dry rot in our civilization. What did that wild-eyed young rebel, Thoreau, say in Concord, Massachusetts? "The majority of men lead lives of quiet desperation."

But this is a subject too daring for a real discussion in our age. I hope I have not shocked you. My remarks should not be taken as a measure of my devotion to home and family. It may be hundreds of years before mankind has the good sense to organize itself in such a way as to enjoy life to the full. So many, now, never taste its nectar from birth to grave.

At present, plural marriage is not discussed openly in Deseret. In fact, it is customary for a Mormon, when questioned, away from his territory, to deny that spiritual marriage is a part of their doctrine. But a blind fool could see that a great many Saints keep a number of wives. Their first marriage is gone through in about the usual way as with "Gentiles": a man's addition of wives, after his first, is described as a "sealing to him." I might comment that they consider their priests to be the only persons on earth truly ordained to perform marriages, hence other unions are null and void. You will recognize, then, that we have been living in sin for years. I hope your slumber remains undisturbed; mine will.

In many cases, several wives occupy the same house, even the same room since a number of houses have only one room, but it is usual to board out the supernumeraries, who often help pay their own way by sewing, cooking, washing, and the like.

The rules governing all this are exceedingly strict. For example, it is a point of personal honor for a man whose wife, daughter or sister has strayed to kill the seducer, and he can always find some like-minded co-religionists to help him. This is known hereabouts as "common mountain law"; taking it into account, no jury will convict the murderer in such cases. A sub-division of this, so stated recently in one of their courts, is that "The man who seduces his neighbor's wife must die, and her nearest relative must kill him."

An anecdote that illustrates the harshness attending this local marriage structure involves an immigrant who resumed, in the Spring, his journey to California. A Mormon woman, with a small child, threw herself on his mercy, relating that a high dignitary to whom she was sealed had neither visited her nor contributed to her upkeep for three years. The immigrant regarded her case sympathetically, added both woman and child to his entourage, and trundled off toward the Elysian fields. Lo and behold, they had not gone a hundred miles before a grim-faced posse of Saints overhauled them and wrenched the screaming woman, with the badly frightened child, from the company and returned her to Salt Lake City. Of her fate thereafter, we have no record.

As to the Mormon contention (on the infrequent occasions when it is mentioned) that plural marriage prevents the "awful licentiousness and the moral and physical degradations in the world," I can only say that the philosophy, to me, has merit. But I cannot become convinced that this was the Saints' original motive. Lieutenant Gunnison's researches, for instance, have turned up some very equivocal material about the high moral tone of Joseph Smith himself. In the Nauvoo phase he was bitterly denounced by "influential and talented" converts, as well as by many of the Gentiles of the area, for "licentiousness, drunkenness and tyranny." Women of the flock accused him of attempted seduction, to which he replied with sanctimonious heat that he was only "testing to see if they were virtuous." This answer failed to satisfy anyone. If several of the intended victims were correct, their virtue would certainly have been jeopardized had they remained in the Saint's presence about five more minutes.

Smith's paper, the *Wasp*, struck out at the dissenters, but a journal begun by the opposition, the *Expositor*, countered with a disturbingly detailed account of "the most offensive debaucheries on the part of the Prophet and his friends."

A footnote to the workability of plural marriage is this comment of Gunnison's, based upon close and impartial scrutiny: "Of all the children that have come under our observation, we must in candor say those of the Mormons are the most lawless and profane."

There you have it. We are each entitled to his opinion, even on such subjects as religion, and it has been my observation that fanatical worship and orgiastic sex are brothers under the skin. But I am prejudiced. I do not believe in stern religions; what is more, my God has never signified his exclusive preference for anyone's organized church. He is not divisible by quarreling sectarians.

Still, I do not mean the above to be an indictment of Mormons, or Mormonism, generally. The sick, feverish compulsion to punish exemplified by Elder Beasely is not, I feel, the prevailing sentiment of this church. Temporarily the Beaselies exert great power; in time, the abuses will vanish and the good remain. It is ever so. And it would be a bigoted fool who could deny that for purpose, enterprise, industry, genius at organization and will to contend against odds, these people are in a class apart. What they have done with this essentially arid, discouraging waste is in itself a miracle.

But they are filled with contradictions, and I wish to chronicle, in closing, the greatest witnessed by us to date.

Saturday last, very late in the evening, when only Coe and I remained awake of our several families, and on a day when the weather—cold, blustery, spitting occasional snow—was so unpleasant that nobody stirred abroad, there came another tapping at our door, very different this time. These occurrences have begun to startle us, who are normally a social and gregarious group. We are wary of the Council; Muller grows more importunate, and Beasely more acid.

So we opened the door no more than a crack at first, admitting a swirl of flakes, and peered out with caution.

I heard a familiar voice. "Doctor McPheeters?"

"*Doctor*," mind you.

"Good evening, Mr. Young," I said. "Pray step in. It's no night to stand freezing on a doorstep."

It was quickly apparent that his manner was very different from the Olympian command of his other visit. Even so, we anticipated trouble, perhaps some kind of ultimatum.

"Sit down, Mr. President," I said; but he looked uneasily about at Coe, as if he wished to have a word with me in private.

"You may think it strange," he said at last, "but I have come to consult you on a personal matter."

"I am at your service, of course."

"You are, I believe, aware of the official position of the Church in regard to treatment of the afflicted."

"I recall that you, ah, mentioned it, on an earlier occasion."

"Officially, diseases are held to be demoniac possessions. Cast out the devil, and the afflicted one is cured. That is the formal view."

"And informally?" I said, beginning to see in which direction the wind blew.

"Mine is a grave responsibility," said Young, with a defensive look of piety. "In my hands have been placed the spiritual and temporal fortunes of thousands, the chosen of God. We can agree that the question of the Prophet's health transcends any rules devised for mortal man."

I waited a moment, as the import of this sank in. Then I said, drily, "Kindly state your symptoms, Mr. Young."

"For more years than I care to remember I have been tortured by the ague."

"Will you please remove your coat," I said, going to fetch my bag.

Can you imagine a more farcical scene? What excellent casuistry! Here is a man whose thunders from the pulpit against conventional medicine have frightened, perhaps even crippled, an entire cult, and what happens when he himself is threatened? He comes sneaking in in the dead of the night to a physician whom he has both warned and abused. I made a promise to keep that unsavory tryst secret, but I have already broken it with the best of cheer. Lieutenant Gunnison has agreed that the paradox of Brigham Young is a fair and just part of any story on the Mormons.

He will include it in his book, but not, *at my request,* unless publication shall take place no sooner than three years from this date.

There is a great deal of good in this movement. There is also some bad. Upon that inconclusive note we shall let matters rest.

I anticipate a crisis in our fortunes here before many weeks have passed. Devotedly yours,

BROTHER SARDIUS MCPHEETERS
(Impious, medical, monogamistic; physician [sub rosa] to God's First Lieutenant)

Chapter XXXII

For several weeks after my father treated Brigham Young we were left in peace about Jennie and Brother Muller. It was a relief not to be visited by that drooling ape; he made everybody nervous. January went by, and part of February, with Mrs. Kissel getting better at last, and then the old thing started up again. Beasely, prodded by Muller, had been working on the Council, and he got downright ugly.

It was too bad, because we had come to like many of these Saints. We even went to their parties, which were merrier than any I'd seen before. One was held in connection with a religious service, where an elder, who was said to be one of their heartiest speakers, arose and lambasted nearly every other form of religion, after which he defended the Mormons, saying, "It is an error, the prevalent opinion that we cleanse the nasal orifice with the big toe, and make tea with holy water. We have among us women who play on the piano and mix French with their talk, and men who like tight boots, and who think more of grammar than the meaning of what they're saying, and who would ask nothing better than to be fed by other people for squaring circles and writing dead languages all their lives—albeit we would not give one good gunsmith's apprentice for the whole of them. And, though we are out-and-out democratic, in spirit and in substance, we have plenty of the hard-to-comb curly-pates of people, of whom the saying is true, that 'we have seen better days,' so that if there is anything we can do, it is to take the measure of sham, half-cut pretensions, and write down their true figures."

He was in a good vein; it was a corker of a speech, and my father took a lot of it down for his Journals. It made you realize that Salt Lake City held cards and spades over most other places, for as he said, "In *our* country, we don't see what the Gentiles look at every day. We don't see old men in the highway picking up manure with their fingers or children in cotton factories dwarfing their little backs before their milk teeth are shed. We don't wear pantaloons sewed at ten cents a pair, and French nose rags brocaded at a hundred dollars apiece.

"We don't have churches laid out in Sunday opera boxes, for fashionable hiring. We don't see men hire other white men to wait on them at table, with bands round their hats, and cockades and uniforms to set off and proclaim their miserable subjections. *Our* men don't see their own species put out their hands to them for alms in the streets, and they don't see what's worse—able-bodied young women, for money, asking the favor God has made man to beg of women, and that even a dog asks of his female . . .

"Heaven be praised, there is not yet a brothel, or a beggar, or a dramshop, or a drunkard, or a thief or a tavernkeeper, or a palace or a prostitute, no, thank God! not one of them yet, in all our settlement."

The people at this celebration, and there must have been hundreds, liked these remarks very well, and nodded to each other with satisfaction, saying things like, "You told the truth, Brother," and "Pitch it in hot, for the Lord's sake."

But when he took to building up Brigham Young, he got the best reception yet. As he said, the Prophet could be just as nice in his person as anybody might wish, perfectly clean and neat, "But he has no mind for some kinds of niffy naffy finical whilly whaling. He has never tried to make himself a Lamb, or a Dandy, or a Lawyer; and therefore neither can I try here to make him out such."

In winding up, he paid tribute to the Prophet's speech and the criticisms some people made of it as being too sprightly.

"As to the language, his 'vehemence,' and 'vulgarity' and 'obscenity,' and as for the language of the Mormons in general, it is our boast that, as we have manners and customs growing up in our Basin that differ from those of people lying across the Beaten Tracks of Travel, so we have already, a style of speaking all our own."

The elder's statements about Mr. Young came because of an unusual tribute the Prophet paid on a recent Sunday to a high official of the United States. From the pulpit, he expressed a wish that this man "become a vagabond afflicted with scab, and be loathsome to himself and all his former friends, wishing for death, without dying, for a long time."

Mormons as a sect, you see, took a downright view of their enemies, and didn't believe in mincing words. Finishing up his talk, the elder said, speaking about disbelievers, "May they be winked at by blind people, kicked across lots by cripples, nibbled to death by young ducks, and carried to hell through the keyhole by bumblebees."

No, sir, if I was out looking for trouble, I wouldn't bother heckling Mormons. There may be some that would enjoy being nibbled by ducks, or carried through a keyhole by bumblebees, but I don't happen to be one of them.

Anyhow, the dinner and frolic that followed made up for everything. These people knew how to have fun and it wasn't any bluenose affair, either. The food came first. I've never seen a spread like that anywhere, even at the church socials in Louisville. The main dishes to start with were roast beef, roast mutton, chicken, roast and boiled veal, roast pig, wild fowl, bear meat, and game pie, along with garden truck and sauce, pies, puddings, preserves, pumpkin butter, and oysters and sardines in cans, from the East. For drink, all the tables had pails of porter and ale, and a few had champagne from the grocery.

When everybody had eaten their fill, the ones that could get on their feet commenced a big figured dance. They did the quadrille, waltzes, minuets, schottisches and the like, and I noticed that the men weren't shy about hugging and squeezing their partners. As music, they had a violin and accordion, but around nine o'clock the Nauvoo Brass Band arrived, and then they made things tune up for sure. I didn't know people could dance so, but Mr. Coe said it came from the strength they got out of the food.

During a couple of intermissions, a Swiss Choir and a Welsh Choir sang several numbers, and did it nobly; they made real music.

Nobody was backward about drinking ale and porter, but there wasn't any rowdyism, if you overlook a bunch of children that were playing tag and upset a table, hitting a very elderly old man with chin whiskers on the head. He rose up from the floor, only a little dazed, not seriously injured at all, except to one of his legs, which was kind of twisted, and caught one of the children, a boy with a mouth so foul that everybody predicted he'd grow up and become a bishop, in the back of the neck with a turkey leg. It was a handsome shot; it would have done credit to a man half his age. Several people got up and congratulated him, and offered him a fresh mug of porter, and after that they carried him to the infirmary.

At twelve o'clock they served refreshments of ice cream, cake, pie, nuts, and more beverages. Then the dancing started up again. It was to go on until two, but my father said Po-Povi and I had been up long enough, so we started home. It was a beautiful night, sharp and frosty, with stars sprinkled all over the sky, close down too, winking and snapping. Beneath our feet the snow lay so dry and cold it gave off a rubbery squeaking, and over in the river you could hear ice booming and bonging, where a crack would appear and run down the line, as if somebody had slid an iron along there. It was a very nice time to be alive. Walking along, Mr. Coe, my father, the Indian girl and I, we took deep breaths of that icy air, good after the food but hurting your nose too, and agreed that things were going tolerably well, now. February would soon be gone and then March, and after the spring thaw we could pack up and resume our way, to California. And at last, of course, the gold. It was exciting.

But when we reached home, there was a sign on the door, with some queer symbols around the edge, and in the middle a sentence written in coarse print:

YOU AND THE GIRL HAVE EXACTLY TWO WEEKS.
—THE DANITES.

Chapter XXXIII

Right after breakfast next morning we held a conference, trying to figure how to proceed. From what we knew of these Danites, they wouldn't balk at anything in the way of terror. Even Coe looked disturbed. But Mr. Kissel was the most cast down, because he felt he and his wife had got us into the trouble by having to stop for a rest. Everybody was in a kind of self-blaming humor. Jennie spoke up to say, "I'm the one he's after. It's my fault, after you took me in like one of your own." She began to dab at her eyes, more angry than sad, as usual. Then she said, "Why doesn't that worthless Coulter turn up the way he promised?"

And after this I'm switched if Po-Povi didn't offer to escape and bring back friends from the Cheyenne nation, only she called them "Paikanavos," which lived somewhere to the southeast. "I belong to the doctor," she said, in a timid but serious way. "Now I can bring much braves."

"Many," observed Coe, who had been keeping up the lessons. "The adjective 'much' is applicable to a *singular* noun, such as 'wheat,' or 'sand'; 'many' is the plural form—'many braves,' 'many horses,' and so on."

I couldn't to save my soul figure any way I was to blame, for once, so I didn't bother to speak. But my father cried, "Oh, poppycock! It's nobody's fault. What's more, these pigheaded ranters aren't going to make us do something we don't want to do. This is still the United States of America, and we're living in the enlightened nineteenth century, not the Dark Ages. I decline to be cowed by the long arm of Sanctimony. If these are God's Apostles, I'm the late Nebuchadnezzar."

This was interesting, but it didn't seem to solve anything, which was customary with my father. Nobody *believed* he was Nebuchadnezzar, so what good did it do to ring in that old skeleton?

And that night he changed his tune a little. We were at supper when came a crash at the window, with a drawn-out tinkle of falling glass, and when we scrambled up to look, a burning arrow was sticking in the center of the floor. My father snatched it out and blew at the flame, then unrolled a coil of paper from near the tip.

" 'Thirteen more days,' " he read, white to his hairline.

"They might have killed somebody," said Mr. Kissel, as if he was only now realizing what all this meant.

We continued supper, but nobody was hungry any more; neither did we talk. And afterwards I saw Jennie and Mr. Kissel whispering together. A few minutes later they excused themselves and went to Mrs. Kissel's room, where they stayed half an hour or so. When they got back, the men discussed the idea of finding Major Bridger's Mormon friend, the one mentioned in his note—Hugh Marlowe. But Mr. Kissel had lost interest. All in all, it was a very poor evening.

In the afternoon of the day following, after the store was closed, my father and Mr. Coe and I saw Jennie and Mr. Kissel coming down the road together toward our house. It seemed odd.

But my father suspected something, for he stepped into the yard and faced them.

"Kissel, what have you done?"

The big fellow looked as shaken as he could get, likely, and Jennie was pale but determined.

"What had to be did, we done—did."

"What do you mean?" cried my father, seizing his arm at the elbow. "In God's name, what *have* you done?"

"We saw the Prophet. If the two of us immerse, he will sanction a sealing of the lass to me."

"In name," said Jennie, looking down at her feet.

346

"Mrs. Kissel begged it so."

"Do you stand there and suggest that you're *joining* this bully-ragging gang and are *marrying* the girl? I may have misunderstood you."

"Until we get free. Bed would in nowise be involved," said Kissel, with an awful grimace of embarrassment.

"My dear friend," said my father, much agitated, "this is a princely and self-sacrificing gesture. But think what's involved. In effect, you are going back on your own faith, and as for the marriage, you'll either be a bigamist or legally bound to two wives of equal station. I urge you to reconsider."

"It's done," said Kissel. "I thought it over first."

"What about you, Jennie?" demanded my father, wheeling around. "Are you anxious to be married as a Mormon?"

"It's our fault, and we've made it up. Anyway, it's only till spring, till we get away."

"You mean *if* we get away. Mark my words," said my father, "this thing will *not* be taken lightly. Not by them. You'll see—not by them."

I thought he was overly harsh, considering they were doing this entirely for us. And I saw Mr. Coe, always polite and thoughtful, go up to Mr. Kissel and say something like, "Very decent, most awfully decent." And then he patted Jennie on the back in a fatherly sort of way, same as he did with Po-Povi, but I didn't seem to mind with this one, somehow.

The second Sunday from this the converts were baptized, along with several others, being dunked backwards, held by the head and waist by two priests, in the font at the Bowery. We all attended, Mrs. Kissel, too, because they said she must be immersed and join like her husband, when she had fully regained her strength. There was a good deal of hocus-pocus along with the ceremony, a communion with wine, a choir of singers, with a band standing behind it, a sermon, and a lot of other tiresome stuff.

When they came to Kissel, the priests had a handful getting him up from the water, but they plopped Jennie in and out in a hurry. You could scarcely hear her responses, her voice shook so.

Well, a day or so later the Council served notice on Kissel that he "must now conform to the rules of tithing," and pay "into the treasury of the Lord," meaning Brigham Young, one tenth of all his worldly goods. And if his goods increased, he must keep paying a tenth right along. What's more, he must donate a tenth of his time to labor on the public works, the community farm (in season), roads, bridges, irrigation canals, and such like.

He discussed it with us, and we concluded to say nothing about the money I'd put up. He turned over what remained of this to me, and I sewed it in the pocket of my jacket. Then, with my father's help, he surrendered a tenth of his goods.

"It's a difficult division to make," my father said, seeing the whole business as ridiculous, and having the time of his life, once he'd got over his rage. "Nobody owns ten of everything, you know. We'll have to pick and choose."

So he selected a tin drinking cup that had sprung a leak, some wormy coffee and flour, two tent stakes that could easily be replaced, a baby shoe with a hole in the bottom, a corset, two bottles of cough syrup, a copy of an I.O.U. for forty dollars that Mr. Kissel owed his wife's father, and a book of Baptist hymns. Mr. Kissel flatly refused to saw off a tenth of his ax handle, on the ground that it would be going too far, and might cause offense.

"Frankly, it doesn't make much of a showing," my father said as he surveyed the pile. "We may have to dicker a little."

He was dead-right. When the tax collectors came around to settle up, they said it was the paltriest offering they'd had to date, and then Mr. Kissel gave up one of the mules we had bought at Fort Bernard. Before they left they assigned him his "tithing labors" for the week.

But if we thought our troubles with the Mormons were over, we were badly mistaken. We'd made an enemy out of Elder Beasely, and Muller, the apelike brewer with adenoids, went kind of crazy in his head from being cheated out of his woman. With some friends, he went to the Apostles and Bishops and tried to get the sealing annulled. I honestly believe if it hadn't been for Brigham Young, and other fair-minded men among the Council, some way would have been found to undo things. As it was, Muller flung taunts at us twice on the street, and another time he overhauled Jennie, whilst shopping, and followed her, making what my father called "lewd suggestions."

Kissel seemed mildly put out when he heard. "That wasn't anything to do," he said, which I figured was about the same as another man's threat of a broken back.

Matters came to a head during a social evening at the Bowery, when they had games and contests. They were always doing something like that, nearly every night. If it wasn't a supper and frolic like before, it was a candy pull or a sleigh ride or a dance or a picnic or a banquet or a round of games. And in the summer, shucking bees and ridge-pole parties, and they customarily put up swings under the cottonwood trees along the river and went fishing and swimming. Or, again, they made horseback excursions to the Great Salt Lake, which was nine miles from the edge of town. But this wasn't always safe, on account of the Utes, or Pah-Utes, as the Indians called themselves.

Tonight at the Bowery they had a number of foolishy contests like pin-on-the-donkey's-tail, but the silliest was a competition between a man and a cat to see which could lap up a saucer of milk the quickest. Everybody was laughing so, the man got to laughing, too, with his nose in the milk, which caused him to choke and fall into a coughing fit, and the cat won. But it was close. People kept telling him he had done very well, and that he certainly looked natural eating that way, and with a little practice would be as good as a cat any day, but he had a reputation as a sore-head, so he got huffy and went home.

Then they laid down a mat for wrestling, and who turned out to be the best wrestler there? Our old friend Muller. He came out dressed in a pair of very tight knee-length pants, without shoes, and did some bend-overs and flexed his muscles. He was built exactly like a gorilla, just as I said, not very tall, or even necessarily broad, but with very long arms, no neck to speak of, sloping shoulders with heavy muscles underneath, and bowlegs, nimble and strong. A person behind us said he always won the matches, and during last summer had crippled the son of an immigrant who tried to recover damages but was driven out of the Valley by Muller's friends.

Elder Ezra T. Benson, the announcer, said Brother Muller, "our popular young brewmaster," would defend his championship against all comers. It was all good-natured, and noisy, and a lot of people called up sarcastic things like, "Where'd you get the bloomers?" and "Why don't somebody rig him a trapeze?" He really *did* look like a monkey, and was partially covered with silky black fur, except for his head, which would be bald as a bullet in a couple of years.

After a good deal of prompting, a group in one corner pushed a candidate up front, a young towheaded farmer who was brick-red with embarrassment. This was exactly what Muller came for. He practically killed that farmer; he made him look as bad as possible, because people said the farmer's girl was there. While the match went on, all the good nature sort of seeped out of things; it wasn't at all funny. Taken all around, these Saints were a bullheaded bunch, but they were human, too, and didn't like to see anybody treated like this. When the farmer put on his shirt and limped back, he had a bloody nose and a sick grin on his face, but he was mad clear through. I could scarcely look at him, with his girl watching and all.

The contest had lasted only two or three minutes, and Muller made the most he could out of winning. He strutted around, grinning and holding up his arms, and then, drat the luck, he spotted Mr. Kissel. The grin dropped off Muller's face in a hurry, but he strode right down from the stage, into the audience.

"Here's a big hunk of blubber," he said, looking at Matt. "Give him a big hand, everybody. Maybe he'll step up, if his liver ain't doing flip-flops."

My father and Mr. Coe leaned over to whisper that we'd prob-

350

ably better go, but Mr. Kissel sat staring up mildly, as if he was thinking it over.

Then Muller made his big mistake.

"He's got his *wife* with him," he said, referring to Jennie. "With a nice piece like that, he don't want to get bunged up none."

Nobody laughed or applauded; in fact, I heard a couple of men say that Muller was a poor loser, and ought to be hushed up.

"I'll wrestle," said Mr. Kissel, getting to his feet and starting for the stage. When he peeled off his shirt, there was a gasp of surprise, and even Muller's cronies, who were likely more afraid of him than fond, took to calling up that he'd better watch his step.

Elder Benson cried, "Begin," and Muller bounded out, feinted to the right and left, then scrambled onto poor Mr. Kissel's back.

"This is farcical," I heard my father say. "Matt hasn't even a rudimentary knowledge of wrestling."

"My apprehensions are along rather different lines," replied Mr. Coe.

No matter what else you might say, Muller *was* a good wrestler, quick as a cat, powerful, too, but right now he wasn't bothering to observe the ordinary rules of sport. It looked more as if he wanted to murder Mr. Kissel. His face was contorted and blotched, and his lungs heaved with pure rage.

Riding Mr. Kissel's back, he got a strangle-hold, and several men near the stage cried, "Foul! Foul!" so Elder Benson stepped in to break it. But when he turned them around, we suddenly saw that Mr. Kissel wasn't discomposed in the slightest. Then the truth dawned over everybody; Muller wasn't able to get Mr. Kissel off his feet. It was ludicrous; lots of people commenced to laugh.

None of our bunch laughed, though. For the first time since we'd known him, including Coulter's scrap with Matlock, Mr. Kissel seemed annoyed. He didn't look mild any more. As my father said later, he gave every appearance of having a bellyful of threats, bad language, insinuations about Jennie, Mormon immersion, tithing, secret societies, plural marriage, arrows burning in the night, and a considerable number of other things, most of them centering on

Muller. It was awesome. Very deliberately he reached up over his shoulder with one arm and seized Muller's head. Then, knotting up his giant's strength, he wrenched that unhappy brewer off his back, turned him a somersault in the air, and slammed him down on the mat. It rattled some dishes on the shelves.

Muller wobbled up to his feet, dazed, and Mr. Kissel stepped forward, grasped his waistband, and ripped the knee-length pants clean off, leaving him standing there bare as the day he was born. But he didn't stand that way long. Mr. Kissel picked him up, crotch and neck, and threw him about thirty feet into an empty row of chairs behind the stage. He went down in a crash of splintered wood, and this time he didn't get up.

"So much for the Danites," said Mr. Kissel loudly, and you could have heard a pin drop. Then people got up and began to file out. There was trouble coming, and very few wanted to be on hand when it started.

We got the new champion dressed, then hustled him home, but an hour later there came a knocking at the door and Brigham Young was standing outside with two grim-faced priests that we didn't know by name.

"This is a bad business, doctor," said Young, coming in.

"Bad enough, I'm afraid," replied my father, with a look of defiance. "First it was Muller hounding Mrs. Brice, then arrows shot through our window, and now, insulting treatment at a public meeting."

"Brother Muller has a broken mandible."

I could see my father itching to make a sarcastic inquiry about the ague, but he held his tongue.

Mr. Kissel had been out of the room, talking to his wife, but now he came back.

"I got riled," he said, regarding Young steadily, not really apologizing. "Commonly, I don't."

"You will appear before the Council tomorrow morning at ten, Brother Kissel," said Young. One of the priests then drew him aside, whereupon the three held a whispered conference. "Yes,"

Young added, "you must bring your sealed one. This is a command from the Prophet and the High Apostles, and is not to be disobeyed, under pain of drastic punishment."

They left, as before, with no further words.

The instant the door slammed, my father cried, "All right, the time's come to get in touch with Marlowe. We can't waste a minute. Our situation here is intolerable."

"I'm mortal sorry," said Matt, and again, in explanation, "I got riled."

Then Coe spoke for us all, I think, when he said, "I must tell you, Kissel, that I don't know when I've enjoyed anything half as much. You were *absolutely splendid!*"

Chapter XXXIV

Things began to move fast now. There was nothing for Kissel and Jennie to do except head for the Council in the morning, but before they left, it being a Sunday, my father jammed on his hat and struck out looking for Brother Marlowe. I went along. I was interested to see how he worked it.

When we got down toward the Bowery, he began nodding to this person and that, wishing them good day in the friendliest tone, and finally spotting one of the rattlebrainedest old biddies in town, he said, "Sister Morganthaler, how nice to see you. I mistook you for your daughter. I wonder if you could give us some information."

"If I'm able, I'll give it and willing, Brother McPheeters."

"We're on the search for Brother Hugh Marlowe. He ordered an elastic stocking, and they've just come in. I promised to let him know."

"Elastic stocking! At his age? I wouldn't thought he had a busted vein in his body, him so skinny."

"It's for his father-in-law. It's a secret, and if you ask me, a very decent gesture. I don't know any more useful gift, when you need one."

"Father-in-law, Brother McPheeters! Why, Brother Marlowe ain't married. Leastways he wasn't last night."

"Of course not," cried my father with a chuckle. "What I meant was, the father of the girl he's courting. There isn't much that escapes you, is there, Sister?"

"I've got good eyes, if I do say so, but I'm bound to admit I didn't know he was courting. Who's the girl?"

"I swore I wouldn't tell," said my father, "but I know I can trust you, Sister Morgenthaler. Will you keep this under your hat?"

"I won't breathe it to a soul, especially Sister Larkin. Last secret I told her, she spread it over town in less than an hour."

"Well, then, what's the name of that farmer out near the University, the fellow with the very pale blonde daughter?"

"You must mean Amos Tillinghast."

"That's the man."

"Well, I'm beat. That daughter of his couldn't be over eleven or twelve at the most. It's a scandal."

"That's exactly what I said, but the next question is, where do I find Marlowe?"

"Right where you'd expect, Brother McPheeters—in the room Brother Thomas rents him, above your store."

"By George, I'd forgotten. He told me so himself. I'm obliged, Sister Morgenthaler. We hope to see you in the Emporium soon."

"And I hope to see *you*, and your boy, in meeting today, Brother McPheeters."

"Absolutely, absolutely," said my father, and when she was out of sight, "Ridiculous old gobbler. A woman on that level of intellect should be boiled down for glue. They're a drag on civilization. Come along, laddie, look sharp, now. It's just down the street."

Reaching Thomas', we waited till nobody was around, then stepped to the rear, where there was an outside stairway, and climbed up in a hurry.

My father knocked, and after a pesky long time, the door opened slowly. I don't know what we expected to see, but I'm blessed if it wasn't the same pale, mischievous young man who had "interpreted" for the woman in church. The one that got up and said, "Melai, meli, melo, melooey."

"Mr. Mar——" my father began, but he interrupted with, "Come in, doctor—been expecting you."

We went inside to a plain, neat room full of books and pictures, and the young man added without preliminaries, "In trouble with the Danites, right?"

"Why, how did you know?"

"My business to know," replied Marlowe, who seemed opposed to wasting time, and speech, on non-essentials. The fact is, everything he said was in a kind of chopped-off, businesslike style, half comic, but soothing on the nerves, too.

"Anyhow, neither here nor there. Question is, how much time?"

My father handed him over our threatening note, then sketched in details of our case, bringing it up to the present, with Kissel and Jennie headed for the Council. While he talked, seated in an uncomfortable-looking chair, the young man paced back and forth, frowning.

"Enough. Got it," he said, cutting my father off in the middle of a gabby sentence. "Too much talk everywhere; not enough action."

"Quite so," said my father, rattled. "I've said so many's the time."

"Probably too many," replied this unusual young man. "Where's your gear? Horses, mules, wagons, furnishings?"

My father began to tell him, but he was so addled by the strange new speech that he began to do it himself.

"Farmer's, mules out of town. Animals boarded, other stuff stored."

"Organize your group. Wait at home for Council's word. If not good, move out tonight. Only way. Seen it before."

"Right," said my father. "Say so myself."

I could see he was itching to ask this Marlowe some questions—what was his part in this Mormon system, why he knew Bridger so well, what was his purpose in helping us, and so on. But he squashed it somehow, and we got up to leave.

Then, all of a sudden, the young man turned human for a second. "Don't worry," he said, clapping my father on the shoulder. "It's a bad business, but don't worry. Leave it all to me. Hate Danites and such. Enjoy outwitting, follow me?"

My father thawed out. "I do, and thank you for your help. We're agitated. The ladies are upset."

"Of course, naturally. Danites a terrible, bloody, murdering

356

bunch. Good Mormons stamp them out someday. Too soon yet. Meanwhile, fight 'em."

"We'll fight," said my father. "We've had enough religious fanaticism for a while." Then, pausing for a second, looking like his old self, he added, "Fed up."

They laughed together, and we moved toward the door, the young man sliding forward nimbly to have a look out first.

"Quick, back!" he cried, and as he did, we heard a stomping of feet on the lower steps.

"In God's name, where?" said my father.

"Under the bed. Nip under, both. *Jump!*"

We rolled under just as a heavy banging commenced on the door. We heard the snick of a lock, then our host saying, "Well, well, Brother Muller. And friends. How pleasant. A Sunday visit?"

"That's enough of your rubbish, Marlowe," said Muller. "The Council's on to you. *And so are some others.* Do you know what I mean?"

"No idea at all. Must ask my Uncle Brigham."

"Being related to Brigham Young ain't going to save your hide forever. You've been skating on thin ice. Where's that doctor and the boy? They was seen heading here."

From under the bed, I could make out four pairs of rough cowhide boots, shuffling from one position to another, and Marlowe's slippered feet. Of them all, only his stood still for a moment.

"Here? Must have come in when I wasn't looking. Let's see, now —sitting here reading, facing east."

"There's another door. Have a look, Ben," said Muller to one of his friends. "You're pretty funny, aren't you, Marlowe? Too good for us Saints, hey?"

"Not good enough for some, too good for others," said the young man in a quiet, different voice.

"What do you mean by that?" I could see a pair of boots come forward two paces until they nearly touched the slippers.

"Nobody's out here. It's a hallway," cried Ben. "Give his nose a pull, and let's get along."

"The Council's just ruled that the girl and old blubber-bag are unsealed. She's going to me. Tell your doctor that, you interfering priss."

"One moment," said Marlowe. "Who are you talking about?"

"Innocent, hey? You know well enough. You'd help them, too, if you was able. Ox-belly, and that big-titty cod-tease he stole."

"You mean the fellow who put that splint on your jaw?"

There was the sound of a very hard slap, then a silence broken only by a coarse chuckle from one of Muller's friends.

"That may turn out to be the very worst mistake you ever made in your coward's life, friend brewer," said Marlowe, sounding perfectly happy and cheerful.

Muller evidently thought he'd gone too far, for he said, "Come on, let's get out—we've got things to do."

When the door slammed, Marlowe snapped the lock and came hopping back. "Up you go, out in the hall, down through the store. Watch close, we can't have a ruckus now. Everything depends on it. Hold on, that door's locked with a key downstairs."

"Aha!" cried my father, digging in his pocket. "I've got the key."

"Splendid. Take it slow down inside stair. No one home—Thomas in church. Hole up till nobody's in sight on the street."

"Tonight?" said my father.

"Bundle up and wait with lights out."

"Most grateful——" began my father, only to be cut off again.

"Enough. No time for talk. Action, remember?"

We tiptoed down into the dark, gloomy store, which could have had an enemy in the shadows behind every box and barrel, and took up a position peering out from under the drawn shades.

"Come to think of it, I've got three dollars due in wages," said my father. "I'll just square the account," and he crossed the room to lift down a handsome new revolving pistol that came in only the week before. It was in a leather holster, on a cartridge belt, and this last he filled all around, then dumped two additional boxes in his pocket. Strapped on, the gun made no noticeable bulge under his coat. This was handy, for our other pistols were ruined in the firing of Kissel's wagon. Just the same, I spoke up; I couldn't help it.

"Father, doesn't that add up to more than three dollars?"

"It works out exactly right," he said. "Three dollars plus the Christmas bonus the old skinflint promised but failed to deliver when the time came. No, it's right on the amount, lacking a few cents, which we can easily settle. Have a piece of candy, son." And he held out a big glass jar.

"I don't mind if I do," I said, grinning. I filled my shirt pocket.

"That's better. I don't like to see a debt go unpaid, and neither does Brother Thomas. It'd plague him if he thought about it."

In ten minutes the street was clear, and we stepped out, walking very brisk and fast toward home. Everybody was waiting for us, Jennie and Kissel sitting down, looking glum, and the others, including Mrs. Kissel, all in the same room, on our side of the house.

"Stir yourselves," said my father, closing the door behind him. "We haven't a minute to lose—we're moving out tonight."

Nobody said a word, but you knew by the way they lit into the packing that we were glad things had finally come to a head.

All was ready long before dark. When night fell, we kept the lamps lit till eight o'clock only, then blew them out. We waited in the darkness.

The night was still, no wind, wholly clear without many stars, cool but not cold, and with that first springy softness in the air that means winter's about gone. I tiptoed through the back door and stood smelling and listening. Already the ice on the canal was broken here and there, where children had thrown rocks in, and you could hear water gurgling below. Pretty soon now the snows would melt in the high mountains, and the river and streams of this valley would be a-bulge with ice water. Even now, they said, there were bare patches on mountain faces where an unusual March sun had beaten down for several days together.

Sidling around, I peered up the street into the darkness. Then I saw something move across the street, a shape blacker than the shadows. I said to myself, what if Muller's got somebody watching the house? We'd never get out.

When I went back to tell the others, Mr. Kissel said, "I'll take a look." He crept out the back, and we tried to watch through the windows, but nobody could see anything but the darkness of the street.

Suddenly, we heard sharp sounds of a scuffle—a scraping of feet on hard ground, a thud, and then a muffled cry. Five minutes later, there came two soft kicks at the back door, and upon our throwing it open, Mr. Kissel was there with one of Muller's friends slung over his shoulder, unconscious.

"I was obliged to invite him in," Mr. Kissel said.

My father and Mr. Coe took bandage strips and trussed the man up, hands and feet; then they strapped a wad of gauze in his mouth for a gag. He appeared to have a fair-sized knot on his forehead, and he was breathing heavy, like a horse that's gone uphill a few miles.

"What did you hit him with?" asked my father in his professional voice, bending down.

"Knuckled him," said Mr. Kissel.

We talked in whispers, and did the tying up to matchlight, that burned a second or two, then flickered out. Now we kept watch in the dark again.

It was just at ten when the door burst open, bringing us scrambling to our feet, and Marlowe shut it quickly behind him.

"Sorry," he said. "Needed to make sure. Ready, all? Well, well, what's this?"

My father told how we had captured Muller's friend, who was slumbering, then he said, "We're packed up, children wrapped in blankets, and itching to get started."

"Then out we go. Leave him here; he'll keep till morning. Single-file after me. Wagons and animals on edge of town."

"How on earth——?"

"Never mind. No time for words."

As nearly as I could see, he led us, Kissel and Mr. Coe and

my father carrying the smallest children, Mrs. Kissel leading the other by the hand, over a back route through the sleeping town and toward the Valley beyond.

In a rocky hollow near the lake we found an Indian boy waiting with the Brice and Coe wagons, loaded with plunder and provisions along with the oxen, mules, and Spot. The moon was up, though veiled over with mist, and things looked ghostly pale as we tumbled children and women into the wagons, packed traps on the mules, which seemed in an agreeable humor for a change, and made the last adjustments of straps and other harness.

"Hurry, hurry, don't dawdle. They'll be on our heels before daylight," said Marlowe, mounted on a horse of his own now, riding up and down beside us.

We cracked the reins and headed off toward the lake, across the Salt Valley, half frozen, patchy with snow, silvery in color under that dull moon.

For hours after reaching the water, we followed the lake shore, crossing some foothills that came right down at one point, with snow to make it hard pulling, and before dawn left the lake to come out on what Marlowe said was the South Trail. Everybody was half dead with tiredness and the animals had that "sobbing" of their sides that my father once put in his Journals.

But we didn't rest long. The animals were fed and watered, we lay down for maybe an hour, until the sky had paled a little across the Wasatch Mountains, then Marlowe was rousting us out. Nobody argued; we knew he told the truth when he said the Danites would pick up the trail by morning. We knew, too, that if caught it meant death for some and a kind of slavery for the rest.

But I don't recollect ever being so played out. We'd been keyed up and nervous for days, and now we had gone all night without sleep. Off and on, I rode Spot a little, but mostly I walked to keep him fresh. Now, with the daylight coming, Po-Povi and I got up, double, for a while and plodded along, nodding and waking, nodding and waking.

When it was full light, we took to looking back over our shoulders.

You do that without knowing it when you think you're being followed. Nothing in sight, but after another rocky range, I noticed Marlowe, on a little peak, studying the low, level waste that stretched out in the shimmering haze behind us.

"Anything?" said my father, when Marlowe got down again.

"Dust cloud—air spiral. Nothing yet."

But he watched more frequently all that day and into the next. And finally, from another rock, studying the back trail, glancing at the sun, and making calculations, he called out:

"So, ho! Company."

We stopped and collected in haste, the women frightened and white. For perhaps the hundredth time that day we stared back at the road we'd come along.

"Other direction," said Marlowe, pointing to the hills.

We whirled round and saw nothing at first but a succession of rocky rills, over which thin clouds drifted, lonely and silent. Then I caught sight of a sun glint on metal, high in the boulders, a glitter followed by several others, spaced out with method.

"Hadn't we better form a defense?" cried my father, more agitated than I'd seen him yet on the trip. "We're exposed on all sides."

"Harmless unless aroused," said Marlowe, pointing up, where a loose, untidy figure carrying a brass-bound telescope was making its leisurely way down.

"Dear me," said my father. He sounded a little shaky in spite of himself. "Major Bridger." And looking again. "Now don't tell me——"

The second man climbing down had the old sarcasticky, familiar look, hair and eyebrows grown back now, and little to show for his burns except two or three ugly white splotches on the backs of his sunburned hands.

"My, my," said Jennie, finding her voice. "We certainly missed you at Christmas. Or did you forget it was mentioned?"

"How's my girl?" said Coulter, unruffled and grinning.

"He arrived at my fort," said Major Bridger to Marlowe, just as

Jennie was getting her back up to do something violent, "and was on his way to Salt Lake when your Injun boy came. We figured to ride up together and pass the time of day."

"We can do without Mr. Coulter," said Jennie. "He's busy with his other interests, in *California*."

"I ain't convinced positive of that, ma'am," said Bridger, pointing at the Valley.

A speck of disturbance, a small roll of dust, moving, this time almost as far distant as the horizon.

"Yep, they're on their way," said Coulter.

"I'd figure about an hour," said Bridger, looking at the sun.

"How many?"

"Look to be eleven or twelve." He gazed through his spyglass. "They seem in a hurry. I hardly ever get in a hurry, myself. It makes you get there ahead of yourself, then you've got to fill in time till you catch up."

"Gentlemen," cried my father, removing his hat to wipe off the band, "we're entirely at your command. It's a great, a very great, pleasure to see you. Had it not been for you, and Brother Marlowe, who, with his cus——"

"Better hop to it," said Marlowe.

"My un-Saintly ear in the Mormon capital," said Bridger, in a kind of introduction. "Buckingham Coulter, apprentice guide."

Coulter shook his hand, then he shook hands with Mr. Coe and Mrs. Kissel and Mr. Kissel and the little Indian girl, and made a mock bow to Jennie, who flushed and afterwards startled everybody by saying, "I don't mind to be kissed hello, if we're going to be killed anyway."

"Good girl," cried Coulter, slapping her on the rump and turning away to Bridger.

Working in a hurry, now, we moved the wagons forward around a bend, where Bridger hid them and tied up the livestock in an opening between boulders. Then we moved the women and children higher, out of sight, and the men took positions that Bridger had already figured out. There was deep snow in the crevices, and a great deal more farther up.

He said, "We'll wait here behind the rocks. When they catch up, we'll hold a little church service."

There were twelve of them; peeping over the rocks, we watched them come on, at a fast trot, the best kind of gait for a burdened horse on a long haul.

We were all nervous, even Coulter, I think, who felt that his responsibility—of getting us to California—was not yet over. And now he had a special interest in seeing Jennie through, too.

"We'll palaver first," said Bridger. "If it ain't unagreeable, hold your fire and leave me do the talking."

In fifteen minutes we could hear the rumble of their hooves; then the jiggling figures were blocked out of view for a minute, hidden between rocks of the curve. When they came out, they were uncomfortably close at hand.

"That's Muller with the bandaged jaw," said my father in a low whisper. "Why not pick him off?"

Bridger spat on one finger, held it up in the air, then nestled his rifle butt against his cheek, I couldn't see the trigger move, but at the crack and puff of smoke, Muller's hat flew off onto the ground. The party pulled up so sharp that one horse reared and spilled its rider.

"Right there'll do," called Bridger. "I wouldn't move none. Now let's make talk."

"We come after the dissenters. Send down that girl and them," cried Muller. "The others can go in peace."

"I don't know as they fancy to return," said Bridger. "Hold on, I'll ask them." He turned to my father and Mr. Kissel and went through some idiotic motions; then called back. "They believe not, but thank you kindly all the same."

"You refusing to chuck them down? Are you standing in the way of the Prophet and the Latter-Day Saints of the Church of Jesus Christ?"

"I don't hear good. You said Brigham Young sent you here his-self?"

The man on the ground suddenly straightened up, holding a pistol, and fired a shot that chipped rock a foot in front of Coulter's face.

I heard him mutter, "Close," and swinging up his rifle he shot the man very nearly in the middle—say an inch to the right—of his forehead.

"There's just a mite of an easterly breeze," observed Bridger.

"I was too mad to take notice."

"Blasphemers! Enemies of God! We'll hunt you down for this if it takes forever," cried Muller in a kind of sob. Then the group scattered in a wild flurry of hooves around the bend and behind the rock.

"Donkey-headed, ain't they?" inquired Bridger.

"What now?" my father asked.

Our men scuttled over the rocks to huddle, and Bridger and Coulter said it was best to stay where we were till dark; then they mentioned something about visiting in the other camp. I didn't understand it fully. But Major Bridger said, "Without pickets, there may be widders before morning."

"I don't like it," said Coulter. "Shoot one of these pious buzzards and you're apt to make *ten* widders. Taken as a whole, the bunch might represent a hundred. Somehow it don't seem right; it's a sacrilege against—hold on, what's that?"

One of the band had thrust a long stick, with what looked like a pair of white drawers, up from behind a rock. Then a forehead rose very cautiously and a voice bellowed out:

"Flag of truce!"

"If you're surrendering, lay down your guns and step out one by one," Bridger called down.

"We're claiming flag of truce for burial. Under the rules of civilized war."

"Never heard of them. Anyhow, we ain't at war. We was on root to California when jumped by bandits."

"You refuse a flag of truce?"

"Our aim is to kill bandits."

"That man lying there requires decent burial in consecrated ground—our religion so ordains."

"Not necessarily—he committed suicide."

Coulter laughed out loud, and there issued from below a string of oaths to peel paint off a stovepipe.

"The madder they are, the poorer the judgment," remarked Bridger. The waiting went on. Presently the underdrawers came out again, and a voice resumed. We didn't think it was Muller's because the truth is that Muller wasn't quite bright, so that others must have done the real thinking.

"Flag of truce for a parley."

"What about?"

"Wish to state our case."

"What case?"

"Grievance against the dissenters."

We held a whispering session, then Bridger cried, "Two step out and advance, unarmed. Walk soft and slow, so the noise won't set off my rifle."

After a puzzling long time, Muller and a man we hadn't seen before approached as far as the first rocks below, maybe fifty yards down, where we had a good look at Muller's bandaged-up face and mean little eyes. He was ugly.

"That'll do. You'll be comfortable there."

"Ain't you going to let us up? Don't tell me we got stand down here in the sun."

"Why no," said Bridger. "You don't need to. Why don't you collect up your Saints and skedaddle back to Salt Lake?"

For some reason, I got the notion they were stalling. They wouldn't speak right out, but kept hemming and hawing. But Muller's companion finally said, "What it amounts to is this. We mean to take that girl. Send her down and the others can do as they please. Now you'll own up that's fair."

"Couldn't ask for fairer," said Bridger. "I'll see if she's ready."

He called out to Jennie, but without waiting for her answer, said, "This places us in a mighty embarrassing position. She ain't ready."

"Very comical," cried Muller, exploding. "Send that trollop down from there, you dried-up old piss-pot, or I'll——" His companion caught his arm roughly, and they withdrew a few feet to talk, turning their backs.

At that moment a pebble rolled down from the heights, bounding a couple of times to hit almost at my feet.

"Mistuh Coe!" yelled Othello from the end of the ledge, and we whirled to see him stand up, grabbing Jennie's pistol, and fire at three men scrambling down from above. A rifle cracked and he fell, screaming; then both Coulter and Bridger dashed over, shooting into the rock and shouting for us to watch the people below.

These now burst into view with a cockadoodle of triumph and fanned out over the sand, firing as they ran. I heard bullets zinging off rocks everywhere around.

With one of the guns from the wagon, I drew a bead on Muller, aiming for his belly, but the second I pulled the trigger, sweat dripped stinging into my eyes and I missed. I could have cried. The trouble was, I wanted it too bad. Any other time, I'd have waited till I could see.

The tables had been reversed all in a twinkling. One minute we'd been sitting up braggy and safe, now we were caught between cross fire. There were too many of them. Of the original twelve or thirteen (it was thirteen, we learned later) one was dead, three were sliding their way down from above, and nine were trying to work up from below, some clawing like madmen at the rocks. Then Jennie let off her double shotgun, from Brice's wagon, and the man with Muller threw his hands over his face, which really wasn't there any more; at the same time, a pistol cracked and one of the Saints spread-eagled on a rock directly above Mrs. Kissel. His head hung down, eyes open and staring, like a man that wanted to say something.

For the moment it was over. The two remaining above got down,

367

from over to one side, and the party below broke off to scramble back out of sight. One was taking it powerfully slow, dragging his left foot, and Coulter shot another in the back before they disappeared. He fell in his tracks like a sack of wheat, heavy, with not so much as a muscle twitch; it wasn't at all pretty to see.

But we had some troubles, too. Othello was breathing in noisy gasps that swelled his chest up and down, and my father bent over one of the Kissels, a yellow-haired tyke about two and a half, with I disremember which name. He was dead, struck in the neck by a ricochet, and hadn't made a sound. None had cried, or even whimpered, during the whole racket. They were good kids; I'd never paid any attention to them before.

"I'm sorry, ma'am," said my father; then he went over to Othello. Coe was on his knees, with his hat off, holding the darky's head. "You promised, Mistuh Coe."

"You're a free man. I pronounce you, Othello Watkins, forever free, in the presence of these witnesses. I'd hoped to say these words in California," said Coe, with tears running down his face. "I should have left you on the auction block in New Orleans."

"Mistuh Coe, I'm—glad—to—be—free."

He made several more gasps, arching up high, then lay still.

Mr. Kissel sat on a rock, chewing a piece of weed, and Mrs. Kissel still held the boy in her arms, rocking back and forth and smoothing his hair. Jennie had taken the other children a few yards away, on the ledge.

Hunched over, Bridger looked crushed, but now he straightened up and made a little speech.

"I reckon I'm to blame. These Mormons ain't Crow Injuns—I won't forget it again. Might be, I've fit Injuns too much—I can't think like a white man any longer."

"Fortunes of war," said Marlowe. "Unhappy but true."

Coulter tightened his gun belt and bent down to pick up his rifle. "Might be, but there's still a few things to settle. I hope to catch up on the trail; if not, remember me to California."

"What are you going to do?" cried Jennie.

"I count eight Saints still waiting for their heavenly reward."

"Come back, you fool!" She put her head in her hands and burst into tears. "I hope I never hear the word California again as long as I live."

"I'll be trailing along," said Bridger. "Here's what—come dark, creep down and get on the move. Harness up, feed the stock, and move out as quiet as you can. *They won't follow.* That's a promise I'll keep. There won't be a blessed one of these sanctified heathens will follow."

"I don't like it," said my father. "The odds aren't what I call suitable. I'll join you."

"Not on this job, doctor. This'll be Injun work, night style, downright ugly. Brother Marlowe will see you up the trail. It's marked plain from here to the Humboldt, and the snow's less than we figured. We'll likely catch up, give a day or so."

We shook hands, and he crawled down the rocks toward Coulter. The sky had boiled up black, with lightning squirting around, and dark would fall in about an hour. Before ten minutes had passed, a regular downpour hit us, probably the last big rain of the winter, according to what Marlowe said. Things here were all topsy-turvy. Commonly no rain fell in the growing season, any time through the summer, but the winters were snowy and rainy, which didn't do a particle of good to a soul.

We hung to our ledge, soaked and shivering, and the storm exploded all around.

"Now!" said Marlowe. "Best time possible. Wonderful cover. Single-file, same as before."

Mr. Kissel and Coe and my father had piled stones over both Othello and the little Kissel boy, so we pried Mrs. Kissel loose and started on down, leaving behind a hard reminder of the Danites.

Chapter XXXV

April 27, 1850

Dear Melissa:

We approach the High Sierras. On the opposite side—California! It seems a decade since Jaimie and I arose on that Spring morning in Kentucky and began our strategic retreat from financial persecution. As previously stated, we had hoped to hear from home and loved ones while in the Mormon capital, but the winter was severe, and the mails presumably did not go through. So, not knowing, we must assume that all is well in Louisville. With any sort of luck, our strike should be made and ourselves well started to rejoin you by autumn.

In my recent missive, I described our tragic brush with the Danites, our flight under cover of storm from the rocks, and our ensuing journey, behind Marlowe, on the "South Trail" across the Great Basin to connect with the main route to California at the Humboldt (or Mary's) River. Far back, bypassed on our Mormon detour, lay the "jumping-off point," the dividing of the ways, where the trails to Oregon and California diverge, near a spot called Soda Springs, where the Oregon immigrants beat toward the watershed of the Snake, and most of those for California strike southwest for the Bear and Humboldt.

In the days after the fight we kept watch for Coulter and Major Bridger, but their absence continued. We are filled with foreboding. There has been no news of either in all the toilsome days of our struggle onward to this much anticipated point. We begin to wonder, did those two men, so contemptuous of danger, miraculously surviving countless set-tos with the aborigines, at last fall victims to a band of religious cranks? If so, will you be so good as to inform the Rev. Carmody? Perhaps he can find a moral here somewhere.

Once back on the main route, at the Humboldt, Marlowe spoke up in his usual elliptical style:

"Well, then. Must say goodbye. Road's plain from here on. Most enjoyable."

I was thunderstruck.

"Surely, you aren't turning *back?*"

"Oh, yes. No interest in gold, you know. Not my line of work."

"See here, friend Marlowe," I said. "There's nothing we'd like more than to make you a member of our family. Perhaps if you came along, we could square our obligation in California."

He looked embarrassed, and when he replied, it was in very close to normal speech. "I appreciate it, of course. But I've got to get back."

"Get back to what? And where?"

"Why, Salt Lake City, of course."

"They'll kill you. You'll be horribly punished."

"Oh, no. They'll try, probably. Make a lot of talk—Councils, and all that. But nothing'll come of it. Seen it before. Uncle's Brigham Young, you know. He doesn't favor the Danites."

I shook my head, saying, "I don't like it. You're taking an awful risk, and all for us."

And then we were startled by his reply.

"I'm a Mormon. Intend to stay a Mormon. But I hope to end the bad things. It's important to get witchcraft out of religion. My job. Mean to convince the Prophet."

A little sadly, we wished him well, and the women crammed his saddle bags full of provisions. Sitting there on his horse, in the mid-afternoon, he looked frail and slight to begin such a journey alone. And he seemed curiously self-conscious about making his farewell. Suddenly he said, "Well, then——" and was off without finishing the sentence. We shouted and waved, but he never turned his head.

I very much doubt that he wanted to return. He simply responded to a sense of duty that is perhaps the essence of his personal religion. I have no idea what view Mormon history will take of Brother Hugh Marlowe, apostle of reason and moderation, but I hope it may prove lenient. When, in the inevitable course of progress, bigotry and narrowness, yes and violence and ugliness, have faded from the minds of these strong-headed people, Brother Marlowe must surely emerge as a milestone of enlightenment.

I shall not attempt to recount the details of our onward plod, with mule and oxen, from the Humboldt to our present position. I'm afraid that, after Marlowe's departure, we made the grave error of taking a northward route, known as Lassen's Cut-Off, which departed from the Humboldt at Lassen's Meadow, proceeded west to Rabbit Hole Spring, thence across Black Rock Desert, and on to the Sierras. Suffice it to say that we have suffered indescribable tortures; in addition, we have prolonged rather than shortened our travel. Certainly we have defeated our basic purpose, that of dodging the privations of the arid Humboldt Sink. Those of the desert we negotiated were worse, we now hear, than anything likely to be encountered on the main trail.

Our supplies being depleted, we have scavenged for food; we are, in effect, living off the country. For days our mouths have been dried up of all saliva, parched for want of water; we have begged flour and sugar from other trains, themselves in distress, we have lost stolen goods to Indians, have fired on Indian skulkers, been ill, exhausted, frozen, burned, starved and harried, and yet we are here, all that remain of us, eager to scale the Pass and come to grips with the Great Adventure beyond . . .

As was his custom in letters home, my father slurred over the worst parts, and that seems too bad, because I started to make a full record of our search for gold in California. So I'd better use some things from his Journals of this Lassen's Cut-Off period, giving it in almost the same sketchy form as he wrote it down, during those days when we were having our very hardest going.

Entries from March 25 to April 29.

Depositing letter for Coulter in barrel post office at Lassen turn-off. This already filled with mail by emigrants who thus leave word of their new route for friends or relatives to follow. Have shuffled through all, nothing for us.

Dust, dust, dust, deep and nasty.

Want of rain makes the soil like a desert, which it really is.

Muskrats [company] have lent us a light wagon. Coe's large blue Santa Fe wagon so very heavy that exhausted oxen could not have hauled it much further.

Pass grave, "E. A. Brown, Louisville." I did not know him.

Twelve men left Muskrat Company yesterday to pack on foot, and left 2 wagons behind. Each took 30 pounds provisions and one blanket.

Still traveling desert-like valley—grass thin and poor.

Sunday—mowed hay for 70-mile desert run. I am tailoring—making my old coat new.

Monday—loaded hay and started, came to bill tacked up on stick: "Provide yourself with hay here for travel of 70 miles. 40 miles from this, take to right to a Spring ½ mile to the left. 12 miles to Hot Springs, 19 miles to Black Rock Wells. Along to Muddy Creek, 7 miles. Sacramento Valley, 32 miles. To Sutter's Fort, 90 miles. Total distance from here to Sutter's Fort, as per above, 270 miles."

Traveling over our old acquaintance, "Ipecacuanha dust"—a powerful emetic in the concentrate.

Wild sage and greasewood, river bottoms very winding all over valley. Enormous dry ditches in which oxen often mire.

Fed oxen chained to the wheels or yoked in the wagons; others fed them loose. The oxen, when they saw the hay, ran to it like hungry dogs.

People we encounter are driving their exhausted cattle behind, or sometimes before, their wagons. When they lie down from exhaustion, people sometimes wait a while for them to rest. At other times they beat them, or set dogs on them, or go through all operations in succession.

Good moonlight tonight from new moon. Oxen stronger.

32 dead oxen, dead horse, passed 4 perfect wagons, 2 carts abandoned.

Are still on Oregon Road, what they call Lassen's Route; *it was ill advised.*

Threw away my old patched coat, also pair of pants bought new at Independence; also a pair of boots.

The women very tired but uncomplaining. Jaimie walks horse and says little. This trial by desert must surely end soon.

Notice tacked up on abandoned wagon: "Water 10½ miles ahead. Grass 12½. This information by a notice ½ mile back. We are just in moving condition and that's all. —C. B. Carr, F. Carmer."

All manner of stuff abandoned. I now sit on excellent leather trunk.

Last night at 9 arrived Hot Springs. 222 dead oxen yesterday.

Cross hot stream to enter a desert with no water for 20 miles. Cut bunch grass as provender for cattle.

My greatest pleasure in traveling through the country is derived from the knowledge that it has seldom been traversed, or at least never been described by any hackneyed tourist; that everything I see or look upon has never been made common by the gaze or description of others. I don't feel the degradation of being charged with the crime of copying the descriptive ideas of others.

We are out of Black Rock Desert but another desert of 20 miles to come.

A St. Louis company has arrived.

We have been out of bacon for some days, and now live on bread or boiled beans and charred coffee without sugar. We have dried apples and peaches in quantity, but seldom boil or stew any.

Sudden cold last night. Ice in coffee cups. Slept in hollow in creek bed to avoid wind.

Muskrats making about 5 to 10 miles daily.

Got 8 pounds sugar, piece of bacon from Muskrats. Godsend.

Played game of "Uca" with Muskrats for provender. Jaimie disapproved. Wolves made tremendous racket last night.

This morning poured coffee from the dregs and sweetened before commencing breakfast, so that no one got more sugar than another.

Learn that grave, of T. E. Carver, Des Moines, is a "cache," containing hidden articles. Many graves are caches. Emigrants hope to retrieve abandoned treasure later. We forced open one cache, had 3 casks of brandy.

Can now see tops of Sierra Nevada.

Met party of men who left wagons to pack. Had made arrangements with another train, in better condition, to bring along their plunder.

Met man from St. Louis who had wandered with pack mules for 14 days in Wind River Mountains—where he ate a mule.

Immense dry lake bed—"mud lake."

Sunday—pass man named Smith with wagons and $1500 worth of dry goods. He, down to 3 yoke of oxen, is burying his dry goods, cloth, calico, etc. He had been on Santa Fe Trail, came north, regretted it.

On the face of the hill above the springs is a row of singularly peaked, whitish pyramids, all shaped like a bishop's mitre. They stand up insulated from one another like the minarets of some extensive monastery.

We leave behind several rifles from Coe's wagon. Burn stocks and bend barrels so Indians will not benefit from them.

Indians stole piece of bacon had obtained from party last night. Fired at noise of men running, around 2 A.M. Indians here very mischievous.

Fine morning, flocks of wild geese. We are nearing the range, spirits rising.

Muskrats, up ahead, sold wagon to a St. Louis company for 115 lbs. flour.

Road here filled with large stones which jar the oxen's shoulders badly.

Dust, sagebrush, made 14 miles today.

17 miles to foot of Sierra Nevada, then north 10 miles, then 3 to Summit.

Grave: "John Kean of St. Louis, aged 70 years."

   "   : "M. Brooker, Va. Aged 31 years."

   "   : "John A. Davison, St. Louis, Mo. Died from eating a poisonous root at the spring."

Within 1½ miles of Sierra Nevada foothills. Hills before us white with snow. Their Eastern face is sprinkled over with small green patches to the top, and the extensive valley at their bottom with grass of all kinds. This is *luxurious* to behold after such a long journey through such an inhospitable and barren wilderness.

We kill antelope, energy *much* recruited by fresh meat. Sunday traded dried fruit for ½ side bacon—no sugar.

April 29: Ready for the ascent. We learn that Governor Smith of California has sent men and supplies for those in need to every pass in these mountains. One of his advance company brought this request of Captain Todd, for perusal of emigrants:

"Notice is hereby given that a Government train sent out by Gov. P. F. Smith, commanding in California, is encamped 8 miles further on than this place. All parties who stand in need of assistance are therefore requested not to camp here but to push on to it as to cause no unnecessary delay. All information as regards this route can be furnished. Inquire for Captain Todd's camp.

ELISHA TODD
Com'd Party"

We are ready for the Summit!

The Journals, you see, came nearer to telling our true condition than my father's letters home did. Still, even in them he couldn't keep his spirits down for long; I remember very well when he wrote that sentence: "We are ready for the Summit!"—though half starved he was as happy as he'd ever been in his life. Anyhow, we were up before daylight, in bitter cold—ice again in the coffee cups—and stirring with excitement, preparing for the climb. The Muskrats were camped nearby, very beat out. Half were planning to pack their goods on the oxen and leave their wagons behind.

My father and Mr. Kissel and Mr. Coe had a conference last night, after drinking a cupful each out of a brandy cask, which my father said appeared to make him stronger. They decided to "double-team" our two wagons to the top, using all mules on one and oxen on the other. It's a waste of time to mix them, because all they do is fight.

We were under way at dawn, wearing anything warm we could find, children wrapped up in blankets in the Brice wagon. Road very rocky, winding in and out, several times crossing an ice-cold stream that was coming down from the snow. The wagons bumped and jarred, and one sprung a tire iron loose, but we let it flop—there wasn't much else we could do.

376

No green but scrubby pines in the crevices, and heaps of snow in the shade. The higher we got (stopping every fifteen minutes to rest) the cloudier it turned, but things were peaceful and still —no storm. I tied Spot to the tail gate of Coe's wagon and walked ahead up the trail. No sound except water dripping off of those icy rocks; you could imagine the mountain was alive and breathing; it had just that little rustle of life. We were getting up toward nine thousand feet. The pass itself was nearly ninety-five hundred, so they said, and my father and Mr. Coe observed that something called the St. Gotthard Pass, in the Alps, wasn't any more than seven thousand.

We got to the top close to noon. It was disappointing, in a way. I think we expected to look down on a kind of paradise—a green valley with running streams, crops growing, and nuggets lying around as big as walnuts. The truth is, all we saw was more rocks, because of the sifty clouds, and when we went down on the other side, hitching animals before and aft to keep the wagons from slipping, there was nothing but the same old desert. We were discouraged, but nobody said a word, even the women.

Davis' settlement was a hundred miles further, the first civilization we would strike in the Sacramento Valley, much of the trip across desert, with Indians stealthier than before. We were still strapped for food, too, but at Goose Lake, a few miles on, got a side of bacon, sugar and flour from a Government wagon parked there. This first wagon crew was fine; they sympathized with our condition and appeared interested when my father said that the Muskrats, back behind us, were worse off yet. But ten miles farther along we met another Government wagon which was selling its commodities at a very stiff price.

My father and the driver, a man wearing a coonskin cap, with his mouth puckered up in a half-moon, exchanged some hot words, after which my father said he was "a typical Government official, slippery, self-serving, and crooked as a snake." He'd forgot about the other wagon, of course. But it gave him something to do, as we walked along, so he lectured to Coe and Kissel on "the tarred brush of politics"—how anybody living off the Government sooner or later loses his fibre, along with his character, and turns into a swine. It passed the time.

That first night down it was deathly cold in the desert. Mr. Coe slept in our tent, and Po-Povi and Jennie in the Brices'. It was really cold, and one reason was, we were hungry. It was necessary to ration both flour and bacon, they said, so we had little to eat before we turned in. Off and on during the night we woke up, and once, while talking, my father said he'd put a piece of jerked buffalo in a sack, several days ago, and now he was blessed if he wasn't going to gnaw it, to keep from freezing. He mooched around in the sack, after kicking the tent pole with his bare foot, and said he'd found it, finally. He offered us some, but we declined.

"I didn't count on it having any flavor," he said, munching away, "but it does seem uncommonly tough. I don't know when I've ever encountered meat so conspicuously painful."

So he struck a light, and what he was chewing was a moccasin, but he'd only eaten just the toe out, so he said it probably wouldn't kill him, but it gave him some powerful stomach cramps during the rest of that night. We heard him taking on. I wasn't surprised; those were a very poor grade of moccasin; I'd worn out two pairs already.

Next day we met another Government wagon, but this time it was for people going through the pass. They refused to sell us anything, food or blankets. My father said, for Government people, he wouldn't "make a poor mouth and beg," so we plodded ahead, the sun rising higher, and hotter, giving us more trouble this way than the cold did at night. No matter how you viewed it, this was mean country; we were dust all over: in our hair, our mouths, our eyes, and our ears—in every part of us, and the women said the same. Our clothes were "varnished" with it, as my father claimed.

We passed a bunch of people with scurvy; their legs were swoll up and blotched and their joints were practically too stiff to move. A pair of Government wagons had refused them food, so we handed out some dried apples, and my father advised them to eat any

378

berries or greenery, even grass, that they could find at a water hole. Near one swampy place we found a grave, a pile of rocks with a headboard that said, "Clayton Reeves, from Tennessee. Shot by Indians. He straggled." With this curious last line at the bottom, "He had more than a dozen arrows in him." Even so, we ourselves never saw any Indians along here; we were lucky that way.

That same day we bought some "pinole" corn meal, no sugar in it, from a wagon and cooked fried mush, which tasted all right but hadn't any strength; I was tired out again in an hour. And that night we bought two loaves of pilot bread, coarse and hard, from an emigrant family which had little more than we did, I'm afraid.

When we got to the Feather River, close to the gold camps, a Government wagon gave us six pounds of beef, without charging anything at all, and later we traded half for bacon, even swap, pound for pound.

On May ninth, my father made this entry in his Journals: "Have at last arrived in Sacramento Valley. Thanks be to God."

Suddenly, everything changed. The weather turned mild, the green grass grew all around, there was water a-plenty to drink and bathe in. We stopped to rest and celebrate. The men toasted each other in cups full of fresh water, with brandy sprinkled in, and the women cried and then fixed up their appearance.

We were in California at last, the way we imagined it, but we cut the celebration short, because we hadn't any food and must push on.

It was like wallowing in pleasure, to roll along in this green, pleasant valley, with a soft breeze on our cheeks. And as for the mules and oxen, we almost had to fight to keep them from stopping every few feet to graze in the thick, rich grass.

At Davis' Rancho—nothing but a few rude log buildings—they were practically out of food, too. Wagons were expected from Sacramento, but they hadn't got in yet. A lot of Indians around were selling wild grapes put up during the past winter, as preserves, along with acorns that Davis' cook made bread from. This Davis had a cook, a yellow-haired woman that swore like a sailor, who he paid fifty cents for every meal she served, and she said she made thirty dollars a day. Mr. Coe insisted that we have supper in the dining room, with him as host, but it wasn't much better than what we could do ourselves, reduced as we were.

So next day we pushed on, after a breakfast of acorns and bacon rind, heading toward Big Butte Creek and what they called "the lower mines," twenty miles distant. Along the way we ran into some men who had "washed" for a day and a half and taken out $123 among them. "It's scarce," they said. "A man's got to scratch like a chicken for worms." But when they gave us two pounds of flour, we stopped and cooked it on the spot, dividing it into four cakes. We passed a big family of Indians that tried to sell us four boys between the ages of five and nine. What they wanted in particular was red flannel shirts.

I felt embarrassed about Po-Povi, but she only stared at them, her face tight and grave. Mr. Coe patted her on the shoulder, and both Jennie and Mrs. Kissel went out of their way to be motherly all the rest of that day. And in the evening, before supper, my father took the girl and me into his tent and said:

"Child," meaning her, "I don't want that scene back there to upset you. Let's understand now and for all—I don't own you any more than I do my own children."

"You bought me, doctor," she said. "By the Indian custom, I am your property, as much as the blanket was."

Mr. Coe had kept up his lessons all winter, so she could talk as well as anybody now, though with a kind of Englishy accent. Mr. Coe said I spoke better, too, but I supposed he was joking, because I'd never talked Indian, and so didn't stand to improve.

"That's nonsense. I 'bought' you, as you insist on calling it, because you seemed unhappy and because we wanted to make you part of the family. Is that clear?"

"If you leave me behind, I must come back. It is the law," said the girl. She had exactly the same kind of mule head as Jennie. I could see that now, and wondered why I hadn't noticed it before.

"Nobody's going to leave you behind. We love you and want you with us. Listen carefully: I now *un*-own you. Savvy? You catchum?"

My father, as I once remarked, could be unusually blockheaded for such a smart man. He continued to take the line that Po-Povi understood mainly Indian talk, and whenever he couldn't get some harebrained notion across, he fell into ridiculous gabble like "catchum."

"Only if you sell me to another."

"Great jumping Jupiter, child! I'm not planning to sell you. I'm not going to own you, either. All right, I'll sell you to Jaimie. How much do you offer? Makee offer."

"I can speak English," I said. "I've spoken it since I was a baby. For that matter, so can she."

"Yes, yes, of course. I was only joking. But let's shuck off this property bugaboo. You offer your barlow knife, all right?"

It seemed silly, but to humor him I handed it over, and he made a show of tucking it in his pocket. Then he told Po-Povi, "Now, you see. Tradee. No longer own you. *I no longer own you.*"

"Jaimie owns me."

"All right, it's gone far enough," I said. "I don't own anybody. I wouldn't care for the responsibility."

My father chuckled and started to leave, saying, "You children hash it out between you. You're brother and sister now."

"Hold on," I said. "I'd like to borrow back my knife. I need it."

"What security can you give?"

The whole thing was such a farce that I said, "I'll put up the girl."

"Fair enough," said my father, and produced the knife. Then he went out, still chuckling, as if he'd had a very good time.

"He's a fool," I said. "But he means well enough. He's just old. All old people act silly one way or another."

"What do you wish me to do?"

It was the first time I'd noticed how she'd grown. And she was only two years younger than me. Then it occurred to me that my birthday, my fourteenth, had gone by and nobody remembered it, not even myself. I couldn't help it; it made me feel bad.

"How's that?"

"You own me, now."

"You own yourself, you poor fish. I've got enough to do to take care of a horse and a goat."

"Men always buy Indian girls for a reason."

To tell the truth, I couldn't figure whether she was pulling my leg or not. She was that deep.

"First chance we get, I'll have a lawyer draw up a quit-claim deed," I said.

"Would you like to go to the stream and have me give you a bath? Squaws bathe the braves in the Cheyenne tribe."

"See here," I said, "let's stop the fooling. We've had some fun, playing together and all, making medicine for my father, exploring around in the woods, but this thing's beginning to get on my nerves. Are you trying to make me mad?"

Her face changed, and she smiled. She had a nice smile; her eyes crinkled up at the sides and the blue part changed color, turning almost purple.

"No, I'm not," she said. "I'm sorry."

"Let's go find some berries."

"I'll find them, you carry them."

She'd had her turn joking me, so I said, "You just think you're smart because you're an Indian."

"I'm not an Indian now; I'm your sister."

That's what I mean. I can't stand women; they've got an answer for everything.

Chapter XXXVI

In two days we reached the Feather River mines, or diggings, buying and scavenging food all along, and such another uproar none of us had seen, even on the trail at its worst.

Jennie said the scum of all creation must have spilled into California. For the most part, they were Americans, of the very roughest kind, but there were lots of Mexicans, and Chileans, and some Australians and English and French, as well as others. Many of these people had come by ship, making a portage across at Panama, and there were even some that had come around the Horn, wherever that was.

Though starved down, we were in high good humor, because the long, long journey was over. Whatever was going to happen to us in California was about to happen. We felt especially fortunate when we talked to others who had fared worse, also when we heard about a party led by Mr. Donner, which was caught by winter storms in the Sierras three years before. A Mr. Montague, who had been with the Frémont expedition but had stayed on to farm, and then to prospect for gold, showed us a clipping from the *California Star*, of April 10, 1847.

"A more shocking scene cannot be imagined, than that witnessed by the party of men who went to the relief of the unfortunate emigrants in the California mountains. The bones of those who had died and been devoured by the miserable ones that still survived, were lying around their tents and cabins. Bodies of men, women, and children, with half the flesh torn from them, lay on every side. A woman sat by the side of the body of her husband, who had just died, cutting out his tongue; the heart she had already taken out, broiled, and ate! The daughter was seen eating the flesh of the father—the mother that of her children—children that of father and mother. The emaciated, wild, and ghastly appearance of the survivors added to the horror of the scene . . .

"After the first few deaths, only the one all-absorbing thought of individual self-preservation prevailed. The fountains of natural affection were dried up. The cords that once vibrated with connubial, parental, and filial affection were rent asunder, and each one seemed resolved, without regard to the fate of others, to escape from the impending calamity. Even the wild, hostile mountain Indians, who once visited their camps, pitied them, and instead of pursuing the natural impulses of their hostile feelings to the whites, and destroying them, as they could easily have done, divided their own scanty supply of food with them.

"So changed had the emigrants become, that when the party sent out arrived with food, some of them cast it aside, and seemed to prefer the putrid human flesh that still remained. The day before the party arrived, one of the emigrants took a child of about four years of age in bed with him, and devoured the whole before morning; and the next day ate another about the same age before noon."

When we read this, we began to think we got off easy, even though we *had* taken some losses. My father said it was a sign we would strike it rich in the mines, which I thought was farfetched but no worse than the generality of his remarks. We camped on a branch of the Feather River, near some other emigrants, not far from a collection of huts called Marysville, where the Yuba River came into the Feather. Sixty miles farther down, this latter emptied into the Sacramento, and the town of Sacramento lay about twenty miles below that. Then, to complete the picture, San Francisco was on down, at the end of the Sacramento, another seventy miles, and across the big San Pablo Bay. That's where we were: up these rivers in Northern California, deep in the middle of the diggings where the gold came from.

Talking to people, we heard how the hullabaloo began. The gold was discovered first by accident, at the mill of a Johann August Sutter, a Swiss gentleman who had come to California by boat in 1839, built a fort and gone into farming. He set up a whopping establishment, fighting Indians singlehanded, then hiring them to work in his fields, and by 1847 he had five hundred employees—farmers, blacksmiths, carpenters, tanners, gunsmiths, vaqueros, gardeners, weavers (for weaving blankets), hunters, sawyers, sheepherders, trappers, and a millwright and a distiller. He was in business in a pretty large way, and devised most all his methods of doing everything. For instance, when it came time to harvest, he turned four hundred Indians loose in a field with pieces of hoop iron, and for threshing, he drove wild horses into a corral where he had grain piled as high as a church. They stomped it and threshed it out.

This Sutter was an important man, filled with energy and resource, my father said, but he lost all his employees overnight. And being extended for credit, he found himself in a first-class pickle. What happened was, his wheelwright, a man named Marshall, recognized gold in Sutter's millrace. We met this Mr. Marshall during our stay on the Feather River, and he said (as my father copied it in the Journals):

"While we were in the habit at night of turning the water through the tail race, I used to go down in the morning to see what had been done through the night; and about half-past seven o'clock on or about the 19th of January—I am not quite certain to a day, but it was between the 18th and 20th of that month—1848, I went down as usual, and after shutting off the water from the race I stepped into it, near the lower end, and there, upon the rock, about six inches beneath the surface of the water, I DISCOVERED THE GOLD. I was entirely alone at the time. I picked up one or two pieces and examined them attentively; and having some general knowledge of minerals, I could not call to mind more than two which in any way resembled this—*sulphuret of iron*, very bright and brittle; and *gold*, bright yet malleable; I then tried it between two rocks, and found that it could be beaten into a different shape, but not broken. Four days afterwards I went to the Fort for provisions, and carried with me about three ounces of the gold, which Capt. Sutter and I tested with *nitric acid.* I then tried it in Sutter's presence by taking three silver dollars and balancing them by the dust in the air, then immersed both in water, and the superior weight of the gold satisfied us both of its nature and value."

That was how it started; now we were in a sweat to get our share. People were strung out up and down all streams, because it was supposed to be there, and in canyons, gulches and ravines. The ravines were favorite places to work, being easy to get at and moderately free of underbrush and rock. A good many "companies," or parties, of men kept passing through. These formed together, pooling their money, and went into the wildest kind of mountains, taking things like provender, cooking utensils, blankets, tools and firearms loaded on mules. If a hole was dug that delivered as much as a quarter's worth of gold, they called that place a "good prospect," so that the word prospecting came out of that. But if the pan showed only very fine grains, too small to save, that was called "finding the color" and wasn't worth pursuing, though it was interesting as a clue.

We parked our wagons, staked out our livestock, set up our tents, and made ready for the grand search. But first my father and Mr. Kissel and I went into Marysville to get supplies—mostly mining tools, since the ones my father bought in Independence had burned with the Kissels' wagon—taking almost the last of our money. Mr. Coe wrote on his book.

This Marysville was no more than temporary structures, a few rough shells of framing, some weather-boarded with clapboards, covered on the inside with domestic cotton, sides and top, over a wood frame. But most of the dwellings were tents, holey and ragged, and lean-tos made of zinc sheets. We came back with lots of stuff packed on mules, after my father had jawed considerable about the prices. To start off, we wanted a good gold washer, with a sieve, but the man asked forty dollars for a secondhand one that had a hole in it where the original owner, now deceased, he told us, "failed to entirely stop a bullet with his stummick." My father blew up; he said you could buy a new one back home for twelve dollars.

The trader, a very smart-aleck-looking fellow with a patch over one eye, said, "I hadn't heerd a man could purchase a new stummick at any price. What locality do you hail from?"

"I mean a washer," said my father sourly. He and Mr. Kissel settled for an ordinary tin washing pan, costing ten dollars, which made him mad all over again. He said you could buy *this* article in a Louisville store for seventy-five cents.

It was an interesting argument. You probably *could* buy a new gold washer for twelve dollars back home, but what good would it do? You could sit on the Ohio River bank for two years, washing out mud, and if you got as much as an old turtle shell you'd be lucky. Or suppose you *sent* for a washer; wrote back home, had a man buy it, bring it out and deliver it. The trip alone would run as high as two hundred dollars, if he made it at all, and by the time he got here, there wouldn't be enough gold in these hills to stuff a tooth with.

Forty dollars seemed cheap to me, and I said so.

Flour, bacon, sugar and coffee were each fifty cents a pound, biscuits ran as high is $1.25, beef was forty cents, and pickled pork a dollar. There was a kind of boardinghouse near us, made of log and clapboards, with a long common table, where a man named Sumner sold "full board" for twenty-one dollars a week or single meals at $1.25 a throw. He had what he called lodging, too, which meant that a body could sleep outside in a tent with several others, furnish his own blanket, for a price of three dollars, "bedbugs and lice at no extra charge," he said, but nobody laughed.

We paid twelve dollars for three picks, eighteen dollars for three shovels, eight dollars for a new pair of shoes for Mr. Kissel, and a dollar a foot for two planks: then we were all but cleaned out.

Mr. Kissel couldn't go right to farming, as he planned to in the beginning, because his stake, including what I'd put up at Laramie, had dwindled down too low. He had some tools but no seed, so he was obliged to join us and hope to make a strike. It was a pity, because my father wrote in his Journals: "Fine places along this river for farmers to squat on, since it is yet unoccupied." As for Mr. Coe, I don't think he had any more interest in gold-mining than he did in raising hogs, but he was observing and annotating, he said, and besides, he wanted to help out. He appeared to have plenty of money, but my father and Mr. Kissel refused to let him pay more than his share, at least at this stage of our adventures.

Well, that night at supper we found that the flour the trader sold us was full of long black worms. My father said a fair exchange would be to go back and fill the trader full of long lead bullets, but we strained the worms out instead, then went ahead and used it. Nobody suffered; the meal was so satisfactory my father swung around to believe that the worms had *improved* the flour, saying they likely "aerated" it, same as they did soil, and he hoped to introduce the idea to millers when he returned home.

Most of this food we bought came from a long way off, the pork and butter clear around Cape Horn from New York, beans and dried fruit from Chile, yams and onions from the Sandwich Islands, and sea gull eggs from someplace called the Farallones. These eggs sold for a dollar each. California was so crazy over gold that nobody was raising any food, you see. People were starved for flavor things like sweet and sour and salt. When we bought our provisions three men were sitting on a log out in front, eating a mixture of vinegar and molasses, sopping it up with bread, wolfing it down like animals.

At dawn we got up and climbed the wooded slopes into the hills. Away from the river proper, there was plenty of ground not spoken for. We found a handy ravine and started to dig, the three men handling picks and me standing by with the pan. We'd left the women and children behind, of course, and given them guns for a precaution, but this wasn't necessary in that spot, because decent people were camped nearby, and a medium-sized yowl would fetch assistance in a jiffy. One of our neighbors, too, had given us a lot of information about gold, so we hoped to fill a sack full of nuggets and cash in at Marysville before dark. First (according to instruction) the men chose a hole about the size of a hat, in the lowest part of the ravine, after rolling away stones on top; then they filled the pan with the dirt taken out. Carrying this to a stream, we washed out the pebbles and dirt, using a kind of circular motion. Mr. Kissel did it first, squatting down beside the stream and holding the pan by both sides. This first dirt was washed several times, but nothing showed in the bottom, so we dug another hole, farther up. Nothing here, either. Altogether, we tried as many as a dozen places and then moved to another ravine.

On the first washing in the new spot we found three or four small black particles, looking like discolored bronze, in the pan. Everybody gave a big whoop, even Mr. Coe, because there's something about gold, looking for it and finding it, that makes you feverish. It's just as they say in the books. It does something funny to you, not all of it good. For instance, when we were digging without luck, we had a fine, enjoyable time, but now we'd washed up say two dollars' worth of gold, we looked around uneasily, as if somebody might burst in and snatch it out of our hands. We had something to *protect*, now, so our free and easy outlook was gone for a little.

But we got busy, on fire to drive ahead, and dug one hole after another. Most had nothing; every fifth or sixth turned up a few bits like the first ones, say as big as very small gravel. These we tucked away in our sack. Some of the washings were little more than dust, not positively gold, but we dumped it in, anyhow, whatever failed to wash out with the dirt and stones. By noon we had what they estimated was better than an ounce, net, which meant that, with gold bringing sixteen dollars an ounce, we'd made about twenty dollars. This wasn't bad; but as my father said toward late afternoon, when the pickings were growing slim, we'd done a square day's work for it. Also, with prices the way they were, we wouldn't pile up much of a backlog at this rate.

We got home early enough to ride into Marysville and have the "dust" weighed out. And right here we got a new shock. It didn't seem to weigh what we'd estimated. Our total haul came to $18.50. Not until several days afterward did we learn that this particular weigher was a known crook. He'd cheated everybody for upwards of a month, but he wasn't due to go on much longer, because in a week a party of sailors from Sacramento, once bit, weighed their next dust first on an honest scale, then took it to this fraud and got the same cheating treatment. So they waltzed him right out of there, down to the riverbank, stripped him, tied him face up on a raft of three logs and shoved him out into the stream. They told him, "Come back and we'll fill you so full of holes you can serve as the underside of a cradle."

After buying more provisions we laid into the diggings early the next day. We'd worked out the good ravine, so we pushed up into the hills. For an hour we got nothing but mud and stones, then we hit more gold, in about the same amount as before. Taking turns at the pick and the pan, we toiled away, adding up our store, one after another calling off how much we thought it was.

"I'd say well over an ounce, maybe two. And if my considerable researches on the subject are correct——"

"Nigh an ounce, not more."

"Oh, come now. We must have two here at least. There might even be three, actually."

"Let's dig another hole," I said.

At suppertime on Saturday, at the end of five days, we went over everything to see how we'd done this first week. The way it shook down was, we'd made plenty to buy provisions and had put away eighty dollars besides.

"The implication is perfectly clear," said my father. "There's gold here, but it's spread out thin. Until we make a real strike, the answer is larger production. I vote to invest in a cradle."

Next morning we scouted around among the traders, hoping for a bargain. It being the Lord's Day, a good many miners had knocked off and came in to visit the saloons and gaming houses. Although they were as rough a crew as you could meet outside of jail—many of them foreigners like Mexicans, Chileans, Chinamen and islander savages—it was interesting that they believed in the Bible lesson of working six days and resting on the seventh. So in they tramped, the mud scraped off their clothes, shaved, too, some of them, except the Chinamen and Indians, which hadn't any beards to start with, and passed the Sabbath getting drunk and shooting craps and fighting, not working even for a minute. It gave me a warmer outlook, and made me wonder if there wasn't something to religion after all. Altogether I saw five fights, except one shouldn't count because both men were so drunk they couldn't exactly see each other, so that one hit an awning post, breaking two knuckles, then fell in the river. I stood by while they fished him out and examined him.

We went into one saloon to talk to the proprietor, who had a cradle for sale. My father, after a look around, a long smell of the sour, yeasty air, and a big sigh, made a drawing of the interior for his Journals on the sly: two very rude tables, a four-legged bench, several wooden food boxes with names of far places printed on them, canvas walls with squares of light ribbing to fix them in place, a pine bar made out of boxboards, an earthenware pitcher of water on top, bartender with scraggly moustache and a low-cornered hat standing behind it with his hands in his pockets, and a row of flimsy shelves behind, holding five or six bottles; two men wearing hats seated at a table examining a sackful of dust; a rough, black-bearded fellow with a hat full of holes leaning against the bar, right foot against a rolled-up blanket on the floor, so as to keep tabs on it, I expect.

The proprietor said he'd "hoped to fetch three ounces"—forty-eight dollars—for the cradle, which though small was in tiptop condition; he'd used it only a few weeks before deciding he could get rich quicker by peddling grog at fifty cents a drink. He was a confidential sort of man, not at all ashamed of swindling the poor, thirsty miners with his outrageous prices. And he said, indicating the ramshackle mess around us, "I've built up a nice place here and I haven't got hardly no overhead except for whiskey and spring water to cut it with."

Being in a testy mood, because of the price, my father made one of his typical jokes. "You haven't even got enough overhead to keep out the rain," and he looked up at the roof, through which the sun was sifting about every few inches.

"It's funny about them holes," said the man. "The water washes right across; it forms a little film. She only leaks in three or four spots—those there the size of your fist, and nary a one of them's over the bar. Anyhow, you take most of my customers, and they're too drunk to notice."

We paid for the cradle and left, and in the morning we tried it on a new ravine where there was very good water trickling down. The way it worked was this: the cradle was an open oblong box about three feet long and half as wide; it was nine inches deep at the upper end and sloped down shallower with the lower end left open. Over the top half fitted another box, a kind of hopper with a bottom of perforated iron—holes half an inch wide and an inch apart—and beneath this was a canvas apron, which was supposed to catch most of the gold. The whole apparatus was placed on a rocker not unlike a child's cradle. When one threw dirt in the hopper, another rocked the cradle, while a third poured in water, using a half-gallon dipper. The water dissolved the dirt, which fell through the holes into the sloping apron and finally into the upper half of the cradle. They had what they called a "riffle bar," an inch or so high, placed crossways at the center, so that what gold left the apron stuck in the top of the cradle, being heavy, as the dirt and stones washed on out.

We spent over an hour getting it set up right in the best place. Then Mr. Kissel began to dig, Mr. Coe shoveled in dirt, and I poured water while my father rocked. It wasn't hard work at all; my father said he preferred it to the rotary motion of panning, which made his head swim.

After two hours we made an inspection and had perhaps half an ounce of dust. This was disappointing, but it wasn't certain we had a good place, so we killed another hour moving farther up, skipping two ravines because a bunch of Chinamen were working a cradle in the first one and some people had a Long Tom going in the second. We ate lunch—sandwiches of pickled pork, as sour as crab apple, biscuits and dried apples—then got back on the job. My father said this ravine looked good; he smelled gold. And he was right for once. It wasn't a strike, but it was rich pay dirt, so good we made three signs and staked out a claim, placing them on upright sticks. Then we really buckled down. By twilight, we'd cradled two leather pouches full of dust—what we figured would run better than four ounces—sixty-four dollars—besides what we had got in the morning.

Mr. Coe expressed the general feeling when he said, "This thing gets in one's blood. Money for nothing; I wouldn't have missed it for a king's ransom. It's precisely what we live for—the incomparable boon of not being bored."

There was a discussion whether we should leave a guard overnight, on account of claim-jumpers, but we hadn't brought blankets or a poncho and it was two miles back to camp. So we stuck our signs in firmer, hid the cradle up in the trees on a hill, covering it over with brush, and went home. The women were hopped up about the gold, specially the prospect of laying in a really fat supply of food. The Kissel children looked white and thin, and Mrs. Kissel said she intended to buy a cow if we struck it rich. Then she thought she might get a proper frock, made out of printed cotton, for Po-Povi.

"Don't you feel the need of anything for yourself, ma'am?" asked Mr. Coe, who always thought she was slighting herself over this thing and that. For instance, he claimed she never took her share of the food.

"Laws, no. I'm too ugly to be improved by adornment."

"As one of my countrymen has remarked, the quality of beauty exists largely in the eye of the beholder. I think I can speak for us all when I say that you don't seem ugly to the members of this party."

Without a doubt, this was the most personal remark we'd heard Mr. Coe make to anybody—that kind of statement doesn't come easy to an Englishman—and he seemed embarrassed, once he'd got it out.

"In that case," she said, smiling around, "maybe I'd better just say I've got everything I want."

To break the ice a little, and show off his knowledge, my father began a gusty discourse on the number of times the word "beauty" occurred in famous poems, and we had supper.

Full of push, we turned out early, having buried our gold at the foot of a tree, and shoved off toward the ravine. But a lot of these ravines look alike, and when we got to what we thought was ours, we didn't see the claim signs anywhere.

"I'm *positive* this is our digging," said my father. "Yet we must be wrong; there's no other answer."

We inspected the next two, and sure enough, we found the signs three hundred yards or so away. But something was mixed up; it just didn't *look* right. And when we went up the hill to uncover our cradle, it was missing. Neither were there signs that it had *been* there. And in the low part of the ravine, we could find no telltale marks of digging, no holes, no rock piles, no muddy spots where a washer had stood.

Facing the others, my father looked grave. "There's been some hanky-panky here. Back we go to the other place."

When we arrived, a party of rascally-looking men were already digging, using two or three pans and a cradle. I recognized one of them; the night before he had come by our camp after supper and asked for a drink of water. And somebody, I forget who— my father, likely—had bragged about our take-out of that day.

We marched on up the hill and went to where we had hid our cradle. The hiding place was there, bushes scattered apart, but the cradle was gone. So we walked down into the ravine, as those villains knocked off to watch. Not a sound, no movement, just a tensed-up waiting by both sides. I didn't care for it. We were outnumbered; there must have been eight or nine of them. Then I saw the leader, a squatty, black-haired Frenchman known as Le Chat, which they said meant The Cat, who had been pointed out to us in town as being the worst bully and villain in all the Feather River diggings. He had on very foppish clothes for a rough-neck, made out of silk, with a filthy brocaded vest, and he wore a rapier in a fancy scabbard, besides two pistols stuck in his belt. His expression was both sly and amused watching us walk up. The others had stopped all work, and now one of them laughed shortly, then spat in the stream.

This Frenchman was some kind of quality gone bad. They said he came from a high family in France, but was the black sheep. Three or four here with him were French; they had come over in his ship, so the talk went, but had run into trouble of some kind; I heard it whispered he'd turned pirate. Whether or not, they didn't arrive at Sacramento in the same ship they left with. People said this was a Spanishman, plain as daylight, very high in the bow and stern.

The Cat wasn't the only quality around here. We met a man named Kelly who was writing a book about the diggings; he'd put in the following paragraph, and let my father copy it out:

"By the end of the week another pack-mule company came in, and several fresh hands from the coast, all the latter of the amateur or dandy class of diggers, in kid gloves and patent leather boots, with flash accoutrements and fancy implements, their polished picks with mahogany handles, and shiny shovels, resembling that presentation class of tools given to lords, baronets, and members of Parliament, to lay a first stone, or turn the first sod on a new line of railway. It was good fun to see those 'gents' nibbling at the useless soil, and then endeavoring to work their pans, with outstretched hands, lest they should slobber their ducks. Subsequently I used to meet members of that school wending back to the coast from the various diggings, 'damning the infernal gold,' and 'cutting the beastly diggins' in disgust."

When we reached this band of ruffians, my father brushed by to inspect the cradle.

"It's ours, all right," he called back to Mr. Kissel and Mr. Coe. "I recognize it from the nick on the left side of the hopper. Our claim, too, of course."

None of the men moved a muscle; all waited for the Frenchman. He had a kind of accent that I won't try to imitate, being no hand at that sort of thing.

"Ah, so," he said, "we have a complaint here, yes?"

In view of the unholy company that now dropped their tools and began to move in, I thought my father spoke up very bravely:

"You might construe it so—this is our cradle and our claim. And I'll ask you to take your helpers and move to another spot."

Coming forward, the Frenchman widened his smile. He had his black hair pulled into a queue behind, like a pirate, all right, and he walked with such easy, flowing motions I began to see where he had got his name.

"Perhaps I have misunderstand. How could this be, your cradle and claim? You see"—he made a pointing-out gesture with his hand —"we use them. Plainly."

"You stole them," said Mr. Kissel in his simple style. "We'll take them back."

I was scared. There was something chilling about this fellow. He was dangerous, and looked especially so right now.

"What was the word you use, my oafish friend?"

Right here, Mr. Coe spoke up, and I think he shocked everybody, including me.

"See here, my good ass, you're nothing but a common thief, you know. I make it a practice not to damn whole races out of hand, even Frogs, but I draw the line at you. In the phrase of our frontier cousins, vamoose. Skedaddle. Drift. *Comprenez?*"

The Frenchman looked as if he'd been slapped. He went absolutely white, and stepped back a pace before he recovered. And in this brief time my father and Mr. Kissel took hold of the cradle, as if they were planning to start work.

In the next few seconds so many things happened they were kind of hazy. The Frenchman screamed something, in his own language, and two men stepped up behind Mr. Kissel. And when my father slipped between them, a fellow wearing an orange sock-cap and blue pantaloons struck him heavily in the face. He went down, Mr. Kissel whirled round very fast for a man of his size, and the other scoundrel swung a pistol barrel heavily against his head. He tottered and reeled, sinking to his knees, not quite unconscious despite the force of the blow.

Then Mr. Coe sang out sharply; I hardly recognized his voice, it was so brisk.

"Hold on there! Enough!"

I saw he had one of those frayed-out white gloves in his right hand. Now, he stepped forward and swung it across the Frenchman's face with a smart whack. It stopped everybody dead in their tracks. My father sat up, looking on, and Mr. Kissel shook his head to clear it, watching the little scene being played out by an Englishman and a Frenchman in this rough American ravine.

The Frenchman's voice was velvet-soft.

"You understand what you do, English swine?"

"Your choice," said Mr. Coe carelessly, drawing on his glove.

"A de Tourville does not play at swords with rabble. I regret, but I must shoot you instead." And he pulled one of the pistols from his belt.

Taking a heavy gold ring from the little finger of his left hand, Mr. Coe tossed it to Le Chat, who inspected it with great curiosity, said "Ah?" and tossed it back.

"The English have always taken an indulgent view of the bar sinister," Mr. Coe said, "hence my generous offer. By the way, I knew your cousin, the legitimate one. Kindly communicate with Doctor McPheeters," indicating my father, "should your courage rise to the occasion."

"Englishman," said Le Chat, "write your letters home, prepare your testament. You have signed your death paper."

Humming, with the best of good cheer, as if he was on the way to a festival, Mr. Coe turned aside and we followed him back toward camp.

Chapter XXXVII

The news spread through the Marysville diggings within a few hours; it was amazing to see how fast people heard. The common feeling was glee that Le Chat had been called to account, for once, and mixed in was pity for Mr. Coe, who was known as a gentle, good and harmless man, but no fit choice to fight a duel.

Everybody waited for the signal, and sure enough, just before supper, one of the Frenchman's band, a sallow, nervous man who might have been a servant once, approached our campfire with his hat in his hand.

"Par-*don*," he said, and held out a note, which my father read aloud, after fixing on his spectacles. " 'If it suits, tomorrow at noon, *épée*, no bandages, *à outrance*, at the glade by what is known as Hawkins' Oak.' "

We knew the place, about a mile away toward town, a green, pasturey dell with a huge gnarled tree in the middle, from one of whose branches a man named Hawkins once was hung for stealing cattle and stirring up Indians.

"Dear me," said Mr. Coe. "I'll have to borrow a sword. One moment," he called to the messenger, and he scribbled a few lines on the back of the note. "There must be no argument whatever about the claim. The winner's a gentleman of property, the loser's a deceased thief. A simple establishment of caste."

All of a sudden, my father exploded.

"It won't do. We won't have it," he told Mr. Coe. "We've been talking this over, and we can't permit you to take any such idiotic risk for a few ounces of gold and a couple of boards knocked together." He laid his arm on Mr. Coe's shoulder. "Believe me, we're touched. But"—he went on briskly—"it simply won't do. With no disrespect to your physical prowess, I see this duel as a case of legalized murder. You aren't the type, Coe, and we have no intention whatever of losing so valuable a friend. So "—snatching up his hat—"I'll just step into town and straighten this mess out. There's no official law around here, but the decent citizens are in the majority, I hope."

"Never mind, doctor," said Mr. Coe. "It's no use, none at all. I seriously doubt if there's any danger. That sort of villain's usually nothing but brag and bounce. I think it highly unlikely that he'll show up at all. Take the note back," he said, repeating it in French, and the messenger scuttled out of the firelight, very evidently delighted to get away.

We made a gloomy supper of it, all but Mr. Coe, who was somewhat more cheerful than usual. But the rest of us were low in our minds, with Mrs. Kissel and Jennie and even Po-Povi sniffling a little now and then, and it took me a poison long time to get to sleep. Way off in the late hours—it must have been midnight—I heard whispering in the Kissel tent, and presently Mr. Kissel crept out, all dressed.

This is curious, I said, and I watched him carefully. He went over to the woodpile and picked up his ax, then hefted it to see that the helve was fastened tightly to the head—it had come off the week before, barely missing Deuteronomy, who was playing on the ground nearby.

It appeared to be on in good shape, so he took up his hat, hunched his shoulders a few times, to get the kinks out, and turned to leave.

On this night, Mr. Coe had placed his blankets and rubber poncho under his wagon; now I heard him say:

"You really mustn't, Kissel. My job entirely."

The talking woke everyone, and we turned out.

"What's this, what's going on?" cried my father.

Mr. Coe smiled. "I'm very much afraid that our esteemed friend,

Matthew Kissel, was about to employ his superb axmanship on an especially foul specimen of the tribe Gallic. I awoke in time."

"What's the meaning of this, Kissel?" said my father.

"Figured to clean out that bunch tonight," replied Mr. Kissel. "Then get on with the digging in the morning."

"I'm glad you didn't get away," said my father, "though I must admit it's tempting. Let's go back to bed. Maybe something will happen before noon."

"I hope not, doctor," said Coe. "It wouldn't do to knock me out of my fun."

He really was a curious fellow. Before I went to sleep, I heard him snoring away under his wagon as calmly as if he was about to be knighted. And what a gaudy to-do the next morning! We'd never seen him so stimulated. I understand now, after the passage of time, that Mr. Coe, a second son, a terrible position under the English system, as my father said, at last felt that he was being of some real use in the world. This was his hour of service, as melancholy as it was when you examined things, and he intended to make the most of it.

Right after breakfast he began to get dolled up in his best clothes. But first he took a bath in the stream; then he put on clean underwear, a white silk shirt, and a pair of fine gray broadcloth trousers, and afterwards he brushed his jacket carefully. He must have spent an hour on his hair and moustaches alone. And all the time he hummed and whistled and even sang, while we sat by feeling miserable.

They had what was called a British Association here, made up mostly of tradesmen and merchants and others of that class, and in the middle of the morning a boy came over with a handsome sword. He also carried a note that said, "Hearing you had none, we took the liberty of finding a meet and proper weapon. Cheerio, best of luck, kindly call on us for any services. Henry Ruxton, Pres. B.A. in Calif."

Mr. Coe drew the blade from the scabbard, poked it here and

there awkwardly, and said, "Capital, capital. I should cut quite a figure."

"See here, Coe," said my father, breaking out again. "I certainly don't mean to be offensive, but have you had *any* experience with this sort of business? Have you done anything athletic at all? Are you a horseman, for example?"

"I never cared for it. Never liked jumping, you know. One always runs the risk of landing on one's neck at a hedge. Never liked games, either, even as a child."

"Well, damn and blast and confound it, what do you mean sailing out there to cross swords with an expert duelist? Doesn't your Church have any feeling about suicide?"

Mr. Coe had hung a piece of broken mirror glass on a tree, and now he inspected his head anxiously, first one side and then the other.

"Immodest, but I rather fancy that hair arrangement. You'll act as second, of course, doctor."

"Very much against my better judgment."

At eleven o'clock, Mr. Coe said, "Well, then," and stood up. He'd been sitting on a log reading from a book of poems to Po-Povi, who sat looking down in silence. "We'd better be getting along."

None of us stayed behind. Jennie and Mrs. Kissel took the children, and Jennie carried a shotgun under her arm, besides. The rest of us had all the weapons we owned, and I reckoned it'd be the last day we'd ever get to use them. I couldn't see anything but trouble in this encounter.

When we got to the glade there was a crowd of nearly two hundred there, miners from the nearby diggings, people from town, wagon-train folk and others, and a number of boys had climbed up the very selfsame oak beneath which the fight was about to take place.

The Frenchman was already on hand, with his seconds. He was dressed entirely in black, and was in fine, merry shape, hopping around and making jokes with those in his vicinity. He had his sleeves rolled up, and his arms were hairy and corded; he reminded me of Brother Muller, but with a lot more polish.

When the people saw Coe coming, a big shout went up, and one of the boys came within an ace of falling out of the tree. The shout was followed by a few titters, and I must admit that he didn't show up to advantage beside Le Chat. To begin with, he couldn't have weighed more than a hundred and fifty pounds.

This Mr. Ruxton of the British Association was there, along with a French doctor, a little less villainous-looking than The Cat. They did some introductions, sober and grave, but nobody shook hands; they only nodded curtly.

My father, for once in his life, wasn't thinking about spreading himself personally but seemed worried and cautious about Mr. Coe's welfare. They discussed the ground, and my father objected to one place that had a furrow in it, and then picked up some trash from another they finally decided on.

"Ordinarily," said the French doctor, who spoke perfectly good English and appeared intelligent, "the code duello would call for black silk bandages to protect the vital organs, but it has been agreed, I understand, to conduct this regrettable affair à outrance."

"Oh, quite," said Coe. "Only way possible as I see it."

My father started to protest, but The Cat said something scornful, then whipped out his weapon and made it sing through the air. It sent a chill clear down my spine. I could feel my heart thumping so hard against my chest I thought others could hear it, too.

"Mr. Coe," called Jennie suddenly. "Don't do this. We ask you to stop it for our sakes."

He waved languidly, and blew her a kiss. I never saw a condemned man enjoy himself with such an outrageous lack of concern.

"Very well, then," said the French doctor. "Take positions, please." Mr. Coe removed his coat, rolled up his sleeves, and picked up his sword. One of the British Association now stepped forward again, in an effort to make what they called "a reconciliation with honor" at the last moment, but Coe dismissed him good-naturedly.

"*En garde!*" said the doctor, looking very serious, and they brought up their blades. I saw Po-Povi turn her back; then came the cry, "Duel! May God attend you."

The Frenchman made a wild lunge and cut savagely across the air, but our frail Mr. Coe wasn't there. That is, he wasn't within range. I rubbed my eyes to be sure I was seeing right. *Was* this our Mr. Coe? He was dancing over the greensward like a man on a ballroom floor, and the blade he had seemed attached to his body. I never saw anything like it, and I realize now, after these years have passed, that I probably never will.

I heard my father breathe, "Lord above! I should have known."

The Frenchman stopped short, and his thick black brows went up in surprise. Then he gritted his teeth and leaped back in to attack. But it was wholly useless. For the first time in his life, probably, he had run up against something he couldn't deal with. The sweat began to pour off his face, and his black shirt clung wetly to his hairy chest. And in a moment he began to pant, almost sobbing in his effort to keep up the pace, and now he made a series of headlong lunges that only kept Mr. Coe dancing back lightly, parrying as if bored, feinting, thrusting halfheartedly, outmaneuvering, outguessing, and outfighting this dishonest bully in every way you could imagine. It was gorgeous, and awesome, too.

The Frenchman screamed something, lunged, stumbled forward, and then dropped his sword. The end of Mr. Coe's blade was sticking out at least a foot from the back of his shoulder, having run him clear through. It was withdrawn quickly and the point placed under his chin.

"Now listen to me, you thieving blackguard. Unless you and your gang have decamped this area by nightfall, never to return, I'll serve you as I ought to serve you this minute. Do you *quite* understand?"

The great roar that went up from that rough crowd made it pretty clear that the conditions would be kept, if they could help it.

I have a feeling that very few people are overly bold when staring death directly in the face. The Cat nodded, still laboring for breath, with one hand on his wound, now, and then turned away, his shoulders slumped in defeat.

The duel was finished.

As many as four dozen people came up to pound Mr. Coe on the back. He was about the biggest hero this area had ever seen. Nearly all of these men had suffered at the hands of the Frenchman, one way or another, and they were tickled to death to see him humbled.

We made a very gay procession home, and that evening at supper we sat around in the highest old humor. And my father, before it started, tramped clear into town and came back with a fine bottle of wine, but the wine dealer refused to let him pay for it, and for once, he didn't start on a drunk—it didn't affect him at all, besides loosening his tongue, which had been on a kind of swivel to start with, you might say. But he made a great number of toasts, and even put a few drops in a glass, with a little sugar, for Po-Povi and me.

"Coe," he said at one point, "it was the greatest exhibition I ever witnessed or hope to witness. Now why in the devil didn't you let us in on it? Why couldn't you tell us you knew how to handle a sword like that?"

"It went off rather well, didn't it?" said Mr. Coe. "On the whole, I'm satisfied. Still, you know, I wasn't certain it would. I never fought an actual duel before, if you know what I mean."

"*Aha*," said my father, chuckling, "you needn't try to tell us you're inexperienced, my boy. In the fencing line, that was *class*, pure and simple. An ignoramus could see it. Why, I'll bet they're drinking your health in every saloon in Marysville this very minute."

"Oh, I've had a good crack, one time and another. Only thing of the sort I actually enjoyed when I was younger. The old gentleman had a tutor around there for several years, a language master, Italian, actually—the old gentleman never could stand him, called him a Dago behind his back—and he showed me how. He was terribly good at it, and I rather think he'd killed a good many people, dueling. Used to hint at it, you know. When I finally got to the point where I could hold my own, my father tried to bribe me to stick him. I remember the scene very well, probably because I never saw much of him, normally. He was standing behind a rosebush and he hissed. Made an actual hiss at me, so he wouldn't be seen. 'See here,' he said when I went over, 'you've been fencing with that Dago, eh, my boy?' I replied that I had, and he pulled out a gold-cornered wallet. 'Tell you what,' he said, 'here's a fiver if you pull the button off and stick him in the stomach.' I must have looked horrified, because he said, 'Oh, don't kill him. Get him over toward the side, near the hipbone—lay him up for a while. Look here—we'll make it an even ten quid. Now what do you say to that?'

"Naturally, I turned it down. You can't go around just sticking people, even Italians."

My father spoke up to inquire, "Coe, if it isn't too prying, what does your father do over there? You've never mentioned it."

"Well, I hate to say so, but he doesn't do much of anything. He just potters around. I suppose you might say he's a farmer by trade."

My father shook his head in sympathy. "Ne'er-do-well, is he? I know the breed, if you don't mind my saying so. Both of my uncles in exactly the same boat, and most of my cousins." He shook his head again, then roused himself to observe, "However run-down your family, Coe, nobody could ever call you, personally, a loafer. You've contributed your share of energy and resolution to this expedition, and more. And I'll just take the liberty of proposing one more round to St. George and his distinguished triumph over the California dragon."

"Amen!" said Mr. Kissel, who had broken his teetotaling custom by drinking a whole glass of wine. "It was a wonder to behold."

After supper we had a setback when Mr. Coe announced that he must make a trip to San Francisco, to pick up the mails. My father sighed and said yes, he himself had been going to suggest that one of us perform that errand soon.

"A year," he said, "one whole year without word from home and loved ones."

They fixed it that Mr. Coe would leave for Sacramento the next day and take a steamer for San Francisco. The entire trip, there and back, would require about two weeks. We would be sorry to see him leave, but it made me excited to think of news from my mother. My father and Mr. Kissel each prepared an "authorization" for Mr. Coe to pick up letters for us, then wrote some letters to be mailed, and I went to bed, homesick all of a sudden. It had been an exhausting day. And a funny thing, I dreamed practically the same dream I had the night before we left—about the prairie, and Indians, and my father practicing medicine—only this time when I awoke, we weren't on our way to California. We were here, and gold lay just up these green wooded valleys.

Chapter XXXVIII

We got our claim signs back up and went on working with the cradle. I rocked while my father and Mr. Kissel poured in the dirt and water. We took upwards of fifty dollars before nightfall—better than three ounces—and nearly that much the day following. But after this the ravine commenced to run thin. We scratched all around up above, where my father said the gold was coming from, but we failed to find anything good near the surface.

The pity of it was, this ravine had more gold in it, but the cradle was so slow we weren't washing enough to justify the time we spent.

"What we need's a Long Tom," my father said. "With that, we can sift ten times as much dirt in the same time."

He and Mr. Kissel talked it over at supper; then we went in the next morning, taking the dust we had saved, and bargained for a used Tom in fair condition, trading in our cradle. It had belonged to some Chileans who had made a new strike in a canyon that had a steep descent, so that they changed over to sluicing.

We set up the Tom in the lowest part of our ravine and attached a piece of canvas hose to it from a spring higher up. These things vary in length, but the one we bought was about twelve feet long, an oblong wooden trough, open at both ends, eight inches deep, narrower at the top than at the middle and lower end. A perforated iron sheet just like the cradle, only heavier, formed about four feet of the lower end and sagged in the middle, making a kind of cup. With, of course, a "riffle box" below to catch the gold. My father and Mr. Kissel spaded in dirt at the upper end of the trough, and

I stood at the lower end to shovel the big stuff, rocks and gravel, off the iron. The sand and fine dirt and gold all fell through into the riffle box, and the worthless part, called the tailings, washed on out the end over the riffle bar, leaving the heavy gold behind.

We could move a lot more dirt this way, and didn't have to rock, because the water from the canvas hose ran down the trough in a steady stream. After a couple of hours, we hauled out the box to check, and had nearly two ounces, which wasn't bad at all. Then we moved to another spot, to make shoveling easier, and pitched in again. Altogether on that first go-round we took out about sixty-five dollars, and called it a pretty square day's work. It was fining out, though. By the end of a week we had nearly two hundred and fifty dollars, but the ravine was emptied, unless you were in a position to sluice it. Of the two hundred and fifty dollars, we spent about a third on supplies, so we had a tidy sum left over. Only thing for it now was to change locations, which we did, but the next two ravines didn't cough up a thing richer than color.

In the third, we struck good dirt, and in three days took out something over two hundred dollars. As my father said, we were making a living, but we certainly weren't making it very fast. Not with the way prices were. But we kept plugging, and always in the air, to keep us going, was the feeling that in that *next* ravine, just over the hill, lay a fortune. This sort of thing can give you a pretty good push of energy, the business of *looking* for something, with the idea of getting it free. It was the same feeling I used to have on the Ohio during spring rise, when we'd nab drift logs from the mills up above, along with boxes full of things, and now and then a skiff or a canoe. It beats making a regular living any time.

On Sunday we knocked off, didn't do a thing. Left our Long Tom standing there with claim signs all around, and went on home to rest up. Mr. Kissel reckoned he'd never get a farm this way, but he said he wasn't complaining, it was the decree of Providence. We had a jolly good breakfast, but missed Mr. Coe; we all said so and talked about him some. He was due back in about four days. It being a Sunday, as stated, I decided to ask permission to wander around, then I remembered they had taken a vote against that sort of thing once before. They said there were so many foreigners here that it mightn't be safe, and particularly Chinamen. "A body can't tell to look at them whether they've been converted or not," Mrs. Kissel said. "I've heard it said that the heathen element smokes dead rats."

"They smoke opium, ma'am," my father said, "and *eat* rats."

"Well, for the Lord's sake, I wouldn't let that boy stir a foot out of this camp," she cried.

I knew about Chinamen, of course. There was a laundryman in Louisville, name of George Yat, and we commonly stopped in the back doorway of his place when traveling up the alley and yelled, "Chink-a-chink-a Chinaman eats dead rats, uses their tails for baseball bats," until my mother heard about it and gave me a licking.

Anyway, I was standing over near the water barrel at the time, under a clump of trees, and concluded that I'd ask permission later, when I got back. That way, there wouldn't be any chance of causing a disturbance, and as my father always said, there's few things more of a nuisance in this world than a troublemaker.

So I threw out the water in my dipper, muttered something about trying to locate my knife, which I'd misplaced, and drifted away, taking care not to stumble over a root. Somehow, I had to get away for a while. To tell the truth, I was a little sick of gold. It was fun to look for, but we'd overdone it. It smelled nice here in the hills. There were pine trees twelve feet and more thick, and birds were just going it every place. This was May, and fine weather, a very good time to be in California. Most all of the miners had gone into Marysville, but about two miles from our camp, up a winding stream, I came out into a beautiful little gulch and there was a tall, lanky, brown-haired man and a tow-haired boy working a cradle. They didn't see me, so I turned to go on, but a rock scudded out from under my foot and went hopping down that piny slope to land right at their feet.

"Well, howdy," said the man, with his eyes kind of squinted up in a humorous look. "Just passing through, stranger?"

"Why, no, sir," I said, gulping a little , because I was intruding here, you know. "It's a Sunday and I was taking a stroll out from camp."

"Come on down, son. Rest yourself. How'd you like a cup of coffee?"

They had a pot hung from a forked stick over a fire that was burning low.

"My father won't let me have it, sir. He claims that taken to excess it will rupture the blood vessels."

"That wouldn't apply in this particular case," said the man. "There ain't enough outright coffee in it to rupture a grasshopper. To haul it down to cases, it's made out of tanbark and sassafras."

I'd been clambering down, holding onto scrub, and I noticed the boy up close for the first time. But he beat me to it and let out a yell that shook the tree branches.

"He's the one with them that killed Ma and Pa! Shoot him, Uncle Ned!"

He began to run lickety-split, crying and yelling, toward a tree where they had a pistol and rifle hanging, and I figured I was about to collect my judgment. I was so scared it took me a minute to muster my wind. I'd seen that boy take a pot shot at Shep Baggott, and he did it handsome, expert and cool. I cried, "Hold on! Stop him! I hadn't anything to do with those scoundrels!"

The boy paid no heed whatever, but yanked the rifle down and swung it up to his shoulder.

Then the man stepped in front, holding me back there with one hand. "Lay that rifle down, Todd. We'll hear his story."

But the boy was sort of frothing at the mouth, he was crying so, and he screamed, "Stand aside, Uncle Ned. If you don't want to get shot through the belly, shove aside so I can kill me a skunk."

"Put that rifle down!"

I was shaking so, they could have heard my knees in Marysville.

The boy hesitated a second, then the man turned around and said easily, "Now, son, come over and set on this log and tell me

410

your account. And make it true, because I'll tell for sure if you're lying."

I didn't need any second instruction, but blurted out, "I was kidnapped! They took me off the trail and tried to ransom me to Pierre Chouteau in St. Louis. I'd shot them myself if I'd had the chance." Then I rushed on and told it all the way it happened; told how they hung Joe Slater, how we'd found John and Shep in Independence, and all about my troubles later in the Pawnee village.

The man never interrupted or even changed expression until I'd finished, and it wasn't any short time, either.

"Joe Slater gave me your father's watch to return you if we ever met up," I said to the boy, and I hauled it out. I'd carried it first in my wagon pouch and then in my pocket from that day to this. It was dented in two or three places, and it wasn't running, but Mr. Coe had said it could be fixed by any reliable jeweler.

The boy brushed his eyes with his sleeve and took the watch, holding it by its chain. Then he opened the back to show the fresh young faces of his father and mother on their wedding day. He looked at them a few moments, blinking back the tears, and said, "I reckon I misjudged it. I don't mind begging your pardon."

"I wish there could have been something to do," I said, and meant it. "But there wasn't, not a blessed thing. I was in the same fix myself."

"Of course there wasn't, boy," said the man. "We'll just thank you for the watch. Now, how are you called?"

"Jaimie, sir."

"Jaimie it is, then. Now what I suggest is this—we'll amble over and meet up with your folks. Pay our respects, like. And maybe your paw'll know something else about those murderers. It don't plague me to acknowledge that I'm about halfway bent on finding them afore I'm done. To go a step further, you might even say we been tracking them. We got wind they were heading this way. But we didn't know all the dee-tails," he added politely.

"Uncle Ned," said the boy, "you promised you wouldn't hog the show, once we caught up."

"You'll get your shot, boy, same as me. A promise is a promise. I don't believe in holding out a delight to a child and then withdrawing it. It's deeleterious for character. No, you take the stout one, being as I'm a mite better shot, and I'll take the skinny. Fair's fair."

Hearing them talk, my blood ran cold. I never heard killing discussed in just those tones. I think maybe any of us could kill somebody, if they get mad enough at the moment, and my father says the same, but these two sounded like they were fixing to butcher a sheep. I wouldn't have been in Shep's and John's shoes for a million dollars, because if this weathered old string bean didn't get them, the boy would; there wasn't any doubt about *that*.

We started back down the woody ravines, the man walking a little behind, and the boy said:

"Don't suppose you care for hunting and fishing and such."

"It's about all I do. Along the Ohio River, at Louisville, Kentucky," I said.

"I don't recall as I've heard it mentioned. Small stream?"

"Small stream, my foot. Haven't you ever been to school?"

"I certainly have," he said warmly. "I was there near about eight weeks three years ago, but my paw tooken me out to help with the crops. I was going back the next fall, but the teacher they had, he stepped on a cottenmouth and it left him kind of addled. It didn't surprise anybody—he was a foreigner anyhow." He said it "furriner."

"Which country?"

"Place called Pennsylvania, so they said."

He was a nice boy, but he seemed uncommonly ignorant, even for a Missourian. For the first time, I was glad I'd taken the trouble to get an education before I started on my travels.

When we reached camp, they were getting ready for the noon meal, with my father and Mr. Kissel fanning away at the fire, coughing as they always did, and the women bustling around with the cooking. I stepped up and said, "These here are some friends from

412

back on the trail in Missouri—the boy named Todd was the one I was telling you about, and this is his Uncle Ned."

My father got up and shook hands grandly, saying:

"We're happy to meet you, sir. If I recall the circumstances correctly, this is quite a coincidence."

"Your boy gave us back the watch," the uncle replied. "We'd be obliged for any further information you might have. I and my nevvy here, who is a fair hand with a squirrel rifle, was hoping to catch the men and talk things over. According to Missouri notions, they done an unfriendly act."

"Unfortunately, we haven't any information whatever. But we'll keep our eye out—we're sorry for your trouble—and in the meantime, we hope you'll join our mess." And he introduced all of our company, with a great deal of style, using the highest-sounding titles he could invent.

This Uncle Ned gave a long sigh, looking at the women's preparations. "To tell the bare truth, I was hoping you'd ask us. I make a mighty poor out at vittling. We'll stop for a bite and grateful, then shuffle ourselves along."

"Nothing of the sort," said my father. "Come join us as often as it suits you. There's plenty of good camping space hereabouts."

We had a good dinner, eating our best meal at noon on a Sunday, and had cornpone, fat bacon, boiled beef, pickled pork, and salad that Jennie and Po-Povi picked in the woods. I never saw a man eat so. And the boy did the same. They were starved down to a point where they were just barely moving and that's all. Every few minutes the man made an apology for "gormandizing" and tackled another plateful. He must have laid in twelve pounds, more or less.

And afterwards, by George if he didn't insist on washing up, he and the boy. They wouldn't let the women touch a thing, shooed everybody right out to the chairs Mr. Kissel had made, and then I'm blessed if they didn't light in and chop about half a cord of firewood. When they finished, toward three o'clock, Uncle Ned came up to Mrs. Kissel with his hat in his hand and said:

"Ma'am, I don't hardly know how to tell you what that meal

signified. We ain't had a thing in any way approaching it for three months. I'll hope to square things up someday."

"Square up!" cried Mrs. Kissel. "Why, you've done a full day's work already. It's we owe you. You'll be back here for supper, or I'll know the reason why."

I may be crazy, but his eyes looked downright damp in the corners. "Ma'am," he said in a voice that shook a little, "you ain't planning to vittle again *today?*"

"Indeed we are—we eat thrice daily. So does everybody, I hope to goodness. Don't you?"

He seemed embarrassed and said, "Here lately, we've had tanbark coffee in the morning, et bacon and greens at noon, and munched acorns for the rest. It serves, but it's right hard to work on."

"Supper's at seven on a Sunday," said Mrs. Kissel. "If you and the boy aren't here, we'll get them to send for you with guns."

The man signaled his nephew, and they took off their coats all over again. Then they chopped up another half cord of firewood.

After this, he sat down and talked with my father and Mr. Kissel about mining, saying they'd had thin luck recently but knew of a slopy place that might be given to sluicing. They discussed it up and down and sideways and agreed to give it a try, since our ravine had run its course. Next morning we went back three miles in the hills, to a place where a stream ran winding along under some pines, then hopped down a series of natural terraces. We'd picked up Todd and his Uncle Ned on the way, and they had seventy feet of sluice boxes they bought during the fall, after cradling some gold. But they hadn't had a chance to use it yet, being shorthanded.

These we carried to the new location, and spent the day setting them up, connecting the narrow end of each box (or trough) to the upper end of the one below it, and placing, altogether, four riffle boxes underneath at the connections. It was like a Long Tom, but you could move a lot more dirt, and you didn't have to knock off and empty out the boxes so often, because there were so many.

By the middle of the afternoon we were able to start work. The stream was directed into the first trough, and the men began throwing in dirt. Todd and I were put to running up and down along the seventy-foot length, spading out rocks and other things that got jammed now and then. In an hour's time we made an inspection and had about two ounces of gold: thirty-two dollars. This was fair pay. When we quit in the evening, Uncle Ned and the boy moved their traps up, so as to camp by the sluice boxes, and we divided the gold fifty-fifty, as we agreed to do at the end of each day.

"I don't know anything underneath the sun that can bust up a friendly relationship like suspicions over gold," said Uncle Ned. "Let's split daily."

My father agreed, in a few thousand words, touching on some famous friendships of the past, including two men named Demon and Pissiest, and others, and suggested it be fifty-fifty, since it was their site and their sluice boxes, though we had the most hands.

So we left it.

In the next few days, Mr. Coe failed to show up and we kept plugging away at the sluice. We took out about three hundred dollars and then, drat the luck, she began running out. It was discouraging. It seemed we couldn't hit on a region that produced any real pay dirt, and Uncle Ned, who his last name was Reeves, said they'd had the same luck time after time, only worse.

My father began to look glum, because we weren't more than holding our own, with these high prices hereabouts, and Mr. Kissel's face suggested that he thought the farm was purely a mirage, now.

But we kept on—they had things organized so well that Todd and I weren't needed all the time, so we wandered off once in a while and played. Everybody said it might be good for us.

This morning we walked through a very heavily wooded place, shooting slingshots and watching out for animals, and pushed into a region of rocky hills and canyons, where there was a dry creek bed with shaly, steep sides. It was interesting. We loafed along, throwing rocks and shooting the slingshot, and coming around a bend, we almost stumbled over a big pile of rattlesnakes. They were coiled all around each other, lying there in the sun, repulsive and slimy. Must have been as many as a dozen or more, wrapped together like eels in a barrel. But they unkinked pretty fast when we began shooting, and disappeared behind a rock and into the black ground somewhere, out of sight.

We went on, but used caution, now, because when you find a place like a creek bed where snakes like to bake, you're apt to run into any number more.

The sun rose high overhead, and we thought we ought to start back to camp. But we sat down a second to rest up and fix my slingshot, which had become unraveled from the forks. It was pleasant here, no lessons to learn, no chores around the house, not even any dirt shoveling for a change, and we made a bargain that we'd never go back to school, ever. If they started to put us back, we'd run off and go to sea, knowing considerable about the water from living on the rivers. Then I said I'd like to see my mother sometime. He fell silent at this, and I felt bad I'd said it, because I knew he was thinking about his folks.

I stared at the opposite side of the creek bed, where the sun was brightest, and spoke up: "That's funny."

"What?"

"Those glints in the wall. It almost looks like——" I got up and went over. "Holy, jumping Jerusalem!" My head spun around so I got almost faint, out of excitement.

There were crevices there that had hunks of gold, solid gold, in them, as big as marbles. They were all up and down as far as you could see, in streaks that ran slantwise from nearly the top to the bottom.

"I never seen anything like it," the boy said. "What do you suppose we ought to do?"

"We'd better fetch the others as fast as we can, before somebody comes along and grabs it. You go, and I'll stand guard. Here, take these hunks, tell them to drop all holds."

I was so nervous, I could hardly get the words out.

As soon as he left, running as hard as he could, I examined the bed in both directions, to see how far the vein went. There was gold plain to the naked eye on around the next bend, thirty yards or so, and no telling how much more farther on. It was a wild and woolly section of country, nothing that the average miner might be attracted to. That is, there were no promising ravines or gullies, and the total absence of water would discourage you from trying anyway. It was desert, and pretty far out, too. Still, you never could tell.

My heart was bumping around again, knocking up against my liver and my lungs, I was in such a sweat to get staked out. I hadn't any pencil, no chalk, nothing. There wasn't even a piece of slate to scratch on bark with.

So, to keep busy, I tried gouging out nuggets with the handle of my slingshot. I got two or three, but it was mighty slow going. What I needed was a metal thing like a spoon or a knife, and I'd mislaid my knife, confound the luck.

It should take an hour before Todd got back. By and by, worn out for the moment, I sat down to think things over, and then I heard something, clumpety-clump, a whole scattering of beats, off to the left, toward the high mountains. And when I ran over, keeping down, to peer through some weeds at the top, sure enough, it was a party of horsemen, five altogether, ugly and rough-looking, too.

I was so sick, I wanted to cry.

"Hold up!" I heard the first one cry, reining in with a jerk. "Have a look in the creek bed for water, Phelps. The horses is lathered up to the busting point."

My palms were so wet I could hardly hang onto the rocks. I believe if I'd had a gun, I'd a shot him.

The others hauled in their mounts, raising a cloud of dust, and the second man, the one called Phelps, said, "There ain't any water over this entire stretch. You could drill to China and raise nothing but sweat for your pains."

"Let's push on," said another. "It couldn't be over three or four miles at the outside."

"Well, I don't like it," said the first man. "Horses don't grow on trees, and I laid out fifty dollars for this one."

"You mean *somebody* did," one of them said, and everybody but the first man laughed. He looked sore for a second, then yanked his horse's head around with an oath, and they clattered off.

I hung on, feeling dizzy. It was about the closest call I could remember, and the most luck we'd had in a long time.

Half an hour later I heard another commotion, downstream, and this time it was my father and the others. They were half running and half walking, beat out but all a-twitter. The raggedy tails of my father's black coat streamed away behind, and he held his hat on with one hand while carrying a light pick in the other. Mr. Kissel had an armful of tools, and so did Uncle Ned.

"My boy," cried my father when he saw me, "is it true? Is it Golconda? Out of the mouths of babes and sucklings——"

He was all but babbling in his excitement, and his voice sounded odd-pitched, high and thin.

"For God's sake," I said—something my mother would have boxed my ears for—"cut out the yammering and get some claim signs up."

"To be sure. Correct in every detail. But be calm, stay calm and collected. You have a tendency to fly off the handle in a crisis. Always remember——"

I didn't pay any attention. I never saw anybody so unstrung. But when Uncle Ned and Mr. Kissel laid into the signs, he quieted down and began to make sense again.

You could hardly blame him. This was what he had quit his practice for, upset his family, dodged his creditors, and toiled away over three thousand miles of wilderness, filled with misery and danger. This, we hoped, was the end of the rainbow, and in about five minutes we meant to open the pot of gold.

Chapter XXXIX

We laid into work with whatever tools we had, and in no time at all had a small heap of particles and chunks. The gold in these was almost pure; they hadn't any black look, but were dull-yellow, very easy on the eyes. But we wanted to be certain, because we didn't care to waste a lot of toil over fool's gold—iron pyrites—or something of the kind, so Uncle Ned took his testing kit and gave it a check. We all crowded around to watch, and nobody said a word. There wasn't any sound except for the rattle of his implements, when something slipped, you know, and a pebble rolling down the bank once in a while.

He had one of these portable assay kits—a tin box with a lamp, a blowpipe, and bottles of acid—that he carried strapped on his back, and said it was worth all the books about gold ever written.

He gave it three tests, the first by the blowpipe. Said he got it from a regular professor that had been in the diggings last summer and struck it rich but turned to guzzling and ended up a bum before they ran him off for being a nuisance, begging. Gold had an "affinity" for oxygen, the professor had said, according to Uncle Ned, while copper, iron, and lead do something called oxidize pretty fast and sink into bone ash when heated. On the other hand, gold and silver, under strong heat, stay on the surface.

Using the blowpipe and a piece of charcoal with a little bone ash bedded in it, he got her going and this metal of ours came through with flags flying.

"We'll give her a quicksilver test and polish off with acid, so hold your breath," he stated.

Then he roasted some of the stuff and pulverized the particles and what he said "triturated" it with quicksilver, which clung to the metal in an amalgam as fast as you could wink.

"So far so good," he said, and we all shifted our positions, letting down a little.

Then he took a weak mixture of nitric and muriatic acids and the metal dissolved right off the bat. In a strong mixture, nothing happened.

"Boys," he said, getting up and slapping his hat against his jeans, "we've got a strike. She came through noble, and probably in a pure state, or I miss my guess. Silver would have dissolved in the strong nitric, and we ruled out all others with the blowpipe. *Yoo-hoo— eee!*"

Everybody shook hands around, and congratulated me on my hawk eyes, just as I'd told my mother that day before we left; then we lit in.

Todd and I used tablespoons; they were equally as good as picks, better for this work, which people around the diggings called "crevicing."

We estimated we took out about eight hundred and fifty dollars that first day, and we hadn't got started yet. It was about the best fun I ever had, and as I told Todd, it was better than getting up early and running old man Burkhardt's trot lines, because this way you didn't have to clean any fish and there wasn't any chance of getting caught, either.

Well, we fetched the women and moved our camp up as close as we could where there was water, and didn't breathe a word to a soul. We left a message with neighbors for Mr. Coe, with another on a bill at the old campsite, and one of us went down every day, looking for him.

Within a week, most of the gold you could see in the ledges was dug out, and we had made, we figured, around forty-eight hundred dollars. It wasn't any fortune, but it was a good stake, and everybody was happy. We were dividing, now, one third to Uncle Ned and two thirds to us, and it was the most money any of us had seen in a long time, or maybe ever. And we weren't through yet.

In the middle of the second week we had well over seven thousand dollars, so we cashed it in with the most honest assayer in Marysville, who only skinned us a few hundred dollars, so Uncle Ned said.

And the next evening at camp we heard a halloo from a ravine below us, and when we ran out to see what the matter was, it was Mr. Coe. He'd bought a horse, a bony one, twenty or thirty years old, sold him by those cheats in Sacramento for a gaudy sum, and he reported that he'd had a mixed-up time trying to locate us. We should have known. In spite of his other good points, he couldn't have found his way from one side of the river to another without a compass. He was the poorest hand that way you ever saw, and the cheerfulest.

"Yes," he said when he'd been introduced and heard our news, "I must have followed the wrong trail up. Note was very explicit, too. But then, where I wasted most of my time was finding the *first* camp. The one down toward Marysville."

"But, Coe," said my father gently, "you couldn't have—that one's right off the road. A child could find it blindfolded."

"Seems odd, doesn't it? I rode right over it, you know. Thinking of something else, I suppose."

He had more than a dozen letters for us; they'd all been marked "Hold" and were waiting at San Francisco. The Kissels had a good many from family and neighbors, and Mr. Coe remarked wryly, in response to a question of my father, that yes, he'd got his, too.

We must have read everything over ten times. My father read me my mother's letters, and we both swabbed out our eyes now and then, but my father said it was a joyous occasion, because now we had money, and knew how to make more, so that soon, very soon, likely, we could begin to think about home.

He read, " 'Mary has her third tooth. Hannah is in Natchez for three weeks, visiting cousins at Cherokee, and I enclose her best souvenirs. She has been paid court by the Gregsons' oldest boy, an empty-headed lout with no prospects of resource within himself and fewer prospects of inheritance, and so I sent her packing. Alas, I fear that she herself, aside from her youth and beauty, is no longer regarded as a "good catch." ' "

He quit reading here and fell to coughing, but presently, by skipping here and there, he got everything out. My mother was making do on her small income from New Orleans, Banker Parsons was pacified for the moment, after an anxious time when he learned we were missing—he had declared briefly his intention of posting a wanted circular but had been talked out of it by friends —and my mother was even making a small payment every month on our debts.

The only real bad news, which seemed to affect me more than my father, was that Sam died. He was a very young goat to go that way, but I understood it better when they said he'd died of undigestion. When I heard that, I wasn't surprised any more, and in fact, you might say he had lived to a ripe old age, if you consider what he ate. In this present case, the farmer had had the foolishness to leave a new harrow within range of his rope, and Sam naturally ate off some of the teeth. The peculiar part was that the farmer insisted on concentrating on his harrow and refused to take any responsibility for the goat.

My father said never mind, he'd make it up somehow. Said he'd get me a pet that it didn't matter what he ate. "I've heard that the python, or anaconda, can swallow anything mechanically capable of passing its jaws. The bodily acids dissolve it in time. There was a case in one of the papers which had to do with a stuffed moose, engorged by error, and it worked out fine. That may be just the ticket."

"I don't want a python," I said, snuffling a little. "I want Sam."

"Well, son, he's expired, and we're simply going to have to bear up and put a brave face on it. Think of it this way—he's gone to frisk and baaa in Goat Heaven, a wonderful, wonderful place for an animal with his disposition. I see it as a very old, littered back yard, full of cans, broken bottles, pieces of rake and umbrella, half-bricks and fresh laundry. He'll browse and munch, selecting this, discarding that. Why, he'll have a perfect picnic of a time. He'll never miss us at all."

No matter what he said, my father never liked Sam after he'd broken into the house and eaten his suitcase. So I didn't listen any more, but took some of the letters and went off by myself.

It wasn't till that evening, when Uncle Ned Reeves and Todd had gone to Marysville to see friends, that Mr. Coe told us what *his* mail had contained.

"The sad truth is, I must leave," he told us, as we sat around the campfire. We made a fuss, and my father said, "If it's a question of money, Coe, it goes without saying that we consider a share of this strike to be yours. As the companion of our misfortunes, you can scarcely be omitted from our triumphs."

Coe smiled. "Thank you, doctor. It isn't a question of money. The trouble is that we've had something of a family crisis. Two of them, in brief, and the consequences are far from pleasant to me."

"Any way we can help, Coe. Any way at all. I've gathered from what you've let slip that they're somewhat beneath you. You have risen above your origins, and I like to think that you've won some influential, and even moneyed, new friends."

"I'm warmly appreciative," said Mr. Coe. "But there isn't any easy solution. No, I've simply got to face the music. There's no two ways about it. You see, I've come into the dukedom—Duke of Blandford—and it isn't the sort of thing I want at all. Never thought it possible, actually. What happened was, the old gentleman toppled over. He had a heart seizure after an argument with some judges at a petunia exhibit, and my elder brother—never could stand him, by the way—took a spill while pursuing the beastly foxes. Rotten bad luck for me. I'm for it, that's all there is to be said."

"Perhaps if you went over it again, a little more slowly, Coe," said my father, and I could see that the words were coming out hard.

"I've got to go back and take charge—manage the estate, lawn fetes, charitable balls, county benefactions, local member, can't imagine a more galling ordeal. I like it out here, too. The life suits me."

"Coe," said my father. "Not a dukedom. Surely you mean baron, or viscount, or even earl or marquis. *Not* a duke, if it's perfectly agreeable."

"Believe me, you have my profoundest apologies. My brother was Lord Hurley, and being the second son, I was 'honourable,' you understand. I never believed in the system at all myself. A title ought to be won, like justice of the peace, or sergeant major. Certainly the old gentleman was never worth shooting, his whole life long, and neither was my brother."

"Why, you must be related to the royal family."

"Cousins—I've forgotten how distant. They've got it written down somewhere around the place."

"The estate's gone to pot, you said?" my father went on hopefully. He'd got to find some flaw here if it killed him. "There probably isn't money enough to keep up appearances? I've seen this sort of thing before; it's common enough."

"No, I believe the governor was considered rather well off, in a comparative way. The estate itself, the house, acres and the like, are entailed, of course. But I believe he has a fairly large amount of money, something like three or four million pounds, somebody said. He didn't make it, of course. His father did. Silly, I mean all that for one man, and him an idiot, practically."

Well, we couldn't think of anything sensible to say. Especially my father, who'd been so free about calling Mr. Coe's family a bunch of ne'er-do-wells. It's funny, but it changed things. The Kissels couldn't take it in, exactly, and Jennie acted like a schoolgirl, never addressing a normal remark to the unhappy fellow from that moment on. It was a crying shame. One day he was a good friend, on the easiest kind of footing, and the next he was something removed forever. And it wasn't any of his doing, either.

"I'd shirk it in a minute if I could," he said gloomily. "But you just don't do that sort of thing in England. I needn't tell you— you probably know it well enough."

424

We had a strained, silent supper, and since everybody was embarrassed to ask Mr. Coe what he should be called, now—knowing, too, that he wouldn't let us change—we didn't call him anything at all, but simply talked without addressing him directly. What's more, I found myself avoiding his eyes, as if one of us had done something dark and shameful. It was crazy.

After supper, he took Po-Povi by the hand and said, including us all, "Now, child, I've been making arrangements with the bank in San Francisco, and if Doctor McPheeters is willing, it would give me pleasure to take you to England and see that you get a proper education. You have a quick, curious mind—that much I've learned from our lessons—and it should be given the chance for knowledge. How does that strike you, doctor?"

My father looked taken aback for an instant; then he said, "Whatever's right for the lass, of course, providing she favors the idea."

The girl looked up, her eyes shining, and then she glanced around at us all, me last. But she didn't need to go throwing herself on my hands; I couldn't make up her mind; it didn't matter two pins to me if she went to the North Pole and sold ice. My father said she was free, and free she was, ungrateful or not.

And later, after they'd talked it over a good deal, she came down to where I was skipping rocks in the stream, and said:

"Doctor thinks I should go. I could be a lady."

"You go right ahead," I said. "Get to be a lady by all means. Yes, Your Worship, no, Your Lordship. Will you have some more punch, Your Honor. I've seen it in books. A collection of capering nincompoops."

"Like Mr. Coe?" she said softly.

"He'll change. You wait. He was wearing white gloves when he came out, and he'll go back to them quick, on the other side."

"Then you think I should *not* go?"

"Who, me? I haven't got any stake in it. It's nothing to me. Charge right on, do just as you please."

"I thought maybe you might miss our fun in the woods. Fishing and hunting for plants, talking together, being friends."

"Fish will bite whether people go to England or stay home. It doesn't make a particle of difference to *them*. Go ahead, if you think you've got to. I don't need any guide in the woods."

She didn't say anything for a minute, then she said, "I'll miss you, anyway. And I'll come back, and be just the same."

"Oh, no. Once you've joined the tea-sippers, you won't have any time for outdoor things. Don't worry about coming back."

"You mean you don't want me to come?"

"I'll be pretty busy," I said, "and digging gold and tea-sipping don't mix. We wouldn't have time to knock off and get the pot going. No, you'd better just count on staying right where you are."

Her eyes suddenly blazed up and turned a kind of fiery purple, the way they did sometimes. Then she whirled around with her head high and started back toward the clearing. I continued to skip rocks, whistling, but I was so mad over her thinking it made any difference to me, I felt sort of choked, and both palms were sweaty. So she was gone. One Indian less. But at the edge of the trees, she stopped and called back, "Jaimee, I will miss *you*. You are my brother." Then she folded her arms in a cross over her bosom, very curious, but it didn't mean a thing to me.

I gave a short laugh, and stood without saying anything until she left. Indians. I kicked a couple of logs, which didn't work out, being barefoot, and sat down on the bank, feeling miserable for some reason.

And I didn't get any sleep that night, either. I was homesick, I guess. Toward dawn I dozed off for a while. When they left, with everybody teary and sad, I stayed to one side, mostly. I said I would write a letter, but didn't mean it. After they were gone, I went down in the woods, and after a while I went to sleep.

Before leaving this part, I want to include a conversation my father had with Mr. Coe apart, after supper the night before. They didn't think I heard, but I happened to be behind a tree, and I failed to entirely avoid listening.

"Coe," said my father, embarrassed. "This is awkward to bring up, and I make my apologies in advance, but is your interest in the little Po-Povi altogether, ah, educational? That is, in an honorable way, of course, do you——?"

"My dear fellow," said Mr. Coe, "you have every right to ask. But I wish you to consider; the child is thirteen; I am nearly forty. What's more, I am tentatively engaged to the Lady Barbara Willing. Nothing could be further from my mind. And as to any sordid intrigue, I can assure you——"

"Please say no more," exclaimed my father, coughing furiously. "I beg you, erase it from your mind. Reduced as I am, I am still able to recognize a gentleman when I see one."

"So am I, doctor," said Mr. Coe, smiling, "and let me tell you now what I am not able to say well—that I feel the richer for having known you all."

"My dear fellow——" began my father, choked up, and they left it at that.

So we lost two companions. It left our hearts heavy. And for my part, I guess I'd better out with it and get it off my chest—in my stupid, cruel, childish way, I let the girl go without a solitary word of kindness. But she hadn't any right saying I'd miss her like that— most of all, she hadn't any right to go.

Chapter XL

We began crevicing in our creek bed again, but we were about through. Uncle Ned thought there was gold down deep in the rock, but it was probably a thin vein there, and not worth the toil. That rock was hard to powder, even for Mr. Kissel.

As it was, we cleaned out everything in sight, up one side and down the other; then we called it a day. Altogether, that creek bed had coughed up better than eight thousand dollars, which was a very good haul, short of an outright strike.

We divided it up and prospected around for more. Everybody could see the Kissels were anxious to put their stake in a farm now, but my father talked them into shooting for more, to "obtain a ranch of princely proportions." So they went along, not because they wanted anything princely, let alone a ranch, but because they wished to be helpful and not leave us shorthanded.

Several days ran by, with us not crevicing enough in the creek beds to pay for our food. We did some dry digging, too, such as people said was popular, near a place called Weber Town, and also used the cradle and sluices on several ravines. But there was very little doing. We hated to see our eight thousand dollars melt away, and got pretty down in the mouth. One evening, a very frail man of about forty-five, gray-black-haired and sickly, with a woman in about the same shape as he was, only worse, stopped by camp to ask for water. Mrs. Kissel took pity on them right away, telling the poor peaked wife she ought not to be traipsing over the hills in her run-down condition but should tent up for a rest. The way they looked, they certainly needed it; they were beat out. Still, raggedy as they

428

were, something about them reminded me of somebody else. It was funny. I racked my brain, but I couldn't place them.

"It's hard," the woman said. "I and Morris have sank everything into getting this far. What's more, we've placed our faith in the dear blessed Jehovah, and we cain't hardly stop when we're this close to Canaan."

The man spoke up in a kind of croaky voice, which would have interested an undertaker with the expectations of doing some business soon, and said, like her, "It's hard, hard. Given one additional month, thirty days, in tolerable health, we could have shoved over the hill, but everything throwed off at once. Bauxie taken down with flux, and then I'm confounded to goodness if I didn't slip on a rock while shoveling and produce a double hernier, totally crippling, both sides, port and starboard."

The man said he had been cook on a small coastal vessel, but had naturally jumped ship when gold was discovered, the year before, and sent for his wife, who was running an eatery in San Francisco.

He looked around uneasily, coughing a little.

"There ain't but one thing to do—sell out before we're thieved out. And us with a fortune in our laps."

"You poor things," cried Mrs. Kissel. "You're churchgoing, you said, back home?"

"Ma'am, it's faith has sustained us this far. Faith, omnium-gatherum, and open bowels."

This omnium-gatherum was a dish of food that a bunch of half-starved Frenchmen had concocted, and the name had spread through the camps, being no more than a potful of whatever they could find hereabouts, mostly frog legs, turtles, woodpecker birds and squirrels, all mixed together.

"Your luck hasn't been all bad, then?" my father asked, politely.

The man looked even uneasier than before; then he said, "All bad, or mediocre, up to five weeks ago, sir."

"Morris, your tongue's a-waggling again."

"These are kind, Christian people," he said. "Even in a den of cutthroat thugs, you can select those worthy of trust, praise be to the infant Jesus." He described how they had been fleeced out of one claim, then told how in another place where they'd dug, a man had been branded on the cheek with a hot iron for claim-jumping, and still another, "only a lad," had been shorn of his ears for pilfering dust out of sacks.

My father smiled. "Whatever secrets you may have are safe with us. We are not yet reduced to preying on our fellow creatures."

Looking all around to establish that no strangers were nearby, the man hauled from his pocket something wrapped in a piece of tissue paper.

"Morris!"

He hesitated a second, then threw the coverings back. We all gasped. Lying there, fat and yellow, was a nugget the size of a walnut. It was pure, solid gold, no quartz blossom, no alloy of any kind —a child could have told it.

"Great Scott!" said my father, and Uncle Ned reached over, with, "Begging your pardon," and held it up to the light.

Showing it, the man was so ashen and sunk in, he looked pitiful, and his wife had tears in her eyes.

"You sweat, starve, sleep in the wet and cold, dig your hands raw, stave off the roughs and the Diggers, and then, when our beloved Saviour showers down His bounty, you're too sick to stand up and respond."

"What exactly do you mean, sir?" inquired my father.

"Morris!"

He had another glance around, and said, "We're rich! We've struck it rich, a gulch that would give us millions—I learned all the signs this past year—and look at us. What can we do? We ain't fit to mine. If I kept my dear wife there another month, she'd been in the ground alongside the gold."

"Morris," broke in the woman. "I'm stouter than you think. I've told you once, and I'll repeat it here—sooner than give up what we've striv this hard for, I'll stand there and dig till I drop. I'd prefer it."

"Not while I call myself a man, Bauxie. No, we've got only the one chance—go in and sell, before the jumpers grab it. And we won't get a fraction of what it's worth, neither. It's hard." I thought he was going to cry.

We felt sorry for them, so we fed them and put them up for the night, since they were traveling light and had only a blanket between them.

Later on, when the others turned in, I saw my father and Uncle Ned getting their heads together, and next morning, up early, he approached the man and said:

"See here, sir, if you have a claim worth selling, we'd take it kindly to have a first look. We haven't struck pay dirt in over a week, and we're anxious to resume work."

"You've befriended us, and we're almighty grateful," he replied, "but I wish you to understand our fix. I'm mortal positive we've got a strike—millions, maybe—so I and Bauxie hoped to get the largest sum we could. To be outright candid, a syndicate in Sacramento——"

"I should have said," my father spoke up quickly, "that we are not entirely without funds. We've had our moments, and rather valuable ones they were."

"We're beholden to you, and should give you first show, but I dislike to make commercial palaver with friends."

"Your attitude does you credit, but let's leave it at this—we'll inspect the claim, explain our financial position, and if we can't get together, there's no harm done whatever."

He wasn't anxious to, it was easy to see that, but my father put so much pressure on that he hadn't much choice. I was embarrassed to watch them. So in the morning after breakfast, the men of our party and this Morris—last named Simpkins—all struck out upcountry, with Todd and me trailing right behind.

It was a comfortable day for a hike, warm but not hot. The country was a series of small hills and dales, same as we'd been digging in, sparsely wooded with scrub pine and such, and we ran across quail, rabbits, and one deer, along with a pair of Digger Indians which jumped up and ran lickety-split. Uncle Ned said he could have shot them easy, but they made a very tough stew. I judged he was joking.

It was nearly three hours—a tolerable long pull, with Mr. Simpkins nearly dead of exhaustion—when we finally got there. A handsome ravine with a scaly creek bed in the bottom, and a long, windy rill leading upwards for a distance of two or three hundred yards into some rocky ledges.

At the edge, before going down, we saw claim signs, a picket fence of them, almost—"Morris Simpkins Claim," and the date staked out.

We stopped on the knoll above, and Mr. Simpkins said, "I think it only upright and honest to tell you gentlemen that I and Bauxie taken out a group of nuggets—maybe a thousand dollars in all—for expenses. I wouldn't care to represent the claim as being wholly unworked."

"Never you mind about that," said my father. "We quite understand. Draining off the visible gold is the most natural thing in the world, once a claim is staked. We've done it ourselves."

"We only creviced it for an hour or so," said Mr. Simpkins. "We stumbled over the claim on root to Sacramento, after Bauxie fell prey to the bloody flux and I'd produced the double hernier."

"You mean you took a thousand dollars in nuggets in an hour's time?" cried my father.

Mr. Simpkins nodded dumbly and then said, "As I cautioned before, I think it's a case for a Sacramento syndicate. There ain't a particle of doubt in my mind it's the biggest strike yet, hereabouts, but if it *was* a dry hole, then we'd be mortally grieved to have mulcted a group of samaritan friends."

He was an honest man, and my father and the others thanked him for coming out so open and forthright about the nuggets. Then they all except Mr. Simpkins, who was having trouble with his hernier, scrambled down the slope, and Todd and I clipped along after.

Well, within seconds, Uncle Ned Reeves had plucked a gold hunk the size of a marble out of a ledge, and the rest of us began picking up particles nearly every place we looked.

My father was as pale as a ghost. He stuffed about three hundred dollars' worth in his pockets, and got the others to knock off searching.

"Hold it!" he said. "Let's pull up. The more we take, the more this claim's apt to cost us. Now we certainly don't want to cheat our friend up there, laid low as he is, but it's only good business to buy as cheap as we can."

"*If* we can buy her at all," said Uncle Ned. "This looks pretty rich for my blood. Let's pool up—how much do you figure we've picked up here in ten minutes?"

We lumped it together, and made a calculation of five or six hundred dollars.

"We've got a fortune, and we might as well have it as a bunch of sharks from Sacramento," said my father. Going on, to make himself feel better, he added, "Moreover, they'll skin him out of every cent, one way or another, as soon as they've paid over the money. Let's go up and negotiate."

Mr. Simpkins was laid out over a log, looking poorly. I felt sorry for him. If he'd had the good health to work this claim, he might have wound up a very wealthy man; everybody was sure of it. There was something familiar about him, too; just as I said, I'd seen him before, but I couldn't to save me spot him exactly. I puzzled over it while they talked.

"Mr. Simpkins, we'll come right down to brass tacks," said my father. "Your claim looks good; there's gold in it. How much, we're not prepared to guess. We'd like to buy you out, if we can afford it."

"I and Bauxie hadn't gone that far in our estimations, doctor. I thought we'd heave down to Sacramento and get her appraised."

"No, no, I wouldn't do that," said my father hastily. "That is, you run the risk of not only claim-jumpers here, but of unscrupulous rascals in Sacramento. Our point is, do you feel like unloading now and getting the matter settled once and for all?"

Mr. Simpkins lay back on the log and shaded his eyes—he *was* sick, and looked so—then he raised up and said, in a sort of quiet, resigned and tired voice, "Let's traipse back and talk it over with Bauxie."

So they left it. But you can bet we hurried him right along. I figured he didn't only have a double hernier when we got there, he probably had a triple at the least, and maybe more. To tell the truth, when we arrived, and they set him in a chair, I slouched over to see if he was breathing. You might have settled it with a mirror in front of his mouth, but I didn't know of any other positive way, not in his case.

By and by, though, when his wife and the other women came up, he roused himself, and Bauxie spoke her piece.

"I say let's sell, and go into a boardinghouse for a rest. I'm tuckered out, and don't mind admitting it freely. Another few days of the flux and I won't know whether to puke or go blind."

Something stirred down deep in my mind, but I couldn't dredge it up to the surface.

Looking nervous, my father asked, "What figure did you good people have in mind?"

"I don't think we'd ever hit on a calculation," replied Mr. Simpkins in his faint voice. "Did we mention a figure, Bauxie?"

"Morris, don't lay it in my lap. You throwed too many things in my lap already. Sell and be done, I say."

"Our situation is this," said my father, sitting down next to Mr. Simpkins, his forehead shining with sweat in his anxiety to get things wound up. "We've got nearly eight thousand dollars altogether, amongst us, every dime we have in the world. Now wouldn't you say seven thousand dollars would be a fair sum, chancy as it is?"

Mr. Simpkins looked a little paler. "It's kinder taken me unawares. We'd reckoned on a tolerable sale."

"Say seventy-five hundred and meet halfway, no harm done to either side."

"Morris, they befriended us."

"Let it go, then," and he sank back down as if it was time to fetch the hearse.

Everybody clasped hands, to seal it, and congratulated each

434

other, and acted well pleased, all except the Simpkinses. The transaction had kind of drawn their last strength, so to speak, and I reckoned that the money would be used to provide them with a decent burial. But the next day, after the papers were signed, we helped them on their ailing way to Marysville. Saying goodbye, I stood watching them go on down toward Vernon as passengers on a Sante Fe wagon, and tried hard to think where I'd seen them. I was getting close—it was right there on the tip of my tongue—but I couldn't pin it down. That's the way of those things. It's like a watched kettle. It might come to me when I wasn't pressing so hard.

In the morning we were filled with bustle and stir. We had a rich claim bought, and couldn't wait to get it delivering up gold. I wished my mother could have seen my father then. There wasn't anything slothful about him, or irresponsible. He was the main leading spirit in getting things organized. When he and Uncle Ned Reeves and Mr. Kissel finally shouldered the tools—we planned to crevice and pan-wash for a starter—Jennie and Mrs. Kissel called good luck, then the Biblical group put in their licks, and we trooped off into the hills. Todd and I ran ahead. The way was easy to find; in fact, they had blazed it coming down. In a few days, we planned to move camp up nearer, but for now we would sleep at the diggings overnight and come back for supper tomorrow.

Todd and I waited on the bank overlooking the site. Everything looked the same; the claim signs were in place; all was ready. My father had written a long letter home last night, and read it through out loud, mentioning things like "Golconda is within our grasp," "a living credit to the glory of Louisville," and "proceed as directed with the McPheeters-California Public Clinic." I'd never been prouder of him. He was right and they were wrong, and that included my mother.

We gave a ringing shout for good luck, then descended into the ravine. Todd and I had spoons, which are very good tools for simple crevicing, and started worrying that creek bed in a hurry.

We didn't turn up anything for five or six minutes, so we shifted places and dug in harder. Then I heard Uncle Ned call out,

435

"Doctor, can you come over here a minute?" It was exactly at the same instant that I remembered where I'd seen those Simpkins. Their name wasn't Simpkins at all—they were the ornery man and wife that had tried to apprentice me, way back on the riverbank in Missouri. They were changed, and they *did* look sick; older, too, but I couldn't to save me think why I hadn't known them at once.

My heart skipped a beat; I felt sick myself. Then I dropped my spoon and ran over to where my father and the others were standing, their faces very grave and concerned.

"Those people," I cried, "that Mr. and Mrs. Simpkins. I know them—they're frauds and cheats!"

"You're a little late, my boy," said my father, sitting down weakly. "We've been robbed of everything. This 'mine' has been salted."

There wasn't an ounce of gold anyplace around, no matter how hard you might search. None of the nuggets so carelessly displayed on our last trip were anywhere to be seen now. They had been deliberately planted there, and those that we had left had been picked up by what my father said was a "confederate."

Well, we *were* crushed. We were so low nobody could think of anything cheerful to say. There just *wasn't* any silver lining.

"It's useless to pursue them," said my father. "They've made their getaway, and been swallowed up long before this."

"Still and all," observed Uncle Ned, "I'd admire to hold a business discussion with them. I'd hope to branch out and conduct a negotiation in hides."

We were several hours getting up the nerve to start back. But the women had to be told, so we did it. Taken all around, this was the mournfulest evening we'd put in yet. After supper, nobody could find a thing to stay up for, so we went to bed early. I could see my father lying across the tent on his back, his eyes open and staring, his hands behind his head, and wished I could think of some way to help. But I couldn't; the words failed to come. After a while, we both went to sleep. Sometimes it's all a person can fall back on in a pinch.

436

Chapter XLI

We were in the summer now, a hot one, steamy and close in this valley of the Sacramento, and our luck had run out. There was grub money left for a while, but no matter how we traipsed these gullies, we took no more than particles the size of a gnat.

It was discouraging to watch our pile dwindle. In July we moved our traps to other diggings, journeying down past the Yuba, beyond the Hock Ranch and some other ranches, past the joining of the Feather and the Sacramento, and dug for a while below the miners' settlement of Vernon.

For two days we stopped at Johnson's Ranch, a mile or two up a tributary of the Feather, called Bear River. This man gave us good greeting, as Mrs. Kissel said. He was a New England sailor who cared nothing for gold and spurned every chance to find it, even when strikes were made almost under his nose. He had left the sea to farm, and his broad fields of wheat, barley and corn, which grew green and high in these Bear River bottoms, extended as far as you could see. I felt sorry for the Kissels, surveying them, their eyes soft with longing.

Johnson lived with Indian servants and workers, in a two-room house of log and adobe, with a doorway of stretched rawhide. Roaming his hills were hundreds of head of cattle, within view of the Sierras, fifty miles away, and the Sacramento off in the other direction. It was a main choice spot, lush and rolling, watered and wooded, and finally I heard Mr. Kissel say, "Here it is, then. When the time's come, we'll stake down in this valley."

No matter how many emigrants stopped by, Johnson provided them with whatever food they needed. I've heard it said he butchered as many as ten steers in a day, to care for the needy. He gave us a supper of beef, cheeses and milk lumpy with cream, biscuits made of flour ground on his hand mill by Indians, and beef tallow in place of lard. And would he take payment? Not so you'd notice it. Along with Captain Sutter, he was the blessedest man in California.

Vernon was even seedier than Marysville, if possible. Almost every house was a "tap," or saloon, and contained, as somebody said, "an apartment consecrated to the god of gambling, where a parcel of hawks, with whetted beaks, were lying in wait for green pigeons."

We got there just after a big organization had tried to drive off the Chileans and Mexicans, which seemed pretty rude to me, and a good deal of brawling was going on over town. We didn't tarry, but struck out for fresh diggings.

In the summer heat we toiled from one dale to another, finding even less than before. And at last, pinched for money, my father and Mr. Kissel and Uncle Ned Reeves hired out as hands to companies. It was heartbreaking, but we had to eat.

For a while, as Todd and I ranged the hills hunting small game to cook, they worked at a flume, where a syndicate had run ten miles of wooden flume troughs out of a steep-sided canyon, with a rushy stream, down over ridges and trees to a dry ravine far below where the gold lay. It was a rich strike, worth all the trouble. There's no telling how long it took to build that water-toting flume; in one place they had it up on a trestle nearly a hundred feet high. When it got down to the gold, the water was led off in a series of ditches and canals, and the precious ore taken out in the same way as sluicing and such. But they needed lots of water.

Another time we signed on to block off a river from its course; we made a new channel, so that mining could commence in the old bed. There were twenty men owned the claim, besides us, which didn't own anything, and what they wanted was to make a race and carry off the water naturally, you might say, but it didn't work; the canyon sides were too steep. The water kept breaking back into the old channel and carrying off valuable tools and gear. So in the end we made a big flume, which carted that whole river right out of its banks and into a new place. Then, by pumping out the mud and puddles, and removing the boulders, they set up sluice boxes and got to work. I saw them take out $5227 from behind one boulder in a single pan of dirt. It made a person hungry. After the flume was done, my father and us weren't needed any more, so we found a new job, at the same old wage of six dollars a day.

Things were so dismal we talked very little around camp now, the way we used to, but generally went straight to bed after supper. And I noticed that my father seldom wrote home, either. I reckon he figured the bundle of nonsense he mailed when we found the nuggets would hold them for a while.

We worked with a gang that found gold at bedrock, nearly a hundred feet down, and needed help to sink a shaft six feet wide, which was made exactly the way people dig a well, with a windlass and bucket above. That is, the dirt from the bottom was brought up bucket-cranked on the windlass. It was dangerous. A good many people were killed by cave-ins, or falling rocks, in those shafts. This job mightn't have lasted very long except that twice on the way down we ran into "leads," or veins of horizontal pay dirt, and opened "drifting" tunnels off in both directions, shoring up the roofs with timber. We tunneled that way when we got to bedrock, too, still sending all dirt up by the windlass-drawn bucket. It was slow but worth while, if the claim was rich, and this one was.

These same people did some outright tunneling into hillsides nearby, which kept us on the job for several more weeks. We had to pick through solid rock for nearly seventy-five feet, although they kept saying they'd sent for blasting powder. We were worn down to a nub when we finished. Todd and I worked on this job, wheelbarrowing light loads of dirt out for washing. Carrying ten hours a day, we got half pay.

Toward the end of summer, eating, living, but with everybody's hopes down to zero, we became so reduced we hooked up first with a party of Mexicans, then Chileans, quartz-mining. And the funny thing was, these foreigners were the nicest bunch we'd met; neither did they haggle nearly so much over the pay. Main trouble was, we couldn't understand a word they said, except for one or two men, and they couldn't understand us.

Some ways, both the Mexicans and Chileans were advanced over anybody in California. Their specialty was quartz-mining, where the gold is blended in with quartz, you know, to form what was called "quartz blossoms."

The Americans we saw quartz-mining had a system so ornamental it wasted most of their time, according to my view. To start with, the position of a quartz lead in a mountain is usually found at an angle of twenty to fifty degrees down from where it crops out at surface. Rather than work from the surface, the Americans went to the nuisance of sinking down a perpendial shaft way back from the outcropping, so they could hit the vein there and work *upward*, lifting the rock from the shaft by windlass, don't ask me why. It was usually so damp down there they had to wear India rubber suits, and use all kinds of other equipment, too.

What's more, their mill that ground the rocks was too complicated. My father and Uncle Ned both said so. It was built around cast-iron "stampers" that weighed up to a thousand pounds and moved up and down like a triphammer, smashing the quartz blocks. There were a bunch of convex arms, and a bedplate, and an amalgamating box, and so on, and altogether there were too many things to get out of whack.

But these Mexicans were foxy. They had what they called a *rastra*, a circular stone track with a post in the middle and a wooden arm that a donkey pulled round and round. It dragged a number of heavy stone blocks, and these smashed up the quartz. Quicksilver was placed in grooves in the stone track, to amalgamate with the gold, which being heavy sought the lowest level. It was just that simple. The amalgam was taken out of the crevices and "retorted," and the bunch we were with then smelted and shaped the gold into ingots before selling it.

The Chileans used the same sort of thing, only they had heavy iron wheels circling the track instead of dragging stone weights. All in all these fellows, both Mexicans and Chileans, were taking out a lot of gold, and it didn't cost them much, either. They would have got rich if the Americans hadn't kept driving them out.

Drifting along all summer, we made our living, but what a comedown from the expectations we'd had of that nugget-strewn creek! And the pity of it was, no matter how we worked now, we never got far ahead on account of the prices.

One day late in September, on a Saturday, at the end of a week with the Chileans, we came home to find Mrs. Kissel as fluffed up as a banty rooster. All of a sudden she was at the end of her tether. For a long time she'd sat back and let these menfolk take the bit, do exactly what they pleased, abandon their farm plans, lose one of her children, and generally lower the family into a misery such as they'd never known before. Now she was ready to take over. With all his ox's strength, there wasn't the slightest use in Kissel's making any opposition, either.

Women are like that, my father said with a sigh. "Basically, they're the stronger sex. We see it in medicine every day. They live longer, do more work, act less afraid—half the men you meet go around with a chip on their shoulder for fear somebody will call them a coward—endure pain better, are more steadfast, and have better instincts. In short, they're closer to nature. Animalistic, they have less intelligence, relying instead upon emotion, but the bald truth is that they're the superior sex by a long sea mile."

So this evening when we came home, here was Mrs. Kissel with fire in her eye, chickens gathered close to her skirts—the pale, wan, skinny little things—and there was that bothersome Jennie, looking plumper and handsomer than she had a right to, standing alongside, ready to back her up.

"Anything wrong, mother?" inquired Mr. Kissel, mildly.

"The gold-pecking is over, Matthew. I've hoped and starved, and made do on nothing long enough. I don't mind a-starving personally, though my daddy wouldn't approve it, but I take objection when my offspring children are roped in likewise. Look at Deuteronomy. His bones stick out where his flesh ought to be. Glance at Leviticus. He don't resemble anything so much as a scarecrow flopping on a pole. *Don't* look at Lamentations. He ain't fit to be seen; I'd ruther we remembered him as he was."

Only the week before, our provisions had dropped so that my father traded a pair of surgical shears for dust enough to get a side of sowbelly, off a disgusted man that was aiming to set up as barber along the Feather River.

Kissel wrinkled up his brows in indecision. He just stood there, waiting.

"Well," he said finally, laying down his pick and scratching his head, "I don't know, exactly——"

"Matthew," said Mrs. Kissel. "Slaughter the Brice oxen."

"And don't argue about it," said Jennie.

"Said what, mother?"

"Slaughter them oxen. I've been talking to neighbors. There's money to be made in the butchery business. Slaughter the steers. We'll get to town with the mules. We're moving camp."

"Now, ladies," cried my father, hopping around anxiously, about to unload some of his guff, "let's be sensible. I'll tell you what we'll do——"

"Doctor," said Mrs. Kissel, "I reckon you're about the finest man we've ever knowed, and the smartest. But there's times when your tongue kind of runs away from your brains and gets out ahead of itself. Jennie and I'll just ask you to take a back seat on this particular occasion, if it ain't too much trouble."

"Of course, of course. I'll be glad to, more than glad." He looked very much the way he always did when my mother jumped him. Agreeable, but ready for travel.

"What was it you wanted done, ma'am?" asked Uncle Ned. He

liked Mrs. Kissel, and would have followed along after her like a dog, as my father once remarked, because of the way she'd fed him that first day.

"Unless I misrecollect, you're handy as a joiner?"

"I've did carpentry, along with soldiering, mining, farming, and unmentionables."

"When we get to town, I'll ask you to knock these wagons apart and build a counter. We can't sell meat under canvas. People want to view it in the open."

Mr. Coe had left us his wagon and mules, together with most of his traps, except for his personal luggage.

"Why, mother, the children——"

"—can sleep in the tent along of us. We'll double up. Mr. Reeves, since your wits ain't turned to wool, I'd be obliged if you'd break camp and hitch up."

"I'd admire to, ma'ma, begging your husband's pardon."

We were on the road in an hour, headed for Vernin, only a short distance away up the river. It was still light when we arrived, but Mrs. Kissel said we could slaughter in the morning. Jennie had four oxen left, and on these prices, they'd bring a sizable sum, sold out cut by cut.

It wasn't any trouble to pick out a good spot to stop, centrally placed but not too near a tap, and Uncle Ned had the wagons half knocked down by dark. Mr. Kissel helped him, finally, but looked pretty glum about it As a farmer born and bred, he hated to see farm things destroyed for the use of another trade.

Early in the morning we were up and doing. Mr. Kissel took his ax and knives, let the oxen back a ways, and commenced work. Todd and I didn't watch. Those animals had been good to us; now it seemed shameful to treat them so. But I guess it had to be done. Poor brutes, the ones waiting their turns took on like the furies, bellowing and stamping, and when Mr. Kissel finally came back, beginning to pack the meat, the tears were running down his face. I thinkthey were the rest of ours, too.

By mid-morning, we had a tidy butcher shop open for business, selling at the customary prices. Mr. Kissel and Uncle Ned were butchers, and Mrs. Kissel bargained with the public, while Jennie minded the children.

My father bustled around, feeling neglected and out of things. But by and by Mrs. Kissel came out during a lull. She said, "Doctor, we've got seven mules and a riding horse, enough to do well packing supplies to the diggings. My neighbors mentioned it as employment, along with the butcher shop. More than that, we'll need a cattle buyer, once this present supply dwindles thin."

I could see him wrestling with his conscience. He felt he ought to stay on, but he'd been pining for months to see San Francisco. He had it fixed in his head that our real future lay there, now, in some mysterious kind of way. So he put her off with some soothery phrases, saying he'd certainly look into it; it sounded interesting. And if it would serve the group best, he'd be certain to do it.

But as things turned out, he got his chance for travel sooner than he expected. To put it in my father's words, good came out of bad, the way children are born out of pain. One morning soon, after he'd actually made a trip with Todd and me up the Bear as far as the ranches, to buy six steers, which we then drove back, Jennie saw a man walking a pinto horse down the street. "Yonder's a customer," she said. It was so early we didn't figure to sell anything till after breakfast, but of course you never could tell. Some of these miners, specially the greenhorns just off the boats, couldn't wait to start. We often had them knock us up in the middle of the night.

"He sits funny, sidewise and careless," said Jennie. "It's almost like——"

"Great jumping Jupiter!" cried my father.

"Coulter's back," said Mr. Kissel.

We ran out into the road, but mostly we stopped in surprise. You couldn't help it. He wasn't hardly the same fellow we'd seen last, but was pale and worn, and his left sleeve was pinned up to his shoulder.

Jennie burst into tears. "Oh, my God," she cried, and then Coulter sang out as chipper and sarcastic as ever:

444

"You call that a way to say howdy to an old friend? I'd better wheel around and vamoose. Ho, boy," jerking the reins, "let's drift."

"Get off that horse," said Jennie. "Oh, your poor arm."

When he slid down, she hung around his neck and cried and cried. My father said later it was the pent-up floodwaters, from wondering, and worrying, and holding it in to herself for so long. We felt awful. I could see my father swiping his hatband again, which was his usual sign of commotion, and even Uncle Ned, who was a perfect stranger to Coulter, worked his Adam's apple up and down.

"This is some better," said Coulter, running his hand over her shiny black hair. "But it isn't all that bad. I'll own up that arm got in my way. I do everything better with my right, and the other was jealous. I'm glad to get shut of it."

"Your poor arm," Jennie kept saying, and touched the sleeve carefully.

We went back to the shop and locked up, then Mrs. Kissel sailed into a breakfast that set some new marks around there. Even Uncle Ned said he'd never seen anything like it, and he'd eaten her cooking for near onto five months. She had corn cakes and eggs and beefsteak and biscuits and liver and coffee and milk and turnip greens along with beef chittlings and sweetbreads and a few other oddities of that sort. Besides bacon and beans, of course. She said Coulter was about forty pounds underweight, and evidently she hoped to pull him up to scratch in one heave, if she could get his co-operation.

But the truth is, he didn't eat much. He'd been deadly sick, and told us about it while we drank our coffee. After we left, he and Bridger had stalked around behind Brother Muller and his Danites, going soft-footed in the rain, and surprising them had killed five outright. Brother Muller was one of the first down. But the remainder made a fight, which scrabbled back and forth over the rocks, and before they had finished—and they *were* finished, every last one of them—Bridger was creased on the scalp and Coulter

445

shot through the upper left arm, the ball smashing the bone and everything around it. Bridger eliminated the surviving Danite by overhauling him, pulling him off his horse, and knifing him through the throat. Then he knotted a shirt around Coulter's arm, loosing now and then, and packed him home to the Fort.

"Jim and his squaws sliced her off near the shoulder," said Coulter, not really seeming to feel bad about it, "but rot set in and I was back-flat for a spell. If you ask me, they did a job of nursing."

My father shook his head. "Coulter, you've given up your arm in the cause of this party. There's no way on earth we can repay you."

"Oh, it might be worked out," said Coulter, looking at Jennie with a grin, but she turned red and then got up and left in a huff.

We went over our adventures, while a number of people pounded on the shop for service. For once, we let them pound.

Within a week, Coulter was looking fit again, gaining weight and taking on color with the good food and rest. We noticed that he'd changed in other ways, too. Whatever it was that had bothered him was gone; he seemed, as my father put it, at peace with himself at last.

The Kissels went on operating the shop, while Uncle Ned and my father, using the mules, worked up a very fair trade packing supplies out to miners. As he mended, Coulter helped with one thing and the other, and Todd and I did the chores.

We were prospering, much better than mining, but one afternoon Coulter and I went into Vernon to get a fresh jug of spring water from a tap owner that bought our meat. When we got inside his place, toward four o'clock of an October day that had a nice blue crackle to it, there was sitting at a table not only the mangy pair from Missouri that had swindled us, but John and Shep besides. They looked prosperous, and meaner than Hades, but John's eyes suggested that if he wasn't outright insane by now, he was very close to it. They were drinking grog. The woman didn't look sickly at all now, but was spruced up and being very friendly with Shep, which didn't appear to put her husband in a better humor.

Except for two elderly whiskerandos standing at the bar, they were the only people in the place.

I sung out, "Lookee there!" and they scrambled back out of their chairs, turning one over with a crash. Coulter stood his ground and watched Shep, with what sounded like a deep breath of satisfaction.

"Those other two are the ones——" I cried, but he interrupted in a perfectly easy voice, "Yes, yes, never mind that right now."

After his first scare, Shep began to get his bluster back, and seeing Coulter's empty sleeve, he said, very bold, "Well, if Buck ain't lost a flipper. Don't tell us you bumped into somebody face to face."

Coulter said, "Come out in the street, Shep."

The two miners at the bar turned around very slow, as if they hadn't heard but were changing their position naturally. They kept talking to one another in a low tone, as if nothing was going on. I knew them slightly; they were rough, hard cases, though old, and very good men at heart.

"Why, Buck," said Shep, but his voice wasn't quite so brash as before, "was you aiming to tackle a grizzly with one fist? I never knowed you to be forward with your old chums. What do you hear from Sandy?"

"I'm done about that," said Coulter. "You're chose. Are you walking out, or do I drag you by the scruff?"

Suddenly I saw John gradually drawing a pistol out of his waist, the same one, I reckon, he used to shoot Todd's mother and father with, a long time ago back there at St. Genevieve.

When it was almost out, being unobserved by anyone but me, I thought, there was head-numbing explosion and a revolver bullet splintered through the floor right at his feet. It didn't miss his left toe a half inch. It was fired by one of the miners standing at the bar, without the gun ever being drawn from its holster, the lead passing out of the open end. Neither did the two men appear to interrupt their conversation, except that the one who fired the shot said, in a friendly enough tone, "Best fight fair, particular when a stranger's rowing with one oar. It's hostile, like."

I thought the knotted-up veins on John's forehead were going to bust, but he lowered his hand, as slowly as he'd raised it, and Shep said, stepping forward a pace, "You want your teeth knocked out and stomped down your gullet, Buck?"

Right then a customer stuck his head in the door, but hauled it back out again fast. He didn't waste a second. I could hear him hollering "Fight! fight!" as he ran up the street.

"You always was scared of me, wasn't you, Shep? You never figured I'd fight, long as you had that about my brother."

One of the miners turned to the other and observed, "I've seed a number of sizable men that wouldn't toe-up when chose. You take many of them, and they run more to mouth than fist."

Shep looked uncertain before, but this was something he could handle. He walked up to the miner, who weighed about a hundred and twenty pounds in his boots, and said, "You looking for a bare-knuckle fuss with me, brother?"

"I wouldn't claim no priority," said the miner, undisturbed. "That gentleman yonder with the absent meat-hook's first in line. I'd admire to take the leavings, though."

"He means me," said Coulter, whirling Shep around and smacking him across one fat red cheek with the back of his open hand.

The bartender, a red-haired Irishman named Costello, hadn't moved a muscle up to this, but now he sailed around with a blackthorn club in his hand, and there was a scramble. This bartender had a prejudice; he didn't allow fighting in his tap—he said it wasn't "genteel." I found myself outside: fifty or sixty other men were there, too, and in the center I saw Coulter and Shep standing face to face, white and ready.

I didn't know what to do. First, I was afraid Coulter might get himself killed, having only one arm, but I wanted to run back and tell the others so we could collar the swindlers as well. Anyhow, I made up my mind too late; the fight was on.

448

Shep stalked him around in a circle, hands working like Matlock's; and his little yellow-black eyes squinted up like a coyote's you've cornered. He was afraid of Coulter, all right, but he'd done a heap of bully-brawling, no doubt about that, and he held all the cards here. He was an ox, almost like Mr. Kissel, and in spite of flabbiness around his middle, he was in generally hard shape. What's more, he was strong as a mule. But he was slow, and it cost him trouble.

Coulter leaped in, struck him smartly with his right fist, and stepped back before either of those hooking arms could reach him. But there was something wrong; without a left arm, he hadn't anywhere near as much leverage. He wasn't quite on balance. The blow lacked the sting that had buckled Matlock's knees.

Shep shook his head, then finding himself damaged but working, commenced to take on confidence.

"It's coming, Bucky boy, it's coming," he said between split, bloody lips. "You'd better say your prayers, you Kentucky mudcat bastard."

Coulter hit him again in the face, then once in the neck and ducked under a roundhouse swing. And when Shep charged in, stung reckless, he kicked him in the stomach with both feet, falling on his back in the dirt. But as he scrambled up, Shep was on him, working both hamlike arms. He hooked him first one side of the face, and then the other, and barely missed closing him in a bear's hug.

I heard several men cry, "Shame!" and "Unfair!—only one arm like that," but Shep, grinning now, rushed in like a bull, ready for the kill and willing to take any punishment involved to make it.

Anybody playing Coulter for done in a fight was running an awful risk, whether one arm or two, and I wasn't surprised to see him twist out of the way, slip beside Shep, and send him sprawling with a hip-and-arm heave. And before he got up, Coulter kicked him flush in the face with the heel of his boot.

But he couldn't win, and everybody knew it. It was only a matter of time. Nose mashed to a pulp, both eyes blacked, and his mouth split, Shep commenced to punish him with those roundhouse blows, first the left and then the right, knocking him down to his knees, down flat, down to his knees again, and finally picking him up so as to knock him down some more. Altogether, he did it seventeen or eighteen times. I couldn't see how a human could stand up under such treatment.

I have no way to tell whether Coulter could have beaten him with one arm if he hadn't been sick. But right now he was in no shape for fighting, not of this sort. Even so, he made a friend of every man there.

The muttering and protesting grew louder and louder until Shep, having his man all but finished, clubbed him down once more and then flopped on top, pulling his head back with both hands locked across the forehead.

"Now, you brother-killing skunk, we'll see if we can't take your ugly knob off by the roots."

It was all I could stand. They lay there, ragged and bloody in the dust, directly at my feet, and I jumped on Shep's back and clawed like a wildcat for his eyes.

Maybe the crowd was only waiting for a signal like this, because as many as a dozen leaped in to snatch me up and haul Shep off, too.

I kicked off my shoes and clipped out down the road. It was just after five; there were a few miners weaving around in the path, but I made good time. When our shop came in view, I could see them staring at me, and when I stumbled up, fighting for breath, Jennie ran out.

"What's the matter? Where's Buck? What's happened?!"

Uncle Ned and Todd had just got in, and before I gasped out my story, Jennie was running back up the street, holding her skirts high in both hands.

Uncle Ned was chewing tobacco, and as I told what happened, he kept on chewing in the same rhythm, only he took out his rifle and gave it a good inspection, then put on his wolfskin cap.

Todd said, "You promised, Uncle Ned."

"Fair's fair, as I remarked previous. I don't withdraw dangled goodies from children."

"Wait a minute," cried my father. "Hold on. What are you fellows planning to do?"

I guess they didn't hear, for a minute later, they got up, taking their rifles, and started up the street, not in any special hurry, with the rest of us trailing after and crying out to stop, that they'd be killed.

Neither one turned around. I was right behind, and could hear them talking.

Uncle Ned said:

"It's uncommon odd how things turn up when you least expect them."

"Uncle Ned, do you favor a belly shot or a head shot with a half-swung-up rifle?"

"It's a matter of taste, son. I've had a power of satisfaction out of head shots, myself. They make a nice spatter. When the person's did you a disservice, that is."

"Hark, now. You said you'd take the thin man and leave the fat one to me. The one I ear-whistled from the wagon."

"I don't want you to feel bad about that, son," said Uncle Ned, kindly. "A rolling-wagon shot is about the toughest kind there is. Seems like a person can't take picks, no matter which way he sprawls."

They sounded as if they were on their way to a turkey-shoot. It was the cold-bloodedest talk I ever heard. And otherwise they were the mildest pair I ever met. The boy, too. When you came down to it, there was no positive proof that both of them wouldn't be killed within the next ten minutes. Because nothing we could do, no amount of pleading, or arguing from the rear ranks, appeared to faze them. They kept right on walking, up the middle of the street.

Seeing them, people fell away to the sides and began to whisper to each other behind their hands. And heads took to popping out of store doors and windows. There wasn't any way to mistake the nature of this dead-march, but it was perfectly easy and quiet, too, if you know what I mean.

The buzz of conversation ran right on up the street, which was fuller, now, on the sides, more of the miners having come in after work. What they left was a wide lane, no interference, no loud talk, only a slammed window or a dog barking to break the silence, clear up to Costello's tap.

Across the way, Coulter was being washed at a horse trough by some men, and Costello stood on the steps of his place, looking worried. From inside, when we got near, I could hear the sound of loud laughter and the clinking of glasses—the buzzards were celebrating—and Shep's bull's voice rising over everything. But when Costello turned to go inside, the noise broke off sharply. There wasn't a sound either there or up and down the street. It was awesome.

Uncle Ned called out in a loud, clear voice:

"There's a pair of murdering dogs in there we'd admire to have step out and meet the people they've wronged."

Still no sound.

Our bunch was down a ways, crouched behind some barrels.

Uncle Ned spoke up again, a little louder this time.

"I'd fret if I had to take and fire the place. No call for innocent to suffer along with the guilty."

Then a scuffle exploded within, and that wild man Murrel burst out, iron-gray hair flying, eyes blazing like a maniac's, with a single-shot pistol swinging in his hand. He stumbled a little before he got down the stairs, but righted himself fast, and cried out to Uncle Ned:

"What's your grievance? Speak up, or by God——"

"Maybe you misrecollect killing this boy's pa and ma in cold blood, back in Missouri. We ain't forgot. When there's a rattle-snake needs squashing, I say squash it."

"So that's it!" cried John in a voice of thunder, staring at Todd. "Then one more won't matter," and he swung up his pistol.

Making no effort to fire the first shot, Uncle Ned wheeled around smartly to present his right side, away from the heart, and covered his head with his arm. The ball raised dust from his shirt, high up on the chest. He made a brief motion of brushing himself off, pulling the cloth out from his body where it began to stick with blood. Then he whipped up his rifle, took a very quick bead, and shot John low in the forehead, just over his nose.

Maniac that he was, he didn't kill easy. A Bible sentence began and died on his lips. " 'The Lord goeth out——' " the glare seemed to fade in his eyes, and he toppled forward on his face.

At almost the same instant, Shep flung out of the tap, beet-red with drink, but when he spied the boy he went all to pieces. I think he'd known from the day on the riverbank that this Todd would finally catch up and undo him. He turned a kind of belly-white, put one hand out as if to ward off something, and said, "I haven't got no g——"

Todd shot his rifle from waist high, the bullet plunking into Shep's stomach with the sound of a paddle slapping a tubful of butter.

Then Shep brought out his right arm from behind him, holding a pistol, so the sentence he hadn't finished was a lie, of course, and a piece of trickery, and tried to bring it up level. But he sat down in the street instead, feeling himself in bewilderment. Then he said, "You've killed me."

"I could have blowed out your brains," said the boy, slobbering, "but I didn't want it fast." He reloaded the rifle, took another aim, and hit Shep in the stomach again, the dust flying out with a little puff.

"The first was for ma, that was pa's."

"You've killed me," said Shep again.

"Sit there and die," said Todd.

As he spoke, Shep fell over sideways. A number of men ran up, and suddenly the street was full of noise. People came out from behind boxes and bales, from inside stores and houses, from about every kind of cover you could find.

"Back! Stand back, give him air," cried a big man in a swallow-tail coat. "Aren't you a doctor?" he said to my father. "Attend this man."

"Not me," replied my father stoutly. It went against his oath, but I don't think he was sorry, afterwards.

Shep still breathed, I could see that from where I knelt between a man's legs, but he was bleeding to death. So, after an oath and the observation, "Killed by a shirttail sprig," he took three or four gasps, as if he couldn't get his lungs full, and choked to death on a big bubble of blood. It wasn't pretty to see; he died hard. Everybody said so several times.

The score was settled.

Chapter XLII

Now began my father's adventures on the streets of San Francisco, a time I won't dwell on, since there wasn't much pleasant about it. Some of it seems funny, though, looking back.

We left a week after the fight, with promises to all (from my father) that we'd find the exact right opportunity and send for them within a month. It had a familiar ring; it sounded like the things he said to my mother nearly two years ago, back in Louisville.

John's bullet had missed Uncle Ned's lungs and various other objects on duty there, but had cracked a rib, then bounced on off and out. He was stiff and sore, but as somebody remarked, wasn't anywhere near as stiff as Murrel, thanks to goodness.

Was it Murrel? Unless the real article should turn up, nobody will ever know. Me, I doubt it. I think this old murderer had been crazy all his life, and had probably branded his own thumb out of craziness, and maybe something like hero worship.

Nobody in town minded the shooting, so there was very little grumbling. For several months, John and Shep had been in and out of Vernon, and wherever they went, making enemies in their easy, effortless style, the people always would have been happy to take up a collection and move them to another place.

Still and all, these miners had their sentimentally side, so they got a bushwhacking preacher out of a tap, held his head in the horse trough to sober him up, and conducted a very nice service. And afterwards, they planted the two scalawags in a new grave-yard that was started only the previous year. I didn't see it myself, but several mentioned it, and two or three thanked Uncle Ned and Todd for making it possible. There was very little decent entertainment around here, and a service like this helped. The only hitch was, the preacher had been so drunk he misunderstood the history of the corpses. So he went praising along about their "good works" and "lives spent in selfless devotion to others" and such other tommyrot, and finished up by saying what a great loss it was to the community but that the Kingdom of Heaven would be the richer. This certainly came as news to me; I was willing to bet next year's salary they were already lodged in the other place. To end up, he led the miners in a hymn that told how sheep along with other farm animals came into a corral when deceased, which seemed pretty far removed from the subject, and after this he knocked off, passed the hat, and went back to the tap.

It sounded a little thick to me, but I've never had any luck making sense out of sermons, funerals included. As far as those swindlers were concerned, they got clean away; we never got a trace of them again from the day of the fight on.

Coulter wasn't much the worse for wear, only bunged up about the head; his spirits were as bouncy as ever. Having only one arm now, he generally wore a revolver strapped to a gun belt, and it gave us a safer feeling to leave them like that. Nobody in his right mind would have reached for a gun facing Coulter, and everybody around here knew it. There were several men in town that had run across him in scouting days, him and Bridger both, along with Kit Carson, mainly on the Santa Fe Trail, and I heard it said he'd backed down some Texas gun slingers in a famous fight there, after plugging two of their best men. After that, they said, troublemakers in that area were very well content to leave him alone.

He and Jennie were going to get married.

"I reckon I'm done roaming," he said. "I never heard of any one-handed trail scouts."

"Oh, you'll roam," Jennie said, "when you get the itch."

He and Uncle Ned and Todd would go on working the mule pack, and the Kissels would operate the butchery. For now, they were all right, and in a month, thirty days, as my father put it, using both measurements every time he mentioned it, as if maybe they weren't clear what a month was, we'd be started toward fortune in San Francisco.

"Think of it!" he cried, fired up with all his old vigor now at the prospect of moving. "A forest of masts in the harbor; ships from the world's farthest ports; the babble of polylinguality in the streets; building and boom everywhere; and gold, gold by the bucketload streaming in from the richest mines yet discovered by man. We'll look around, we'll spot the missing link in this golden chain of commerce, and we'll charge forward to found our concern. With any kind of luck, we'll be rolling in wealth by Christmas."

This "concern" was something that had crept into his speech, but was a mystery to me. I think he'd fixed his notions on building up some kind of business, but he hadn't let us in on what it was. Like the McPheeters-California Public Clinic, it flourished entirely in his head.

That evening before we left, I took Todd back where I kept Spot tied to a tree, and said, "I'll leave him with you. You take care of him, hear? He sidles to the right if he sees something white in the path."

We were going down to Sacramento by the boats.

Todd rubbed his muzzle.

"Not anxious to. I never had any friend before. Back home, there wasn't any neighbor in rifle sound; Pa liked things solitary. He was a woodsy man."

"I'll be seeing you and old Spot in a month."

"Uncle Ned says not. He says your pa's one of them with dreams always in their heads. He says your pa's got to chase his dreams all of his life. But he says it makes things kind of beautiful for backwoods people like us. Said we must pick him up if he stumbles. Uncle Ned ain't an altogether ignorant man in some ways."

"He's fine," I said, feeling bad. "You both are."

"I'm not forgetting about the watch. How you toted it all them miles."

Right here it struck me that everything I liked was going. Mr. Coe had gone, and Po-Povi—and now we were leaving Jennie and the Kissels and Coulter and Uncle Ned and Todd. I hurt inside. Another part of our adventure was over, and even then, I realized that nothing ever comes back again quite the same. Things roll on, new sights take the place of the old, and the only way you can do it over is remember. So, after a lecture from Jennie about minding my manners, along with a quick hug and kiss, I went to bed, sore at my father, refusing to answer when he called, "Good night, son."

But nothing looks very bad in the morning, when you're a boy. For I was a boy still, though on the edge of manhood, as my father had said, studying me over as if he hadn't seen me for a while. We were up and off long before breakfast, eating some biscuits on the way, and spinning down the river by nine.

The boat was a two-master belonging to a syndicate of Chileans that had hired a captain who described himself as a "Yankee." In fact, he described himself this way about every five minutes, and took a nip out of a bottle to reinforce it. On board, besides, was a poor sort of immigrant group, but we concentrated on watching the river.

This passage had cost us six dollars for my father and four dollars for me, "deck passage," without meals, as far as Sacramento, where the boat was headed. We had altogether about a hundred dollars and a little over from what was left of our money. The distance was upwards of twenty miles, down a green and fertile valley. Being a sailor, when the wind took a rest the boat commenced to drift broadside. The captain had gone below, drunk, and when they told him the fix we were in, he raised up from his bunk—I was there—and said, "Be we headed downstream?"

One of the men spoke up sharply. "Naturally, you fool."

"Ain't floating against the current?"

Somebody snorted in disgust, and he said, "Then we're laying the right course. If she begins to float contrary to the drift, roust me out."

There wasn't a thing could be done with him, he was in too happy a humor, and when we left, with some mutters and threats, he raised up again to take another snort and cried, "If you strike Sacramento, heave the anchor."

No matter what, our situation was far from pleasant—there were other boats in this river, along with debris, "sawyers" (or big trees), sand bars, and other obstacles, and two of our Chilean hands managed to say, mainly with sign talk, that we'd better break out a boat and tow the bow downstream. So we did it, nearly all of the men taking a turn, including my father. There was a very hard-bitten Australian passenger on board, a rough, seamy-faced fellow with a soiled blue sash tied around his waist, and he suggested, perfectly serious, that they fix a line to one of the captain's legs and "keelhaul" him.

"They done it to a cobber of mine, and it worked wonders, lads, wonders."

I got the idea that what they did was toss him overboard at the bow, bring the free end of the line back along the opposite side, and then, amidships, haul him under and up.

"It's the barnacles perform the miracle," he said. "Flogging ain't in it."

But he was overruled, on the grounds that it wouldn't be humane, and besides, treatment like that might come under the heading of mutiny, whether he was drunk or not.

It was nearly dark when we reached Sacramento, which was on the west side of the river, and we dinghied ashore but could find no chance of lodging. Then we heard of a place on the out-skirts of town, and when we got there, it was run by a Mr. Harris that had been an original member of our wagon team from In-dependence. He was glad to see us, and made shakedowns on the front-room floor, because everything else was jammed. But he wouldn't take money, and next morning he gave us a good break-fast, too.

Back in town, we sought passage on down to San Francisco. It seemed a lively place, with the usual half-finished frame and zinc houses, and mud nearly every place you stepped. It was a curiosity to me that those Mormons, working under the worst kind of conditions, in a desert without water and on ground so ugly nobody else would have dreamed of settling there, yet had managed to build a city that was handsome and neat and *planned*. It had no points of resemblance to this ramshackle pile of lumber and clay. Salt Lake City was a place you could take pride in, as far as the looks of it went.

Still, Sacramento stirred with a kind of bubbling excitement. It was a-rise like a loaf of bread that's got out of control. And in the harbor there were all manner of craft, including two steamboats, a number of many-masted vessels, and a scattering around like ducks of open boats and skiffs. We looked for somebody to talk to about passage, but there were only two or three sleepy-eyed hands lolling about, so early in the day, and these told us the captains and officers were all to be found uptown, in the coffeehouses (which actually were nothing but grogshops), the Empire and United States Hotel.

In the last, we found two fiddlers asleep on the gambling tables lined up along one side, and a red-faced man in captain's dress stood at the bar, sucking down great gollops of coffee with rum poured in it. He said he'd take us to San Francisco, starting in an hour, for twelve dollars apiece, in a brig, the money to be paid on delivery at San Francisco.

"It ain't in me to cheat, never was," he said, blowing his horrible breath at us, "and I may turn too drunk to get there. I've did it before," he went on, chuckling. "Lodged on a island and stuck there two days. Have some gut-wash? You, sir? Boy?"

"At this hour?" said my father, still exasperated over the troublesome voyage down from Vernon.

"I overslept," said the captain, in a kind of apology. Apparently, he'd misunderstood.

It was a full two hours before we got aboard the brig. A filthier ship would be hard to imagine. Broken casks lay about, garbage was strewn over the decks, several deck hands leaned over the rail, bleary and unshaven, and from below there floated up snatches of drunken song. Eight passengers had arranged transportation, besides us; we all stood looking around with distaste.

This ship was a square-rigged two-master, though a small one, and about half of the rigging appeared unfit for use. But when the captain came on board, reeling slightly, just like the man on the boat from Vernon, he began to bray orders through a ridiculous kind of brass-rimmed horn, as if this was the grandest ship on the ocean. For about five minutes, nobody paid the least attention, then three of the hands sullenly took to hauling on this line, and loosing that, and the lower sails on both masts finally got up; we were under way.

I won't go through the details of that trip, but it was considerably worse than the other, except that the captain stayed on deck. It was about seventy miles to San Pablo Bay, plus forty miles across the Bay to the city. Throughout, he never once managed to get the drunken singers down below on the job, though he went to the companionway several times to shout through his horn: "All hands on deck. Lay to, there." And once, in an aggrieved tone, "All right, Bilters. You and Jones ain't going to get a cent of whiskey money out of me. You'll see. Not this trip." The singing broke off, but nobody appeared, and presently it started up again.

In places the river was very broad and we sailed before a mild breeze for several hours; then, rounding a bend thirty miles below Sacramento, a fresh wind sprung up and blew us on shore. Well, we were in a fix, worse than the last one. The captain roused himself up and said we'd put a line to the other shore and haul off. But none of the hands would row over without grumbling. After a good many threats, they finally tumbled in a skiff, cursing, and made the trip. Then they put a tackle block on a tree, took a turn with the rope, and heaved, but the line was too weak, so it broke, and there we stayed, right where we were, stuck fast.

"What's to be done here?" my father demanded of the captain, having worked up a peeve by talking to the other passengers.

"Well, sir, I wish I knew. Tell you the truth, I been trying to sell my interest in her, but she needs touching up here and there. The brightwork's gone green."

"Touching *up!*" cried my father. "It's a floating pigsty, and I don't mind saying so."

"Floating *now,*" said the captain, with a shrewd look. "We'll see what she's doing by morning." At this, my father stamped off, so red in the face I thought he'd explode.

"That scoundrel's no more a seaman than I am," he told the other passengers.

But when evening came, the wind died down and we hauled off to recommence our float-and-sail downstream. And at dark, we tied up at the foot of an island for the night.

Off early the next morning, the captain walking the deck with a cup of coffee, probably full of rum. It was an interesting trip, and stirred you up. We began to pass all manner of ships—schooners, steamers, brigs, barkentines and the like—and along shore we occasionally saw Indian villages. Saw one at a place called "the Slew," then we got to the junction of the Sacramento and Joaquin rivers, where there was a town called New York, with six or seven houses, and after that, when we'd gone through some rough water at Hills Cook, I'm blessed if *this* ship didn't swing around and take to floating stern first. It was so much of a coincidence that my father threw his hat down on deck and stamped on it.

"That ends it," he said. "We'll never get to San Francisco."

But to give him credit, this captain did his best possible; at least he was on duty, which I thought was quite an improvement. Just as before, we cracked out a boat and towed the bow till the wind blew up again.

This far down, the river was strongly affected by tide, so we went aground around about dark, but the tide floated us off by midnight, and we kept right on booming, it being moonlight, bright and clear.

We slept on deck and had our meals, $1.50 apiece, in a bad-smelling saloon below. The food was so painful—biscuits like leather, pork rancid, coffee like mud—that my father and some others called in the cook to congratulate him. Afterward, we came to find out he'd never cooked before, but had just signed on, being busted as a miner, to get down the river.

"On behalf of the passengers," said my father acidly, "I want to thank you for the most indigestible presentation of swill it has ever been our pleasure to reject." I never saw him in a worse humor.

This cook was a big, lanky man wearing a ridiculous white hat like a mushroom to keep the hair out of the food, somebody explained, as if it would make any difference; and I thought he might get sore.

But he only grinned. "Fierce, ain't it? I durn near puked on it myself."

It was fifteen miles from New York to Benicia, which was a brand-new town where they had a Government Army Post, and five miles after that we entered San Pablo Bay, all sparkling in the strong sunlight, water a pale blue-green, choppy with white-caps peeling off, grassy hills rolling up from the sides, with cattle grazing there, and altogether a very fine sight to behold. I couldn't get enough of that fresh salt bay air in my lungs. But it was nippy, too.

We reached the city in the afternoon and went ashore, to the racketiest uproar we'd seen since Independence. Everywhere you looked, but mostly going up the hills, were tents of all shapes and sizes, and scattered over the rough, uneven ground were shiny new frame houses, houses of tin, zinc, galvanized iron, brick tiles, and others with parts made of each.

Somebody told us later that the city was in a period of "rapid transition." My father wrote the remarks down in his diary. Only a few months before, it had been nothing more than a nasty, dirty, raviney, sandhilly, clayey place on one side and a great rocky hill covered with earth on the other. And not a good house in town, the best of them a kind of plank cow stable, with the greater number made of canvas or calico, using any old wood for frame studs. The streets were so miry all winter it was hard to get up and down, and the first sidewalks were barrel staves nailed end to end, in a couple of the "squares."

Now everything was being improved. They had sawed plank and board coming down from Oregon, and bricks unloading from other ships, and the streets were taking on a fresh look. The main thing that helped build the city was three monster fires, or conflagrations, as they said, which burned down the trashy stuff around Portsmouth Square, which was the main square, so that they hadn't any choice but to replace it with better.

Also filling in gullies, leveling sand hills, and planning a wharf to extend out a half a mile into the Bay. They had started grading the streets, too, and later they meant to put down planking for pavement.

The city lay five miles across the Bay from the entrance to the ocean, and a better harbor would be difficult to find, for the tidal ebb and flow brought big ships right in and out, to anchor directly in front of the city, without needing the slightest breeze; they could make it even with the wind smack in their face.

All in all, there were some that predicted the city, so situated, had a tolerable chance to grow; and one man, who they laughed at, because you *can* go too far in these things, said he figured to see it at a population of a hundred thousand, before he "handed in his bucket."

Once ashore, we hiked to the post office after mail, and I found out that Po-Povi had left me a letter behind. Funny thing was, it didn't bother me. I wouldn't say I missed her, because nobody can really miss an Indian, but I found myself seeing things on that trip we would have talked about, and it's perfectly possible I might have missed her if she'd been white. She had a kind of way about her, almost wise, never answering you right off, but

464

thinking things over first so as not to talk a lot of nonsense. Most important, she wasn't like Jennie; there wasn't anything bossy about her, or sassy like that. And she was nowhere near as ugly as she could have been. Not only in the face, with her plain black hair and dusky-pale skin, but all over, because I'd seen her bathing in the stream, just like Pretty Walker, and then walking out, and she looked like a slim piece of statuary out of a garden, standing there in the grass. But don't let slim fool you—she was grown. It was interesting to see how she wasn't a child any longer, being somehow larger undressed than dressed, both forward and rear. To be honest about it, this was the first time I'd noticed how she looked especially.

She said, "Dear Jaimie: How nice that I have learned to make letters in the English tongue. We leave tomorrow on a great ship, with white wings like a bird. I am to be a lady. Mr. Coe has told me that I shall stand the country squires on their heads. I do not know exactly what he means, or who these are, but it will be very funny to see them so.

"He is a kind and good man; I must prepare myself to serve him in any way he desires. But I know him very little. He has beautiful yellow hair that ripples like the waters of a brook. I recall that your hair is stiff, the color of sand, and that it is not combed very often.

"I am lonely for the people who bought me from the A-rap-a-hoe. Do you please take care of the doctor, that his great and foolish heart shall not lead him into trouble. He is a child's spirit imprisoned in the body of a man. How I shall miss you all! I have cried in my sleep from this sorrow.

"Now you must write a letter to your sister. Dear Jaimie, think of me sometimes when you wander in the woods.

Po-Povi"

It made my head dizzy for a few minutes, when I read that. It was just what you'd expect from an Indian. She was sorrowful, now she was leaving, and after everybody had practically begged her to stay, too. As for Mr. Coe and his beautiful hair—that exhibit

465

would look uncommonly well hanging from the tip of a Crow spear.

I read it over, itching to write an answer right away, so as to straighten some things out. But I wasn't quite so mad when I read it a second time. She had learned to write very well. There were a good many girls in my grade in Louisville, specially Daisy Coontz, who could chin herself, all right, but would never know the difference between the Greeks and the Spartans if she lived to be a hundred, that couldn't do anywhere near as well. I'm not the best writer in the world, but I've read most of the books back home, certainly all those about robbery and murder, and I could see that this Indian girl had shot right ahead. Once she'd got onto using a few long words, and dropped all those short ones, she'd be a credit to her race. It's off the subject, but she had the same trouble that way as the Bible, which my mother read from in the evenings. I hate to knock something religious, because those old Hebrews likely put in a lot of time on it and hoped it would succeed, but the book lacked style. It hadn't any words that amounted to a hill of beans, and alongside a work like *The Last Days of Captain Kidd*, by Morton E. Jenkins, it was mighty thin stuff. No, in some ways, the Bible was a very ignorant book.

While my father stood in the post office door, reading a letter from Mr. Coe, I went over her remarks again. I didn't like that part about her crying in her sleep. It was a coincidence, for many and many a night since they left, I lay in our tent feeling very blue, lonesome for my mother, I reckon. This Indian girl *was* my sister, red or white, and I didn't think I'd have much trouble thinking about her when I wandered in the woods. I'd done it already. All of a sudden I began to wonder if I hadn't lost something. I didn't feel so good; I had a hollow in my stomach, and went over and sat down on a box. I had this funny idea that maybe I was going to throw up.

But there's something I forgot to tell. When collecting our mail a few minutes before, a strange thing happened. The man in the window looked up sharply and said, "Doctor Sardius McPheeters, formerly of Louisville?"

Astonished, my father replied, "That is correct, sir. May I ask how you know?"

The man looked embarrassed. "There was an inquiry. We had a note here about it. Would you mind very much to say where you are stopping here?"

"Why——" my father began, and I could see he was about to give out a high-sounding address, but he was handicapped, not knowing any, so he said, "We aren't settled in, sir. Not as yet."

"When do you expect to come in for mail again?"

"I'll call at ten tomorrow."

"Thank you, sir," said the clerk, and scribbled a memorandum on the note he had.

"Most mysterious, most mysterious indeed," my father said, as we walked down the street. "But in no way uncivil. No doubt one of the old wagon train, desirous of renewing our acquaintance."

We walked around, looking the place over and keeping an eye out for "opportunities," but none appeared to arise, so that night we paid three dollars to share a small, lumpy, ill-smelling bed in a mean lodginghouse. Neither of us slept much, because my father was in one of his snoring humors, which sounds like a cross cut saw ripping into a nail, and my legs have the habit of twitching, or kicking, as the muscles get rested and smooth out. "I don't know when I've taken such a hiding," he said when we got up, both pretty grouchy. "I'm black and blue from ankle to thigh. It was an interesting experience, not unlike being shut up in a four-foot stall with an especially vicious donkey."

I mumbled something just as surly, and we got dressed.

Out early to have breakfast in a coffeehouse, and killed time till ten, when we went back to the post office. There wasn't any more mail, of course, but the clerk seemed glad to see us, and said, "The gentleman was here only a moment ago. I believe he will make himself——"

"Good morning, sir," cried a very dapper little man, with a beaming smile, who had come up behind us. He was soberly dressed, almost with elegance, though businesslike, and had on striped

467

pants, a frock coat, and a bowler hat. His nose was long and thin, his eyes very sharp and black, and his mouth a perfect straight line across, with what seemed like no lips at all, unless he broke into a smile, which for some reason I thought was made for reasons of business.

"May I introduce myself—Junius T. Peters, on commission for a client who must, at the moment, remain anonymous."

"I'm afraid I don't understand, sir," said my father, a trifle warily.

"Dear me," said Mr. Peters, "it *is* awkward, is it not? For I have nothing to say, nothing at all, except to request, with apologies, that you be so good as keep the Government post office apprised of your address, by word if in the city, by dispatch should removal occur."

"Mr. Peters," said my father, growing slightly nettled, "I have no wish to be rude, but this is most unusual. A less patient man might regard it as an intrusion. Will you kindly state the nature of your business."

"I *quite* understand," said Mr. Peters, keeping pace with us, as we had all begun to walk away from the building. He made a ridiculous figure, for he hopped around like a tomcat in a patch of briers, trying to stay in step, shifting first to match my father and then me, hoping, it appeared, to draw us all in line. But he never did; I saw to that, not having much else to do at the moment.

"Yes," he said, "your attitude is quite what one would expect. Doctor Sardius McPheeters," he went on, with a shrewd, sidelong look, "of *Louisville?*"

"Precisely."

"Son Jaimie, diminutive of James. Aged fourteen?"

The humor of this odd little man began to appeal to my father, who realized now he was nothing but a harmless lunatic, so he said, "Wife Melissa, age unstated."

Instead of being offended, Mr. Peters cried, "Aha! That was a fact I didn't have, sir," and whipping out a notebook, he wrote it down carefully.

468

At the end of the square, he stopped with an air of great decision, working his business smile again, and said, "In *my* mind, sir, identity is fully established, but when Client remains *in absentia,* as he must, all possible caution should be maintained."

Suddenly my father spoke up, serious again, to say, "There's something I think you owe us in this—tell me, if you will, should we expect *trouble* or *benefit* from your attentions?"

I could see the business smile opening and closing like a fish's gills as the little man thought it over, wrestling with his conscience. Finally he gave a sigh, looking almost human, and asked, with a sharp glance:

"Sir, do you enjoy sound and restful sleep?"

My father started to nod yes, and Mr. Peters said briskly, "Client would not wish it disturbed. Good day, sir"—lifting his hat—"we shall meet from time to time."

We watched him go, trim and proper, filled with respectability. At last, my father burst into a merry laugh. "Probably, I should resent it, but you know, somehow I couldn't. The fact is, I *like* him."

"So do I," I said. "I really think he wanted to do better."

"He did, didn't he?"

On this odd note, we took up our life in San Francisco. Later in the day, we checked and found we had only ten dollars and a few pennies left. Plus a picayune that my father found in an otherwise empty gold sack back near Marysville.

Having to do something quick, we commenced a search for employment, but it was a discouraging job. I remember those first days as ones of endless street trudging, polite inquiries at first, anxious ones as the time passed, and then, after a week, something approaching despair.

Leaving the lodginghouse, we slept in a tent with four sailors. Our food was mostly biscuit and coffee, but in loitering around the waterfront, we often were given bits from the galleys, when friendly Scotsmen or Englishmen heard our story. The grand opportunity that my father had mentioned seemed disinclined to turn up.

For two days in the second week we made six dollars a day wheeling dirt on the city streets, where gullies and ditches and ruts the size of a wagon were being filled in.

Then we visited the British Consul, who eyed my father's garments sourly and said he would "place on file" our request for clerical work. But neither of us believed him, and we never heard from him again. Next day, we called on a Mr. Gillespie, the president of the New Wharf Company, which was building a bigger landing wharf for ships, forty feet long, but when my father, "pleading his Scotch name," requested employment and wanted to show his papers, Mr. Gillespie "spurned them with cool civility," as I find written in the Journals.

To make things worse, the sailors in the tents where we slept began to row about keeping us on. Two men said it was all right, but the others, whiny, oafish fellows, said we weren't "making enough of a contribution." So my father, leaving me behind so as not to witness his disgrace, went to call on a Mr. Austin, a Scottish baker, and came back with to loaves of bread, which he had begged, of course, and put the sailors in good temper for a while.

This tent of theirs not only was patchy but it was full of pinprick holes besides, and the canvas was worn so thin that a touch of your hand underneath caused the rain to come dripping through. It rained sheets one night and we lay miserable and shivery. It had got to be early November now, and while this San Francisco weather was never severe, you could suffer sleeping in a tent. The nights were often cold. Already on the sunny tops of the mountains, in plain sight beyond the city, a white eagle's cap of snow could be seen on some mornings.

They said the climate here was unlike any other about, being entirely local. During the summer and fall, the wind blew from the west or northwest, directly in from the ocean. Then the mornings were warm and calm, but around noon, as a general thing, the ocean wind lifted to a regular gale, driving dust and paper and filth over the streets so thick you had to shield your eyes. And always, at sunset, it died away to nothing, leaving a time of peaceful quiet. The early evenings were pleasant but after dark it turned so cool you could wear woolen clothing nearly any old time you chose. In the winter, they said, there was nothing but soft, gentle breezes from the southeast, with temperatures always mild, the thermometer rarely sinking below 50.

When the wind blew in from the ocean the rains seldom came, but when it blew from the land, in both winter and spring, showers were very common, just like April and May back home. From the standpoint of climate, San Francisco wasn't any bad place to be destitute on the streets in this autumn of 1850.

Chapter XLIII

I'll say this for my father, he tried hard in those first weeks. No matter how low we got, he was up early and off to make his rounds, calling on this merchant and that, trying for honest work. Until lately the commerce of the city had been largely in the hands of a very few families, a Mr. Leidesdorff, from Denmark, a Mr. Grimes, Mr. Davis, and a Mr. Frank Ward, from New York. Their houses did a bustling business, using very large sailing ships, with Oregon, the southern Pacific coast, and the Sandwich Islands. From Oregon they brought lumber, flour, salmon and cheese, and from the Islands, sugar, coffee and preserved tropical fruits. The main articles traded in return were hides and tallow.

Before these gentlemen, California hadn't any trade to speak of. Commercial houses of Boston and New York had hogged it all for years, sending out ships loaded with dry goods and knickknacks that did a retail business going from port to port, holding auctions right on deck when the rancheros came in from their back-country places. They charged some pretty fancy prices, too; common brown cotton cloth, for example, sold for a dollar a yard.

With the finding of gold, everything changed, of course. New businesses sprang up everywhere, money rolled in by the wagon-load, and probably the most noticeable, and worst, difference was the gambling halls. These now stood all over town, dancing a gay tune, to a silvery, golden tinkle, and there was trouble in them a-plenty. Often in the evenings, having nothing better to do, my father led me from one to another—the El Dorado, United States, Parker House—saying it would prove "educational." But the truth is, he was drawn by the excitement and the lights and the fiddler music and the sight of people gambling. They were noisy places; a body could see how they might get to be a habit. Most of them were combination hotel and casinos, their walls spread over with the splendidest kind of paintings—women, mainly, minus their shifts—the tables along both sides stacked high with gold and silver coins, musicians on a platform in the rear, polished plank in a corner near the entrance, where a "gentleman of the bar," or bartender, served out what they called "the needful," and several circles of men drinking each other's health in that foolish-formal, over-warm complimentary way, likely hoping down inside that nobody would slop over and hit them.

Crowds were always streaming in and out, and rouged women with sweet faces were on hand everywhere, to act as a sort of mother, I reckon, although when one chucked me under the chin and said, "Here's a saucy duckling," my father pushed her away. He was downright rude, after she'd taken the trouble to introduce herself that way. The rackety laughter, shrill curses, shouts, money chinking, feet stamping, fiddles scraping, glasses pounding on the bar, and dealers crying out numbers was enough to flatten your eardrums.

One night a wholly innocent man was stabbed to death in a scuffle, right before me, and on another, half of the ceiling fell down where we were. Being nothing but calico tacked up, the rising night wind got between it and the roof. But it made a gaudy mess with drunks trying to crawl free, women screaming and busting out of their low-front dresses, dust everywhere, and a number of men that didn't get hit laughing fit to kill.

In the daytime we continued our search for work. The old word of "opportunity," which was to mean a big fortune in a hurry, hadn't been mentioned for a while. What we worried about instead was keeping body and soul together. It sounds complainy, but I don't remember once not being hungry along in that period.

We called on a Colonel Collier, head of the Customs House, who was very kind and said he would help us find something soon, after my father showed him his medical documents and others. When we left, he said if a vessel arrived tomorrow, he could put us both on the payroll. Then we called on Mr. Edwin Bryant, who was formerly the alcalde of San Francisco, now a judge, and I don't think we'd met such a good and interested man since we left home. He insisted on hearing every detail of my father's story, after which he made us drink a glass of claret and loaned us five dollars. Leaving his house, my father had recovered a lot of his pomp and good cheer. But when we returned to the tent, those four sailors wouldn't let us in any more. They threw out our ponchos and gear, and said, "Shift for yourselves; we've got troubles of our own." That night we slept on a pile of shavings, collected from a half-built house, in a corner of an alley protected from the wind. Two days later we moved into an empty shed that the owner, a merchant named Dobbs, was planning to knock down for lumber but mightn't get around to for upwards of a month yet.

Then, out of a clear sky, we made $13.50 working on the streets and returned Mr. Bryant the five dollars we owed him. My father said this was important, because it always paid to keep your credit alive, so we bought two comforts for four dollars, had two cups of coffee apiece at twelve and a half cents a cup, bought some cooking utensils for $3.10, bought some meal and sugar for $1.20, got a cloth cap for me for twenty-five cents and bought two razors for my father for fifty cents. Then we borrowed back the five dollars from Mr. Bryant. I began to see how finance, as my father called it, worked, and when he explained it, he got carried away so far he began to talk about opening a bank. But they already had a bank here.

Sleeping and cooking in the shed, picking up work on the streets, but not enough, and making the rounds the rest of the time, we hung on, but I still failed to see any signs of Opportunity turning up.

One evening down by Pacific Wharf, we ran across this man William Ebersohl, who was a street preacher. He was standing on some unloaded cargo, to be exact a brandy keg, and we stopped to listen.

He was a large-framed man, whose clothes, minister's black, hung loosely on his large body, and had a whity-gray mane of long hair, a moustache and beard, a string tie, bushy black eyebrows, the bluest and clearest eyes I ever saw, a ruddy, outdoors complexion, strong, hawklike nose, and a wide mouth with a look of great determination. In spite of his gray hair, you didn't get the feeling he was particularly old. He just grew that way.

Well, he had a fair-sized crowd, mostly hecklers, and he said, just as I find it in the Journals, "Gentlemen, I'm no croaker. I'm not here to bind and chafe, or make injudicious attacks on Romanism. I've been preaching regularly in the streets for more than ten years, seven of them among California gamblers and rum-sellers. Now I'd like to call your attention to the difference between a decent, well-behaved sinner and a violent, outbreaking sinner. Gentlemen, I stand on what I suppose to be a cask of brandy. Keep it bunged and spiled, and it is entirely harmless; nay, it answers some very good purposes; it even makes a good pulpit. But draw that spile and fifty men will be down here to drink up its spirit and wallow in the gutter, and before ten o'clock tonight will carry sorrow and desolation to the hearts of fifty families. A case in point is a congregation man we had at the Powell Street Methodist Church, a previous sinner, black as tar, with a history to shame a cutthroat criminal. But he'd heard the sweet word of Jesus, through your humble servant, and he straightened up like a sergeant, though his tripes burned for rum as a wolf ravens after gore——"

There was an interruption here when one of the hecklers sung out, "You ort to be ashamed, pinching off his mother's milk like that."

"—for six months he held up, a model of virtue, happy in his situation, dry as chalk, blaspheming not, stiff-backed and tail high, whilst the angels caroled in heaven——"

"Reverend," cried a man, "could you slip a fellow a dram? I just loaned my last drop to your bishop."

The preacher waited for the laughter to quiet, then he said, calmly, "And what happened? A ring-tailed misled hyena like our friend here"—pointing at the last heckler—"drew him off and led him astray. Lured him to a gambling hell and spooned *spiritus frumenti* into his sarsaparilla, solely on the Devil's mission. You ask what happened? *Within two months, that man was the dregs of San Francisco!* And he died reviling his Saviour's name. Gentlemen," cried the preacher in a lion's voice, *"somebody pulled out his spile!"*

Of a sudden, so that it dratted near scared everybody to death, he laid back his head and burst into song so loud the watch hands commenced flocking to the ship rails out in the harbor. I never heard anything like it for sheer, outright volume. No matter what else you might claim, this Reverend Ebersohl was a champion musician. They used to say that when the wind lay right, they could hear him in Sacramento, but I reckon that was an exaggeration.

With a melodious bray, like that of a full-grown jackass, he now tucked into a very nice hymn—some of them *are* nice, you know, and tend to cool down what's bothering you—but a bunch of drunks behind began to sing, "Old Uncle Ned, with the Hair off His Head," some of them hitting the tune now and then, and others not even trying, but soaring way up over everything in a kind of woman's voice, and one fellow, taking turns singing and doubling up to laugh, stepped on a wooden boat roller and fell off into the Bay. They fished him out, still singing, and soon after that the meeting broke up.

My father pushed forward, angry about the drunks, and introduced himself, along with me. "I enjoyed your sermon, sir. A very delicate parallel. As for the rest of those vill——"

"It *did* go off well, did it not?" He rearranged the cargo he'd been using as a pulpit, carefully brushed his coat, and gazed at us earnestly, his eyes so deep, steady, and innocent that I realized, with a shock, that nothing would ever seriously disturb him, not on *this* earth, at least. When he came near, we saw his clothes were frayed and shiny, and I had a feeling that the white shirt collar was only a collar, and nothing more.

"Yes," he said, "I feel that I held them safe in the clasp of Jesus tonight. I'll tell you something, sir—Doctor McPheeters?—you would hardly credit it, but there are times when an unseemly levity, or boisterousness, has made it downright difficult for me to proceed."

Was he joking? I saw my father start then, looking at him, recover and fall into the same vein.

"You surprise me, Reverend."

"As you remarked, sir, tonight's was a meeting to remember. It would not astonish me for a moment if some of this selfsame audience—I trust you noted the ardor of their singing—if some of this selfsame audience appeared at the Powell Street Church and put in a letter for membership tomorrow."

"Doubtless, and I shouldn't hesitate for a second to reject it," said my father, who was going to make a joke or bust. "Tell me, Reverend Ebersohl, do you preach at the church as well as here on the street? And why don't you take up a collection, if you don't mind my asking?"

"Not at all," he replied, gathering together his traps, which included three signs—actually they were no more than scrolls of cotton cloth with runny block letters painted on them: "Reverend William Ebersohl, Disciple of Jesus"; "Repent—at Methodist Church (Powell St.)"; and "Jesus of Nazareth was a Toteetaler." "I never plate-pass on the streets, the people resent it. In addition, Satan puts mischief in their heads. When I first tried, I collected up three rocks, a broken padlock, a shoehorn, a discarded opium pipe, and a very small but active rattlesnake, some five inches in length. As to preaching, I deliver three bully sermons in church on Sunday, but have plenty of strength left over, praise God, for a minimum of two each evening on the street."

Noticing his signs, my father said, "Did you fashion the displays yourself, Reverend?"

"You mean the misspelling, of course. I've been planning to correct it. A convert, a half-cast native from the Sandwich Islands—our Lord's color-blind, sir, did you realize that?—wrought them for me, and do you know, some people at the church contend he misspelled teetotaler on purpose, as a prank. They will never make me believe it, never!"

We walked up the street together. It was the only time in my life I ever saw my father cordial to a preacher. But he had a kind of animal's sense about people—you've likely observed that a dog's uncommonly selective about who it bites?—and he recognized this Reverend William Ebersohl as an authentic saint. He was, too. Getting to know him, we realized that there wasn't any way on earth he could be made to believe that a person was outright bad. At the worst, they were "misled." The tougher a case a man was, the harder Reverend Ebersohl worked to save him. And when he was let down the worst, he only stuck his chin out farther and said that he himself was at fault, because he'd slacked on the job—"the Devil had got hold of his coattails."

When we reached our shed, having given a quick account of our adventures, Reverend Ebersohl looked around sadly. "I wish I could offer you better accommodations, I really do. It grieves me. But my own, being a grass mattress in the loft of the church, are far from elegant." He straightened up. "I prefer them that way, of course. I doubt if Jesus, himself so patient on the Cross, also born in a manger, would expect me to live like a nabob and sleep amidst silks and downs."

Then, seeing an untidy pile in the corner, he said, "What's that yonder, doctor?"

My father looked shamefaced, and I was astonished to hear him tell the unvarnished truth for a change, without ornating it up any. "Well, I guess that's our laundry. What with one thing and another we haven't had time to do it."

Reverend Ebersohl gathered it up and tucked it under his arm. "Thanks be to Jesus, there's one problem solved. I'll do it myself in the morning."

"You'll *what?*" cried my father, horrified.

"Back in the evening, if it's good drying weather. And now I'm off; the day's only begun."

478

"But where are you going? Surely not back again at this hour!"

The Reverend Ebersohl looked grave. "The Devil's work is going forward on all sides of Portsmouth Square. As long as I'm here, Jesus is unrepresented. Good night. Never fear for your laundry. I'm able with both board and iron."

We couldn't help it; we crept out later and snuck up to the Square, and there standing on a box before the El Dorado, with the lights and the shouts and a merry old turmoil going on inside, and a few men gathered around outside, happily heckling, the Reverend Ebersohl roared out his thunders.

When we arrived, he had a firm toe-hold on the devil, and as he told the crowd, meant to chase him right on out of California and over the Canadian border. "The population's scarcer there," he said. "There aren't so many opportunities." He was downer on the devil than anybody I ever met. Then he started off with something about "the carnal gas of enmity toward God," and we left.

Right on schedule the next evening, while we were eating bread and molasses and two cups of chocolate we'd bought off a ship, Reverend Ebersohl appeared with our laundry. It was done up in a neat bundle and tied with a string. My father paid him elaborate thanks and persuaded him to share the chocolate, then take a piece of bread. But he said he'd consumed a very hearty meal around one o'clock, of "forest greens," meaning grass, I reckon, and goat's milk, but would try to choke down a bite to be courteous. Then he took a snap, though perfectly mannerly, at that bread and it disappeared from the public view forever. Watching him carefully, my father said, "Reverend, what happens to the money you take up in collecting?"

"Spent on the church and the everlasting glory of God."

"Take last Sunday, specifically."

"Bought a wood-burning stove, six-foot section of stovepipe, with elbow, two pieces of fireproof paper, and a clamp."

"Sounds interesting," said my father, "but there isn't much nourishment in it." Then he added, "See here, Reverend, you'll have to buy yourself some proper food now and then if you wish to keep up your strength. The devil's in tiptop condition. Look at you, the clothes hang from your frame like a scarecrow's."

"It's true I often forget to eat, but my parishioners, though poor, are exceedingly thoughtful and generous. It may tax your credulity, but it was a genuine Irishman, a reformed Romanist, who brought me the pail of goat's milk only this morning."

"Goat milk's fine," said my father. "It has proved especially efficacious for goats. But a man doing your kind of work needs a square meal."

Reverend Ebersohl said, "Last year, I attempted to augment my collections by operating a small stand in the streets. It was a means of sustenance, but it was time stolen from our Lord."

"Where is it? The physical property, I mean."

"Out behind the Powell Street Church, forty dollars' worth altogether—lumber, nails and paint."

"Reverend," said my father, "I suggest a partnership. We'll go halves—you furnish the stand, we'll run the business, share and share alike."

At noon that day we got a drayman to cart the stand down to the Square, and my father made a sign: "McPheeters and Ebersohl, Sundries." We only had about a dollar, but we sunk this in tea, also bought off a boat, and for two days I tended stand while my father barrowed for pay on the streets, so as to buy stock.

Sunday came and went, and Reverend Ebersohl put in $3.40 from his collection. He would have laid out more, he stated, but he had to buy twelve new hymnals. Also he'd given two dollars to a backslid convert named Turnipseed. (This last was money wasted; I took the trouble to check up. As soon as he got the cash, Turnipseed had a very beneficial prayer session on his knees with Reverend Ebersohl, then cried and signed a pledge. And after he'd got up, he headed for the Parker House, hurrying pretty fast, because he'd been delayed longer than he intended, tossed down two snorts to warm up, won twelve dollars playing faro, had seven or eight more snorts, then went back and lost every cent on the wheels. When morning came, they found him drunk in a ditch, but he was on fire to be converted again, because he said his luck couldn't run bad like that *all* the time.)

For the stand, we bought coffee and chocolate and sugar, and more tea, and had a very good run selling it for twelve and a half cents a cup. People around there liked my father, and they often asked questions of me—what we were doing there, and all. We bought a quart of molasses for fifty cents, and ten pounds of biscuits at $1.50. And the next week, we got a barrel of pickled pork, costing thirty-five dollars. So we were very well off for edibles, and before long we began to lay in some real sundries, just anything these busted miners and gamblers were trying to get rid of cheap. We acquired a very fine set of chessmen, carved from ivory and beautiful woods from the Orient, for five dollars, and sold them the same day to a Catholic priest for ten. We got a case of expert mathematical instruments for $3.25 and turned it over for five dollars even before the week was out. A Chinaman sold us a quart of sperm oil, but we kept this and used it for a lamp. To protect the stand, we had to buy a tent, to be pitched alongside, and in the same transaction we got some more cooking utensils, meal, sugar, and chocolate, all for sixteen dollars.

The business was going very well. My father said this was the identical same way all big merchants got started and he aimed to build a two-storey building the next year and maybe buy a schooner. He hadn't hopped around with so much importance for months. His experience as clerk for Brother Thomas, back in Deseret, stood him useful now, because whenever the opportunity arose to practically steal something, or to sell at a sharp bargain, he just gritted his teeth and went ahead, same as Brother Thomas did, only the latter didn't have to grit his teeth, not that skinflint.

We were eating regular now, of course, and felt stronger. And the Reverend Ebersohl, striking by early from his church, would lay into a handsome breakfast along with us, but he always apologized for it, noting that the dear beloved Jesus would have fasted, instead of gorged, to put His appetite down in its place, and would have been "nourished on spiritual fodder" instead. By now, I'm morally convinced that every dime Reverend Ebersohl took out of the stand was frittered right away on those worthless humbugs that came whining around, begging for salvation.

He probably never knew it, but many of the petty gamblers at the casinos were kept rolling by Reverend Ebersohl, with the money he intended for just the opposite use. There was no way to tell him. What good would it do? He'd only find some way to excuse them, and predict that the next time up, they'd win the Battle against Temptation. He did all our laundry, did most of the lugging of stock up from the ships, often pitched in at the stand, and took far less than his share at the end of each week. And how he bullied and badgered the devil! He hardly gave him any rest at all.

They said he preached a sermon one night from the deck of the steamship *Union* (it was on a day when he'd knuckled under to his appetite to eat a pound of pickled pork) that resulted in a kind of mass convulsion. There wasn't a soul on board that didn't come forward at the end and give himself to Jesus, and this included the captain, who'd already given himself to Jesus only the trip before, as well as several times before that, along with the Chinese cook, who didn't understand a word that was said. What fetched him was the singing, they found out later. But the odd thing was, that the cook carried right on through, joined up, through an interpreter, swore off opium, though he turned a kind of turkey-skin purple for a while, became a respected member of the Powell Street congregation, passing the plate on Sundays, and remains so to this day. He was the only hundred per cent Chinese Methodist in San Francisco.

People around the Square knew my father was a doctor; they called him "Doc," but they never took it very seriously. They figured him for some kind of horse doctor, or a doctor that had got in a jam somewhere. This was the only condition they fully understood. It required a shipwreck to get him started off in medicine in San Francisco. The steamship traffic was very brisk now, with big boats like the *Independence* and the *Panama* coming in every few days, carrying several hundred passengers. We were at the stand on a morning in mid-December, a bright, sunny day after a rain the previous evening, selling off ten purses that my father had fashioned out of buckskin, when a man dashed across the Plaza, waving his hat wildly, and cried, "Shipwreck! Shipwreck! The *Liberty*'s run aground on Santa Rosa Island!"

In no time, a crowd had collected to hear the news. People poured out of the El Dorado and United States, the women looking not quite so motherly in the strong sunlight, but chalky-white and played out, and there was an ear-splitting racket of shouting and running. Then somebody down the street cried, "They're bringing in survivors on the *City of Sacramento!*"

The crowd scattered pell-mell for the wharves, my father threw our wares in the underneath part of the stand, and we picked up our heels, too. There was that awful, hurrying, white-faced air of calamity, women snatching children out of the way, dogs barking, horses rearing and men cursing because they were excited, and maybe a little scared, too.

At the wharves the *City of Sacramento* was coming down the Bay, and we could see everybody crowded to the rails; then we saw stretcher cases laid out on deck, and as soon as she steamed up within hailing, the captain came out on the bridge, holding a horn, and bawled: "We've got a hundred and fifty burned, half drowned and suffocated. We need carriages and blankets."

Now a number of men on shore jumped into skiffs, turning one over, and rowed for the *Sacramento* as she came in, and you could hear women crying everywhere, and a terrible hubbub going on.

"Shore ahoy!" the captain shouted again. "Have you prepared hospitaling?"

Then I saw Mr. Edwin Bryant speak to my father and send two men running, one to the City Hospital and the other to the State Marine Hospital. And by this time, the *Sacramento* was warping close in, with lines coming onto the wharf, missing, mostly out of hurry and nervousness, then finally she was in and the gangplank rattled down in a hurry.

I heard Mr. Bryant sing out, "This way, doctor, come aboard."

My father had his medical bag along, though he'd sold a few things out from time to time, so now he ran down the dock and was swallowed up in the crowd.

So many people were fighting back and forth, lots of them with friends or relatives on the *Liberty*, that it looked like a regular stampede. These spectators were almost totally out of control. And then, by gum, if there didn't rise up over everything the old familiar bullfrog voice of the Reverend Ebersohl, who'd jumped up on a barrel and begun to sing, and in just about thirty seconds, he had that crowd in hand. He had taken his hat off, and his gray-white hair streamed out behind in the breeze. "Stand back, my friends, make way, make a lane from the gangplank—no, no don't try to go aboard, sir—Blessud Jesus, meek and mild (this last in song) Calm the wicked, rude and wild——"

He was a wonder. The people listened to him—they couldn't exactly help it, to tell you the truth; his voice drowned everything else out; the captain tried a couple of hoots of the whistle against it, then threw in the sponge—and order was put right back into this mess, with the Reverend Ebersohl running everything on shore.

When they commenced to carry down the injured, I climbed up a rope to the deck. I wanted to see, and thought I might bear a hand, too. It was a sickening sight up there. Rows of people horribly burned and otherwise maimed were laid out almost shoulder to shoulder, covered with blankets and comforts, and their faces, some of them, turned to a kind of reddish-brown crust, like a baked ham, the hair and eyebrows all burned off.

A few were unconscious but others were moaning or screaming in pain. Somebody said that a lot more would be screaming, except that the burned cases were still in shock, and couldn't feel a thing, the way Coulter had been, I guess. They would die, but it might take several days, and the last days, out of shock, would be frightful. The *Sacramento's* passengers tended them all up and down the line. I saw one woman passenger throw up on deck, and a man, a steward, sat down suddenly and put his face in his hands. A little girl rose up out of her blankets, just as I arrived, and tried to crawl to the rail, not having the slightest idea where she was. She would have gone right on over if I hadn't caught her. One of her legs was burned all up and down, her clothes were a soggy mass of char, and her face was bandaged so that you couldn't see any features real well.

An officer in uniform sent me below to fetch more water, and for an hour after that I was busy running errands. I watched four people die while being lifted ashore, and once I encountered my father, bending over with another doctor, white as a sheet, and remembered how he hated this sort of thing.

What had happened was, the *Liberty* struck a reef, which caused a bad leak. A sail had then been drawn over the hole and the ship headed for shore, with the idea of grounding her, a four-mile run. They made it, too, but the first boat sent ashore with a line swamped in the heavy breakers. The second made it, carrying a hawser in, but by now the water had risen in the *Liberty* to the place where her lower flues were stopped, and the fire came washing out of the furnace doors. In almost no time, a number of explosions followed, and the ship was all over fire. After that, the scene on top was a perfect nightmare. Hundreds jumped overboard, and some of these, hanging to floating spars and things, made it in through the surf. Rich men, they said, were offering great sums of money to be taken off, but nobody paid them any mind. I'm afraid the fact is that a very big proportion of the crew just minded themselves, and let the others go hang.

Before the day was out, I heard a lot of stories. As the flames crept up, a sick man begged from his cabin to be carried to the rail and dropped, but when he hit the water, he never appeared again; went straight to the bottom, and then they remembered he had a heavy metal cast bandaged to one leg. A mother drew her child from the fire, and jumped, holding him in her arms, and they didn't come up again either. A Captain Taylor took his little boy between his teeth and his wife under his arm, and flung himself into the sea at the stern. But the shock separated the boy, which drowneded, and the wife died of injuries on shore.

Passengers that jumped clung from one end to the other of that hawser the second boat managed to get ashore, but one of the officers, thinking it might break, ordered it slackened, and everybody dipped under. Almost all of them drowned. Altogether, about a hundred and fifty died in the first hour or two, but of the four hundred and fifty total, nearly everybody was injured, one way or another.

By nightfall the City Hospital and State Marine Hospital had the bad cases under care, and my father stayed on to help. Most all the carting had been done by people at the gambling halls, in carriages tied up there; they did a bang-up job; everybody said so. And the hospitals being full, the lighter cases were taken not only to the churches but the gambling houses, too, and given a patching-up. After that, they were provided with lodging wherever it could be found.

It's interesting how the worst scum in a city will turn to in times of emergency. Some of those gamblers hadn't taken any exercise in years, and would have walked past a starving beggar without giving him a glance. But let a public calamity arise and they half killed themselves to help. And felt good about it. I heard men jabbering away in conversation that night who didn't utter a dozen words on an average day. Everybody was brought together and made friendly for a while, by seeing how much worse off it was possible for them to be. No, sir, when it comes to cheering people up, and making them feel warm inside, nothing can do it like a catastrophe.

After dark I went by the City Hospital and found my father. The place was stacked up with patients, and a good-sized crowd, relatives and such, thronged around in the corridors. But the grief and commotion of the first hours had quietened down, and lots of people even were talking in whispers.

In one room, at a bed, my father was seated talking to a man who was burned all over, everywhere you could see—face, arms, feet —all the same baked-brown color, the skin hardened like a crust but unwrinkled, no blood, not much of anything except that un-

486

real changed color and hardness. It was impossible to tell how old he was, because the hair was gone and his skin hadn't any look of a particular age any more. Too, it was covered over, now, with a yellowish kind of salve.

His eyes were bloodshot but open and alert, trapped undamaged in his ruined body, peering out like an animal's from the depths of a hole.

My father tapped on the brown-red crust of his chest.

"Do you feel that?"

"No, not a thing."

"Are you conscious of any pain at all?"

"I feel fine. Are you a doctor? I guess I got off lucky."

"Do you remember what happened?"

"Oh, yes, very clearly. We'd put in at Acapulco and had a nice run up. Then we went aground, and after that the explosions."

"Do you remember in your own case?"

"Not very well; it isn't clear. I got off lucky. When will I be up and around?"

The eyes showed a sudden alarm. He tried to rise up to his elbows.

"Where's my wife?"

My father pushed him back gently. "She's well taken care of. You'll be seeing her soon."

"It's funny—I don't feel sleepy or anything. What happened to me?"

"You suffered certain burns."

"Will I feel anything later?"

"You'll notice it more later."

When my father got up and saw me, he steered me out to the hall and said, "Go on back to the tent. I'll be here all night." His face was an old man's gray, and looked shrunken.

"That man in there; he'll die, won't he?"

"He's dead now. But he'll come to life for about three days before the Almighty makes it official. He'll spend them screaming unless there's morphine enough."

I stared at him, uneasy in my mind. All the promise and humbug and good cheer seemed to have drained out of his face. In addition, he looked the way he used to in Louisville when he needed a drink of whiskey. "Maybe we should have stayed in the hills," I said. "Away from the cities, and hospitals, and such." I couldn't seem to find the exact words for it. "A person has the right to do what he wants——"

"No, I don't think so, son. I used to. I thought it was possible to run fast and leave it all behind. But running faster only completes the circle sooner. This is my job, and maybe always will be. You trot on back to the tent."

For now, at least, all his hope was gone. I walked on out, past the quiet people talking in the halls, the ones sitting down weeping, past open rooms with the scorched patients inside, into the street and down toward the Plaza. I was fed clear up with what I'd seen and smelled and heard. The fact is, I felt older myself, and had a hard, curious itch to get rid of the misery in one quick thrust and shudder.

In the El Dorado, survivors from the *Liberty* were being arranged on shakedowns. Everybody talked in low tones, no gambling going on, the same as they talked, now, at the hospital. The women were busy fixing bandages and getting drinks of water and being motherly and good, and this one, this plump one of around forty, with the too-yellow hair, a kindly-appearing woman, rouge and powder run over from tears, and a most awfully tired expression in her eyes, came up and said, "Were you looking for someone, honey?"

I said no, I'd only stopped in because I wasn't ready to sleep and wondered if I could find something to do. Then one of the gamblers called out, "A couple of you kids get more sheets, will you?" and she said, "Come along, honey, you can carry mine." Things seemed to dance around as we went up the stairs, the ten-foot paintings of naked women, fat and pink, either sprawled on their bellies or seated with a gauzy something between their legs, the curlicue gold of the frames, bloody basins on the floor below, bandages, cotton, gambling tables, fiddles leaning silent against the piano: things that didn't go together, disturbing things, and sounds that belonged in different rooms.

She closed the door behind me, and stripped the sheets from a white-painted iron bed; then she sat down, with two tears started on her cheeks.

"I had a boy, he'd be just your age."

The room was bothersome, I didn't know why. Its red-checkered wallpaper, the lamp with the frill underneath, the picture of Madonna and Child, spangled clothes in the closet, white nightgowns, Bible on a stand, Teddy bear on the pillow, crockery pitcher and funny kind of chamber on the floor all spun around in a crazy revolving pattern. I felt about burst, all tightened up, and a little faint, too.

She said, sounding tearful and worn out with excitement, "I could have been your mother." It confused me, as dizzy as I felt. I knew she wasn't, of course, but she might have been, and besides, it had been two years since I'd seen her. Pulling me down on the bed, she slid her dress off her shoulders and put one of her great breasts in my mouth. She rocked that way for a while, and, then I don't exactly remember what happened, but it took some little time and was a comfort to us both.

Back in the tent, late, with the lamp trimmed down and feeling very fresh and clear, I wrote: "Dear Po-Povi: I got your letter. Things have been lonely around here too. My father and I are in San Francisco trying to make our fortune, but I guess he never will. I think he's always got to have some kind of rainbow in the sky, but I don't believe there's any pot of gold at the end. It came to me tonight that what he's chasing is the rainbow itself; it's more fun for him that way. I miss the wandering around we used to do in the woods. There hasn't been any fun at all here lately. We had a big boat explosion here today; a lot of people were killed and hurt. I don't know how to say it, exactly, but it sort of woke me up.

Tell you something—if you came back, I wouldn't mind. Not just a sister, either. The main thing that came to me tonight was that I used to not be very smart, but I am now. It wouldn't be at all bad if you came back. My father once said that you were just as white as I am, inside. I see what he means now. When he said that was not in my smart period.

As stated, kindly come back as soon as convenient. (In a few days.)

Sincerely yours,
JAIMIE (McPHEETERS)

P.S. You don't owe Mr. Coe anything, don't pay him anything. (Frankly, to be candid, I always thought he had very ugly hair.)

Chapter XLIV

In the next few days we got letters from the people at Vernon, in reply to ones we'd mailed out earlier. All hands were well and happy. The butchery was thriving, and Coulter had taken a real interest in helping Uncle Ned Reeves build up the mule-packing service. In their hearts, Jennie said, they hoped we wouldn't strike it rich in San Francisco, because they had no wish to leave, now. Instead, why didn't we come on back? She and Buck Coulter were to be married Christmas morning.

"Let's go!" I burst out at my father, standing in front of the post office. "If we leave now we can get there for the wedding. We've got money enough, too."

"Son," he said, looking determined but sad, "when we left home I promised to make a fortune in California. To date, we have failed, through no fault of our own. Gold-mining had its chance, and missed fire. The butchery business is for butchers; mule-packing opens glorious vistas for mules, a chance for travel and refreshment. But for us, San Francisco remains, despite its essentially hostile attitude, the city of Opportunity, a western Philadelphia in embryo, stirring, swelling, a rare commercial bud on the threshold of blossom. My intention is to grow with the city. And in that line, we'll give it a year, no matter if we starve on the streets in the process."

"Never mind," I said wearily, "let's get back to the stand."

But our situation at the stand never was the same again. Because of his work with the shipwreck, my father began to get some medical trade. It shook him. His hands started trembling every time somebody appeared at the stand and asked for help. Mostly the better element didn't bother to pay, but the gambler bunch were very prompt and generous. It's an odd thing, but here he was in San Francisco, with almost identically the same kind of custom as he had back home. Only now the gamblers were in fancy hotels, what the Reverend Ebersohl called "gambling hells," instead of being on shantyboats. Otherwise, nothing was changed. Still, some of the doctors took to throwing him cases they didn't care for—baby deliveries and that, where it called for visits at late hours.

So, much as he hated it, he was back doctoring.

And what happened?

One afternoon he came in from a case and seemed in fine spirits, very worked up about the treatment he'd prescribed. This was unusual, because he generally didn't care to mention any of them at all. Throwing his bag on the stand, which I ran in his absence, he said, "I'd suspected this right along, in spite of what Wilkins [Dr. Wilkins of the City Hospital] maintained. The woman has catarrhal gastritis, *not* a stricture of the pylorus. Her symptoms were plain as a signpost: uneasiness, heat, pain at the epigastrium, flatulence and distension, ropy vomit, greenish bile. Sallow circle around the eyes, a loaded tongue, sense of anxiety at the praecordia, bowels costive, urine scanty, an intense loathing of animal foods. Now what does that mean to you?"

While he'd talked, the Reverend Ebersohl came up and sat down to listen, his clear, deep innocent eyes touched with sympathy.

"It adds up to one thing, one only," he said in his booming voice, not able to fight the subject he was hipped on. "I don't need to, but I'll spell it out—D-E-V-I-L. For reasons denied to the lowly mortal, Beelzebub crept into that poor woman's intestines."

"If so, my examination failed to uncover him," said my father, who was a little flushed now, but even more talkative than before. Feeling sick, I sat dumbly, realizing I should have expected it, under the circumstances.

"—in cases of these kinds, it's always well to open the bowels with an enema—pint of salt water, two if she can retain it. If no nausea, Compound powder of Jalap ʒiJ to Water Oss. *Then,* an infusion of the bark of the Peach tree to control irritation, taken *only* from the young limbs. After *that,* teaspoon of Mint Water and Bismuth every half hour. And finally, a mild stomachic to restore digestion—Hydrastis, or something of the sort. I'll see to it tomorrow. Yes, tomorrow and tomorrow and tomorrow. What a day is tomorrow——"

He began to sing, and when I could face it, I looked up at the Reverend Ebersohl. He hadn't turned a hair, but sat regarding my father steadily, not disappointed or shocked or set back in any way. The excuses had already taken hold automatically.

"Your father's been under a great strain," he said aside to me. "Who among us, God's poor servants, can measure the sensitivity of another? Come on, my boy, we'll get him into bed."

And when my father was stretched out in the tent, making a fuss because he said he had a date to go sailing with the Mayor, Reverend Ebersohl sank to his knees and offered up a genuine crusher of a prayer. But did he pray for my father to straighten up and behave? Not so you could notice it. His remarks were along the line of abusing himself, for being so busy with other work, and so blind, that he'd failed to take note of his friends.

And all the time, his voice rising up in competition, but not winning, my father was singing "Angus McGregor, Helpless in the Heather."

It was embarrassing.

This began a long series of such ruckuses and was when we began to go seriously downhill in San Francisco. Days went by when he wouldn't take a drink at all; then, set off by somebody's medical troubles, usually a child's, he would reel home drunk. Never angry or troublesome, you know, but released from his worries. And, of course, no good to himself or anybody else. Again, he mightn't come home at all but would go to the United States or El Dorado and gamble away whatever he had on him. If the Reverend Ebersohl was handy, he helped me straighten him out, not ever with a reproach, nor a mark of impatience, but only an increased resolve to get at the real culprit, who he said was the Devil.

"Never fear, my boy," he cried one day when the people at the United States brought my father home, "we'll get him in the end. This poor suffering physician, our honored friend and parent, is only the hapless instrument. It's the Devil has done it. We'll get him; we'll flay him right out of the state."

Reverend Ebersohl got so exercised over the Devil on this occasion that he did something he rarely ever tried; he went right into the United States and, standing on a table, preached a sermon on Temperance. Now that gambler crowd liked my father, and they liked Reverend Ebersohl too, though they ragged him some, so they knocked off as polite as pie to let him preach. A few quiet games of seven-up and such continued in the corners; otherwise people listened.

At the beginning, Mr. Wilcox, the proprietor of the United States, "guaranteed" Reverend Ebersohl silence for half an hour, and he kept his word.

It was a powerful sermon, though I've got to admit that many and many a time I failed to entirely get Reverend Ebersohl's drift, much as I admired him. My father said the same: "He's a great man, with a lion's heart. Smart, too, but the messages come out addled." I disagreed with him there; it wasn't so much addled as he got off the point. The point here tonight was temperance, but it wriggled out of his grip.

After knocking rum in a general way, along with the people who sold it, while holding out hope that it might be mainly the Devil, he said, "As I look over this group of sinners, I see upwards of two dozen men that I've saved with regularity ever since I came to San Francisco. Yes, and I'll save them that many more before I'm done. I'm thinking of one citizen—naming no names—as my gaze sweeps around, a man of great potential, educated, accomplished, handsome in appearance, *and it was not a week ago* that he appeared on his knees before me to promise, 'So help me God, I'll never drink another drop!' Two days later, I found him drunk on the streets. For shame!

"Another such came to me a short time ago, and after relating the sad tale of his sorrows, asked to sign the pledge. I gave him a pledge and he signed it, saying, 'There it is; my name is there for once and all. Henceforth I'm the living spirit of sobriety.' The next day, as I passed up California Street, I saw him with a demijohn in his hand. 'Why, my friend, what are you doing with that stuff?' said I. 'Oh,' said he, 'I thought since I was knocking off for good this time, I'd just take one more nip in farewell.'

"My dear friends," cried Reverend Ebersohl, "such is the bondage to your prevailing sins, whatever they may be. Chains of habit are stronger than chains of steel; you cannot break them without help from Jesus.

"At the moment when I was talking to that poor fellow mentioned before, a candidate for the chain gang was conducted along the street, with a heavy shackle around his leg. Said I to the crowd, 'Look at that miserable creature. How gladly would he kick off that heavy chain and be free! He cannot break it. And yet he is no more a prisoner today, under that heavy chain, in the hands of his keeper, than you are under the chains of awful habit, in the hands of *your* keeper, the Devil, by whom you are led, captive by his will.'

"Then a man under the Devil's influence had the effrontery to speak up from the rear and say, 'Oh, well, if that be true, it's no use to try to straighten up. You might as well leave us alone!'"

Reverend Ebersohl was going at his best clip, and the crowd appreciated it, calling out "Amen," and "Give it to 'em, Reverend," to emphasize points. They weren't ragging, either. They saw the sense to what he said, so far, and were with him every inch of the way.

So he said, "The Holy Spirit is looking at each of you now"—a man in a black suit tried to crawl under a table here; I don't know whether he was skylarking or not—"and listening to every pulsation of your moral heart. And were He to reveal what has passed there this day, how shocking a revelation He would make!

495

It is not by the professions of the mouth, but by the conduct of men, that we learn the orthodoxy of their hearts. A miserable gambler said to me only a short time ago, 'I came to California with exactly twenty-five cents, but I had good luck playing cards and set up a monte table, and thanks be to God, I have been very successful.'

"What priceless insolence! But wait a minute, hold your horses, that isn't the worst. A wretched rumseller over here on Jackson Street filched the pockets of a poor fellow, wrecked his constitution, blighted all his hopes for time and eternity, unstrung his nervous system, and drove him into delirium tremens; and when his poor victim was dying, I'm blessed if he didn't come to me and say, 'Reverend, I'll ask you to step round and pray for so-and-so's soul. *I'm worried about him.*' Can you believe it?

"Why, these gamblers on the Plaza here, whenever they shoot a fellow, go right off for a preacher to pray over their dead. One who came for me to preach at the funeral of C.B., who was shot the night before just there in that large saloon, said, 'We thought it would be a pity to bury the man without religious ceremonies. It will be a comfort to his friends, too, to know that he had a decent Christian burial.'

"Get thee behind me, Satan. Or come out and fight in the open."

Everybody cried "A-a-a-amen," and "If you're aiming to fight the Reverend, fight fair," relishing every word. But I'll be a baboon if Reverend Ebersohl didn't switch off here and commence to explain about the "techniques" of street preaching. He told some of his early struggles, how he had to compete with other entertainments, and said, "If by a cry of fire, or otherwise, your congregation is scattered, do not be discouraged, but watch your opportunity. Set your sails to take the breeze, and you will probably double or quadruple your congregation in five minutes.

"Once, in Belair Market, Baltimore City, I was half through my discourse when a large funeral procession passed by, accompanied by a band of music. Now that band was unfair competition; I saw it so then, and I still do. The melody took the ears of my audience, and when they broke loose to join, I roared 'Brethren, we can make better music than that'; and struck up the very best song at my command. I hesitate, in modesty before our Lord, to tell you the result. A friend with a good view of everything said at least a hundred of the procession shook loose and came to the preaching. What he said, more specifically, was, and I ask you to take it with a pinch of salt, 'Reverend, we didn't leave anything of that funeral except the horses and the corpse.' "

Reverend Ebersohl stopped a second, beaming, because he *did* have a good audience tonight, and said, "Gentlemen, where was I?"

"You were speaking on the general subject of Temperance," said one man drily.

"Oh, yes, Temperance. On another occasion, some rough fellows next to my stand got up a dogfight, in the way of providing competition of *that* sort, and off they went, hissing and whooping. I cried, 'Run, boys, run! *There's* a rare opportunity! A glorious entertainment, that! What an intellectual feast it must be to enlightened, high-minded American gentlemen to see a couple of dogs fight!' By that time, I'd recaptured the last man of them, so the good-natured dogs, having nobody to prod them, trotted away in a comradely spirit. I said, 'Boys, I don't blame you for seeking enjoyment and trying to be happy. God, who made us and endowed us with wonderful powers of intellect and heart, designed us to be happy, hence this insatiable thirst for happiness that constitutes the mainspring of human actions. The difference between us is in regard to the source whence we derive happiness. You have tried many sources, money-making and money spending, rum drinking and gambling, with occasional boy and dogfights. Bills were posted all through your streets last week, promising a rich treat for immortal souls on Sunday in American Valley. The intellectual feast to commence with a fight between a bull and a grizzly bear. The second course to consist of a magnificent dinner, and as much whiskey as could be desired at two bits a nip. The third course to consist of music and dancing among the men (ladies being scarce), which might be protracted till every soul was satisfied.' "

I'm telling this speech of the Reverend Ebersohl in detail, as I remember it and from his notes which he showed me, because it gives a better picture of him than what I could do, also a view of San Francisco in those days, particularly from his closing comments on Temperance, which went as follows:

"I give it as my candid opinion that your throat and lungs will suffer less in the pure open air than they do in the carbonized, sickly atmosphere of crowded churches. I am accustomed to listen to the same clear voices in the streets three hundred and sixty-five days in each year: 'Fish! fish! fresh salmon!' 'Eggs! eggs! fresh California eggs!' 'Candy! Here's your celebrated cough candy! Everybody buys it; now's your chance!' 'Here's your fresh California pears, apples, oranges, and peaches! Only two bits a pound! Buy 'em up!' 'Latest news from the East! Arrival of the *John L. Stephens!* here's your New-York *Herald*, New-York *Tribune*, and New-Orleans *True Delta!*' Who ever heard of a fish, egg, candy, or fruit 'crier' or newsboy taking the bronchitis? An auctioneer will stand in the street and cry at the top of his voice for two hours every day, yet we never heard of an auctioneer taking the bronchitis.

"If you will not bind your neck with a tight cravat, if you will stand erect, head up, speak naturally, and not strain your voices, you will experience an improvement in the quality and power of voice; you will also find greater facility in natural utterance by regular street preaching. Ten years ago, preaching two sermons in church and one in the streets caused me hoarseness of voice, along with weariness of body; but now, with three sermons in church and two in the streets each Sabbath, I have no hoarseness, and but little weariness. Before I commenced street preaching, I was subject to violent colds and soreness of throat and lungs; but I have known nothing of 'sore throat' or 'sore lungs' for years. I would not intimate that I am invulnerable, but I do believe that the danger is lessened, at least fifty per cent, by outdoor preaching."

Having said this, Reverend Ebersohl looked around, with a little frown of annoyance between his brows, as if he was trying to remember something. Then the line cleared away and he said briskly, "That concludes my remarks for this evening on the subject of Temperance."

There was a perfect thunder of applause, as both men and women looked at each other and said how good it was. And a half dozen or more sang out, "Drinks for the House!" Everybody agreed it was the best lecture they ever heard on Temperance, even including Reverend Ebersohl's sermon aboard the *Union*, when he converted everybody in sight, along with the Chinese cook. But Mr. Wilcox, the proprietor, jumped up on the bar and cried, "Hold on—nobody's going to buy a drink for the House here except the House. Step up, gentlemen, name your poison."

And as Reverend Ebersohl climbed down to roll up his signs, one after another at the bar turned and toasted him, sober and courteous, thanking him for the Temperance lecture, and said things like, "Your health, sir," and "Strength to your voice, Reverend," and "A splendid effort—both moving and convincing."

"*Hear me!*" cried Reverend Ebersohl, jarred but not quite done yet. "This being a lecture on Temperance, I'll ask which among you would care to sign the pledge? In the interest of shaming the Devil and saving your souls." He held up a piece of paper and a quill.

I honestly thought there was going to be a riot. They practically fought to sign up, and you could hear things like, "Quit shoving, will you?", "See, here, I was in line first," and "That isn't fair—you've signed twice already. Give somebody else a show."

Everybody put their name down at least once and some as many as four or five times. Then they had a whole new round of toasts, and thanked him again for the opportunity to sign the pledge, being glad, as they said, that he hadn't forgot it before the lecture was closed.

Mr. Wilcox said the next day that the meeting had stirred people up so, he'd sold twenty-two per cent more whiskey than on any other evening of the previous twelve months. There was talk of trying to put Reverend Ebersohl on the regular payroll, along with the fiddlers and chorus girls, but nothing came of it.

I walked out with Reverend Ebersohl when he left. He was just a trifle discouraged, the first time I'd seen him so. But it didn't last over a minute. "There must be *some* way to make them stop drinking," he said. "Bound to be, it stands to reason. But I'm obliged to say that up to now, I've been sniffing away at the wrong scent. If nothing else works, it may be necessary, along with the late, lamented Samson, to employ the jawbone of an ass."

Chapter XLV

No change in our living through December and January. My father would drink for a few days, then sober up and work like the furies for a while. Either way, he never mentioned his condition, the lapses or the good parts. It was a secret between us, something shameful that wouldn't be in good taste to bring out in the open.

I ran the stand, helped by Reverend Ebersohl. By now I figured out the things to buy—food, mainly—and let my father handle his medical calls and other problems. I served coffee and tea and chocolate, twelve and a half cents a cup, and sometimes sandwiches and cakes, bread and molasses. I'd established a good business selling whale oil, too, that I got from the Chinaman.

You might have called it living, but there was precious little fun in it. We had plenty to eat, what with the money from the stand and from doctoring, but nothing was left over. Because whatever my father got his hands on, from any source, he gambled away in a hurry. Sometimes he won a little; not often. To be fair, none of the people in the El Dorado or United States wanted him to drink or gamble. They knew our condition, but of course they couldn't keep him out.

What I missed most was companionship. On days like Christmas, that meant something back home, I was so low I had to fight tears when I went to bed. I had Christmas dinner by myself, off pickled pork and cold biscuit, my father being drunk somewhere, and in the afternoon, about dead from loneliness, I went to Reverend Ebersohl's church service. Afterwards he gave me some cake a woman had brought him and seemed so anxious and concerned and fatherly that it only made me bluer, somehow. He was a good man. I missed Po-Povi, and I missed Todd, too. Herbert Swann and the boys in Louisville seemed a long, long, time ago; I couldn't get them straightened out in my mind any more. I wanted to see my mother of course, but what I missed most right now was our family of the wagon train. Even Jennie.

You could say there was excitement here a-plenty, but not for a boy, unless he wanted to grow up fast and forget he'd been a boy. Still, that fight the Reverend Ebersohl mentioned in his speech, between the bull and the grizzly bear, was interesting for about two minutes, for the way the animals took to each other. Reading the handbills and hearing the talk, my father closed the stand, during one of his sober spells, and we got a ride to the American Valley, where they had this high, spiked corral built, to keep the bull in. A whopping big crowd was there, in a drunken, noisy humor, and the promoter made a pile of money selling tickets at a dollar a head, half price for children under twelve, and infants free.

Then the time came, they rolled the grizzly out in his cage, with a chain fastened to a ring in his nose, and turned him loose in the pen. The bull came charging up with a spine-jangling bellow, but when he saw who it was, only a grizzly bear, he acted like his peeve had been a case of mistaken identity. The bear stood on his hind legs and smelled the bull over, bow and stern, then seemed pleased to have made this attractive new friend. They ambled over the turf together, the bull grazing, the bear searching for grubs and ants, for all I know steering each other to the choice tidbits.

A number of men cried, "Sold!" and threatened to put the promoter in the corral with the animals, but they finally let him off. Even a drunk man could see it wasn't his fault.

Dogfights were a favored amusement on the Plaza, and the scabbier men occasionally got up what they called a "boy fight," sicking two boys of about equal size onto each other, making them fight so as not to be called cowards. Usually these were fixed up between boys of different races—American and Mexican for the most part—with the representation that they were fighting for the glory of their country. Often, these poor, ignorant, ragged, dirty boys were made to fight until they had knocked one or the other's teeth out, along with torn-up ears, and twice I saw boys of around twelve blinded in one eye. My father said "nothing could be more contemptible" and claimed that the men who started these things likely wouldn't fight if you kicked them in the stomach, unless it was a midget or a tubercular woman.

In February he had a long session of soberness, and some doctors at the City Hospital put him up for a steady job there, with the title of Assistant Physician. The salary would be twenty-five hundred dollars a year. Hearing about it, he was almost cheerful over something to do with medicine, for a change. It was an honor, and the salary being, as he said, princely, it would enable us to move into a house, buy a carriage and horses, send for Jennie and them, if they'd come, and then send for the folks at Louisville later on. He was all worked up about it, though it seemed to me only swapping an unhappy situation in Louisville for the same kettle of fish in San Francisco.

In any case, it didn't matter, for on the first ballot taken by the Board, five votes were cast for my father and three for a Dr. Hunter, and then, when they ran it off in other ballots, Dr. Hunter won out.

This crushed my father down as bad as anything that had happened. He even began to neglect his occasional practice he'd built up, and took to spending his time serving on juries, making three or four dollars a day. I ran the stand, Reverend Ebersohl helped as usual, also helped with my father, and we floundered along.

On one of the worst days, in late March, I was steering him across the Plaza (as he'd fallen into a ditch after coming out of the Courthouse) when I heard a familiar, "Dear me, dear me, I hope there's nothing wrong," and it was the spry little cricket, Mr.

Peters, who'd insisted on knowing our address in San Francisco.

My father straightened up with dignity, slapped some of the mud off of his trousers, brushed his hat, which was now a wreck, with the lid busted loose so that your hand would slide through, and said, "Wrong? wrong? Perhaps you'll explain yourself, sir."

Mr. Peters was a hoppity little rabbit of a man, but he was not easily cowed. He stood surveying my father, one forefinger on his upper lip, then shook his head in distress. He was dressed in the same professional way, fussy, prim, neat, even more businesslike than before, if possible.

"Oh, this won't do, it really won't—and seven months yet to go" (consulting his notebook) "till October twentieth, to be exact. Client would be *most* disturbed."

It's hard to admit, but my father was far from sober. To put it plainly, he didn't entirely make sense. But he drew himself up like the grandest kind of actor on a stage, jammed on his hat with a beautiful flourish, causing the lid to pop up on one side and stay there, then said, "I am not accostomed to being accused in the public thoroughfare, like a common footpad. Kindly consult me at my office, sir. Make an appointment. Any afternoon will do; I generally sleep it off in the mornings."

"Oh, my!" said Mr. Peters. "This *is* serious, is it not? How fickle is fortune! I never dreamed—— Surely you remember me, sir. Junius T. Peters, of the inquiry at the post office?"

My father gave him a very keen look, then he said, "It won't do you a particle of good to masquerade under an alias. I'm onto that dodge. Now suppose you sit yourself down there"—we had reached the stand—"and state your symptoms like a man."

"My dear sir, I am *not* ill! I really must protest——"

My father had reached underneath the counter, removed his heart cone, and applied it to Mr. Peters' chest. Listening gravely, still with his hat on, he said, "You should have come in sooner. I cannot stress too strongly the importance of a periodic check, especially at your age." Then he straightened up with an air of decision. "Your case is simple, Mr. Streeter. You've either swallowed a cheap watch or you haven't over a month to live. In any event, I'd like to call in another opinion before resorting to surgery."

I have no idea how much of this nonsense was done on purpose, from being in a gay mood, and how much was dumb, drunken talk. Once alcohol removed his cautions, he was sometimes given to carrying on very elaborate, silly jokes, to make up for all the seriousness he had to go through, and hated, about medicine. I'd seen him do it often before.

Mr. Peters tried to struggle to his feet, but he was pushed back firmly and a wooden spatula inserted in his mouth.

"Ah," said my father. "Say 'Ah.' No, no, not 'Ugh'—'Ah.' Better, that's better. You're coming along fine. We'll lick this thing yet. The trick is to get them at their source. *Great jumping Jehosophat!*"—peering into his mouth—"this is shocking. Mr. Streeter, I hate to say so, but I'm afraid you've been drinking."

Mr. Peters opened his mouth to protest again, having got rid of the spatula, but my father sat down beside him and said, in a sympathetic tone—he *did* have a fine bedside manner; everybody noticed it, "To understand this case more fully, I'll have to ask a few routine questions, to get your history, that is. Now, first of all, has there been any serious insanity in your family? On either side."

Right here I want to pay tribute to one of the most admirable men, large or small, it's ever been my good fortune to know. In these years, while I've been writing down our adventures, I never go to San Francisco without calling at his home, and he, in turn, often comes to see us.

Instead of blowing up, as he was wholly entitled to do, from this outrage, Mr. Peters said, "Both my mother and my father, sir, were certifiable idiots."

I could see my father's face working, and realized that the answer had gone pretty far toward getting him back to normal. Suddenly he took a bottle out of his pocket, fetched two small tumblers from under the stand, poured them half full, then broke the bottle on the end boards.

"Mr. Peters, I'm going to prescribe a remedy that should do you a world of good. It's the only known specific for patience during a medical consultation of this kind. Your health, sir."

Mr. Peters inclined his head slightly, then tossed off that raw whiskey without so much as a twitch.

"Thank you, sir. One good turn deserves another, so if I may, I'll just suggest a prescription for you." He picked up a tin lying in view on the stand. "Known pharmacologically as Tea."

My father sat down and had a look at himself, his torn and muddied trousers, his threadbare coat, his hat (removing it to work the lid up and down with his hand) and at last, the stand itself, together, it seemed, with our miserable circumstance in general.

"A shabby old man in defeat. Not pretty, Mr. Peters."

"Oh, come, sir," cried Mr. Peters with great good cheer, "it isn't all that bad. We must take steps, we must dedicate ourselves toward, as it were, reconstruction. It's a matter of business. First, as stated, the Tea." (I'd got our spirit-pot going and now began to pour out three cups.) "Then the question of attire. I dislike to sound picayune, but there are certain features of your present costume which fall below the level of strictly good usage. I suggest——"

"You've struck a snag there." My father produced a handful of silver. "I have exactly $2.40, the bulk of it supplied by an inebriated miner for whom I splinted up a leg, quite possibly the wrong one."

"Then there appears only one thing to do. We must visit my personal tailor. And we must visit him at once."

"Do you mean to say you wish to outfit me from your own purse? Why?"

"I assure you, sir, it's business. Purely business. We must remember that I have a certain responsibility to Client." He acted a trifle embarrassed, as if, indeed, his actions were *not* good business. But he'd made up his mind, so after an exchange in which my father unsuccessfully tried to learn the name of Mr. Peters' client, then gave some of his usual hogwash about how he insisted on making a "note of hand" for the debt, we struck out down the street. They'd laid plank sidewalks along here the month before, and Mr. Peters, for some reason, seemed dead-set against stepping on the cracks. They weren't easy to miss. He skipped, teetering this way and that, balanced, hopped, fell back, and danced the tightrope, and altogether, before we arrived, I was as nervous as a cat. Tired, too. I'd have been happy to see him go back to the former oddity of trying to keep everybody in step. That one was comparatively easy to handle.

At the tailor's, some measurements were taken on my father for a new coat and trousers, by a very sissified man that acted as if he didn't relish the job. Then Mr. Peters left us, to disappear into wherever he came from. Before he did, standing there on the sidewalk, looking first at me and then at my father, switching his expression back and forth from the perfectly tight line of his mouth to his business smile, he finally sighed, and let his face go slack. Despite his manner, I had the idea that he wasn't a natural-born businessman at all, but had to work at it pretty hard.

"Doctor," he said in a different voice. "This procedure of living in a tent on the public square. Is it good? Is it wise? And what about the boy?"

"Business?" inquired my father, wrinkling up the corners of his eyes.

"Sir, from the cradle to the grave, everything is business, in one sense or another. My father, a banker of prominence, drilled that point home to me each year of my childhood, and he was correct, absolutely correct. My inquiry is based on business."

"Mr. Peters," said my father, "you're a humbug. I don't think you care any more about business than I do. It's only a triumph of will over instinct. I've never understood your interest in us, but we feel that it is, in some way, benign. So I'll answer what would appear, in another, to be impertinence. We are going back to our tent, Jaimie and I, put our house, or tent, in order, resume the practice of medicine, wearing your clothes, attending to duty, forswearing all games of chance and intoxicants, and find proper lodgings as soon as prosperity permits. Does that suit you?"

Mr. Peters sighed. "I wish I could make available my address, in case the need arose. But it would be in direct violation of my injunction by Client. That would never do."

"Unbusinesslike," said my father.

"I'll bid you good day," said Mr. Peters, stiffly. We had the impression that he was professionally, but not personally, offended.

We walked down the street toward our tent, my father and I, in the warm but blustery March weather, and neither of us could find much to say. I felt a little down, and wished we were back at Vernon. Besides, I wasn't exactly proud of my father. So I just walked along.

At the stand, he said, "Sit down a minute, laddie. Let's have a talk."

I wasn't in the humor, but I perched on the edge of the bench and sat staring off across the Plaza. For some reason, I couldn't get up the interest to look at him.

"Son," he said, "how would you like to go back home?"

"To the diggings?"

"To Louisville."

Then I *did* look at him, because this was about the *last* thing I expected. It made me kind of sore, and I spoke up in a way I'd never done before.

"You falling down on that, too?"

It shook him; he turned a couple of shades paler, which wasn't easy to tell because of the stubble, sprinkled through with gray now, that covered his chin.

"I don't mind your saying that. I hate to *hear* you say it, but you've got the right. I suppose there isn't a single thing I haven't botched from start to finish."

"Up to lately, you've done fine. Nobody could have worked harder."

"Well, you've heard the old saying about throwing good money after bad. Maybe the simplest thing to do is face reality, admit defeat, grow up—me, I mean—troop back to Louisville, and dig in, whatever the pain. It's quite possible I've been running long enough. In all truth, your mother was right, she always has been.

Here's what we can do, boy. We can take the Santa Fe Trail, the southerly route, new country, new adventures, maybe a little hike over to Mexico—always wanted to see it—and who knows how we'll wind up? Why"—his face began to take on a very familiar look— "we're apt to stumble across a fortune! Opp——"

I got up abruptly and opened the stand.

I said, "I worked a wheelbarrow for some Mexicans up near Vernon, three dollars for ten hours. Down where *they* lived—in Mexico, that is—they'd heard about the opportunities in California. I'll be right here, in San Francisco. I don't mind saying I'd like to see my mother and Hannah and Mary and Aunt Kitty, but we said we'd give it a year, and that's what I'm giving it. Now you do just what you please."

There was a silence, then he said, "Son, what have you done these last weeks? I can't seem to pick any one day out of the rest."

"Run the stand, hid what money I could so as to eat, talked, and worked, with Reverend Ebersohl, and slept in a tent. Is there something better?"

I'm not proud of those words, for he looked terrible. He arose and said, "Put on some hot water; I need a shave." And in a minute, while scraping away with his razor, he said, "There's no use in saying I'm ashamed. It won't solve anything. Deeds speak louder than words. John Barleycorn is buried as of today. We *will* stick out our year. I'll work up a practice you'll be proud of. And we'll have the family here by Christmas. Son, reach in my medical bag and hand me that bottle of whiskey. Right there, that's it, the one that says Back Liniment on the label."

"What a wonderful start——"

"—as a lotion after shaving," he went on, turning the bottle up in his hand and slapping the liquid over his face, "it can't be beat. Ah, yes, very efficacious; the only disagreeable feature is the smell. Dear me, I'm afraid it's too acute; I'll never get used to it." He poured the rest on the ground, then, stepping over a few yards beside a bush, scooped up a mound of dirt and stuck the bottle upside down at the head. "Behold—John Barleycorn's grave. We'll decorate it daily."

He'd got going now, and to give him credit, he spruced himself up handsome. He repaired the hat, cleaned his shoes, cleaned off his clothes and had them pressed by a Chinaman, and washed out what laundry the Reverend Ebersohl hadn't already done. Then he straightened up the tent from stem to stern and came out with pride in his eyes. I'd never seen him look quite so officious. It was as clear as daylight he'd come to some kind of decision. But I wasn't entirely convinced; I'd been here before.

We had to stop and serve figs and molasses and sassafras tea to four English sailors off a ship in the harbor. They said both their food and water had turned weevily, and their teeth were loose in their heads from scurvy. It was close on to six o'clock.

"Shut her up for the day, my boy," cried my father when they left. "We have an errand to do."

Call me crazy, but he said we were going up to the Powell Street Methodist Church and sign the pledge.

"*I'm* not signing a pledge," I said. "I haven't any reason to, and never will, if I can help it."

"I've never believed in that cant myself, but there is a tide in the affairs of men which, taken at the flood, leads on to fortune, especially in San Francisco. I mean to strike while the iron's hot."

As we turned to go, a man with a wooden leg that my father had become acquainted with, from the Sandwich Islands, a Mr. Hobson, perfectly white, came thump-thumping up and cried, "Come on, doc, they're empaneling veniremen to try Bill McGurn. He's guilty as hell. Being as I saw the whole thing, I'm unprejudiced by idle talk, so we can sleep right through."

"Friend Hobson," said my father. "I am no longer a career juror. That belonged to my Barleycorn period. I am now a physician only."

"Why, doc, you'll drink up all your painkiller."

"If you'll excuse us, we have an appointment to keep. Call in at my office any time."

"Best of luck, doc," Mr. Hobson called out cheerfully. He was a good enough fellow, and you could excuse him for drinking. He'd been on a trading trip through the southerly islands and been captured by some cannibals that cut off his leg, boiled it and ate it right in front of him, while he was conscious and watched them serve it out in pieces. Before they were finished, another bunch of outriggers pulled up, full of friendlies, and he was rescued. So now he was alive, though drunk, but he had a wooden leg. It was all written up in the *Alta Californian*, under the heading of "A Grisly Ordeal." He carried the clipping around with him, and showed it to anybody that would look, after which he commonly mooched the price of a drink. People were very glad to pay it, in order to get away and think about something else.

When we reached the church, Reverend Ebersohl was preparing to leave for his evening street preaching. And when he heard why we'd come, he didn't seem happy. Anybody else, he'd a signed them up in a hurry, but with my father, he hated to see him demean himself in that way.

"If I know the Lord, and I think I do, He'll be glad to take the will for the deed."

"Reverend," said my father, "kindly produce your paper. I've turned over a new leaf, and I'd like it authenticated in writing. Who knows? The document may eventually assume historical importance."

Chapter XLVI

For a number of weeks my father pitched into his practice like a man reformed forever. We had letters from home, several from Vernon, and wrote some back, including one to Louisville which hinted that we practically owned San Francisco by now, and suggesting that my mother be "alerted" to join us when he gave the signal. I could see her face when she read it.

Medically, he picked up a very fair number of cases, because people recognized that he was skilled at his job when sober, no matter how much he disliked it. I won't come out and say he was happy—being a doctor was a strain on him—but he kept plugging away, and in this period, after a lapse of time, he began to write in his Journals again. He wrote up many of his cases, and I'll tell some, to show how good and careful he was at doctoring when he really buckled down.

April 5, 1851:

Called on a Mrs. Oscar Theobald, aged 40. Symtoms: extensive warmth of rectum, sharp, lancinating pain near anus, red, modulating mass protruding from same, also uneasiness, constitutional disturbance. Diagnosis: Haemorrhoids exterior of the sphincter ani. Treatment: application of ice water, tannic acid, Persulphate of Iron; lessening of constipation by having patient drink several glasses water in morning, also kneading of abdomen, thighs and pelvis plus salt hip bath to relax perineal structures. Lastly, anointed Haemorrhoids locally by introducing wet cigar in rectum.

April 7, 1851:

Called on Swen Nordlund, widower, aged 73. Symptoms: dizziness, sensation of anxiety at praecordia, vertigo, singing in the ears, abnormal pulse—hard, sharp, quick, dicrotous, intermittent; tenderness on pressure over first and second cervical vertebrae; complaint of dull, aching pain in back of head. Problem: whether symptoms from dyspepsia, chronic inflammation of lungs, severe mental labor, troubled mind from want of success, or sexual excesses, notably masturbation. Diagnosis: irregular heart from last-named cause. Treatment: tincture of Cactus, teaspoon every four hours, together with recommendation patient move from his boardinghouse, where the 17-year-old daughter of proprietor undresses and lolls Narcissistically on bed, nude, within patient's view from window each evening upon retirement.

I should say here, before continuing, that these cases are exactly the way my father wrote them, but now and then, as only a fool could help but see, he was unable to avoid touching on the humor of certain ones. I think he tried not to, but it crept in, though I'm convinced he kept everything wholly accurate and in line, because I'm sure he felt that people were going to read these Journals someday.

For instance:

April 7, 1851:
Called upstairs to United States Hotel, patient, "Slick" Carstairs, aged around 35, occupation cardsharp. Symptoms: absence of heartbeat, small round blue hole in center of forehead. Diagnosis: Dead. (Of revolver bullet.) Treatment: Placed 3-cent copper coins on eyelids, folded arms on chest, summoned undertaker.

And:

April 17, 1851:
Called on Ralph Kobler, aged 45, well-known journalist and poet of this city. Symptoms: excitement of nervous system proceeding to prostration, pulse slow, acute thirst, no appetite, anxiety and dejection, frequent sighs, increasing restlessness and vigilance. Condition complicated by patient's insistence that a devil with a

red nose and dragon's tail is sitting on end of bed prodding him with pitchfork. In short passage of time, tongue dry and furred, tremor of muscles, wild threshing of limbs, persecution of patient heightened when devil reinforced by several parti-colored snakes, a Chinese mandarin, 2 lizards, racoon answering to name of Shakespeare, 1 alligator, Gila monster, Unicorn, and a three-legged fox.

Diagnosis: Delirium tremens. Treatment: Iodine pill every three hours, Iron, Quinine and Strychnine in powder, beef-tea enema, small dosage of whiskey (doled out) plus Chloroform if Kobler grows in violence.

Sometimes these San Francisco gamblers and miners tried to play pranks on my father, being rough, frolicsome men, and he went right ahead and wrote up such cases along with the others:

April 20, 1851:
Visited at tent by 2 seamen, Second Mate and Bosun of trading schooner *Voluta*. They carrying parcel in brown paper and said,

"Doc, are you acquainted with a disease called 'itchycosis'?"
"Ichthyosis," I replied, "an ailment in which the skin becomes scaly and fishlike."

"We hearn about it in the islands," they said. "And on the way home, dog if our old mate Bill didn't tune up with just such an eruption. It wasn't hardly human; he only lingered about a week. We feel right bad about it, doc. We'd perk up if you'd figure out what caused him to go like that. And so would his folks. Natcherly we didn't have the refrigeration to keep him intact, but we peeled off a stretch of skin, some of the scaliest part, and applied salt. Look her over, will you, doc, and see if you can run it down. Bill was a robust man till this turned up and blistered his hull."

One of these worthies then had the effrontery to take out a faded bandana and conceal a tear, after which he sniffed loudly.

"I see," I replied with what I hope was a wary look. "I'll be happy to give the case my best attention."

Upon their return, two days later, they said, "What is it, doc? Did you track her down?"

"According to my diagnosis, confirmed by two other physicians and a scallop dragger, it is, or was, a silver tarpon, a very nice specimen, probably weighing around 140 pounds. That will be two dollars, if you please."

April 29, 1851:
   Called to home of Mr. and Mrs. Ivor Beddows, parents of patient, Franklin, aged 9.
   Symptoms diffuse, child poorly nourished, muscles soft and flabby, leaded tongue, bad breath, derangement of secretions. Fever paroxysms afternoon and evening, skin hot and dry, pulse fast, marked irritability and restlessness, frequent voracious appetite, occasional convulsion. Also sleeps poorly, abdomen tumid, frequent picking of nose, swelling of upper lip, and white line appearing around mouth, together with itching of arms. Also, more infrequently, abdominal spasms, convulsive cough, disordered digestion, irregular evacuation, vertigo, defects in speech, upward undulatory movement of abdomen.
   Diagnosis: Reached result after several visits, proceeding by method of *exclusion*, passing the entire system in review, using ordinary *nosological* classification, analyzing by the standard of *excess, defect,* and *perversion.*
   Final diagnosis: Examination of faeces showed positive presence of 4 species of intestinal worms: *ascaris lumbricoides,* or long round worm, *ascaris vermicularis,* small threadworm, *tricocephalus dispar,* long threadworm, and *taenia solium,* tapeworm. All species presumably introduced into intestines through eating of raw pork, possibly bacon.
   Treatment: For first-named species, infusion of Pink and Senna plus vermifuge Oil of Wormwood, causing worms to leave nest in bowels. Then Santonate of Soda followed by Castor Oil sprinkled on bread and butter. Follow with Jalap and Senna.
   For tapeworm, Turpentine beaten up in yolks of 3 eggs, followed by Castor Oil. Also Pomegranate bark (*Punica granatum*) boiled in water. Also Male Fern in mucilage. Also Pumpkin Seed in sugar and water. Tapeworm heads appeared in faeces after 3 days, followed by other portions day later. Full recovery indicated.

   The main trouble with doctoring was, nobody really felt inclined to pay their bill. It was the last thing on their list. And just like Louisville, my father hadn't any stomach to send out statements. Finally, urged on by friends in the casinos, he got some forms printed up, by a man with a hand press in a basement that was used mainly to print a small, blackmail newspaper he was slipping under people's doors in the mornings. Everyone knew who it was, but it made such enjoyable reading that nobody cared to stop it.

Anyway, my father had the forms, but he often didn't bother putting them to use, so we still had to make out mainly from the stand. Even so, he was inching along, and hoped to have a good paying practice soon.

Then, on May fourth, the most profitable part of our lives here came to an end. We were asleep in our tent, and shortly after dawn, of an unusually windy morning, heard a cry from across the Plaza of "Fire! fire!" Now San Francisco had already had several fires in the last few years, some of them destructive, but this one put the clincher on everything.

We piled out in a hurry, jumping into our clothes, but before we were halfway across the Plaza, we saw that nothing was going to work—bucket line, wet blankets, hose pump, anything. These buildings around the Square were pasteboard-flimsy, and with the wind to fan things, we had a roarer going in about fifteen minutes. People were yelling and running whichever way, and others piled out of the hotels, wearing anything they could grab, even curtains in some cases. All that day (and it was about the worst in the city's history) nobody got any more serious a hurt than singed eyebrows or skinned-up elbows, though I heard somebody say a man had broken his leg by jumping out of a second-storey window into a mortar box which looked wet but wasn't—that concrete had been standing there two weeks and was harder than iron.

The fire broke out on the east side of the Square; before eight o'clock it had wiped out the four main gambling halls, and one of the biggest boardinghouses. By afternoon the Square was, as the paper said next day, reduced to ashes except for two houses of 72-foot frontage at the southwest corner and a solitary brick house at the northeast corner. That wind did zip along! From Washington Street down to Montgomery, all leveled off—gambling houses, stores, residences, everything. Sparks and burning cloth swept over the Plaza on a level line close to the ground, like a blizzard of snow, and you had to look sharp to keep from getting your clothes afire. My father wrote in his Journals: "It was an awful and sublime scene. The smoke made the brilliant sun as though seen through a piece of black bottle glass."

I guess it was around noon, with the sky all dark that way and burning bits swirling past, when we thought about the stand. I don't know why it hadn't occurred to us before, except that our things were a hundred yards away from the main area of flames. But when we got there, the tent was all but gone and the stand was on fire in three places. We kicked it over, and my father snatched up his bag, but we couldn't stamp out the flames. A big piece of burning calico—a ceiling from somewhere, likely—had blown against it, giving it a very good start. We'd lost everything except the clothes we stood up in, but they included my father's new suit, thanks to goodness.

By twilight, the Square was like something out of a nightmare. Where before rickety wooden buildings had reared up on all four sides, ugly but familiar and warm and homey, now only chimneys were standing, along with that solitary brick building shell. Everything else was a mass of tumbled-down char, smoking, with now and then a little crash as something settled deeper, sending a plume of sparks, and even flame, shooting upward. All across the Plaza people stood and talked, uneasy, the gamblers and women distressed maybe the worst of all, because their reputation wasn't so good, you see, and none of the "decent" element was anxious to take them in. Piles of furniture every few feet, especially on Jackson and Washington streets down to Montgomery, where a few sticks had been hauled out in a hurry, but not many, because this fire had gone very fast, like a blaze sweeping over dry prairie, once it started. And where *did* it start? That was a mystery. The best reports said that a man who had turned in late at the United

States smoked a last cigar of the night and went to sleep with it hanging from his fingers. But he declined to admit it later, so I guess they'll never know.

One dead. The man that jumped into the mortar trough developed complications on the third day and died of pneumonia. With nothing better to do, we and everyone else trooped up to the public burying grounds, two miles off, and laid him to rest. The Reverend Ebersohl preached the funeral sermon, from the text, "O Generation of Vipers, who hath warned you to flee from the wrath to come?" and did a good, careful job, only referring to gambling directly four or five times and whiskey not at all, except once, and didn't dwell on it. The only awkwardness came when nobody knew the man's name. He had checked into one of the hotels, a silent, unfriendly fellow, and the register burned. At the City Hospital he'd said, "Just call me Slim," and refused to amplify things. So Reverend Ebersohl made his death kind of stand for the death of gambling halls in San Francisco and merely referred to him, when necessary, as "our late, esteemed friend of the mortar box," or "him who lies here," and finally, having worked those threadbare, just used the handier "Corpse," as if it was a name.

One thing the sermon accomplished, it cleared up who was to blame for the fire. Reverend Ebersohl had taken some little trouble to run it down, and it was the Devil.

Viewed from all angles, it was a very satisfactory sermon, and put the capper on the great fire of May fourth.

The people went back to work to build up bigger and better structures, and life hurried on.

But not so good for us. We moved into a back room of the Powell Street Church, but we hadn't any stand, now, and no money to get a new one made, or buy provisions with. So it was up to my father to go it alone for a while. All the responsibility was his; everything depended on medicine. His face grew more and more haggard, and his hopes were ground down into the dirt. He never talked much in this period; he seemed to have run entirely out of Plans. But he gritted his teeth and held on. I was proud of him, and to help out got a number of odd jobs, wheeling dirt on the streets and such like.

Then one afternoon in late June he came home whistling, his face pink and happy, swinging his bag and kicking a tin along. He was drunk. Who could blame him? Not me, not this time; I was growing up a little, I guess. And not the Reverend Ebersohl, either. He only looked sorrowful, and quiet, and said, "My friend, let's sleep it away. Out of sight and out of mind. One swallow does not a summer make, nor even a habit of drinking."

But it wasn't any use. From that day forward he went steadily downhill. And the same as before, he never mentioned it; got up every morning cheerful, even a little pompous, but never again came home quite sober. He'd stopped the really bad times, the outright drunkenness and the gambling, but he was working on whiskey now and not on nerve. And of course, he lost most of his custom. The gamblers and miners still called him in, and generally paid off, but the others no longer cared to chance a man with whiskey on his breath. Moreover, there was a suggestion of a scandal, having to do with a baby delivery that he may have bungled while drinking; everybody felt bad about it, but they were a little suspicious, too.

The summer ran along. Often I had barely enough to eat. Reverend Ebersohl worked like a draft horse to take care of us, and himself, and his congregation, and keep the devil off at the same time, but it was toilsome going. Twice, Mr. Peters dropped in, both times in the morning when my father seemed sober, so he didn't stay long, though he looked puzzled, or at least uncertain. And each time he consulted his notebook before he left, as if he was checking dates for some reason.

On several occasions that summer, all we ate was what I bought from working on the streets. Summer is a poor time for church, as Reverend Ebersohl admitted. "The people fall listless," he said.

"Warm weather drives the Devil from their minds, so they *think*. But he's there, back in the shadows, deep in the caverns of the soul, waiting for his Chance to Spring." The turnouts at his church were scarce, and the collections worse. And what money he got, he put back into hymnals or repairs, instead of laying in food. His clothes flapped loosely on his great frame, but his eyes, made brilliant by overwork and fasting, shone out with more fire than ever.

August dragged by, and September. My father didn't look like himself any more. His hair was shot through with gray, and his complexion was blotched. His hands trembled, and his new suit was shiny; he wore it every day.

I got a letter from Po-Povi:

Dear Jaimie: Perhaps it is very wrong, but I'm *glad* you feel lonely for your sister. Mr. Coe says I 'repine' for the forests and streams and hills of my land back home. And (dear, wise friend that he is) for my people who bought me. But I am greatly educated. What a solemn procession of tutors, music masters and ladies of ruined fortune has come to fill my mind, guiding my fingers over strings and keys, showing me the arts of society. These are strange people, the English of Mr. Coe's. They make a religion of indifference, and often, indeed, the manner of these men, if shown among the Indians of my tribe, would have sent them to work among the squaws. But woe to those who mistake their foppery for an infirm purpose. From reading their history, and from what my eyes have seen, I believe there is no way to convince them of defeat.

Shall I come home? You must write and say the words quite openly.

Po-Povi

The twentieth of October was one of those sharp days with an indigo sky and air so clear you could make out each separate clapboard on houses a mile away. In the Bay, the riffled-up waves looked like something seen through a spyglass, and the islands were closer in to the mainland. Still, it was just another day, a poor one for me because rain fell yesterday and no work was to be had on the streets. Same kind of a day as usual for my father, who arose slowly, trying to muster good cheer, shaved, moving the piece of mirror to a corner so dark he was unable to see his face clearly, fixed up his clothes, then stepped behind a partition where he thought he wasn't seen and had a nip out of a bottle. He refused a breakfast of cold biscuits and tea without sugar; then he took up his kit to leave, when there came a knocking at our back door.

"*Good* morning, sirs," cried Mr. Peters as we opened it. "It is, as you perceive from this newspaper, the twentieth of October. October twenty, exactly a year from the day you arrived in San Francisco."

So it was, to be sure. Another year of our adventures was gone, a year of failure and disappointment, a year wasted.

My father sat down weakly. He looked pitiful; his hands shook so at Mr. Peters' unexpected interruption that he put them out of sight under his coat.

"Then we are to hear at last?"

"I have Client's instructions," said Mr. Peters. "Everything executed and in order."

"Excuse me a moment," my father said, and stepped behind the partition again. I saw Mr. Peters' eye gleam with something more than business, but he coughed, to bring himself back to normal, and opened his portfolio. Taking out some legal-looking papers, he said: "First of all, to ease your anxiety, although the procedure is not, strictly speaking, professional, I will depose that you have come into a handsome estate, *most* handsome. And in that connection, I am to give you, at this beginning stage of the transaction, a letter. Will you, doctor, be so good as to read it aloud?"

My father took it and put on his spectacles, but he had to take them off and wipe them. Then he handed it back to Mr. Peters. The simple truth is that his hands shook so much he couldn't do

521

the job. "If you don't mind—I'm not feeling well this morning. I dined injudic——"

" 'Cherished friends of the Trail,' " Mr. Peters read, trying not to enjoy himself but failing. " 'I am taking the liberty of leaving behind a reminder of a companion who would use this selfish means of staying on with you in spirit. Perhaps by now you have made that rich strike which we sought for so many, to me, pleasurable months. If true, I shall be deprived of my gesture. If not, I shall spend many happy hours thinking of you, content in your glorious California. It seems unlikely that we shall meet again. The responsibilities of my new role do not admit of much travel. It is not a bad role, by the way. For better or worse, this is the England that bred me, and I find the matter of discharging my debt in many ways rewarding. Would you, doctor, compress your buoyant spirit into a few pages of correspondence once each year, at Christmas time, to help me to renew my memory of a period that I shall ever regard as among the most priceless treasures of my life?

God bless you all; may good fortune attend your ventures.

BLANDFORD

(Henry T. Coe)

Postscript: I must add that it would be quite useless for you to refuse; the property is yours, whether or not you wish actively to manage it.

H.T.C.' "

Mr. Peters' face appeared to have strayed from business for a moment. He blew his nose. "To proceed to the point, His Grace, the Duke of Blandford, has seen fit, through the Bank, for which I act as agent, to place on deposit, soon to be in Trust, the sum of ten thousand pounds—approximately fifty thousand dollars—for the purpose of buying, stocking, equipping and Perpetuating—you will kindly note the clause 'Perpetuating,' for it has a bearing on the Trust provisions—an estate, or ranch, of not less than six thousand acres, the ownership to be divided among the parties hereinafter named, subject, again, to Trust (for a period of years), the management to be effectuated by any method you decide upon, once again, within the limitations of Trust.

"That, in brief, is the commission which I am herewith, ah, able, or, as it were, pleased, or even happy, though the viewpoint is unprofessional, to discharge.

"Doctor McPheeters," said Mr. Peters, arising, "my congratulations, speaking entirely personally, you understand. You are a wealthy man. I wish you and your son and your colleagues the very best of luck!"

My father sat there like a stone. "It's too late," he said finally. "Look at me, a drunken ruin, my family split, hearts broken, hopes dashed, my son's education knocked into a cocked hat, and by whom? By me, and me alone."

"Permit me to say—Nonsense!" cried Mr. Peters. "I ask you to look upon me as a friend. The main business is over and finished. I think I may flatter myself that it has been carried out in a way that would have done credit to my father, who was, as stated, a banker of import. I don't wish to seem unfilial, but I believe a case might be made that he was *all* business.

"What remains is trivial, principally a matter of counsel, advice, assistance. I shall be working with you on behalf of the Bank. Speaking for myself, and *not* for the Bank, I feel that you will, with no difficulty, rise to this great occasion."

My father looked up, and said, "What do *you* think, son? Do you suppose you could ever believe another promise of mine?"

They'd said I was grown now, and I *felt* grown after this past year of starving and looking after my father and wheeling dirt on the streets of San Francisco.

I stooped down, trying not to notice the gray hair and veiny skin and the flesh hanging slack and purplish on his cheeks.

"You kept us together on this trip, however bad things got," I said. "Strong or not, it wasn't Mr. Kissel, nor was it Buck Coulter, tough as he is. It has to do with what Mr. Coe wrote in his letter, the part about spirit. And I don't think a thing like that ever dies out. The way I see it," I went on, "this is just about the perfect example of Opportun——"

"Mr. Peters," my father said suddenly, getting up and brushing off his hat, and having to hold onto a table, a little, for support, "what's next in the order of business?"

Chapter XLVII

At the bank we learned that the actual transfer of the funds would be done only after it was certain that none of us—the Kissels, Coulter and them—had made a big strike up to October twentieth. But they hadn't; we knew that, because they weren't prospecting any more, and besides, we'd heard from them only a few days since.

Came a morning soon when my father and Mr. Peters and I boarded a sailing vessel bound upriver for Sacramento. We had a farewell dinner with the Reverend Ebersohl, using real food at a hotel for a change, which Mr. Peters insisted on paying for, though making it clear the money would come out of Administration. When my father and I begged Reverend Ebersohl to join us in our new life, he declined, with a wistful but determined shake of the head, saying that his real work lay in San Francisco, because the devil had clamped a grip on this region that might take forty years to unhook. Still, he promised that, if he and his associates *did* get the upper hand, through day and night campaigning, he would come to see us, wherever we were.

He stood on the wharf when we sailed, waving his hat, bareheaded, smiling, half starved, filled with courage and duty, a great man, as my father said, by every measure known.

We'd posted letters of thanks to Mr. Coe and a long one home, a letter that had a real ring of truth for once. Then I'd written a note to Po-Povi, but I won't tell what I said; I'm not much good at that mushy stuff. Before we reached Vernon—actually by Sacramento—my father had begun to take on a fresher look. During the days riding up the river, he never mentioned whiskey, although some gentlemen in the saloon were drinking freely every night. For several nights he lay wide awake, though. I knew it well enough because he had an upper bunk, with me in the lower, and I heard him tossing around. By now, I could guess how he suffered. In the moonlight that shone through our door, I saw his hand gripping the outside of the bunk, the skin white, tight-drawn over the knuckles. There wasn't a thing could be done; Mr. Peters knew it, too. So we kept quiet and waited.

The miserable part was that his pomp and bluster were gone. He'd lost most of that bubbling-up confidence, the real honest feeling that Fortune lay just round the corner. I hated to see him so. But standing day after day on deck in the sun and wind and spray toughened him up and helped his appearance some. The gray hair was there, and would stay, but the blotchiness was disappearing fast. Hard going or not, he was on the mend, and before Vernon his appetite had come back almost to normal.

Disembarking at last, we started down the street, me with a nervous fluttering in my stomach. It *had* been a long time. But there it was, standing right in the same old place. The identical exact butchery stand, though added to considerable, and a little house, with a number of rambling rooms built out behind. The sun was in my eyes, so I shaded them with my hand, trying to make out who I saw. Then I heard Jennie's happy cry, and the next minute she was flying up the road, holding her petticoats as usual. Her soft, starchy, sweet-smelling hug somehow made up for the whole year of pauperdom. Then it was Mrs. Kissel, and her brood, and, finally, the usual bear's grip from her husband, confound him; he was dangerous when carried away by good feeling, and my father said the same.

We all had a good cry, even Mr. Peters, who had, as he stated several times, no more than a business interest in the reunion; so that he was, as he told us (blowing his nose) uninvolved in any emotional way. For which he was thankful, since he doubted if his late father would have approved of the other.

And later that day, when Coulter and Uncle Ned and Todd came in from a trip to the mines, we did it all over again.

Then we told about Mr. Coe and the ranch, and nobody could take it in, it was so awesome. But I guess the most affected were the Kissels. Mr. Kissel said five or six times, so as to pound it in, "He was a farmer born; I always felt it," and Mrs. Kissel went aside to hide her face in her apron, but later on she came back to say she would send him some tomatoes out of the very first stand that was raised.

The only flaw in our good feeling was that everybody seemed embarrassed by my father's new manner. They hated to see him so quiet and abject. I watched Coulter at dinner—we had it indoors, now, instead of around the old campfire—and afterward, when he got my father aside, I followed out of curiosity. I found me a handy place behind a tree.

"Doc," said Coulter, taking my father's elbow, "you did me a favor once that I'm not apt to forget. Far as I can see, my turn appears to have come. It might be you're feeling like a failure right now, blaming yourself for hardships and losses. No, don't interrupt. Likely you don't feel so good about drinking, either. Well, you're in the same boat I was in when you gave me the preaching." My father started to speak again, but Coulter waved him down.

"I ask you—who's responsible for Mr. Coe and this thing he's done? Me? a backwoods ignoramus that can't more than sign his name? Matt Kissel, who couldn't hook three sentences together to save himself from drowning? Mrs. Kissel? Jennie? No, it was you all down the line. Doc, you're the backbone of this party, and always was. There was a kind of poetry in all those stories you spun around the campfire. I don't think anybody entirely *believed* all your fancy dreams, but we enjoyed hearing them told, and what's more, they kept us going. Uncle Ned Reeves and I were talking about it the other day. Doc, you made us feel good; it's something that can't be bought. We miss it, and hope it comes back soon."

My father turned away and walked off toward the river. But the next morning, when we got up, he seemed to have undergone a change; he didn't look hangdog any more.

"About the location for the ranch," he said, putting on his spectacles and removing a booklet from his pocket, "I've been doing some research and feel that Opportunity, the real opportunity, lies in the Sandwich Islands, coming to be known more commonly as Hawaii, the vowels to be pronounced independently for strictly pure usage.

"During the course of my practice in San Francisco, I had reason to converse with a number of people from there. The climate is salubrious, the land fertile and cheap, the mineral situation largely unexplored. To go a step further, news of a gold strike in that area at any minute would not surprise me.

"*However,* the point of particular interest is this: the present native ruler, King Kamehameha III, is a confirmed sot"—he had the good grace to wince slightly when he got the word out—"and in truth appears at Court functions almost invariably carrying a brandy bottle under his arm. This is not hearsay; it is factual material that will soon appear in the book of an English acquaintance of mine.

"*Most* important from our standpoint is this: the king is completely under the domination *of a Scottish minister!*

"Now, can you not envision the preferential treatment we must enjoy with such a racial tie at Court? I allude, of course, to my own Scottish origins.

"So—there is no question in my mind of geography. Fortune, probably wealth undreamed of on the mainland, lies in Hawaii."

He paused here and took off his spectacles; then he said briskly, "Boat passage may be booked from San Francisco every fortnight."

It was pleasant to hear him; his remarks were downright musical, and made about as much sense as before; that is, there was certainly something in them, but not much. Anyhow, he had returned to normal, and everybody looked glad.

Coulter said, with a smile, "Let's save Hawaii to use as the other side of the fence, doc. It'll be there to think on. We can keep it permanent, like, for when we get restless."

"There's land," said Matt Kissel. "Green rolling land, with thick black dirt underneath, along the Bear River. I've bore it in mind this last year."

Nobody questioned him. Any time he made a statement of that length, it amounted to pronouncing the benediction.

So, I'll move along—these adventures have taken up too much space already—and say that, by depending on Mr. Peters' shrewd, calculating eye, we sold out the butchery and the mules and found our way, early in November, into a well-watered valley lying north of the Bear River bottoms; a succession of richly green and fertile fields, with woodlands, that rolled up from the bottoms to the foot-hills of the mountains above. Meadows with good pastures, and groves of black oak with mistletoe clumped in their branches, creek beds full of yellow willows, and digger pines, black and twin-trunked, in the high reaches. Flowering trees and shrubs such as we hadn't seen since the prairies: dogwood and climbing grape, berries, wild peas and manzanitas—"little apples"—and nuts very sweet to the taste.

My father wrote in his Journals: "There is room here for the great cattle ranches that we mean to create out of this overflowing wilderness. This valley of ours comes close, I believe, to a Paradise on earth."

The arrangements had all been made. We'd scouted it thoroughly, and not bought it on the spur of the moment, as my father urged of each new piece inspected. This land itself cost next to nothing; in fact, you might have grabbed it by squatting, but Mr. Peters insisted on "unclouding" some Spanish land-grant titles and some claims made by Indians, too. It was free and clear, over seven thousand acres, ownership divided equally between those of us together on the trip, divided in three, that is, with a section and home for Todd and Uncle Ned, with advantages to get them started and assistance to buy more if they chose.

Our houses were on their way up before Christmas. We had fenced pastures, but had left most unwooded acres as open range. Then we'd bought cattle from people like Captain Sutter, Mr.

Johnson, of Johnson Ranch down the Bear River, Mr. Yount and Mr. Chiles, in Napa Valley, and General Vallejo and his brother, Colonel Salvador Vallejo, both fine, generous men, at Sonoma.

Matt Kissel, still determined to farm crops, along with raising cattle, had laid in wheat, corn and barley, and now waited impatiently for the spring.

Altogether we had hired about a dozen Indians to help out with the work, and now we made things move. I never before saw my father so hard put. But something remained missing; he wanted the family out. He'd written letters saying he was coming home to fetch them, and now he could hardly wait. So, after a very merry Christmas spent in the Kissels' half-finished house, of timber and adobe brick, we bade him farewell. I was to stay behind, living with Buck and Jennie, to keep the work going on our place.

We gathered early one morning in the Kissels' front yard, with those smoky-blue mountains in the background, and hallooed him off. Mr. Peters was there, too, on one of his trips out to supervise the buying.

Giving me an embrace, my father shook hands with Mr. Kissel and Coulter and Uncle Ned and Todd, and kissed the women on the cheek.

"Six months, eight at the most," he cried, swinging up into the saddle. "We'll be reunited and wander no more." Then he called to Jennie, "Take care of the future Governor of California," which was his way of mentioning the baby they were going to have that summer.

I will remember him as he looked that morning. He was healthy; the gray hair now seemed more dignified than old, and his face, tanned and taut, had the appearance of a man who has finally come close to finding what he wants. He held his hat in his hand, and his eyes shone with the fun of starting out on a new venture. The Santa Fe Trail. Who could tell, there might be a fortune in it. Opportunity, opportunity . . .

Standing there watching him, I was glad he had never grown up.

Probably I should have been sad, because I had an uneasy feeling that we would never see him again. But I couldn't help smiling instead. It was all right. The pot of gold, the real strike, his dream run to earth, lay somewhere up ahead, around the next bend of the trail. It was all right. That next bend *was* my father's pot of gold, just as I'd said in my letter. I wondered how long he could have lasted before those beckoning hills stirred the old restlessness. How many months before the ranch itself was his enemy, and, the first crack had appeared that told of trouble coming? We waved goodbye, and I watched him ride away to keep his appointment with Fortune.

Spring had arrived—the willows were budding along the creek beds and snow was melting in the high ranges—when a solitary rider covered with dust walked his horse up to the Coulters' doorstep late one evening. Hearing him, we stepped out, and he said, "Can you direct me to James, or Jaimie, McPheeters?"

Somehow, without asking, I knew he brought news of my father. When I spoke up, he dismounted and handed over an envelope.

I took it indoors, to lantern light, and examined the contents, which were twofold: a short note of condolence from Mr. Peters and a dispatch, containing a report, from the Bishop of Zacatecas, in Mexico. It appeared that, without notifying us first and perhaps causing needless alarm, Mr. Peters had started inquiries after receiving by mail a number of papers (in which his name and address were mentioned) that my father carried when he left. The dispatch from the Bishop of Zacatecas read as follows:

Mr. Junius T. Peters
Miners, and Seamen's Bank Trust Co.
San Francisco, California
Sir:
I received your letter of March 15, but have delayed my reply as I was waiting for information I had requested from the Rector of the Colotlán. His report has now reached me and reads as follows:

"*Most Excellent Sir:* Desiring to satisfy the wishes of Your Holiness about the assassination of Dr. McPheeters, I have the honor to make the following statement: Dr. McPheeters was wounded on Tuesday, February 3, in an abandoned house on the outskirts of this city where he had been taken on the pretext of calling on a patient, by a man disguised as a woman, who came between 9 and 10 at night to Mr. James Dwyer's house, in which Dr. McPheeters was living.

"The Doctor accompanied the disguised man to the house of the supposed patient, and having gone as far as the patio, was surrounded by three men, one of whom stabbed him in the chest with a dagger and struck his head with a stick, inflicting seven serious head wounds. The police found the dying man there, being guided by his moans. He was carried to his residence, which was the same as Mr. James Dwyer's (an American quack), and lingered there in bed till the fifth, then was buried the same day in the cemetery which lies south of this city.

"According to the records of the trial, which I have before me in giving this information to Your Holiness, the assassins did not have the time to rob him, as he lost only his hat, cane and a ring of slight worth. It seems, then, and appears from the records, that the assassins were paid by the quack Dwyer to put him to death so as to get possession of some funds of the deceased, for from the statement of Maria Sostenes Banuelos, who attended him, it appears that he always wore a sort of vest which she herself made for him, holding a few ounces of gold, and that in addition to this quantity, the deceased had in a leather belt five small money bags which would hold about $20 or more each. This money disappeared, though the police were active in trying to clear up the crime. The records bring to light facts that lead one to regard Dwyer as the instigator of the crime, with Petronilo Raigosa and Antonio Gonzalez as the executors of the homicide.

"The trial is still undecided. The record consists of 117 large sheets, yet in spite of the fact that in it the defendants are declared under arrest, they are nevertheless at liberty, and Mr. Dwyer free on bail, which he broke and lives undisturbed at the Chachihuitee mine, where he has gone so far in his disservice and wickedness as to present a claim to Washington against Mexico for damages and injuries for the time he was held in this city on account of his horrible crime. May God our Lord guard Your Holiness for many years.

(*signed*) PABLO SANCHEZ CASTELLANOS"

I believe the foregoing will satisfy your wishes, at least so far as I am able to do so.

Placing myself at your service, I am

Faithfully yours, J. M. DEL REFUGIO
Bishop of Zacatecas

The rest of my father's Journals were sent along later. The last word of the last entry he made, obviously in haste, was, "Tomorrow," with three dots: ". . ."

The Reverend Ebersohl arrived a week after the letter. Seeing his duty to be removed for a while from San Francisco, devil or no devil, he had worked his way upriver by manual toil, and walked or ridden wagon trains as far as the ranch. It would be hard to say just how glad we were to see him. Sitting on the Kissels' porch after supper—Coulter and Jennie and Uncle Ned and Todd and the Kissels—Reverend Ebersohl forgot he was a preacher for a while. He even drank a glass of wine; I couldn't have been more staggered if he'd hung up a notice praising the devil. Then he sat talking about my father until midnight. I'd never heard him make so much sense; he said the old things, but he said them well.

"Doctor placed his trust in the future. That way, it might be said that he had more faith than all of us put together. He believed in the green pastures, the beacon on the hill. And I think he died feeling he had found it. Probably he never realized that, to hold it, to savor fully what was nothing but a poor ghost, he must release it soon, keep moving, hurry on, push forward on a search that, for him, could never end. You mustn't grieve, son.

He's safe in his illusory world, rid of his private demons. And we've all been enriched by his wonderful faults and foolishness."

I wrote a letter to my mother, and in due time an answer came back. The house was sold and my father's debts paid; there was enough left over for her and Hannah and Mary to come to California, by way of Panama, then by steamer to San Francisco. During the winter, Aunt Kitty had died, having failed to cure a case of pneumonia with a broth made of possum liver and sanctified spunk water (and refusing to co-operate with a doctor who was summoned). Clara and Willie had both been freed, given a present of money, and jobs found them in the neighborhood.

My mother was putting Louisville behind her for good. I knew how she hated to leave, but I was glad she was coming. At no place in her letter did she mention my father in any way. I think that for her in these years, left alone as she was, his letters drying up for long periods, he had almost ceased to exist. She had shut him out with such firmness that he no longer had any power to hurt her.

Months would pass before they could arrive. Meanwhile the ranches grew, our crops were planted, we prospered. But the times were not peaceful entirely. People had begun to sense the value of these lands, and ruffians had twice tried to take possession. On one terrible day, Coulter, tired of trying to pit reason against force (very much against his nature to start off with) buckled on his gun, looking like the black-jowled roughneck of the trail, and killed three men in a glade not far from his house, letting each draw first, in accordance with his reputation. After that, when word got out clear up and down the coast exactly who he was, the side-kick of Bridger and Kit Carson, the man they couldn't run out of Texas, the land-hawks let us alone. One unhappy feature of the incident was that it caused bad blood for a few days between him and Uncle Ned, who claimed that, with odds of three to one, Coulter had a moral obligation to let him in on the entertainment. Coulter promised to reform, and it passed off.

534

Autumn has come, and I am on my way to San Francisco. I have a new suit. I am going on seventeen years old. I am scarcely aware of the river, or the boats, or, finally, the city where I lived in hardship for so long. There is a little stab of pain when I see the spot where the sailors' tent stood, and think of my father's plans in those days. But a ship is coming in toward the wharf; the lines are out; men are running up and down; a skiff picks out a lead line that falls short in the water; and the steam winches make a great noise.

And on deck, strange in her English clothes and smart manner, is my sister who can be a sister no longer. For a second, she folds her arms across her breasts in the Indian sign I had not understood that day in the grove when she left; then she gives a gay smile and waves.

The gangplank is down, and I am up in a rush, my heart thumping in my chest.

"You look—different. Is it really you?"

"Oh, Jaimie, it *is* me!"

She places her hand in mine, and we walk away into that fine bright future that my father always knew existed, our present, in which I shall now believe forever.

ACKNOWLEDGMENT

The author wishes to acknowledge his indebtedness to Sterling Memorial Library, at Yale University, and in particular to the curator of the Library's collection of Western Americana, Dr. Archibald Hanna, whose patient guidance and help made possible the research here involved.

Thanks also are extended to the Public Library of Louisville, Kentucky, and to the Medical College of Edinburgh University.

It should be noted that the journals of Dr. Joseph Middleton, upon which much of this material is very loosely based, are occasionally quoted verbatim, and that the letter from the Bishop of Zacatecas, in the final chapter, is substantially the same as one written after the death of Dr. Middleton in Mexico. The early San Francisco street sermons of Reverend William Taylor are twice drawn upon with minor alterations; several paragraphs are similarly used from J. M. Grant's The Truth for the Mormons, *published in the middle 1800's; and two paragraphs followed closely from the collected journals of Edwin Bryant,* What I Saw in California, *published in London in 1849.*

The author is, of course, especially grateful to his wife, whose assistance throughout the preparation of this book and whose cheerful encouragement in the face of depressing odds were far beyond the call of marital duty.

R.L.T.

PRINCIPAL BIBLIOGRAPHY

American Notes, by Charles Dickens

George W. Applegate: Letters from him and his father, Lisbon Applegate, about their journey to California by Panama and life in California and at the mines, 1849 to 1891

John Wodehouse Audubon and Others: Memorandum of an agreement made, January 27, 1849, relating to the organization of an overland company, leaving New York for California, February 7, 1849

Roger Sherman Baldwin: Letters to his family and other correspondence, written during his journey from New York to California by Nicaragua, and his stay in California, 1849 to 1856

The Book Needed for the Times, Containing the Latest Well-Authenticated Facts from the Gold Mines, by Daniel Walton

A Brief Biographical Sketch of James Bridger, by John B. Colton

The California and Australia Gold Rushes, by Amos S. Pittman

California and Its Gold Regions, by Fayette Robinson

California as It Is, and as It May Be, or, A Guide to the Gold Region, by Felix Paul Wierzbicki

Capture and Escape, or Life among the Sioux, by Mrs. Sarah Larimer

Capture and Rescue of Rebecca J. Fisher (by Rebecca Fisher)

Captured and Branded by the Camanche Indians, by Edwin Eastman

Captured by the Indians, by Mrs. Minnie Carrigan

The Child Captives, by Margaret Hosmer

The City of Saints, by Richard Burton

René August Chouteau: Two letters, in French, to William Grant

Damon's Trip to Lower Oregon and Upper California

Death Valley in 1849, by William Lewis

Der Deutsche Answanderer nach den Verinigten Staaten von Nordamerika, by Alexander Ziegler

News, The Deseret, 1850 to 1898

Diary of a Journey from Burlington, Vermont, to St. Louis, and across the Plains to Sacramento; and of His Stay in California, 1849 to

1851, by Gurdon Backus

Diary of a Journey from Iowa, Overland to California, 1849; Experiences at the Mines, and the Voyage Home by the Isthmus, 1851, by P. C. Tiffany

Diary of a Journey from Warren, Pennsylvania, to California, 1849, by Philip Badman

Diary of a Physician in California, by James Lawrence Tyson

Diary of an Overland Journey from Independence, Missouri, to Weaverville, California, 1850, by Abram Krill

Diary of an Overland Journey to Great Salt Lake City, 1849, by Robert Bond

Diary of Rev. Edward J. Willis, Giving Account of Travell from Independence, Missouri, to California in 1849, across the Plains

Down the Century with Stewart's (STEWART DRY GOODS CO.) *1846–1946,* by Isabel McLennan McMeekin

Simon Doyle: Journals and letters describing his overland journeys from Illinois to California in 1849 and 1854, his life in the mines, and his return journey in 1856 by Panama

Eclectic Practice of Medicine, by John M. Scudder, M.D. (from the personal library of the author's grandfather, Dr. Hodge Scott Taylor, of Golconda, Illinois)

Eighteen Years Captivity among the Indians, by Joseph Barney

The Emigrants' Guide to California, by Joseph E. Ware

The Emigrant's Guide to the Gold Mines, by Henry I. Simpson

En Route to California, 1850, by Caleb Booth

An Excursion to California, over the Prairie, Rocky Mountains, and Great Sierra Nevada, with a Stroll through the Diggings and Ranches of That Country, by William Kelley, J. P.

Exploration and Survey of the Valley of the Great Salt Lake of Utah, Including a Reconnaissance of a New Route through the Rocky Mountains, in 1849, by Howard Stansbury, Captain Corps Topographical Engineers, U. S. Army

A Few Choice Samples of Mormon Practices and Sermons

Filings from an Old Saw—Reminiscences of San Francisco, by Joseph T. Downey

President Millard Fillmore: Reports to Him from Judges Sent to Utah

Fort Bridger, by Col. Albert G. Brackett

Four Months among the Gold-Finders in Alta California, by Henry Vizetelly

A Frenchman in the Gold Rush, by Ernest de Massey

Friend, The Honolulu

Fruits of Mormonism, or a Fair and Candid Statement of Facts Illustrative of Mormon Principles, Mormon Policy and Mormon Character, by More than 40 Eye-Witnesses, by Nelson Slater

Geographical Memoir upon Upper California, by John Charles Frémont

Girl Captives of the Cheyennes, by Mrs. Grace E. Meredith

Gleanings by the Way, by J. A. Clark

The Gold Places of California, by Samuel Augustus Mitchell

The Gold Regions of California, by George Foster

The Gold-Seeker's Manual, by David Thomas Ansted

Granville Company Diary, from Zanesville, Ohio, to the Feather River Valley, 1849

Great Salt Lake City: ordinances passed by the Legislative Council and ordered to be printed

Grey-Hawk: John Tanner's Captivity among the Indians

Guide to California, and the Mines, with a General Description of the Country, by G. S. Isham

Haldeman's Picture of Louisville, by Peabody Poor (directory and business advertiser)

History of Kentucky, by R. H. Collins

History of Louisville, by Ben Casseday

History of the Ohio Falls Cities and Their Counties

Hooper's Medical Dictionary

In Captivity, the Experience, Privations, and Dangers of Samuel J. Brown and Others While Prisoners of the Hostile Sioux During the Massacre and War of 1862

The Indian Captive, by Matther Brayton

Indian Horrors of the Fifties, by Jesse H. Alexander

Instructions For Collecting, Testing, Melting and Assaying Gold, with a Description of the Process for Distinguishing Native Gold, by Edward N. Kent

William Henry Jackson: Indian names from his Indian portraits

Journal of a Voyage to California, and Life in the Gold Diggings. And Also of a Voyage from California to the Sandwich Islands, by Albert Lyman

Journal of an Overland Journey from Indiana to California, 1852, by D. B. Andrews

Journal of an Overland Journey from Rochester, Wisconsin, to Georgetown, California, 1850, by Abial Whitman

Journal of John Wood, as Kept by Him while Traveling from Cincinnati to the Gold Diggings in California, in the Spring and Summer of 1850

A Journal of the Overland Route to California and the Gold Mines, by Lorenzo D. Aldrich

Journal of the Suffering and Hardships of Capt. Parker H. French's Overland Expedition to California, Which Left New York City, May 13, 1850, and Arrived at San Francisco, Dec. 14, by William Miles

Journal of Travel across the Plains to California and Guide to Future Emigrants, by J. Shepherd

Journal of Travels over the Rocky Mountains, by Joel Palmer

A Journal of Travels to and from California, with Full Details of the Hardships and Privations, also a Description of the Country, Mines, Cities, Towns, etc., by John T. Clapp

Journal on & of the Route to California, by F. D. Everts

A Journal to Salt Lake City, by Jules Rémy

Latter-Day Saints in Utah, by Franklin Dewey Richards

Letters from the East and from the West, by Frederick Hall

Letters of a California Pioneer, by Moses Ellis

Life & Adventures among the Indians of the Far West in 1829, by Mrs. Gertrude Morgan

Life and Adventures of William Filley, Who Was Stolen from His Home in Jackson, Michigan, by the Indians, August 3rd, 1837, and His Safe Return from Captivity, Oct. 19, 1866, after an Absence of Twenty-nine Years (by William Filley)

A Live Woman in the Mines, by Alonzo Delano

Louisville, Her Commercial, Manufacturing and Social Advantages, by Richard Deering

Louisville, 1780–1892, by Paul B. Woodlief

Louisville, the Gateway City, by I. M. McMeekin

Louisville Directory, 1848–1849, by J. B. Jegli

Memoirs of L. C. McKeeby, 1809, containing a description of his journey to California in 1850

Memorial History of Louisville, by J. S. Johnston

Men and Manners, by Thomas Hamilton

Dr. Joseph Middleton: (of Louisville, Kentucky) His letters and journal

The Miner's Own Book

Expositor, The Mormon

The Mormons; or Latter-Day Saints, by Henry Mayhew

The Mormons, or Latter-Day Saints, in the Valley of the Great Salt Lake, by Lt. J. W. Gunnison of the Topographical Engineers

Mormon Sacred Hymns

Mormon Way-Bill to the Gold Mines, by Joseph Cain

Mrs. Huggins' Account as a Minnesota Captive

Three Years in California, by Reverend Walter Colton, USN

A Thrilling Narrative of Indian Captivity, by Mary Renville Butler

A Trip across the Plains, in the Spring of 1850, by James Abbey

A Trip across the Plains and Life in California, by George Kelley

The Truth for the Mormons, by J. M. Grant

A Visit to Salt Lake; Being a Journey across the Plains and a Residence in the Mormon Settlements at Utah, by William Chandless

A Vocabulary of Words in Hancock's Harbor Language, on the North West Coast of N. America, by Abraham Waters

Wake of the Prairie Schooner, by Irene D. Paden

Westward America, by Howard R. Driggs

What I Saw in California, Being the Journal of a Tour in the Years 1846, 1847, by Edwin Bryant

Brigham Young: Original manuscript letters to W. H. Hooper

Brigham Young: Sermons

544